DESPERATE STRUGGLE

The Forged one had doubled back. From behind a great stump he leaped at us. He was big and muscled like a smithy. Unlike other Forged ones I had encountered, this one's size and strength had kept him fed and well clothed. The boundless anger of a hunted animal was his. He seized me, lifting me clear off my feet, and then fell upon me with one knotty fore-arm crushing my throat. He landed atop me, barrel chest on my back, pinning my chest and one arm to the earth below him. I reached back, to sink my knife twice into a meaty thigh. He roared with anger and increased the pressure. He pressed my face into the frozen earth. Black dots spotted my vision, and Nighteyes was a sudden addition to the weight on my back. I thought my spine would snap. Nighteyes slashed at the man's back with his fangs, but the Forged one only drew his chin into his chest and hunched his shoulders against the attack. He knew he was killing me; time enough to deal with the wolf when I was dead. . . .

Bantam Books

by Robin Hobb

The Farseer: Assassin's Apprentice

The Farseer: Royal Assassin

The Farseer: Assassin's Quest

The Liveship Traders: Ship of Magic

The Liveship Traders: Mad Ship

The Liveship Traders: Ship of Destiny

The Tawny Man: Fool's Errand

The Tawny Man: Golden Fool

The Tawny Man: Fool's Fate

THE FARSEER

Royal Assassin

Robin Hobb

BANTAM BOOKS

New York   Toronto   London   Sydney   Auckland

THE FARSEER: ROYAL ASSASSIN
A Bantam Spectra Book

PUBLISHING HISTORY
Bantam trade paperback edition published May 1996
Bantam mass market edition / March 1997

SPECTRA and the portrayal of a boxed "s" are trademarks
of Bantam Books,
a division of Random House, Inc.

For information regarding prints and poster reproductions of the
artwork of Michael Whelan, contact Glass Onion Graphics, Post
Office Box 88, Brookfield, CT 06804, USA. Phone/Fax: (203) 798-
6063. And look for *The Art of Michael* Whelan wherever Bantam
Books are sold.

ISBN 0-553-57341-1

Published simultaneously in the United States and Canada

Bantam Books are published by Bantam Books, a division of Random
House, Inc. Its trademark, consisting of the words "Bantam Books"
and the portrayal of a rooster, is Registered in U.S. Patent and
Trademark Office and in other countries. Marca Registrada.
Bantam Books, New York, New York.

PRINTED IN THE UNITED STATES OF AMERICA
OPM   20

For Ryan

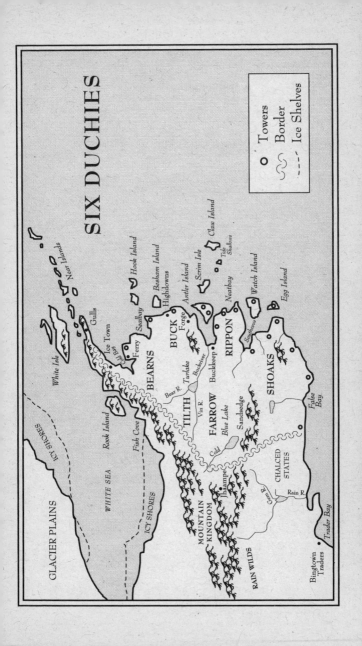

SIX DUCHIES

Towers ○
Border
Ice Shelves - - -

GLACIER PLAINS

ICY SHORES

WHITE SEA

White Isle

Rook Island

Fish Cove

Near Islands

Gulls

Ice Town

Gull Bay

Ferry

Sedbay

Hook Island

BEARNS

Beaham Island

Highdowns

Forge

BUCK

Antler Island

Scrim Isle

Claw Island

Turlake

Buckkeep

Buckkeep

Bear R.

Neatbay

RIPPON

Tide Shallows

TILTH

Vin R.

Southcove

Watch Island

Blue Lake

FARROW

Sandsedge

Egg Island

Cold

SHOAKS

MOUNTAIN
KINGDOM

Jhaampe

False Bay

Gem R.

CHALCED
STATES

Rain R.

RAIN WILDS

Bingtown
Traders

Trader Bay

Prologue

Dreams and Awakenings

WHY IS IT *forbidden to write down specific knowledge of the magics? Perhaps because we all fear that such knowledge would fall into the hands of one not worthy to use it. Certainly there has always been a system of apprenticeship to ensure that specific knowledge of magic is passed only to those trained and judged worthy of such knowledge. While this seems a laudable attempt to protect us from unworthy practitioners of arcane lore, it ignores the fact that the magics are not derived from this specific knowledge. The predilection for a certain type of magic is either inborn or lacking. For instance, the ability for the magics known as the Skill is tied closely to blood relationship to the royal Farseer line, though it may also occur as a "wild strain" among folk whose ancestors came from both the inland tribes and the Outislanders. One trained in the Skill is able to reach out to another's mind, no matter how distant, and know what he is thinking. Those who are strongly Skilled can influence that thinking, or have converse with that person. For the conducting of a battle, or the gathering of information, it is a most useful tool.*

Folklore tells of an even older magic, much despised now,

known as the Wit. Few will admit a talent for this magic, hence it is always said to be the province of the folk in the next valley, or the ones who live on the other side of the far ridge. I suspect it was once the natural magic of those who lived on the land as hunters rather than as settled folk; a magic for those who felt kinship with the wild beasts of the woods. The Wit, it is said, gave one the ability to speak the tongues of the beasts. It was also warned that those who practiced the Wit too long or too well became whatever beast they had bonded to. But this may be only legend.

There are the Hedge magics, though I have never been able to determine the source of this name. These are magics both verified and suspect, including palm reading, water gazing, the interpretation of crystal reflections, and a host of other magics that attempt to predict the future. In a separate un-named category are the magics that cause physical effects, such as invisibility, levitation, giving motion or life to inanimate objects—all the magics of the old legends, from the Flying Chair of the Widow's Son to the North Wind's Magic Tablecloth. I know of no people who claim these magics as their own. They seem to be solely the stuff of legend, ascribed to folk living in ancient times or distant places, or beings of mythical or near-mythical reputation: dragons, giants, the Elderlings, the Others, pecksies.

⇒═►

I pause to clean my pen. My writing wanders from spidery to blobbish on this poor paper. But I will not use good parchment for these words; not yet. I am not sure they should be written. I ask myself, why put this to paper at all? Will not this knowledge be passed down by word of mouth to those who are worthy? Perhaps. But perhaps not. What we take for granted now, the knowing of these things, may be a wonder and a mystery someday to our descendants.

There is very little in any of the libraries on magic. I work laboriously, tracing a thread of knowledge through a patchwork quilt of information. I find scattered references, passing allusions, but that is all. I have gathered it, over these last few years, and stored it in my head, always intending to commit my knowledge to paper. I will put down what I know from my own experience, as well as what I have ferreted out. Perhaps to provide answers for some other poor fool, in times to come, who might find himself as battered by the warring of the magics within him as I have been.

But when I sit down to the task, I hesitate. Who am I to set my will against the wisdom of those who have gone before me? Shall I set down in plain lettering the methods by which a Wit-gifted one can expand her range, or can bond a creature to himself? Shall I detail the training one must undergo before being recognized as a Skilled one? The Hedge wizardries and legendary magics have never been mine. Have I any right to dig out their secrets and pin them to paper like so many butterflies or leaves collected for study?

I try to consider what one might do with such knowledge, unjustly gained. It leads me to consider what this knowledge has gained for me. Power, wealth, the love of a woman? I mock myself. Neither the Skill nor the Wit has ever offered any such to me. Or if they did, I had not the sense nor ambition to seize them when offered.

Power. I do not think I ever wanted it for its own sake. I thirsted for it, sometimes, when I was ground down, or when those close to me suffered beneath ones who abused their powers. Wealth. I never really considered it. From the moment that I, his bastard grandson, pledged myself to King Shrewd, he always saw that all my needs were fulfilled. I had plenty to eat, more education than I sometimes cared for, clothes both simple and those annoyingly fashionable, and often enough a coin or two of my own to spend. Growing up in Buckkeep, that was wealth enough and more than most boys in Buckkeep Town could claim. Love? Well. My horse Sooty was fond enough of me, in her own placid way. I had the truehearted loyalty of a hound named Nosy, and that took him to his grave. I was given the fiercest of loves by a terrier pup, and it was likewise the death of him. I wince to think of the price willingly paid for loving me.

Always I have possessed the loneliness of one raised amid intrigues and clustering secrets, the isolation of a boy who cannot trust the completeness of his heart to anyone. I could not go to Fedwren, the court scribe, who praised me for my neat lettering and well-inked illustrations, and confide that I was already apprenticed to the royal assassin, and thus could not follow his writing trade. Nor could I divulge to Chade, my master in the Diplomacy of the Knife, the frustrating brutality I endured trying to learn the ways of the Skill from Galen the Skill Master. And to no one did I dare speak openly of my emerging proclivity for the Wit, the ancient beast magic, said to be a perversion and a taint to any who used it.

Not even to Molly.

Molly was that most cherished of items: a genuine refuge. She had absolutely nothing to do with my day-to-day life. It was not just that she was female, though that was mystery enough to me. I was raised almost entirely in the company of men, bereft not only of my natural mother and father, but of any blood relations that would openly acknowledge me. As a child, my care was entrusted to Burrich, the gruff stablemaster who had once been my father's right-hand man. The stable hands and the guards were my daily companions. Then as now, there were women in the guard companies, though not so many then as now. But like their male comrades, they had duties to perform, and lives and families of their own when they were not on watch. I could not claim their time. I had no mother, nor sisters or aunts of my own. There were no women who offered me the special tenderness said to be the province of women.

None save Molly.

She was but a year or two older than myself, and growing the same way a sprig of greenery forces its way up through a gap in the cobblestones. Neither her father's near-constant drunkenness and frequent brutality nor the grinding chores of a child trying to maintain the pretense of both home and family business could crush her. When I first met her, she was as wild and wary as a fox cub. Molly Nosebleed she was called among the street children. She often bore the marks of the beatings her father gave her. Despite his cruelty, she cared for him. I never understood that. He would grumble and berate her even as she tottered him home after one of his binges and put him to bed. And when he awoke, he never had any remorse for his drunkenness and harsh words. There were only more criticisms: Why hadn't the chandlery been swept and fresh strewing herbs put on the floor? Why hadn't she tended the beehives, when they were nearly out of honey to sell? Why had she let the fire go out under the tallow pot? I was mute witness more times than I care to remember.

But through it all, Molly grew. She flowered, one sudden summer, into a young woman who left me in awe of her capable ways and womanly charms. For her part, she seemed totally unaware of how her eyes could meet mine and turn my tongue to leather in my mouth. No magic I possessed, no Skill, no Wit, was proof against the accidental touch of her hand against mine, nor could defend me against the awkwardness that overwhelmed me at the quirk of her smile.

Should I catalog her hair flowing with the wind, or detail how the color of her eyes shifted from dark amber to rich brown depending on her mood and the color of her gown? I would catch a glimpse of her scarlet skirts and red shawl among the market throng, and suddenly be aware of no one else. These are magics I witnessed, and though I might set them down on paper, no other could ever work them with such skill.

How did I court her? With a boy's clumsy gallantries, gaping after her like a simpleton watching the whirling disks of a juggler. She knew I loved her before I did. And she let me court her, although I was a few years younger than she, and not one of the town boys and possessed of small prospects as far as she knew. She thought I was the scribe's errand boy, a part-time helper in the stables, a Keep runner. She never suspected I was the Bastard, the unacknowledged son that had toppled Prince Chivalry from his place in the line of succession. That alone was a big enough secret. Of my magics and my other profession, she knew nothing.

Maybe that was why I could love her.

It was certainly why I lost her.

I let the secrets and failures and pains of my other lives keep me too busy. There were magics to learn, secrets to ferret out, men to kill, intrigues to survive. Surrounded by them, it never occurred to me that I could turn to Molly for a measure of the hope and understanding that eluded me everywhere else.

She was apart from these things, unsullied by them. I carefully preserved her from any touch of them. I never tried to draw her into my world. Instead, I went to hers, to the fishing and shipping port town where she sold candles and honey in her shop, and shopped in the market, and, sometimes, walked on the beaches with me. To me, it was enough that she existed for me to love. I did not even dare to hope she might return that feeling.

There came a time when my training in the Skill ground me into a misery so deep I did not think I could survive it. I could not forgive myself for being unable to learn it; I could not imagine that my failure might not matter to others. I cloaked my despair in surly withdrawal. I let the long weeks pass, and never saw her or even sent her word that I thought of her. Finally, when there was no one else that I could turn to, I sought her. Too late. I arrived at the Beebalm Chandlery in Buckkeep Town one afternoon, gifts in hand, in time to see her leaving. Not alone. With Jade, a fine broad-chested seaman, with a bold earring in one ear and the sure masculinity of his superior years. Unnoticed, defeated, I slunk away and watched them walk off arm in arm. I watched her go, and I let her go, and in the months that followed, I tried to convince myself that my heart had let her go as well. I wonder what would have happened if I had run after them that afternoon, if I had begged one last word of her. Odd, to think of so many events turning upon a boy's misplaced pride and his schooled acceptance of defeats. I set her out of my thoughts, and spoke of her to no one. I got on with my life.

King Shrewd sent me as his assassin with a great caravan of folk going to witness the pledging of the Mountain Princess Kettricken as Prince Verity's bride. My mission was to quietly cause the death of her older brother, Prince Rurisk, subtly of course, so that she would be left the sole heir to the Mountain throne. But what I found when I arrived there was a web of deceit and lies engineered by my youngest uncle, Prince Regal, who hoped to topple Verity from the line of succession and claim the Princess as his own bride. I was the pawn he would sacrifice for this goal; and I was the pawn who instead toppled the game pieces around him, bringing his wrath and vengeance down on myself, but saving the crown and the Princess for Prince Verity. I do not think this was heroism. Nor do I think it was petty spite wreaked on one who had always bullied and belittled me. It was the act of a boy becoming a man, and doing what I had sworn to do years before I comprehended the cost of such an oath. The price was my healthy young body, so long taken for granted.

Long after I had defeated Regal's plot, I lingered in a sickbed in the Mountain Kingdom. But finally a morning came when I awoke and believed that my long illness was finally over. Burrich had decided I was recovered enough to begin the long journey back home to the Six Duchies. Princess Kettricken and her entourage had left for Buckkeep weeks before, when the weather was still fine. Now winter snows already smothered the higher parts of the Mountain Kingdom. If we did not leave Jhaampe soon, we would be forced to winter there. I was up early that morning, doing my final packing, when the first small tremors began. Resolutely, I ignored them. I was just shaky, I told myself, with not having eaten breakfast yet, and the excitement of the journey home. I donned the garments that Jonqui had furnished for our winter journey through the Mountains and across the plains. For me there was a long red shirt, padded with wool quilted into it. The quilted trousers were green, but embroidered with red at the waist and cuffs. The boots were soft, almost shapeless until my feet were laced inside them. They were like sacks of soft leather, padded with sheared wool and trimmed with fur. They fastened to the feet with long wrappings of leather strips. My trembling fingers made tying them a difficult task. Jonqui had told us they were wonderful for the dry snow of the mountains, but to beware of getting them wet.

There was a looking glass in the room. At first, I smiled at my reflection. Not even King Shrewd's fool dressed as gaily as this. But above the bright garments, my face was thin and pale, making my dark eyes too large, while my fever-shorn hair, black and bristly, stood up like a dog's hackles. My illness had ravaged me. But I told myself I was finally on my way home. I turned aside from the mirror. As I packed the few small gifts I had selected to take home to my friends, the unsteadiness grew in my hands.

For the last time Burrich, Hands, and I sat down to break fast with Jonqui. I thanked her once again for all she had done toward healing me. I picked up a spoon for the porridge, and my hand gave a twitch. I dropped it. I watched the silvery shape fall and fell after it.

The next thing I remember is the shadowy corners of the bedroom. I lay for a long time, not moving or speaking. I went from a state of emptiness to knowing I had had another seizure. It had passed; both body and mind were mine to command once more. But I no longer wanted them. At fifteen years old, an age when most were coming into their full strength, I could no longer trust my body to perform the simplest task. It was damaged, and I rejected it fiercely. I felt savagely vindictive toward the flesh and bone that enclosed me, and wished for some way to express my raging disappointment. Why couldn't I heal? Why hadn't I recovered?

"It's going to take time, that's all. Wait until half a year has passed since the day you were damaged. Then assess yourself." It was Jonqui the healer. She was sitting near the fireplace, but her chair was drawn back into the shadows. I hadn't noticed her until she spoke. She rose slowly, as if the winter made her bones ache, and came to stand beside my bed.

"I don't want to live like an old man."

She pursed her lips. "Sooner or later you will have to. At least, I so wish that you will survive that many years. I am old, and so is my brother King Eyod. We do not find it so great a burden."

"I should not mind an old man's body if the years had earned it for me. But I can't go on like this."

She shook her head, puzzled. "Of course you can. Healing is tedious sometimes, but to say that you cannot go on . . . I do not understand. It is, perhaps, a difference in our languages?"

I took a breath to speak, but at that moment Burrich came in. "Awake? Feeling better?"

"Awake. Not feeling better," I grumbled. Even to myself, I sounded like a fretful child. Burrich and Jonqui exchanged glances over me. She came to the bedside, patted my shoulder, and then left the room silently. Their obvious tolerance was galling, and my impotent anger rose like a tide. "Why can't you heal me?" I demanded of Burrich.

He was taken aback by the accusation in my question. "It's not that simple," he began.

"Why not?" I hauled myself up straight in the bed. "I've seen you cure all manner of ailments in beasts. Sickness, broken bones, worms, mange . . . you're stablemaster, and I've seen you treat them all. Why can't you cure me?"

"You're not a dog, Fitz," Burrich said quietly. "It's simpler with a beast, when it's seriously ill. I've taken drastic measures, sometimes, telling myself, well, if the animal dies, at least it's not suffering anymore, and this may heal it. I can't do that with you. You're not a beast."

"That's no answer! Half the time the guards come to you instead of the healer. You took the head of an arrow out of Den. You laid his whole arm open to do it! When the healer said that Greydin's foot was too infected and she'd have to lose it, she came to you, and you saved it. And all the time the healer was saying the infection would spread and she'd die and it would be your fault."

Burrich folded his lips, quelling his temper. If I'd been healthy, I'd have been wary of his wrath. But his restraint with me during my convalescence had made me bold. When he spoke, his voice was quiet and controlled. "Those were risky healings, yes. But the folk who wanted them done knew the risks. And," he said, raising his voice to cover the objection I'd been about to utter, "they were simple things. I knew the cause. Take out the arrowhead and haft from his arm and clean it up. Poultice and draw the infection from Greydin's foot. But your sickness isn't that simple. Neither Jonqui nor I really know what's wrong with you. Is it the aftermath of the poison Kettricken fed you when she thought you had come to kill her brother? Is this the effects of the poisoned wine that Regal arranged for you? Or is it from the beating you took afterward? From being near drowned? Or did all those things combine to do this to you? We don't know, and so we don't know how to cure you. We just don't know."

His voice clenched on his last words, and I suddenly saw how his sympathy for me overlay his frustration. He paced a few steps, then halted to stare into the fire. "We've talked long about it. Jonqui has much in her Mountain lore that I have never heard of before. And I've told her of cures I know. But we both agreed the best thing to do was give you time to heal. You're in no danger of dying that we can see. Possibly, in time, your own body can cast out the last vestiges of the poison, or heal whatever damage was done inside you."

"Or," I added quietly, "it's possible that I'll be this way the rest of my life. That the poison or the beating damaged something permanently. Damn Regal, to kick me like that when I was trussed already."

Burrich stood as if turned to ice. Then he sagged into the chair in the shadows. Defeat was in his voice. "Yes. That is just as possible as the other. But don't you see we have no choice? I could physick you to try to force the poison out of your body. But if it's damage, not poison, all I would do was weaken you, so that your body's own healing would take that much longer." He stared into the flames, and lifted a hand to touch a streak of white at his temple. I was not the only one who'd fallen to Regal's treachery. Burrich himself was but newly recovered from a skull blow that would have killed anyone less thickheaded than he. I knew he had endured long days of dizziness and blurred vision. I did not recall he had complained at all. I had the decency to feel a bit of shame.

"So what do I do?"

Burrich started as if roused from dozing. "What we've been doing. Wait. Eat. Rest. Be easy on yourself. And see what happens. Is that so terrible?"

I ignored his question. "And if I don't get better? If I just stay like this, where the tremors or fits can come over me at any time?"

His answer was slow in coming. "Live with it. Many folk have to live with worse. Most of the time you're fine. You're not blind. You're not paralyzed. You've your wits, still. Stop defining yourself by what you can't do. Why don't you consider what you didn't lose?"

"What I didn't lose? What I didn't lose?" My anger rose

like a covey of birds taking flight and likewise driven by panic. "I'm helpless, Burrich. I can't go back to Buckkeep like this! I'm useless. I'm worse than useless, I'm a waiting victim. If I could go back and batter Regal into a pulp, that might be worth it. Instead, I will have to sit at table with Prince Regal, to be civil and deferential to a man who plotted to overthrow Verity and kill me as an added spice. I can't endure him seeing me tremble with weakness, or suddenly fall in a seizure. I don't want to see him smile at what he has made me; I don't want to watch him savor his triumph. He will try to kill me again. We both know that. Perhaps he has learned he is no match for Verity, perhaps he will respect his older brother's reign and new wife. But I doubt he will extend that to me. I'll be one more way he can strike at Verity. And when he comes, what shall I be doing? Sitting by the fire like a palsied old man, doing nothing. Nothing! All I've been trained for, all Hod's weaponry instruction, all Fedwren's careful teachings about lettering, even all you've taught me about taking care of beasts! All a waste! I can do none of it. I'm just a bastard again, Burrich. And someone once told me that a royal bastard is only kept alive so long as he is useful." I was practically shouting at him as I said the last words. But even in my fury and despair, I did not speak aloud of Chade and my training as an assassin. At that, too, I was useless now. All my stealth and sleight of hand, all the precise ways to kill a man by touch, the painstaking mixing of poisons, all were denied me by my own rattling body.

Burrich sat quietly, hearing me out. When my breath and my anger ran out and I sat gasping in my bed, clasping my traitorously trembling hands together, he spoke calmly.

"So. Are you saying we don't go back to Buckkeep?"

That put me off balance. "We?"

"My life is pledged to the man who wears that earring. There's a long story behind that, one that perhaps I'll tell you someday. Patience had no right to give it to you. I thought it had gone with Prince Chivalry to his grave. She probably thought it just a simple piece of jewelry her husband had worn, hers to keep or to give. In any wise, you wear it now. Where you go, I follow."

I lifted my hand to the bauble. It was a tiny blue stone
caught up in a web of silver net. I started to unfasten it.

"Don't do that," Burrich said. The words were quiet,
deeper than a dog's growl. But his voice held both threat and
command. I dropped my hand away, unable to question him on
this at least. It felt strange that the man who had watched over
me since I was an abandoned child now put his future into my
hands. Yet there he sat before the fire and waited for my words.
I studied what I could see of him in the dance of firelight. He
had once seemed a surly giant to me, dark and threatening, but
also a savage protector. Now, for perhaps the first time, I studied him as a man. The dark hair and eyes were prevalent in
those who carried Outislander blood, and in this we resembled
each other. But his eyes were brown, not black, and the wind
brought a redness to his cheeks above his curling beard that
bespoke a fairer ancestor somewhere. When he walked, he
limped, very noticeably on cold days. It was the legacy of
turning aside a boar that had been trying to kill Chivalry. He
was not so big as he had once seemed to me. If I kept on
growing, I would probably be taller than he before another year
was out. Nor was he massively muscled, but instead had a
compactness to him that was a readiness of both muscle and
mind. It was not his size that had made him both feared and
respected at Buckkeep, but his black temper and his tenacity.
Once, when I was very young, I had asked him if he had ever
lost a fight. He had just subdued a willful young stallion and
was in the stall with him, calming him. Burrich had grinned,
teeth showing white as a wolf's. The sweat had stood out in
droplets on his forehead and was running down his cheeks into
his dark beard. He spoke to me over the side of the stall. "Lost
a fight?" he'd asked, still out of breath. "The fight isn't over
until you win it, Fitz. That's all you have to remember. No
matter what the other man thinks. Or the horse."

I wondered if I were a fight he had to win. He'd often told
me that I was the last task Chivalry had given him. My father
had abdicated the throne, shamed by my existence. Yet he'd
given me over to this man, and told him to raise me well.
Maybe Burrich thought he hadn't finished that task yet.

"What do you think I should do?" I asked humbly. Neither the words nor the humility came easily.

"Heal," he said after a few moments. "Take the time to heal. It can't be forced." He glanced down at his own legs stretched toward the fire. Something not a smile twisted his lips.

"Do you think we should go back?" I pressed.

He leaned back into the chair. He crossed his booted feet at the ankle and stared into the fire. He took a long time answering. But finally he said, almost reluctantly, "If we don't, Regal will think he has won. And he will try to kill Verity. Or at least do whatever he thinks he must to make a grab for his brother's crown. I am sworn to my king, Fitz, as are you. Right now that is King Shrewd. But Verity is king-in-waiting. I don't think it right that he should have waited in vain."

"He has other soldiers, more capable than I."

"Does that free you from your promise?"

"You argue like a priest."

"I don't argue at all. I merely asked you a question. And one other. What do you forsake, if you leave Buckkeep behind?"

It was my turn to fall silent. I did think of my king, and all I had sworn to him. I thought of Prince Verity, and his bluff heartiness and open ways with me. I recalled old Chade and his slow smile when I had finally mastered some arcane bit of lore. Lady Patience and her maid Lacey, Fedwren and Hod, even Cook and Mistress Hasty the seamstress. There were not so many folk that had cared for me, but that made them more significant, not less. I would miss all of them if I never went back to Buckkeep. But what leaped up in me like an ember rekindled was my memory of Molly. And somehow, I found myself speaking of her to Burrich, and him just nodding as I spilled out the whole story.

When he did speak, he told me only that he had heard that the Beebalm Chandlery closed when the old drunkard that owned it had died in debt. His daughter had been forced to go to relatives in another town. He did not know what town, but he was certain I could find it out, if I were determined. "Know your heart before you do, Fitz," he added. "If you've nothing to offer her, let her go. Are you crippled? Only if you decide so. But if you're determined that you're a cripple now, then perhaps you've no right to go and seek her out. I don't think you'd want her pity. It's a poor substitute for love.'' And then he rose and left me, to stare into the fire and think.

Was I a cripple? Had I lost? My body jangled like badly tuned harp strings. That was true. But my will, not Regal's, had prevailed. My prince Verity was still in line for the Six Duchies throne, and the Mountain Princess was his wife now. Did I dread Regal smirking over my trembling hands? Could I not smirk back at he who would never be king? A savage satisfaction welled up in me. Burrich was right. I had not lost. But I could make sure that Regal knew I had won.

If I had won against Regal, could I not win Molly as well? What stood between her and me? Jade? But Burrich had heard she had left Buckkeep Town, not wed. Gone penniless to live with relatives. Shame upon him, had Jade let her do so. I would seek her out, I would find her and win her. Molly, with her hair loose and blowing, Molly with her bright red skirts and cloak, bold as a red-robber bird, and eyes as bright. The thought of her sent a shiver down my spine. I smiled to myself, and then felt my lips set like a rictus, and the shiver become a shuddering. My body spasmed and the back of my head rebounded sharply off the bedstead. I cried out involuntarily, a gargling wordless cry.

In an instant Jonqui was there, calling Burrich back, and then they were both holding down my flailing limbs. Burrich's body weight was flung atop me as he strove to restrain my thrashing. And then I was gone.

I came out of blackness into light, like surfacing from a deep dive into warm waters. The deep down of the feather bed cradled me, the blankets were soft and warm. I felt safe. For a moment all was peaceful. I lay quiescently, almost feeling good.

''Fitz?'' Burrich asked, leaning over me.

The world came back. I knew myself a mangled, pitiful thing, a puppet with half its strings tangled or a horse with a severed tendon. I would never be as I was before; there was no place left for me in the world I had once inhabited. Burrich had said pity is a poor substitute for love. I wanted pity from none of them.

"Burrich."

He leaned closer over me. "It wasn't that bad," he lied. "Just rest now. Tomorrow—"

"Tomorrow you leave for Buckkeep," I told him.

He frowned. "Let's take it slowly. Give yourself a few days to recover, and then we'll—"

"No." I dragged myself up to a sitting position. I put every bit of strength I had into the words. "I've made a decision. Tomorrow you will go back to Buckkeep. There are people and animals waiting for you there. You're needed. It's your home and your world. But it's not mine. Not anymore."

He was silent for a long moment. "And what will you do?"

I shook my head. "That's no longer your concern. Or anyone's, save mine."

"The girl?"

I shook my head again, more violently. "She's taken care of one cripple already, and spent her youth doing so, only to find that he left her a debtor. Shall I go back and seek her out, like this? Shall I ask her to love me so I can be a burden to her like her father was? No. Alone or wed to another, she's better off now as she is."

The silence stretched long between us. Jonqui was busy in a corner of the room, concocting yet another herbal draft that would do nothing for me. Burrich stood over me, black and lowering as a thundercloud. I knew how badly he wanted to shake me, how he longed to cuff the stubbornness from me. But he did not. Burrich did not hit cripples.

"So," he said at last. "That leaves only your king. Or do you forget you are sworn as a King's Man?"

"I do not forget," I said quietly. "And did I believe myself a man still, I would go back. But I am not, Burrich. I am a liability. On the game board, I have become but one of those tokens that must be protected. A hostage for the taking, powerless to defend myself or anyone else. No. The last act I can make as a King's Man is to remove myself, before someone else does and injures my king in the doing."

Burrich turned aside from me. He was a silhouette in the dim room, his face unreadable by the firelight. "Tomorrow we will talk," he began.

"Only to say farewell," I interrupted. "My heart is firm on this, Burrich." I reached up to touch the earring in my ear.

"If you stay, then so must I." There was a fierceness in his low voice.

"That isn't how it works," I told him. "Once, my father told you to stay behind, and raise a bastard for him. Now I tell you to leave, to go to serve a King who still needs you."

"FitzChivalry, I don't—"

"Please." I don't know what he heard in my voice. Only that he was suddenly still. "I am so tired. So damnably tired. The only thing I know is that I can't live up to what everyone else thinks I should do. I just can't do it." My voice quavered like an old man's. "No matter what I ought to do. No·matter what I am pledged to do. There isn't enough of me left to keep my word. Maybe that's not right, but that's how it is. Everyone else's plans. Everyone else's goals. Never mine. I tried, but . . ." The room rocked around me as if someone else were speaking, and I was shocked at what he was saying. But I couldn't deny the truth of his words. "I need to be alone now. To rest," I said simply.

Both of them just looked at me. Neither one of them spoke. They left the room, slowly, as if hoping I would relent and call them back. I did not.

But after they had gone, and I was alone, I permitted myself to breathe out. I felt dizzy with the decision I had made. I wasn't going back to Buckkeep. What I was going to do, I had no idea. I had swept my broken bits of life from the game table. Now there was room to set out anew what pieces I still had, to plot a new strategy for living. Slowly, I realized I had no doubts. Regrets warred with relief, but I had no doubts. Somehow it was much more bearable to move forward into a life where no one would recall who I had once been. A life not pledged to someone else's will. Not even my king's. It was done. I lay back in my bed, and for the first time in weeks, I relaxed completely. Farewell, I thought wearily. I would have liked to wish them all farewell, to stand one last time before my king and see his brief nod that I had done well. Perhaps I could have made him understand why I did not wish to go back. It was not to be. It was done now, all done. ''I am sorry, my king,'' I muttered. I stared into the dancing flames in the hearth until sleep claimed me.

Siltbay

To be the *King-in-Waiting, or the Queen-in-Waiting, is to firmly straddle the fence between responsibility and authority. It is said the position was created to satisfy the ambitions of an heir for power, while schooling him in the exercising of it. The eldest child in the royal family assumes this position upon the sixteenth birthday. From that day on, the King- or Queen-in-Waiting assumes a full share of responsibility for the running of the Six Duchies. Generally, he immediately assumes such duties as the ruling monarch cares least for, and these have varied greatly from reign to reign.*

Under King Shrewd, Prince Chivalry first became king-in-waiting. To him, King Shrewd ceded over all that had to do with the borders and frontiers: warfare, negotiations and diplomacy, the discomforts of extended travel and the miserable conditions often encountered on the campaigns. When Chivalry abdicated and Prince Verity became king-in-waiting, he inherited all the uncertainties of the war with the Outislanders, and the civil unrest this situation created between the Inland and Coastal Duchies. All of these tasks were rendered more difficult in that, at any time, his decisions could be overridden by the King. Often he was left to cope with a situation not of his creating, armed only with options not of his choosing.

Even less tenable, perhaps, was the position of Queen-in-

*Waiting Kettricken. Her Mountain ways marked her as a for-
eigner in the Six Duchies court. In peaceful times, perhaps she
would have been received with more tolerance. But the court at
Buckkeep seethed with the general unrest of the Six Duchies.
The Red-Ships from the Outislands harried our shoreline as
they had not for generations, destroying far more than they
stole. The first winter of Kettricken's reign as queen-in-waiting
saw also the first winter raiding we had ever experienced. The
constant threat of raids, and the lingering torment of Forged
ones in our midst rocked the foundations of the Six Duchies.
Confidence in the monarchy was low, and Kettricken had the
unenviable position of being an unadmired king-in-waiting's
outlandish queen.*

*Civil unrest divided the court as the Inland Duchies voiced
their resentment at taxes to protect a coastline they did not
share. The Coastal Duchies cried out for warships and soldiers
and an effective way to battle the Raiders that always struck
where we were least prepared. Inland-bred Prince Regal
sought to gather power to himself by courting the Inland Dukes
with gifts and social attentions. King-in-Waiting Verity, convinced that his Skill was no longer sufficient to hold the Raiders at bay, put his attentions to building warships to guard the
Coastal Duchies, with little time for his new queen. Over all,
King Shrewd crouched like a great spider, endeavoring to keep
power spread among himself and his sons, to keep all in balance and the Six Duchies intact.*

⤙⊚⛭

I awakened to someone touching my forehead. With an
annoyed grunt, I turned my head aside from the touch. My
blankets were weltered around me; I fought my way clear of
their restraint and then sat up to see who had dared disturb me.
King Shrewd's fool perched anxiously on a chair beside my
bed. I stared at him wildly, and he drew back from my look.
Uneasiness assailed me.

The Fool should have been back in Buckkeep, with the
King, many miles and days from here. I had never known him
to leave the King's side for more than a few hours or a night's
rest. That he was here boded no good. The Fool was my friend,

as much as his strangeness allowed him to be friends with anyone. But a visit from him always had a purpose, and such purposes were seldom trivial or pleasant. He looked as weary as I had ever seen him. He wore an unfamiliar motley of greens and reds and carried a fool's scepter with a rat's head on it. The gay garments contrasted too strongly with his colorless skin. They made him a translucent candle wreathed in holly. His clothing seemed more substantial than he did. His fine pale hair floated from the confines of his cap like a drowned man's hair in seawater, while the dancing flames of the fireplace shone in his eyes. I rubbed my gritty eyes and pushed some of the hair back from my face. My hair was damp; I'd been sweating in my sleep.

"Hello," I managed. "I didn't expect to see you here." My mouth felt dry, my tongue thick and sour. I'd been sick, I recalled. The details seemed hazy.

"Where else?" He looked at me woefully. "For every hour you've slept, the less rested you seem. Lie back, my lord. Let me make you comfortable." He plucked at my pillows fussily, but I waved him away. Something was wrong here. Never had he spoken me so fair. Friends we were, but the Fool's words to me were always as pithy and sour as half-ripened fruit. If this sudden kindness was a show of pity, I wanted none of it.

I glanced down at my embroidered nightshirt, at the rich bedcovers. Something seemed odd about them. I was too tired and weak to puzzle it out. "What are you doing here?" I asked him.

He took a breath and sighed. "I am tending you. Watching over you while you sleep. I know you think it foolish, but then, I am the Fool. You know then that I must be foolish. Yet you ask me this same thing every time you awake. Let me then propose something wiser. I beg you, my lord, let me send for another healer."

I leaned back against my pillows. They were sweat damp, and smelled sour to me. I knew I could ask the Fool to change them and he would. But I would just sweat anew if he did. It was useless. I clutched at my covers with gnarled fingers. I asked him bluntly, "Why have you come here?"

He took my hand in his and patted it. "My lord, I mistrust this sudden weakness. You seem to take no good from this healer's ministrations. I fear that his knowledge is much smaller than his opinion of it."

"Burrich?" I asked incredulously.

"Burrich? Would that he were here, my lord! He may be the stablemaster, but for all that, I warrant he is more of a healer than this Wallace who doses and sweats you."

"Wallace? Burrich is not here?"

The Fool's face grew graver. "No, my king. He remained in the Mountains, as well you know."

"Your king," I said, and attempted to laugh. "Such mockery."

"Never, my lord," he said gently. "Never."

His tenderness confused me. This was not the Fool I knew, full of twisting words and riddles, of sly jabs and puns and cunning insults. I felt suddenly stretched thin as old rope, and as frayed. Still, I tried to piece things together. "Then I am in Buckkeep?"

He nodded slowly. "Of course you are." Worry pinched his mouth.

I was silent, plumbing the full depth of my betrayal. Somehow I had been returned to Buckkeep. Against my will. Burrich had not even seen fit to accompany me.

"Let me get you some food," the Fool begged me. "You always feel better after you have eaten." He rose. "I brought it up hours ago. I've kept it warm by the hearth."

My eyes followed him wearily. At the big hearth he crouched, to coach a covered tureen away from the edge of the fire. He lifted the lid and I smelled rich beef stew. He began to ladle it into a bowl. It had been months since I'd had beef. In the Mountains, it was all venison and mutton and goat's flesh. My eyes wandered wearily about the room. The heavy tapestries, the massive wooden chairs. The heavy stones of the fireplace, the richly worked bed hangings. I knew this place. This was the King's bedchamber at Buckkeep. Why was I here, in the King's own bed? I tried to ask the Fool, but another spoke with my lips. "I know too many things, Fool. I can no longer stop myself from knowing them. Sometimes it is as if another

controlled my will, and pushed my mind where I would rather it did not go. My walls are breached. It all pours in like a tide.''
I drew a deep breath, but I could not stave it off. First a chill tingling, then as if I were immersed in a swift flowing of cold water. ''A rising tide,'' I gasped. ''Bearing ships. Red-keeled ships . . .''

The Fool's eyes widened in alarm. ''In this season, Your Majesty? Surely not! Not in winter!''

My breath was pressed tight in my chest. I struggled to speak. ''The winter has crept in too softly. She has spared us both her storms and her protection. Look. Look out there, across the water. See? They come. They come from the fog.''

I lifted my arm to point. The Fool came hastily, to stand beside me. He crouched to peer where I pointed, but I knew he could not see. Still, he loyally placed a hesitant hand on my thin shoulder, and stared as if he could will away the walls and the miles that stood between him and my vision. I longed to be as blind as he. I clasped the long-fingered pale hand that rested on my shoulder. For a moment I looked down at my withered hand, at the royal signet ring that clung to a bony finger behind a swollen knuckle. Then my reluctant gaze was drawn up and my vision taken afar.

My pointing hand indicated the quiet harbor. I struggled to sit up taller, to see more. The darkened town spread out before me like a patchwork of houses and roads. Fog lay in hollows and was thick upon the bay. Weather change coming, I thought to myself. Something stirred in the air that chilled me, cooling the old sweat on my skin so that I shivered. Despite the blackness of the night and the fog, I had no difficulty in seeing everything perfectly. Skill watching I told myself, and then wondered. I could not Skill, not predictably, not usefully.

But as I watched, two ships broke out of the mists and emerged into the sleeping harbor. I forgot what I could or could not do. They were sleek and trim, those ships, and though they were black under the moonlight, I knew their keels were red. Red-Ship Raiders from the Outislands. The ships moved like knives through the wavelets, cutting their way clear of the fog, slicing into the protected water of the harbor like a thin blade slicing into a pig's belly. The oars moved silently, in perfect unison, oarlocks muffled with rags. They came alongside the docks as boldly as honest merchants come to trade. From the first boat, a sailor leaped lightly, carrying a line to make fast to a piling. An oarsman fended her off the dock until the aft line was thrown and made fast as well. All so calmly, so blatantly. The second ship was following their example. The dreaded Red-Ships had come into town, bold as gulls, and tied up at their victims' home dock.

No sentry cried out. No watchman blew a horn, or threw a torch onto a waiting heap of pitchpine to kindle a signal fire. I looked for them, and instantly found them. Heads on chests, they were idling at their posts. Good woolen homespun had gone from gray to red sopping up the blood of their slit throats. Their killers had come quietly, overland, sure of each sentry post, to silence every watcher. No one would warn the sleeping town.

There had not been that many sentries. There was not much to this little town, scarce enough to deserve a dot on the map. The town had counted on the humbleness of its possessions to shelter it from raids such as this. Good wool they grew there, and they spun a fine yarn, it was true. They harvested and smoked the salmon that came right up their river, and the apples here were tiny but sweet, and they made a good wine. There was a fine clam beach to the west of town. These were the riches of Siltbay, and if they were not great, they were enough to make life treasured by those who lived here. Surely, though, they were not worth coming after with a torch and a blade. What sane man would think a keg of apple wine or a rack of smoked salmon worth a raider's time?

But these were Red-Ships, and they did not come to raid for wealth or treasures. They were not after prize breeding cattle or even women for wives or boys for galley slaves. The wool-fat sheep would be mutilated and slaughtered, the smoked salmon trampled underfoot, the warehouses of fleeces and wines torched. They would take hostages, yes, but only to Forge them. The Forge magic would leave them less than human, bereft of all emotions and any but the most basic thoughts. The Raiders would not keep these hostages, but would abandon them here, to work their debilitating anguish upon those who had loved them and called them kin. Stripped of every human sensitivity, Forged ones would scour their homeland as pitilessly as wolverines. This setting of our own kin to prey upon us as Forged ones was the Outislanders' cruelest weapon. This I already knew as I watched. I had seen the aftermath of other raids.

I watched the tide of death rise to inundate the little town. The Outislander pirates leaped from the ship to the docks and flowed up into the village. They trickled silently up the streets in bands of twos and threes, as deadly as poison unfurling in wine. Some few paused to search the other vessels tied to the dock. Most of the boats were small open dories, but there were two larger fishing vessels and one trader. Their crews met swift death. Their frantic struggles were as pathetic as fowl flapping and squawking when a weasel gets into the chicken house. They called out to me with voices full of blood. The thick fog gulped their cries greedily. It made the death of a sailor no more than the keening of a seabird. Afterward, the boats were torched, carelessly, with no thought to their value as spoils. These Raiders took no real booty. Perhaps a handful of coins if easily found, or a necklace from the body of one they had raped and killed, but little more than that.

I could do nothing except watch. I coughed heavily, then found a breath to speak. "If only I could understand them," I said to the Fool. "If only I knew what they wanted. There is no sense to these Red-Ships. How can we fight those who war for a reason they will not divulge? But if I could understand them . . ."

The Fool pursed his pale lips and considered. "They partake of the madness of he who drives them. They can only be understood if you share that madness. I myself have no wish to understand them. Understanding them will not stop them."

"No." I did not want to watch the village. I had seen this nightmare too often. But only a heartless man could have turned away as if it were a poorly staged puppet show. The least I could do for my people was watch them die. It also was the most I could do for them. I was sick and a cripple, an old man far away. No more could be expected from me. So I watched.

I watched the little town awaken from soft sleep to the rough grip of a strange hand on the throat or breast, to a knife over a cradle, or the sudden cry of a child dragged from sleep. Lights began to flicker and glow throughout the village; some were candles kindled on hearing a neighbor's outcry; others were torches or burning houses. Although the Red-Ships had terrorized the Six Duchies for over a year, for this folk it became completely real tonight. They had thought they were prepared. They had heard the horror stories, and resolved never to let it happen to them. But still the houses burned and the screams rose to the night sky as if borne on the smoke.

"Speak, Fool," I commanded hoarsely. "Remember forward for me. What do they say about Siltbay? A raid on Siltbay, in winter."

He took a shuddering breath. "It is not easy, nor clear," he hesitated. "All wavers, all is change still. Too much is in flux, Your Majesty. The future spills out in all directions there."

"Speak any you can see," I commanded.

"They made a song about this town," the Fool observed hollowly. He gripped my shoulder still; through my nightshirt, the clutch of his long, strong fingers was cold. A trembling passed between us and I felt how he labored to continue standing beside me. "When it is sung in a tavern, with the refrain hammered out to the beat of ale mugs upon a table, none of this seems so bad. One can imagine the brave stand these folk made, going down fighting rather than surrendering. Not one, not one single person, was taken alive and Forged. Not one." The Fool paused. A hysterical note mingled with the levity he forced into his voice. "Of course, when you're drinking and singing, you don't see the blood. Or smell the burning flesh. Or hear the screams. But that's understandable. Have you ever tried to find a rhyme for 'dismembered child'? Someone once tried 'remembered wild' but the verse still didn't quite scan." There is no merriment in his banter. His bitter jests can shield neither him nor me. He falls silent once more, my prisoner doomed to share his painful knowledge with me.

I witness in silence. No verse would tell of a parent pushing a poison pellet into a child's mouth to keep him from the

Raiders. No one could sing of children crying out with the cramps of the swift, harsh poison, or the women who were raped as they lay dying. No rhyme nor melody could bear the weight of telling of archers whose truest arrows slew captured kinfolk before they could be dragged away. I peered into the interior of a burning house. Through the flames, I watched a ten-year-old boy bare his throat for the slash of his mother's knife. He held the body of his baby sister, strangled already, for the Red-Ships had come, and no loving brother would give her to either the Raiders or the voracious flames. I saw the mother's eyes as she lifted her children's bodies and carried them into the flames with her. Such things are better not remembered. But I was not spared the knowledge. It was my duty to know these things, and to recall them.

Not all died. Some fled into the surrounding fields and forests. I saw one young man take four children under the docks with him, to cling in the chill water to the barnacled pilings until the Raiders left. Others tried to flee and were slain as they ran. I saw a woman in a nightgown slip from a house. Flames were already running up the side of the building. She carried one child in her arms and another clung to her skirts and followed her. Even in the darkness, the light from the burning huts woke burnished highlights in her hair. She glanced about fearfully, but the long knife she carried in her free hand was up and at the ready. I caught a glimpse of a small mouth set grimly, eyes narrowed fiercely. Then, for an instant, I saw that proud profile limned against firelight. "Molly!" I gasped. I reached a clawed hand to her. She lifted a door and shooed the children down into a root cellar behind the blazing home. She lowered the door silently over them all. Safe?

No. They came around the corner, two of them. One carried an ax. They were walking slowly, swaggering and laughing aloud. The soot that smeared their faces made their teeth and the whites of their eyes stand out. One was a woman. She was very beautiful, laughing as she strode. Fearless. Her hair was braided back with silver wire. The flames winked red in it. The Raiders advanced to the door of the root cellar, and the one swung his ax in a great arcing blow. The ax bit deep into the wood. I heard the terrified cry of a child. "Molly!" I shrieked.

I scrabbled from my bed, but had no strength to stand. I crawled toward her.

The door gave way, and the Raiders laughed. One died laughing as Molly came leaping through the shattered remnants of the door to put her long knife into his throat. But the beautiful woman with the shining silver in her hair had a sword. And as Molly struggled to pull her knife clear of the dying man, that sword was falling, falling, falling.

At that instant something gave way in the burning house with a sharp crack. The structure swayed and then fell in a shower of sparks and an upburst of roaring flames. A curtain of fire soared up between me and the root cellar. I could see nothing through that inferno. Had it fallen across the door of the root cellar and the Raiders attacking it? I could not see. I lunged forth, reaching out for Molly.

But in an instant, all was gone. There was no burning house, no pillaged town, no violated harbor, no Red-Ships. Only myself, crouching by the hearth. I had thrust my hand into the fire and my fingers clutched a coal. The Fool cried out and seized my wrist to pull my hand from the fire. I shook him off, then looked at my blistered fingers dully.

"My king," the Fool said woefully. He knelt beside me, carefully moved the tureen of soup by my knee. He moistened a napkin in the wine he had poured for my meal, and folded it over my fingers. I let him. I could not feel the burned skin for the great wound inside me. His worried eyes stared into mine. I could scarcely see him. He seemed an insubstantial thing, with the faltering flames of the fireplace showing in his colorless eyes. A shadow like all the other shadows that came to torment me.

My burned fingers throbbed suddenly. I clutched them in my other hand. What had I been doing, what had I been thinking? The Skill had come on me like a fit, and then departed, leaving me as drained as an empty glass. Weariness flowed in to fill me, and pain rode it like a horse. I struggled to retain what I had seen. "What woman was that? Is she important?"

"Ah." The Fool seemed even wearier, but struggled to gather himself. "A woman at Siltbay?" He paused as if racking his brains. "No. I have nothing. It is all a muddle, my king. So hard to know."

"Molly has no children," I told him. "It could not have been her."

"Molly?"

"Her name is Molly?" I demanded. My head throbbed. Anger suddenly possessed me. "Why do you torment me like this?"

"My lord, I know of no Molly. Come. Come back to your bed, and I will bring you some food."

He helped me to my feet and I tolerated his touch. I found my voice. I floated, the focus of my eyes coming and going. One moment I could feel his hand on my arm, the next it seemed as if I dreamed the room and the men who spoke there. I managed to speak. "I have to know if that was Molly. I have to know if she is dying. Fool, I have to know."

The Fool sighed heavily. "It is not a thing I can command, my king. You know that. Like your visions, mine rule me, not the reverse. I cannot pluck a thread from the tapestry, but must look where my eyes are pointed. The future, my king, is like a current in a channel. I cannot tell you where one drop of water goes, but I can tell you where the flow is strongest."

"A woman at Siltbay," I insisted. Part of me pitied my poor fool, but another part insisted. "I would not have seen her so clearly if she were not important. Try. Who was she?"

"She is significant?"

"Yes. I am sure of it. Oh, yes."

The Fool sat cross-legged on the floor. He put his long thin fingers to his temples and pressed as if trying to open a door. "I know not. I don't understand. . . . All is a muddle, all is a crossroads. The tracks are trampled, the scents gone awry. . . ." He looked up at me. Somehow I had stood, but he sat on the floor at my feet, looking up at me. His pale eyes goggled in his eggshell face. He swayed from the strain, smiled foolishly. He considered his rat scepter, went nose to nose with it. "Did you know any such Molly, Ratsy? No? I didn't think you would. Perhaps he should ask someone more in a position to know. The worms, perhaps." A silly giggling seized him. Useless creature. Silly riddling soothsayer. Well, he could not help what he was. I left him and walked slowly back to my bed. I sat on the edge of it.

I found I was shaking as if with an ague. A seizure, I told myself. I must calm myself or risk a seizure. Did I want the Fool to see me twitching and gasping? I didn't care. Nothing mattered, except finding out if that was my Molly, and if so, had she perished? I had to know. I had to know if she had died, and if she had died, how she had died. Never had the knowing of something been so essential to me.

The Fool crouched on the rug like a pale toad. He wet his lips and smiled at me. Pain sometimes can wring such a smile from a man. "It's a very glad song,' the one they sing about Siltbay," he observed. "A triumphant song. The villagers won, you see. Didn't win life for themselves, no, but clean death. Well, death anyway. Death, not Forging. At least that's something. Something to make a song about and hold on to these days. That's how it is in Six Duchies now. We kill our own so the Raiders can't, and then we make victory songs about it. Amazing what folk will take comfort in when there's nothing else to hold on to."

My vision softened. I knew suddenly that I dreamed. "I'm not even here," I said faintly. "This is a dream. I dream that I am King Shrewd."

He held his pale hand up to the firelight, considered the bones limned so plainly in the thin flesh. "If you say so, my liege, it must be so. I, too, then, dream you are King Shrewd. If I pinch you, perhaps, shall I awaken myself?"

I looked down at my hands. They were old and scarred. I closed them, watched veins and tendons bulge beneath the papery surface, felt the sandy resistance of my own swollen knuckles. I'm an old man now, I thought to myself. This is what it really feels like to be old. Not sick, where one might get better. Old. When each day can only be more difficult, each month is another burden to the body. Everything was slipping sideways. I had thought, briefly, that I was fifteen. From somewhere came the scent of scorching flesh and burning hair. No, rich beef stew. No, Jonqui's healing incense. The mingling scents made me nauseous. I had lost track of who I was, of what was important. I scrabbled at the slippery logic, trying to surmount it. It was hopeless. "I don't know," I whispered. "I don't understand any of this."

"Ah," said the Fool. "As I told you. You can only understand a thing when you become it."

"Is this what it means to be King Shrewd, then?" I demanded. It shook me to my core. I had never seen him like this, racked by the pains of age but still relentlessly confronted by the pains of his subjects. "Is this what he must endure, day after day?"

"I fear it is, my liege," the Fool replied gently. "Come. Let me help you back into your bed. Surely, tomorrow you will feel better."

"No. We both know I will not." I did not speak those terrible words. They came from King Shrewd's lips, and I heard them, and knew that this was the debilitating truth King Shrewd bore every day. I was so terribly tired. Every part of me ached. I had not known that flesh could be so heavy, that the mere bending of a finger could demand a painful effort. I wanted to rest. To sleep again. Was it I, or Shrewd? I should let the Fool put me to bed, let my king have his rest. But the Fool kept holding that one key morsel of information just above my snapping jaws. He juggled away the one mote of knowledge I must possess to be whole.

"Did she die there?" I demanded.

He looked at me sadly. He stooped abruptly, picked up his rat scepter again. A tiny pearl of a tear trickled down Ratsy's cheek. He focused on it and his eyes went afar again, wandering across a tundra of pain. He spoke in a whisper. "A woman in Siltbay. A drop of water in the current of all the women of Siltbay. What might have befallen her? Did she die? Yes. No. Badly burned, but alive. Her arm severed at the shoulder. Cornered and raped while they killed her children, but left alive. Sort of." The Fool's eyes became even emptier. It was as if he read aloud from a roster. His voice had no inflection. "Roasted alive with the children when the burning structure fell on them. Took poison as soon as her husband awoke her. Choked to death on smoke. And died of an infection in a sword wound only a few days later. Died of a sword thrust. Strangled on her own blood as she was raped. Cut her own throat after she had killed the children while Raiders were hacking her door down. Survived, and gave birth to a Raider's child the next summer. Was found wandering days later, badly burned, but recalling nothing. Had her face burned and her hands hacked off, but lived a short—''

"Stop!" I commanded him. "Stop it! I beg you, stop."

He paused and drew a breath. His eyes came back to me, focused on me. "Stop it?" He sighed. He put his face into his hands, spoke through muffling fingers. "Stop it? So shrieked the women of Siltbay. But it is done already, my liege. We cannot stop what's already happening. Once it's come to pass, it's too late." He lifted his face from his hands. He looked very weary.

"Please," I begged him. "Cannot you tell me of the one woman I saw?" I suddenly could not recall her name, only that she was very important to me.

He shook his head, and the small silver bells on his cap jingled wearily. "The only way to find out would be to go there." He looked up at me. "If you command it, I shall do so."

"Summon Verity," I told him instead. "I have instructions for him."

"Our soldiers cannot arrive in time to stop this raid," he reminded me. "Only to help to douse the fires and assist the folk there in picking from the ruins what is left to them."

"Then so they shall do," I said heavily.

"First, let me help you return to your bed, my king. Before you take a chill. And let me bring you food."

"No, Fool," I told him sadly. "Shall I eat and be warm, while the bodies of children are cooling in the mud? Fetch me instead my robe and buskins. And then be off to find Verity."

The Fool stood his ground boldly. "Do you think the discomfort you inflict on yourself will give even one child another breath, my liege? What happened at Siltbay is done. Why must you suffer?"

"Why must I suffer?" I found a smile for the Fool. "Surely that is the same question that every inhabitant of Siltbay asked tonight of the fog. I suffer, my fool, because they did. Because I am king. But more, because I am a man, and I

saw what happened there. Consider it, Fool. What if every man
in the Six Duchies said to himself, 'Well, the worst that can
befall them has already happened. Why should I give up my
meal and warm bed to concern myself with it?' Fool, by the
blood that is in me, these are my folk. Do I suffer more tonight
than any one of them did? What is the pain and trembling of
one man compared with what happened at Siltbay? Why
should I shelter myself while my folk are slaughtered like
cattle?"

"But two words are all I need say to Prince Verity." The
Fool vexed me with more words. " 'Raiders' and 'Siltbay,' and
he knows as much as any man needs to. Let me rest you in your
bed, my lord, and then I shall race to him with those words."

"No." A fresh cloud of pain blossomed in the back of my
skull. It tried to push the sense from my thoughts, but I held
firm. I forced my body to walk to the chair beside the hearth. I
managed to lower myself into it. "I spent my youth defining
the borders of the Six Duchies to any who challenged them.
Should my life be too valuable to risk now, when there is so
little left of it, and all of that riddled with pain? No, Fool. Fetch
my son to me at once. He shall Skill for me, since my own
strength for it is at an end this night. Together, we shall consider what we see, and make our decisions as to what must be
done. Now go. GO!"

The Fool's feet pattered on the stone floor as he fled.

I was left alone with myself. Myselves. I put my hands to
my temples. I felt a painful smile crease my face as I found
myself. *So, boy. There you are.* My king slowly turned his
attention to me. He was weary, but he reached his Skill toward
me to touch my mind as softly as blowing spiderweb. I reached
clumsily, attempting to complete the Skill bond and it all went
awry. Our contact tattered, fraying apart like rotten cloth. And
then he was gone.

I hunkered alone on the floor of my bedchamber in the
Mountain Kingdom, uncomfortably close to the hearth fire. I
was fifteen, and my nightclothes were soft and clean. The fire
in the hearth had burned low. My blistered fingers throbbed
angrily. The beginnings of a Skill headache pulsed in my temples.

I moved slowly, cautiously as I rose. Like an old man? No. Like a young man whose health was still mending. I knew the difference now.

My soft, clean bed beckoned, like a soft clean tomorrow.

I refused them both. I took the chair by the hearth and stared into the flames, pondering.

When Burrich came at first light to bid me farewell, I was ready to ride with him.

2

The Homecoming

BUCKKEEP HOLD OVERLOOKS the finest deep-water harbor in the Six Duchies. To the north, the Buck River spills into the sea, and with its waters carries most of the goods exported from the interior Duchies of Tilth and Farrow. Steep black cliffs provide the seat for the castle, which overlooks the river mouth, the harbor, and the waters beyond. The town of Buckkeep clings precariously to those cliffs, well away from the great river's floodplain, with a good portion of it built on docks and quays. The original stronghold was a log structure built by the original inhabitants of the area as a defense against Outislander raids. It was seized in ancient time, by a raider named Taker, who with the seizing of the fort became a resident. He replaced the timber structure with walls and towers of black stone quarried from the cliffs themselves, and in the process sank the foundations of Buckkeep deep into the stone. With each succeeding generation of the Farseer line, the walls were fortified and the towers built taller and stouter. Since Taker, the founder of the Farseer line, Buckkeep has never fallen to enemy hands.

❧━═━❧

Snow kissed my face, wind pushed the hair back from my forehead. I stirred from a dark dream to a darker one, to a

winterscape in forestland. I was cold, save where the rising
heat of my toiling horse warmed me. Beneath me, Sooty was
plodding stolidly along through wind-banked snow. I thought I
had been riding long. Hands the stable boy was riding before
me. He turned in his saddle and shouted something back to me.

Sooty stopped, not abruptly, but I was not expecting it, and
I nearly slid from the saddle. I caught at her mane and steadied
myself. Steadily falling flakes veiled the forest around us. The
spruce trees were heavy with accumulated snow, while the
interspersed birches were bare black silhouettes in the clouded
winter moonlight. There was no sign of a trail. The woods were
thick around us. Hands had reined in his black gelding in front
of us, and that was why Sooty halted. Behind me Burrich sat
his roan mare with the practiced ease of the lifelong horseman.

I was cold, and shaky with weakness. I looked around
dully, wondering why we had stopped. The wind gusted
sharply, snapping my damp cloak against Sooty's flank. Hands
pointed suddenly. "There!" He looked back at me. "Surely
you saw that?"

I leaned forward to peer through snow that fell like fluttering lace curtains. "I think so," I said, the wind and falling
snow swallowing my words. For an instant I had glimpsed tiny
lights. They had been yellow and stationary, unlike the pale
blue will o' the wisps that still occasionally plagued my vision.

"Do you think it's Buckkeep?" Hands shouted through
the rising wind.

"It is," Burrich asserted quietly, his deep voice carrying
effortlessly. "I know where we are now. This is where Prince
Verity killed that big doe about six years ago. I remember
because she leaped when the arrow went in, and tumbled down
that gully. It took us the rest of the day to get down there and
pack the meat out."

The gully he gestured to was no more than a line of brush
glimpsed through the falling snow. But suddenly it all snapped
into place for me. The lay of this hillside, the types of trees, the
gully there, and so Buckkeep was that way, just a brief ride
before we could clearly see the fortress on the sea cliffs overlooking the bay and Buckkeep Town below. For the first time in
days, I knew with absolute certainty where we were. The heavy

overcast had kept us from checking our course by the stars, and the unusually deep snowfall had altered the lay of the land until even Burrich had seemed unsure. But now I knew that home was but a brief ride away. In summer. But I picked up what was left of my determination.

"Not much farther," I told Burrich.

Hands had already started his horse. The stocky little gelding surged ahead bravely, breaking trail through the banked snow. I nudged Sooty and the tall mare reluctantly stepped out. As she leaned into the hill I slid to one side. As I scrabbled futilely at my saddle Burrich nudged his horse abreast of mine. He reached out, seized me by the back of my collar, and dragged me upright again. "It's not much farther," he agreed. "You'll make it."

I managed a nod. It was only the second time he'd had to steady me in the last hour or so. One of my better evenings, I told myself bitterly. I pulled myself up straighter in the saddle, resolutely squared my shoulders. Nearly home.

The journey had been long and arduous. The weather had been foul, and the constant hardships had not improved my health. Much of it I remembered like a dark dream; days of jolting along in the saddle, barely cognizant of our path, nights when I lay between Hands and Burrich in our small tent and trembled with a weariness so great I could not even sleep. As we had drawn closer to Buck Duchy I had thought our travel would become easier. I had not reckoned on Burrich's caution.

At Turlake, we had stopped a night at an inn. I had thought that we'd take passage on a river barge the next day, for though ice might line the banks of the Buck River, its strong current kept a channel clear year-round. I went straight to our room, for I had not much stamina. Burrich and Hands were both anticipating hot food and companionship, to say nothing of ale. I had not expected them to come soon to the room. But scarcely two hours had passed before they both came up to ready themselves for bed.

Burrich was grim and silent, but after he had gone to bed, Hands whispered to me from his bed how poorly the King was spoken of in this town. "Had they known we were from Buckkeep, I doubt they would have spoken so freely. But clad as we are in Mountain garments, they thought us traders or merchants. A dozen times I thought Burrich would challenge one of them. In truth, I do not know how he contained himself. All complain about the taxes for defending the coast. They sneer, saying that for all the taxes they bleed, the Raiders still came unlooked for in autumn, when the weather lasted fine, and burned two more towns.'' Hands had paused, and uncertainly added, ''But they speak uncommonly well of Prince Regal. He passed through here escorting Kettricken back to Buckkeep. One man at the table called her a great white fish of a wife, fit for the coast King. And another spoke up, saying that at least Prince Regal bore himself well despite his hardships, and looked ever as a Prince should. Then they drank to the Prince's health and long life.''

A cold settled in me. I whispered back, ''The two Forged villages. Did you hear what ones they were?''

''Whalejaw up in Bearns. And Siltbay in Buck itself.''

The darkness settled darker around me, and I lay watching it all night.

The next morning we left Turlake. On horseback. Overland. Burrich would not even let us keep to the road. I had protested in vain. He listened to me complain, then took me aside, to fiercely demand, ''Do you want to die?''

I looked at him blankly. He snorted in disgust.

''Fitz, nothing has changed. You're still a royal bastard, and Prince Regal still regards you as an obstacle. He's tried to be rid of you, not once, but twice. Do you think he's going to welcome you back to Buckkeep? No. Even better for him if we never make it back at all. So let's not make easy targets of ourselves. We go overland. If he or his hirelings want us, they'll have to hunt us through the woods. And he's never been much of a hunter.''

''Wouldn't Verity protect us?'' I asked weakly.

''You're a King's Man, and Verity is king-in-waiting,'' Burrich had pointed out shortly. ''You protect your king, Fitz. Not the reverse. Not that he doesn't think well of you, and would do all he could to protect you. But he has weightier matters to attend. Red-Ships. A new bride. And a younger brother who thinks the crown would sit better on his own head.

No. Don't expect the King-in-Waiting to watch over you. Do that for yourself.''

All I could think of was the extra days he was putting between me and my search for Molly. But I did not give that reason. I had not told him of my dream. Instead, I said, ''Regal would have to be crazy to try to kill us again. Everyone would know he was the murderer.''

''Not crazy, Fitz. Just ruthless. Regal is that. Let's not ever suppose that Regal abides by the rules we observe, or even thinks as we do. If Regal sees an opportunity to kill us, he'll take it. He won't care who suspects so long as no one can prove it. Verity is our king-in-waiting. Not our king. Not yet. While King Shrewd is alive and on the throne, Regal will find ways around his father. He will get away with many things. Even murder.''

Burrich had reined his horse aside from the well-traveled road, plunged off through drifts and up the unmarked snowy hillside beyond, to strike a straight course for Buckkeep. Hands had looked at me as if he felt ill. But we had followed. And every night when we had slept, bundled all together in a single tent for warmth instead of in beds in a cozy inn, I had thought of Regal. Every floundering step up each hillside, leading our horses more often than not, and every cautious descent, I had thought of the youngest Prince. I tallied every extra hour between Molly and me. The only times I felt strength surge through me were during my daydreams of battering Regal into ruin. I could not promise myself revenge. Revenge was the property of the crown. But if I could not have revenge, Regal would not have satisfaction. I would return to Buckkeep, and I would stand tall before him, and when his black eye fell upon me, I would not flinch. Nor, I vowed, would Regal ever see me tremble, or catch at a wall for support, or pass a hand before my blurry eyes. He would never know how close he had come to winning it all.

So at last we rode to Buckkeep, not up the winding sea-coast road, but from the forested hills behind her. The snow dwindled, then ceased. The night winds blew the clouds aside, and a fine moon made Buckkeep's stone walls shine black as jet against the sea. Light shone yellow in her turrets and beside the side gate. "We're home," Burrich said quietly. We rode down one last hill, struck the road at last, and rode around to the great gate of Buckkeep.

A young soldier stood night guard. He lowered his pike to block our way and demanded our names.

Burrich pushed his hood back from his face, but the lad didn't move. "I'm Burrich, the stablemaster!" Burrich informed him incredulously. "The stablemaster here for longer than you've been alive, most likely. I feel I should be asking you what your business is here at my gate!"

Before the flustered lad could reply, there was a tumble and rush of soldiers from the guardhouse. "It *is* Burrich!" the watch sergeant exclaimed. Burrich was instantly the center of a cluster of men, all shouting greetings and talking at once while Hands and I sat our weary horses at the edge of the hubbub. The sergeant, one Blade, finally shouted them to silence, mostly so he could speak his own comments easily. "We hadn't looked for you until spring, man," the burly old soldier declared. "And even then, we was told you might not be the man that left here. But you look good, you do. A bit cold, and outlandishly dressed, and another scar or two, but yourself for all that. Word was that you was hurt bad, and the Bastard like to die. Plague or poison, the rumors was."

Burrich laughed and held out his arms that all might admire his Mountain garb. For a moment I saw Burrich as they must have seen him, his purple-and-yellow quilted trousers and smock and buskins. I no longer wondered at how we had been challenged at the gate. But I did wonder at the rumors.

"Who said the Bastard would die?" I demanded curiously.

"Who's asking?" Blade demanded in return. He glanced over my garments, looked me in the eye, and knew me not. But as I sat up straighter on my horse, he gave a start. To this day, I believe he knew Sooty and that was how he recognized me. He did not cover his shock.

"Fitz? There's hardly half of you left! You look like you've had the Blood Plague." It was my first inkling of just how bad I looked to those who knew me.

"Who said I had been poisoned, or afflicted with plague?" I repeated the question quietly.

Blade flinched and glanced back over his shoulder. "Oh, no one. Well, no one in particular. You know how it is. When you didn't come back with the others, well, some supposed this and some that, and pretty soon it was almost like we knew it. Rumors, guardroom talk. Soldiers gossip. We wondered why you didn't come back, that was all. No one believed anything that was said. We spread too many rumors ourselves to give gossip any credence. We just wondered why you and Burrich and Hands hadn't come back."

He finally realized he was repeating himself and fell silent before my stare. I let the silence stretch long enough to make it plain that I didn't intend to answer this question. Then I shrugged it away. "No harm done, Blade. But you can tell them all the Bastard isn't done for yet. Plagues or poisons, you should have known Burrich would physick me through it. I'm alive and well; I just look like a corpse."

"Oh, Fitz, lad, I didn't mean it that way. It's just that—"

"I said, no harm done, Blade. Let it go."

"Good enough, sir," he replied.

I nodded, and looked at Burrich to find him regarding me strangely. When I turned to exchange a puzzled glance with Hands, I met the same startlement on his face. I could not guess the reason.

"Well, good night to you, Sergeant. Don't chide your man with the pike. He did well to stop strangers at Buckkeep's gate."

"Yes, sir. Good night, sir." Blade gave me a rusty salute and the great wooden gates swung wide before us as we entered the keep. Sooty lifted her head and some of the weariness fell from her. Behind me, Hands's horse whinnied softly and Burrich's snorted. Never before had the road from the keep wall to the stables seemed so long. As Hands dismounted, Burrich caught me by the sleeve and held me back. Hands greeted the drowsy stable boy who appeared to light our way.

"We've been some time in the Mountain Kingdom, Fitz," Burrich cautioned me in a low voice. "Up there, no one cares what side of the sheets you were born on. But we're home now. Here, Chivalry's son is not a Prince, but a bastard."

"I know that." I was stung by his directness. "I've known it all my life. Lived it all my life."

"You have," he conceded. A strange look stole over his face, a smile half-incredulous and half-proud. "So why are you demanding reports of the sergeant, and giving out commendations as briskly as if you were Chivalry himself? I scarce believed it, how you spoke, and how those men came to heel. You didn't even take notice of how they responded to you, you didn't even realize you'd stepped up and taken command away from me."

I felt a slow flush creep up my face. All in the Mountain Kingdom had treated me as if I were a Prince in fact, instead of a Prince's bastard. Had I so quickly accustomed myself to that higher station?

Burrich chuckled at my expression, then quickly grew sober. "Fitz, you need to find your caution again. Keep your eyes down and don't carry your head like a young stallion. Regal will take it as a challenge, and that's something we aren't ready to face. Not yet. Maybe not ever."

I nodded grimly, my eyes on the churned snow of the stable yard. I had become careless. When I reported to Chade, the old assassin would not be pleased with his apprentice. I would have to answer for it. I had no doubt that he would know all about the incident at the gate before he next summoned me.

"Don't be a sluggard. Get down, boy." Burrich interrupted my musings abruptly. I jumped to his tone and realized that he, too, was having to readjust to our comparative positions at Buckkeep. How many years had I been his stable boy and ward? Best that we resume those roles as closely as possible. It would save kitchen gossip. I dismounted and, leading Sooty, followed Burrich into his stables.

Inside it was warm and close. The blackness and cold of the winter night were shut outside the thick stone walls. Here was home, the lanterns shone yellow and the stalled horses breathed slow and deep. But as Burrich passed, the stables came to life. Not a horse or a dog in the whole place didn't catch his scent and rouse to give greeting. The stablemaster was home, and he was greeted warmly by those who knew him best. Two stable boys soon trailed after us, rattling off simultaneously every bit of news concerning hawk or hound or horse. Burrich was in full command here, nodding sagely and asking a terse question or two as he absorbed every detail. His reserve only broke when his old bitch hound Vixen came walking stiff to greet him. He went down on one knee to hug and thump her and she wiggled puppyishly and tried to lick his face. "Now, here's a real dog," he greeted her. Then he stood again, to continue his round. She followed him, hindquarters wobbling with every wag of her tail.

I lagged behind, the warmth robbing the strength from my limbs. One boy came hurrying back to leave a lamp with me, and then hastened away to pay court to Burrich. I came to Sooty's stall and unlatched the door. She entered eagerly, snorting her appreciation. I set my light on its shelf and looked about me. Home. This was home, more than my chamber up in the castle, more than anywhere else in the world. A stall in Burrich's stable, safe in his domain, one of his creatures. If only I could turn back the days, and burrow into the deep straw and drag a horse blanket over my head.

Sooty snorted again, this time rebukingly. She'd carried me all those days and ways, and deserved every comfort I could give her. But every buckle resisted my numbed and weary fingers. I dragged the saddle down from her back and very nearly dropped it. I fumbled at her bridle endlessly, the bright metal of the buckles dancing before my eyes. Finally I closed them and let my fingers work alone to take her bridle off. When I opened my eyes, Hands was at my elbow. I nodded at him, and the bridle dropped from my lifeless fingers. He glanced at it, but said nothing. Instead he poured for Sooty the bucket of fresh water he had brought, and shook out oats for her and fetched an armful of sweet hay with much green still to it. I had taken down Sooty's brushes when he reached past me and took them from my feeble grip. "I'll do this," he said quietly.

"Take care of your own horse first," I chided him.

"I already did, Fitz. Look. You can't do a good job on her. Let me do it. You can barely stand up. Go get some rest." He added, almost kindly, "Another time, when we ride, you can do Stoutheart for me."

"Burrich will have my hide off if I leave my animal's care for someone else."

"No, he won't. He wouldn't leave an animal in the care of someone who can barely stand," Burrich observed from outside the stall. "Leave Sooty to Hands, boy. He knows his job. Hands, take charge of things here for a bit. When you've done with Sooty, check on that one spotted mare at the south end of the stables. I don't know who owns her or where she came from, but she looks sick. If you find it so, have the boys move her away from the other horses and scrub out the stall with vinegar. I'll be back in a bit after I see FitzChivalry to his quarters. I'll bring you food, and we'll eat in my room. Oh. Tell a boy to start us a fire there. Probably cold as a cave up there."

Hands nodded, already busy with my horse. Sooty's nose was in her oats. Burrich took my arm. "Come along," he said, just as he spoke to a horse. I found myself unwillingly leaning on him as we walked the long row of stalls. At the door he picked up a lantern. The night seemed colder and darker after the warmth of the stables. As we walked up the frozen path to the kitchens, the snow began falling again. My mind went swirling and drifting with the flakes. I wasn't sure where my feet were. "It's all changed, forever, now," I observed to the night. My words whirled away with the snowflakes.

"What has?" Burrich asked cautiously. His tone bespoke his worry that I might be getting feverish again.

"Everything. How you treat me. When you aren't thinking about it. How Hands treats me. Two years ago he and I were friends. Just two boys working in the stables. He'd never have offered to brush down my horse for me. But tonight, he treated me like some sickly weakling . . . not even someone he can insult about it. Like I should just expect him to do things like that for me. The men at the gate didn't even know me. Even you, Burrich. Six months or a year ago, if I took sick, you'd have dragged me up to your loft and dosed me like a hound. And if I'd complained, you'd have had no tolerance for it. Now you walk me up to the kitchen doors and—"

"Stop whining," Burrich said gruffly. "Stop complaining

and stop pitying yourself. If Hands looked like you do, you'd do the same for him." Almost unwillingly he added, "Things change, because time passes. Hands hasn't stopped being your friend. But you are not the same boy who left Buckkeep at harvest time. That Fitz was an errand boy for Verity, and had been my stable boy, but wasn't much more than that. A royal bastard, yes, but that seemed of small importance to any save me. But up at Jhaampe in the Mountain Kingdom, you showed yourself more than that. It doesn't matter if your face is pale, or if you can barely walk after a day in the saddle. You move as Chivalry's son should. That is what shows in your bearing, and what those guards responded to. And Hands." He took a breath and paused to shoulder the heavy kitchen door open. "And I, Eda help us all," he added in a mutter.

But then, as if to belie his own words, he steered me into the watch room off the kitchen and unceremoniously dumped me at one of the long benches beside the scarred wooden table. The watch room smelled incredibly good. Here was where any soldier, no matter how muddy or snowy or drunk, could come and find comfort. Cook always kept a kettle of stew simmering over the fire here, and bread and cheese waited on the table, as well as a slab of yellow summer butter from the deep larder. Burrich served us up bowls of hot stew thick with barley and mugs of cold ale to go with the bread and butter and cheese.

For a moment I just looked at it, too weary to lift a spoon. But the smell tempted me to one mouthful and that was all it took. Midway through, I paused to shoulder out of my quilted smock and break off another slab of bread. I looked up from my second bowl of stew to find Burrich watching me with amusement. "Better?" he asked.

I stopped to think about it. "Yes." I was warm, fed, and though I was tired, it was a good weariness, one that might be cured by simple sleep. I lifted my hand and looked at it. I could still feel the tremors, but they were no longer obvious to the eye. "Much better." I stood, and found my legs steady under me.

"Now you're fit to report to the King."

I stared at him in disbelief. "Now? Tonight? King Shrewd's long abed. I won't get past his door guard."

"Perhaps not, and you should be grateful for that. But you must at least announce yourself there tonight. It's the King's decision as to when he will see you. If you're turned away, then you can go to bed. But I'll wager that if King Shrewd turns you aside, King-in-Waiting Verity will still want a report. And probably right away."

"Are you going back to the stables?"

"Of course." He smiled in wolfish self-satisfaction. "Me, I'm just the stablemaster, Fitz. I have nothing to report. And I promised Hands I'd bring him something to eat."

I watched silently as he loaded a platter. He sliced the bread lengthwise and covered two bowls of the hot stew with a slab of it, and then loaded a wedge of cheese and a thick slice of yellow butter onto the side of it.

"What do you think of Hands?"

"He's a good lad," Burrich said grudgingly.

"He's more than that. You chose him to stay in the Mountain Kingdom and ride home with us, when you sent all the others back with the main caravan."

"I needed someone steady. At that time you were . . . very ill. And I wasn't much better, truth to tell." He lifted a hand to a streak of white in his dark hair, testimony to the blow that had nearly killed him.

"How did you come to choose him?"

"I didn't, really. He came to me. Somehow he found where they'd housed us, and then talked his way past Jonqui. I was still bandaged up and scarce able to make my eyes focus. I felt him standing there more than saw him. I asked him what he wanted, and he told me that I needed to put someone in charge, because with me sick and Cob gone, the stable help were getting sloppy."

"And that impressed you."

"He got to the point. No idle questions about me, or you, or what was going on. He had found the thing he could do and come to do it. I like that in a man. Knowing what he can do, and doing it. So I put him in charge. He managed it well. I kept him when I sent the others home because I knew I might need a man who could do that. And also to see for myself what he was. Was he all ambition, or was there a genuine understanding of what a man owes a beast when he claims to own him? Did he want power over those under him, or the well-being of his animals?''

"What do you think of him now?"

"I am not so young as I once was. I think there still may be a good stablemaster in Buckkeep stables when I can no longer manage an ill-tempered stallion. Not that I expect to step down soon. There is still much he needs to be taught. But we are both still young enough, him to learn and me to teach. There is a satisfaction in that."

I nodded. Once, I supposed, he had planned that spot for me. Now we both knew it would never be.

He turned to go. "Burrich," I said quietly. He paused. "No one can replace you. Thank you. For all you've done these last few months. I owe you my life. Not just that you saved me from death. But you gave me my life, and who I am. Ever since I was six. Chivalry was my father, I know. But I never met him. You've fathered me day in and day out, over a lot of years. I didn't always appreciate—"

Burrich snorted and opened the door. "Save speeches like that for when one of us is dying. Go report, and then go to bed."

"Yes, sir," I heard myself say, and knew that he smiled even as I did. He shouldered the door open and bore Hands's dinner out to the stables for him. He was home there.

And this, here, was my home. Time I dealt with that. I took a moment to straighten my damp clothing and run a hand through my hair. I cleared our dishes from the table and then folded my wet smock over my arm.

As I made my way from the kitchen to the hall, and then to the Great Hall, I was mystified by what I saw. Did the tapestries glow more brightly than they once had? Had the strewing herbs always smelled so sweet, the carved woodwork by each doorway always gleamed so warmly? Briefly I put it down to my relief at finally being home. But when I paused at the foot of the great stair to take up a candle to light my way up to my chamber, I noticed that the table there was not bespattered with wax, and more, that an embroidered cloth graced it. Kettricken.

There was a Queen at Buckkeep now. I found myself
smiling foolishly. So. This great fortress castle had had a go-
ing-over in my absence. Had Verity bestirred himself and his
folk before her arrival, or had Kettricken herself demanded this
vast scrubbing out? It would be interesting to find out.

As I climbed the great staircase I noticed other things. The
ancient soot marks above each sconce were gone. Not even
the corners of the steps held dust. There were no cobwebs. The
candelabra at each landing were full and bright with candles.
And a rack at each landing held blades, ready for defense. So
this was what it meant to have a Queen in residence. But even
when Shrewd's queen had been alive, I didn't recall that
Buckkeep had looked or smelled so clean or been so brightly
lit.

The guard at King Shrewd's door was a dour-faced veteran I had known since I was six. A silent man, he peered at me
closely, then recognized me. He allowed me a brief smile as he
asked, "Anything critical to report, Fitz?"

"Only that I'm back," I said, and he nodded sagely. He
was used to my coming and going here, often at some very odd
hours, but he was not a man to make assumptions or draw
conclusions, or even speak to those who might. So he stepped
quietly inside the King's chamber, to pass the word to someone
that Fitz was here. In a moment the word came back that the
King would summon me at his convenience, but also that he
was glad I was safe. I stepped quietly away from his door,
making more of his message than if those words had come
from any other man. Shrewd never mouthed polite nothings.

Farther down the same corridor were Verity's chambers.
Here again I was recognized, but when I requested the man let
Verity know I was back and wished to report, he replied only
that Prince Verity was not within his chamber.

"In his tower, then?" I asked, wondering what he would
be watching for at this time of year. Winter storms kept our
coast safe from Raiders for at least these few months of the
year.

A slow smile stole over the guard's face. When he saw my
puzzled glance, it became a grin. "Prince Verity is not in his
chambers just now," he repeated. And then added: "I shall see

that he gets your message as soon as he awakes in the morning.''

For a moment longer I stood, stupid as a post. Then I turned and walked quietly away. I felt a sort of wonder. This, too, was what it meant for there to be a Queen in Buckkeep.

I climbed another two flights of stairs, and went down the hall to my own chamber. It smelled stale, and there was no fire in the hearth. It was cold with disuse, and dusty. No touch of a woman's hand here. It seemed as bare and colorless as a cell. But it was still warmer than a tent in the snow, and the feather bed was as soft and deep as I remembered it. I shed my travel-stained garments as I walked toward it. I fell into it and sleep.

3

Renewing Ties

THE OLDEST REFERENCE *to the Elderlings in the Buckkeep library is a battered scroll. Vague discolorations upon the vellum suggest that it came from a parti-colored beast, one mottled in a way unfamiliar to any of our hunters. The lettering ink is one derived from squid ink and bell root. It has stood the test of time well, much better than the colored inks that originally supplied illustrations and illuminations for the text. These have not only faded and bled, but in many places have drawn the attentions of some mite that has gnawed and stiffened the once-supple parchment, making parts of the scroll too brittle to unroll.*

Unfortunately, the damage was concentrated most at the innermost parts of the scroll, which deal with portions of King Wisdom's quest that were not recorded elsewhere. From these fragmented remains, one can glean that sore need drove him to seek the homeland of the Elderlings. His troubles are familiar ones; ships raided his coastline mercilessly. Tatters hint that he rode off toward the Mountain Kingdom. We don't know why he suspected that way would lead him to the home of the mythical Elderlings. Unfortunately the final stages of his journey and his encounter with the Elderlings seem to have been richly illustrated, for here the parchment is reduced to a lacy web of tantalizing word bits and body parts. We do not know anything of this first encounter. Nor have we even an inkling as to how he induced the Elderlings to become his allies. Many songs, rich in metaphor, tell how the Elderlings descended, like "storms," like "tidal waves," like "vengeance gone gold," and "wrath embodied in flesh of stone" to drive the Raiders away from our shores. Legends also tell that they swore to Wisdom that if ever the Six Duchies had need of their aid, they would rise again to our defense. One may conjecture; many have, and the variety of legends that surround this alliance are proof of that. But King Wisdom's scribe's recounting of the event has been lost to mildew and worms forever.

My chamber had a single tall window that looked out over the sea. In winter a wooden shutter closed out the storm winds, and a tapestry hung over that gave my room an illusion of cozy warmth. So I awakened to darkness, and for a time lay quietly finding myself. Gradually the subtle sounds of the Keep filtered in to me. Morning sounds. Very early-morning sounds. Home, I realized. Buckkeep. And in the next instant, "Molly," I said aloud to the darkness. My body was weary and aching still. But not exhausted. I clambered from my bed into the chill of my room.

I stumbled to my long-disused hearth and kindled a small fire. I needed to bring up more firewood soon. The dancing flames lent the room a fickle yellow light. I took clothing from the chest at the foot of my bed, only to find the garments oddly ill-fitting. My long illness had wasted the muscle from my frame, but I had still somehow managed to grow longer in the legs and arms. Nothing fit. I picked up my shirt from yesterday, but a night in clean bedding had refreshed my nose. I could no longer abide the smell of the travel-stained garment. I dug in my clothes chest again. I found one soft brown shirt that had once been too long in the sleeve for me, and now just fit. I put it on with my green quilted mountain trousers and buskins. I had no doubt that as soon as I encountered the Lady Patience or Mistress Hasty, I would be attacked and the situation remedied. But not, I hoped, before breakfast and a trip into Buckkeep

Town. There were several places there where I might get word of Molly.

I found the castle stirring but not yet fully awake. I ate in the kitchen as I had when a child, finding that there, as always, the bread was freshest and the porridge sweetest. Cook exclaimed to see me, one minute commenting on how much I had grown, and the next lamenting how thin and worn I looked. I surmised that before the day was out, I would be heartily sick of these observations. As traffic in the kitchen increased I fled, carrying off a thick slice of bread well buttered and laden with rose-hip preserves. I headed back toward my room to get a winter cloak.

In every chamber I passed through, I found more and more evidence of Kettricken's presence. A sort of tapestry, woven of different-colored grasses and representing a mountain scene, now graced the wall of the Lesser Hall. There were no flowers to be had this time of year, but in odd places I encountered fat pottery bowls full of pebbles, and these held bare but graceful branches, or dried thistles and cattails. The changes were small but unmistakable.

I found myself in one of the older sections of Buckkeep, and then climbing the dusty steps to Verity's watchtower. It commanded a wide view of our seacoast, and from its tall windows Verity kept his summer vigil for raiding ships. From here he worked the Skill magic that kept the Raiders at bay, or at least gave us some warning of their coming. It was a thin defense at times. He should have had a coterie of underlings trained in the Skill to assist him. But I myself, despite my bastard blood, had never been able to control my random Skill abilities. Galen, our Skill master, had died before he had trained more than a handful in the Skill. There was no one to replace him, and those he had trained lacked a true communion with Verity. So Verity Skilled alone against our enemies. It had aged him before his time. I worried that he would overspend himself upon it, and succumb to the addicting weakness of those who Skilled too much.

By the time I reached the top of the spiraling tower steps, I was winded and my legs ached. I pushed at the door and it gave easily on oiled hinges. From long habit, I stepped quietly as I

entered the room. I had not really expected to find Verity or
anyone else there. The sea storms were our watchmen in winter, guarding our coasts from Raiders. I blinked in the sudden
gray light of morning that was flooding in from the unshuttered
tower windows. Verity was a dark silhouette against a gray
storm sky. He did not turn. "Shut the door," he said quietly.
"The draft up the stairs makes this room as windy as a chimney."

I did so, and then stood shivering in the chill. The wind
brought the scent of the sea with it, and I breathed it in as if it
were life itself. "I had not expected to find you here," I said.

He kept his eyes on the water. "Didn't you? Then why did
you come?" There was amusement in his voice.

It jolted me. "I don't really know. I headed back to my
room. . . ." My voice dwindled away as I tried to recall why I
had come here.

"I Skilled you," he said simply.

I stood silent and thought. "I felt nothing."

"I didn't intend that you should. It is as I told you a long
time ago. The Skill can be a soft whisper in a man's ear. It
doesn't have to be a shout of command."

He slowly turned to face me, and as my eyes adjusted to
the light my heart leaped with joy at the change I saw in the
man. When I had left Buckkeep at harvest time, he had been a
withered shadow, worn thin by the weight of his duties and his
constant watchfulness. His dark hair was still salted with gray,
but there was muscle once more on his stocky frame, and
vitality snapped in his dark eyes. He looked every bit a King.

"Marriage seems to agree with you, my prince," I said
inanely.

That flustered him. "In some ways," he conceded as a
boyish flush rose on his cheeks. He turned back quickly to his
window. "Come and see my ships," he commanded.

It was my turn to be baffled. I stepped to the window
beside him and looked out over the harbor, and then over the
sea itself. "Where?" I asked in bewilderment. He took me by
the shoulders and turned me toward the shipyard. A long barn
of a building of new yellow pine had been erected there. Men
were coming and going from it as smoke rose from chimneys

and forges there. Dark against the snow were several of the immense timbers that had been Kettricken's bride offering to him.

"Sometimes, when I stand up here on a winter morning, I look out to sea and I can almost see the Red-Ships. I know they must come. But sometimes, too, I can see the ships we shall have to meet them. They will not find their prey so helpless this spring, my boy. And by next winter I intend to teach them what it is to be raided." He spoke with a savage satisfaction that would have been frightening, had I not shared it. I felt my grin mirror his as our eyes met.

And then his look changed. "You look terrible," he offered. "As bad as your clothes. Let's go somewhere warmer and find you some mulled wine and something to eat."

"I've eaten," I told him. "And I'm much better than I was a few months ago, thank you."

"Don't be prickly," he admonished me. "And don't tell me what I already know. Nor lie to me. The climb up the stairs has exhausted you, and you're shivering as you stand there."

"You're using the Skill on me," I accused him, and he nodded.

"I've been aware of your approach for some days now. I tried several times to Skill to you, but could not make you aware of me. I was concerned when you left the road, but I understand Burrich's concern. I am pleased that he has looked after you so well; not just in bringing you home safe, but in all that went on at Jhaampe. I am at a loss as to how to reward him. It would have to be subtle. Given who was involved, a public recognition would not do. Have you any suggestions?"

"Your word of thanks would be all he would accept. He would bridle that you thought he needed more. My own feelings are that no object you gave him would be a match for what he did for me. The way to handle him is to tell him to take his pick of the likely two-year-olds, for his horse is growing old. He'd understand that." I considered it carefully. "Yes. You might do that."

"Might I?" Verity asked me dryly. There was an acid edge to the amusement in his voice.

I was suddenly amazed at my own boldness. "I forgot myself, my prince," I said humbly.

A smile curved his lips and his hand fell on my shoulder in a heavy pat. "Well, I asked you, did I not? For a moment I would have sworn it was old Chivalry instructing me in handling my men, rather than my young nephew. Your trip to Jhaampe has quite changed you, boy. Come. I meant what I said about a warmer spot and a glass of something. Kettricken will be wanting to see you later in the day. And Patience, too, I imagine."

My heart sank as he heaped the tasks before me. Buckkeep Town pulled at me like a lodestone. But this was my king-in-waiting. I bowed my head to his will.

We left the tower and I followed him down the stairs, speaking of inconsequential things. He told me to tell Mistress Hasty I needed new clothes; I asked after Leon, his wolfhound. He stopped a lad in the corridor and asked him to bring wine and meat pies to his study. I followed him, not up to his chambers, but to a lower room at once familiar and strange. The last time I had been in it, Fedwren the scribe had been using it to sort and dry herbs and shells and roots for the making of his inks. All signs of that had been cleared from it. A fire burned low in the small hearth. Verity poked this up and added wood as I looked around. There was a large carved oak table and two smaller ones, a variety of chairs, a scroll rack, and a battered shelf littered with miscellaneous objects. Spread out on the table was the beginnings of a map of the Chalced States. The corners of it were weighted with a dagger and three stones. Various scraps of parchment that littered the tabletop were covered with Verity's hand and preliminary sketches with notes scratched across them. The friendly litter that covered the two smaller tables and several of the chairs seemed familiar. After a moment I recognized it as the layer of Verity's possessions that had previously been scattered about his bedchamber. Verity rose from awakening the fire and smiled ruefully at my raised eyebrows. "My queen-in-waiting has small patience with clutter. 'How,' she asked me, 'can you hope to create precise lines in the midst of such disorder?' Her own chamber has the precision of a military encampment. So I hide myself away down here, for I quickly found that in a clean and sparse chamber I could get no work done at all. Besides, it gives me a place for quiet talk, where not all know to seek me.''

He had scarcely finished speaking when the door opened to admit Charim with a tray. I nodded to Verity's serving man, who not only seemed unsurprised to see me, but had added to Verity's request a certain type of spice bread that I had always enjoyed. He moved about the room briefly, making perfunctory tidying motions as he shifted a few books and scrolls to free a chair for me, and then vanished again. Verity was so accustomed to him he scarce seemed to notice him, save for the brief smile they exchanged as Charim left.

''So,'' he said, as soon as the door was fairly shut. ''Let's have a full report. From the time you left Buckkeep.''

This was not a simple recounting of my journey and the events of it. I had been trained by Chade to be a spy as well as an assassin. And since my earliest days Burrich had always demanded that I be able to give a detailed account of anything that went on in the stables in his absence. So as we ate and drank I gave Verity an accounting of all I had seen and done since I had left Buckkeep. This was followed by my summation of what I had concluded from my experiences, and then by what I suspected from what I had learned. By then, Charim had returned with another meal. While we consumed this Verity limited our talk to his warships. He could not conceal his enthusiasm for them. ''Mastfish has come down to supervise the building. I went up to Highdowns myself to fetch him. He claimed to be an old man now. 'The cold would stiffen my bones; I can't build a boat in winter anymore,' that was the word he sent me. So I set the apprentices work, and I myself went to fetch him. He could not refuse me to my face. When he got here, I took him down to the shipyards. And I showed him the heated shed, big enough to house a warship, built so he might work and not be cold. But that was not what convinced him. It was the white oak that Kettricken brought me. When he saw the timber, he could not wait to put a drawknife to it. The grain is straight and true throughout. The planking is well begun already. They will be lovely ships, swan-necked, sinuous as snakes upon the water.'' Enthusiasm spilled from him. I could already imagine the rising and falling of the oars, the bellying of the square masts when they were under way.

Then the dishes and oddments were pushed to one side, and he began to quiz me upon the events in Jhaampe. He forced me to reconsider each separate incident from every possible perspective. By the time he was finished with me, I had relived the entire episode and my anger at my betrayal was fresh and vivid once more.

Verity was not blind to it. He leaned back in his chair to reach for another log. He flipped it onto the fire, sending a shower of sparks up the chimney. "You have questions," he observed. "This time you may ask them." He folded his hands quietly into his lap and waited.

I tried to master my emotions. "Prince Regal, your brother," I began carefully, "is guilty of the highest treason. He arranged the killing of your bride's elder brother, Prince Rurisk. He attempted a plot that would have resulted in your death. His aim was to usurp both your crown and your bride. As little more than a spice, he twice tried to kill me. And Burrich." I paused to breathe, forcing my heart and voice back to calmness.

"You and I both accept those things as true. They would be difficult for us to prove," Verity observed mildly.

"And he relies upon that!" I spat out, and then turned my face aside from Verity until I could master my anger. The very intensity of it frightened me, for I had not allowed myself to feel it until now. Months ago, when I was using all my wits to stay alive, I had pushed it aside to keep my mind clear. There had followed the wasting months of convalescence as I recovered from Regal's botched poisoning attempt. Not even to Burrich had I been able to tell all, for Verity had made it clear that he wished no one to know any more about the situation than could be helped. Now I stood before my prince and trembled with the force of my own anger. My face spasmed suddenly in a violent series of twitches. That dismayed me enough that I was able to force calm upon myself once more.

"Regal relies upon it," I said more quietly. All this while Verity had not budged nor changed expression despite my outburst. He sat gravely at his end of the table, his work-scarred hands composed before him, watching me with dark eyes. I looked down at the tabletop and traced with a fingertip the carved scrollwork on the corner. "He does not admire you, that you keep the laws of the kingdom. He sees it as a weakness, as a way to circumvent justice. He may try to kill you again. Almost certainly, he will make an attempt upon me."

"Then we must be careful, we two, mustn't we?" Verity observed mildly.

I lifted my eyes to look him in the face. "That is all you say to me?" I asked tightly, choking down my outrage.

"FitzChivalry. I am your prince. I am your king-in-waiting. You are sworn to me, as much as to my father. And, if it comes to it, you are sworn to my brother as well." Verity rose suddenly to take a pace around the room. "Justice. There's a thing we shall ever thirst after, and ever be parched. No. We content ourselves with law. And this is only more true, the higher a man's rank rises. Justice would put you next in line for the throne, Fitz. Chivalry was my elder brother. But law says you were born outside of wedlock, and hence can never make any claim to the crown. Some might say I had snatched the throne from my brother's son. Should I be shocked that my younger brother should want to grab it from me?"

I had never heard Verity speak like this, his voice so even but so fraught with emotion. I kept silent.

"You think I should punish him. I could. I need not prove his wrongdoing to make life unpleasant for him. I could send him as emissary to Cold Bay, on some contrived errand, and keep him there, in uncomfortable conditions, far from court. I could all but banish him. Or I could keep him here at court, but so load him with unpleasant duties that he has no time for that which amuses him. He would understand he was being punished. So would every noble with half a wit. Those who sympathize with him would rally to his defense. The Inland Duchies could contrive some emergency in his mother's land that demanded the presence of her son. Once there, he could build further support for himself. He might very well be able to foment the civil unrest he sought before, and found an inland kingdom loyal only to him. Even if he did not achieve that end, he could cause enough unrest to steal the unity I must have if I am to defend our kingdom.''

He stopped speaking. He lifted his eyes and glanced around the room. I followed his gaze. The walls were hung with his maps. There was Bearns, there was Shoaks, and here was Rippon. On the opposite wall, Buck, Farrow, and Tilth. All done in Verity's precise hand, every river blue-inked, every town named. Here were his Six Duchies. He knew them as Regal never would. He had ridden those roads, helped set the markers of those boundaries. Following Chivalry, he had treated with the folk who bordered our lands. He had swung a sword in defense of it, and known when to set down that sword and negotiate a peace. Who was I to be telling him how to rule at home?

''What will you do?'' I asked quietly.

''Keep him. He is my brother. And my father's son.'' He poured himself more wine. ''My father's most cherished, youngest son. I have gone to my father, the King, and suggested that Regal might be more content with his lot if he had more to do with the running of the kingdom. King Shrewd has consented to this. I expect to be much occupied with defending our land from the Red-Ships. So to Regal will fall the task of raising the revenues we shall need, and he will also be dealing with any other internal crises that may arise. With a circle of nobles to assist him, of course. He is full welcome to deal with their bickering and dissensions.''

''And Regal is content with this?''

Verity smiled a thin smile. ''He cannot say he is not. Not if he wishes to keep the image of a young man adept at ruling and but waiting for opportunity to prove himself.'' He lifted his wineglass and turned to stare into the fire. The only sound in the room was the snapping of the flames as they consumed the wood. ''When you come to me tomorrow,'' he began.

''Tomorrow I must have for myself,'' I told him.

He set down his wineglass and turned to look at me. ''Must you?'' he asked in an odd tone.

I looked up and met his eyes. I swallowed. I brought myself to my feet. ''My prince,'' I began formally. ''I would ask your kind permission to be excused from duties tomorrow, that I might . . . pursue errands of my own.''

He let me stand for a moment. Then: ''Oh, sit down, Fitz. Petty. I suppose that was petty of me. Thinking of Regal puts me in such a frame of mind. Certainly you can have the day, boy. If anyone asks, you are on my business. Might I ask what this urgent errand is?''

I looked into the fire at the leaping flames. ''My friend was living in Siltbay. I need to find out—''

''Oh, Fitz.'' There was more sympathy in Verity's voice than I could withstand.

A sudden wave of weariness washed over me. I was glad to sit again. My hands began to tremble. I put them below the table and clasped them to still them. I still felt the tremors, but at least no one could see my weakness now.

He cleared his throat. ''Go to your room and rest,'' he said kindly. ''Do you want a man to ride with you to Siltbay tomorrow?''

I shook my head dumbly, suddenly and miserably certain of what I would discover. The thought made me sick. Another shudder went through me. I tried to breathe slowly, to calm myself and edge back from the fit that threatened. I could not abide the thought of shaming myself that way before Verity.

''Shame to me, not you, to have ignored how ill you have been.'' He had arisen silently. He set his glass of wine before me. ''The damage you took was taken for me. I am appalled by what I allowed to befall you.''

I forced myself to meet Verity's eyes. He knew all that I tried to conceal. Knew it, and was miserable with guilt.

''It is not often this bad,'' I offered him.

He smiled at me, but his eyes did not change. ''You are an excellent liar, Fitz. Do not think your training has gone awry. But you cannot lie to a man who has been with you as much as I have, not just these last few days, but often during your illness. If any other man says to you, 'I know just how you feel,' you may regard it as a politeness. But from me accept it as truth. And I know that with you it is as it is with Burrich. I shall not offer you the pick of the colts a few months hence. I do offer you my arm, if you wish it, to get back to your room.''

"I can manage," I said stiffly. I was aware of how he honored me, but also of how plainly he saw my weakness. I wanted to be alone, to hide myself.

He nodded, understanding. "Would that you had mastered the Skill. I could offer you strength, just as I have too often taken it from you."

"I could not," I muttered, unable to mask how distasteful I would find the drawing off of another man's strength to replace my own. I instantly regretted the moment of shame I saw in my prince's eyes.

"I, too, could once speak with such pride," he said quietly. "Go get some rest, boy." He turned slowly aside from me. He busied himself setting out his inks and his vellum once more. I left quietly.

We had been closeted for the whole day. Outside, it was full dark. The castle had the settled air of a winter's evening. The tables cleared, the folk would be gathered about the hearths in the Great Hall. Minstrels might be singing, or a puppeteer moving his gangly charges through a story. Some folk would watch while fletching arrows, some would be plying needles, children would be spinning tops or matching markers or drowsing against their parents' knees or shoulders. All was secure. Outside, the winter storms blew and kept us safe.

I walked with a drunkard's caution, avoiding the common areas where folk had gathered for the evening. I folded my arms and hunched my shoulders as if chilled, and so stilled the trembling in my arms. I climbed the first flight of stairs slowly, as if lost in thought. On the landing I permitted myself to pause for a count of ten, then forced myself to begin the next flight.

But as I set my foot to the first step, Lacey came bounding down. A plump woman more than a score of years older than myself, she still moved down the steps with a child's skipping gait. As she reached the bottom she seized me with a cry of "There you are!" as if I were a pair of shears she'd misplaced from her sewing basket. She clutched my arm firmly and turned me toward the hall. "I've been up and down those stairs a dozen times today if I've been once. My, you've gotten taller. Lady Patience has not been at all herself and it's your fault. At first she expected you to tap on the door any moment. She was so pleased you were finally home.'' She paused to look up at me with her bright bird eyes. ''That was this morning,'' she confided. Then: ''You *have* been ill! Such circles under your eyes.''

Without giving me a chance to reply, she went on, ''By early afternoon, when you hadn't arrived, she began to be insulted and a bit cross. By dinner she was in such a temper over your rudeness she could scarcely eat. Since then, she's decided to believe the rumors about how sick you've been. She's sure that you've either collapsed somewhere, or that Burrich has kept you down in the stables cleaning up after horses and dogs despite your health. Now, here we are, in you go, I have him, my lady.'' And she whisked me into Patience's chambers.

Lacey's chatter had an odd undertone to it, as if she avoided something. I entered hesitantly, wondering if Patience herself had been ill or if some misfortune had befallen her. If either were so, then it hadn't affected her living habits at all. Her chambers were much as they always were. All her greenery had grown and twined and dropped leaves. A new layer of sudden interests overlay all the discarded ones in the room. Two doves had been added to her menagerie. A dozen or so horseshoes were scattered about the room. A fat bayberry candle burned on the table, giving off a pleasant scent, but dripping wax onto some dried flowers and herbs on a tray beside it. Some oddly carved little sticks in a bundle were also threatened. They appeared to be fortune-telling sticks such as the Chyurda used. As I entered, her tough little terrier bitch came up to greet me. I stooped to pat her, then wondered if I could stand again. To cover my delay, I carefully picked up a tablet from the floor. It was a rather old one, and probably rare, on the use of the fortune-telling sticks. Patience turned away from her loom to greet me.

''Oh, get up and stop being ridiculous,'' she exclaimed at seeing me crouch. ''Going down on one knee is idiocy. Or did you think it would make me forget how rude you've been in not coming to see me right away. What's that you've brought me? Oh, how thoughtful! How did you know I'd been studying them? You know, I've searched all the castle's libraries and not found much on the predicting sticks at all!''

She took the tablet from my hand and smiled up at me at the supposed gift. Over her shoulder, Lacey winked at me. I gave a minuscule shrug in return. I glanced back at Lady Patience, who set the tablet atop a teetering stack of tablets. She turned back to me. For a moment she regarded me warmly, then she called up a frown to her face. Her brows gathered over her hazel eyes, while her small straight mouth held a firm line. The effect of her reproving look was rather spoiled by the fact that she came just to my shoulder now, and that she had two ivy leaves stuck in her hair. ''Excuse me,'' I said, and boldly plucked them from the unruly dark curls. She took them from my hand seriously, as if they were important, and set them atop the tablet.

''Where have you been, all these months, when you were needed here?'' she demanded. ''Your uncle's bride arrived months ago. You've missed the formal wedding, you've missed the feasting and the dancing and the gathering of the nobles. Here I am, expending all my energies to see that you are treated as the son of a Prince, and there you are, avoiding all your social obligations. And when you do get home, you don't come to see me, but go all about the Keep where anyone else might talk to you, dressed like a ragged tinker. Whatever possessed you to cut your hair like that?'' My father's wife, once horrified to discover that he had sired a bastard before they were wed, had gone from abhorring me to aggressively bettering me. Sometimes that was more difficult to deal with than if she had ostracized me. Now she demanded, ''Had you no thought that you might have social duties here that were more important than gallivanting about with Burrich looking at horses?''

''I am sorry, my lady.'' Experience had taught me never to argue with Patience. Her eccentricity had delighted Prince Chivalry. It drove me to distraction on a good day. Tonight I felt overwhelmed by it. ''For a time I was ill. I did not feel well enough to travel. By the time I recovered, the weather delayed us. I am sorry to have missed the wedding.''

''And that was all? That was the sole reason for your

delay?'' She spoke sharply, as if suspecting some heinous deception.

"It was,'' I answered gravely. "But I did think of you. I have something for you, out in my packs. I haven't brought them up from the stable yet, but I will tomorrow.''

"What is it?'' she demanded, curious as a child.

I took a deep breath. I desperately wished for my bed. "It's a sort of an herbal. A simple one, for they are delicate, and the more ornate ones would not have stood up to the trip. The Chyurda don't use tablets or scrolls for teaching herbs, as we do. Instead, this is a wooden case. When you open it, you will discover tiny wax models of the herbs, tinted to the correct colors and scented with each herb to make it easier to learn them. The lettering is in Chyurda, of course, but I still thought you would enjoy it.''

"It sounds quite interesting,'' she said, and her eyes shone. "I look forward to seeing it.''

"Shall I bring him a chair, my lady? He does look as if he has been ill,'' Lacey interjected.

"Oh, of course, Lacey. Sit down, boy. Tell me, what was your illness?''

"I ate something, one of the foreign herbs, and had a strong reaction to it.'' There. That was truthful. Lacey brought me a small stool and I sat gratefully. A wave of weariness passed through me.

"Oh. I see.'' She dismissed my illness. She took a breath, glanced about, then suddenly demanded, "Tell me. Have you ever considered marriage?''

The abrupt change in subject was so like Patience that I had to smile. I tried to put my mind to the question. For a moment I saw Molly, her cheeks reddened with the wind that teased her dark hair loose. Molly. Tomorrow, I promised myself. Siltbay.

"Fitz! Stop that! I won't have you staring through me as if I were not here. Do you hear me? Are you well?''

With an effort I called myself back. "Not really,'' I answered honestly. "It's been a tiring day for me. . . .''

"Lacey, fetch the boy a cup of elderberry wine. He does look worn. Maybe this isn't the best time for talk,'' Lady

Patience decided falteringly. For the first time she really looked at me. Genuine concern grew in her eyes. "Perhaps," she suggested softly, after a moment, "I do not know the full tale of your adventures."

I looked down at my padded mountain buskins. The truth hovered inside me, then fell and was drowned in the danger of her knowing all that truth. "A long journey. Bad food. Dirty inns with sour beds and sticky tables. That sums it up. I don't think you really want to hear all the details."

An odd thing happened. Our eyes met, and I knew she saw my lie. She nodded slowly, accepting the lie as necessary, and looked aside. I wondered how many times my father had told her similar lies. What did it cost her to nod?

Lacey put the cup of wine into my hand firmly. I lifted it, and the sweet sting of the first sip revived me. I held it in both hands and managed to smile at Patience over it. "Tell me," I began, and despite myself, my voice quavered like an old man's. I cleared my throat to steady it. "How have you been? I imagine that having a Queen here at Buckkeep has made your life much busier. Tell me of all I have missed."

"Oh," she said, as if pricked with a pin. Now it was Patience's turn to look aside. "You know what a solitary creature I am. My health is not always strong. To stay up late, dancing and talking, leaves me abed for two days afterward. No. I have presented myself to the Queen and sat at table with her a time or two. But she is young and busy and caught up in her new life. And I am old and odd, and my life is full of my own interests. . . ."

"Kettricken shares your love of growing things," I ventured. "She would probably be most interested—" A sudden tremor rattled my bones and my teeth chattered to stillness. "I am just . . . a bit cold." I excused myself and lifted my wine cup again. I took a gulp instead of the sip I had intended. My hands shook and wine sloshed over my chin and down my shirtfront. I jumped up in dismay and my traitorous hands let go the cup. It struck the carpet and rolled away, leaving a trail of dark wine like blood. I sat down again abruptly and clasped my arms around myself to try to still my shaking. "I am very tired," I attempted.

Lacey came at me with a cloth and dabbed at me until I took it from her. I wiped my chin and blotted most of the wine from my shirt. But when I crouched down to mop up what had spilled, I almost pitched forward onto my face.

"No, Fitz, forget the wine. We can tidy up. You are tired, and half-sick. Just take yourself up to bed. Come and see me when you've rested. I've something serious to discuss with you, but it will keep another night. Now off you go, boy. Off to bed."

I stood, grateful for the reprieve, and made my cautious courtesies. Lacey saw me as far as the door, and then stood watching after me anxiously as far as the landing. I tried to walk as if the walls and floors weren't wavering. I paused at the stairs to give her a small wave, and then started up them. Three steps up and out of her sight, I stopped to lean on the wall and catch my breath. I lifted my hands to shield my eyes from the brilliant candlelight. Dizziness was washing over me in waves. When I opened my eyes, my vision was wreathed in rainbow fogs. I closed them tight and pressed my hands to them.

I heard a light step coming down the stairs toward me. It paused two steps above me. "Are you all right, sir?" someone asked uncertainly.

"A bit too much to drink," I lied. Certainly the wine I had dumped over myself made me smell like a drunk. "I'll be fine in a moment."

"Let me help you up the stairs. A stumble here might be dangerous." There was starched disapproval in the voice now. I opened my eyes and peered through my fingers. Blue skirts. Of the sensible fabric that all the servants wore. No doubt she'd had to deal with drunks before.

I shook my head, but she ignored that, just as I would have in her position. I felt a strong hand grip my upper arm firmly, while her other arm encircled my waist. "Let's just get you up the stairs," she encouraged me. I leaned on her, not wanting to, and stumbled up to the next landing.

"Thank you," I muttered, thinking she would leave me now, but she kept her grip.

"Are you sure you belong on this level? The servants' quarters are the next flight up, you know."

I managed a nod. "Third door. If you don't mind."

She was silent for longer than a moment. "That's the Bastard's room." The words were flung like a cold challenge.

I did not flinch to the words as I would have once. I did not even lift my head. "Yes. You may go now." I dismissed her as coldly.

Instead she stepped closer. She seized my hair, jerked my head up to face her. "Newboy!" she hissed in fury. "I should drop you right here."

I jerked my head up. I could not make my eyes focus on her eyes, but all the same, I knew her, knew the shape of her face and how her hair fell forward on her shoulders, and her scent, like a summer afternoon. Relief crashed over me like a wave. It was Molly, my Molly the candlemaker. "You're alive!" I cried out. My heart leaped in me like a hooked fish. I took her in my arms and kissed her.

At least, I attempted to. She stiff-armed me away, saying gruffly, "I shall never kiss a drunk. That's one promise I've made to myself and shall always keep. Nor be kissed by one." Her voice was tight.

"I'm not drunk, I'm . . . sick," I protested. The surge of excitement had made my head spin more than ever. I swayed on my feet. "It doesn't matter anyway. You're here and safe."

She steadied me. A reflex she had learned taking care of her father. "Oh. I see. You're not drunk." Disgust and disbelief mingled in her voice. "You're not the scriber's boy, either. Nor a stable hand. Is lying how you always begin with people? It seems to be how you always end."

"I didn't lie," I said querulously, confused by the anger in her voice. I wished I could make my eyes meet hers. "I just didn't tell you quite . . . it's too complicated. Molly, I'm just so glad you're all right. And here in Buckkeep! I thought I was going to have to search . . ." She still gripped me, holding me on my feet. "I'm not drunk. Really. I did lie just now, because it was embarrassing to admit how weak I am."

"And so you lie." Her voice cut like a whip. "You should be more embarrassed to lie, Newboy. Or is lying permitted to a Prince's son?"

She let go of me and I sagged against a wall. I tried to get a grip on my whirling thoughts while keeping my body vertical. "I'm not a Prince's son," I said at last. "I'm a bastard. That's different. And yes, that was too embarrassing to admit, too. But I never told you I wasn't the Bastard. I just always felt, when I was with you, I was Newboy. It was nice, having a few friends who looked at me and thought, 'Newboy' instead of 'the Bastard.' "

Molly didn't reply. Instead she grabbed me, much more roughly than before, by my shirtfront, and hauled me down the hall to my room. I was amazed at how strong women were when they were angry. She shouldered the door open as if it were a personal enemy and propelled me toward my bed. As soon as I was close, she let go and I fell against it. I righted myself and managed to sit down. By clutching my hands tightly together and gripping them between my knees, I could control my trembling. Molly stood glaring at me. I couldn't precisely see her. Her outline was blurred, her features a smear, but I could tell by the way she stood that she was furious.

After a moment I ventured, "I dreamed of you. While I was gone."

She still didn't speak. I felt a bit braver. "I dreamed you were at Siltbay. When it was raided." My words came out tight with my effort to keep my voice from shaking. "I dreamed of fires, and Raiders attacking. In my dream, there were two children you had to protect. It seemed like they were yours." Her silence held like a wall against my words. She probably thought I was ten kinds of an idiot, babbling about dreams. And why, oh why, of all the people in the world who could have seen me so unmanned, why did it have to be Molly? The silence had grown long. "But you were here, at Buckkeep and safe." I tried to steady my quavering voice. "I'm glad you're safe. But what are you doing at Buckkeep?"

"What am I doing here?" Her voice was as tight as mine. Anger made it cold, but I thought it was hedged with fear, too. "I came looking for a friend." She paused and seemed to strangle for a bit. When she spoke again, her voice was artificially calm, almost kind. "You see, my father died and left me a debtor. So my creditors took my shop from me. I went to stay with relatives, to help with the harvest, to earn money to start gain. In Siltbay. Though how you came to know of it, I cannot ven guess. I earned a bit and my cousin was willing to loan me he rest. The harvest had been good. I was to come back to uckkeep the next day. But Siltbay was raided. I was there, ith my nieces. . . .'' Briefly, her voice trailed away. I remembered with her. The ships, the fire, the laughing woman ith the sword. I looked up at her and could almost focus on er. I could not speak. But she was looking off, over my head. he spoke on calmly.

''My cousins lost everything they owned. They counted hemselves lucky, for their children survived. I couldn't ask hem to loan me money still. Truth was, they couldn't even ave paid me for the work I had done, if I had thought to ask. o I came back to Buckkeep, with winter closing in, and no lace to stay. And I thought, I've always been friends with Tewboy. If there's anyone I could ask to loan me money to tide he over, it would be him. So I came up to the Keep, and asked or the scriber's boy. But everyone shrugged and sent me to edwren. And Fedwren listened as I described you, and owned, and sent me to Patience.'' Molly paused significantly. tried to imagine that meeting, but shuddered away from it. She took me on as a lady's maid,'' Molly said softly. ''She aid it was the least she could do, after you had shamed me.''

''Shamed you?'' I jerked upright. The world rocked round me and my blurry vision dissolved into sparks. ''How? ow shamed you?''

Molly's voice was quiet. ''She said you had obviously won y affections, and then left me. Under my false assumption hat you would someday be able to marry me, I'd let you court he.''

''I didn't . . .'' I faltered, and then: ''We were friends. I idn't know you felt any more than that. . . .''

''You didn't?'' She lifted her chin; I knew that gesture. Six ears ago she would have followed it with a punch to my tomach. I still flinched. But she just spoke more quietly when he said, ''I suppose I should have expected you to say that. It's n easy thing to say.''

It was my turn to be nettled. ''You're the one who left me, ith not even a word of farewell. And with that sailor, Jade. Do

you think I don't know about him? I was there, Molly. I saw
you take his arm and walk away with him. Why didn't you
come to me, then, before leaving with him?''

She drew herself up. "I had been a woman with prospects.
Then I became, all unwittingly, a debtor. Do you imagine that
knew of the debts my father had incurred, and then ignored
Not till after he was buried did the creditors come knocking.
lost everything. Should I have come to you as a beggar, hoping
you'd take me in? I'd thought that you'd cared about me.
believed that you wanted . . . El damn you, why do I have to
admit this to you!" Her words rattled against me like flung
stones. I knew her eyes were blazing, her cheeks flushed. ''
thought you did want to marry me, that you did want a future
with me. I wanted to bring something to it, not come to you
penniless and prospectless. I'd imagined us with a little shop
me with my candles and herbs and honey, and you with your
scriber's skills. . . . And so I went to my cousin, to ask to
borrow money. He had none to spare, but arranged for my
passage to Siltbay, to talk to his elder brother Flint. I've told
you how that ended. I worked my way back here on a fishing
boat, Newboy, gutting fish and putting them down in salt.
came back to Buckkeep like a beaten dog. And I swallowed my
pride and came up here that day, and found out how stupid
was, how you'd pretended and lied to me. You are a bastard
Newboy. You are.''

For a moment I listened to an odd sound, trying to com
prehend what it was. Then I knew. She was crying, in little
catches of her breath. I knew if I tried to stand and go to her
I'd fall on my face. Or I'd reach her, and she'd knock me flat
So stupidly as any drunk, I repeated, "Well, what about Jade
then? Why did you find it so easy to go to him? Why didn't you
come to me first?''

"I told you! He's my cousin, you moron!" Her anger
flared past her tears. "When you're in trouble, you turn to your
family. I asked him for help, and he took me to his family's
farm, to help out with the harvest." A moment of silence
Then, incredulously: "What did you think? That I was the type
of woman who could have another man on the side?" Icily
"That I would let you court me, and be seeing someone else?"

"No. I didn't say that."

"Of course you would." She said it as if it suddenly all made sense. "You're like my father. He always believed I lied, because he told so many lies himself. Just like you. 'Oh, I'm not drunk,' when you stink of it and you can barely stand. And your stupid story: 'I dreamed of you at Siltbay.' Everyone in town knew I went to Siltbay. You probably heard the whole story tonight, while you were sitting in some tavern."

"No, I didn't, Molly. You have to believe me." I clutched at the blankets on the bed to keep myself upright. She had turned her back on me.

"No. I don't! I don't have to believe anyone anymore." She paused, as if considering something. "You know, once, a long time ago, when I was a little, little girl. Before I even met you." Her voice was getting oddly calmer. Emptier, but calmer. "It was at Springfest. I remember when I asked my daddy for some pennies for the fair booths, he slapped me and said he wouldn't waste money on foolish things like that. And then he locked me in the shop and went drinking. But even then I knew how to get out of the shop. I went to the fair booths anyway, just to see them. One was an old man telling fortunes with crystals. You know how they do. They hold the crystal to a candle's light, and tell your future by how the colors fall across your face." She paused.

"I know," I admitted to her silence. I knew the type of hedge wizard she meant. I'd seen the dance of colored lights across a woman's close-eyed face. Right now I only wished I could see Molly clearly. I thought if I could meet her eyes, I could make her see the truth inside me. I wished I dared stand, to go to her and try to hold her again. But she thought me drunk, and I knew I'd fall. I would not shame myself in front of her again.

"A lot of the other girls and women were getting their fortunes told. But I didn't have a penny, so I could only watch. But after a bit the old man noticed me. I guess he thought I was shy. He asked me if I didn't want to know my fortune. And I started crying, because I did, but I didn't have a penny. Then Brinna the fishwife laughed, and said there was no need for me to pay to know it. Everyone knew my future already. I was the daughter of a drunk, I'd be the wife of a drunk, and the mother of drunks.'' She whispered, "Everyone started laughing. Even the old man.''

"Molly," I said. I don't think she even heard me.

"I still don't have a penny," she said slowly. "But at least I know I won't be the wife of a drunk. I don't think I even want to be friends with one."

"You have to listen to me. You're not being fair!'' My traitorous tongue slurred my words. "I—''

The door slammed.

"—didn't know you liked me that way," I said stupidly to the cold and empty room.

The shaking overtook me in earnest. But I wasn't going to lose her that easily again. I rose and managed two strides before the floor rocked beneath me and I went to my knees. I remained there a bit, head hanging like a dog. I didn't think she'd be impressed if I crawled after her. She'd probably kick me. If I could even find her. I crawled back to my bed instead, and clambered back onto it. I didn't undress, but just dragged the edge of my blanket over me. My vision dimmed, closing in black from the edges, but I didn't sleep right away. Instead, I lay there and thought what a stupid boy I had been last summer. I had courted a woman, thinking that I was walking out with a girl. Those three years' difference in age had mattered so much to me, but in all the wrong ways. I had thought she had seen me as a boy, and despaired of winning her. So I had acted like a boy, instead of trying to make her see me as a man. And the boy had hurt her, and yes, deceived her, and in all likelihood, lost her forever. The dark closed down, blackness everywhere but for one whirling spark.

She had loved the boy, and foreseen a life together for us. I clung to the spark and sank into sleep.

4

Dilemmas

*A*S REGARDS THE *Wit and the Skill, I suspect that every human has at least some capacity. I have seen women rise abruptly from their tasks to go into an adjacent room where an infant is just beginning to awake. Cannot this be some form of the Skill? Or witness the wordless cooperation that arises among a crew that has long tended the same vessel. They function, without spoken words, as closely as a coterie, so that the ship becomes almost a beast alive, and the crew her life force. Other folk sense an affinity for certain animals, and express it in a crest or in the names they bestow upon their children. The Wit opens one to that affinity. The Wit allows awareness of all animals, but folklore insists that most Wit users eventually develop a bond with one certain animal. Some tales recount that users of the Wit eventually took on the ways and finally the form of the beasts they bonded to. These tales, I believe, we can dismiss as scare tales to discourage children from Beast magic.*

❦

I awoke in the afternoon. My room was cold. No fire at all. My sweaty clothes clung to me. I staggered downstairs to the kitchen, ate something, went out to the bathhouse, began trembling, and went back up to my room. I got back into my bed, shaking with cold. Later someone came in and talked to me. I don't remember what was said, but I do remember being shaken. It was unpleasant, but I could ignore it and did.

I awoke in early evening. There was a fire in my hearth, and a neat pile of firewood in the hod. A little table had been drawn up near my bed, and some bread and meat and cheese was set out on a platter atop an embroidered cloth with tatted edges. A fat pot with brewing herbs in the bottom was waiting for water from the very large kettle steaming over the fire. A washtub and soap were set out on the other side of the hearth. A clean nightshirt had been left across the foot of my bed; it wasn't one of my old ones. It might actually fit me.

My gratitude outweighed my puzzlement. I managed to get out of bed and take advantage of everything. Afterward I felt much better. My dizziness was replaced by a feeling of unnatural lightness, but that quickly succumbed to the bread and cheese. The tea had a hint of elfbark in it; I instantly suspected Chade and wondered if he was the one who'd tried to wake me. But no, Chade only summoned me at night.

I was dragging the clean nightshirt over my head when the door opened quietly. The Fool came slipping into my room. He was in his winter motley of black and white, and his colorless skin seemed even paler because of it. His garments were made of some silky fabric, and cut so loosely that he looked like a stick swathed in it. He'd gotten taller, and even thinner, if that were possible. As always, his white eyes were a shock, even in his bloodless face. He smiled at me, and then waggled a pale pink tongue derisively.

"You," I surmised, and gestured 'round. "Thank you."

"No," he denied. His pale hair floated out from beneath his cap in a halo as he shook his head. "But I assisted. Thank you for bathing. It makes my task of checking on you less onerous. I'm glad you're awake. You snore abominably."

I let his comment pass. "You've grown," I observed.

"Yes. So have you. And you've been sick. And you slept quite a long time. And now you are awake and bathed and fed. You still look terrible. But you no longer smell. It's late afternoon now. Are there any other obvious facts you'd like to review?"

"I dreamed about you. While I was gone."

He gave me a dubious look. "Did you? How touching. I can't say I dreamed of you."

"I've missed you," I said, and enjoyed the brief flash of surprise on the Fool's face.

"How droll. Does that explain why you've been playing the fool yourself so much?"

"I suppose. Sit down. Tell me what's been happening while I was gone."

"I can't. King Shrewd is expecting me. Rather, he isn't expecting me, and that is precisely why I must go to him now. When you feel better, you should go and see him. Especially if he isn't expecting you." He turned abruptly to go. He whisked himself out the door, then leaned back in abruptly. He lifted the silver bells at the end of one ridiculously long sleeve and jingled them at me. "Farewell, Fitz. Do try to do a bit better at not letting people kill you." The door closed silently behind him.

I was left alone. I poured myself another cup of tea and sipped at it. My door opened again. I looked up, expecting the Fool. Lacey peeked in and announced, "Oh, he's awake," and then, more severely, demanded, "Why didn't you say how tired you were? It's fair scared me to death, you sleeping a whole day 'round like that." She did not wait to be invited, but bustled into the room, clean linens and blankets in her arms and Lady Patience on her heels.

"Oh, he is awake!" she exclaimed to Lacey, as if she had doubted it. They ignored my humiliation at confronting them in my nightshirt. Lady Patience seated herself on my bed while Lacey fussed about the room, putting it to rights. There was not much to do in my bare chamber, but she stacked my dirty dishes, poked at my fire, tsk-tsked over my dirty bathwater and scattered garments. I stood at bay by the hearth while she stripped my bed, made it up fresh, gathered my dirty clothes over her arm with a disdainful sniff, glanced about, and then sailed out the door with her plunder.

"I was going to tidy that up," I muttered, embarrassed, but Lady Patience didn't appear to notice. She gestured imperiously at the bed. Reluctantly I got into it. I don't believe I have ever felt more at a disadvantage. She emphasized it by leaning over and tucking the covers around me.

"About Molly," she announced abruptly. "Your behavior that night was reprehensible. You used your weakness to lure her to your room. And upset her no end with your accusations. Fitz, I will not allow it. If you were not so sick, I would be furious with you. As it is, I am gravely disappointed. I cannot think what to say about how you deceived that poor girl, and led her on. So I will simply say that it will happen no more. You shall behave honorably to her, in every way."

A simple misunderstanding between Molly and me had suddenly become a serious matter. "There's been a mistake here," I said, trying to sound competent and calm. "Molly and I need to straighten it out. By talking together, privately. I assure you, for your peace of mind, that it is not at all what you seem to think it is."

"Bear in mind who you are. The son of a Prince does not—"

"Fitz," I reminded her firmly. "I am FitzChivalry. Chivalry's bastard." Patience looked stricken. I felt again how much I had changed since I had left Buckkeep. I was not a boy anymore for her to supervise and correct. She had to see me as I was. Still, I tried to soften my tone as I pointed out, "Not the proper son of Prince Chivalry, my lady. Only your husband's bastard."

She sat on the foot of my bed and looked at me. Her hazel eyes met mine squarely and held. I saw past her giddiness and distractibility, into a soul capable of more pain and vaster regret than I had ever suspected. "How do you think I could ever forget that?" she asked quietly.

My voice died in my throat as I sought for an answer. I was rescued by Lacey's return. She had recruited two serving men and a couple of small boys. The dirty water from my bath and my dishes was whisked away by them while Lacey set out a tray of small pastries and two more cups, and measured out fresh brewing herbs for another pot of tea. Patience and I were silent until the serving folk left the room. Lacey made the tea, poured cups for all, and then settled herself with her ever-present tatting.

"It is precisely because of who you are that this is more than a misunderstanding." Patience launched back into the topic, as if I had never dared interrupt. "If you were just Fedwren's apprentice, or a stable hand, then you would be free to court and marry however you wished. But you are not, FitzChivalry Farseer. You are of the royal blood. Even a bastard"—she stumbled slightly on the word—"of that line must observe certain customs. And practice certain discretions. Consider your position in the royal household. You must have the King's permission to marry. Surely you are aware of that. Courtesy to King Shrewd demanded that you inform him of your intention to court so that he might consider the case's merits, and tell you if it pleased him or not. He would consider it. Is it a good time for you to wed? Does it benefit the throne? Is the match an acceptable one, or is it likely to cause scandal? Will your courting interfere with your duties? Are the lady's bloodlines acceptable? Does the King wish you to have offspring?"

With each question she posed, I felt the shock go deeper. I lay back on my pillows and stared at the bed hangings. I had never really set out to court Molly. From a childhood friendship, we had drifted to a deeper companionship. I had known how my heart wished it to go, but my head had never stopped to consider it. She read my face plainly.

"Remember, too, FitzChivalry, that you have already sworn an oath to another. Your life belongs to your king already. What would you offer Molly if you wed her? His leavings? The bits of time that he did not demand? A man whose duty is sworn to a King has little time for anyone else in his life." Tears stood suddenly in her eyes. "Some women are willing to take what such a man can honestly offer, and content themselves with it. For others, it is not enough. Could never be enough. You must . . ." She hesitated, and it seemed as if the words were wrung from her. "You must consider that. One horse cannot bear two saddles. However much he may wish to . . ." Her voice dwindled off on the last words. She closed her eyes as if something hurt her. Then she took a breath and went on briskly, as if she had never paused, "Another consideration, FitzChivalry. Molly is, or was, a woman of prospects.

She has a trade, and knows it well. I expect she will be able to reestablish herself, after a time of hiring out. But what about you? What do you bring to her? You write a fair hand, but you cannot claim a full scriber's skills. You are a good stable hand, yes, but that is not how you earn your bread. You are a Prince's bastard. You live in the Keep, you are fed, you are clothed. But you have no fixed allowance. This could be a comfortable chamber, for one person. But did you expect to bring Molly here to live with you? Or did you seriously believe the King would grant you permission to leave Buckkeep? And if he did, then what? Will you live with your wife and eat the bread she earns with the work of her hands, and do naught? Or would you be content to learn her trade, and be a help to her?''

She finally paused. She did not expect me to answer any of her questions. I did not try. She took a breath and resumed. ''You have behaved as a thoughtless boy. I know you meant no harm, and we must see that no harm comes of it. To anyone. But most especially to Molly. You have grown up amidst the gossip and intrigues of the royal court. She has not. Will you let it be said she is your concubine, or worse, a Keep whore? For long years now, Buckkeep has been a man's court. Queen Desire was . . . the Queen, but she did not hold court as Queen Constance did. We have a Queen at Buckkeep again. Already, things are different here, as you will discover. If you truly hope to make Molly your wife, she must be brought into this court a step at a time. Or she will find herself an outcast among politely nodding people. I am speaking plainly to you, FitzChivalry. Not to be cruel to you. But far better I am cruel to you now than that Molly live a lifetime of casual cruelty.'' She spoke so calmly, her eyes never leaving my face.

She waited until I asked hopelessly, ''What must I do?''

For a moment she looked down at her hands. Then she met my eyes again. ''For now, nothing. I mean exactly that. I have made Molly one of my serving women. I am teaching her, as best I can, the ways of the court. She is proving an apt student, as well as a most pleasant teacher for me in the matters of herbs and scent making. I am having Fedwren teach her letters, something she is most eager to learn. But for now, that is all that must be happening. She must be accepted by the women of the court as one of my ladies—not the Bastard's woman. After a time you may begin to call upon her. But for now it would be unseemly for you to see her alone, or even seek to see her at all.''

''But I need to speak to her alone. Just once, just briefly, then I promise I'll abide by your rules. She thinks I deliberately deceived her, Patience. She thinks I was drunk last night. I have to explain. . . .''

But Patience was shaking her head before the first sentence was out of my mouth, and continued until I faltered to a halt. ''We have already had a sprinkling of rumors, because she came here seeking you. Or so the gossip was. I have crushed it, assuring everyone that Molly came to me because she was facing difficulties and her mother had been a tiring woman to Lady Heather during the time of Queen Constance's court. Which is true, and hence she does have the right to seek me out, for was not Lady Heather a friend to me when first I came to Buckkeep?''

''Did you know Molly's mother?'' I asked curiously.

''Not really. She had left, to marry a chandler, before I came to Buckkeep. But I did know Lady Heather, and she was kind to me.'' She dismissed my question.

''But couldn't I come to your chambers, and speak to her there, privately, and—''

''I will not have a scandal!'' she declared firmly. ''I will not tempt a scandal. Fitz, you have enemies at court. I will not let Molly become their victim for their aims of hurting you. There. Have I spoken plainly enough at last?''

She had spoken plainly, and of things I had believed her ignorant. How much did she know of my enemies? Did she think it merely social? Though that would be enough at court. I thought of Regal, and his sly witticisms, and how he could turn and speak softly to his hangers-on at a feast and all would smirk to one another and add soft-voiced comments to the Prince's criticism. I thought how I would have to kill him.

''By the set of your jaw, I see you understand.'' Patience arose, setting her teacup on the table. ''Lacey. I believe we should leave FitzChivalry to rest now.''

''Please, at least tell her not to be angry with me,'' I

begged. ''Tell her I wasn't drunk last night. Tell her I never meant to deceive her, or to cause her any harm.''

''I will carry no such message! Nor shall you, Lacey! Don't think I didn't see that wink. Both of you, I insist that you will be decorous. Remember this, FitzChivalry. You do not know Molly. Mistress Chandler. She does not know you. It is how it must be. Now come, Lacey. FitzChivalry, I expect you to get some rest tonight.''

They left me. Although I tried to catch Lacey's eyes and win her alliance, she refused to glance at me. The door closed behind them and I leaned back on my pillows. I tried not to let my mind rattle against the restrictions Patience had set upon me. Annoying as it was, she was right. I could only hope that Molly would see my behavior as thoughtless rather than deceitful or conniving.

I arose from my bed and went to poke at the fire. Then I sat on the hearth and looked about my chamber. After my months in the Mountain Kingdom, it seemed a bleak place indeed. The closest my chamber came to decoration was a rather dusty tapestry of King Wisdom befriending the Elderlings. It had come with the chamber, as had the cedar chest at the foot of my bed. I stared up at the tapestry critically. It was old and moth-eaten; I could see why it had been banished to here. When I had been younger, it had given me nightmares. Woven in an old style, King Wisdom appeared strangely elongated, while the Elderlings bore no resemblance to any creatures I had ever seen. There was a suggestion of wings on their bulging shoulders. Or perhaps that was meant to be a halo of light surrounding them. I leaned back on the hearth to consider them.

I dozed. I awakened to a draft on my shoulder. The secret door beside the hearth that led up to Chade's domain was wide-open and beckoning. I arose stiffly, stretched, and went up the stone stairs. Thus had I first gone, so long ago, clad then as I was now in just my nightshirt. I had followed a frightening old man with a pocked visage and eyes sharp and bright as a raven's. He had offered to teach me to kill people. He had also offered, wordlessly, to be my friend. I had accepted both offers.

The stone steps were cold. Here there were still cobwebs and dust and soot above the sconces on the walls. So the housecleaning hadn't extended to this staircase. Nor to Chade's quarters. They were as chaotic, disreputable, and comfortable as ever. At one end of his chamber was his working hearth, bare stone floors and an immense table. The usual clutter overflowed it: mortars and pestles, sticky dishes of meat scraps for Slink the weasel, pots of dried herbs, tablets and scrolls, spoons and tongs, and a blackened kettle, still sending a reeking smoke curling into the chamber.

But Chade was not there. No, he was at the other end of the chamber, where a fatly cushioned chair faced a hearth with a dancing fire. Carpets overlay one another over the floor there, and an elegantly carved table held a glass bowl of fall apples and a decanter of summer wine. Chade was ensconced in the chair, a partially unrolled scroll held to the light as he read it. Did he hold it farther from his nose than once he had, and were his spare arms more desiccated? I wondered if he had aged in the months I had been away, or if I had simply not noticed before. His gray woolen robe looked as well-worn as ever, and his long gray hair overlay its shoulders and seemed the same color. As always, I stood silent until he deigned to look up and recognize my presence. Some things changed, but some things did not.

He finally lowered the scroll and looked my way. He had green eyes, and their lightness was always surprising in his Farseer face. Despite the poxlike scars that stippled his face and arms, his bastard bloodlines were almost as plain-marked as mine. I suppose I could have claimed his as a great-uncle, but our apprentice-to-master relationship was closer than a blood tie. He looked me over and I self-consciously stood straighter under his scrutiny. His voice was grave as he commanded, "Boy, come into the light."

I advanced a dozen steps and stood apprehensively. He studied me as intently as he had studied the scroll. "Were we ambitious traitors, you and I, we would make sure folk marked your resemblance to Chivalry. I could teach you to stand as he stood; you already walk as he did. I could show you how to add lines to your face to make you appear older. You have most of his height. You could learn his catchphrases, and the way he laughed. Slowly, we could gather power, in quiet ways, with none even recognizing what they were conceding. And one day, we could step up and take power.''

He paused.

Slowly I shook my head. Then we both smiled, and I came to sit on the hearthstones by his feet. The warmth of the fire on my back felt good.

''It's my trade, I suppose.'' He sighed and took a sip of his wine. ''I have to think of these things, for I know that others will. One day, sooner or later, some petty noble will believe it an original idea and approach you with it. Wait and see if I am not right.''

''I pray you are wrong. I have had enough of intrigues, Chade, and not fared as well at that game as I had expected to.''

''You did not do badly, with the hand you were dealt. You survived.'' He looked past me into the fire. A question hung between us, almost palpably. Why had King Shrewd revealed to Prince Regal that I was his trained assassin? Why had he put me in the position of reporting to and taking orders from a man who wished me dead? Had he traded me away to Regal, to distract him from his other discontents? And if I had been a sacrificial pawn, was I still being dangled as bait and a distraction to the younger Prince? I think not even Chade could have answered all my questions, and to ask any of them would have been blackest betrayal of what we were both sworn to be: King's Men. Both of us long ago had given our lives into Shrewd's keeping, for the protection of the royal family. It was not for us to question how he chose to spend us. That way lay treason.

So Chade lifted the summer wine and filled a waiting glass for me. For a brief time we conversed of things that were of no import to any save us, and all the more precious for that. I asked after Slink the weasel, and he haltingly offered sympathy over Nosy's death. He asked a question or two that let me know he was privy to everything I had reported to Verity, and a lot of stable gossip as well. I was filled in on the minor gossip of the Keep, and all the doings I had missed among the lesser folk while I was gone. But when I asked him what he thought of Kettricken, our queen-in-waiting, his face grew grave.

"She faces a difficult path. She comes to a Queenless court, where she herself is and yet is not the Queen. She comes in a time of hardship, to a kingdom facing both raiders and civil unrest. But most difficult for her is that she comes to a court that does not understand her concept of royalty. She has been besieged with feasts and gatherings in her honor. She is used to walking out among her own people, to tending her own gardens and looms and forge, to solving disputes and sacrificing herself to spare her people hardship. Here, she finds, her society is solely the nobility, the privileged, the wealthy. She does not understand the consumption of wine and exotic foods, the display of costly fabrics in dress, the flaunting of jewels that are the purpose of these gatherings. And so she does not 'show well.' She is a handsome woman, in her way. But she is too big, too heartily muscled, too fair amongst the Buckkeep women. She is like a charger stabled among hunters. Her heart is good, but I do not know if she will be sufficient to the task, boy. In truth, I pity her. She came here alone, you know. Those few who accompanied her here have long since returned to the Mountains. So she is very alone here, despite those who court her favor."

"And Verity," I asked, troubled. "He does nothing to allay that loneliness, nothing to teach her of our ways?"

"Verity has little time for her," Chade said bluntly. "He tried to explain this to King Shrewd before the marriage was arranged, but we did not listen to him. King Shrewd and I were beguiled with the political advantages she offered. I forgot there would be a woman here, in this court, day after day. Verity has his hands full. Were they just a man and a woman, and given time, I think they could genuinely care for one another. But here and now, they must devote all their efforts to appearance. Soon an heir will be demanded. They have no time to get to know one another, let alone care for one another." He must have seen the pain in my face, for he added, "That's how it has always been for royalty, boy. Chivalry and Patience were the exception. And they bought their happiness at the cost of political advantages. It was unheard of, for the King-in-Waiting to marry for love. I'm sure you've heard over and over how foolish a thing it was."

"And I'd always wondered if he'd cared."

"It cost him," Chade said quietly. "I don't think he regretted his decision. But he was king-in-waiting. You don't have that latitude."

Here it came. I'd suspected he'd know everything. And useless to hope he'd say nothing. I felt a slow flush steal up my face. "Molly."

He nodded slowly. "It was one thing when it was down in town, and you were more or less a boy. That could be ignored. But now you're being seen as a man. When she came here asking after you, it started tongues wagging and folk speculating. Patience was remarkably agile at hushing the rumors and taking charge of the situation. Not that I'd have kept the woman here, had it been left to me. But Patience handled it well enough."

"The woman . . ." I repeated, stung. If he'd said "the whore" I couldn't have felt it more sharply. "Chade, you misjudge her. And me. It began as a friendship, a long time ago, and if anyone was at fault in . . . how things went, it was me, not Molly. I'd always thought that the friends I made in town, that the time I spent there as 'Newboy' belonged to me." I faltered to a halt, hearing only the foolishness of my words.

"Did you think you could lead two lives?" Chade's voice was soft but not gentle. "We belong to the King, boy. King's Men. Our lives belong to him. Every moment, of every day, asleep or awake. You have no time for your own concerns. Only his."

I shifted slightly, to look into the fire. I considered what I knew of Chade in that light. I met him here, by darkness, in these isolated chambers. I had never seen him out and about around Buckkeep. No one spoke his name to me. Occasionally, disguised as Lady Thyme, he ventured forth. Once we had ridden together through the night, to that first awful Forging at Forge. But even that had been at the King's command. What did Chade have for a life? A chamber, good food and wine, and a weasel for a companion. He was Shrewd's older brother. But for his bastardy, he would be upon the throne. Was his life a foreshadowing of what mine was to be?

"No."

I hadn't spoken, but as I looked up into Chade's face he guessed my thoughts. "I chose this life, boy. After a mishandled potion exploded and scarred me. I was handsome, once. And vain. Almost as vain as Regal. When I ruined my face, I wished myself dead. For months I did not stir out of my chambers. When I finally went forth, it was in disguises, not Lady Thyme, not then, no. But disguises that covered my face and my hands. I left Buckkeep. For a long time. And when I came back, that handsome young man I had been was dead. I found myself more useful to the family, now that I was dead. There is much more to that story, boy. But know that I chose the way I live. It was not something Shrewd forced me into. I did it myself. Your future may be different. But do not imagine it is yours to command."

Curiosity prodded me. "Is that why Chivalry and Verity knew of you, but not Regal?"

Chade smiled in an odd way. "I was a sort of a kindly step-uncle to the two older boys, if you can believe it. I watched over them, in some ways. But once I was scarred, I kept myself even from them. Regal never knew me. His mother had a horror of the pox. I think she believed all the legends of the Pocked Man, harbinger of disaster and misfortune. For that matter, she had an almost superstitious dread of anyone who was not whole. You see it in Regal's reaction to the Fool. She would never keep a clubfooted maid or even a serving man with a missing finger or two. So. When I returned, I was never introduced to the lady, or the child she bore. When Chivalry became king-in-waiting to Shrewd, I was one of the things revealed to him. I was shocked to find he recalled me, and had missed me. He brought Verity to see me that evening. I had to scold him over that. It was difficult to make them understand they could not come calling on me anytime they chose. Those boys." He shook his head and smiled at his memories. I can not explain the twinge of jealousy I felt. I called the conversation back to myself.

"What do you think I should do?"

Chade pursed his lips, sipped his wine, and thought. "For now, Patience has given you good advice. Ignore or avoid Molly, but not obviously. Treat her as if she were a new scullery maid; courteously, if you encounter her, but not familiarly. Do not seek her out. Devote yourself to the Queen-in-Waiting. Verity will be glad of your distracting her. Kettricken will be glad of a friendly face. And if your intent is to win permission to marry Molly, the Queen-in-Waiting could be a powerful ally. As you divert Kettricken, watch over her as well. Bear in mind there are those whose interests do not support Verity having an heir. Those same ones who would not be enthused about your having children. So be wary and alert. Keep your guard up.''

"Is that all?'' I asked, daunted.

"No. Get some rest. Deadroot was what was used on you, by Regal?'' I nodded and he shook his head, narrowing his eyes. Then he looked me squarely in the face. "You are young. You may be able to recover, mostly. I've seen one other man survive it. But he trembled the rest of his life. I see the small signs of it on you yet. It will not show much, except to those who know you well. But do not overtire yourself. Weariness will bring on tremblings and blurred vision. Push yourself, and you will have fits. You do not want anyone to know you have a weakness. The best course is to conduct your life in such a way that the weakness never shows.''

"Was that why there was elfbark in the tea?'' I asked needlessly.

He raised an eyebrow at me. "Tea?''

"Perhaps it was the Fool's doing. I awoke to food and tea in my room. . . .''

"And if it had been Regal's doing?''

It took a moment for the realization to dawn. "I could have been poisoned.''

"But you weren't. Not this time. No, it was neither I nor the Fool. It was Lacey. There is someone deeper than you credit. The Fool discovered you, and something possessed him to tell Patience. While she was flustering, Lacey quietly ordered it all done. I think that privately she considers you as scatterbrained as her mistress. Give her the slightest opening, and she will move in and organize your life. Good as her intentions are, you cannot allow that, Fitz. An assassin needs privacy. Get a latch for your door.''

"Fitz?" I wondered aloud.

"It is your name. FitzChivalry. As it seems to have lost its sting with you, I will use it now. I was beginning to weary of 'boy.' "

I bowed my head. We went on to talk of other things. It was an hour or so until morning when I left his windowless chambers and returned to my own. I went back to bed, but sleep eluded me. I had always stifled the hidden anger I felt at my position at court. Now it smoldered within me, so I could not rest. I threw off my blankets and dressed in my outgrown clothes, left the Keep, and walked down into Buckkeep Town.

The brisk wind off the water blew damp cold like a wet slap in the face. I pulled my cloak more tightly around myself and tugged up my hood. I walked briskly, avoiding icy spots on the steep roadway down to town. I tried not to think, but I found that the brisk pumping of my blood was warming my anger more than my flesh. My thoughts danced like a reined-in horse.

When I had first come to Buckkeep Town, it had been a busy, grubby little place. In the last decade it had grown and adopted a veneer of sophistication, but its roots were only too plain. The town clung to the cliffs below Buckkeep Castle, and when those cliffs gave way to the rocky beaches, the warehouses and sheds were built out on docks and pilings. The good deep anchorage that sheltered below Buckkeep attracted merchant vessels and traders. Farther to the north, where the Buck River met the sea, there were gentler beaches, and the wide river to carry trading barges far inland to the Inland Duchies. The land closest to the river mouth was susceptible to flooding, and the anchorage unpredictable as the river shifted in its course. So the folk of Buckkeep Town lived crowded together on the steep cliffs above the harbor like the birds on Egg Bluffs. It made for narrow, badly cobbled streets that wound back and forth across the steepness as they made their way down to the water. The houses, shops, and inns clung humbly to the cliff face, endeavoring to offer no resistance to the winds that were almost constant there. Higher up the cliff face, the more ambitious homes and businesses were of timber, with their foundations cut into the stone of the cliffs themselves. But I knew little of that stratum. I had run and played as a child among the humbler shops and sailors inns that fronted almost on the water itself.

By the time I reached this area of Buckkeep Town, I was ironically reflecting that both Molly and I would have been better off had we never become friends. I had compromised her reputation, and if I continued my attentions, she would most likely become a target for Regal's malice. As for myself, the anguish I had felt at believing she had blithely left me for another was but a scratch compared with the bleeding now at knowing she thought I had deceived her.

I came out of my bleak thoughts to realize that my traitor-ous feet had carried me to the very door of her chandlery. Now it was a tea-and-herb shop. Just what Buckkeep Town needed; another tea-and-herb shop. I wondered what had become of Molly's beehives. It gave me a pang to realize that for Molly the sense of dislocation must be ten times—no, a hundred times worse. I had so easily accepted that Molly had lost her father, and with him her livelihood and her prospects. So easily accepted the change that made her a servant in the Keep. A servant. I clenched my teeth and kept walking.

I wandered the town aimlessly. Despite my bleak mood, I noticed how much it had changed in the last six months. Even on this cold winter day, it bustled. The construction of the ships had brought more folk, and more folk meant more trade. I stopped in a tavern where Molly, Dirk, Kerry, and I had used to share a bit of brandy now and then. The cheapest blackberry brandy was usually what we got. I sat by myself and drank my short beer in silence, but around me tongues wagged and I learned much. It was not just the ship construction that had bolstered Buckkeep Town's prosperity. Verity had put out a call for sailors to man his warships. The call had been amply answered, by men and women from all of the Coastal Duchies. Some came with a grudge to settle, to avenge those killed or Forged by the Raiders. Others came for the adventure, and the hope of booty, or simply because in the ravaged villages, they had no other prospects. Some were from fisher or merchant families, with sea time and water skills. Others were the former shepherds and farmers of ravaged villages. It mattered little.

All had come to Buckkeep Town, eager to shed Red-Ship blood.

For now, many were housed in what had once been warehouses. Hod, the Buckkeep weaponsmaster, was giving them weapons training, winnowing out those she thought might be suitable for Verity's ships. The others would be offered hire as soldiers. These were the extra folk that swelled the town and crowded the inns and taverns and eating places. I heard complaints, too, that some of those who came to man the warships were immigrant Outislanders, displaced from their own land by the very Red-Ships that now menaced our coasts. They, too, claimed to be eager for revenge, but few Six Duchies folk trusted them, and some businesses in town would not sell to them. It gave an ugly charged undercurrent to the busy tavern. There was a snickering discussion of an Outislander who had been beaten on the docks the day before. No one had called the town patrol. When the speculation became even uglier, that these Outislanders were all spies and that burning them out would be a wise and sensible precaution, I could no longer stomach it, and left the tavern. Was there nowhere I could go to be free of suspicions and intrigues, if only for an hour?

I walked alone through the wintry streets. A storm was blowing up. The merciless wind prowled the twisting streets, promising snow. The same angry cold twisted and churned inside me, switching from anger to hatred to frustration and back to anger again, building to an unbearable pressure. They had no right to do this to me. I had not been born to be their tool. I had a right to live my life freely, to be who I was born to be. Did they think they could bend me to their will, use me however they would, and I would never retaliate? No. A time would come. My time would come.

A man hurried toward me, face shrouded in his hood against the wind. He glanced up and our eyes met. He blanched and turned aside, to hurry back the way he had come. Well, and so he might. I felt my anger building to an unbearable heat. The wind whipped at my hair and sought to chill me, but I only strode faster, and felt the strength of my hatred grow hotter. It lured me and I followed it like the scent of fresh blood.

I turned a corner and found myself in the market. Threatened by the coming storm, the poorer merchants were packing up their goods from their blankets and mats. Those with stalls were fastening their shutters. I strode past them. People scuttled out of my way. I brushed past them, not caring how they stared.

I came to the animal vendor's stall, and stood face-to-face with myself. He was gaunt, with bleak dark eyes. He glared at me balefully, and the waves of hatred pulsing out from him washed over me in greeting. Our hearts beat to the same rhythm. I felt my upper lip twitch, as if to snarl up and bare my pitiful human teeth. I straightened my features, battered my emotion back under control. But the caged wolf cub with the dirty gray coat stared up at me, and lifted his black lips to reveal all his teeth. *I hate you. All of you. Come, come closer. I'll kill you. I'll rip out your throat after I hamstring you. I'll feast on your entrails. I hate you.*

"You want something?"

"Blood," I said quietly. "I want your blood."

"What?"

I jerked my eyes from the wolf up to the man. He was greasy and dirty. He stank, by El, how he reeked. I could smell sweat and rancid food and his own droppings on him. He was swaddled in poorly cured hides, and the stench of them hung about him as well. He had little ferret eyes, and cruel dirty hands, and an oak stick bound in brass that hung at his belt. It was all I could do to keep from seizing that hated stick and splattering his brains out with it. He wore thick boots on his kicking feet. He stepped too close to me and I gripped my cloak to keep from killing him.

"Wolf," I managed to get out. My voice sounded guttural, choking. "I want the wolf."

"You certain, boy? He's a mean one." He nudged the cage with his foot and I sprang at it, clashing my teeth against the wooden bars, bruising my muzzle again, but I didn't care, if I could get just one grip on his flesh, I'd tear it loose or never let go.

No. Get back, get out of my head. I shook my head to clear it. The merchant regarded me strangely. "I know what I want." I spoke flatly, refusing the wolf's emotions.

"Do you, eh?" The man stared at me, judging my worth. He'd charge what he thought I could afford. My outgrown clothes didn't please him, nor my youth. But I surmised he'd had the wolf for a while. He'd hoped to sell him as a cub. Now, with the wolf needing more food and not getting it, the man would probably take whatever he could get. As well for me. I didn't have much. "What do you want him for?" the man asked casually.

"Pits," I said nonchalantly. "He's scrawny, but there might be a bit of sport left in him."

The wolf suddenly flung himself against the bars, jaws wide, teeth flashing. *I'll kill them, I'll kill them all, rip their throats out, tear their bellies open. . . .*

Be silent, if you want your freedom. I mentally gave him a push and the wolf leaped back as if stung by a bee. He retreated to the far corner of his cage and cowered there, teeth bared, but tail down between his legs. Uncertainty flooded him.

"Dog fights, eh? Oh, he'll put up a good fight." The merchant nudged at the cage again with a thick boot, but the wolf didn't respond. "He'll win you a lot of coin, this one will. He's meaner than a wolverine." He kicked the cage, harder. The wolf cowered smaller.

"Oh, he certainly looks as if he will," I said disdainfully. I turned aside from the wolf as if I'd lost interest. I studied the caged birds behind him. The pigeons and doves looked as if they were cared for, but two jays and a crow were crowded into a filthy cage littered with rotting scraps of meat and bird droppings. The crow looked like a beggar man in black tatters of feathers. *Pick at the bright bug,* I suggested to the birds. *Perhaps you'll find a way out.* The crow perched wearily where he was, head sunk deep in his feathers, but one jay fluttered to a higher perch and began to tap and tug at the metal pin that held the cage fastened. I glanced back at the wolf.

"I hadn't intended to fight him anyway. I was only going to throw him to the dogs to warm them up. A bit of blood primes them for a fight."

"Oh, but he'd make you a fine fighter. Here, look at this. This is what he done to me but a month gone. And me trying to give him food when he went for me."

He rolled back a sleeve to bare a grimy wrist striped with livid slashes, but half-healed still.

I leaned over as if mildly interested. "Looks infected. Think you'll lose your hand?"

" 'S not infected. Just slow healing, that's all. Look here, boy, a storm's coming up. I got to put my wares in my cart and haul off before it hits. Now, you going to make me an offer for that wolf? He'll make you a fine fighter."

"He might make bear bait, but not much more than that. I'll give you, oh, six coppers." I had a grand total of seven.

"Coppers? Boy, we're talking silvers here, at least. Look, he's a fine animal. Feed him up a bit, he'll get bigger and meaner. I could get six coppers for his hide alone, right now."

"Then you'd best do it, before he gets any mangier. And before he decides to take your other hand off." I leaned closer to the cage, *pushing* as I did so, and the wolf cowered more deeply. "Looks sick to me. My master would be furious with me if I brought him in and the dogs got sick from killing him." I glanced up at the sky. "Storm is coming. I'd better be off."

"One silver, boy. And that's giving him to you."

At that moment the jay succeeded in pulling the pin. The cage door swung open and he hopped to the door's edge. I casually stepped between the man and the cage. Behind me, I heard the jays hop out to the top of the pigeons' cage. *Door's open,* I pointed out to the crow. I heard him rattle his pathetic feathers. I caught up the pouch at my belt, hefted it thoughtfully. "A silver? I don't have a silver. But it's no matter, really. I just realized I've no way to cart him home with me. Best I don't buy him."

Behind me, the jays took flight. The man blazed out a curse and lunged past me toward the cage. I managed to get entangled with him so that we both fell. The crow had made it as far as the cage door. I shook myself clear of the merchant and jumped to my feet, jarring the cage to spook the bird out into the free air. He beat his wings laboriously, but they carried him to the roof of a nearby inn. As the merchant lumbered to his feet the crow opened his threadbare wings and cawed derisively.

"There's a whole cageful of my wares gone!" he began

accusingly, but I caught up my cloak and pointed to a tear in it. "My master's going to be angry over this!" I exclaimed, and matched him glare for glare.

He glanced up at the crow. The bird had huffed its feathers against the storm and sidled into the shelter of a chimney. He'd never catch that bird again. Behind me, the wolf whined suddenly.

"Nine coppers!" the merchant offered suddenly, desperately. He'd sold nothing that day, I'd wager.

"I told you, I've no way to take him home!" I countered. I tugged up my hood, glanced at the sky. "Storm's here," I announced as the thick wet flakes began to fall. This would be nasty weather, too warm to freeze, too cold to melt. By daylight, the streets would be shining with ice. I turned to go.

"Give me your six damned coppers, then!" the merchant bellowed in frustration.

I fumbled them out hesitatingly. "And will you cart him to where I live?" I asked as he snatched them out of my hand.

"Carry him yourself, boy. You've robbed me and you know it."

With that, he seized up his cage of doves and pigeons and heaved it into the cart. The empty crow's cage followed. He ignored my angry remonstrance as he climbed up on the seat and shook the pony's reins. The old beast dragged the creaking cart off, into the thickening snow and dusk. The market around us was abandoned. The only traffic now were folk hurrying home through the storm, collars and cloaks tight against the wet wind and blowing snow.

"Now what am I to do with you?" I asked the wolf.

Let me out. Free me.

I can't. Not safe. If I turned a wolf loose here in the heart of town, he'd never find his way to the woods alive. There were too many dogs that would pack up to bring him down, too many men who would shoot him for his hide. Or for being a wolf. I bent toward the cage, intending to heft it and see how heavy it was. He lunged at me, teeth bared.

Get back! I was instantly angry. It was contagious.

I'll kill you. You're the same as he was, a man. You'd keep me in this cage, would you? I'll kill you, I'll rip your belly out and tussle with your guts.

You'll get back*!* I *pushed* at him, hard, and he cowered away again. He snarled and whined his confusion at what I had done, but he shrank away from me into the corner of his cage. I seized the cage, lifted it. It was heavy, and the frantic shifting of his weight didn't make it any easier. But I could carry it. Not very far, and not for long. But if I took it in stages, I could get him out of the town. Full grown, he'd probably weigh as much as I did. But he was skinny, and young. Younger than I had guessed at first glance.

I heaved the cage up, held it against my chest. If he went for me now, he could do some damage. But he only whined and cowered back from me into the far corner. It made it very awkward to carry him.

How did he catch you?

I hate you.

How did he catch you?

He remembered a den, and two brothers. A mother who brought him fish. And blood and smoke and his brothers and mother became smelly hides for the boot man. He was dragged out last and thrown into a cage that smelled like ferrets, and kept alive on carrion. And hate. Hate was what he had throve upon.

You were whelped late, if your mother was feeding you on the fish runs.

He sulked at me.

All the roads were uphill, and the snow was starting to stick. My worn boots slid on the icy cobbles, and my shoulders ached with the awkward burden of the cage. I feared I would start trembling. I had to stop frequently to rest. When I did, I firmly refused to think about what I was doing. I told myself that I would not bond with this wolf, or any other creature. I had promised myself. I was just going to feed this cub up and then turn him loose somewhere. Burrich need never know. I would not have to face his disgust. I hefted the cage up again. Who would have thought such a mangy little cub could be so heavy?

Not mangy. Indignant. *Bugs. The cage is full of bugs.*

So I wasn't imagining that itching on my chest. Wonderful. I'd have to bathe again tonight, unless I wanted to share my bed with fleas the rest of the winter.

I had reached the edge of Buckkeep Town. From here, there were only a scattering of houses, and the road would be steeper. Much steeper. Once again I lowered the cage to the snowy ground. The cub huddled in it, small and miserable without anger and hate to sustain him. He was hungry. I made a decision.

I'm going to take you out. I'm going to carry you.

Nothing from him. He watched me steadily as I worked the catch on the cage and swung the door open. I had thought he would charge past me and vanish into the night and the falling snow. Instead he crouched where he was. I reached into the cage and seized him by the scruff to drag him out. In a flash he was on me, driving into my chest, jaws going wide for my throat. I got my arm up just in time to shove my forearm crossways into his jaws. I kept my grip on the scruff of his neck and pushed my arm hard into his mouth, deeper than he liked. His hind legs tore at my belly, but my jerkin was thick enough to divert most of the damage. In an instant we were rolling over and over in the snow, both snapping and snarling like mad things. But I had the weight and the leverage and the experience of tussling with dogs for years. I got him on his back and held him there, helpless, while his head thrashed back and forth and he called me vile names that humans have no words for. When he had exhausted himself I leaned forward over him. I gripped his throat and leaned down to stare into his eyes. This was a physical message he understood. I added to it. *I am the Wolf. You are the Cub. You* will *obey me!*

I held him there staring into his eyes. He quickly looked away, but still I held him, until he looked back up at me and I saw the change in them. I let go of him and stood up and stepped away. He lay still. *Get up. Come here.* He rolled over and came to me, belly low to the ground, tail between his legs. When he got close to me, he fell over on his side and then showed his belly. He whined softly.

After a moment I relented. *It's all right. We just had to understand each other. I don't intend to hurt you. Come with me now.* I reached over to scratch his chest, but when I touched him, he yelped. I felt the red flash of his pain.

Where are you hurt?

I saw the brass-bound club of the cage man. *Everywhere.*

I tried to be gentle as I felt him over. Old scabs, lumps on his ribs. I stood, and kicked the cage savagely aside from our path. He came and leaned against my leg. *Hungry. Cold. So tired.* His feelings were bleeding over into mine again. When I touched him, it was difficult to separate my thoughts from his. Was it my outrage over how he had been treated, or his own? I decided it didn't matter. I gathered him up carefully and stood. Without the cage, held close to my chest, he didn't weigh nearly as much. He was mostly fur and long growing bones. I regretted the force I'd used on him, but also knew that it was the only language he would have recognized. "I'll take care of you," I forced myself to say aloud.

Warm, he thought gratefully, and I took a moment to pull my cloak over him. His senses were feeding mine. I could smell myself, a thousand times stronger than I wanted to. Horses and dogs and wood smoke and beer and a trace of Patience's perfume. I did my best to block out my awareness of his senses. I snugged him to me and carried him up the steep path to Buckkeep. I knew of a disused cottage. An old pig man had once lived in it, out back behind the granaries. No one lived there now. It was too tumbledown, and too far from everyone else at Buckkeep. But it would suit my purposes. I'd put him there, with some bones to gnaw and some boiled grain, and some straw to bed down in. A week or two, maybe a month, and he'd be healed up and strong enough to care for himself. Then I'd take him out west of Buckkeep and turn him loose.

Meat?

I sighed. *Meat,* I promised. Never had any beast sensed my thoughts so completely, or expressed his own to me so clearly. It was good that we would not be around one another for long. Very good that he'd be leaving soon.

Warm, he contradicted me. He set his head atop my shoulder and fell asleep, his muzzle snuffling damply against my ear.

5

Gambit

CERTAINLY THERE IS *an ancient code of conduct, and certainly its customs were harsher than ours today. But I would venture that we have not wandered so far from those customs so much as put a veneer over them. A warrior's word is still his bond, and among those who serve side by side, there is nothing so foul as one who lies to his comrades, or leads them into dishonor. The laws of hospitality still forbid those who have shared salt at a man's table to shed blood on his floor.*

Winter deepened around Buckkeep Castle. The storms came in off the sea, to pound us with icy fury and then depart. Snow usually fell in their wake, great dumps of it that iced the battlements like sweet paste on nut cakes. The great darks of the long nights grew longer, and on clear nights the stars burned cold over us. After my long journey home from the Mountain Kingdom, the ferocity of the winter didn't threaten me as it once had. As I went my daily rounds to the stable and to the old pig hut, my cheeks might burn with cold and my eyelashes cling together with frost, but I always knew that home and a warm hearth were close by. The storms and the

deep colds that snarled at us like wolves at the door were also
the watch beasts that kept the Red-Ships away from our shores.

Time dragged for me. I called on Kettricken each day, as
Chade had suggested, but our restiveness was too much alike
for us. I am sure I irritated her as much as she did me. I dared
not spend too many hours with the cub, lest we bond. I had no
other fixed duties. There were too many hours to the day, and
all were filled with my thoughts of Molly. Nights were the
worst, for then my sleeping mind was beyond my control, and
my dreams were full of my Molly, my bright red-skirted candlemaker, now gone so demure and drab in serving-girl blue. If
I could not be near her by day, my dreaming self courted her
with an earnestness and energy that my waking self had never
mustered the courage for. When we walked the beaches after a
storm, her hand was in mine. I kissed her competently, without
uncertainty, and met her eyes with no secrets to hide. No one
could keep her from me. In my dreams.

At first, Chade's training of me seduced me into spying
upon her. I knew which room on the servants' floor was hers, I
knew which window was hers. I learned, without intention, the
hours of her comings and goings. It shamed me to stand where
I might hear her step upon the stairs and catch a brief glimpse
of her going out on her market errands, but try as I might, I
could not forbid myself to be there. I knew who her friends
were among the serving women. Though I might not speak to
her, I could greet them, and have a chance bit of talk with
them, hoping always for some stray mention of Molly. I
yearned after her hopelessly. Sleep eluded me, and food held
no interest for me. Nothing held any interest for me.

I was sitting one evening in the guardroom off the kitchen.
I had found a place in the corner where I could lean against the
wall and prop my boots up on the opposite bench to discourage
company. A mug of ale that had gone warm hours ago sat in
front of me. I lacked even the ambition to drink myself into a
stupor. I was looking at nothing, attempting not to think, when
the bench was jerked out from under my propped feet. I nearly
fell from my seat, then recovered to see Burrich seating himself
opposite me. "What ails you?" he asked without niceties. He

leaned forward and pitched his voice for me alone. "Have you had another seizure?"

I looked back at the table. I spoke as quietly. "A few trembling fits, but no real seizures. They only seem to come on me if I strain myself."

He nodded gravely, then waited. I looked up to find his dark eyes on me. The concern in them touched something in me. I shook my head, my voice suddenly gone. "It's Molly," I said after a moment.

"You haven't been able to find where she went?"

"No. She's here, at Buckkeep, working as a maid for Patience. But Patience won't let me see her. She says . . ."

Burrich's eyes had widened at my first words. Now he glanced around us, then tossed his head at the door. I arose and followed him as he led me back to his stables, and then up to his room. I sat down at his table, before his hearth, and he brought out his good Tilth brandy and two cups. Then he set out his leather-mending tools. And his perpetual pile of harness to be mended. He handed me a halter that needed a new strap. For himself, he laid out some fancy work on a saddle skirt. He drew up his own stool and looked at me. "This Molly. I've seen her then, in the washer courts with Lacey? Carries her head proud? Red glint to her coat?"

"Her hair," I corrected him grudgingly.

"Nice wide hips. She'll bear easily," he said with approval.

I glared at him. "Thank you," I said icily.

He shocked me by grinning. "Get angry. I'd rather you were that than self-pitying. So. Tell me."

And I told him. Probably much more than I would have in the guardroom, for here we were alone, the brandy went warm down my throat, and the familiar sights and smells of his room and work were all around me. Here, if anywhere in my life, I had always been safe. It seemed safe to reveal to him my pain. He did not speak or make any comments. Even after I had talked myself out, he kept his silence. I watched him rub dye into the lines of the buck he had incised in the leather.

"So. What should I do?" I heard myself ask.

He set down his work, drank off his brandy, and then

refilled his cup. He looked about his room. "You ask me, of course, because you have noted my rare success at providing myself with a fond wife and many children?"

The bitterness in his voice shocked me, but before I could react to it, he gave a choked laugh. "Forget I said that. Ultimately, the decision was mine, and done a long time ago. FitzChivalry, what do you think you should be doing?"

I stared at him morosely.

"What made things go wrong in the first place?" When I did not reply, he asked me, "Did not you yourself just tell me that you courted her as a boy, when she considered your offer a man's? She was looking for a man. So don't go sulking about like a thwarted child. Be a man." He drank down half his brandy, then refilled both our cups.

"How?" I demanded.

"The same way you've shown yourself a man elsewhere. Accept the discipline, live up to the task. So you cannot see her. If I know anything of women, it does not mean she does not see you. Keep that in mind. Look at yourself. Your hair looks like a pony's winter coat, I'll wager you've worn that shirt a week straight, and you're thin as a winter foal. I doubt you'll regain her respect that way. Feed yourself up, groom yourself daily, and in Eda's name, get some exercise instead of moping about the guardroom. Set yourself some tasks and get onto them."

I nodded slowly to the advice. I knew he was right. But I could not help protesting, "But all of that will do me no good if Patience will still not permit me to see Molly."

"In the long run, my boy, it is not about you and Patience. It is about you and Molly."

"And King Shrewd," I said wryly.

He glanced up at me quizzically.

"According to Patience, a man cannot be sworn to a King and give his heart fully to a woman as well. 'You cannot put two saddles on one horse,' she told me. This from a woman who married a King-in-Waiting, and was content with whatever time he had for her." I reached to hand Burrich the mended halter.

He did not take it. He had been in the act of lifting his

brandy cup. He set it down on the table so sharply that the liquid leaped and slopped over the edge. "She said that to you?" he asked me hoarsely. His eyes bored into mine.

I nodded slowly. "She said it would not be honorable to expect Molly to be content with whatever time the King left to me as my own."

Burrich leaned back in his chair. A chain of conflicting emotions dragged across his features. He looked aside into the hearthfire, and then back at me. For a moment he seemed on the verge of speaking. Then he sat up, drank off his brandy in one gulp, and abruptly stood. "It's too quiet up here. Let's go down to Buckkeep Town, shall we?"

⊷⊨

The next day I arose and ignored my pounding head to set myself the task of not behaving like a lovesick boy. A boy's impetuosity and carelessness were what had lost her to me. I resolved to attempt a man's restraint. If biding my time was my only path to her, I would take Burrich's advice and use that time well.

So I arose each day early, before even the morning cooks were up. In the privacy of my room, I stretched and then worked through sparring drills with an old stave. I would work myself into sweat and dizziness, and then go down to the baths to steam myself. Slowly, very slowly, my stamina began to return. I gained weight and began to rebuild the muscle on my bones. The new clothing that Mistress Hasty had inflicted on me began to fit. I was still not free of the tremors that sometimes assailed me. But I had fewer seizures, and always managed to return to my rooms before I could shame myself by falling. Patience told me that my color was better, while Lacey delighted in feeding me at every opportunity. I began to feel myself again.

I ate with the guards each morning, where quantity consumed was always of more importance than manners. Breakfast was followed with a trip to the stables, to take Sooty out for a snowy canter to keep her in condition. When I returned her to the stables, there was a homey comfort in taking care of her myself. Before our misadventures in the Mountain Kingdom, Burrich and I had been on bad terms over my use of the Wit. I had been all but barred from the stables. So there was more than satisfaction in rubbing her down and seeing to her grain myself. There was the busyness of the stables, the warm smells of the beasts, and the gossip of the Keep as only the stable hands could tell it. On fortunate days, Hands or Burrich would take time to stop and talk with me. And on other days, busy days, there was the bittersweet satisfaction of seeing them conferring over a stallion's cough, or doctoring the ailing boar that some farmer had brought up to the Keep. On those days they had little time for pleasantries and, without intending it, excluded me from their circle. It was as it had to be. I had moved on to another life. I could not expect the old one to be held ajar for me forever.

That thought did not prevent a pang of guilt as I slipped away each day to the disused cottage behind the granaries. Wariness always stalked me. My new peace with Burrich had not existed so long that I took it for granted; it was only too fresh in my memory exactly how painful losing his friendship had been. If Burrich ever suspected that I had returned to using the Wit, he would abandon me just as swiftly and completely as he had before. Each day I asked myself exactly why I was willing to gamble his friendship and respect for the sake of a wolf cub.

My only answer was, I had no choice. I could no more have turned aside from Cub than I could have walked away from a starved and caged child. To Burrich, the Wit that some-times left me open to the minds of animals was a perversion, a disgusting weakness that no true man indulged. He had all but admitted to the latent ability for it, but staunchly insisted that he never used it himself. If he did, I had never caught him at it. The opposite was never true. With uncanny perception, he had always known when I was drawn to an animal. As a boy, my indulgence in the Wit with a beast had usually led to a rap on the head or a sound cuff to rouse me back to my duties. When I had lived with Burrich in the stables, he had done everything in his power to keep me from bonding to any animal. He had succeeded always, save twice. The keen pain of losing my bond companions had convinced me Burrich was right. Only a fool would indulge in something that inevitably led to such loss. So I was a fool, rather than a man who could turn aside from the plea of a beaten and starved cub.

I pilfered bones and meat scraps and crusts, and did my best that no one, not even Cook or the Fool, knew of my activity. I took elaborate pains to vary the times of my visits each day, and to take every day a different path to avoid creating too beaten a trail to the back cottage. Hardest had been smuggling clean straw and an old horse blanket out of the stables. But I had managed it.

No matter when I arrived, I found Cub waiting for me. It was not just the watchfulness of an animal awaiting food. He sensed when I began my daily hike to the back cottage behind all the granaries and awaited me. He knew when I had ginger cakes in my pocket, and too quickly became fond of them. Not that his suspicions of me had vanished. No. I felt his wariness, and how he shrank in on himself each time I stepped within reach of him. But every day that I did not strike him, every bit of food I brought him was one more plank of trust in the bridge between us. It was a link I did not want to establish. I tried to be sternly aloof from him, to know him through the Wit as little as possible. I feared he might lose the wildness that he would need to survive on his own. Over and over I warned him, "You must keep yourself hidden. Every man is a danger to you, as is every hound. You must keep yourself within this structure, and make no sound if anyone is near."

At first it was easy for him to obey. He was sadly thin, and would fall immediately upon the food I brought and devour it all. Usually he was asleep in his bedding before I left the cottage, or jealously eyeing me as he lay gnawing a treasured bone. But as he was fed adequately, and had room to move, and lost his fear of me, the innate playfulness of a cub began to reassert itself. He took to springing upon me in mock attacks as soon as the door was opened, and expressing delight in knuckly beef bones with snarls and tusslings inflicted on them. When I rebuked him for being too noisy, or for the tracks that betrayed his night romp in the snowy field behind the cottage, he would cower before my displeasure.

But I noted as well the masked savagery in his eyes at

those times. He did not concede mastery to me. Only a sort of pack seniority. He bided his time until his decisions should be his own. Painful as it was sometimes, it was as it needed to be. I had rescued him with the firm intent of returning him to freedom. A year from now, he would be but one more wolf howling in the distance at night. I told him this repeatedly. At first, he would demand to know when he would be taken from the smelly Keep and the confining stone walls that fenced it. I would promise him soon, as soon as he was fed to strength again, as soon as the deepest snows of winter were past and he could fend for himself. But as weeks passed, and the storms outside reminded him of the snugness of his bed and the good meat filled out on his bones, he asked less often. Sometimes I forgot to remind him.

Loneliness ate at me from inside and out. At night I would wonder what would happen if I crept upstairs and knocked at Molly's door. By day I held myself back from bonding to the small cub who depended so completely on me. There was only one other creature in the Keep who was as lonely as I was.

⇥≡⇤

"I am sure you have other duties. Why do you come to call on me each day?" Kettricken asked me in the forthright Mountain way. It was midmorning, on a day following a night of storm. Snow was falling in fat flakes, and despite the chill, Kettricken had ordered the window shutters opened so she might watch it. Her sewing chamber overlooked the sea, and I thought she was fascinated by the immense and restless waters. Her eyes were much the same color as the water that day.

"I had thought to help time pass more pleasantly for you, my queen-in-waiting."

"Passing time." She sighed. She cupped her chin in her hand and leaned on her elbow to stare pensively out at the falling snow. The sea wind tangled in her pale hair. "It is an odd language, yours. You speak of passing time as in the Mountains we speak of passing wind. As if it were a thing to be gotten rid of."

Her little maid Rosemary, seated at her feet, giggled into her hands. Behind us, her two ladies tittered apprehensively, then bent their heads industriously over their needlework again. Kettricken herself had a large embroidery frame set up, with the beginning of mountains and a waterfall in it. I had not noticed her making much progress on it. Her other ladies had not presented themselves today, but had sent pages with excuses as to why they could not attend her. Headaches, mostly. She did not seem to understand that she was being slighted by their inattention. I did not know how to explain it to her, and on some days I wondered if I should. Today was one of those days.

I shifted in my chair and crossed my legs the other way. "I meant only that in winter, Buckkeep can become a tedious place. The weather keeps us within doors so much; there is little that is amusing."

"That is not the case down at the shipwrights' sheds," she informed me. Her eyes got a strangely hungry look. "There it is all a bustle, with every bit of daylight used in the setting of the great timbers and the bending of the planks. Even when the day is dim or wild with storm, within the sheds shipbuilders are still hewing and shaping and planing wood. At the metal forges, they make chains and anchors. Some weave stout canvas for sails, and others cut and sew it. Verity walks about there, overseeing it all. While I sit here with fancywork, and prick my fingers and strain my eyes to knot in flowers and birds' eyes. So that when I am finished, it can be set aside with a dozen other prettyworks."

"Oh, not set aside, no, never, my lady," one of her women burst in impulsively. "Why, your needlework is much treasured when you gift it out. In Shoaks there is a framed bit in Lord Shemshy's private chambers, and Duke Kelvar of Rippon—"

Kettricken's sigh cut short the woman's compliment. "I would I worked at a sail instead, with a great iron needle or a wooden fid, to grace one of my husband's ships. There would be a work that was worthy of my time, and his respect. Instead, I am given toys to amuse me, as if I were a spoiled child that did not understand the value of time well spent." She turned back to her window. I noticed then that the smoke rising from the shipyards was as easily visible as the sea. Perhaps I had mistaken the direction of her attention.

"Shall I send for tea and cakes, my lady?" one of her ladies inquired hopefully. Both of them sat with their shawls pulled up over their shoulders. Kettricken did not appear to notice the chill sea air spilling in the open window, but it could not have been pleasant for those two to sit and ply their needles in it.

"If you wish them," Kettricken replied disinterestedly. "I do not hunger or thirst. Indeed, I fear I will grow fat as a penned goose, sitting at needlework and nibbling and sipping all day. I long to do something of significance. Tell me true, Fitz. If you did not feel required to call upon me, would you be sitting idly in your chambers? Or doing fancywork at a loom?"

"No. But then, I am not the Queen-in-Waiting."

"Waiting. Ah, I understand well now that part of my title." A bitterness I had never heard from her before crept into her voice. "But Queen? In my land, as well you know, we do not say Queen. Were I there now, and ruling instead of my father, I would be called Sacrifice. More, I would be Sacrifice. To whatever was to the good of my land and my people."

"Were you there now, in the deep of winter, what would you be doing?" I asked, thinking only to find a more comfortable area of conversation. It was a mistake.

She grew silent and stared out the window. "In the Mountains," she said softly, "there was never time to be idle. I was the younger of course, and most of the duties of Sacrifice fell upon my father and my older brother. But, as Jonqui says, there is always enough work to go 'round and some to spare. Here, in Buckkeep, all is done by servants, out of sight, and one sees only the results, the tidied chamber, the meal on the table. Perhaps it is because this is such a populous place."

She paused a moment and her eyes went afar. "In Jhaampe, in winter, the hall and the town itself grow quiet. Snows fall thick and heavy, and great cold closes in on the land. The lesser-used trails disappear for the winter. Wheels are replaced by runners. Visitors to the city have long gone home by now. In the palace at Jhaampe, there is only the family, and those who choose to stay and help them. Not serve them, no, not exactly. You have been to Jhaampe. You know there are no ones who only serve, save for the royal family. In

Jhaampe, I would rise early, to fetch the water for the household porridge, and to take my turn at the stirring of the kettle. Keera and Sennick and Jofron and I would make the kitchen lively with talk. And all the young ones dashing about, bringing in the firewood and setting out the plates and talking of a thousand things.'' Her voice faltered, and I listened to the silence of her loneliness.

After a bit she went on: ''If there was work to be done, heavy or light, we all joined in it. I have helped to bend and lash the branches for a barn. Even in the deep of winter, I have helped to clear snow and raise new roof arches for a family devastated by a fire. Do you think a Sacrifice cannot hunt down a cranky old bear that has turned to killing goats, or strain against a rope to help brace a bridge battered by floodwaters?'' She looked at me with real pain in her eyes.

''Here, in Buckkeep, we do not risk our queens,'' I told her simply. ''Another shoulder can brace a rope, we have dozens of hunters who would vie for the honor of dispatching a cattle killer. We have but one Queen. There are things a Queen can do that no other can.''

Behind us in the room, her ladies had all but forgotten her. One had summoned a page, and he had returned with sweet cakes and steaming tea in a pot. They chatted together, warming their hands about their teacups. Briefly I looked at them, to remember well what ladies had chosen to attend their queen. Kettricken, I was coming to see, might not be the easiest of Queens to attend upon. Kettricken's little maid, Rosemary, sat on the floor by the tea-table, dreamy-eyed, a sweet cake clasped in her small hands. I suddenly wished I were eight years old again and could join her there.

''I know what you speak of,'' Kettricken said bluntly. ''I am here to bear an heir to Verity. It is a duty I do not avoid, for I do not consider it a duty, but a pleasure. I only wish I were sure my lord shared my sentiments. Always he is away and about the town on business. I know where he is today; down there, watching his ships arise from planks and timbers. Could I not be with him with no danger to myself? Surely, if only I can bear his heir, only he can sire it. Why must I be confined here while he immerses himself in the task of protecting our people? That is a task I should be sharing as Sacrifice for the Six Duchies.''

Accustomed as I had become to Mountain forthrightness in my time there, I was still shocked at how bluntly she spoke. It made me overbold in my reply. I found myself rising to lean past her and pull the shutters tight over the drafty window. I took advantage of the closeness to whisper fiercely, ''If you think that is the only duty that our queens bear, you are gravely mistaken, my lady. To speak as plainly as you have, you neglect your duties to your ladies, who are here this day only to attend upon you and converse with you. Think. Could they not be doing this same needlework in the coziness of their own chambers, or in the company of Mistress Hasty? You sigh after what you perceive as a more important task; but before you is a task the King himself cannot do. You are here to do it. Rebuild the court at Buckkeep. Make it a desirable and attractive place to be. Encourage his lord and ladies to vie for his attention; make them eager to support him in his endeavors. It has been long since there was a congenial Queen in this castle. Instead of looking down at a ship that other hands are more capable of building, take up the task you are given, and suit yourself to it.''

I finished redraping the tapestry that covered the shutters and helped to seal out the cold of the sea storms. I then stepped back and met my queen's eyes. To my chagrin, she was as chastened as if she were a milkmaid. Tears stood in her pale eyes, and her cheeks were as red as if I had slapped her. I glanced at her ladies, who were still taking tea and chatting. Rosemary, unwatched, was taking the opportunity to poke at the tarts carefully to see what was inside them. No one appeared to have noticed anything amiss. But I was learning rapidly how adept court ladies were at such dissimulation, and feared speculation as to what the Bastard might have said to the Queen-in-Waiting to bring tears to her eyes.

I cursed my clumsiness, and reminded myself that however tall Kettricken might be, she was not much older than myself, and in a foreign place alone. I should not have spoken to her, but should instead have presented the problem to Chade, and let him manipulate someone into explaining it to her. Then it dawned on me that he had already selected someone to explain such things to her. I met her eyes again and ventured a nervous smile. Quickly she followed my glance to the ladies, and as swiftly returned decorum to her face. My heart surged with pride in her.

"What do you suggest?" she asked quietly.

"I suggest," I said humbly, "that I am ashamed at how boldly I have spoken to my queen. I ask her forgiveness. But I suggest, also, that she show these two loyal ladies some especial mark of royal favor, to reward them for their faithfulness."

She nodded her comprehension. "And that favor might be?" she asked softly.

"A private gathering with their queen in her personal chambers, perhaps for a special minstrel or puppeteer. It matters not what entertainment you provide; only that those who have not chosen to attend you as faithfully be excluded."

"That sounds like something Regal would do."

"Probably. He is very adept at creating lackeys and hangers-on. But he would do it spitefully, to punish those who had not danced attendance upon him."

"And I?"

"And you, my Queen-in-Waiting, you do it as a reward to those who have. With no thought of punishing those who have not, but only of enjoying the company of those who obviously reciprocate that feeling."

"I see. And the minstrel?"

"Mellow. He has a most gallant way of singing to every lady in the room."

"Will you see if he is free this evening?"

"My lady." I had to smile. "You are the Queen-in-Waiting. You honor him to request his presence. He will never be too busy to attend upon you."

She sighed again, but it was a smaller sigh. She nodded her dismissal of me and rose to advance smiling upon her ladies, begging them to excuse her wandering thoughts this morning, and then asking if they might also attend her this evening in her own chambers. I watched them exchange glances and smile, and knew we had done well. I noted their names to myself: Lady Hopeful and Lady Modesty. I bowed my way out of the room, my departure scarcely noticed.

So I came to be adviser to Kettricken. It was not a role I relished, to be companion and instructor, to be the whisperer that told her what steps she next must dance. In truth, it was an uncomfortable task. I felt I diminished her by my chiding, and that I corrupted her, teaching her the spidery ways of power in the web of the court. She was right. These were Regal's tricks. If she worked them with higher ideals and kinder ways than Regal did, my intentions were selfish enough for both of us. I wanted her to gather power into her hands, and with it bind the throne firmly to Verity in the minds of one and all.

Early each evening, I was expected to call on Lady Patience. She and Lacey both took these visits quite seriously. Patience considered me completely at her disposal, as if I were her page still, and thought nothing of requiring me to copy some ancient scroll for her onto her precious reed paper, or to demand that I show her my improvement in playing the sea pipes. She always took me to task for not showing enough effort in that area, and would spend the better part of an hour confusing me whilst attempting to instruct me in it. I tried to be tractable and polite, but felt entrapped in their conspiracy to keep me from seeing Molly. I knew the wisdom of Patience's course, but wisdom does not allay loneliness. Despite their efforts to keep me from her, I saw Molly everywhere. Oh, not her person, no, but in the scent of the fat bayberry candle burning so sweetly, in the cloak left draped over a chair, even the honey in the honey cakes tasted of Molly to me. Will you think me a fool that I sat close by the candle and smelled its scent, or took the chair that I might lean against her snow-damped cloak as I sat? Sometimes I felt as Kettricken did, that I was drowning in what was required of me, and that there was nothing left in my life that was for me alone.

I reported weekly to Chade upon Kettricken's progress in court intrigue. Chade it was who warned me that suddenly the ladies most enamored of Regal were courting favor with Kettricken as well. And so I must warn her, whom to treat courteously, but no more than that, and whom to genuinely smile upon. Sometimes I thought to myself that I would rather be quietly killing for my king than to be so embroiled in all these secretive schemes. But then King Shrewd summoned me.

The message came very early one morning, and I made haste to dress myself to attend my king. This was the first time he had summoned me to his presence since I had returned to Buckkeep. It had made me uneasy to be ignored. Was he displeased with me, over what had happened at Jhaampe? Surely he would have told me so directly. Still. Uncertainty gnawed me. I tried to make great haste to wait upon him, and yet to take special care with my appearance. I ended up doing poorly at both. My hair, shorn for fever when I was in the Mountains, had grown back as bushy and unmanageable as Verity's. Worse, my beard was beginning to bristle as well. Twice Burrich had told me that I had better decide to wear a beard, or to attend more closely to my shaving. As my beard came in as patchy as a pony's winter coat, I diligently cut my face several times that morning, before deciding that a bit of bristle would be less noticeable than all the blood. I curried my hair back from my face and wished I could bind it back in a warrior's tail. I set into my shirt the pin that Shrewd had so long ago given me to mark me as his. Then I hurried to attend my king.

As I strode hastily down the hall to the King's door, Regal stepped abruptly from his own doorway. I halted not to run into him, and then felt trapped there, staring at him. I had seen him, several times since I had returned. But it had always been across a hall, or a passing glimpse of him while I was engaged in some task. Now we stood, scarce an arm's length apart, and stared at one another. Almost, we could have been mistaken for brothers, I realized with shock. His hair was curlier, his features finer, his bearing more aristocratic. His garments were peacock's feathers compared with my wren colors, I lacked silver at my throat and on my hands. Still the stamp of the Farseers was plain on us both. We shared Shrewd's jaw and the fold of his eyelids and the curve of his lower lip. Neither of us would ever compare with Verity's widely muscled build, but I would come closer than he would. Less than a decade of years separated our ages. Only his skin separated me from his blood. I met his eyes and wished I could spill his guts upon the clean-swept floor.

He smiled, a brief showing of white teeth. "Bastard," he greeted me pleasantly. His smile grew sharper. "Or, that is, Master Fits. A *fitting* name you've taken to yourself." His careful pronunciation left no room for doubting his insult.

"Prince Regal," I replied, and let my tone make the words mean the same as his. I waited with an icy patience I had not known I owned. He had to strike me first.

For a time we held our positions, eyes locked. Then he glanced down, to flick imaginary dust from his sleeve. He strode past me. I did not step aside for him. He did not jostle me as once he would have. I took a breath and walked on.

I did not know the guardsman at the door, but he waved me into the King's chamber. I sighed and set myself another task. I would learn names and faces again. Now that the court was swelling with folk come to see the new Queen, I found myself being recognized by people I didn't know. "That'd be the Bastard, by the look of him," I'd heard a bacon monger say to his apprentice the other day outside the kitchen doors. It made me feel vulnerable. Things were changing too fast for me.

King Shrewd's chamber shocked me. I had expected to find the windows ajar to the brisk winter air, to find Shrewd up and dressed and alert at table, as keen as a captain receiving reports from his lieutenants. Always he had been so, a sharp old man, strict with himself, an early riser, shrewd as his name. But he was not in his sitting room at all. I ventured to the entry of his bedchamber, peered within the open door.

Inside, the room was half in shadow still. A servant rattled cups and plates at a small table drawn up by the great curtained bed. He glanced at me, then away, evidently thinking I was a serving boy. The air was still and musty, as if the room were disused or had not been aired in a long time. I waited a time for the servant to let King Shrewd know I had come. When he continued to ignore me, I advanced warily to the edge of the bed.

"My king?" I made bold to address him when he did not speak. "I have come as you bid me."

Shrewd was sitting up in the curtained shadows of his bed, well propped with cushions. He opened his eyes when I spoke.

"Who . . . ah. Fitz. Sit, then. Wallace, bring him a chair. A cup and plate, too." As the servant moved to his bidding King Shrewd confided to me, "I do miss Cheffers. With me for so many years, and I never had to tell him anymore what I wanted done."

"I remember him, my lord. Where is he, then?"

"A cough took him. He caught it in the fall, and it never left him. It slowly wore him away, until he couldn't take a breath without wheezing."

I recalled the servant. He had not been a young man, but not so old either. I was surprised to hear of his death. I stood silently, wordless, while Wallace brought the chair and a plate and cup for me. He frowned disapprovingly as I seated myself, but I ignored it. He would soon enough learn that King Shrewd designed his own protocol. "And you, my king? Are you well? I cannot recall that I ever knew you to keep to your bed in the morning?"

King Shrewd made an impatient noise. "It is most annoying. Not a sickness really. Just a giddiness, a sort of dizziness that sweeps down upon me if I move swiftly. Every morning I think it gone, but when I try to rise, the very stones of Buckkeep rock under me. So I keep to my bed, and eat and drink a bit, and then rise slowly. By midday I am myself. I think it has something to do with the winter cold, though the healer says it may be from an old sword cut, taken when I was not much older than you are now. See, I bear the scar still, though I thought the damage long healed." King Shrewd leaned forward in his curtained bed, lifting with one shaky hand a sheaf of his graying hair from his left temple. I saw the pucker of the old scar and nodded.

"But, enough. I did not summon you for consultations about my health. I suspect you guess why you are here?"

"You would like a complete report of the events at Jhaampe?" I guessed. I glanced about for the servant, saw Wallace hovering near. Cheffers would have departed to allow Shrewd and me to talk freely. I wondered how plainly I dared speak before this new man.

But Shrewd waved it aside. "It is done, boy," he said heavily. "Verity and I have consulted. Now we let it go. I do not think there is much you could tell me that I do not know, or guess already. Verity and I have spoken at length. I . . . regret . . . some things. But. Here we are, and here is always the place we must start from. Eh?''

Words swelled in my throat, nearly choking me. Regal, I wanted to say to him. Your son who tried to kill me, your bastard grandson. Did you speak at length with him, also? And was it before or after you put me into his power? But, as clearly as if Chade or Verity had spoken to me, I knew suddenly I had no right to question my king. Not even to ask if he had given my life over to his youngest son. I clenched my jaws and held my words unuttered.

Shrewd met my eyes. His eyes flickered to Wallace. ''Wallace. Take yourself to the kitchens for a bit. Or wherever you wish that is not here.'' Wallace looked displeased, but he turned with a sniff and departed. He left the door ajar behind him. At a sign from Shrewd, I arose and shut it. I returned to my seat.

''FitzChivalry,'' he said gravely. ''This will not do.''

''Sir.'' I met his eyes for a moment, then looked down.

He spoke heavily. ''Sometimes, ambitious young men do foolish things. When they are shown the error of their ways, they apologize.'' I looked up suddenly, wondering if he expected an apology from me. But he went on. ''I have been tendered such an apology. I have accepted it. Now we go on. In this, trust me,'' he said, and he spoke gently but it was not a request. ''Least said is soonest mended.''

I leaned back in my chair. I took a breath, sighed it carefully out. In a moment I had mastered myself. I looked up at my king with an open face. ''May I ask why you have called me, my king?''

''An unpleasantness,'' he said distastefully. ''Duke Brawndy of Bearns thinks I should resolve it. He fears what may follow if I do not. He does not think it . . . political to take direct action himself. So I have granted the request, but grudgingly. Have not we enough to face with the Raiders at our doorstep, without internal strife? Still. They have the right to ask it of me, and I the duty to oblige any who asks. Once more you will bear the King's justice, Fitz.''

He told me concisely of the situation in Bearns. A young woman from Sealbay had come to Ripplekeep to offer herself to Brawndy as a warrior. He had been pleased to accept her, for she was both well muscled and adept, skilled at staves, bows, and blades. She was beautiful as well as strong, small and dark and sleek as a sea otter. She had been a welcome addition to his guard, and soon was a popular figure in his court as well. She had, not charm, but that courage and strength of will that draws others to follow. Brawndy himself had grown fond of her. She enlivened his court and instilled new spirit in his guard.

But lately she had begun to fancy herself a prophetess and soothsayer. She claimed to have been chosen by El the sea god for a higher destiny. Her name had been Madja, her parentage unremarkable, but now she had renamed herself, in a ceremony of fire, wind, and water, and called herself Virago. She ate only meat she had taken herself, and kept in her rooms nothing that she had not either made herself or won by show of arms. Her following was swelling, and included some of the younger nobles as well as many of the soldiers under her command. To all she preached the need to return to El's worship and honor. She espoused the old ways, advocating a rigorous, simple life that glorified what a person could win by her own strength.

She saw the Raiders and Forging as El's punishment for our soft ways, and blamed the Farseer line for encouraging that softness. At first she had spoken circumspectly of such things. Of late, she had become more open, but never so bold as to voice outright treason. Still, there had been bullock sacrifices on the sea cliffs, and she had blood-painted a number of young folk and sent them out on spirit quests as in the very old days. Brawndy had heard rumors that she sought a man worthy of herself, who would join her to throw down the Farseer throne. They would rule together, to begin the time of the Fighter and put an end to the days of the Farmer. According to Bearns, quite a number of young men were ready to vie for that honor. Brawndy wished her stopped, before he himself had to accuse her of treason, and force his men to choose between Virago and himself. Shrewd offered the opinion that her following would probably drop off drastically, were she to be bested at arms, or have a severe accident or become victim to a wasting illness that depleted her strength and beauty. I was forced to agree that was probably so, but observed that there were many cases where folks who died became like gods afterward. Shrewd said certainly, if the person died honorably.

Then, abruptly, he changed the topic. In Ripplekeep, on Sealbay, there was an old scroll that Verity wished copied, a listing of all those from Bearns who had served the King in the Skill, as coterie members. It was also said that at Ripplekeep there was a relic from the days of the Elderling defense of that city. Shrewd wished me to leave on the morrow, to go to Sealbay and copy the scrolls and to view the relic and bring him a report of it. I would also convey to Brawndy the King's best wishes and his certainty that the Duke's unease would soon be put to rest.

I understood.

As I stood to leave, Shrewd raised a finger to bid me pause. I stood, waiting.

"And do you feel I am keeping my bargain with you?" he asked. It was the old question, the one he had always asked me after our meetings when I was a boy. It made me smile.

"Sir, I do," I said as I always had.

"Then see that you keep your end of it as well." He paused, then added, as he never had before, "Remember, FitzChivalry. Any injury done to one of my own is an injury to me."

"Sir?"

"You would not injure one of mine, would you?"

I drew myself up. I knew what he asked for, and I ceded it to him. "Sir, I will not injure one of yours. I am sworn to the Farseer line."

He nodded slowly. He had wrung an apology from Regal, and from me my word that I would not kill his son. He probably believed he had made peace between us. Outside his door, I paused to push the hair back from my eyes. I had just made a promise, I reminded myself. I considered it carefully and forced myself to look at what it could cost me to keep it. Bitterness flooded me, until I compared what it would cost me should I break it. Then I found the reservations in myself, crushed them firmly. I formed a resolve, to cleanly keep my promise to my king. I had no true peace with Regal, but at least I could have that much peace with myself. The decision left me feeling better, and I strode purposefully down the hall.

I had not replenished my stocks of poisons since I had returned from the Mountains. Nothing green showed outside now. I'd have to steal what I needed. The wool dyers would have some I might use, and the healer's stock would yield me others. My mind was busy with this planning as I started down the stairs.

Serene was coming up the stairs. When I saw her, I halted where I was. The sight of her made me quail as Regal had not. It was an old reflex. Of all Galen's coterie, she was now the strongest. August had retired from the field, gone far inland to live in orchard country and be a gentleman there. His Skill had been entirely blasted out of him during the final encounter that marked the end of Galen. Serene was now the key Skill-user of the coterie. In summers, she remained at Buckkeep, and all the other members of the coterie, scattered to towers and keeps up and down our long coast, channeled all their reports to the King through her. During winter, the entire coterie came to Buckkeep, to renew their bonds and fellowship. In the absence of a Skill Master, she had assumed much of Galen's status at Buckkeep. She had also assumed, with great enthusiasm, Galen's passionate hatred of me. She reminded me too vividly of past abuses, and inspired in me a dread that would not yield to logic. I had avoided her since my return, but now her gaze pinned me.

The staircase was more than sufficiently wide to allow two people to pass. Unless one person deliberately planted herself in the middle of a step. Even looking up at me, I felt she had the advantage. Her bearing had changed since we had been Galen's students together. Her whole physical appearance reflected her new position. Her midnight-blue robe was richly embroidered. Her long black hair was bound back intricately with burnished wire strung with ivory ornaments. Silver graced her throat and ringed her fingers. But her femaleness was gone. She had adopted Galen's ascetic values, for her face was thinned to bone, her hands to claws. As he had, she burned with self-righteousness. It was the first time she had directly accosted me since Galen's death. I halted above her, with no idea of what she wanted from me.

"Bastard," she said flatly. It was a naming, not a greeting. I wondered if that word would ever lose its sting with me.

"Serene," I said, as tonelessly as I could manage.

"You did not die in the Mountains."

"No. I did not."

Still she stood there, blocking my way. Very quietly she said, "I know what you did. I know what you are."

Inside, I was quivering like a rabbit. I told myself it was probably taking every bit of Skill strength she had to impose this fear on me. I told myself that it was not my true emotion, but only what her Skill suggested I should feel. I forced words from my throat.

"I, too, know what I am. I am a King's Man."

"You are no kind of a man at all," she asserted calmly. She smiled up at me. "Someday everyone will know that."

Fear feels remarkably like fear, regardless of the source. I stood, making no response. Eventually, she stepped aside to allow me to pass. I made a small victory of that, though in retrospect there was little else she could have done. I went to ready things for my trip to Bearns, suddenly glad to leave the Keep for a few days.

I have no good memories of that errand. I met Virago, for she was herself a guest at Ripplekeep while I was there doing my scribe tasks. She was as Shrewd had described her, a handsome woman, well muscled, who moved lithe as a little hunting cat. She wore the vitality of her health like a glamour. All eyes followed her when she was in a room. Her chastity challenged every male who followed her. Even I felt myself drawn to her, and agonized about my task.

Our very first evening at table together, she was seated across from me. Duke Brawndy had made me very welcome indeed, even to having his cook prepare a certain spicy meat dish I was fond of. His libraries were at my disposal, and the services of his lesser scribe. His youngest daughter had even extended her shy companionship to me. I was discussing my scroll errand with Celerity, who surprised me with her soft-spoken intelligence. Midway through the meal, Virago remarked quite clearly to her dining companion that at one time bastards were drowned at birth. The old ways of El demanded it, she said. I could have ignored the remark, had she not leaned across the table to smilingly ask me, "Have you never heard of that custom, bastard?"

I looked up to Duke Brawndy's seat at the head of the table, but he was engaged in a lively discussion with his eldest daughter. He didn't even glance my way. "I believe it is as old as the custom of one guest's courtesy to another at their host's table," I replied. I tried to keep my eyes and voice steady. Bait. Brawndy had seated me across the table from her as bait. Never before had I been so blatantly used. I steeled myself to it, tried to set personal feelings aside. At least I was ready.

"Some would say it was a sign of the degeneracy of the Farseer line, that your father came unchaste to his wedding bed. I, of course, would not speak against my king's family. But tell me. How did your mother's people accept her whoredom?"

I smiled pleasantly. I suddenly had fewer qualms about my task. "I do not recall much of my mother or her kin," I offered conversationally. "But I imagine they believed as I do. Better to be a whore, or the child of a whore, than a traitor to one's king."

I lifted my wineglass and turned my eyes back to Celerity. Her dark blue eyes widened and she gasped as Virago's belt knife plunged into Brawndy's table but inches from my elbow. I had expected it and did not flinch. Instead, I turned to meet her eyes. Virago stood in her table place, eyes blazing and nostrils flared. Her heightened color enflamed her beauty.

I spoke mildly. "Tell me. You teach the old ways, do you not? Do you not then hold to the one that forbids the shedding of blood in a house where you are a guest?"

"Are you not unbloodied?" she asked by way of reply.

"As are you. I would not shame my duke's table by letting it be said that he had allowed guests to kill one another over his bread. Or do you care as little for your courtesy to your duke as you do your loyalty to your king?"

"I have sworn no loyalty to your soft Farseer king," she hissed.

Folk shifted, some uncomfortably, some for a better vantage. So some had come to witness her challenge me, at Brawndy's table. All of this had been as carefully planned as any battle campaign. Would she know how well I had planned also? Did she suspect the tiny package in my cuff? I spoke boldly, pitching my voice to carry. "I have heard of you. I think that those you tempt to follow you into treachery would be wiser to go to Buckkeep. King-in-Waiting Verity has issued a call for those skilled in arms to come and man his new warships and bear those arms against the Outislanders, who are enemy to us all. That, I think, would be a better measure of a warrior's skill. Is not that more honorable a pursuit than to turn against leaders one has sworn to, or to waste bull's blood down a cliffside by moonlight, when the same meat might go to feed our kin despoiled by Red-Ships?"

I spoke passionately, and my voice grew in volume as she stared at how much I knew. I found myself caught up in my own words, for I believed them. I leaned across the table, over Virago's plate and cup, to thrust my face close to hers as I asked, "Tell me, brave one. Have you ever lifted arms against one who was not your own countryman? Against a Red-Ship crew? I thought not. Far easier to insult a host's hospitality, or maim a neighbor's son, than to kill one who came to kill our own."

Words were not Virago's best weapon. Enraged, she spat at me.

I leaned back, calmly, to wipe my face clean. "Perhaps you would care to challenge me, in a more appropriate time and place. Perhaps a week hence, on the cliffs where you so boldly slew the cow's husband? Perhaps I, a scribe, might present you more of a challenge than your bovine warrior did?"

Duke Brawndy suddenly deigned to notice the disturbance. "FitzChivalry! Virago!" he rebuked us. But our gazes remained locked, my hands planted to either side of her place setting as I leaned to confront her.

I think the man beside her might have challenged me also, had not Duke Brawndy then slammed his salt bowl against the table, near shattering it, and reminded us forcefully that this was his table and his hall and he'd have no blood shed in it. He, at least, was capable of honoring both King Shrewd and the old ways at once, and suggested we attempt to do the same. I apologized most humbly and eloquently, and Virago muttered her "sorrys." The meal resumed, and the minstrels sang, and over the next few days I copied the scroll for Verity and viewed the Elderling relic, which looked like nothing to me so much as a glass vial of very fine fish scales. Celerity seemed more impressed with me than I was comfortable with. The other side of that coin was facing the cold animosity in the faces of those who sided with Virago. It was a long week.

I never had to fight my challenge, for before the week was out, Virago's tongue and mouth had broken out in the boils and sores that were the legendary punishment for one who lied to arms companions and betrayed spoken vows. She scarce was able to drink, let alone eat, and so disfiguring was her affliction that all those close to her forsook her company for fear it spread to them as well. Her pain was such that she could not go forth into the cold to fight, and there was no one willing to stand her challenge for her. I waited on the cliffs, for a challenger who never came. Celerity waited with me, as did perhaps a score of minor nobles that Duke Brawndy had urged to attend me. We made casual talk, and drank entirely too much brandy to keep ourselves warm. As evening fell, a messenger from the keep came to tell us that Virago had left Ripplekeep, but not to face her challenger. She had ridden away, inland. Alone. Celerity clasped her hands together, and then astonished me with a hug. We returned chilled but merry to enjoy one more meal at Ripplekeep before my departure for Buckkeep. Brawndy sat me at his left hand, and Celerity beside me.

"You know," he observed to me, toward the end of the meal. "Your likeness to your father becomes more remarkable every year."

All of the brandy in Bearns could not have defeated the chill his words sent through me.

6

Forged Ones

THE TWO SONS of Queen Constance and King Shrewd were Chivalry and Verity. Only two years separated their births, and they grew up as close as two brothers can be. Chivalry was the eldest, and the first to assume the title King-in-Waiting on his sixteenth birthday. He was almost immediately dispatched by his father to deal with a border dispute with the Chalced States. From that time on, he was seldom at Buckkeep for more than a few months at a time. Even after Chivalry had married, he was seldom allowed to spend his days at rest. It was not so much that there were so many border uprisings at that time as that Shrewd seemed intent on formalizing his boundaries with all his neighbors. Many of these disputes were settled with the sword, though as time went on, Chivalry became more astute at employing diplomacy first.

Some said that assigning Chivalry to this task was the plot of his stepmother, Queen Desire, who hoped to send him to his death. Others say it was Shrewd's way of putting his eldest son out of his new queen's sight and authority. Prince Verity, condemned by his youth to remain at home, made formal application to his father every month to be allowed to follow his brother. All of Shrewd's efforts to interest him in responsibilities of his own were wasted. Prince Verity performed the tasks given him, but never let anyone think for a moment that he

would not rather be with his older brother. At last, on Verity's
twentieth birthday, after six years of requesting monthly to be
allowed to follow his brother, Shrewd reluctantly conceded to
him.

From then, until the day four years later when Chivalry
abdicated and Verity assumed the title King-in-Waiting, the two
Princes worked as one in formalizing boundaries, treaties, and
trade agreements with the lands bordering the Six Duchies.
Prince Chivalry's talent was for dealing with people, as individuals or as a folk. Verity's was for the detail of agreements,
the precise maps that delineated agreed borders, and the supporting of his brother in his authority both as a soldier and as
a prince.

Prince Regal, youngest of Shrewd's sons and his only child
with Queen Desire, spent his youth at home at court, where his
mother made every effort to groom him as a candidate for the
throne.

<hr />

I traveled home to Buckkeep with a sense of relief. It was
not the first time I had performed such a task for my king, but I
had never developed a relish for my work as an assassin. I was
glad at how Virago had insulted me and baited me, for it had
made my task bearable. And yet, she had been a very beautiful
woman, and a skilled warrior. It was a waste, and I took no
pride in my work, save that I had obeyed my king's command.
Such were my thoughts as Sooty carried me up the last rise
toward home.

I looked up the hill, and scarce could believe what I saw.
Kettricken and Regal on horseback. They rode side by side.
Together. They looked like an illustration from one of Fedwren's best vellums. Regal was in scarlet and gold with glossy
black boots and black gloves. His riding cloak was flung back
from one shoulder, to display the brilliant contrast of the colors
as they billowed in the morning wind. The wind had brought a
redness of the outdoors to his cheeks, and tousled his black hair
from its precise arrangement of curls. His dark eyes shone.
Almost, he looked a man, I thought, astride the tall black horse
that carried itself so well. He could be this if he chose, rather

than the languid prince with always a glass of wine in hand and
a lady beside him. Another waste.

Ah, but the lady beside him was another matter. Compared
with the entourage that followed them, she showed as a rare
and foreign blossom. She rode astride in loose trousers, and no
Buckkeep dyeing vat had produced that crocus purple. Her
trousers were adorned with intricate embroideries in rich colors, and tucked securely into her boot tops. Her boots came
almost to her knee; Burrich would have approved that practi-
cality. She wore, not a cloak, but a short jacket of voluminous
white fur, with a high collar to shield her neck from the wind.
A white fox, I guessed, from the tundra on the far side of the
Mountains. Her hands were gloved in black. The wind had
played with her long yellow hair, streaming it out and tangling
it over her shoulders. Atop her head was a knitted cap of every
bright color I could imagine. She sat her horse high and forward, in the Mountain style, and it made Softstep think she
must prance instead of walk. The chestnut mare's harness was
a-jingle with tiny silver bells, ringing sharp as icicles in the
brisk morning. Compared with the other women in their voluminous skirts and cloaks, she looked agile as a cat.

She brought to mind an exotic warrior from a northern
clime or an adventurer from some ancient tale. It set her apart
from her ladies, not as a highborn and well-adorned woman
shows her status among those less royal, but almost as a hawk
would appear caged with songbirds. I was not sure she should
show herself so to her subjects. Prince Regal rode at Kettricken's side, smiling and talking to her. Their conversation
was lively, spiced often with laughter. As I approached closer I
let Sooty slow her pace. Kettricken reined in, smiling, and
would have stopped to give me greeting, but Prince Regal
nodded icily and kneed his horse to a trot. Kettricken's mare,
not to be left behind, tugged at her bit and kept pace with him.
I received as brisk a greeting from those who trailed after the
Queen and Prince. I halted to watch them pass, and then continued up to Buckkeep with an uneasy heart. Kettricken's face
had been animated, her pale cheeks pink with the cold air, and
her smile at Regal had been as genuinely merry as the occa-

sional smiles she still gave me. Yet I could not believe she would be so gullible as to trust him.

I pondered this while I unsaddled Sooty and rubbed her down. I had bent down to check her hooves when I felt Burrich watching me over the wall of the stall. I asked him, "For how long?"

He knew what I was asking.

"He began a few days after you left. He brought her down here one day, and spoke me fair, saying he thought it quite a shame that the Queen was spending all her days shut up in the Keep. She was used to such an open and hearty life up in the Mountains. He claimed he had allowed her to persuade him to teach her to ride as we rode here in the lower lands. Then he had me saddle Softstep with the saddle Verity had made for his queen, and off they went. Well, what was I to do or say?" he asked me fiercely as I turned to look at him questioningly. "It is as you have said before. We are King's Men. Sworn. And Regal is a Prince of the Farseer house. Even if I were faithless enough to refuse him, there was my queen-in-waiting, expecting me to fetch her horse for her and saddle her."

A slight motion of my hand reminded Burrich that his words sounded close to treason. He stepped into the stall beside me, to scratch behind Sooty's ears pensively as I finished with her.

"You could do nothing else," I conceded. "But I must wonder what his real intent is. And why she suffers him."

"His intent? Perhaps just to wriggle his way back into favor with her. It is no secret that she pines in the castle. Oh, she is fair-spoken to all. But there is too much honesty in her for her to make others believe she is happy when she is not."

"Perhaps," I conceded grudgingly. I lifted my head as suddenly as a dog does when his master whistles. "I have to go. King-in-Waiting Verity . . ." I let the words trail away. I did not have to let Burrich know I had been summoned by the Skill. I slung my saddlebags with the arduously copied scrolls inside to my shoulder and headed up to the castle.

I did not pause to change my clothes, or even to warm myself at the kitchen fires, but went straight to Verity's map room. The door was ajar, and I tapped once and then entered.

Verity leaned over a map secured to his table. He scarcely glanced up to acknowledge me. Steaming mulled wine already awaited me, and a generous platter of cold meats and bread stood on a table near the hearth. After a bit he straightened up.

"You block too well," Verity said by way of a greeting. "I have been trying to get you to hurry for the past three days, and when do you finally know you are Skilled? When you are standing in my own stables. I tell you, Fitz, we must find time to teach you some sort of control over your Skill."

But I knew even as he spoke that there would never be that time. Too many other things demanded his attention. As always, he immediately plunged into his concern. "Forged ones," he said. I felt a chill of foreboding run up my spine.

"The Red-Ships have struck again? This deep in winter?" I asked incredulously.

"No. At least we are still spared that. But it seems that the Red-Ships can leave us and go home to their hearths, and still leave their poison among us." He paused. "Well, go on. Warm yourself and eat. You can chew and listen at the same time."

As I helped myself to the mulled wine and food, Verity lectured me. "It is the same problem as before. Reports of Forged ones, robbing and despoiling, not just travelers, but isolated farms and houses. I have investigated, and must give credence to the reports. Yet the attacks are happening far from the sites of any raids; and in every case the folk claim there are not one or two Forged ones, but groups of them, acting in concert."

I considered for a moment, swallowed, then spoke. "I don't think Forged ones are capable of acting in bands or even as partners. When one encounters them, one finds they have no sense of . . . community. Of shared humanity. They can speak, and reason, but only selfishly. They are as wolverines would be if given human tongues. They care for nothing but their own survival. They see each other only as rivals for food or comfort of any kind." I refilled my mug, grateful for the spreading warmth of the wine. At least it pushed aside the physical cold. The chill thought of the bleak isolation of the Forged ones it could not touch.

It was the Wit that had let me discover this about Forged

ones. So deadened were they to all sense of kinship with the world that I could scarcely sense them at all. The Wit gave me a certain access to that web that bound all creatures together, but the Forged ones were separate from that net, as isolated as stones, as hungry and merciless as an unthinking storm or a river in flood. To encounter one unexpectedly was as startling to me as if a stone rose up to attack me.

But Verity only nodded thoughtfully. "Yet even wolves, animals as they are, attack as a pack. As do tearfish on a whale. If these animals can band together to bring down food, why not the Forged ones?"

I set down the bread I had picked up. "Wolves and tearfish do as they do by their nature, and share the flesh with their young. They do not kill, each for his own meat, but for meat for the pack. I have seen Forged ones in groups, but they do not act together. The time I was attacked by more than one Forged one, the only thing that saved me was that I was able to turn them against each other. I dropped the cloak they desired, and they fought over it. And when they came after me again, they more got in one another's way than helped one another." I fought to keep my voice steady as the memory of that night rose up in me. Smithy had died that night, and I had first killed. "But they do not fight together. That is what is beyond the Forged ones; the idea of cooperating so that all might benefit."

I looked up to find Verity's dark eyes full of sympathy. "I had forgotten that you had had some experience fighting them. Forgive me. I don't dismiss it. There is just so much besieging me lately." His voice dwindled away and he seemed to be listening to something far away. After a moment he came back to himself. "So. You believe they cannot cooperate. And yet it seems to be happening. See, here," and he brushed his hand lightly over a map spread out on his table. "I have been marking the places of the complaints, and keeping track of how many are said to be there. What do you think of this?"

I went to stand beside him. Standing next to Verity was now like standing next to a different sort of hearth. The strength of the Skill radiated from him. I wondered if he strove to hold it in check, if it always threatened to spill out of him and spread his consciousness over the whole kingdom.

"The map, Fitz," he recalled me, and I wondered how much he knew of my thoughts. I forced myself to concentrate on the task at hand. The map showed Buck, done in wondrous detail. Shallows and tide flats were marked along the coast, as well as inland landmarks and lesser roads. It was a map made lovingly, by a man who had walked and ridden and sailed the area. Verity had used bits of red wax as markers. I studied them, trying to see what his real concern was.

"Seven different incidents." He reached to touch his markers. "Some within a day's ride of Buckkeep. But we have had no raids that close, so where would these Forged ones be coming from? They might be driven away from their home villages, true, but why would they converge upon Buckkeep?"

"Perhaps these are desperate people pretending to be Forged ones when they go out to steal from their neighbors?"

"Perhaps. But it is troubling that the incidents are happening closer and closer to Buckkeep. There are three different groups, from what the victims say. But each time there is a report of a robbery or a barn broken into or a cow butchered in the field, the group responsible seems to have moved closer to Buckkeep. I can think of no reason for Forged ones to do such a thing. And"—he halted me as I began to speak—"the descriptions of one group match those of another attack, reported over a month ago. If these are the same Forged ones, they have come a long way in that time."

"It does not seem like Forged ones," I said, and then carefully, I asked, "Do you suspect a conspiracy of some kind?"

Verity snorted bitterly. "Of course. When do I not suspect conspiracies anymore? But for this, at least, I think I can look further afield than Buckkeep to find the source." He halted abruptly, as if hearing how bluntly he had spoken. "Look into it for me, Fitz, will you? Ride out and about a bit, and listen. Tell me what they say in the taverns, and tell me what sign you find on the roads. Gather gossip of other attacks, and keep track of the detail. Quietly. Can you do that for me?"

"Of course. But why quietly? It seems to me that if we alerted folk, we would hear more swiftly of what goes on."

"We would hear more, that's true. More of rumors, and

much more of complaint. So far these are individual complaints. I am the only one, I think, who has put together a pattern from them. I do not want Buckkeep itself up in arms, complaining that the King cannot even protect his capital city. No. Quietly, Fitz. Quietly.''

"Just look into it quietly." I did not voice it as a question.

Verity gave his broad shoulders a small shrug. But it was more like a man shifting a burden than dislodging a load. ''Put a stop to it where you can.'' His voice was small and he looked into the fire. ''Quietly, Fitz. Very quietly.''

I nodded slowly. I had had these kinds of assignments before also. Killing Forged ones did not bother me as much as killing a man did. Sometimes I tried to pretend I was laying a restless soul to peace, putting a family's anguish to a final end. I hoped I would not become too adept at lying to myself. It was a luxury an assassin could not afford. Chade had warned me that I must always remember what I truly was. Not an angel of mercy, but a killer who worked for the good of the King. Or the King-in-Waiting. It was my duty to keep the throne secure. My duty. I hesitated, then spoke.

"My prince. As I was coming back I saw our Queen-in-Waiting Kettricken. She was riding out with Prince Regal.''

"They make a handsome pair, do they not? And does she sit her horse well?'' Verity could not entirely keep bitterness from his voice.

"Aye. But in the Mountain style still.''

"She came to me, saying she wished to learn to ride our tall lowland horses better. I commended the idea. I did not know she would choose Regal as a riding master.'' Verity leaned over his map, studying detail that was not there.

"Perhaps she hoped you would teach her.'' I spoke thoughtlessly, to the man, not the Prince.

"Perhaps.'' He sighed suddenly. ''Oh, I know she did. Kettricken is lonely, sometimes. Often.'' He shook his head. "She should have been married to a younger son, to a man with time on his hands. Or to a King whose kingdom was not on the verge of war and disaster. I do not do her justice, Fitz. I know this. But she is so . . . young. Sometimes. And when she is not being so young, she is so fanatically patriotic. She

burns to sacrifice herself for the Six Duchies. Always I have to
hold her back, to tell her that is not what the Six Duchies need.
She is like a gadfly. There is no peace in her for me, Fitz.
Either she wants to be romped like a child, or she is quizzing
me on the very details of some crisis I am trying to set aside for
a few moments.''

I thought suddenly of Chivalry's single-minded pursuit of
the frivolous Patience, and caught a glimpse of his motives. A
woman who was an escape for him. Who would Verity have
chosen, had he been allowed to choose for himself? Probably
someone older, a placid woman possessed of inner self-worth
and peace.

''I grow so tired,'' Verity said softly. He poured himself
more mulled wine and stepped to the hearth to sip at it. ''Do
you know what I wish?''

It wasn't really a question. I didn't even bother to reply.

''I wish your father were alive, and king-in-waiting. And I
his right-hand man still. He would be telling me what tasks I
must tackle, and I would be doing as he asked. I would be at
peace with myself, no matter how hard my work, for I would be
sure he knew best. Do you know how easy it is, Fitz, to follow
a man you believe in?''

He looked up at last to meet my eyes.

''My prince,'' I said quietly. ''I believe I do.''

For a moment Verity was very still. Then: ''Ah,'' he said.
He held my eyes with his, and I did not need the warmth of his
Skilling to feel the gratitude he sent me. He stepped away from
the hearth, drew himself up straighter. My king-in-waiting
stood before me once more. He dismissed me with a tiny
motion, and I went. As I climbed the stairs to my room, for the
first time in my life I wondered if I should not be grateful to
have been born a bastard.

7

Encounters

*I*T HAD ALWAYS *been the custom and the expectancy that when a King or Queen of Buckkeep wed, the royal spouse would bring an entourage of his or her own as attendants. Such had been the case with both of Shrewd's queens. But when Queen Kettricken of the Mountains came to Buckkeep, she came as Sacrifice, as was her country's custom. She came alone, with no women or men to attend her, not even a maid to be a confidante. No person in Buckkeep was there to give the comfort of familiarity to her in her new home. She began her reign surrounded completely by strangers, not just at her own social level, but extending down to servants and guards as well. As time progressed she gathered friends to her, and found servants as well who suited her, though at first the idea of having a person whose lifework was to wait on her was a foreign and distressing concept to her.*

❧

Cub had missed my company. Before I departed for Bearns, I had left him the carcass of a deer, well frozen and concealed behind the hut. It should have been ample to feed him for the time I was gone. But in true wolf fashion, he had gorged, and slept, and gorged and slept again, until the meat was gone. *Two days ago,* he informed me, leaping and dancing about me. The interior of the hut was a litter of well-gnawed bones. He greeted me with frantic enthusiasm, doubly informed by the Wit and his nose of the fresh meat I brought. He fell upon it ravenously and paid me no mind at all as I gathered his chewed bones into a sack. Too much of this type of litter would draw rats, and the Keep rat hounds would follow. I couldn't chance that. I watched him surreptitiously as I tidied, saw the rippling of muscles in his shoulders as he braced his forefeet against the chunk of meat and tore a piece of flesh free. I noted, too, that all but the thickest deer bones had been cracked and licked clean of marrow. This was cub's play no longer, but the work of a powerful young animal. The bones he had cracked were thicker than the bones in my arm.

But why would I turn on you? You bring the meat. And ginger cakes.

His thought was laden with meaning. This was the way of a pack. I, an elder, brought meat to feed Cub, a young one. I was the hunter, bringing him back a portion of my kill. I quested toward him and found that, for him, our separateness was fading. We were pack. It was a concept I had never encountered before, going deeper than companion or partner. I feared that to him it meant what bonding did to me. I could not permit it.

''I am a human. You are a wolf.'' I spoke the words aloud, knowing he would get their meaning from my thoughts, but trying to force him to know in all his senses our differences.

Outwardly. Inside, we are pack. He paused and licked his nose complacently. Blood dotted his forepaws.

''No. I feed you and protect you here. But only for a time. When you are able to hunt for yourself, I will take you to a far place and leave you there.''

I have never hunted.

''I will teach you.''

That, too, is of the pack. You will teach me, and I will hunt with you. We will share many kills and much rich meat.

I will teach you to hunt, and then I will set you free.

I am already free. You do not hold me here, save that I will it. He lolled his tongue out over white teeth, laughing at my assumption.

You are arrogant, Cub. And ignorant.

So teach me. He turned his head sideways to let his back teeth scissor meat and tendon from the bone he was working on. *It is your pack duty.*

We are not pack. I have no pack. My allegiance is to my king.

If he is your leader, then he is mine also. We are pack. As his belly filled he was becoming more and more complacent about it.

I changed tactics. Coldly I told him, *I am of a pack that you cannot be part of. In my pack, all are humans. You are not a human. You are a wolf. We are not pack.*

A stillness welled in him. He did not try to reply. But he felt, and what he felt chilled me. Isolation, and betrayal. Loneliness.

I turned and left him there. But I could not hide from him how hard it was for me to leave him like that, nor conceal the deep shame at refusing him. I hoped he sensed also that I believed it was what was best for him. Much, I reflected, as Burrich had felt it was best for me when he took Nosy away from me because I had bonded to the puppy. The thought burned me and I did not just hasten away, I fled.

Evening was falling as I returned to the Keep and made my way up the stairs. I visited my room for certain bundles I had left there, and then made my way downstairs again. My traitorous feet slowed as I passed the second landing. I knew that very shortly Molly would be coming this way, bearing away the tray and dishes from Patience's meal. Patience seldom chose to dine in the hall with the other lords and ladies of the Keep, preferring the privacy of her own rooms and Lacey's easy companionship. Her shyness had begun to take on overtones of reclusiveness lately. But it was not concern over that which kept me loitering on the stairs. I heard the tap of Molly's feet coming down the hall; I knew I should move on, but it had been days since I had even glimpsed her. Celerity's shy flirtations had only made me more acutely aware of how I missed Molly. Surely it could not be too much for me simply to wish her good evening as I might any other servant girl. I knew I should not, I knew that if Patience heard of it, I would be rebuked. And yet . . .

I pretended to be studying a tapestry on the landing, a tapestry that had hung there since before I had ever come to Buckkeep. I heard her footsteps approaching, I heard them slow. My heart was thundering high in my chest, the palms of my hands were moist with sweat as I turned to see her. "Good evening," I managed, between a squeak and a whisper.

"Good evening to you," she said with great dignity. Her head went up a notch higher, her chin firmed. Her hair had been tamed into two thick braids and pinned about her head like a crown. Her dress of simple blue had a collar of delicate white lace, and there were lace cuffs to it as well. I knew whose fingers had worked that scalloped pattern. Lacey treated her well and gifted her with the work of her hands. That was good to know.

Molly did not falter as she passed me. Her eyes skittered sideways to me once, and I could not forbear to smile, and at my smile a blush so warm suffused her face and throat that almost I felt the heat of it. Her mouth went into a firmer line. As she turned and descended the stairs her scent wafted back to me, lemon balm and ginger riding on the sweeter scent that was simply Molly's own.

Female. Nice. Vast approval.

I leaped as if stung and spun about, expecting foolishly to discover Cub behind me. He was not, of course. I quested out, but he was not with me in my mind. I quested farther, found him dozing on his straw in the hut. *Don't do that,* I warned him. *Stay out of my mind, unless I bid you be with me.*

Consternation. *What is it you bid me do?*

Do not be with me, except when I wish you to.

Then how would I know when you wished me to be with you?

I will seek your mind when I want you.

A long quiet. *And I shall seek yours when I want you,* he offered. *Yes, this is pack. To call when one needs help, and to be always ready to hear such a call. We are pack.*

No! That is not what I am telling you. I am saying you

*must keep out of my mind when I do not wish you to be there. I
do not wish to be always sharing thoughts with you.*

*You make no sense at all. Shall I only breathe when you
are not snuffing the air? Your mind, my mind, it is all the pack
mind. Where else shall I think, but here? If you do not wish to
hear me, do not listen.*

I stood dumbfounded, trying to make sense of the thought.
I realized I was staring off into space. A serving boy had just
wished me good evening, and I had offered no response.
"Good evening," I replied, but he had already passed me. He
glanced back in puzzlement, to see if he was summoned, but I
waved him on. I shook my head to clear it of cobwebs and
started down the hall to Patience's room. I would discuss it
with Cub later, and make him understand. And soon he would
be off on his own, out of touch, out of mind. I pushed the
experience aside.

I tapped at Patience's door and was admitted. I saw that
Lacey had gone on one of her periodic rampages and restored a
sort of order to the room. There was even a cleared chair to sit
upon. They were both glad to see me. I told them of my trip to
Bearns, avoiding any mention of Virago. I knew that eventually
Patience would hear of it, and confront me about it, and I
would then assure her that gossip had greatly exaggerated our
encounter. I hoped that would work. In the meantime I had
brought gifts back with me. Tiny ivory fish, drilled to be strung
as beads or attached to a garment for Lacey, and for Patience
amber-and-silver earrings. An earthenware pot of wintergreen
berries preserved and sealed with a lid of wax.

"Wintergreen? I've no taste for wintergreen," Patience
puzzled when I offered it to her.

"Haven't you?" I feigned puzzlement as well. "I thought
you told me it was a flavor and scent you missed from your
childhood. Did not you have an uncle who brought you wintergreen?"

"No. I recall no such conversation."

"Perhaps it was Lacey, then?" I asked sincerely.

"Not I, master. Stings my nose to taste it, though it has a
nice scent in the air."

"Ah, well, then. My mistake." I set it aside on the table.

"What, Snowflake? Not pregnant again?" This I addressed to Patience's white terrier who had finally decided to come forth and sniff at me. I could sense her doggy little mind puzzling over Cub's scent on me.

"No, she's just getting fat," Lacey interjected for her, stooping to scratch her behind the ears. "My lady leaves sweetmeats and cookies about on plates, and Snowflake is always getting at them."

"You know you shouldn't let her. It's very bad for her teeth and coat," I rebuked Patience, and she replied that she knew it, but Snowflake was too old to be taught better. The conversation rambled from there, and it was another hour before I stretched and told them I must be going, to try once more to report to the King.

"I was earlier turned aside from his door," I mentioned. "Though not by any guard. His man Wallace came to the door when I knocked, to refuse me entry. When I asked why there was no guard on the King's door, he said they had been relieved of that duty. He had assumed it himself, the better to keep things quiet for the King."

"The King's not well, you know," Lacey offered. "I've heard that he's seldom seen out of his chambers before noon. Then, when he comes forth, he is like a man possessed, full of energy and appetite, but by early evening, he fades again, and begins to shuffle and mumble his words. He takes his dinner in his rooms, and cook says the tray comes back as full as it went up. It's quite a worry."

"It is," I agreed, and made my departure, almost dreading to hear more. So the King's health was now talk for the Keep. That was not good. I must ask Chade about it. And I must see for myself. In my earlier attempt to report to the King, I had encountered only the officious Wallace. Wallace had been most brusque with me, as if I were come simply to pass the time of day, rather than to report after a mission. He behaved as if the King were the most delicate of invalids and took it upon himself to keep anyone from bothering him. Wallace, I decided, had not been very well taught as to what the duties of his position were. He was a most annoying man. As I tapped I was wondering how long it would take Molly to find the wintergreen. She must know I had meant it for her; it was a taste she had always been greedy for when we were children.

Wallace came to the door and opened it a crack to peer out. He frowned at discovering me. He swung the door wider, but filled the opening with his body, as if my glimpsing the King might do him harm. He gave me no greeting, only demanded, "Did not you come before, earlier today?"

"Yes. I did. At that time you told me King Shrewd slept. And so I have come again, to make my report." I tried to keep my tone civil.

"Ah. It is important, this report?"

"I think the King can judge if it is, and send me away if he thinks I waste his time. I suggest you tell him I am here." I smiled belatedly, trying to soften the sharpness of my tone.

"The King has little energy. I try to see that he expends it only where it is needed." He wasn't moving from the door. I found myself sizing him up, wondering if I could just shoulder past him. That would create a commotion, and if the King were ill, I did not wish that. Someone tapped on my shoulder, but when I turned to look, no one was there. Turning back, I found the Fool in front of me, between Wallace and me.

"Are you his physician, then, to make such judgments?" The Fool took up my conversation for me. "For surely, you would be an excellent one. You physick me merely with your looks, and your words dispel your wind as well as mine. How physicked then must our dear king be, who languishes all day in your presence?"

The Fool bore a tray covered with a napkin. I smelled good beef broth and egg bread warm from the oven. His winter motley of black and white he had made merry with enameled bells and a garland of holly banded his cap. His fool's scepter was tucked up under his arm. A rat again. This one had been set atop the wand as if prancing. I had observed him holding long conversations with it in front of the Great Hearth, or on the steps before the King's throne.

"Begone, Fool! You've been in here twice today already. The King has already gone to his bed. He has no need of you." The man spoke sternly. But Wallace was the one who retreated, without intending to. I saw he was one of those people who

could not meet the Fool's pale eyes, and quailed from the touch
of his white hand.

"Twice shall be thrice, Wall Ass, dear, and your presence
replaced with my presents. Toddle off hence, and tell Regal all
your tattling. If walls have ears, then so must you, for you've
already the Wall's Ass. Such ears are filled to overflowing with
the King's business. You might physick our dear prince while
you enlighten him. For the darkness of his glance, methinks,
betokens that his bowels have backed up so far as to blind
him."

"Dare you speak so of the Prince?" Wallace sputtered.
The Fool was already inside the door and I on his heels. "He
shall hear of this."

"Speak so? Speak, sow. I doubt not that he hears all that
you do. Do not vent your wind at me, Wall Ass dear. Save that
for your prince, who delights in such puffing. He is at his
smokes now, I believe, and you might gust at him and he shall
drowse and nod and think you speak wisely and your airs most
sweet."

The Fool continued his advance as he nattered on, the
laden tray like a shield before him. Wallace gave ground
readily, and the Fool forced him back, through the sitting room
and into the King's bedchamber. There the Fool set the tray
down at the King's bedside while Wallace retreated to the other
door of the chamber. The Fool's eyes grew brighter.

"Ah, not abed at all, our king, unless you've hidden him
under coverlets, Wall Ass, my sweet. Come out, come out, my
king, my Shrewd one. King Shrewd you are, not king of shrews
to hide and creep about the walls and under the bedding." The
Fool began to poke so assiduously among the obviously empty
bed and coverlets, and to send his rat scepter peeping up
among the bed curtains, that I could not contain my laughter.

Wallace leaned back against the inner door, as if to guard
it from us, but at that instant it opened from within, and he all
but tumbled into the King's arms. He sat down heavily on the
floor. "Mind him!" the Fool observed to me. "See how he
seeks to put himself in my place before the King's feet, and to
play the fool with his clumsy pratfalls. Such a man deserves
the title Fool, but not the post!"

Shrewd stood there, robed as for rest, a frown of vexation on his face. He looked down in puzzlement at Wallace on the floor, and up at the Fool and me waiting for him, and then dismissed whatever the situation was. He spoke to Wallace as he scrabbled to his feet. "This steam does me no good at all, Wallace. It but makes my head ache all the more, and leaves a foul taste in my mouth as well. Take it away, and tell Regal I think his new herb might drive flies away, but not sickness. Take it away now, before it stinks up this room as well. Ah, Fool, you are here. And Fitz, you have finally come to report as well. Come in, sit down. Wallace, do you hear me? Remove that wretched pot! No, do not bring it through here, take it out the other way." And with a wave of his hand, Shrewd swatted the man away as if he had been an annoying fly.

Shrewd shut the door to his bathing room firmly, as if to keep the stink from spreading into his bedchamber, and came to take a straight-backed chair by the fire. In a moment the Fool had drawn a table up beside it, the cloth covering the food had become a tablecloth, and he had set out food for the King as prettily as any serving maid could have done. Silverware and a napkin appeared, a sleight of hand that had even Shrewd smiling, and then the Fool folded himself up on the hearth, knees nearly to his ears, chin cupped in his long-fingered hands, pale skin and hair picking up red tones from the fire's dancing flames. His every move was as graceful as a dancer's and the pose he struck now was artful as well as comical. The King reached down to smooth his flying hair as if the Fool were a kitten.

"I told you I was not hungry, Fool."

"That you did. But you did not tell me not to bring food."

"And if I had?"

"Then I should tell you this is not food, but a steaming pot such as Wall Ass afflicts you with, to fill your nostrils with a scent at least more pleasing than his. And this be not bread, but a plaster for your tongue, which you should apply at once."

"Ah." King Shrewd drew his table a bit closer and took up a spoonful of the soup. Barley shouldered against bits of carrot and meat in it. Shrewd tasted, and then began to eat.

"Am I not at least as good a physician as Wall Ass?" the Fool purred, well pleased with himself.

"Well you know Wallace is not a physician, but simply my servant."

"Well I know it, and well do you, but Wall Ass knows it not, and hence you are not well."

"Enough of your nattering. Step up, Fitz, don't stand there grinning like a simpleton. What have you to tell me?"

I glanced at the Fool, and then decided I would insult neither King nor Fool by asking if I could report freely in front of him. So I did, a simple report, with no mention of my more clandestine actions other than their results. Shrewd listened gravely, and at the end he had no comment, other than to rebuke me mildly for poor manners at the Duke's table. He then asked if Duke Brawndy of Bearns seemed well and content with the peace in his Duchy. I replied that he had when I left. Shrewd nodded. Then he requested the scrolls I had copied. These I took out and displayed for him, and was rewarded by a compliment on the gracefulness of my handiwork. He told me to take them to Verity's map room, and be sure Verity knew of them. He asked if I had viewed the Elderling's relic. I described it to him in detail. And all the while the Fool perched on the hearthstones and watched us silent as an owl. King Shrewd ate his soup and bread under the Fool's watchful eyes as I read the scroll aloud to him. When I was finished, he sighed and leaned back in his chair. "So, let's see this scroll-work of yours," he commanded, and puzzled, I surrendered it to him. Once more he looked it over carefully, then rerolled it. As he gave it back to me he said, "You've a graceful way with a pen, boy. Well lettered and well done. Take it to Verity's map room, and see that he knows of it."

"Of course, my king." I faltered, confused. I did not understand his motive in repeating himself, and was unsure if he were waiting for some other response from me. But the Fool was rising, and I caught from him something less than a glance; not quite the lift of an eyebrow, not quite the turn of a lip, but enough to bid me to silence. The Fool gathered up the dishes, all the while making merry talk with the King, and then both of us were dismissed together. As we left, the King was staring into the flames.

Out in the hall, we exchanged glances more openly. I began to speak, but the Fool commenced to whistle, and did not cease until we were halfway down the stairs. Then he paused and caught at my sleeve, and we halted on the stairway, betwixt floors. I sensed he had chosen this spot carefully. None could see or hear us speak here, save that we saw them also. Still, it was not even the Fool that spoke to me, but the rat atop the scepter. He brought it up before my nose and squeaked in the rat's voice, "Ah, but you and I, we must remember whatever he forgets, Fitz, and keep it safe for him. It costs him much to show as strong as he did tonight. Do not be deceived about that. What he said to you, twice, you must cherish and obey, for it means he held it twice as hard in his mind to be sure he would say it to you."

I nodded and resolved to deliver the scroll that very night to Verity. "I do not much care for Wallace," I commented to the Fool.

"'Tis not Wall's Ass you should have a care for, but Wall's Ears," he replied solemnly. Abruptly he balanced the tray on one long-fingered hand and lofted it high over his head, and went capering off down the stairs before me, leaving me alone to think.

I delivered the scroll that night, and in the days that followed, I took up the tasks Verity had assigned me earlier. I used fat sausage and smoked fish as the vehicles for my poisons, wrapped in small bundles. These I might easily scatter as I fled, in the hopes there would be sufficient for all who pursued me. Each morning I studied the map in Verity's map room, and then saddled Sooty and took myself and my poisons out where I thought it most likely I would be set upon by Forged ones. Remembering my previous experiences, I carried a short sword on these riding expeditions, something that afforded both Hands and Burrich some amusement at first. I gave it out that I was scouting for game in case Verity wished to plan a winter hunt. Hands accepted it easily, Burrich with a tightened mouth that showed he knew I lied, and knew also that I could not tell him the truth. He did not pry, but neither did he like it.

Twice in ten days I was set upon by Forged ones, and twice fled easily, letting my poisoned provisions tumble from my saddlebags as I went. They fell upon them greedily, scarcely unwrapping the meat before stuffing it into their mouths. I returned to each site the following day, to document for Verity how many I had slain and the details of their appearances. The second group did not match any description we had received. We both suspected this meant there were more Forged ones than we had heard.

I did my task, but I took no pride in it. Dead, they were even more pitiful than alive. Ragged, thin creatures, frostbitten and battered by their fights among themselves they were, and the savagery of the quick harsh poisons I used twisted their bodies into caricatures of men. Frost glistened on their beards and eyebrows, and the blood from their mouths made red clumps like frozen rubies in the snow. Seven Forged ones I killed this way, and then heaped the frozen bodies with pitchpine, and poured oil on them and set them aflame. I cannot say what I found most distasteful, the poisoning, or the concealing of my deed. Cub had initially begged to go with me when he understood that I was riding out each day after feeding him, but at one point, as I stood over the frozen stickmen I had slain, I heard, *This is not hunting, this. This is no pack's doing. This is man's doing.* His presence was gone before I could rebuke him for intruding into my mind again.

Evenings I returned to the Keep, to hot fresh food and warm fires, dry clothes and a soft bed, but the specters of those Forged ones stood between me and those comforts. I felt myself a heartless beast that I could enjoy such things after spreading death by day. My only comfort was a prickly one, that at night when I slept, I dreamed of Molly, and walked and talked with her, unhaunted by Forged ones or their frost-rimed bodies.

Came a day I rode out later than I had intended, for Verity had been in his map room and had kept me overlong in talk. A storm was coming up, but it did not seem too severe of one. I had not intended to go far that day. But I found fresh sign instead of my prey, and sign of a larger group of them than I had expected. And so I rode on, ever at the alert with my five senses, for the sixth of the Wit was no help at all in finding Forged ones. The gathering clouds stole the light from the sky more swiftly than I had expected and the sign led me down game trails where Sooty and I found it slow going. When I finally glanced up from my tracking, admitting that they had eluded me this day, I found myself much farther from Buckkeep than I had intended and well off any traveled road.

The wind began to blow, a nasty cold one that foretold snow to follow. I wrapped my cloak more tightly about myself and turned Sooty's head toward home, relying on her to pick her path and pace. Darkness fell before we'd gone far, and snow with it. Had I not traversed this area so frequently of late, I would surely have been lost. But we pressed on, going always, it seemed, into the teeth of the wind. The cold soaked right through me, and I began to shiver. I feared the shivering might actually be the beginnings of trembling and a fit such as I had not suffered for a long time.

I was grateful when the winds finally tore a rent in the cloud cover, and moonlight and starlight leaked through to gray our way. We made a better pace then, despite the fresh snow that Sooty waded through. We broke out of a thin birch forest, onto a hillside that lightning had burned off a few years ago. The wind was stronger here with nothing to oppose it, and I gathered my cloak and turned up the collar again. I knew that once I crested the hill, I would see the lights of Buckkeep, and that another hill away and a vale would find a well-used road to take me home. So I was of better cheer as we cut our way across the hill's smooth flank.

Sudden as thunder, I heard the hoofbeats of a horse struggling to make speed, but somehow encumbered. Sooty slowed, then threw back her head and whinnied. At the same moment I saw a horse and rider break out of the cover, downhill of me and to the south. The horse carried a rider, and two other people clung to it, one to its breast strap and one to the rider's leg. Light glinted on a blade that rose and fell, and with a cry the man clutching at the rider's leg fell away to wallow and shriek in the snow. But the other figure had caught the horse's headstall, and as he tried to drag the beast to a halt, two other pursuers burst from the trees to converge on the struggling horse and rider.

The moment of recognizing Kettricken is inseparable from the moment I set heels to Sooty. What I saw made no sense to me, but that did not prevent my responding. I did not ask myself what my queen-in-waiting was doing out here, at night, unaccompanied and set upon by robbers. Rather, I found myself admiring how she kept her seat and set her horse to wheeling as she kicked and slashed at the men who tried to drag her down. I drew my sword as we closed on the struggle, but I do not recall that I made any sound. My recollection of the whole struggle is a strange one, a battle of silhouettes, done in black and white like a mountain shadow play, soundless save for the grunts and cries of the Forged ones as one after another they fell.

Kettricken had slashed one across the face, blinding him with blood, but still he clung to her and tried to drag her from the saddle. The other ignored the plight of his fellows, tugging instead at saddlebags that probably carried no more than a bit of food and brandy packed for a day's ride.

Sooty took me in close to the one gripping Softstep's headstall. I saw it was a woman and then my sword was into her and out again, as soulless an exercise as chopping wood. Such a peculiar struggle. I could sense Kettricken and me, the fright of her horse and Sooty's battle-trained enthusiasm, but from her attackers, nothing. Nothing at all. No anger throbbed, no pain of their wounds shrieked for attention. To my Wit, they were not there at all, any more than the snow or the wind that likewise opposed me.

I watched as in a dream as Kettricken seized her attacker by the hair and leaned his head back that she might cut his throat. Blood spilled black in the moonlight, drenching her coat and leaving a sheen on the chestnut's neck and shoulder before he fell back to spasm in the snow. I swung my short sword at the last one, but missed. Kettricken did not. Her short knife danced in, and punched through jerkin and rib cage and into his lung, and out again as swift. She kicked him away. "To me!" she said simply into the night, and put heels to her chestnut, driving Softstep straight up the hill. Sooty ran with her nose at Kettricken's stirrup, and so we crested the hill together, glimpsing the lights of Buckkeep briefly before we plunged down the other side.

There was brush at the bottom of the slope, and a creek hidden by the snow, so I kicked Sooty into the lead and turned Softstep before she could blunder into it and fall. Kettricken said nothing as I turned her horse, but let me take the lead as we entered the forest on the other side of the stream. I moved us as swiftly as I dared, expecting always figures to shout and leap out at us. But we made the road at last, just as the clouds closed up again, stealing the moonlight from us. I slowed the horses and let them breathe. For some time we traveled in silence, both intently listening for any sounds of pursuit.

After a time we felt safer, and I heard Kettricken let out her pent breath in a long, shaky sigh. "Thank you, Fitz," she said simply, but could not keep her voice quite steady. I made no comment, half expecting that at any moment she would burst into weeping. I would not have blamed her. Instead she gradually gathered herself, tugging her clothes straight, wiping her blade on her pants and then resheathing it at her waist. She leaned forward to pat Softstep's neck and murmur words of praise and comfort to the horse. I felt Softstep's tension ease and admired Kettricken's skill to have so swiftly gained the confidence of the tall horse.

"How came you here? Seeking me?" she asked at last.

I shook my head. Snow was beginning to fall again. "I was out hunting, and went farther than I had intended. It was but good fortune that brought me to you." I paused, then ventured, "Did you get lost? Will there be riders searching for you?"

She sniffed, and took a breath. "Not exactly," she said in a shaky voice. "I went out riding with Regal. A few others rode with us, but when the storm began to threaten, we all turned back to Buckkeep. The others rode on before us, but Regal and I came more slowly. He was telling me a folktale from his home Duchy, and we let the others ride ahead, that I should not have to hear it through their chatter." She took a breath and I heard her swallow back the last of the night's terror. Her voice was calmer when she went on.

"The others were far ahead of us, when a fox started up suddenly from the brush by the path. 'Follow me, if you'd like to see real sport!' Regal challenged me, and he turned his horse from the path and set off after the animal. Whether I would or no, Softstep sprang after them. Regal rode like a mad thing, all stretched out on his horse, urging it on with a quirt." There was consternation, and wonder, but also a stain of admiration in her voice as she described him.

Softstep had not answered the rein. At first she had been fearful of their pace, for she did not know the terrain and feared that Softstep would stumble. So she had tried to rein in her mount. But when she had realized that she could no longer see the road or the others, and that Regal had gotten far ahead of her, she had given Softstep her head, in the hopes of catching up. With the predictable result that as the storm closed in she had lost her way completely. She had turned back to retrace her trail to the road, but the falling snow and blowing wind had quickly erased it. At last she had given Softstep the bit, trusting her horse to find her way home. Probably she would have, if those wild men had not set upon her. Her voice dwindled away into silence.

"Forged ones," I told her quietly.

"Forged ones," she repeated in a wondering voice. Then, more firmly: "They have no hearts left. So it was explained to me." I felt more than saw her glance. "Am I so poor a Sacrifice that there are folk who would kill me?"

In the distance we heard the winding of a horn. Searchers.

"They would have set upon any that crossed their paths," I told her. "For them, there was no thought that it was their queen-in-waiting they attacked. I doubt greatly that they knew who you were at all." I closed my jaws firmly before I could add that such was not the case with Regal. If he had not intended her harm, neither had he kept her from coming to it. I did not believe he had ever intended to show her "sport" in chasing a fox across snowy hills in the twilight. He had meant to lose her. And done so handily.

"I think my lord will be very wroth with me," she said,

woeful as a child. As if in answer to her prediction, we rounded the shoulder of the hill and saw men on horseback bearing torches coming toward us. We heard the horn again, more clearly, and in a few moments we were among them. They were the forerunners of the main search party, and a girl set out at once galloping back to tell the King-in-Waiting that his queen had been found. In the light of the torches, Verity's guards exclaimed and swore over the blood that glinted yet on Softstep's neck, but Kettricken kept her composure as she assured them that none of it was hers. She spoke quietly of the Forged ones who had set upon her and what she had done to defend herself. I saw admiration of her growing among the soldiers. I heard then for the first time that the boldest attacker had dropped out of a tree upon her. Him she had slain first.

"Four she done, and not a scratch upon her!" exulted one grizzled veteran, and then: "Begging your pardon, my lady queen. No disrespect meant!"

"It might have been a different tale had not Fitz come to free my horse's head," Kettricken said quietly. Their respect for her grew as she did not glory in her triumph, but made sure I received my due as well.

They congratulated her loudly, and spoke angrily of scouring the woods tomorrow all about Buckkeep. "It shames us all as soldiers, that our own queen cannot ride forth safely!" declared one woman. She set her hand to the hilt of her blade and swore on it to have it blooded with Forged blood by the morrow. Several others followed her example. The talk grew loud, bravado and relief at the Queen's safety fueling it. It became a triumphal procession home, until Verity arrived. He came at a dead gallop, on a horse lathered by both distance and speed. I knew then that the search had not been a brief one, and could only guess at how many roads Verity had traveled since he had received word his lady was missing.

"How could you be so foolish as to go so far astray!" were his first words to her. His voice was not tender. I saw her head lose its proud lift, and heard the muttered comments of the man closest to me. From there nothing went well. He did not scold her before his men, but I saw him wince as she told him plainly what had become of her and how she had killed to defend herself. He was not pleased to have her speak so plainly of a band of Forged ones, brave enough to attack the Queen, and scarce out of Buckkeep's shadow. That which Verity had sought to keep quiet would be on everyone's lips tomorrow, with the added fillip that it had been the Queen herself they'd dared to attack. Verity shot me a murderous glance, as if it were all my doing, and roughly commandeered fresh horses from two of his guard to take himself and his queen back to Buckkeep. He whisked her away from them, carrying her back to Buckkeep at a gallop as if arriving there sooner would somehow make the breach of safety less real. He seemed not to realize he had denied his guard the honor of bringing her safely home.

I myself rode back slowly with them, trying not to hear the disgruntled words of the soldiers. They did not quite criticize the King-in-Waiting, but complimented the Queen more on her spirit and thought it sad she'd not been welcomed back with an embrace and a kind word or two. If any gave thought to Regal's behavior, they did not speak it aloud.

Later that night, in the stables, after I'd seen to Sooty, I helped Burrich and Hands put Softstep and Truth, Verity's horse, to rights. Burrich grumbled at how hard both beasts had been used. Softstep had taken a minor scratch during the attack, and her mouth was sore, bruised from fighting for her head, but neither animal would take permanent hurt. Burrich sent Hands off to fix a warm mash of grain for them both. Only then did he quietly tell how Regal had come in, given his horse over for stabling, and gone up to the Keep without so much as mentioning Kettricken. Burrich himself had been alerted by a stable boy, asking where Softstep was. When Burrich had set about to find out, and made so bold as to ask Regal himself, Regal had replied that he had thought Kettricken had stayed on the road and come in with her attendants. So Burrich had been the one to sound the alarm, with Regal very vague as to where he had actually left the road, and what direction the fox had led him, and presumably Kettricken. "He's covered his tracks well," Burrich muttered to me as Hands came back with the grain. I knew he did not refer to the fox.

My feet were leaden as I made my way up to the Keep that

night, and my heart as well. I did not want to imagine what Kettricken was feeling, nor did I care to consider what the talk was in the guardroom. I pulled off my clothes and fell into bed, and instantly into a sleep. Molly was waiting for me in my dreams, and the only peace I knew.

I was awakened a short time later, by someone pounding on my latched door. I arose and opened it to a sleepy page, who'd been sent to fetch me to Verity's map room. I told him I knew the way and sent him back to bed. I dragged on my clothes hastily and raced down the stairs, wondering what disaster had befallen us now.

Verity was waiting for me there, the hearthfire almost the only light in the room. His hair was rumpled, and he had thrown a robe on over his nightshirt. Plainly he had just come from his bed himself, and I braced myself for whatever news he'd received. "Shut the door!" he commanded me tersely. I did and then came to stand before him. I could not tell if the glint in his eyes was anger or amusement as he abruptly demanded, "Who is Lady Red-Skirts, and why do I dream of her every night?"

I could not find my tongue. Desperately I wondered just how privy to my dreams he had been. Embarrassment dizzied me. Had I stood naked before the whole court, I could not have felt more exposed.

Verity turned his face aside and gave a cough that might have started as a chuckle. "Come, boy, it is not as if I cannot understand. I did not wish to be privy to your secret; rather you have thrust it upon me, especially so these last few nights. And I need my sleep, not to start up in bed fevered with your . . . admiration for this woman." He stopped speaking abruptly. My flaming blush was warmer than any hearthfire.

"So," he said uncomfortably. Then abruptly: "Sit down. I am going to teach you to guard your thoughts as well as you guard your tongue." He shook his head. "Strange, Fitz, that you can block my Skilling so completely from your mind at times, but spill your most private desires out like a wolf howling into the night. I suppose it springs from what Galen did to you. Would we could undo that. But as we can't, I shall teach you what I can, whenever I can."

I had not moved. Suddenly neither of us could look at the other. "Come here," he repeated gruffly. "Sit down here with me. Look into the flames."

And in the space of an hour, he gave me an exercise to practice, one that would keep my dreams to myself, or more likely, ensure that I had no dreams at all. With a sinking heart I realized I would lose even the Molly of my imagination as surely as I'd lost the real one. He sensed my glumness.

"Come, Fitz, it will pass. Keep a rein on yourself and endure. It can be done. May come a day when you will wish your life to be as empty of women as it is now. As I do."

"She didn't mean to get lost, sir."

Verity shot me a baleful glance. "Intentions cannot be exchanged for results. She is queen-in-waiting, boy. She must always think, not once, but thrice, before she takes action."

"She told me that Softstep followed Regal's horse, and would not respond to the rein. You can fault Burrich and I for that; we're supposed to have trained that horse."

He sighed suddenly. "I suppose so. Consider yourself re-buked, and tell Burrich to find my lady a less spirited horse to ride until she is a better horsewoman." He sighed again, deeply. "I suppose she will consider that a punishment from me. She will look at me sadly with those great blue eyes, but speak not a word against it. Ah, well. It cannot be helped. But did she have to kill, and then to speak of it so blithely? What will my people think of her?"

"She scarcely had a choice, sir. Would it have been better for her to die? As to what folk will think . . . well. The soldiers who first found us thought her plucky. And capable. Not bad qualities for a Queen, sir. The women, especially, in your guard spoke warmly of her as we returned. They see her as their queen now, much more than if she were a weeping, quailing thing. They will follow her without question. In times like these, perhaps a Queen with a knife will give us more heart than a woman who drapes herself in jewels and hides behind walls."

"Perhaps," Verity said quietly. I sensed he did not agree. "But now all shall know, most vividly, of the Forged ones who are gathering about Buckkeep."

"They shall know, too, that a determined person can defend herself from them. And from the talk of your guard as we came back, I think there shall be far fewer Forged ones a week hence."

"I know that. Some will be slaying their own kin. Forged or not, it is Six Duchies blood we are shedding. I had sought to avoid having my guard kill my own people."

A small silence fell between us as we both reflected he had not scrupled to set me to that same task. Assassin. That was the word for what I was. I had no honor to preserve, I realized.

"Not true, Fitz." He answered my thought. "You preserve my honor. And I honor you for that, for doing what must be done. The ugly work, the hidden work. Do not be shamed that you work to preserve the Six Duchies. Do not think I do not appreciate such work simply because it must remain secret. Tonight, you saved my queen. I do not forget that either."

"She needed little saving, sir. I believe that even alone, she would have survived."

"Well. We won't wonder about that." He paused, then said awkwardly, "I must reward you, you know."

When I opened my mouth to protest, he held up a forbidding hand. "I know you require nothing. I know, too, that there is already so much between us that nothing I could give you would be sufficient for my gratitude. But most folk know nothing of that. Will you have it said in Buckkeep Town that you saved the Queen's life, and the King-in-Waiting acknowledged you not at all? But I am at a loss to know what to gift you with . . . it should be something visible, and you must carry it about with you for a while. That much I know of statecraft, at least. A sword? Something better than that piece of iron you were carrying tonight?"

"It's an old blade Hod told me to take to practice with," I defended myself. "It works."

"Obviously. I shall have her select a better one for you, and do a bit of fancywork on the hilt and scabbard. Would that do it?"

"I think so," I said awkwardly.

"Well. Let's back to bed, shall we? And I shall be able to

sleep now, won't I?'' There was no mistaking the amusement in his voice now. My cheeks burned anew.

''Sir. I have to ask. . . .'' I fumbled the hard words out. ''Do you know who I was dreaming about?''

He shook his head slowly. ''Do not fear you have compromised her honor. I know only that she wears blue skirts, but you see them as red. And that you love her with an ardency that is appropriate to youth. Do not struggle to stop loving her. Only to stop Skilling it about at night. I am not the only one open to such Skilling, though I believe I am the only one who would recognize your signature on the dream so plain. Still, be cautious. Galen's coterie is not without Skill, even if they use it clumsily and with little strength. A man can be undone when his enemies learn what is dearest to him from his Skill dreams. Keep your guard up.'' He gave an inadvertent chuckle. ''And hope your Lady Red-Skirts has no Skill in her blood, for if she does at all, she must have heard you all these many nights.''

And having put that unsettling thought into my head, he dismissed me back to my chambers and bed. I did not sleep again that night.

8

The Queen Awakes

Oh, some folk ride to the wild-boar hunt
Or for elk they nock their arrows.
But my love rode with the Vixen Queen
To lay to rest our sorrows.

She did not dream of fame that day
Nor fear what pain might find her.
She rode to heal her people's hearts
And my love rode behind her.

—''The Vixen Queen's Hunt''

The whole Keep was astir early the next day. There was a fevered, almost festival air in the courtyard as Verity's personal guard and every warrior who had no scheduled duties that day massed for a hunt. Tracking hounds bayed restively, while the pull-down dogs with their massive jaws and barrel chests huffed excitedly and tested their restraints. Bets were already being set on who would hunt the most successfully. Horses pawed the earth, bowstrings were checked, while pages ran helter-skelter everywhere. Inside the kitchen, half the cooking staff was busy putting up packages of food for the hunters to take with them. Soldiers young and old, male and female, strutted and laughed aloud, bragging of past confrontations, comparing weapons, building spirit for the hunt. I had seen this a hundred times, before a winter hunt for elk, or bear. But now there was an edge to it, a rank smell of bloodlust on the air. I heard snatches of conversations, words that made me queasy:

". . . no mercy for that dung . . .", ". . . cowards and traitors, to dare to attack the Queen . . .", ". . . shall pay
dearly. They don't deserve a swift death. . . ." I ducked hastily back into the kitchen, threaded my way through an area
busy as a stirred anthill. Here, too, I heard the same sorts of
sentiments voiced, the same craving for revenge.

I found Verity in his map room. I could tell he had washed
and dressed himself afresh this day, but he wore last night as
plainly as a dirty robe. He was attired for a day inside, among
his papers. I tapped lightly at the door, although it stood ajar.
He sat in a chair before the fire, his back to me. He nodded, but
did not look up at me as I entered. For all his stillness, there
was a charged air to the room, the gathering of a storm. A tray
of breakfast rested on a table beside his chair, untouched. I
came and stood quietly beside him, almost certain I had been
Skilled here. As the silence grew longer I wondered if Verity
himself knew why. At length I decided to speak.

"My prince. You do not ride with your guard today?" I
ventured.

It was as if I had opened a floodgate. He turned to look at
me; the lines in his face had been graven deeper overnight. He
looked haggard, sickened. "I do not. I dare not. How could I
countenance such a thing, this hunting down of our own folk
and kin! And yet what is my alternative? To hide and mope
within the Keep walls while others go out to avenge this insult
to my queen-in-waiting! I dare not forbid my men to uphold
their honor. So I must behave as if I am unaware of what goes
on in the courtyard. As if I am a simpleton, or a laggard, or a
coward. There will be a ballad written about this day, I doubt it
not. What shall it be called? 'Verity's Massacre of the Wit-
less'? Or 'Queen Kettricken's Sacrifice of the Forged'?" His
voice rose on every word, and before he was half-done, I had
stepped to the door and shut it firmly. I looked about the room
as he ranted, wondering who else besides myself was hearing
these words.

"Did you sleep at all, my prince?" I asked when he had
run down.

He smiled with bleak amusement. "Well you know what

put an end to my first attempt at rest. My second was less . . . engaging. My lady came to my chamber.''

I felt my ears begin to warm. Whatever he was about to tell me, I did not want to hear it. I had no wish to know what had passed between them last night. Quarrel or amendment, I wanted to know nothing of it. Verity was merciless.

''Not weeping, as you might think she would. Not for comfort. Not to be held against night fears, or reassured of my regard. But sword stiff as a rebuked sergeant, to stand at the foot of the bed and beg my pardon for her transgressions. Whiter than chalk and hard as oak . . .'' His voice trailed off, as if he realized he betrayed too much of himself. ''She foresaw this hunting mob, not I. She came to me in the middle of the night, asking what must we do. I had no answer for her, any more than I do now—''

''At least she foresaw this,'' I ventured, hoping to bring some respite from his anger for Kettricken.

''And I did not,'' he said heavily. ''She did. Chivalry would have. Oh, Chivalry would have known it would happen from the moment she went missing, and would have had all sorts of contingency plans. But I did not. I thought only to bring her swiftly home, and hope not too many heard of it. As if such a thing could be! And so today I think to myself that if ever the crown does come to rest on my brow, it will be in a most unworthy place.''

This was a Prince Verity I had never seen before, a man with his confidence in tatters. I finally saw how poor a match Kettricken was for him. It was not her fault. She was strong, and raised to rule. Verity often said himself he had been raised as a second son. The right sort of woman would have steadied him like a sea anchor, helped him rise to assume his kingship. A woman who had come weeping to his bed, to be cuddled and reassured, would have let him arise certain he was a man and fit to be a King. Kettricken's discipline and restraint made him doubt his own strength. My prince was human, I suddenly perceived. It was not reassuring.

''You should at least come out and speak to them,'' I ventured.

''And say what? 'Good hunting'? No. But you go, boy. Go

and watch and bring me word of what is happening. Go now.
And shut my door. I have no desire to see anyone else until you
return with word of what goes on.''

I turned and did as he bid me. As I left the Great Hall and
went down the passage to the courtyard, I encountered Regal.
He was seldom up and about this early, and he looked as if his
arising this morning had been no choice of his. His clothing
and hair were well arranged, but all the tiny primping touches
were missing: no earring, no carefully folded and pinned silk at
his throat, and the only jewelry was his signet ring. His hair
was combed, but not scented and curled. And his eyes were
networked in red. Fury rode him. As I sought to pass him he
seized me and jerked me to face him. That, at least, was his
intention. I did not resist, but merely laxed my muscles. And
found, to my delight and amazement, that he could not move
me. He turned to face me, eyes blazing, and found out that he
must look up, ever so slightly, to glare at me eye to eye. I had
grown and put on weight. I had known that, but had never
considered this delightful side effect. I stopped the grin before
it reached my mouth, but it must have showed in my eyes. He
gave me a violent shove, and I allowed it to rock me. A bit.

''Where's Verity?'' he snarled.

''My prince?'' I queried, as if not grasping what he desired.

''Where is my brother? That wretched wife of his—'' He
broke off, strangling on his anger. ''Where is my brother usually at this time of day?'' he finally managed.

I did not lie. ''Some days he goes early to his tower. Or he
may be breakfasting, I suppose. Or in the baths . . .'' I offered.

''Useless bastard,'' Regal dismissed me, and whirled, to
hurry off in the direction of the tower. I hoped the climb would
amuse him. As soon as he was out of sight, I broke into a run,
not to waste the precious time I had gained.

The moment I entered the courtyard, the reason for Regal's fury was made clear. Kettricken stood atop a wagon seat,
and every head was turned up toward her. She wore the same
clothes she had the night before. By daylight, I could see how a
spray of blood had marked the sleeve of the white fur jacket,

and how a heavier plume of it had soaked and stained her purple trousers. She was booted and hatted, ready to ride. A sword was buckled at her hip. Dismay rose in me. How could she? I glanced about, wondering what she had been saying. Every face was turned to her, eyes wide. I had emerged into a moment of utter silence. Every man and woman seemed to be holding breath, awaiting her next words. When they came, they were uttered in a speaking voice, calmly, but so silent was the crowd that her clear voice carried in the cold air.

"This is not a hunt, I say," Kettricken repeated gravely. "Put aside your merriment and boasts. Remove from your bodies every bit of jewelry, every sign of rank. Let your hearts be solemn and consider what we do."

Her words were accented still with the flavor of the Mountains, but a cool part of my mind observed how carefully chosen was each word, how balanced each phrase.

"We do not go to hunt," she repeated. "But to claim our casualties. We go to lay to rest those the Red-Ships have stolen from us. The Red-Ships have taken the hearts of the Forged ones, and left their bodies to stalk us. Nonetheless, those we put down today are of the Six Duchies. Our own.

"My soldiers, I ask of you that no arrow be loosed today, no blow struck save for a clean kill. I know you skilled enough to do this. We have all suffered enough. Let each death today be as brief and merciful as we can manage, for all our sakes. Let us clench our jaws, and remove that which infects us, with as much resolve and regret as if we severed a maimed limb from a body. For such is what we do. Not vengeance, my people, but surgery, to be followed by a healing. Do as I say, now."

For some few minutes she stood still and looked down at us all. As in a dream, folk began to move. Hunters removed feathers and ribbons, tokens and jewelry from their garments and handed them to pages. The mood of merriment and boasting had evaporated. She had stripped that protection away, forced all to consider truly what they were about to do. No one relished it. All were poised, waiting to hear what she would say next. Kettricken kept her absolute silence and stillness, so that each eye was perforce drawn back to her. When she saw she had the attention of all, she spoke again.

"Good," she praised us quietly. "And now heed my words well. I desire horse-drawn litters, or wagons . . . whatever you of the stable judge best. Pad them well with straw. No body of our folk will be left to feed foxes or be pecked by crows. They will be brought back here, names noted if known, and prepared for the pyre that is the honor of those fallen in battle. If families be known and be near, they shall be summoned to the mourning. To those who live far, word will be sent, and the honors due those who have lost their blood kin as soldiers." Tears ran unchecked, untouched down her cheeks. They glinted in the early-winter sunlight like diamonds. Her voice thickened as she turned to command another group. "My cooks and serving folk! Set all tables in the Great Hall and prepare a funeral feast. Set the Lesser Hall with water and herbs and clean garments that we may prepare the bodies of our folk for burning. All others, leave your ordinary duties. Fetch wood and build a pyre. We shall return, to burn our dead and mourn them." She gazed about, meeting every eye. Something in her face set. She drew the sword from her belt and pointed it aloft in an oath. "When we have done with our grieving, we shall make ready to avenge them! Those who have taken our folk shall know our wrath!" Slowly she lowered her blade, sheathed it cleanly. Again her eyes commanded us. "And now we ride, my folk!"

My flesh stood up in goose bumps. Around me, men and women were mounting horses and a hunt was forming up. With impeccable timing, Burrich was suddenly beside the wagon, with Softstep saddled and awaiting her rider. I wondered where he had gotten the black-and-red harness, the colors of grief and vengeance. I wondered if she had ordered it, or if he had simply known. She stepped down, onto her horse's back, then settled into the saddle, and Softstep stood steady despite the novel mount. She lifted her hand, and it held a sword. The hunt surged forth behind her.

"Stop her!" hissed Regal behind me, and I spun to find that both he and Verity stood at my back, completely unnoticed by the crowd.

"No!" I dared to breathe aloud. "Cannot you feel it? Do not spoil it. She's given them all something back. I don't know what it is, but they have been sore missing it for a long time."

"It is pride," Verity said, his deep voice a rumble. "What we have all been missing, and I most of all. There rides a Queen," he continued in soft amazement. Was there a shade of envy there as well? He turned slowly and went quietly back into the Keep. Behind us a babble of voices arose, and folk hastened to do as she had bidden them. I walked behind Verity, near stunned by what I had witnessed. Regal pushed past me, to leap in front of Verity and confront him. He was quivering with outrage. My prince halted.

"How can you have allowed this to happen? Have you no control over that woman at all? She makes mockery of us! Who is she, to thus issue commands and take out an armed guard from the Keep! Who is she, to decree all this so high-handedly!" Regal's voice cracked in his fury.

"My wife," Verity said mildly. "And your queen-in-waiting. The one you chose. Father assured me you would choose a woman worthy to be a Queen. I think you picked better than you knew."

"Your wife? Your undoing, you ass! She undermines you, she cuts your throat as you sleep! She steals their hearts, she builds her own name! Cannot you see it, you dolt? You may be content to let that Mountain vixen steal the crown, but I am not!"

I turned aside hastily and bent to retie my shoe so I could not witness that Prince Verity struck Prince Regal. I did hear something very like the crack of an openhanded blow to a man's face and a bitten off cry of fury. When I looked up, Verity was standing as quietly as before, while Regal hunkered forward with a hand over his nose and mouth. "King-in-Waiting Verity will brook no insults to Queen-in-Waiting Kettricken. Or even to himself. I said my lady had reawakened pride in our soldiers. Perhaps she has stirred mine as well." Verity looked mildly surprised as he considered this.

"The King will hear of this!" Regal took his hand away from his face, looked aghast at the blood on it. He held it up, shaking, to show Verity. "My father will see this blood you

have shed!'' he quavered, and choked on the blood coursing
from his nose. He leaned forward slightly and held his bloody
hand away from himself so as not to spoil his clothing with a
stain.

''What? You intend to bleed all the way to this afternoon,
when our father arises? If you can manage that, come and show
me as well!'' To me: ''Fitz! Have you nothing better to do than
stand about gaping? Be off with you. See that my lady's commands are well obeyed!''

Verity turned and strode off down the corridor. I made
haste to obey and to take myself out of Regal's range. Behind
us, he stamped and cursed like a child in the midst of a tan-
trum. Neither of us turned back to him, but I at least hoped that
no servants had marked what had transpired.

It was a long and peculiar day about the Keep. Verity made
a visit to King Shrewd's rooms, and then kept himself to his
map room. I know not what Regal did. All folk turned out to do
the Queen's bidding, working swiftly, but almost silently, gos-
siping quietly among themselves as they prepared the one hall
for food and the other for bodies. One great change I marked.
Those women who had been most faithful to the Queen now
found themselves attended, as if they were shadows of Kettricken. And these nobly born women suddenly did not scruple
to come themselves to the Lesser Hall, to supervise the preparing of the herb-scented water and the laying out of towels and
linens. I myself helped with the fetching of wood for the required pyre.

By late afternoon, the hunt returned. They came quietly,
riding in solemn guard around the wagons they escorted. Kettricken rode at their head. She looked tired, and frozen in a way
that had nothing to do with the cold. I wanted to go to her, but
did not steal the honor as Burrich came to take her horse's
head and assist her dismount. Fresh blood spattered her boots
and Softstep's shoulders. She had not ordered her soldiers to
do that which she would not do herself. With a quiet command,
Kettricken dismissed the guard to wash themselves, to comb
hair and beards, and to return freshly clothed to the hall. As
Burrich led Softstep away Kettricken stood briefly alone. A

sadness grayer than anything I had ever felt emanated from her. She was weary. So very weary.

I approached her quietly. "If you have need, my lady queen," I said softly.

She did not turn. "I must do this myself. But be close, in case I need you." She spoke so quietly I am sure none heard her but myself. Then she moved forward, and the waiting Keep folk parted before her. Heads bobbed as she acknowledged them gravely. She walked silently through the kitchens, nodding at the food she saw prepared, and then paced through the Great Hall, once more nodding approval of all she saw there. In the Lesser Hall, she paused, then removed her gaily knit cap and her jacket, to reveal underneath a simple soft shirt of purple linen. The cap and jacket she gave over to a page, who looked stunned by the honor. She stepped to the head of one of the tables and began to fold her sleeves back. All movement in the hall ceased as heads turned to watch her. She looked up to our amazed regard. "Bring in our dead," she said simply.

The pitiful bodies were carried in, a heartbreaking stream of them. I did not count how many. More than I had expected, more than Verity's reports had led us to believe. I followed behind Kettricken, and carried the basin of warm scented water as she moved from body to body, and gently bathed each ravaged face and closed tormented eyes forever. Behind us came others, a snaking procession as each body was undressed gently, completely bathed, hair combed, and wound in clean cloth. At some point I became aware that Verity was there, a young scribe beside him, going from body to body, taking down the names of those few who were recognized, writing briefly of every other.

One name I supplied him myself. Kerry. The last Molly and I had known of this street boy, he had gone off as a puppeteer's apprentice. He'd ended his days as little more than a puppet. His laughing mouth was stilled forever. As boys, we'd run errands together, to earn a penny or two. He'd been beside me the first time I got puking drunk, and laughed until his own stomach betrayed him. He'd wedged the rotten fish in the trestles of the tavernkeeper's table, the one who had accused us of stealing. The days we had shared I alone would remember now. I suddenly felt less real. Part of my past, Forged away from me.

When we were done, and stood silently looking at the tables of bodies, Verity stepped forward, to read his tally aloud in the silence. The names were few, but he did not neglect those unknown. "A young man, newly bearded, dark hair, the scars of fishing on his hands . . ." he said of one, and of another, "A woman, curly-haired and comely, tattooed with the puppeteers' guild sign." We listened to the litany of those we had lost, and if any did not weep, they had hearts of stone. As a people, we lifted our dead and carried them to the funeral pyre, to set them carefully atop this last bed. Verity himself brought the torch for the kindling, but he handed it off to the Queen, who waited beside the pyre. As she set flame to the pitch-laden boughs, she cried out to the dark skies, "You shall not be forgotten!" All echoed her with a shout. Blade, the old sergeant, stood beside the pyre with shears, to take from every soldier a finger's-length lock of hair, a symbol of the mourning for a fallen comrade. Verity joined the queue, and Kettricken stood behind him, to offer up a pale lock of her own hair.

There followed a night such as I had never known. Most of Buckkeep Town came to the Keep that night, and were admitted without question. All followed the Queen's example and kept a watching fast until the pyre had burned itself to ash and bone. Then the Great Hall and the Lesser were filled, and planks laid as tables outside in the courtyard for those who could not crowd within. Kegs of drink were rolled out, and such a setting out of bread and roasted meat and other viands as I had not even imagined that Buckkeep possessed. Later I was to learn that much of it had simply come up from the town, unsought but offered freely.

The King descended, as he had not for some weeks, to sit in his throne at the high table and preside over the gathering. The Fool came, too, to stand beside and behind his chair and accept from his plate whatever the King offered. But this night he made not merry for the King; his fool's prattle was stilled, and even the bells on his cap and sleeves had been tied in strips of fabric to mute them. Only once did our eyes meet that night, but for me, the glance carried no discernible message. To the

King's right was Verity, to his left Kettricken. Regal was there, too, of course, in so sumptuous a costume of black that only the color denoted any sort of mourning. He scowled and sulked and drank, and I suppose for some his surly silence passed for grieving. For me, I could sense the anger seething within him, and knew that someone, somewhere would pay for what he saw as insult to himself. Even Patience was there, her appearance as rare as the King's, and I sensed the unity of purpose we displayed.

The King ate but little. He waited until those at the High Table were filled before he arose to speak. As he spoke, his words were repeated at the lower tables, and in the Lesser Hall, and even outside in the courtyard by minstrels. He spoke briefly of those we had lost to the Red-Ships. He said nothing of Forging, or of the day's task of hunting down and killing the Forged ones. He spoke instead as if they had but recently died in a battle against the Red-Ships, and said only that we must remember them. Then, pleading fatigue and grief, he left the table to return to his own chambers.

Then it was that Verity arose. He did little more than repeat Kettricken's words of earlier, that we grieved now, but when the grieving was over, we must make ready our vengeance. He lacked the fire and impassionment of Kettricken's earlier speech, but I could see all at table responding to it. Folk nodded and began to talk among themselves, while Regal sat and glowered silently. Verity and Kettricken left the table late that night, she on his arm, and they made sure that all marked how they left together. Regal remained, drinking and muttering to himself. I myself slipped away shortly after Verity and Kettricken left, to seek my own bed.

I made no attempt to fall asleep, but only flung myself on my bed to stare into the fire. When the concealed door opened, I rose immediately to ascend to Chade's chambers. I found him a-jitter with an infectious excitement. There was even a pinkness to his pale cheeks about his pock scars. His gray hair was wild, his green eyes glittered like gems. He was pacing about his chambers, and as I entered he actually seized me in a rough embrace. He stepped back and laughed aloud at my shocked expression.

"She was born to rule! Born to it, and somehow now she has awakened to it! It could not have come at a better time! She may yet save us all!"

His exultation was unholy in its glee.

"I know not how many folk died today," I rebuked him.

"Ah! But not in vain! At least not in vain! Those were not wasted deaths, FitzChivalry. By El and Eda both, Kettricken has the instinct and the grace! I had not suspected it in her. Now had we still your father alive, boy, and him paired with her on the throne, we could have a pair as could cup the whole world in their hands." He took another sip of his wine and paced again about his chambers. I had never seen him so elated. He all but capered. A covered basket rested on a table close to hand, and its contents had been set out on a cloth. Wine, cheese, sausages, pickles, and bread. So even here in his tower, Chade shared the funeral feast. Slink the weasel popped up from the other side of the table, to regard me past the food with avaricious eyes. Chade's voice broke me from my thoughts.

"She has an ample share of what Chivalry had. The instinct for seizing the moment and turning it to advantage. She took an unavoidable, unmentionable situation and made high tragedy of what might have been simple slaughter in lesser hands. Boy, we have a Queen, a Queen again at Buckkeep!"

I felt slightly repulsed by his joy. And, for an instant, cheated. Hesitantly, I asked, "Do you think, really, that the Queen did as she did for show? That it was all a calculated political move?"

He halted in his tracks, considered briefly. "No. No, FitzChivalry, I believe she acted from her heart. But that does not make it any less tactically brilliant. Ah, you think me heartless. Or callous in my ignorance. The truth is, I know only too well. Know far better than you what today meant to us. I know men died today. I even know that six of our own force took injuries, mostly minor, in today's action. I can tell you how many Forged ones fell, and within a day or so, I expect to know most of their names. Names already listed by me, included in the tallies of all the Red-Ships have done to us. It will be I, boy, who sees that the purses of blood gold are paid to surviving kin. Those families will be told the King regards their fallen as the equals of any of his soldiers who fall in battle with the Red-Ships. And entreats their aid in taking vengeance for them. They will not be pleasant letters to pen, Fitz. But pen them I shall, in Verity's own hand, for Shrewd's signature. Or did you think I did naught but kill for my king?''

"I beg pardon. It was just that you seemed so merry when first I entered—" I began.

"And merry I am! As you should be. We have been rudderless and drifted, pounded by the waves and pushed by every wind. And now, comes a woman, to take the tiller and cry the course. I find it a course full to my liking! As shall everyone in the kingdom who has sickened these past years from being always on our knees. We rise, boy, we rise to fight!''

I saw then how his ebullience was borne on the wave of his fury and his grief. I remembered the expression he had worn when first we rode into Forge town on that black day and saw what the Raiders had left of our folk. He had told me then that I would learn to care, that it was in my blood. With a rush I felt the rightness of his sentiment, and seized up a glass to join him. Together we toasted our queen. Then Chade grew more sober, and divulged the reason for his summons. The King, Shrewd himself, had once more repeated his order that I watch over Kettricken.

"I've been meaning to speak to you about that; that Shrewd sometimes now repeats an order already given or a comment already made.''

"I'm aware enough of that, Fitz. What can be done, is. But the King's health is another topic for another time. For now, I myself assure you that his repetition was not the rattling of a sickly mind. No. The King made this request again today as he was preparing himself to descend to dinner. He repeats it to make sure your efforts will be redoubled. He sees, as I do, that by arousing folk to follow her, the Queen puts herself more at risk. Though he would not speak it so plain. Be on your guard for her safety.''

"Regal," I snorted.

"Prince Regal?'' Chade queried.

"He is who we have to fear, especially now that the Queen has taken a place of power."

"I said nothing of the kind. Nor should you," Chade observed quietly. His voice was calm but his face was severe.

"Why not?" I challenged him. "Why may not we, at least once, speak plain to one another?"

"To one another, we might, if we were entirely alone and it concerned only you and me. But such is not the case. We are King's Men sworn, and King's Men do not entertain even thoughts of treason, let alone . . ."

There was a gagging noise, and Slink disgorged himself. On the table, beside the food basket. He snorted, spraying drops of moisture.

"Greedy little wretch! Choked yourself, did you?" Chade rebuked him unconcernedly.

I found a rag to clean up the mess. But when I got there, Slink was lying on his side, panting, while Chade poked at the vomit with a skewer. I nearly retched myself. He waved my rag aside, picking up Slink instead and handing me the shivering creature. "Calm him, and get water down him," he directed me tersely. "Go on, old man, go to Fitz, he'll see to you." This to the weasel.

I carried him over by the fire, where he promptly puked all down my shirt. At closer range, the smell was overpowering. As I set him down and pulled my shirt off, I caught an underlying scent, more bitter than vomit even. Even as I opened my mouth to speak Chade confirmed my suspicions. "Varta leaves. Crushed fine. The spiciness of the sausage would conceal the taste well. Let's hope the wine wasn't poisoned as well, or we're both dead."

Every hair on my body stood up in horror. Chade looked up to see me frozen, and pushed gently past me to pick Slink up. He offered him a saucer of water and looked pleased when Slink sampled it. "I think he'll live. The little pig stuffed his mouth full, and got a better taste of it than a human would have. Up it came. The stuff on the table looks chewed, but not digested. I think the taste made him gag, not the poison."

"I hope so," I said faintly. Every one of my nerves was tuned to an inner waiting. Had I been poisoned? Did I feel sleepy, nauseous, dizzy? Was my mouth numb, dry, watering? I broke out in a sudden sweat and began to tremble. Not again.

"Stop it," Chade said quietly. "Sit down. Drink some water. You're doing this to yourself, Fitz. That bottle was well sealed with an old cork. If the wine was poisoned, it was done years ago. I know of few men with the patience to poison a bottle of wine, and then age it. I think we're fine."

I drew a shaky breath. "But such was not someone's intent. Who brought your food?"

Chade gave a snort. "I prepared my own food, as always. But that on the table was from a gift basket left for Lady Thyme. From time to time folk seek to curry favor with her, as it is rumored she has the King's ear. I did not think my masquerade woman a likely target for poison."

"Regal," I said again. "I told you he believes she is the King's poisoner. How could you have been so careless? You know he blames Lady Thyme for his mother's death! Shall we be so polite as to let him kill us all? He will not stop until the throne is his."

"And I tell you again, I will hear nothing of treason!" Chade all but shouted the words. He sat down in his chair and cradled Slink in his lap. The little beast sat up, tidied his whiskers, and then curled up again to compose himself for sleep. I watched Chade's pale hand, the standing tendons, the paper skin, as he stroked his small pet. He looked only at the weasel, his face closed. After a moment he spoke more calmly. "I think our king was right. We should all redouble our caution. And not just for Kettricken. Or ourselves." He lifted tortured eyes to mine. "Watch over your women, boy. Neither innocence nor ignorance is any protection against this night's work. Patience, Molly, even Lacey. Find a way, a subtle way, to give Burrich warning as well." He sighed, asked of no one, "Have we not enemies enough outside our walls?"

"Aplenty," I assured him. But I said no more of Regal to him.

He shook his head. "This is an ill way for me to begin a journey."

"A journey? You?" I was incredulous. Chade never left the Keep. Almost. "Where?"

"Where I need to go. Now I think I need almost as much to stay." He shook his head to himself. "Take care of yourself while I'm gone, boy. I won't be about to watch over you." And that was as much as he would tell me.

When I left him, he was still staring into the fire, his lax hands sheltering Slink. I went down the stairs on jelly legs. The attempt on Chade had shaken me more than anything ever had. Not even the secret of his existence had been enough to shield him. And there were other, easier targets, just as close to my heart.

I damned the bravado that had earlier let me make Regal aware of how much stronger I had grown. I had been a fool to tempt him to attack me; I should have known he would find a less obvious target. In my room, I changed hastily into fresh clothing. Then I left my chamber, climbed the stairs, and went straight to Molly's bedchamber. I tapped lightly on the door.

No answer. I did not tap louder. It lacked but an hour or two until dawn; most of the Keep was exhausted, abed. Still, I had no desire to rouse the wrong person to see me at Molly's door. Yet I had to know.

Her door was latched, but it was a simple one. I slipped it in a matter of seconds and made note to myself that she would have a better one before tomorrow night. Soft as shadow, I entered her room and drew the door closed behind me.

A fire had burned low in the hearth. Its lingering embers cast an uncertain haze of light. I stood still a moment, letting my eyes adjust, then I moved carefully into the room, staying away from the hearth light. I could hear the steady sleep rhythm of Molly's breath from her bed. It should have been enough for me. But I teased myself that she might be fevered and sinking even now into a death sleep from poison. I promised myself that I would do no more than touch her pillow, just to see if skin was fevered or normal. No more than that. I drifted to the bedside.

Beside the bed I stood motionless. I could just make out her shape under the covers in the dim light. She smelled heathery and warm and sweet. Healthy. No feverish poison victim slept here. I knew I should go. "Sleep well," I breathed.

Silently she sprang up at me. The ember light ran red

along the blade in her hand. "Molly!" I cried as I parried her knife hand aside with the back of my forearm. She froze, her other hand drawn back in a fist, and for an instant all in the room was silent and motionless. Then: "Newboy!" she hissed furiously, and punched me in the belly with her left hand. As I doubled over, gasping for air, she rolled from the bed. "You idiot! You frightened me to death! What do you think you're about, rattling at my latch and sneaking about in my room! I should call the Keep guardsmen to put you out!"

"No!" I begged as she threw wood on the fire, and then kindled a candle at it. "Please. I'll go. I meant no harm or offense. I just wanted to be sure you were all right."

"Well, I'm not!" she stormed in a whisper. Her hair was confined for the night into two thick braids, reminding me sharply of the little girl I had met so long ago. A girl no longer. She caught me staring at her. She threw a heavier robe about her shoulders and belted it at her waist. "I'm a shaking wreck! I shan't sleep another wink tonight! You've been drinking, haven't you? Are you drunk, then? What do you want?"

She advanced on me with the candle as if it were a weapon. "No," I assured her. I drew myself upright and tugged my shirt straight. "I promise you, I'm not drunk. And truly, I had no bad intentions. But . . . something happened tonight, something that made me worry that something bad might happen to you, so I thought I had best come and make sure you were all right, but I knew Patience would not approve, and I certainly didn't want to go waking up the whole Keep, so I thought I would just slip in and—"

"Newboy. You're babbling," she informed me icily.

It was true. "I'm sorry," I said again, and sat down on the corner of the bed.

"Don't get comfortable," she warned me. "You were just leaving. Alone, or with the Keep guards. Your choice."

"I'll go," I promised, standing hastily. "I just wanted to be sure you were all right."

"I'm fine," she said testily. "Why wouldn't I be fine? I'm as fine tonight as I was last night, as I have been for the last thirty nights. On none of them were you inspired to come and inspect my health. So why tonight?"

I took a breath. "Because on some nights threats are more obvious than others. Bad things happen, that make me take stock of what worse things could happen. On some nights, it is not the healthiest thing to be the beloved of a bastard."

The lines of her mouth went as flat as her voice as she asked, "What is that supposed to mean?"

I took a breath, determined that I would be as honest with her as I was able. "I cannot tell you what happened. Only that it made me believe you might be in danger. You will have to trust—"

"That isn't the part I meant. What do you mean, beloved of a bastard? How do you dare to call me that?" Her eyes were bright with anger.

I swear that my heart thudded to a halt in my chest. The cold of death swept through me. "It is true, I have no right," I said haltingly. "But neither is there any way I could stop caring for you. And whether or not I have the right to name you my beloved would not deter those who might seek to injure me by striking at you. How can I say I love you so much that I wish I did not love you, or at least could refrain from showing that I loved you, because my love puts you in such danger, and have those words be true?" Stiffly, I turned to go.

"And how could I possibly dare to say I made sense of your last statement and have it be true?" Molly wondered aloud.

Something in her voice made me turn around. For a moment we just looked at one another. Then she burst out laughing. I stood, affronted and grim, as she came to me, still laughing. Then she put her arms around me. "Newboy. You take a most roundabout path to finally declare you love me. To break into my room, and then to stand there, tying your tongue in knots about the word 'love.' Could not you simply have said it, a long time ago?"

I stood stupid in the circle of her arms. I looked down at her. Yes, I realized dully, I had grown that much taller than her.

"Well?" she prompted, and for a moment I was puzzled.

"I love you, Molly." So easy to say, after all. And such a relief. Slowly, cautiously, I put my arms around her.

She smiled up at me. "And I love you."

So, finally, I kissed her. In the moment of that kiss, somewhere near Buckkeep a wolf lifted up his voice in a joyous ululation that set every hound to baying and every dog to barking in a chorus that rang against the brittle night sky.

9

Guards and Bonds

O FTENTIMES I UNDERSTAND *and commend Fed-*
wren's stated dream. Had he his way, paper would be as
common as bread, and every child would learn his letters before
he was thirteen. But even were it so, I do not think this would
bring to pass all he hopes. He mourns of all the knowledge that
goes into a grave each time a man dies, even the commonest of
men. He speaks of a time to come when a blacksmith's way of
setting a shoe, or a shipwright's knack for pulling a drawknife
would be set down in letters, that any who could read could
learn to do as well. I do not believe it is so, or ever will be. Some
things may be learned from words on a page, but some skills are
learned first by a man's hands and heart, and later by his head.
I have believed this ever since I saw Mastfish set the fish-shaped
block of wood that he was named after into Verity's first ship.
His eyes had seen that mastfish before it existed, and he set his
hands to shaping what his heart knew must be. This is not a
thing that can be learned from words on a page. Perhaps it
cannot be learned at all, but comes, as does the Skill or the Wit,
from the blood of one's forebears.

⊷⊨⊱

I returned to my own chamber and sat watching the dying
embers in my hearth, waiting for the rest of the Keep to

awaken. I should have been exhausted. Instead, I almost trembled with the energy rushing through me. I fancied that if I sat very still, I could still feel the warmth of Molly's arms around me. I knew precisely where her cheek had touched mine. A very faint scent of her clung to my shirt from our brief embrace, and I agonized over whether to wear the shirt that day, to carry that scent with me, or to set it aside carefully in my clothing chest, to preserve it. I did not think it a foolish thing at all to care so much about that. Looking back, I smile, but it is at my wisdom, not my folly.

Morning brought storm winds and falling snow to Buckkeep Castle, but to me it only made all inside the cozier. Perhaps it would give us all a chance to recover ourselves from yesterday. I did not want to think about those poor ragged bodies, or bathing the still, cold faces. Nor of the roaring flames and heat that had consumed Kerry's body. We could all use a quiet day inside the Keep. Perhaps the evening would find all gathered about the hearths, for storytelling, music, and conversation. I hoped so. I left my chambers to go to Patience and Lacey.

I tormented myself, knowing well the exact moment when Molly would descend the stairs to fetch a breakfast tray for Patience, and also when she would ascend the stairs carrying it. I could be on the stairs or in the hallway as she passed. It would be a minor thing, a coincidence. But I had no question that there were those who had been set to watching me, and they would make note of such "coincidences" if they occurred too often. No. I had to heed the warnings that both the King and Chade had given me. I would show Molly I had a man's self-control and forbearance. If I must wait before I could court her, then I would.

So I sat in my room and agonized until I was sure that she would have left Patience's chambers. Then I descended, to tap upon the door. As I waited for Lacey to open it I reflected that redoubling my watch upon Patience and Lacey was easier said than done. But I had a few ideas. I had begun last night, by extracting a promise from Molly that she would bring up no food she had not prepared herself, or taken fresh from the common serving pots. She had snorted at this, for it had come after a most ardent good-bye. "Now you sound just like Lacey," she had rebuked me, and gently closed the door in my face. She opened it a moment later, to find me still staring at it. "Go to bed," she chided me. Blushing, she added, "And dream of me. I hope I have plagued your dreams lately as much as you have mine." Those words sent me fleeing down to my room, and every time I thought of it, I blushed again.

Now, as I entered Patience's room, I tried to put all such thoughts from my mind. I was here on business, even if Patience and Lacey must believe it a social call. Keep my mind on my tasks. I cast my eyes over the latch that had secured the door and found it well to my liking. No one would be slipping that with a belt knife. As for the window, even if anyone had scaled the outer wall to it, they must burst through not only stoutly barred wooden shutters, but a tapestry, and then rank upon rank of pots of plants, soldiered in rows before the closed window. It was a route no professional would willingly choose. Lacey resettled herself with a bit of mending while Patience greeted me. Lady Patience herself was seemingly idle, seated on the hearth before the fire as if she were but a girl. She poked at the coals a bit. "Did you know," she asked me suddenly, "that there is a substantial history of strong Queens at Buckkeep? Not just those born as Farseers, either. Many a Farseer Prince has married a woman whose name came to overshadow his in the telling of deeds."

"Do you think Kettricken will become such a Queen?" I asked politely. I had no idea where this conversation would lead.

"I do not know," she said softly. She stirred the coals idly again. "I only know that I would not have been one." She sighed heavily, then lifted her eyes to say almost apologetically, "I am having one of those mornings, Fitz, when all that fills my head is what might have been and what could have been. I should never have allowed him to abdicate. I'd wager he'd be alive today, if he had not."

There seemed little reply I could make to such a statement. She sighed again, and drew on the hearthstones with the ash-coated poker. "I am a woman of longings today, Fitz. While everyone else yesterday was stirred to amazement at what Kettricken did, it awakened in me the deepest discontent with myself. Had I been in her position, I would have hidden away in my chamber. Just as I do now. But your grandmother would not have. Now there was a Queen. Like Kettricken in some ways. Constance was a woman who spurred others to action. Other women especially. When she was queen, over half our guard was female. Did you know that? Ask Hod about her sometime. I understand that Hod came with her when Constance came here to be Shrewd's queen.'' Patience fell silent. For a few moments she was so quiet I thought she was finished speaking. Then she added softly, "She liked me, Queen Constance did.'' She smiled almost shyly.

"She knew I did not care for crowds. So, sometimes, she would summon me, and only me, to come and attend her in her garden. And we would not even speak much, but only work quietly in the soil and the sunlight. Some of my pleasantest memories of Buckkeep are of those times.'' She looked up at me suddenly. "I was just a little girl then. And your father was just a boy, and we had not ever really met. My parents brought me to Buckkeep, the times they came to court, even though they knew I did not much care for all the folderol of court life. What a woman Queen Constance was, to notice a homely, quiet little girl, and give her of her time. But she was like that. Buckkeep was a different place then; a much merrier court. Times were safer, and all was more stable. But then Constance died, and her infant daughter with her, of a birth fever. And Shrewd remarried a few years later, and . . .'' She paused and sighed again suddenly. Then her lips firmed. She patted the hearth beside her.

"Come and sit here. There are things we must speak of.''

I did as she bid me, likewise sitting on the hearthstones. I had never seen Patience so serious, nor so focused. All of this, I felt, was leading up to something. It was so different from her usual fey prattle that it almost frightened me. Once I was seated, she motioned me closer. I scooted forward until I was nearly in her lap. She leaned forward and whispered, "Some things are best not spoken of. But there comes a time when they must be spoken of. FitzChivalry, my dear, do not think me mean-spirited. But I must warn you that your uncle Regal is not as well disposed toward you as you might believe.''

I couldn't help it. I laughed.

Patience was instantly indignant. ''You must attend me!'' she whispered more urgently. ''Oh, I know he is gay and charming and witty. I know what a flatterer he can be, and I have marked well how all the young women of the court flutter their fans at him, and how all the young men mimic his clothes and mannerisms. But underneath those fine feathers there is much ambition. And I am afraid there is suspicion there, and jealousy, also. I have never told you this. But he was totally opposed to my undertaking your schooling, as well as to your learning to Skill. Sometimes I think it is as well that you failed at that, for had you succeeded, his jealousy would have known no bounds.'' She paused, and finding that I was listening with a sober face, she went on: ''These are unsettled times, Fitz. Not just because of the Red-Ships that harry our shores. It is a time when any b . . . born as you were should be careful. There are those who smile fairly at you, but may be your enemy. When your father was alive, we relied on the fact that his influence would be enough to shelter you. But after he was . . . he died, I realized that as you grew you would be more and more at risk, the closer you came to manhood. So, when I decently could, I forced myself to come back to court, to see if there truly was need. I found there was, and I found you worthy of my help. So I vowed to do all I could to educate and protect you.'' She allowed herself a brief smile of satisfaction.

''I would say I had done fairly well by you so far. But''— and she leaned closer—''comes a time when even I will not be able to protect you. You must begin to take care of yourself. You must recall your lessons from Hod, and review them with her often. You must be cautious of what you eat and drink, and be wary of visiting isolated places alone. I hate to put these fears into you, FitzChivalry. But you are almost a man now, and must begin to think of such things.''

Laughable. Almost a farce. So I could have seen it, to have this sheltered, reclusive woman speaking to me so earnestly of the realities of the world I had survived in since I was six.

Instead, I found tears stinging the corners of my eyes. I had always been mystified as to why Patience had come back to Buckkeep, to live a hermit's life in the midst of a society she obviously did not care for. Now I knew. She had come for me, for my sake. To protect me.

Burrich had sheltered me. So had Chade, and even Verity in his way. And of course Shrewd had claimed me as his own, very early. But all of them, in one way and another, had stood to gain by my survival. Even Burrich would have seen it as a great loss of pride if someone had managed to murder me while I was under his protection. Only this woman, who by all rights should have abhorred me, had come to shelter me for my sake only. She was so often foolish and meddlesome and some-times most annoying. But as our eyes met I knew she had breached the final wall I had kept between us. I greatly doubted that her presence had done anything to deter bad will toward me; if anything, her interest in me must have been a constant reminder to Regal of who had fathered me. But it was not the deed, but the intention that moved me. She had given up her quiet life, her orchards and gardens and woods, to come here, to a damp castle of stone on the sea cliffs, to a court full of folk she cared nothing about, to watch over her husband's bastard.

"Thank you," I said quietly. And meant it with all my heart.

"Well." She turned aside from my look quickly. "Well. You are welcome, you know."

"I know. But the truth was, I came here this morning thinking that perhaps someone should warn you and Lacey to be careful of yourselves. Times are unstable here, and you might be seen as an . . . obstacle."

Now Patience laughed aloud. "I! I? Funny, dowdy, foolish old Patience? Patience, who cannot keep an idea fixed in her head for more than ten minutes? Patience, all but made mad by her husband's death? My boy, I know how they talk of me. No one perceives me as a threat to anyone. Why, I am but another fool here at the court, a thing to be made sport of. I am quite safe, I assure you. But, even if I were not, I have the habits of a lifetime to protect me. And Lacey."

"Lacey?" I could not keep incredulity from my voice nor

a grin from my face. I turned to exchange a wink with Lacey.
Lacey glared at me as if affronted by my smile. Before I could
even unfold from the hearth, Lacey sprang up from her rocking
chair. A long needle, stripped of its eternal yarn, prodded my
jugular vein, while the other probed a certain space between
my ribs. I very nearly wet myself. I looked up at a woman I
suddenly knew not at all, and dared not make a word.

"Stop teasing the child," Patience rebuked her gently.
"Yes, Fitz, Lacey. The most apt pupil that Hod ever had, even
if she did come to Hod as a grown woman." As Patience spoke
Lacey took her weapons away from my body. She reseated
herself, and deftly rethreaded her needles into her work. I
swear she didn't even drop a stitch. When she was finished, she
looked up at me. She winked. And went back to her knitting. I
remembered to start breathing again.

A very chastened assassin left their apartments sometime
later. As I made my way down the hall I reflected that Chade
had warned me I was underestimating Lacey. I wondered
wryly if this was his idea of humor, or of teaching me greater
respect for seemingly mild folk.

Thoughts of Molly pushed their way into my mind. I resolutely refused to give in to them, but could not resist lowering
my face to catch that faint scent of her on the shoulder of my
shirt. I took the foolish smile from my face and set off to locate
Kettricken. I had duties.

I'm hungry.

The thought intruded without warning. Shame flooded me.
I had taken Cub nothing yesterday. I had all but forgotten him
in the sweep of the day's events.

*A day's fast is nothing. Besides, I found a nest of mice
beneath a corner of the cottage. Do you think I cannot care for
myself at all? But something more substantial would be pleasing.*

Soon, I promised him. *There is a thing I must do first.*

In Kettricken's sitting chamber, I found only two young
pages, ostensibly tidying, but giggling as I came in. Neither of
them knew anything. I next tried Mistress Hasty's weaving
room, as it was a warm and friendly chamber where many of
the Keep women gathered. No Kettricken, but Lady Modesty

was there. She told me that her mistress had said she needed to speak with Prince Verity this morning. Perhaps she was with him.

But Verity was not in his chambers, nor his map room. Charim was there, however, sorting through sheets of vellum and separating them by quality. Verity, he told me, had arisen very early and immediately set out for his boat shed. Yes, Kettricken had been there this morning, but it had been after Verity left, and once Charim had told her he was gone, she, too, had departed. Where? He was not certain.

By this time I was starving, and I excused my trip to the kitchens on the grounds that gossip always grew thickest there. Perhaps someone there would know where our queen-in-waiting had gone. I was not worried, I told myself. Not yet.

The kitchens of Buckkeep were at their best on a cold and blustery day. Steam from bubbling stews mingled with the nourishing aroma of baking bread and roasting meat. Chilled stable boys loitered there, chatting with the kitchen help and pilfering fresh-baked rolls and the ends of cheeses, tasting stews and disappearing like mist if Burrich appeared in the door. I cut myself a slab of cold meal pudding from the morning's cooking, and reinforced it with honey and some bacon ends that Cook was rendering down for cracklings. As I ate I listened to the talk.

Oddly enough, few people spoke directly of the previous day's events. I grasped it would take a while for the Keep to come to terms with all that had happened. But there was something there, a feeling almost of relief. I had seen that before, in a man who had had his maimed foot removed, or the family that finally finds their drowned child's body. To finally confront the worst there is, to look it squarely in the face and say, ''I know you. You have hurt me, almost to death, but still I live. And I will go on living.'' That was the feeling I got from the folk of the Keep. All had finally acknowledged the severity of our injuries from the Red-Ships. Now there was a sense that we might begin to heal, and to fight back.

I did not wish to make direct inquiries down here as to where the Queen might be. As luck would have it, one of the stable boys was speaking of Softstep. Some of the blood I had seen on the horse's shoulder the previous day had been her own, and the boys were talking of how the horse had snapped at Burrich when he tried to work on her shoulder, and how it had taken two of them to hold her head. I wangled my way into the conversation. "Perhaps a horse of less temperament would be a better mount for the Queen?" I suggested.

"Ah, no. Our queen likes Softstep's pride and spirit. She said so herself, to me, when she was down in the stables this morning. She came herself, to see the horse, and to ask when she might be ridden again. She spoke directly to me, she did. So I told her, no horse wanted to be ridden on a day such as this, let alone with a gashed shoulder. And Queen Kettricken nodded, and we stood talking there, and she asked how I had lost my tooth."

"And you told her a horse had thrown his head back when you were exercising him! Because you didn't want Burrich to know we'd been wrestling up in the hayloft and you'd fallen into the gray colt's stall!"

"Shut up! You're the one who pushed me, so it was your fault as much as mine!"

And the two were off, pushing and scuffling with each other, until a shout from Cook sent them tumbling from the kitchen. But I had as much information as I needed. I headed out for the stables.

I found it a colder and nastier day outside than I had expected. Even within the stables, the wind found every crack and came shrieking through the doors each time one was opened. The horses' breath steamed in the air, and stable mates leaned companionably close for the warmth they could share. I found Hands, and asked where Burrich was.

"Cutting wood," he said quietly. "For a funeral pyre. He's been drinking since dawn, too."

Almost this drove my quest from my mind. I had never known such a thing to be. Burrich drank, but in the evenings, when the day's work was done. Hands read my face.

"Vixen. His old bitch hound. She died in the night. Yet I have never heard of a pyre for a dog. He's out behind the exercise pen now."

I turned toward the pen.

"Fitz!" Hands warned me urgently.

"It will be all right, Hands. I know what she meant to him. The first night he had care of me, he put me in a stall beside her, and told her to guard me. She had a pup beside her, Nosy . . ."

Hands shook his head. "He said he wanted to see no one. To send him no questions today. No one to talk to him. He's never given me an order like that."

"All right." I sighed.

Hands looked disapproving. "As old as she was, he should have expected it. She couldn't even hunt with him anymore. He should have replaced her a long time ago."

I looked at Hands. For all his caring for the beasts, for all his gentleness and good instincts, he couldn't really know. Once, I had been shocked to discover my Wit sense as a separate sense. Now to confront Hands's total lack of it was to discover his blindness. I just shook my head and dragged my mind back to my original errand. "Hands, have you seen the Queen today?"

"Yes, but it was a while ago." His eyes scanned my face anxiously. "She came to me and asked if Prince Verity had taken Truth out of the stables and down to town. I told her no, that the Prince had come to see him, but had left him in the stables today. I told her the streets would be all iced cobbles. Verity would not risk his favorite on a surface like that. He walks down to Buckkeep Town as often as not these days, though he comes through the stable almost every day. He told me it's an excuse to be out in the air and the open."

My heart sank. With a certainty that was like a vision, I knew that Kettricken had followed Verity into Buckkeep Town. On foot? With no one accompanying her? On this foul day? While Hands berated himself for not foreseeing the Queen's intention, I took Sidekick, a well-named but surefooted mule, from his stall. I dared not take the time to go back to my room for warmer clothes. So I borrowed Hands's cloak to supplement mine and dragged the reluctant animal out of the stables and into the wind and falling snow.

Are you coming now?

Not now, but soon. There is something I must see to.

May I go, too?

No. It isn't safe. Now be quiet and stay out of my thoughts.

I stopped at the gate to question the guard most bluntly. Yes, a woman on foot had come this way this morning. Several of them, for there were some whose trades made this trip necessary, no matter the weather. The Queen? The men on watch exchanged glances. No one replied. I suggested perhaps there had been a woman, heavily cloaked, and hooded well? White fur trimming the hood? A young guard nodded. Embroidery on the cloak, white and purple at the hem? They exchanged uncomfortable glances. There had been a woman like that. They had not known who she was, but now that I suggested those colors, they should have known. . . .

In a coldly level voice, I berated them as dolts and morons. Unidentified folk passed unchallenged through our gates? They had looked on white fur and purple embroidery, and never even guessed it might be the Queen? And none had seen fit to accompany her? None chose to be her guard? Even after yesterday? A fine place was Buckkeep these days, when our queen had not even a foot soldier at her heels when she went out walking in a snowstorm down to Buckkeep Town. I kicked Sidekick and left them settling blame among themselves.

The going was miserable. The wind was in a fickle mood, changing directions as often as I found a way to block it with my cloak. The snow not only fell, the wind caught up the frozen crystals from the ground and swirled it up under my cloak at every opportunity. Sidekick was not happy, but he plodded along through the thickening snow. Beneath the snow, the uneven trail to town was glazed with treacherous ice. The mule became resigned to my stubbornness and trudged disconsolately along. I blinked the clinging flakes from my eyelashes and tried to urge him to greater speed. Images of the Queen, crumpled in the snow, the blowing flakes covering her over, kept trying to push into my mind. Nonsense! I told myself firmly. Nonsense.

I was on the outskirts of Buckkeep Town before I overtook her. I knew her from behind, even if she had not been wearing her purple and white. She strode through the drifting snow with a fine indifference to it, her Mountain-bred flesh as immune to the cold as I was to salt breeze and damp. "Queen Kettricken! Lady! Please, wait for me!"

She turned and, as she caught sight of me, smiled and waited. I slid from Sidekick's back as I came abreast of her. I had not realized how worried I was until the relief flooded through me at seeing her unharmed. "What are you doing out here, alone, in this storm?" I demanded of her, and belatedly added, "My lady."

She looked about her as if just noticing the falling snow and gusting wind, then turned back to me with a rueful grin. She was not the least bit chilled or uncomfortable. To the contrary, her cheeks were rosy with her walk, and the white fur around her face set off her yellow hair and blue eyes. Here, in this whiteness, she was not pale and colorless, but tawny and pink, blue eyes sparkling. She looked more vital than I had seen her in days. Yesterday she had been Death astride a horse, and Grief washing the bodies of her slain. But today, here, in the snow, she was a merry girl, escaped from Keep and station to go hiking through the snow. "I go to find my husband."

"Alone? Does he know you are coming, and like this, afoot?"

She looked startled. Then she tucked her chin and bridled just like my mule. "Is he not my husband? Do I need an appointment to see him? Why should not I go afoot and alone? Do I seem so incompetent to you that I might become lost on the road to Buckkeep Town?"

She set off walking again, and I was forced to keep pace with her. I dragged the mule along with me. Sidekick was not enthused. "Queen Kettricken," I began, but she cut me off.

"I grow so weary of this." She halted abruptly and turned to face me. "Yesterday, for the first time in many days, I felt as if I were alive and had a will of my own. I do not intend to let that slip away from me. If I wish to visit my husband at his work, I shall. Well do I know that not one of my ladies would care for this outing, in this weather and afoot, or otherwise. So I am alone. And my horse was injured yesterday, and the footing here is not kind to a beast anyway. So I do not ride. All of this makes sense. Why have you followed me and why do you question me?"

She had chosen bluntness as the weapon, so I took it up as well. But I took a breath and tuned my voice to courtesy before I began. "My lady queen, I followed to be sure you had not come to any harm. Here, with only a mule's ears to hear us, I will speak plainly. Have you so swiftly forgotten who tried to topple Verity from the throne in your own Mountain Kingdom? Would he hesitate to plot here as well? I think not. Do you believe it an accident you were lost and astray in the woods two nights ago? I do not. And do you think that your actions yesterday were pleasing to him? Quite the contrary. What you do for the sake of your people, he sees as your ploy to take power to yourself. So he sulks and mutters and decides you are a greater threat than before. You must know all this. So why do you set yourself out as a target, here where an arrow or a knife could find you with such ease and no witnesses?"

"I am not so easy a target as that," she defied me. " 'T would take an excellent archer indeed to make an arrow fly true in these shifting winds. As for a knife, well, I've a knife, too. To strike me, one must come where I can strike back." She turned and strode off again.

I followed relentlessly. "And where would that lead? To your killing a man. And all the Keep in an uproar, and Verity chastising his guard, that you could be so endangered? And what if the killer were better with a knife than you? What consequence for the Six Duchies if I were now pulling your body out of a drift?" I swallowed and added, "My queen."

Her pace slowed, but her chin was still up as she asked softly, "What consequence for me if I sit day after day in the Keep, growing soft and blind as a grub? FitzChivalry, I am not a game piece, to sit my space on the board until some player sets me in motion. I am . . . there's a wolf watching us!"

"Where?"

She pointed, but he had vanished like a swirl of snow, leaving only a ghostly laughter in my mind. A moment later a trick of the wind brought his scent to Sidestep. The mule snorted and tugged at his lead rope. "I did not know we had wolves so near!" Kettricken marveled.

"Just a town dog, my lady. Probably some mangy, homeless beast out to sniff and paw through the village trash heap. He is nothing to fear.''

You think not? I'm hungry enough to eat that mule.

Go back and wait. I shall come soon.

The trash heap is nowhere near here. Besides, it's full of seagulls and stinks of their droppings. And other things. The mule would be fresh and sweet.

Go back, I tell you. I'll bring you meat later.

''FitzChivalry?'' This from Kettricken, warily.

I snapped my eyes back to her face. ''I beg pardon, my lady. My mind wandered.''

''Then that anger in your face is not for me?''

''No. Another has . . . crossed my will this day. For you, I have concern, not anger. Will not you mount Sidekick and let me take you back to the Keep?''

''I wish to see Verity.''

''My queen, it will not please him, to see you come so.''

She sighed and grew a bit smaller inside her cloak. She looked aside from me as she asked more quietly, ''Have you never wished to pass your time in someone's presence, Fitz, whether they welcomed you or not? Cannot you understand my loneliness . . . ?''

I do.

''To be his queen-in-waiting, to be sacrifice for Buckkeep, this I know I must do well. But there is another part of me . . . I am woman to his man and wife to his husbanding. To that I am sworn as well, and am more willing than dutiful to it. But he comes seldom to me, and when he does, he speaks little and leaves soon.'' She turned back to me. Tears sparkled suddenly on her eyelashes. She dashed them away and a note of anger crept into her voice. ''You spoke once of my duty, of doing what only a Queen can do for Buckkeep. Well, I shall not get with child lying alone in my bed night after night!''

''My queen, my lady, please,'' I begged her. Heat rose in my face.

She was merciless. ''Last night, I did not wait. I went to his door. But the guard claimed he was not there. That he had gone to his tower.'' She looked aside from me. ''Even that work is preferable to how he must labor in my bed." Not even that bitterness could cover the hurt under her words.

I reeled with the things I did not want to know. The cold of Kettricken alone in her bed. Verity, drawn to Skill at night. I did not know what was worse. My voice shook as I said, "You must not tell me these things, my queen. To speak of this to me is not right—"

"Then let me go and speak to him. He is the one who needs to hear this, I know. And I am going to speak it! If he will not come to me for his heart's sake, then he must come for his duty."

This makes sense. She is the one who must bear if the pack is to increase.

Stay out of this. Go home.

Home! A derisive bark of laughter in my mind. *Home is a pack, not a cold empty place. Listen to the female. She speaks well. We should all go, to be with him who leads. You fear foolishly for this bitch. She hunts well, with a keen tooth, and her kills are clean. I watched her yesterday. She is worthy of he who leads.*

We are not pack. Be silent.

I am. At the corner of my eye, I caught a flash of movement. I turned quickly, but there was nothing there. I turned back to find Kettricken standing silent before me still. But I sensed the spark of anger that had spirited her was now damped in pain. It bled her resolve from her.

I spoke quietly through the wind. "Please, lady, let me take you back to Buckkeep."

She did not reply, but pulled her hood up around her face and tightened it to hide most of her face. Then she walked to the mule and mounted and suffered me to lead the beast back to Buckkeep. It seemed a longer, colder walk in her subdued silence. I was not proud of the change I had wrought in her. To take my mind from it, I quested out about me carefully. It did not take me long to find Cub. He stalked and shadowed us, drifting like smoke through the tree cover, using the wind-blown drifts and falling snow to hide himself. I could never once actually swear that I saw him. I caught motion from the

orner of my eye, of a tiny bit of his scent on the wind. His
nstincts served him well.

Think you I am ready to hunt?

Not until you are ready to obey. I made my reply severe.

What then shall I do when I hunt alone, packless one? He
was stung, and angry.

We were drawing near to the outer wall of Buckkeep. I
wondered how he had gotten outside the Keep without passing
through a gate.

Shall I show you? A peace offering.

Perhaps later. When I come with meat. I felt his assent. He
was no longer pacing us, but had raced off ahead, and would be
at the cottage when I got there. The guards at the gate abash-
dly challenged me. I identified myself formally, and the ser-
eant had the wit not to insist that I identify the lady with me.
In the courtyard I halted Sidekick that she might dismount and
ffered her my hand. As she climbed down I all but felt eyes on
me. I turned, and saw Molly. She carried two buckets of water
resh drawn from the well. She stood still, looking at me,
oised like a deer before flight. Her eyes were deep, her face
ery still. When she turned aside, there was a stiffness to her
arriage. She did not glance at us again as she crossed the
ourtyard and went toward the kitchen entrance. I felt a cold
oreboding inside me. Then Kettricken let go of my hand and
athered her cloak more closely about herself. She did not look
at me either, but only said softly, "Thank you, FitzChivalry."
he walked slowly toward the door.

I returned Sidekick to the stable and saw to him. Hands
ame by and raised an eyebrow at me. I nodded, and he went
n about his work. Sometimes, I think that was what I liked
est about Hands, his ability to leave alone that which was not
is concern.

I made bold my heart for that which I did next. I went out
ehind the exercise pens. There was a thin trail of smoke rising
nd a nasty scent of scorching meat and hair. I walked toward
. Burrich stood next to the fire, watching it burn. The wind
nd snow kept trying to put it out, but Burrich was determined
 would burn well. He glanced at me as I came up but would
ot look at me or speak to me. His eyes were black hollows full

of dumb pain. It would turn to anger if I dared speak to him.
But I had not come for him. I took my knife from my belt and
cut from my head a finger's-length lock of hair. I added it to
the pyre, and watched as it burned. Vixen. A most excellent
bitch. A memory came to me and I spoke it aloud. "She was
there the first time Regal ever looked at me. She lay beside me
and snarled up at him."

After a moment Burrich nodded to my words. He, too, had
been there. I turned and slowly walked away.

My next stop was the kitchen, to filch a number of meaty
bones left over from yesterday's wake. They were not fresh
meat, but they'd have to do. Cub was right. He'd have to be put
out on his own soon, to hunt for himself. Seeing Burrich's pain
had renewed my resolve. Vixen had lived a long life, for a
hound, but still too short for Burrich's heart. To bond to any
animal was to promise oneself that future pain. My heart had
been broken sufficient times already.

I was still pondering the best way to do this as I approached the cottage. I lifted my head suddenly, getting only
the briefest precognition, and then his full weight hit me. He
had come, swift as an arrow, speeding over the snow, to fling
his weight against the backs of my knees, shouldering me down
as he passed. The force of his momentum threw me onto my
face in the snow. I lifted my head and got my arms under me as
he wheeled tightly and raced up to me again. I flung up an arm
but he plowed over me again, sharp claws digging into my flesh
for purchase as he ran. *Got you, got you, got you!* Glorious
exuberance.

Halfway to my feet, and he hit me again, full in my chest. I
flung up a forearm to shield my throat and face and he seized it
in his jaws. He growled deeply as he mock-worried it. I lost my
balance under his attack and went down in the snow. This time
I kept a grip on him, hugging him to me, and we rolled over
and over and over. He nipped me in a dozen places, some
painful, and all the time *Fun, fun, fun, got you, got you, and got
you again! Here, you're dead, here, I broke your forepaw, here,
your blood runs out! Got you, got you, got you!*

Enough! Enough! And finally: "Enough!" I roared, and
he let go of me and leaped away. He fled over the snow,

bounding ridiculously, to fling himself in a circle and come racing back at me. I flung my arms up to shelter my face, but he only seized my bag of bones and raced off with it, daring me to follow. I could not let him win so easily. So I leaped after him, tackling him, seizing the bag of bones, and it degenerated into a tugging match, at which he cheated by letting go suddenly, nipping me on the forearm hard enough to numb my hand, and then grabbing the bag again. I gave chase again.

Got you. A tug on the tail. *Got you!* I kneed his shoulder, pushing him off balance. *Got the bones!* and for an instant I had them and was running. He hit me full square in the back, all four paws, and drove me facedown in the snow, seized the trove, and was off again.

I do not know how long we played. We had flung ourselves finally down in the snow to rest and lay panting together in thoughtless simplicity. The sacking of the bag was torn in places, the bones peeking through, and Cub seized one, to shake and drag it from the clinging folds. He set to upon it, scissoring the meat and then pinning the bone down with his paws as his jaws cracked the knuckly cartilage on the end. I reached for the sack and tugged at a bone, a good meaty one, a thick marrow bone, and drew it forth.

And abruptly was a man again. Like awaking from a dream, like the popping of a soap bubble, and Cub's ears twitched and he turned to me as if I had spoken. But I had not. I had only separated my self from his. Abruptly I was cold, snow had gotten inside the tops of my boots and at my waist and collar. There were standing welts on my forearms and hands where his teeth had dragged over my flesh. My cloak was torn in two places. And I felt as groggy as if I were just coming out of a drugged sleep.

What's wrong? Real concern. *Why did you go away?*

I can't do this. I can't be like this, with you. This is wrong.

Puzzlement. *Wrong? If you can do it, how can it be wrong?*

I am a man, not a wolf.

Sometimes, he agreed. *But you don't have to be all the time.*

Yes, I must. I don't want to be bonded with you like this.

We cannot have this closeness. I have to set you free, to live the life you were meant to live. I must live the life I was meant for.

A derisive snort, a sneer of fangs. *This is it, brother. We are as we are. How can you claim to know what life I was meant to lead, let alone threaten to force me into it? You cannot even accept what you are meant to be. You deny it even as you are it. All your quibbling is nonsense. As well forbid your nose to snuff, or your ears to hear. We are as we do. Brother.*

I did not drop my guard. I did not give him leave. But he swept through my mind like a wind sweeps through an unshuttered window and fills a room. *The night and the snow. Meat in our jaws. Listen, snuff, the world is alive tonight and so are we! We can hunt until dawn, we are alive and the night and the forest are ours! Our eyes are keen, our jaws are strong, and we can run down a buck and feast before morning. Come! Come back to what you were born to be!*

A moment later I came to myself. I was on my feet, standing, and I was trembling from head to foot. I lifted my hands and looked at them, and suddenly my own flesh seemed foreign and confining, as unnatural as the clothes I wore. I could go. I could go, now, tonight, and travel far to find our own kind, and no one would ever be able to follow us, let alone find us. He offered me a moonlit world of blacks and whites, of food and rest, so simple, so complete. Our eyes were locked, and his were lambent green and beckoning to me. *Come. Come with me. What have the likes of us to do with men and all their petty plotting? There is not one mouthful of meat to be had in all their wrangling, no clean joys in their scheming, and never a simple pleasure taken unthinkingly. Why do you choose it? Come, come away!*

I blinked. Snowflakes clung to my eyelashes, and I was standing in the dark, chilled and shaking. A short distance from me, a wolf stood up and shook himself all over. Tail out flat, ears up, he came to me, and rubbed his head along my leg and with his nose gave my cold hand a flip. I went down on one knee and hugged him, felt the warmth of his ruff against my hands, the solidity of his muscle and bone. He smelled good, clean and wild. ''We are what we are, brother. Eat well,'' I told him. I rubbed his ears briefly, and then stood. As he picked up the sack of bones to drag them into the den he'd scuffed out under the cottage, I turned away. The lights of Buckkeep were almost blinding, but I went toward them anyway. I could not have said why just then. But I did it.

10

Fool's Errand

*I*N TIMES OF *peace, the teaching of the Skill was re-
stricted to those of royal blood, to keep the magic more
exclusive and reduce the chance of it being turned against the
King. Thus, when Galen became apprentice to Skill Master
Solicity, his duties consisted of assisting in completing the
training of Chivalry and Verity. No others were receiving instruction at that time. Regal, a delicate child, was judged by his
mother to be too sickly to withstand the rigors of the Skill
training. Thus, after Solicity's untimely death, Galen came to
the title of Skill Master, but had few duties. Some, at least, felt
that the time he had served as apprentice to Solicity was insuf-
ficient to be the full training of a Skill Master. Others have
averred that he never possessed the Skill strength necessary to
be a true Skill Master. In any case, during those years he had
no opportunity to prove himself, and disprove his critics. There
were no young Princes or Princesses to train during the years
that Galen was Skill Master.*

*It was only with the Red-Ship raids that it was decided that
the circle of those trained in the Skill must be expanded. A
proper coterie had not existed for years. Tradition tells us that
in previous troubles with the Outislanders, it was not unusual
for three, or even four coteries to exist. These usually consisted
of six to eight members, mutually chosen, well suited to be*

bonded among themselves, and with at least one member possessing a strong affinity with the reigning monarch. This key member reported directly to the monarch all that his coterie members relayed to him, if they were a messaging, or information-gathering coterie. Other coteries existed to pool strength and extend to the monarch their Skilling resources as he might need them. The key members in these coteries were often referred to as a King's or Queen's Man or Woman. Very rarely, such a one existed independent of any coterie or training, but simply as one who had such an affinity for the monarch that strength could be tapped, usually by a physical touch. From this key member, the monarch could draw endurance as needed to sustain a Skilling effort. By custom, a coterie was named after its key member. Thus we have legendary examples such as Crossfire's coterie.

Galen chose to ignore all tradition in the creation of his first and only coterie. Galen's coterie came to be named after the Skill Master who fashioned it, and retained that name even after his death. Rather than creating a pool of Skilled ones and letting a coterie emerge from it, Galen himself selected those who would be members of it. The coterie lacked the internal bonding of the legendary groups, and their truest affinity was to the Skill Master rather than to the King. Thus, the key member, initially August, reported to Galen fully as often as he reported to King Shrewd or King-in-Waiting Verity. With the death of Galen and the blasting of August's Skill sense, Serene rose to be key member of Galen's coterie. The other surviving members of the group were Justin, Will, Carrod, and Burl.

⇥⊨⇤

By night I ran as a wolf.

The first time I thought it a singularly vivid dream. The wide stretch of white snow with the inky tree shadows spilled on it, the elusive scents on the cold wind, the ridiculous fun of bounding and digging after shrews that ventured out of their winter burrows. I awoke clear-minded and good-tempered.

But the next night I dreamed again so vividly. I awoke knowing that when I blocked from Verity and hence myself my dreams of Molly, I left myself wide to the wolf's night thoughts. Here was a whole realm where not Verity nor any Skilled one could follow me. It was a world bereft of court intrigues or plotting, of worries and plans. My wolf lived in the present. I found his mind clean of the cluttering detail of memories. From day to day, he carried only that necessary to his survival. He did not remember how many shrews he had killed two nights ago, but only larger things, such as which game trails yielded the most rabbits to chase or where the spring ran swift enough that it never iced over.

This, then, was when and how I first showed him how to hunt. We did not do so well at first. I still arose very early each morning to take him food as needed. I told myself that it was but a small corner of my life that I kept for myself. It was as the wolf had said, not a thing I did, but something I was. Besides, I promised myself, I would not let this joining become a full bond. Soon, very soon, he would be able to hunt for himself, and I would send him away to be free. Sometimes I told myself that I only permitted him into my dreams that I might teach him to hunt, the sooner to set him free. I refused to consider what Burrich would think of such a thing.

I returned from one of my early-morning expeditions to find two soldiers sparring with one another in the kitchen yard. They had staves and were good-naturedly insulting one another as they huffed and shifted and traded whacks in the cold clear air. The man I did not know at all, and for a moment I thought both were strangers. Then the woman of the pair caught sight of me. ''Ho! FitzChivalry. A word with you!'' she called, but without retiring her stave.

I stared at her, trying to place her. Her opponent missed a parry and she clipped him sharply with her stave. As he hopped she danced back and laughed aloud, an unmistakable high-pitched whinny. ''Whistle?'' I asked incredulously.

The woman I had just addressed flashed her famous gap-toothed smile, caught her partner's stave a ringing blow, and danced back again. ''Yes?'' she asked breathlessly. Her sparring partner, seeing her occupied, courteously lowered his stave. Whistle immediately darted hers at him. With so much skill he almost looked lazy, his stave leaped up to counter hers. Again she laughed and held up her hand to ask a truce.

"Yes," she repeated, this time turning to me. "I've come . . . that is, I've been chosen to come and ask a favor of you."

I gestured at the clothes she wore. "I don't understand. You've left Verity's guard?"

She gave a tiny shrug, but I could see the question delighted her. "But not to go far. Queen's guard. Vixen badge. See?" She tugged the front of the short white jacket she wore to hold the fabric taut. Good sensible woolen homespun, I saw, and saw, too, the embroidered snarling white fox on a purple background. The purple matched the purple of her heavy woolen trousers. The loose pants cuff had been tucked into knee boots. Her partner's garb matched hers. Queen's guard. In light of Kettricken's adventure, the uniform made sense.

"Verity decided she needed a guard of her own?" I asked delightedly.

The smile faded a bit from Whistle's face. "Not exactly," she hedged, and then straightened as if reporting to me. "We decided she needed a Queen's guard. Me and some of the others that rode with her the other day. We got to talking about . . . everything, later. About how she handled herself out there. And back here. And how she came here, all alone. We talked about it then, that someone should get permission to form up a guard for her. But none of us really knew how to approach it. We knew it was needed, but no one else seemed to be paying much attention . . . but then last week, at the gate, I heard you got pretty hot about how she'd gone out, on foot and alone, and no one at her back. Well, you did! I was in the other room, and I heard!"

I bit back my protest, nodded curtly, and Whistle went on: "So. Well, we just did. Those of us who felt we wanted to wear the purple and white just said so. It was a pretty even split. It was time to take in some new blood anyway; most of Verity's guard was getting a bit long in the tooth. And soft, from too much time in the Keep. So we re-formed, giving rank to some who should have made it long ago, if there'd been any openings to fill, and taking in some recruits to fill in where needed. It all worked out perfectly. These newcomers will give us something to hone our skills on while we teach them. The

Queen will have her own guard, when she wants one. Or needs one.''

''I see.'' I was beginning to get an uneasy feeling. ''And what was the favor you wanted of me?''

''Explain it to Verity. Tell the Queen she has a guard.'' She said the words simply and quietly.

''This walks close to disloyalty,'' I said just as simply. ''Soldiers of Verity's own guard, setting aside his colors to take on his queen's . . .''

''Some might see it that way. Some might speak it that way.'' Her eyes met mine squarely, and the smile was gone from her face. ''But you know it is not. It's a needed thing. Your . . . Chivalry would have seen it, would have had a guard for her before she even arrived here. But King-in-Waiting Verity . . . well, this is no disloyalty to him. We've served him well, because we love him. Still do. This is those who've always watched his back, falling back and re-forming to watch his back even better. That's all. He's got a good Queen, is what we think. We don't want to see him lose her. That was all. We don't think any the less of our king-in-waiting. You know that.''

I did. But still. I looked away from her plea, shook my head, and tried to think. Why me? a part of me demanded angrily. Then I knew, that in the moment I'd lost my temper and berated the guard for not protecting their queen, I'd volunteered for this. Burrich had warned me about not remembering my place. ''I will speak to King-in-Waiting Verity. And to the Queen, if he approves this.''

Whistle flashed her smile again. ''We knew you'd do it for us. Thanks, Fitz.''

As quickly she was spinning away from me, stave at the ready as she danced threateningly toward her partner, who gave ground grudgingly. With a sigh, I turned away from the courtyard. I had thought Molly would be fetching water at this time. I'd hoped for a glimpse of her. But she was not, and I left feeling disappointed. I knew I should not play at such games, but some days I could not resist the temptation. I left the courtyard.

The last few days had become a special sort of self-torture

for me. I refused to allow myself to see Molly again, but could not resist shadowing her. So I was in the kitchen but a moment after she had left, fancying I could still catch the trace of her perfume in the air. Or I stationed myself in the Great Hall of an evening, and tried to be where I could watch her without being noticed. No matter what amusement was offered, minstrel or poet or puppeteer, or just folk talking and working on their handicrafts, my eyes would be drawn always to wherever Molly might be. She looked so sober and demure in her dark blue skirts and blouse, and she had never a glance for me. Always she spoke with the other Keep women, or on the rare evenings when Patience chose to descend, she sat beside her and attended to her with a focus of attention that denied I even existed. Sometimes I thought my brief encounter with her had been a dream. But at night I could go back to my room and take out the shirt I had hidden in the bottom of my clothes chest, and if I held it close to my face, I fancied I could still smell the faint trace of her perfume upon it. And so I endured.

A number of days had passed since we had burned the Forged ones on their funeral pyre. In addition to the formation of the Queen's guard, other changes were afoot within and without the Keep. Two other master boatbuilders, unsummoned, had come to volunteer their skills for the building of the ships. Verity had been delighted. But even more so had Queen Kettricken been moved, for it was to her that they presented themselves, saying that they desired to be of service. Their apprentices came with them, to swell the ranks of those working in the shipyards. Now the lamps burned both before dawn and after the sun's setting, and work proceeded at a breakneck pace. So Verity was away all the more, and Kettricken, when I called on her, was more subdued than ever. I tempted her with books or outings to no avail. She spent most of her time sitting near idly at her loom, growing more pale and listless with every passing day. Her dark mood infected those ladies who attended her, so that to visit her room was as cheery as keeping a deathwatch.

I had not expected to find Verity in his study, and was not disappointed. He was down at the boat sheds, as always. I left word with Charim to ask that I be summoned whenever Verity might have the time to see me. Then, with a resolve to keep myself busy and to do as Chade had suggested, I returned to my room. I took both dice and tally sticks with me, and headed for the Queen's chambers.

I had resolved to teach her some of the games of chance that the lords and ladies were fond of, in the hopes that she might expand her circle of entertainments. I also hoped, with less expectations, that such games might draw her to socialize more widely and to depend less on my companionship. Her bleak mood was beginning to burden me with its oppressiveness, so that I often heartily wished to be away from her.

"Teach her to cheat first. Only, just tell her that's how the game is played. Tell her the rules permit deception. A bit of sleight of hand, easily taught, and she could clean Regal's pockets for him a time or two before he dared suspect her. And then what could he do? Accuse Buckkeep's lady of cheating at dice?"

The Fool, of course. At my elbow, companionably pacing alongside me, his rat scepter jouncing lightly on his shoulder. I did not startle physically, but he knew that once more, he had taken me by surprise. His amusement shone in his eyes.

"I think our queen-in-waiting might take it amiss if I so misinformed her. Why do you not come with me instead, to brighten her spirits a bit? I shall set aside the dice, and you can juggle for her," I suggested.

"Juggle for her? Why, Fitz, that is all I do, all day long, and you see it as but my foolery. You see my work and deem it play, while I see you work so earnestly at playing games you have not yourself devised. Take a Fool's advice on this. Teach the lady not dice, but riddles, and you will both be the wiser."

"Riddles? That's a Bingtown game, is it not?"

" 'Twere one played well at Buckkeep these days. Answer me this one, if you can. How does one call a thing when one does not know how to call it?"

"I have never been any good at this game, Fool."

"Nor any other of your bloodline, from what I have heard. So answer this. What has wings in Shrewd's scroll, a tongue of flame in Verity's book, silver eyes in the Relltown Vellums, and gold-scaled skin in your room?"

"That's a riddle?"

He looked at me pityingly. "No. A riddle is what I just asked you. That's an Elderling. And the first riddle was, how do you summon one?"

My stride slowed. I looked at him more directly, but his eyes were always difficult to meet.

"Is that a riddle? Or a serious question?"

"Yes." The Fool was grave.

I stopped in midstride, completely bemuddled. I glared at him. In answer, he went nose to nose with his rat scepter. They simpered at one another. "You see, Ratsy, he knows no more than his uncle or his grandfather. None of them know how to summon an Elderling."

"By the Skill," I said impetuously.

The Fool looked at me strangely. "You know this?"

"I suspect it is so."

"Why?"

"I don't know. Now that I consider it, I do not think it likely. King Wisdom made a long journey to find the Elderlings. If he could simply have Skilled to them, why didn't he?"

"Indeed. But sometimes there is truth in impetuosity. So riddle me this, boy. A King is alive. Likewise a Prince. And both are Skilled. But where are those who trained alongside the King, or those who trained before him? How come we to this, this paucity of Skilled ones at a time when they are so grievously needed?"

"Few are trained in times of peace. Galen didn't see fit to train any, up until his last year. And the coterie he created . . ." I paused suddenly, and though the corridor was empty, I suddenly did not want to speak anymore about it. I had always kept whatever Verity told me about the Skill in confidence.

The Fool pranced in a sudden circle about me. "If the shoe does not fit, one cannot wear it, no matter who made it for you," he declared.

I nodded grudgingly. "Exactly."

"And he who made it is gone. Sad. So sad. Sadder than

hot meat on the table and red wine in your glass. But he who is gone was made by someone in turn.''

"Solicity. But she is also gone.''

"Ah. But Shrewd is not. Nor Verity. It seems to me that if there are two she created still breathing, there ought to be others. Where are they?''

I shrugged. "Gone. Old. Dead. I don't know.'' I forced my impatience down, tried to consider his question. "King Shrewd's sister, Merry. August's mother. She would have been trained, perhaps, but she is long dead. Shrewd's father, King Bounty, was the last to have a coterie, I believe. But very few folk of that generation are still alive.'' I halted my tongue. Verity had once told me that Solicity had trained as many in the Skill as she could find the talent in. Surely there must be some of them left alive; they would be no more than a decade or so older than Verity. . . .

"Dead, too many of them, if you ask me. I do know.'' The Fool interjected an answer to my unspoken question. I looked at him blankly. He stuck his tongue out at me, waltzed away from me a bit. He considered his scepter, chucked the rat lovingly under the chin. "You see, Ratsy. It is as I told you. None of them know. None of them are smart enough to ask.''

"Fool, cannot you ever speak plain?'' I cried out in frustration.

He halted as suddenly as if struck. In midpirouette, he lowered his heels to the floor and stood like a statue. "Would it help any?'' he asked soberly. "Would you listen to me if I came to you and did not speak in riddles? Would that make you pause and think and hang upon every word, and ponder those words later, in your chamber? Very well then. I shall try. Do you know the rhyme 'Six Wisemen went to Jhaampe-town'?''

I nodded, as confused as ever.

"Recite it for me.''

" 'Six Wisemen went to Jhaampe-town, climbed a hill and never came down, turned to stone and flew away. . . .' '' The old nursery rhyme eluded me suddenly. "I don't recall it all. It's nonsense anyway, one of those rhyming things that sticks in your head but means nothing.''

"That, of course, is why it is enscrolled with the knowledge verses," the Fool concluded.

"I don't know!" I retorted. I suddenly felt irritated beyond endurance. "Fool, you are doing it again. All you speak is riddles, ever! You claim to speak plain, but your truth eludes me."

"Riddles, dear Fitzy-fitz, are supposed to make folk think. To find new truth in old saws. But, be that as it may. . . . Your brain eludes me. How shall I reach it? Perhaps if I came to you, by dark of night, and sang under your window:

" *'Bastard Princeling, Fitz my sweet,*
You waste your hours to your own defeat.
You work to stop, you strive to refrain,
When all your effort should go to a gain.' "

He had flung himself to one knee, and plucked nonexistent strings on his scepter. He sang quite lustily, and even well. The tune belonged to a popular love ballad. He looked at me, sighed theatrically, wet his lips, and continued mournfully:

" *'Why does a Farseer look never afar,*
Why dwells he completely in things as they are?
Your coasts are besieged, your people beset.
I warn and I urge, but they all say, "not yet!"
O Bastard Princeling, gentle Fitz,
Will you delay until chopped to bits?' "

A passing servant girl paused to stand bemused and listen. A page came to the door of one chamber and peeped out at us, grinning widely. A slow flush began to heat my cheeks, for the Fool's expression was both tender and ardent as he looked up at me. I tried to walk casually away from him, but he followed me on his knees, clutching at my sleeve. I was forced to stand, or engage in a ridiculous struggle to free myself. I stood, feeling foolish. He simpered a smile up at me. The page giggled, and down the hall I heard two voices conferring in amusement. I refused to lift my eyes to see who was so enjoying my dis-

comfort. The Fool mouthed a kiss up at me. He let his voice
sink to a confidential whisper as he sang on:

>   " 'Will fate seduce you to her will?
>   Not if you struggle with all your Skill.
>   Summon your allies, locate the trained,
>   Consummate all from which you've refrained.
>   There's a future not yet fashioned,
>   Founded by your fiery passions.
>   If you use your Wits to win,
>   You'll save the Duchies for your kin.
>   Thus begs a Fool, on bended knee,
>   Let not a darkness come to be.
>   Let not our peoples go to dust
>   When Life in you has placed this trust.' "

He paused, then sang loudly and jovially:

>   " 'And if you choose to let this pass
>   Like so much farting from your ass,
>   Behold my reverence for thee,
>   Feast eyes on what men seldom see!' "

He suddenly released my cuff, to tumble away from me in
a somersault that somehow reached a finish with his presentation of his bare buttocks to me. They were shockingly pale, and
I could conceal neither my amazement nor affront. The Fool
vaulted to his feet, suitably clothed again, and Ratsy on his
scepter bowed most humbly to all who had paused to watch my
humiliation. There was general laughter and a scattering of
applause. His performance had left me speechless. I looked
aside and tried to walk past him, but with a bound the Fool
blocked my passage once again. The Fool abruptly assumed a
stern stance and addressed all who still grinned.

"Fie and shame upon you all, to be so merry! To giggle
and point at a boy's broken heart! Do not you know the Fitz has
lost one most dear to him? Ah, he hides his grief beneath his
blushes, but she has gone to her grave and left his passion
unslaked. That most stubbornly chaste and virulently flatulent

of maidens, dear Lady Thyme, has perished. Of her own stench, I doubt it not, though some say it came of eating spoiled meat. But spoiled meat, you say, has a most foul odor, to warn off any from consuming it. Such we can say of Lady Thyme also, and so perhaps she smelled it not, or deemed it but the perfume of her fingers. Mourn not, poor Fitz, another shall be found for you. To this I shall devote myself, this very day! I swear it, by Sir Ratsy's skull. And now I bid you hasten on your tasks, for in truth I have delayed mine much too long. Farewell, poor Fitz. Brave, sad heart! To put so bold a face on your desolation! Poor disconsolate youth! Ah, Fitz, poor poor Fitz . . .''

And he wandered off down the hall from me, shaking his head woefully, and conferring with Ratsy as to which elderly dowager he should court on my behalf. I stared in disbelief after him. I felt betrayed, that he could make so public a spectacle of me. Sharp-tongued and flighty as the Fool could be, I had never expected to be the public butt of one of his jokes. I kept waiting for him to turn around and say some last thing that would make me understand what had just happened. He did not. When he turned a corner, I perceived that my ordeal was finally at an end. I proceeded down the hallway, fuming with embarrassment and dazed with puzzlement at the same time. The doggerel of his rhymes had stored his words in my head, and I knew that I would ponder his love song much in days to come, to try to worry out the meanings hidden there. But Lady Thyme? Surely he would not say such a thing, were it not ''true.'' But why would Chade allow his public persona to die in such a way? What poor woman's body would be carried out as Lady Thyme, no doubt to be carted off to distant relatives for burial? Was this his method of beginning his journey, a way to leave the Keep unseen? But again, why let her be dead? So that Regal might believe he had succeeded in his poisoning? To what end?

Thus bemused, I finally came to the doors of Kettricken's chamber. I stood in the hall a moment, to recover my aplomb and compose my face. Suddenly the door across the hall flung open and Regal strode into me. His momentum jostled me aside, and before I could recover myself, he grandly offered,

"It's all right, Fitz. I scarcely expect an apology from one so bereaved as yourself." He stood in the hallway, straightening his jerkin as the young men following him emerged from his chamber, tittering in amusement. He smiled 'round at them, and then leaned close to me to ask, in a quietly venomous voice, "Where will you suckle up now that the old whore Thyme is dead? Ah, well. I am sure you will find some other old woman to coddle you. Or are you come to wheedle up to a younger one now?" He dared to smile at me, before he wheeled on his heel and strode off in a fine flutter of sleeves, trailed by his three sycophants.

The insult to the Queen poisoned me into rage. It came with a suddenness such as I had never experienced. I felt my chest and throat swell with it. A terrible strength rushed through me; I know my upper lip lifted in a snarl. From afar I sensed, *What? What is it? Kill it! Kill it! Kill it!* I took a step, the next would have been a spring, and I know my teeth would have sunk into the place where throat meets shoulder.

But: "FitzChivalry," said a voice, full of surprise.

Molly's voice! I turned to her, my emotions wrenching from rage to delight at seeing her. But as swiftly she was turning aside, saying, "Beg pardon, my lord," and brushing past me. Her eyes were down, her manner that of a servant.

"Molly?" I called, stepping after her. She paused. When she looked back at me, her face was empty of emotion, her voice neutral.

"Sir? Had you an errand for me?"

"An errand?" Of course. I glanced about us, but the corridor was empty. I took a step toward her, pitched my voice low for her ears only. "No. I've just missed you so. Molly, I—"

"This is not seemly, sir. I beg you to excuse me." She turned, proudly, calmly, and walked away from me.

"What did I do?" I demanded, in angry consternation. I did not really expect an answer. But she paused. Her blue-clothed back was straight, her head erect under her tatted hair-cloth. She did not turn back to me, but said quietly, to the corridor, "Nothing. You did nothing at all, my lord. Absolutely nothing."

"Molly!" I protested, but she turned the corner and was

gone. I stood staring after her. After a moment I realized I was
making a sound somewhere between a whine and a growl.

Let us go hunting instead.

Perhaps, I found myself agreeing, *that would be the best
thing. To go hunting, to kill, to eat, to sleep. And to do no more
than that.*

Why not now?

I don't really know.

I composed myself and knocked at Kettricken's door. It
was opened by little Rosemary, who dimpled a smile at me as
she invited me in. Once within, Molly's errand here was evident. Kettricken was holding a fat green candle under her nose.
On the table were several others. "Bayberry," I observed.

Kettricken looked up with a smile. "FitzChivalry. Welcome. Come in and be seated. May I offer you food? Wine?"

I stood looking at her. A sea change. I felt her strength,
knew she stood in the center of herself. She was dressed in a
soft gray tunic and leggings. Her hair was dressed in her cus-
tomary way. Her jewelry was simple, a single necklace of
green and blue stone beads. But this was not the woman I had
brought back to the Keep a few days ago. That woman had
been distressed, angry, hurt, and confused. This Kettricken
welled serenity.

"My queen," I began hesitantly.

"Kettricken," she corrected me calmly. She moved about
the room, setting some of the candles on shelves. It was almost
a challenge in that she did not say more.

I came farther into her sitting room. She and Rosemary
were the only occupants. Verity had once complained to me
that her chambers had the precision of a military encampment.
It had not been an exaggeration. The simple furnishings were
spotlessly clean. The heavy tapestries and rugs that furnished
most of Buckkeep were missing here. Simple mats of straw
were on the floor, and frames supported parchment screens
painted with delicate sprays of flowers and trees. There was no
clutter at all. In this room, all was finished and put away, or not
yet begun. That is the only way I can describe the stillness I felt
there.

I had come in a roil of conflicting emotions. Now I stood

still and silent, my breathing steadying and my heart calming. One corner of the chamber had been turned into an alcove walled with the parchment screens. Here there was a rug of green wool on the floor, and low padded benches such as I had seen in the mountains. Kettricken placed the green bayberry candle behind one of the screens. She kindled it with a flame from the hearth. The dancing candlelight behind the screen gave the life and warmth of a sunrise to the painted scene. Kettricken walked around to sit on one of the low benches within the alcove. She indicated the bench opposite hers. "Will you join me?"

I did. The gently lit screen, the illusion of a small private room, and the sweet scent of bayberry surrounded me. The low bench was oddly comfortable. It took me a moment to recall the purpose of my visit. "My queen, I thought you might like to learn some of the games of chance we play at Buckkeep. So you could join in when the other folk are amusing themselves."

"Perhaps another time," she said kindly. "If you and I wish to amuse ourselves, and if it would please you to teach me the game. But for those reasons only. I have found the old adages to be true. One can only walk so far from one's true self before the bond either snaps, or pulls one back. I am fortunate. I have been pulled back. I walk once more in trueness to myself, FitzChivalry. That is what you sense today."

"I don't understand."

She smiled. "You don't need to."

She fell silent again. Little Rosemary had gone to sit by the hearth. She took up her slate and chalk as if to amuse herself. Even that child's normal merriment seemed placid today. I turned back to Kettricken and waited. But she only sat looking at me, a bemused smile on her face.

After a moment or two, I asked, "What are we doing?"

"Nothing," Kettricken said.

I copied her silence. After a long time she observed, "Our own ambitions and tasks that we set for ourselves, the framework we attempt to impose upon the world, is no more than a shadow of a tree cast across the snow. It will change as the sun moves, be swallowed in the night, sway with the wind, and when the smooth snow vanishes, it will lie distorted upon the uneven earth. But the tree continues to be. Do you understand that?'' She leaned forward slightly to look into my face. Her eyes were kind.

"I think so," I said uneasily.

She gave me a look almost of pity. "You would if you stopped trying to understand it, if you gave up worrying about why this is important to me, and simply tried to see if it is an idea that has worth in your own life. But I do not bid you to do that. I bid no one do anything here."

She sat back again, a gentle loosening that made her straight spine seem effortless and restful. Again she did nothing. She simply sat across from me and unfurled herself. I felt her life brush up against me and flow around me. It was but the faintest touching, and had I not experienced both the Skill and the Wit, I do not think I would have sensed it. Cautiously, as softly as if I assayed a bridge made of cobweb, I overlay my senses on hers.

She quested. Not as I did, toward a specific beast, or to read what might be close by. I discarded the word I had always given to my sensing. Kettricken did not seek after anything with her Wit. It was as she said, simply a being, but it was being a part of the whole. She composed herself and considered all the ways the great web touched her, and was content. It was a delicate and tenuous thing and I marveled at it. For an instant I, too, relaxed. I breathed out. I opened myself, Wit wide to all. I discarded all caution, all worry that Burrich would sense me. I had never done anything to compare it with before. Kettricken's reaching was as delicate as droplets of dew sliding down a strand of spiderweb. I was like a dammed flood, suddenly released, to rush out to fill old channels to overflowing and to send fingers of water investigating the lowlands.

Let us hunt! The Wolf, joyfully.

In the stables, Burrich straightened from cleaning a hoof, to frown at no one. Sooty stamped in her stall. Molly shrugged away and shook out her hair. Across from me, Kettricken started and looked at me as if I had spoken aloud. A moment more I was held, seized from a thousand sides, stretched and expanded, illuminated pitilessly. I felt it all, not just the human folk with their comings and goings, but every pigeon that fluttered in the eaves, every mouse that crept unnoticed behind the wine kegs, every speck of life, that was not and never had been a speck, but had always been a node on the web of life. *Nothing alone, nothing forsaken, nothing without meaning, nothing of no significance, and nothing of importance.* Somewhere, someone sang, and then fell silent. A chorus filled in after that solo, other voices, distant and dim, saying, *What? Beg pardon? Did you call? Are you here? Do I dream*? They plucked at me, as beggars pluck at strangers' sleeves, and I suddenly felt that if I did not draw away, I could come unraveled like a piece of fabric. I blinked my eyes, sealing myself inside myself again. I breathed in.

No time had passed. A single breath, a wink of an eye. Kettricken looked askance at me. I appeared not to notice. I reached up to scratch my nose. I shifted my weight.

I resettled myself firmly. I let a few more minutes pass before I sighed and shrugged apologetically. "I do not understand the game, I am afraid," I offered.

I had succeeded in annoying her. "It is not a game. You don't have to understand it, or 'do' it. Simply stop all else, and be."

I made a show of making another effort. I sat still for several moments, then fidgeted absently with my cuff until she looked at me doing it. Then I cast my eyes down as if ashamed. "The candle smells very sweet," I complimented her.

Kettricken sighed and gave up on me. "The girl who makes them has a very keen awareness of scents. Almost she can bring me my gardens and surround me with their fragrances. Regal brought me one of her honeysuckle tapers, and after that I sought out her wares myself. She is a serving girl here, and does not have the time or resources to make too many. So I count myself fortunate when she brings them to offer to me."

"Regal," I repeated. Regal speaking to Molly. Regal knowing her well enough to know of her candlemaking. Everything inside me clenched with foreboding. "My queen, I think I distract you from what you wish to be doing. That is not my desire. May I leave you now, to return again when you wish to have company?''

"This exercise does not exclude company, FitzChivalry."
She looked at me sadly. ''Will not you try again to let go? For a moment I thought . . . No? Ah, then, I let you go.'' I heard regret and loneliness in her voice. Then she straightened herself. She took a breath, breathed it out slowly. I felt again her consciousness thrumming in the web. She has the Wit, I thought to myself. Not strong, but she has it.

I left her room quietly. There was a tiny bit of amusement to wondering what Burrich would think if he knew. Much less amusing to recall how she had been alerted to me when I quested out with the Wit. I thought of my night hunts with the wolf. Would soon the Queen begin to complain of strange dreams?

A cold certainty welled up in me. I would be discovered. I had been too careless, too long. I knew that Burrich could sense when I used the Wit. What if there were others? I could be accused of Beast magic. I found my resolve and hardened myself to it. Tomorrow, I would act.

11

Lone Wolves

THE FOOL WILL *always remain one of Buckkeep's great mysteries. It is almost possible to say that nothing is definitely known of him. His origin, age, sex, and race have all been the subject of conjecture. Most amazing is how such a public person maintained such an aura of privacy. The questions about the Fool will always outnumber the answers. Did he ever truly possess any mystical powers, any prescience, any magic at all, or was it merely that his quick wits and razor tongue made it seem as if he knew all before it came to pass? If he did not know the future, he appeared to, and by his calm assumption of foreknowledge, he swayed many of us to help him shape the future as he saw fit.*

⋅━■▝⋅

White on white. An ear twitched, and that minute movement betrayed all.

You see? I prompted him.

I scent.

I see. I flicked my eyes toward the prey. No more a movement than that. It was sufficient.

I see! He leaped, the rabbit started, and Cub went floundering after it. The rabbit ran lightly over the unpacked snow, while Cub had to surge and bound and leap through it. The rabbit darted elusively, this way, that way, around the tree, around the clump of bushes, into the brambles. Had he stayed in there? Cub snuffed hopefully, but the density of the thorns turned his sensitive nose back.

It's gone, I told him.

Are you sure? Why didn't you help?

I can't run down game in loose snow. I must stalk and spring only when one spring is sufficient.

Ah. Enlightenment. Consideration. *There are two of us. We should hunt as a pair. I could start game and drive it toward you. You could be ready to leap out and snap its neck.*

I shook my head slowly. *You must learn to hunt alone, Cub. I will not always be with you, in mind or in flesh.*

A wolf is not meant to hunt alone.

Perhaps not. But many do. As you will. But I did not intend that you should start with rabbits. Come on.

He fell in at my heels, content to let me lead. We had left the Keep before winter light had even grayed the skies. Now they were blue and open, clear and cold above us. The trail we were following was no more than a soft-shouldered groove in the deep snow. I sank calf-deep at every step. About us, the forest was a winter stillness, broken only by the occasional dart of a small bird, or the far-off cawing of a crow. It was open forest, mostly saplings with the occasional giant that had survived the fire that had cleared this hillside. It was good pasturage for goats in summer. Their sharp little hooves had cut the trail we were now following. It led to a simple stone hut and a tumbledown corral and shelter for the goats. It was only used in summer.

Cub had been delighted when I went to get him this morning. He had shown me his roundabout path for slipping past the guards. An old cattle gate, long bricked up, was his egress. Some shift of the earth had unsettled the stone and mortar blocking it, creating a crack wide enough for him to slip through. The beaten-down snow showed me that he had used it often. Once outside the walls, we had ghosted away from the Keep, moving like shadows in the not-light of stars and moon on white snow. Once safely away from the Keep, Cub had turned the expedition into stalking practice. He raced ahead to lie in wait, to spring out and tag me with a splayed paw or a sharp nip, and then race away in a great circle, to attack me from behind. I had let him play, welcoming the exertion that warmed me, as well as the sheer joy of the mindless romping. Always, I kept us moving, so that by the time the sun and light found us, we were miles from Buckkeep, in an area seldom visited during the winter. My spotting of the white rabbit against the white snow had been pure happenstance. I had even humbler game in mind for his first solo hunt.

Why do we come here? Cub demanded as soon as we came in sight of the hut.

To hunt, I said simply. I halted some distance away. The cub sank down beside me, waiting. *Well, go ahead,* I told him. *Go check for game sign.*

Oh, this is worthy hunting, this. Sniffing about some man den for scraps. Disdainful.

Not scraps. Go look.

He surged forward, and then angled toward the hut. I watched him go. Our dream hunts together had taught him much, but now I wished him to hunt entirely independently of me. I did not doubt that he could do it. I chided myself that demanding this proof was just one more procrastination.

He stayed in the snowy brush as much as he could. He approached the hut cautiously, ears alert and nose working. *Old scents. Humans. Goats. Cold and gone.* He froze an instant, then took a careful step forward. His motions now were calculated and precise. Ears forward, tail straight, he was totally intent and focused. *MOUSE!* He sprang and had it. He shook his head, a quick snap, and then let the little animal go flying. He caught it again as it came down. *Mouse!* he announced gleefully. He flipped his kill up into the air and danced up after it on his hind legs. He caught it again, delicately, in his small front teeth, and tossed it up again. I radiated pride and approval at him. By the time he had finished playing with his kill, the mouse was little more than a sodden rag of fur. He gulped it down finally in a single snap and came bounding back to me.

Mice! The place is riddled with them. Their smell and sign are everywhere all about the hut.

I thought there would be plenty here. The shepherds complain about them, that the mice overrun this place and spoil their provisions in the summer. I guessed they would winter here, too.

Surprisingly fat, for this time of year, Cub opined, and was off again with a bound. He hunted with frantic enthusiasm, but only until his hunger was sated. Then it was my turn to approach the hut. Snow had drifted up against the rickety wooden door, but I shouldered it open. The interior was dismal. Snow had sifted in through the thatched roof and lay in streaks and stripes on the frozen dirt floor. There was a rudimentary hearth and chimney, with a kettle hook. A stool and a wooden bench were the only furnishings. There was still a bit of firewood left beside the hearth, and I used it to build a careful fire on the blackened stones. I kept it small, just enough to warm myself and to thaw the bread and meat I had packed with me. Cub came for a taste of that, more for the sharing than for any hunger. He made a leisurely exploration of the hut's interior. *Lots of mice!*

I know. I hesitated, then forced myself to add, *You won't starve here.*

He lifted his nose abruptly from the corner he'd been sniffing. He advanced a few steps toward me, then stopped, standing stiff-legged. His eyes met mine and held. The wilds were in their darkness. *You're abandoning me here.*

Yes. There is food in plenty here. In a while I will come back, to be sure you are all right. I think you will be fine here. You will teach yourself to hunt. Mice at first, and then larger game . . .

You betray me. You betray pack.

No. We are not pack. I am setting you free, Cub. We are becoming too close. That is not good, for either of us. I warned you, long ago, that I would not bond. We can have no part of each other's lives. It is better for you to go off, alone, to become what you were meant to be.

I was meant to be a member of a pack. He leveled his stare at me. *Will you tell me that there are wolves near here, ones who will accept an intruder into their territory and make me part of their pack?*

I was forced to look aside from him. *No. There are no wolves here. One would have to travel many days to come to a place wild enough for wolves to run freely.*

Then what is there here for me?

Food. Freedom. Your own life, independent of mine.

Isolation. He bared his teeth at me, and then abruptly turned aside. He circled past me, a wide circle as he went to the door. *Men.* He sneered. *Truly you are not pack, but man.* He paused in the open door to look back at me. *Men it is who think they can rule others' lives but have no bonds to them. Do you think that to bond or not to bond is for you alone to decide? My heart is my own. I give it where I will. I will not give it to one who thrusts me aside. Nor will I obey one who denies pack and bond. Do you think I will stay here and snuff about this men's lair, to snap at the mice who have come for their leavings, to be like the mice, things that live on the droppings of men? No. If we are not pack, then we are not kin. I owe you nothing, and least of all obedience. I shall not stay here. I shall live as I please.*

A slyness to his thoughts. He was hiding something, but I guessed it. *You shall do as you wish, Cub, but for one thing. You shall not follow me back to Buckkeep. I forbid it.*

You forbid? You forbid? Forbid the wind to blow past your stone den, then, or the grass to grow in the earth around it. You have as much right. You forbid.

He snorted and turned away from me. I hardened my will, and spoke a final time to him. "Cub!" I said in my man voice. He turned back to me, startled. His small ears went back at my tone. Almost he sneered his teeth at me. But before he could, I *repelled* at him. It was a thing I had always known how to do, as instinctively as one knows to pull the finger back from the flame. It was a force I had used but seldom, for once Burrich had turned it against me, and I did not always trust it. This was not a push, such as I had used on him when he was caged. I put force into it, the mental repulsing becoming almost a physical thing as he recoiled from me. He leaped back a stride then stood splay-legged on the snow, ready for flight. His eyes were shocked.

"GO!" I shouted at him, man's word, man's voice, and at

the same time *repelled* him again with every bit of Wit I had. He fled, not gracefully, but leaping and scrabbling away through the snow. I held myself within myself, refusing to follow him with my mind and make sure that he did not stop. No. I was done with that. The *repelling* was a breaking of that bond, not only a withdrawing of myself from him, but a pushing back of every tie he had to me. Severed. And better to let them remain that way. Yet as I stood staring at the patch of brush where he had disappeared, I felt an emptiness that was very like to cold, a tingling itch of something lost, something missing. I have heard men speak so of an amputated limb. A physical groping about for a part gone forever.

I left the hut and began my hike home. The farther I walked, the more I hurt. Not physically, but that is the only comparison I have. As raw and flayed as if stripped of skin and meat. It was worse than when Burrich had taken Nosy, for I had done it to myself. The waning afternoon seemed chillier than the dark of dawn had. I tried to tell myself that I did not feel ashamed. I had done what was necessary. As I had with Virago. I pushed that thought aside. No. Cub would be fine. He would be better off than if he were with me. What life would it be for that wild creature, skulking about, always in danger of discovery, by the Keep dogs or hunters or anyone who might spot him? He might be isolated, he might be lonely, but he would be alive. Our connection was severed. There was an insistent temptation to quest out about me, to see if I could sense him still, to grope and find if his mind still touched mine at all. I sternly resisted it, and sealed my thoughts against his as firmly as I could. Gone. He would not follow me. Not after I had *repelled* him like that. No. I tramped on and refused to look back.

Had I not been so deep in thought, so intent on remaining isolated inside myself, I might have had some warning. But I doubt it. The Wit was never any use against Forged ones. I do not know if they stalked me, or if I blundered right past their hiding place. The first I knew of them was when the weight hit my back and I went down face-first in the snow. At first I thought it was Cub, come back to challenge my decision. I rolled and came almost to my feet before another one seized hold of my shoulder. Forged ones, three males, one young, two large and once well muscled. My mind recorded it all quickly, categorizing them as neatly as if this were one of Chade's exercises. One big one with a knife, the others had sticks. Torn and filthy clothing. Faces reddened and peeling from the cold, filthy beards, shaggy hair. Faces bruised and cut. Did they fight among themselves, or had they attacked someone else before me?

I broke the one's grip and leaped back, trying to get as clear of them as I could. I had a belt knife. It was not a long blade, but it was all I had. I had thought I would not need any weapon today; I had thought there were no more Forged ones anywhere near Buckkeep. They circled wide of me, keeping me in the center of their ring. They let me get my knife clear. It didn't seem to worry them.

"What do you want? My cloak?" I undid the catch and let it fall. One's eyes followed it down, but none of them leaped for it as I had hoped. I shifted, turning, trying to watch all three at once, trying to have none of them completely behind me. It wasn't easy. "Mittens?" I stripped them from my hands, tossed them as a pair toward the one who appeared youngest. He let them fall at his feet. They grunted as they shuffled, rocking on their feet, watching me. No one wanted to be the first to attack. They knew I had a knife; whoever went first would meet the blade. I took a step or two toward an opening in the ring. They shifted to block my escape.

"What do you want?" I roared at them. I spun around, trying to look at each of them, and for a moment locked eyes with one. There was less in his eyes than there had been in Cub's. No clean wildness, only the misery of physical discomfort and want. I stared at him and he blinked.

"Meat." He grunted as if I had wrung the word from him.

"I have no meat, no food at all. You'll get nothing from me but a fight!"

"You," huffed another, in a parody of laughter. Mirthless, heartless. "Meat!"

I had paused a moment too long, looked too long at one, for another sprang suddenly to my back. He flung his arms around me, pinning one of my arms, and then suddenly, horribly, his teeth sank into my flesh where my neck met my shoulder. Meat. Me.

A horror beyond thought engulfed me and I fought. I fought just as I had the first time I had battled Forged ones, with a mindless brutality that rivaled their own. The elements were my only ally, for they were ravaged by cold and privation. Their hands were clumsy with cold, and if we were all powered by the frenzy for survival, at least mine was new and strong within me while theirs had been worn down by the brutality of their current existence. I left flesh in the mouth of that first attacker, but tear myself free I did. That I recall. The rest is not so clear. I cannot put it in order. I broke off my knife in the young one's ribs. I recall a thumb gouging into my eye, and the snap when I dislocated it from its socket. Locked in a struggle with one, another pounded me across the shoulders with his stick, until I managed to turn his mate to meet the blow. I don't recall that I felt the pain of that pounding, and the torn flesh at my neck seemed but a warm spot where blood flowed. I had no sense of damage to myself, no daunting of my desire to kill them all. I could not win. There were too many. The young one was down in the snow, coughing blood, but one was throttling me while the other tried to jerk the sword free from its entanglement in my flesh and sleeve. I was kicking and flailing, trying uselessly to inflict any sort of damage on my attackers while the edges of the world grew black and the sky began to spin.

Brother!

He came, slashing teeth and weight hitting our tangled struggle like a battering ram. We all went down in the snow then, and the impact loosened the Forged one's grip enough that I caught a whistle of air into my lungs. My head cleared, and suddenly I had heart to fight again, to ignore pain and damage, to fight! I swear I saw myself, face purpled from strangling, the rich blood streaming and soaking and the smell so maddening. I bared my teeth. Then Cub bore the one down and away from me. He attacked him with a speed no man could match, slashing and snapping and leaping clear before the grasping hands could seize his coat. He darted back in suddenly.

I know that I knew when Cub's jaws closed in his throat. I felt that death rattle in my own jaws and the swift spurting blood that drenched my muzzle and flowed out over my jowls. I shook my head, my teeth tearing flesh, setting all the life loose to run free down his stinking garments.

Then was a time of nothing.

Then I was sitting in the snow, back against a tree. Cub was lying in the snow not far from me. His forepaws were dappled with blood. He was licking his legs clean, a careful, slow, thorough licking.

I lifted my sleeve to my mouth and chin. I wiped away blood. It was not mine. I knelt suddenly forward in the snow, to spit out beard hairs, and then to vomit, but not even the acid taste of my bile could cleanse the dead man's flesh and blood from my mouth. I glanced at his body, looked away. His throat was torn out. For a terrible instant I could recall how I had chewed down, the tendons of his throat taut against my teeth. I shut my eyes tight. I sat very still.

Cold nose against my cheek. I opened my eyes. He sat beside me, regarding me. *Cub.*

Nighteyes, he corrected me. *My mother named me Nighteyes. I was the last of my litter to get my eyes open.* He snuffed, then sneezed suddenly. He looked around at the fallen men. I followed his gaze unwillingly. My knife had taken the young one, but he had not died quickly. The other two . . .

I killed faster, Nighteyes observed quietly. *But I have not the teeth of a cow. You did well, for your kind.* He stood up and shook himself. Blood, both cold and warm, spattered my face. I gasped and wiped it away, then realized the significance.

You're bleeding.

So are you. He pulled the blade out of you to put it in me. Let me look at it.

Why?

The question hung between us in the cold air. Night was about to find us. Overhead the tree branches had gone black against the evening sky. I did not need the light to see him. I did not even need to see him. Do you need to see your ear to know it is part of you? As useless to deny that part of my flesh was mine as to deny Nighteyes.

We are brothers. We are pack, I conceded.

Are we?

I felt a reaching, a groping, a tugging for my attention. I let myself recall that I had felt this before and denied it. Now I did not. I gave him my focus, my undivided attention. Nighteyes was there, hide and tooth, muscle and claw, and I did not avoid him. I knew the sword thrust in his shoulder and felt how it had gone between two big muscles there. He held his paw curled to his chest. I hesitated, and then felt his hurt that I would hesitate. So I paused no longer, but reached out to him as he had to me. *Trust is not trust until it is complete.* So close were we, I do not know which of us offered this thought. For an instant I had a double awareness of the world as Nighteyes' perceptions overlay my own, his scenting of the bodies, his hearing telling me of scavenger foxes already creeping closer, his eyes making no difficulty of the fading light. Then the duality was gone, and his senses were mine, and mine his. We were bonded.

Cold was settling, on the land and into my bones. We found my cloak, clotted with frost, but I shook it out and put it on. I did not try to fasten it, but kept it wide away from where I had been bitten. I managed to drag my mittens on despite my injured forearm. ''We'd better go,'' I told him softly. ''When we get home, I'll see to cleaning and bandaging us. But first, we'd better get there and get warm.''

I felt his assent. He walked beside me as we went, not behind me. He lifted his nose once, to snuff deeply of the fresh air. A cold wind had come up. Snow began to fall. That was all. His nose brought me the knowledge that I need fear no more Forged ones. The air was clean save for the stench of those behind us, and even that was fading, turning into carrion smell, mingling with the scavenger foxes come to find them.

You were wrong, he observed. *Neither of us hunts very well alone.* Sly amusement. *Unless you thought you were doing well before I came along?*

''A wolf is not meant to hunt alone,'' I told him. I tried for dignity.

He lolled his tongue at me. *Don't fear, little brother. I'll be here.*

We continued walking through the crisp white snow and

the stark black trees. *Not much farther to home,* he comforted
me. I felt his strength mingling with mine as we limped on.

⇥=⊨

It was nearly noon when I presented myself at Verity's
map-room door. My forearm was snugly bandaged and invisible inside a voluminous sleeve. The wound itself was not that
severe, but it was painful. The bite between my shoulder and
neck was not so easily concealed. I had lost flesh there, and it
had bled profusely. When I had seen it with a looking glass the
night before, I was nearly sick. Cleaning it had made it bleed
even more profusely; there was a chunk of me gone. Well, and
if Nighteyes had not intervened, more of me would have followed that mouthful. I cannot explain how sickening I found
that thought. I had managed to get a dressing on it, but not a
very good one. I had pulled my shirt high and fastened it in
place to conceal the bandaging. It chafed painfully against the
wound, but it concealed it. Apprehensively, I tapped on the
door, and was clearing my throat as it opened.

Charim told me Verity was not there. There was a worry
deep in his eyes. I tried not to share it. "He can't leave the
boatbuilders to that work, can he?"

Charim shook his head to my banter. "No. Up in his
tower," the old servant said shortly. I turned aside as he slowly
shut the door.

Well, Kettricken had told me as much. I had tried to forget
that part of our conversation. Dread crept through me as I
sought the tower stairs. Verity had no reason to be in this tower.
This tower was where he Skilled from in summers, when the
weather was fine and the Raiders harried our shores. There was
no reason to be up there in winter, especially with the wind
howling and the snow dropping as it was today. No reason save
the terrible attraction of the Skill itself.

I had felt that lure, I reminded myself as I gritted my teeth
and began the long climb to the top. I had known, for a time,
the heady exuberance of the Skill. Like the clotted memory of
long-ago pain, Galen the Skill Master's words came back to
me. "If you are weak," he had threatened us, "if you lack
focus and discipline, if you are indulgent and inclined to plea-

sure, you will not master the Skill. Rather, the Skill will master you. Practice the denial of all pleasures to yourself; deny all weaknesses that tempt you. Then, when you are as steel, perhaps you will be ready to encounter the lure of the Skill and turn aside from it. If you give in to it, you will become as a great babe, mindless and drooling.'' Then he had schooled us, with privations and punishments that went far past any sane level. Yet when I had encountered the Skill joy, I had not found it the tawdry pleasure Galen had implied. Rather, it had been the same rush of blood and thunder of heart that sometimes music brought to me, or a sudden flight of bright pheasant in an autumn wood, or even the pleasure of taking a horse perfectly over a difficult jump. That instant when all things come into balance, and for a moment turn together as perfectly as birds wheeling in flight. The Skill gave that to one, but not for just a moment. Rather it lasted for as long as a man could sustain it, and became stronger and purer as one's ability with the Skill refined. Or so I believed. My own abilities with the Skill had been permanently damaged in a battle of wills with Galen. The defensive mental walls I had erected were such that not even someone as strongly Skilled as Verity could always reach me. My own ability to reach out of myself had become an intermittent thing, skittish and flighty as a spooky horse.

I paused outside Verity's door. I took a very deep breath, then breathed it out slowly, refusing to let the blackness of spirit settle on me. Those things were done, that time was gone. No sense railing to myself about it. As was my old habit, I entered without knocking, lest the noise break Verity's concentration.

He should not have been Skilling. He was. The shutters of the window were open and he leaned out on the sill. Wind and snow swirled throughout the room, speckling his dark hair and dark blue shirt and jerkin. He was breathing in deep, long steady breaths, a cadence somewhere between a very deep sleep and that of a runner at rest and catching his wind. He seemed oblivious of me. ''Prince Verity?'' I said softly.

He turned to me, and his gaze was like heat, like light, like wind in my face. He Skilled into me with such force that I felt driven out of myself, his mind possessing mine so completely that there was no room left to be myself in it. For a moment I was drowning in Verity, and then he was gone, withdrawing so rapidly that I was left stumbling and gasping like a fish deserted by a high wave. In a step he was beside me, catching my elbow and steadying me on my feet.

"I'm sorry," he apologized. "I was not expecting you. You startled me."

"I should have knocked, my prince," I replied, and then gave a quick nod to him that I could stand. "What's out there, that you watch so intently?"

He glanced aside from me. "Not much. Some boys on the cliffs, watching a pod of whales sporting. Two of our own boats, fishing halibut. Even in this weather, though not enjoying it much."

"Then you are not Skilling for Outislanders. . . ."

"There are not any out there, this time of year. But I keep a watch." He glanced down at my forearm, the one he had just released, and changed the subject. "What happened to you?"

"That's what I came to see you about. Forged ones attacked me. Out on the face of the ridge, the one where the spruce-hen hunting is good. Near the goatherd's shed."

He nodded quickly, his dark brows knitting. "I know the area. How many? Describe them."

I quickly sketched my attackers for him and he nodded briefly, unsurprised. "I had a report of them, four days ago. They should not be this close to Buckkeep this soon; not unless they are consistently moving in this direction, every day. Are they finished?"

"Yes. You expected this?" I was aghast. "I thought we had wiped them out."

"We wiped out the ones who were here then. There are others, moving in this direction. I have been keeping track of them by the reports, but I had not expected them to be so close so soon."

I struggled briefly, got my voice under control. "My prince, why do we simply keep track of them? Why do not we . . . take care of this problem?"

Verity made a small noise in his throat and turned back to his window. "Sometimes one has to wait, and let the enemy complete a move, in order to discover what the full strategy is. Do you understand me?''

"The Forged ones have a strategy? I think not, my prince. They were—"

"Report to me in full," Verity directed me without looking at me. I hesitated briefly, then launched into a complete retelling. Toward the end of the struggle, my account became a bit incoherent. I let the words die on my lips. "But I did manage to break his grip on me. And all three of them died there."

He did not take his eyes from the sea. "You should avoid physical struggles, FitzChivalry. You always seem to get hurt in them."

"I know, my prince," I admitted humbly. "Hod did her best with me—"

"But you were not really trained to be a fighter. You have other talents. And those are the ones you should be putting to use to preserve yourself. Oh, you're a competent swordsman; but you've not the brawn and weight to be a brawler. At least, not yet. And that is what you always seem to revert to in a fight."

"I was not offered the selection of weapons," I said, a bit testily, and then added, "my prince."

"No. You won't be." He seemed to speak from afar. A slight tension in the air told me that he Skilled out even as we spoke. "Yet I'm afraid I must send you out again. I think you are perhaps right. I have watched what is happening long enough. The Forged ones are converging on Buckkeep. I cannot fathom why, and yet perhaps knowing that is not as important as preventing them from attaining their goal. You will again undertake the removal of this problem, Fitz. Perhaps this time I can keep my own lady from becoming involved in it. I understand that if she wishes to go riding, she now has a guard of her own?"

"As you have been told, sir," I told him, cursing myself for not coming to speak to him sooner of the Queen's guard.

He turned to regard me levelly. "The rumor I heard was that you had authorized the creation of such a guard. Not to steal your glory, but when such rumor reached me, I let it be supposed that I had requested it of you. As, I suppose, I did. Very indirectly.''

"My prince," I said, and had the good sense to keep quiet.

"Well. If she must ride, at least she is guarded now. Though I would greatly prefer she had no more encounters with Forged ones. Would I could think of something to busy her," he added wearily.

"The Queen's Garden," I suggested, recalling Patience's account of it.

Verity cocked his eye at me.

"The old ones, atop the tower," I explained. "They have been unused for years. I saw what was left of them, before Galen ordered us to dismantle them to clear space for our Skill lessons. It must have been a charming place at one time. Tubs of earth and greenery, statuary, climbing vines."

Verity smiled to himself. "And basins of water, too, with pond lilies in them, and fish, and even tiny frogs. The birds came there often in summer, to drink and to splash. Chivalry and I used to play up there. She had little charms hung on strings, made of glass and bright metal. And when the wind stirred them, they would chime together, or flash like jewels in the sun." I could feel myself warming with his memory of that place and time. "My mother kept a little hunting cat, and it would lounge on the warm stone when the sun struck it. Hisspit; that was her name. Spotted coat and tufted ears. And we would tease her with string and tufts of feathers, and she would stalk us among the pots of flowers. While we were supposed to be studying tablets on herbs. I never properly learned them. There was too much else to do there. Except for thyme. I knew every kind of thyme she had. My mother grew a lot of thyme. And catmint." He was smiling.

"Kettricken would love such a place," I told him. "She gardened much in the Mountains."

"Did she?" He looked surprised. "I would have thought her occupied with more . . . physical pastimes."

I felt an instant of annoyance with him. No, of something more than annoyance. How could it be that I knew more of his wife than he did? "She kept gardens," I said quietly. "Of many herbs, and knew all the uses of those that grew therein. I have told you of them myself.''

''Yes, I suppose you have.'' He sighed. ''You are right, Fitz. Visit her for me, and tell her of the Queen's Garden. It is winter now, and there is probably little she can do with it. But come spring, it would be a wondrous thing to see it restored. . . .''

''Perhaps, you yourself, my prince,'' I ventured, but he shook his head.

''I haven't the time. But I trust it to you. And now, downstairs. To the maps. I have things I wish to discuss with you.''

I turned immediately toward the door. Verity followed more slowly. I held the door for him and on the threshold he paused and looked back over his shoulder at the open window. ''It calls me,'' he admitted to me, calmly, simply, as if observing that he enjoyed plums. ''It calls to me, at any moment when I am not busied. And so I must be busy, Fitz. And too busy.''

''I see,'' I said slowly, not at all sure that I did.

''No. You don't.'' Verity spoke with great certainty. ''It is like a great loneliness, boy. I can reach out and touch others. Some, quite easily. But no one ever reaches back. When Chivalry was alive . . . I still miss him, boy. Sometimes I am so lonely for him; it is like being the only one of something in the world. Like the very last wolf, hunting alone.''

A shiver went down my spine. ''What of King Shrewd?'' I ventured to ask.

He shook his head. ''He Skills seldom now. His strength for it has dwindled, and it taxes his body as well as his mind.'' We went down a few more steps. ''You and I are the only ones now to know that,'' he added softly. I nodded.

We went down the stairs slowly. ''Has the healer looked at your arm?'' he queried.

I shook my head.

''Nor Burrich.''

He was stating this as fact, already knowing it was true.

I shook my head again. The marks of Nighteyes' teeth were too plain upon my skin, although he had given those bites in play. I could not show Burrich the marks of the Forged ones without betraying my wolf to him.

Verity sighed. "Well. Keep it clean. I suppose you know as well as any how to keep an injury clean. Next time you go out, remember this, and go prepared. Always. There may not always be one to step in and aid you."

I came to a slow stop on the stairs. Verity continued down. I took a deep breath. "Verity," I asked quietly. "How much do you know? About . . . this."

"Less than you do," he said jovially. "But more than you think I do."

"You sound like the Fool," I said bitterly.

"Yes. Sometimes. He is another one who has a great understanding of aloneness, and what it can drive a man to do." He took a breath, and almost I thought he might say that he knew what I was, and did not condemn me for it. Instead, he continued, "I believe the Fool had words with you, a few days ago."

I followed him silently now, wondering how he knew so much about so many things. The Skilling, of course. We came to his study and I followed him in. Charim, as ever, was already waiting for us. Food was set out, and mulled wine. Verity set upon it with a great appetite. I sat across from him, mostly watching him eat. I was not very hungry, but it built my appetite to watch how much he enjoyed this simple, robust meal. In this he was still a soldier, I thought. He would take this small pleasure, this good, well-served food when he was hungry, and relish it while he could. It gave me much satisfaction to see him with this much life and appetite to him. I wondered how he would be next summer, when he would have to Skill for hours every day, keeping watch for Raiders off our coast, and using the tricks of his mind to set them astray while giving our own folk early warning. I thought of Verity as he had been last summer by harvest time: worn to thinness, face lined, without the energy to eat save that he drank the stimulants that Chade put in his tea. His life had become the hours he spent Skilling. Come summer, his hunger for the Skilling would replace every other hunger in his life. How would Kettricken react to that? I wondered.

After we had eaten, Verity went over his maps with me. There was no longer any mistaking the pattern that emerged.

Regardless of what obstacles, forest or river or frozen plains, the Forged ones were moving toward Buckkeep. It made no sense to me. The ones I had encountered seemed all but bereft of their senses. I found it difficult to believe that any one of them would conceive of traveling overland, despite hardships, simply to come to Buckkeep. "And these records you've kept indicate that all of them have. All of the Forged ones that you've identified seem to be moving toward Buckkeep."

"Yet you have difficulty seeing it as a coordinated plan?" Verity asked quietly.

"I fail to see how they could have any plan at all. How have they contacted each other? And it doesn't seem a concerted effort. They aren't meeting up and traveling here in bands. It simply seems that each and every one sets out this way, and some of them fall in together."

"Like moths drawn to a candle flame," Verity observed.

"Or flies to carrion," I added sourly.

"The ones to fascination, the others to feed," Verity mused. "I wish I knew which it is that draws the Forged ones to me. Perhaps another thing entirely."

"Why do you think you must know why they come? Do you think you are their target?"

"I do not know. But if I find out, I may understand my enemy. I do not think it chance that all the Forged ones make their way to Buckkeep. I think they move against me, Fitz. Perhaps not of their own will, but it is still a move against me. I need to understand why."

"To understand them, you must become them."

"Oh." He looked less than amused. "Now who sounds like the Fool?"

The question made me uneasy and I let it slip by me. "My prince, when the Fool mocked me the other day . . ." I hesitated, still stung by the memory. I had always believed the Fool to be my friend. I tried to push the emotion aside. "He put ideas in my mind. In his teasing way. He said, if I understand his riddles aright, that I should be seeking for others who are Skilled. Men and women from your father's generation, trained by Solicity before Galen became Skill Master. And he seemed also to say that I should be finding out more about the

Elderlings. How are they summoned, what can they do? What are they?''

Verity leaned back in his chair and steepled his fingers over his chest. ''Either of those quests might be enough for a dozen men. And yet, neither is even sufficient for one, for the answers to either question are so scarce. To the first, yes, there should yet be Skilled ones amongst us, folk older than my father even, trained for the old wars against the Outislanders. It would not have been common folk knowledge as to who was trained. Training was done privately, and even those in a cote- rie might know of few outside their own circle. Still, there should have been records. I am sure there were, at one time. But what has become of them, no one can say. I imagine that they were passed from Solicity down to Galen. But they were not found in his room or among his things after he . . . died.'' _

It was Verity's turn to pause. We both knew how Galen had died, in a sense had both been there, though we had never spoken much of it. Galen had died a traitor, in the act of trying to Skill-tap Verity's strength and drain it off and kill him. Instead, Verity had borrowed my strength to aid him in drain- ing Galen. It was not a thing either of us enjoyed recalling. But I spoke boldly, trying to keep all emotion from my voice.

''Do you think Regal would know where such records are?''

''If he does, he has said nothing of it.'' Verity's voice was as flat as my own, putting an end to that topic. ''But I have had some small success in uncovering a few Skilled ones. The names, at least. In every case, those I have managed to discover have either already died or cannot be located now.''

''Um.'' I recalled hearing something of this from Chade some time ago. ''How did you discover their names?''

''Some my father could recall. The members of the last coterie, who served King Bounty. Others I knew vaguely, when I was very small. A few others I discovered by talking to some of the very old folk in the Keep, asking them to recall what rumors they could of who might have been trained in the Skill. Though of course I did not ask in so many words. I did not, and still do not, wish my quest to be known.''

"May I ask why?"

He frowned and nodded toward his maps. "I am not as brilliant as your father was, my boy. Chivalry could make leaps of intuition that seemed nothing short of magical. What I discover are patterns. Does it seem likely to you that every Skilled one I can discover should be either dead, or unfindable? It seems to me that if I find one, and his name is known as a Skilled one, it might not be healthy for him."

For a time we sat in silence. He was letting me come to my own conclusions. I was wise enough not to voice them aloud. "And Elderlings?" I asked at last.

"A different sort of riddle. At the time they were written about, all knew what they were. So I surmise. It would be the same if you went to find a scroll that explained exactly what a horse was. You would find many passing mentions of them, and a few that related directly to shoeing one, or to one stallion's bloodline. But who amongst us would see the need to devote the labor and time to writing out exactly what a horse is?"

"I see."

"So, again, it is a sifting out of detail. I have not had the time required to devote myself to such a task." For a moment he sat looking at me. Then he opened a little stone box on his desk and took out a key. "There is a cabinet in my bedchamber," he said slowly. "I have gathered there what scrolls I could find that made even a passing mention of the Elderlings. There are also some related to the Skill. I give you leave to pore through them. Ask Fedwren for good paper, and keep notes of what you discover. Look for patterns among those notes. And bring them to me, every month or so."

I took the little brass key in my hand. It weighed strangely heavy, as if attached to the task the Fool had suggested and Verity had confirmed. Look for patterns, Verity had suggested. I suddenly saw one, a web woven from me to the Fool to Verity and back again. Like Verity's other patterns, it did not seem to be an accident. I wondered who had originated the pattern. I glanced at Verity, but his thoughts had gone afar. I rose quietly to go.

As I touched the door he spoke to me. "Come to me. Very early tomorrow morning. To my tower."

"Sir?"

"Perhaps we may yet discover another Skilled one, unsuspected in our midst."

12

Tasks

ERHAPS THE MOST *devastating part of our war with the Red-Ships was the sense of helplessness that overpowered us. It was as if a terrible paralysis lay over the land and its rulers. The tactics of the Raiders were so incomprehensible that for the first year we stood still as if dazed. The second year of raiding, we tried to defend ourselves. But our skills were rusty; for too long they had been employed only against the chance Raiders, the opportunistic or the desperate. Against organized pirates who had studied our seacoasts, our watchtower positions, our tides and currents, we were like children. Only Prince Verity's Skilling provided any protection for us. How many ships he turned aside, how many navigators he muddled or pilots he confused, we will never know. Because his people could not grasp what he did for them, it was as if the Farseers did nothing. Folks saw only the raids that were successful, never the ships that went onto the rocks or sailed too far south during a storm. The people lost heart. The Inland Duchies bridled at taxes to protect a coastline they didn't share; the Coastal Duchies labored under taxes that seemed to make no difference. So if the enthusiasm for Verity's warships was a fickle thing, rising and falling with the folk's current assessment of him, we cannot really blame the people. It seemed the longest winter of my life.*

I went from Verity's study to Queen Kettricken's apartments. I knocked and was admitted by the same little page girl as previously. With her merry little face and dark curly hair, Rosemary reminded me of some pool sprite. Within, the atmosphere of the room seemed subdued. Several of Kettricken's women were there, and they all sat on stools around a frame holding a white linen cloth. They were doing edgework on it, flowers and greenery done in bright threads. I had witnessed similar projects in Mistress Hasty's apartments. Usually these activities seemed merry, with tongues wagging and friendly banter, needles flashing as they dragged their tails of bright thread through the heavy cloth. But here, it was near silent. The women worked with their heads bent, diligently, skillfully, but without gay talk. Scented candles, pink and green, burned in each corner of the room. Their subtle fragrances mingled scents over the frame.

Kettricken presided over the work, her own hands as busy as any. She seemed the source of the stillness. Her face was composed, even peaceful. Her self-containment was so evident I could almost see the walls around her. Her look was pleasant, her eyes kind, but I did not sense she was really there at all. She was like a container of cool still water. She was dressed in a long simple robe of green, more of the mountain style than of Buckkeep. She had set her jewelry aside. She looked up at me and smiled questioningly. I felt like an intruder, an interruption to a group of studying pupils and their master. So instead of simply greeting her, I tried to justify my presence. I spoke formally, mindful of all the watching women.

"Queen Kettricken. King-in-Waiting Verity has asked me to bring a message to you."

Something seemed to flicker behind her eyes, and then was still again. "Yes," she said neutrally. None of the needles paused in their jumping dance, but I was sure that every ear waited for whatever tidings I might be bringing.

"Atop a tower, there was once a garden, called the Queen's Garden. Once, King Verity said, it had pots of greenery, and ponds of water. It was a place of flowering plants, and fish, and wind chimes. It was his mother's. My queen, he wishes you to have it.''

The stillness at the table grew profound. Kettricken's eyes grew very wide. Carefully, she asked, ''Are you certain of this message?''

''Of course, my lady.'' I was puzzled by her reaction. ''He said it would give him a great deal of pleasure to see it restored. He spoke of it with great fondness, especially recalling the beds of flowering thyme.''

The joy in Kettricken's face unfurled like the petals of a flower. She lifted a hand to her mouth, took a shivering breath through her fingers. Blood flushed through her pale face, rosing her cheeks. Her eyes shone. ''I must see it,'' she exclaimed. ''I must see it now!'' She stood abruptly. ''Rosemary? My cloak and gloves, please.'' She beamed about at her ladies. ''Will not you fetch your cloaks and gloves also, and accompany me?''

''My queen, the storm is most fierce today. . . .'' one began hesitantly.

But another, an older woman with a motherly cast to her features, Lady Modesty, stood slowly. ''I shall join you on the tower top. Pluck!'' A small boy who had been drowsing in the corner leaped to his feet. ''Dash off and fetch my cloak and gloves. And my hood.'' She turned back to Kettricken. ''I recall that garden well, from Queen Constance's days. Many a pleasant hour I spent there in her company. I will take joy in its restoration.''

There was a heartbeat's pause, and then the other ladies were taking similar action. By the time I had returned with my own cloak, they were all ready to go. I felt distinctly peculiar as I led this procession of ladies through the Keep, and then up the long climb to the Queen's Garden. By then, counting the pages and the curious, there were nearly a score of people following Kettricken and me. As I led the way up the steep stone steps, Kettricken was right on my heels. The others trailed out in a long tail behind us. As I pushed on the heavy door, forcing it open against the layer of snow outside it, Kettricken asked softly, ''He's forgiven me, hasn't he?''

I paused to catch my breath. Shouldering the door open

was doing the injury on my neck no good at all. My forearm throbbed dully. "My queen?" I asked in reply.

"My lord Verity has forgiven me. And this is his way of showing it. Oh, I shall make a garden for us to share. I shall never shame him again." As I stared at her rapt smile she casually put her own shoulder to the door and shoved it open. While I stood blinking in the chill and the light of the winter day, she walked out onto the tower top. She waded through crusted snow calf-deep, and paid it no mind at all. I looked around the barren tower top and wondered if I had lost my mind. There was nothing here, only the blown and crusted snow under the leaden sky. It had drifted up over the discarded statuary and pots along one wall. I braced for Kettricken's disappointment. Instead, in the center of the tower top, as the wind swirled the falling flakes around her, she stretched out her arms and spun in a circle, laughing like a child. "It's so beautiful!" she exclaimed.

I ventured out after her. Others came behind me. In a moment Kettricken was by the tumbled piles of statuary and vases and basins that were heaped along one wall. She brushed snow from a cherub's cheek as tenderly as if she were its mother. She swept a load of snow from a stone bench, and then picked up the cherub and set it atop it. It was not a small statue, but Kettricken used her size and strength energetically as she extricated several other pieces from the drifted snow. She exclaimed over them, insisting that her women come and admire them.

I stood a little apart from them. The cold wind blew past me, awakening the pain in my injuries and bringing me hard memories. Here I had stood once, near naked to the cold, while Galen had tried to hammer the Skill ability into me. Here I had stood, in this very spot, while he beat me as if I were a dog. And here I had struggled with him and, in the struggle, burned and scarred over whatever Skill I had once had. This was a bitter place to me still. I wondered if any garden, no matter how green and peaceful, could charm me if it stood atop this stone. One low wall beckoned me. Had I gone to it and looked over the edge, I knew I would look down on rocky cliffs below. I did not. The quick end that fall had once offered me would never tempt me again. I pushed Galen's old Skill suggestion aside. I turned back to watch the Queen.

Against the white backdrop of snow and stone, her colors came alive. There is a flower called a snowdrop, that sometimes blooms even as the banked snows of winter are retreating. She reminded me of one. Her pale hair was suddenly gold against the green cloak she wore, her lips red, her cheeks pink as the roses that would bloom here again. Her eyes were darting blue jewels as she excavated and exclaimed over each treasure. In contrast, her dark-tressed ladies with eyes of black or brown were cloaked and hooded against the winter chill. They stood quietly, agreeing with their queen and enjoying her enjoyment, but also rubbing chilled fingers together, or holding cloaks tightly closed against the wind. This, I thought, this is how Verity should see her, glowing with enthusiasm and life. Then he could not help but love her. Her vitality burned, even as his did when he hunted or rode. Or had once.

"It is, of course, quite lovely," one Lady Hope ventured to say. "But very cold. And there is little that can be done here until the snow melts and the wind grows kinder."

"Oh, but you are wrong!" Queen Kettricken exclaimed. She laughed aloud as she straightened up from her treasures, walked again to the center of the tower top. "A garden begins in the heart. I must sweep the snow and ice from the tower top tomorrow. And then, all these benches and statues and pots must be set out. But how? Like the spokes of a wheel? As a charming maze? Formally, by variation of height and theme? There are a thousand ways they could be arranged, and I must experiment. Unless, perhaps, my lord will remember it for me just as it once was. Then I shall restore it to him, the garden of his childhood!"

"Tomorrow, Queen Kettricken. For the skies grow dark, and colder," advised Lady Modesty. I could see what the climb followed by standing in the cold had cost the older woman. But she smiled kindly as she spoke. "I could, perhaps, tell you tonight what I remember of this garden."

"Would you?" Kettricken exclaimed, and clasped both of her hands in her own. The smile she shed on Lady Modesty was like a blessing.

"I should be glad to."

And on those words we slowly began to file from the rooftop. I was the last to go. I pulled the door closed behind me and stood for a moment letting my eyes adjust to the darkness in the tower. Below me, candles bobbed as the others descended. I blessed whatever page had thought to run and fetch them. I followed more slowly, my whole arm, from bite to sword cut, throbbing nastily. I thought of Kettricken's joy, and was glad of it, even as I guiltily reflected that it was built on a false foundation. Verity had been relieved at my suggestion to turn the garden over to Kettricken, but the act had not the significance to him that it did to Kettricken. She would attack this project as if she were building a shrine to their love. I doubted that by the morrow Verity would even recall he had gifted her with it. I felt traitorous and foolish both as I descended the steps.

I went to the evening meal thinking I wished to be alone. So I avoided the hall and took myself instead to the guardroom off the kitchen. There I encountered both Burrich and Hands at their meal. When they invited me to join them, I could not refuse. But once I was seated, it was as if I were not there. They did not exclude me from their conversation. But they spoke of a life I no longer shared. The immensely rich detail of all that went on in the stables and mews eluded me now. They discussed problems with the confident briskness of men who shared an intimate background knowledge. More and more, I found myself nodding at their words, but contributing nothing. They got along well. Burrich did not speak down to Hands. But Hands did not conceal his respect for a man he clearly regarded as his superior. Hands had learned much from Burrich in a short time. He had left Buckkeep as a lowly stable boy last fall. He now spoke competently of the hawks and dogs and asked solid questions concerning Burrich's breeding choices for the horses. I was still eating when they got up to leave. Hands was concerned about a dog that had been kicked by a horse earlier in the day. They wished me good evening, and were still talking together as they went out the door.

I sat quietly. There were others about me, guards and soldiers, eating and drinking and talking. The pleasant sounds

of talk, of spoon against the pot's side, the thud as someone cut
a wedge of cheese from a wheel was like a music. The room
smelled of food and folk, of the wood fire and spilled ale and
the rich stew bubbling. I should have felt content, not restless.
Nor melancholy. Not alone.

Brother?

Coming. Meet me at the old pig shed.

Nighteyes had been hunting afar. I was there first, and I
stood in the darkness and waited for him. There was a pot of
unguent in my pouch, and I bore a sack of bones as well. The
snow whirled around me, an endless dance of winter sparks.
My eyes probed the darkness. I sensed him, felt him near, but
he still managed to spring out and startle me. He was merciful,
giving me no more than a nip and a shake on my uninjured
wrist. We went inside the hut. I kindled the stump of a candle
and looked at his shoulder. I had been weary last night, and in
pain, so I was pleased to see I had done a good job. I had
sheared the dense hair and undercoat close to his hide around
the cut and wiped the injury with clean snow. The scab on it
was thick and dark. I could tell it had bled a bit more today. But
not much. I smeared my unguent over it in a thick greasy layer.
Nighteyes winced slightly, but suffered my ministrations. Afterward, he turned his head and gave a questioning sniff to the
spot.

Goosegrease, he observed, and began to lick at it. I let
him. Nothing in the medicine would harm him, and his tongue
would push it into the wound better than my fingers could.

Hungry? I asked.

Not really. There are mice in plenty along the old wall.
Then, as he got a whiff of the bag I'd brought: *But a bit of beef
or venison would be just as welcome.*

I tumbled the bones out in a heap for him and he flung
himself down beside them to possess them. He snuffed them
over, then picked out a meaty knuckle to work on. *We hunt
soon?* He imaged Forged ones for me.

*In a day or so. I want to be able to wield a sword the next
time.*

*I don't blame you. Cow's teeth are not much of a weapon.
But don't wait too long.*

Why is that?

Because I saw some today. Senseless ones. They had found a winter-killed buck on a stream bank and were eating it. Fouled, stinking meat, and they were eating it. But it won't hold them for long. Tomorrow, they'll be coming closer.

Then we hunt tomorrow. Show me where you saw them. I closed my eyes, and recognized the bit of creek bank that he recalled for me. *I did not know you ranged that far! Did you go all that way today, with an injured shoulder?*

It was not so far. I sensed a bit of bravado in that answer. *And I knew we would be seeking them. I can travel much faster alone. Easier for me to find them out alone, and then take you to them for the hunting.*

It is scarcely hunting, Nighteyes.

No. But it is a thing we do for our pack.

I sat with him for a while in companionable silence, watching him gnaw on the bones I had brought him. He had grown well this winter. Given a good diet and freed from the confines of a cage, he had put on weight and muscle. Snow might fall on his coat, but the thicker black guard hairs interspersed throughout his gray coat shed the snowflakes and kept any moisture from reaching his skin. He smelled healthy, too, not the rank dogginess of an overfed canine kept inside and unexercised, but a wild, clean scent. *You saved my life, yesterday.*

You saved me from a death in a cage.

I think that I had been alone so long, I had forgotten what it meant to have a friend.

He stopped chewing his bone and looked up at me in mild amusement. *A friend? Too small a word for it, brother. And in the wrong direction. So do not look at me like that. I will be to you what you are to me. Bond brother, and pack. But I am not all you will ever need.* He went back to chewing his bone, and I sat chewing over what he had just advised.

Sleep well, brother, I told him as I left.

He snorted. *Sleep? Hardly. The moon may yet break through this overcast and give me some hunting light. But if not, I may sleep.*

I nodded and left him to his bones. As I walked back to the

castle I felt less dismal and alone than I had before. But I also had a twinge of guilt that Nighteyes would so adapt his life and will to mine. It did not seem a clean thing for him to do, this snuffing out of Forged ones.

For the pack. This is for the good of the pack. The sense-less ones are trying to come into our territory. We cannot allow it. He sounded comfortable with it, and surprised that it should bother me. I nodded to ourselves in the dark and pushed my way through the kitchen door, back into yellow light and warmth.

I climbed the stairs to my room, thinking of what I had wrought over the past few days. I had resolved to set the cub free. Instead, we had become brothers. I was not sorry. I had gone to warn Verity of new Forged ones near Buckkeep. Instead, I had found he already knew about them, and had gained for myself the task of studying the Elderlings and trying to discover other Skilled ones. I had asked him to give the garden to Kettricken, to busy her mind away from her hurts. Instead, I had deceived her, and bound her more to her love for Verity. I paused to catch my breath on a landing. Perhaps, I reflected, we all danced to the Fool's tune. Had not he suggested some of these very things to me?

I felt again the brass key in my pocket. Now was as good a time as any. Verity was not in his bedchamber, but Charim was. He had no qualms about allowing me to come in and use the key. I took an armload of the scrolls I found there; there were more than I had expected. I bore them back to my room and set them down on my dressing chest. I built up the fire in the fireplace. I peeked at the dressing on the bite on my neck. It was an ugly wad of cloth, saturated with blood. I knew I should change it. I dreaded pulling it loose. In a while. I put more wood on my fire. I sorted through the scrolls. Spidery little writing, faded illustrations. Then I lifted my eyes and looked around my room.

A bed. A chest. A small stand by the bed. A ewer and bowl for wash water. A truly ugly tapestry of King Wisdom conferring with a yellowish Elderling. A branch of candles on the mantel. It had scarcely changed in the years I had lived here from the first night I had moved into it. It was a bare and dreary room, devoid of imagination. Suddenly I was a bare and dreary person, devoid of imagination. I fetched and I hunted and I killed. I obeyed. More hound than man. And not even a favored hound, to be petted and praised. One of the working pack. When was the last time I had heard from Shrewd? Or Chade. Even the Fool mocked me. What was I, anymore, to anyone, except a tool? Was there anyone left who cared for me, myself? Suddenly I could no longer abide my own company. I set down the scroll I had picked up and left my room.

When I knocked at the door of Patience's room, there was a pause. "Who is it?" came Lacey's voice.

"Only FitzChivalry."

"FitzChivalry!" A bit of surprise in the tone. It was late for a visit from me. Usually I came during the day. Then I was comforted to hear the sound of a bar being removed, and a latch worked. She had paid attention to what I had told her, I thought. The door opened slowly and Lacey stepped back to admit me, smiling dubiously.

I stepped in, greeting Lacey warmly, and then glanced about for Patience. She was in the other chamber, I surmised. But in a corner, eyes lowered over needlework, sat Molly. She did not look up at me or acknowledge my presence at all. Her hair was tidied back in a bun under a lacy little cap. On another woman, her blue dress might have been simple and modest. On Molly it was drab. Her eyes stayed down on her work. I glanced at Lacey to find her regarding me levelly. I looked at Molly again and something inside me gave way. It took me four steps to cross the room to her. I knelt beside her chair and as she drew back from me, I seized her hand and carried it to my lips.

"FitzChivalry!" Patience's voice behind me was outraged. I glanced at her framed in the doorway. Her lips were set flat in anger. I turned away from her.

Molly had turned her face aside from me. I held her hand and spoke quietly. "I cannot go on like this anymore. No matter how foolish, no matter how dangerous, no matter what any other may think. I cannot be always apart from you."

She pulled her hand away from me, and I let it go not to hurt her fingers. But I grasped at her skirt and clutched a fold of it like a stubborn child. "At least speak to me," I begged her, but it was Patience who spoke.

"FitzChivalry, this is not seemly. Stop it at once."

"It was not seemly, nor wise, nor appropriate for my father to court you as he did, either. But he did not hesitate. I suspect he felt much as I do right now." I did not look away from Molly.

That won me a moment of startled silence from Patience. But it was Molly who set aside her needlework and rose. She stepped away, and when it became clear that I must let go or tear the fabric of her skirt, I released it. She stepped clear of me. "If my lady Patience will excuse me for the evening?"

"Certainly," Patience replied, but her voice was not at all certain.

"If you go away, there is nothing for me." I knew I sounded too dramatic. I was still on my knees by her chair.

"If I stay, there is still nothing for you." Molly spoke levelly as she took off her apron and hung it on a hook. "I am a serving girl. You are a young noble, of the royal family. There can never be anything between us. I've come to see that, over the last few weeks."

"No." I rose and stepped toward her, but forbore to touch her. "You are Molly and I am Newboy."

"Maybe. Once," Molly conceded. Then she sighed. "But not now. Do not make this harder for me than it is, sir. You must leave me in peace. I have nowhere else to go; I must stay here and work, at least until I earn enough. . . ." She shook her head suddenly. "Good evening, my lady. Lacey. Sir." She turned aside from me. Lacey stood silently. I noticed she did not open the door for Molly, but Molly did not pause there. The door shut very firmly behind her. A terrible silence welled up in the room.

"Well," Patience breathed at last. "I am glad to see that at least one of you has some sense. What on earth were you thinking, FitzChivalry, to barge in here and all but attack my maid?"

"I was thinking that I loved her," I said bluntly. I dropped into a chair and put my head into my hands. "I was thinking that I am very weary of being so alone."

"That is why you came here?" Patience sounded almost offended.

"No. I came here to see you. I did not know she would be here. But when I saw her, it just came over me. It's true, Patience. I cannot go on like this."

"Well, you'd better, because you're going to have to." The words were hard, but she sighed as she said them.

"Does Molly speak of it . . . of me? To you. I must know. Please." I battered at their silence and exchanged looks. "Does she truly wish me to leave her alone? Have I become so despised of her? Have I not done all you demanded of me? I have waited, Patience. I have avoided her, I have taken care not to cause talk. But when is an end to it? Or is this your plan? To keep us apart until we forget each other? It cannot work. I am not a babe, and this is not some bauble you hide from me, to distract me with other toys. This is Molly. And she is my heart and I will not let her go."

"I am afraid you must." Patience said the words heavily.

"Why? Has she chosen another?"

Patience batted my words away as if they were flies. "No. She is not fickle, not that one. She is smart and diligent and full of wit and spirit. I can see how you lost your heart to her. But she also has pride. She has come to see what you refuse. That you come, each of you, from places so far apart that there can be no meeting in the middle. Even were Shrewd to consent to a marriage, which I very much doubt, how would you live? You cannot leave the Keep, to go down to Buckkeep Town and work in a candle shop. You know you cannot. And what status would she enjoy if you kept her here? Despite her goodness, people who did not know her well would see only the differences in your rank. She would be seen as a low appetite you had indulged. 'Oh, the Bastard, he had an eye for his stepmother's maid. I fancy he caught her around the corner one time too many, and now he has to pay the piper.' You know the kind of talk I mean."

I did. "I don't care what folk would say."

"Perhaps you could endure it. But what of Molly? What of your children?"

I was silent. Patience looked down at her hands idle in her

lap. "You are young, FitzChivalry." She spoke very quietly, very soothingly. "I know you do not believe it now. But, you may meet another. One closer to your station. And she may also. Maybe she deserves that chance at happiness. Perhaps you should draw back. Give yourself a year or so. And if your heart has not changed by then, well . . ."

"My heart will not change."

"Nor will hers, I fear." Patience spoke bluntly. "She cared for you, Fitz. Not knowing who you really were, she gave her heart to you. She has said as much. I do not wish to betray her confidences to me, but if you do as she asks and leave her alone, she can never tell you herself. So I will speak, and hope you hold me harmless for the pain I must give you. She knows this can never be. She does not want to be a servant marrying a noble. She does not want her children to be the daughters and sons of a Keep servant. So she saves the little I am able to pay her. She buys her wax and her scents, and works still at her trade, as best as she is able. She means to save enough, somehow, to begin again, with her own chandlery. It will not be soon. But that is her goal." Patience paused. "She sees no place in that life for you."

I sat a long time, thinking. Neither Lacey nor Patience spoke. Lacey moved slowly through our stillness, brewing tea. She pushed a cup of it into my hand. I lifted my eyes and tried to smile at her. I set the tea carefully aside. "Did you know, from the beginning, that it would come to this?" I asked.

"I feared it," Patience said simply. "But I also knew there was nothing I could do about it. Nor can you."

I sat still, not even thinking. Under the old hut, in a scratched-out hollow, Nighteyes was dozing with his nose over a bone. I touched him softly, not even waking him. His calm breathing was an anchor. I steadied myself against him.

"Fitz? What will you do?"

Tears stung my eyes. I blinked, and it passed. "What I am told," I said heavily. "When have I ever done otherwise?"

Patience was silent as I got slowly to my feet. The wound on my neck was throbbing. I suddenly wanted only to sleep. She nodded to me as I excused myself. At the door I paused. "Why I came this evening. Besides to see you. Queen Kettricken will be restoring the Queen's Garden. The one on top of the tower. She mentioned she would like to know how the garden was originally arranged. In Queen Constance's time. I thought perhaps you could recall it for her.''

Patience hesitated. ''I do recall it. Very well.'' She was quiet for a moment, then brightened. ''I will draw it out for you, and explain it. Then you could go to the Queen.''

I met her eyes. ''I think you should go to her. I think it would please her very much.''

''Fitz, I have never been good with people.'' Her voice faltered. ''I am sure she would find me odd. Boring. I could not—'' Her voice stuttered to a halt.

''Queen Kettricken is very alone,'' I said quietly. ''There are ladies around her, but I do not think she has real friends. Once, you were queen-in-waiting. Cannot you recall what it was like?''

''Very different for her than it was for me, I should think.''

''Probably,'' I agreed. I turned to go. ''For one thing, you had an attentive and loving husband.'' Behind me Patience made a small shocked sound. ''And I do not think Prince Regal was as . . . clever then as he is now. And you had Lacey to support you. Yes, Lady Patience. I am sure it is very different for her. Much harder.''

''FitzChivalry!''

I paused at the door. ''Yes, my lady?''

''Turn about when I speak to you!''

I turned slowly and she actually stamped the floor at me. ''This ill becomes you. You seek to shame me! Think you that I do not do my duty? That I do not know my duty?''

''My lady?''

''I shall go to her, tomorrow. And she will think me odd and awkward and flighty. She will be bored with me and wish I had never come. And then you shall apologize to me for making me do it.''

''I am sure you know best, my lady.''

''Take your courtier's manners and go. Insufferable boy.'' She stamped her foot again, then whirled and fled back into her bedchamber. Lacey held the door for me as I left. Her lips were folded in a flat line, her demeanor subdued.

"Well?" I asked her as I left, knowing she had words left to say to me.

"I was thinking that you are very like your father," Lacey observed tartly. "Except not quite as stubborn. He did not give up as easily as you have." She shut the door firmly behind me.

I looked at the closed door for a while, then headed back to my room. I knew I had to change the dressing on my neck wound. I climbed the flight of stairs, my arm throbbing at every step. I halted on the landing. For a time I watched the candles burning in their holders. I climbed the next flight of stairs.

I knocked steadily for several minutes. A yellow candle-light had been coming out the crack under her door, but as I knocked, it suddenly winked out. I took out my knife and experimented, loudly, with the latch on her door. She'd changed it. There seemed to be a bar as well, a heavier one than the tip of my blade would lift. I gave it up and left.

Down is always easier than up. In fact, it can be too much easier, when one arm is already injured. I looked down at the waves breaking like white lace on the rocks far away. Night-eyes had been right. The moon had managed to come out for a bit. The rope slipped a bit through my gloved hand and I grunted as my injured arm had to take my weight. Only a little more, I promised myself. I let myself down another two steps.

The ledge of Molly's window was narrower than I had hoped it would be. I kept the rope in a wrap around my arm as I perched there. My knife blade slipped easily into the crack between the shutters; they were very poorly fitted. The upper catch had yielded and I was working on the lower one when I heard her voice from inside.

"If you come in, I shall scream. The guards will come."

"Then you'd best put on tea for them," I replied grimly, and went back to wriggling at the lower catch.

In a moment Molly snatched the shutters open. She stood framed in the window, the dancing light of the fire on the hearth illuminating her from behind. She was in her nightdress, but she hadn't braided her hair back yet. It was loose and gleaming from brushing. She had thrown a shawl over her shoulders.

"Go away," she told me fiercely. "Get out of here."

"I can't," I panted. "I haven't the strength to climb back up, and the rope isn't long enough to reach to the base of the wall."

"You can't come in," she repeated stubbornly.

"Very well." I seated myself on the windowsill, one leg inside the room, the other dangling out the window. Wind gusted past me, stirring her night robe and fanning the flames of the fire. I said nothing. After a moment she began to shiver.

"What do you want?" she demanded angrily.

"You. I wanted to tell you that tomorrow I am going to the King to ask permission to marry you." The words came out of my mouth with no planning. I was suddenly giddily aware that I could say and do anything. Anything at all.

Molly stared a moment. Her voice was low as she said, "I do not wish to marry you."

"I wasn't going to tell him that part." I found myself grinning at her.

"You are intolerable!"

"Yes. And very cold. Please, at least let me come in out of the cold."

She did not give me permission. But she did stand back from the window. I jumped lightly in, ignoring the jolt to my arm. I closed and fastened the shutters. I walked across the room. I knelt by her hearth and built up the fire well with logs to chase the chill from the room. Then I stood, thawing my hands at it. Molly said not a word. She stood sword straight, her arms crossed on her chest. I glanced over at her and smiled.

She didn't smile. "You should go."

I felt my own smile fade. "Molly, please, just talk to me. I thought, the last time we spoke, that we understood each other. Now you don't speak to me, you turn away. . . . I don't know what changed, I don't understand what is happening between us."

"Nothing." She suddenly looked very fragile. "Nothing is happening between us. Nothing can happen between us. FitzChivalry"—and that name sounded so strange on her lips—"I've had time to think. If you had come to me, like this, a week ago, or a month ago, impetuous and smiling, I know I would have been won over." She permitted herself the ghost of a sad smile. As if she were remembering the way a dead child had skipped on some long-ago summer day. "But you didn't. You were correct and practical, and did all the right things. And foolish as it may sound, that hurt me. I told myself that if you loved me as deeply as you had declared you did, nothing—not walls, not manners or reputation or protocol—would get in the way of your seeing me. That night, when you came, when we . . . but it changed nothing. You did not come back."

"But it was for your sake, for your reputation—" I began desperately.

"Hush. I told you it was foolish. But feelings do not have to be wise. Feelings just are. Your loving me was not wise. Nor my caring for you. I've come to see that. And I've come to see that wisdom must overrule feelings." She sighed. "I was so angry when your uncle first spoke to me. So outraged. He made me defiant, he gave me a steel resolve to stay in spite of everything that stood between us. But I am not a stone. Even if I were, even a stone can be worn away by the constant cold drip of common sense."

"My uncle? Prince Regal?" I was incredulous at the betrayal.

She nodded slowly. "He wished me to keep his visit to myself. Nothing, he said, could be gained by your knowing of it. He needed to act in his family's best interests. He said I should understand that. I did, but it made me angry. It was only over time that he made me see that it was in my own best interests as well." She paused and brushed a hand over her cheek. She was crying. Silently, just the tears running as she spoke.

I walked across the room to her. Tentatively, I took her into my arms. She didn't resist, and that surprised me. I held her carefully, as if she were a butterfly that might be crushed too easily. She leaned her head forward, so that her forehead barely rested on my shoulder, and spoke into my chest. "In a few more months, I will have saved enough that I can start out on my own again. Not open a business, but rent a room somewhere, and find work to sustain me. And begin to start saving for a shop. That's what I intend to do. Lady Patience is kind, and Lacey has become a real friend to me. But I do not like being a servant. And I will do it no longer than I have to.'' She stopped speaking and stood still in my arms. She was trembling lightly, as if from exhaustion. She seemed to have run out of words.

"What did my uncle say to you?" I asked carefully.

"Oh." She swallowed, and moved her face lightly against me. I think she wiped tears on my shirt. "Only what I should have expected him to say. When first he came to me, he was cold and aloof. He thought me a . . . street whore, I suppose. He warned me sternly that the King would tolerate no more scandals. He demanded to know if I was with child. Of course, I was angry. I told him it was impossible that I should be. That we had never . . ." Molly paused and I could feel how shamed she had been that anyone could even ask such a question. "So then he told me that if that was so, it was good. He asked what I thought I deserved, as reparation for your deceptions."

The word was like a little knife twisted in my guts. The fury I felt was building, but I forced myself to keep silent that she might speak it all out.

"I told him I expected nothing. That I had deceived myself as much as you had deceived me. So then he offered me money. To go away. And never speak of you. Or what had happened between us."

She was having trouble speaking. Her voice kept getting higher and tighter on each phrase. She fought for a semblance of calm I knew she didn't feel. "He offered me enough to open a chandlery. I was angry. I told him I could not be paid to stop loving someone. That if the offer of money could make me love, or not love, then I was truly a whore. He grew very angry, but he left." She gave a sudden shuddering sob, then held herself still. I moved my hands lightly over her shoulders, feeling the tension there. I stroked her hair; softer than any horse's mane, and sleeker. She had fallen silent.

"Regal makes mischief," I heard myself say. "He seeks to injure me by driving you away. To shame me by hurting you." I shook my head to myself, wondering at my stupidity. "I should have foreseen this. All I thought was that he might whisper against you. Or arrange for physical harm to befall you. But Burrich is right. The man has no morals, he is bound by no rules.''

"He was cold, at first. But never coarsely rude. He came only as the King's messenger, he said, and came himself to save scandal, that no more should know of it than needed to. He sought to avoid talk, not make it. Later, after we had talked a few times, he said he regretted to see me cornered so, and that he would tell the King it was not of my devising. He even bought candles of me, and arranged for others to know what I had to sell. I believe he is trying to help, FitzChivalry. Or so he sees it.''

To hear her defend Regal cut me deeper than any insult or rebuke she could level at me. My fingers tangled in her soft hair and I unwound them carefully. Regal. All the weeks I had gone alone, avoiding her, not speaking to her lest it cause scandal. Leaving her alone, so that Regal could come in my stead. Not courting her, no, but winning her with his practiced charm and studied words. Chopping away at her image of me while I was not there to contradict anything he said. Making himself out to be her ally while I was left voiceless to become the unthinking callow youth, the thoughtless villain. I bit my tongue before I spoke any more ill of him to her. It would only sound like a shallow angry boy striking back at one who sought to deny his will.

"Have you ever spoken of Regal's visits to Patience or Lacey? What did they say of him?''

She shook her head, and the movement loosed the fragrance of her hair. "He cautioned me not to speak of it. 'Women talk' he said, and I know that is true. I should not even have spoken of it to you. He said that Patience and Lacey would respect me more if it seemed I had reached this decision on my own. He said, also . . . that you would not let me go . . . if you thought the decision came from him. That you must believe that I turned away from you on my own.''

"He knows me that well,'' I conceded to her.

"I should not have told you,'' she murmured. She pushed a little away from me, to look up into my eyes. "I don't know why I did.''

Her eyes and her hair were the colors of a forest. "Perhaps you did not want me to let you go?" I ventured.

"You must," she said. "We both know there is no future for us."

For an instant all was stillness. The fire crackled softly to itself. Neither of us moved. But somehow I stepped to another place, where I was achingly aware of every scent and touch of her. Her eyes and the herb scents of her skin and hair were one piece with the warmth and suppleness of her body under the soft woolen night robe. I experienced her as if she were a new color suddenly revealed to my eyes. All concerns, even all thoughts, were suspended in that sudden awareness. I know I trembled, for she put her hands on my shoulders and clasped them, to steady me. Warmth flowed through me from her hands. I looked down into her eyes and wondered at what I saw there.

She kissed me.

That simple act, of offering up her mouth to mine, was like the opening of a floodgate. What followed was a seamless continuation of her kiss. We did not pause to consider wisdom or morality, we did not hesitate at all. The permission we gave each other was absolute. We ventured together into that newness, and I cannot imagine a deeper joining than our shared amazement brought us. We both came whole to that night, unfettered by expectations or memories of others. I had no more right to her than she had to me. But I gave and I took and I swear I shall never regret it. The memory of that night's sweet awkwardness is the truest possession of my soul. My trembling fingers jumbled the ribbon at the neck closure of her nightgown into a hopeless knot. Molly seemed wise and sure as she touched me, only to betray her surprise with her sharply indrawn breath when I responded. It did not matter. Our ignorance yielded to a knowing older than us both. I strove to be both gentle and strong, but found myself amazed at her strength and gentleness both.

I have heard it called a dance, I have heard it called a battle. Some men speak of it with a knowing laugh, some with a sneer. I have heard the sturdy market women chuckling over it like hens clucking over bread crumbs; I have been approached by bawds who spoke their wares as boldly as peddlers hawking fresh fish. For myself, I think some things are beyond words. The color blue can only be experienced, as can the scent of jasmine or the sound of a flute. The curve of a warm bared shoulder, the uniquely feminine softness of a breast, the startled sound one makes when all barriers suddenly yield, the perfume of her throat, the taste of her skin are all but parts, and sweet as they may be, they do not embody the whole. A thousand such details still would not illustrate it.

The fireplace logs burned down to dark red embers. The candles had long since guttered out. It seemed we were in a place we had entered as strangers, and discovered to be home. I think I would have given away all the rest of the world, just to remain in the drowsy nest of tousled blankets and feather quilts, breathing her warm stillness.

Brother, this is good.

I leaped like a hooked fish, jolting Molly out of her drowsing reverie. "What is it?"

"A cramp in my calf," I lied, and she laughed, believing me. So simple a fib, but I was suddenly shamed by the lie, by all the lies I had ever spoken and all the truths I had made into lies by leaving them unspoken. I opened my lips to tell her all. That I was the royal assassin, the King's killing tool. That the knowledge of her that she had given me that night had been shared by my brother the wolf. That she had given herself so freely to a man who killed other men and shared his life with an animal.

It was unthinkable. To tell her those things would hurt and shame her. She would have felt permanently dirtied by the touch we had shared. I told myself that I could stand to have her despise me, but I could not stand to have her despise herself. I told myself that I clenched my lips shut because it was the nobler thing to do, to keep these secrets to myself was better than to let the truth destroy her. Did I lie to myself, then?

Don't we all?

I lay there, with her arms twined warm around me, with the length of her body warming my side, and promised myself that I would change. I would stop being all those things, and then I would never need tell her. Tomorrow, I promised myself,

I would tell Chade and Shrewd that I would no longer kill for them. Tomorrow, I would make Nighteyes understand why I must sever my bond with him. Tomorrow.

But today, in this day that was already beginning to dawn, I had to go forth with the wolf at my side, to hunt the Forged ones and slay them. Because I wanted to go to Shrewd with a fresh triumph, to put him in the mood to grant the boon I would ask. This very evening, when my killing was done, I would ask him to allow Molly and me to marry. I promised myself that his permission would mark the beginning of my new life as a man who would no longer have to keep secrets from the woman he loved. I kissed her forehead, then set her arms softly aside from me.

"I have to leave you," I whispered as she stirred. "But I pray it will not be for long. Today I go to Shrewd, to ask permission to marry you."

She stirred and opened her eyes. She watched in a sort of wonder as I went naked from her bed. I put more wood on the fire, then avoided her gaze as I gathered my scattered clothes and put them on. She was not so shy, for as I looked up from fastening my belt, I found her eyes upon me, smiling. I blushed.

"I feel we are wed already," she whispered. "I cannot imagine how the speaking of any vows could make us more truly joined."

"Nor I." I came to sit on the edge of her bed, to take her hands in mine once again. "But there will be great satisfaction to me in letting all know of it. And that, my lady, requires a wedding. And a public speaking of all my heart has already vowed to you. But for now, I must go."

"Not yet. Stay awhile yet. I am sure we have some small time left before anyone else begins to stir."

I leaned over her to kiss her. "I have to go now, to retrieve a certain rope that is hanging from the battlements to my lady's window. Otherwise, it might excite comment."

"At least stay long enough to let me change the dressings on your arm and neck. However did you hurt yourself so? I meant to ask you last night, but . . ."

I smiled down at her. "I know. There were more interesting things to pursue. No, my dear. But I promise you I shall take care of it this morning, in my room." To call her "my dear" made me feel a man as no words ever had before. I kissed her, promising myself that I would go immediately afterward, but found myself lingering to her touch on my neck. I sighed. "I do have to go."

"I know. But you have not told me how you injured yourself."

I could hear in her voice that she did not think my hurts were serious, but only tried to use the subject to detain me at her side. But still it shamed me, and I tried to make the lie as harmless as possible. "Dog bites. A bitch in the stable with pups. I guess I did not know her as well as I had thought. I bent to pick up one of her pups, and she went for me."

"Poor boy. Well. Are you sure you cleaned it well? Animal bites infect very easily."

"I'll clean it again when I dress it. Now. I must go." I covered her over with the feather quilt, but not without a twinge of regret at leaving that warmth. "Get what little sleep is left for you before day breaks."

"FitzChivalry!"

I paused at the door, turned back. "Yes?"

"Come to me tonight. Regardless of what the King may say."

I opened my mouth to protest.

"Promise me! Otherwise, I shall not survive this day. Promise me you will return to me. For no matter what the King may say, know this. I am your wife now. And always will be. Always."

My heart stood still in me at that gift, and I could do no more than dumbly nod. My look must have been enough, for the smile she bestowed on me was bright and golden as midsummer sunshine. I lifted the bar and unhooked the latch of the door. Easing it open, I peered out into the darkened hallway. "Be sure you lock up after me," I whispered, and then I slipped away from her into the little that was left of the night.

Hunting

THE SKILL, LIKE *any other discipline, can be taught in a number of ways. Galen, Skill Master under King Shrewd, used techniques of deprivation and enforced hardship to break down a student's inner walls. Once reduced to a level of cowering survival, the student was susceptible to Galen's invasion of his mind and his enforced acceptance of Galen's Skilling techniques. While the students who survived his training and went on to become his coterie could all Skill reliably, none were especially strong of talent. Galen reportedly congratulated himself at taking students of little talent, and teaching them to Skill reliably. This may be the case. Or perhaps he took students with great potential, and ground them down to adequate tools.*

One may contrast Galen's techniques with that of Solicity, Skill Mistress before him. She supplied the initial instruction to the then young Princes Verity and Chivalry. Verity's account of his instruction indicates much was accomplished by gentleness and lulling her students into lowering their barriers. Both Verity and Chivalry emerged from her training as adept and strong Skill users. Her death unfortunately occurred before their full adult instruction was complete, and before Galen had advanced to a journey status as a Skill instructor. One can only wonder how much knowledge of the Skill went to her grave

*with her, and what potentials of this royal magic may never be
rediscovered.*

⤖⊨

I spent little time in my room that morning. The fire had
gone out, but the chill I felt there was more than that of an
unwarmed room. This room was an empty shell of a life soon
to be left behind. It seemed more barren than ever. I stood,
bared to the waist, and shivered as I washed myself with unwarmed water, and belatedly changed the bandaging on my
arm and neck. I did not deserve for those wounds to look as
clean as they did. Nonetheless, they were healing well.

I dressed warmly, a padded mountain shirt going on under
a heavy leather jerkin. I pulled on heavy leather overtrousers
and laced them close to my legs with strips of leather. I took
down my work blade and armed myself with a short dagger as
well. From my working kit, I took a small pot of powdered
death's cap. Despite all this, I felt unprotected, and equally
foolish, as I left my room.

I went straight to Verity's tower. I knew he would be
awaiting me, expecting to work with me on Skilling. Somehow
I would have to convince him that I needed to hunt Forged ones
this day. I climbed the stairs swiftly, wishing this day were
over. All of my life was presently focused on the moment when
I could knock on King Shrewd's door and ask his permission
to marry Molly. The mere thought of her flooded me with such
a strange combination of unfamiliar feelings that my strides on
the stairs slowed as I tried to consider them all. Then I gave it
over as useless. "Molly," I said aloud, but softly, to myself.
Like a magic word, it strengthened my resolve and spurred me
on. I stopped outside the door and rapped loudly.

I felt rather than heard Verity's permission to enter. I
pushed open the door and went inside. I shut the door behind
me.

Physically, the room was still. A cool breeze sprang in
from the open window and Verity sat enthroned before it on his
old chair. His hands rested idly on the windowsill and his eyes
were fixed on the distant horizon. His cheeks were pink, his
dark hair mussed by the wind's fingers. Save for the soft cur-

rent from the window, the room was still and silent. Yet I felt as
if I had stepped into a whirlwind. Verity's consciousness
washed against me and I was drawn into his mind, swept
along with his thoughts and his Skilling far out to sea. He
carried me with him on a dizzying tour of every ship within the
range of his mind. Here we brushed the thoughts of a merchant
captain, ". . . if the price is good enough, load up with oil for
the return trip. . . ." and then skipped from him to a net
mender patching hastily, her fid flying, grumbling to herself as
the captain railed at her to be faster about her task. We found a
pilot worrying about his pregnant wife at home, and three
families out digging clams in the dim morning light before the
tide came in to cover the beds again. These and a dozen others
we visited before Verity suddenly recalled us to our own bodies
and place. I felt as giddy as a small boy who has been boosted
aloft by his father to perceive the whole chaos of the fair before
being returned to his own feet and his child's view of knees
and legs.

I approached the window to stand beside Verity. He still
stared out over the water to the horizons. But I suddenly understood his maps and why he created them. The network of lives
he had touched so briefly for me were as if he had opened his
palm to reveal he cupped a handful of priceless gems. People.
His people. It was not some rocky coast or rich pastureland that
he stood watch over. It was these folk, these bright glimpses of
other lives unlived by him, but cherished all the same. This was
Verity's kingdom. Geographical boundaries marked on parchment enclosed them for him. For a moment I shared his baffle-
ment that anyone could wish harm on these people, and shared,
too, his fierce determination that not one more life should be
lost to the Red-Ships.

The world steadied around me, as vertigo passing, and all
was still in the tower top. Verity did not look at me as he spoke.
"So. Hunting today."

I nodded, not caring that he did not see the gesture. It
didn't matter. "Yes. The Forged ones are closer than we suspected even."

"Do you expect to fight them?"

"You told me to go prepared. I will try the poison first.

But they may not be as eager to gobble it down. Or they may still try to attack me. So I'm taking my blade, in case.''

"So I surmised. But take this one instead.'' He lifted a sheathed sword from beside his chair and gave it into my hands. For a moment I could only look at it. The leather was fancifully tooled, the hilt had that beautiful simplicity possessed by weapons and tools made by a master. At Verity's nod, I drew the blade in his presence. The metal gleamed and shimmered, the hammering and folding that had given it strength recalled as a watery rippling of light down its length. I held it out and felt it perch in my hand, weightless and waiting. It was a much finer sword than my skill deserved. "I should present it to you with pomp and ceremony, of course. But I give it to you now, lest for the lack of it you can't return later. During Winterfest, I might ask it back of you so that I may present it to you properly.''

I slipped it back into its sheath, then drew it out, swift as an indrawn breath. I had never possessed anything so finely made. "I feel as if I should swear it to you or something,'' I said awkwardly.

Verity permitted himself a smile. "No doubt Regal would require some such oath. As for me, I don't think a man need swear his sword to me when he has already sworn me his life.''

Guilt assaulted me. I took my courage in both hands. "Verity, my prince. I go forth today to serve you as an assassin.''

Even Verity was taken aback. "Direct words,'' he mused guardedly.

"It is time for direct words, I think. That is how I serve you today. But my heart has grown weary of it. I have sworn my life to you, as you say, and if you command it, so must I continue. But I ask that you find for me another way to serve you.''

Verity was silent for what seemed a long time. He rested his chin on his fist and sighed. "Were it only I you were sworn to, perhaps I could answer swiftly and simply. But I am only king-in-waiting. This request must be made of your king. As must your request to wed.''

The silence in the room now grew very wide and deep,

making a distance between us. I could not break it. Verity spoke at last. "I showed you how to ward your dreams, FitzChivalry. If you neglect to enclose your mind, you cannot blame others for what you divulge."

I pushed down my anger and swallowed it. "How much?" I asked coldly.

"As little as possible, I assure you. I am well used to guarding my own thoughts, less so to blocking out those of others. Especially the thoughts of one as strongly, if erratically Skilled, as yourself. I did not seek to be privy to your . . . assignation."

He was silent. I did not trust myself to speak. It was not just that my own privacy had been so badly betrayed. But Molly! How I was ever to explain this to Molly, I could not imagine. Nor could I tolerate the idea of yet another silence masking an unspoken lie between us. As always, Verity was as true as his name. The carelessness had been mine. Verity was speaking, very quietly.

"Truth to tell, I envy you, boy. Were it my choice, you should be wed today. If Shrewd denies you permission today, hold this in your heart, and impart it to Lady Red-Skirts: when I am king, you will be free to marry when and where you choose. I will not do to you what was done to me."

I think then that I grasped all that had been taken from Verity. It is one thing to sympathize with a man whose wife was chosen for him. It is another to come from the bed of one's beloved, and suddenly realize that a man you care for will never know the fullness of what I had experienced with Molly. How bitter must it have been to glimpse what Molly and I shared, and what he must be forever denied.

"Verity. Thank you," I told him.

He met my eyes briefly and gave me a wan smile.

"Well. I suppose." He hesitated. "This is not a promise, so do not take it as such. There may be something I can do about the other as well. You might not have time to function as a . . . diplomat, if you were given other duties. Duties more valuable to us."

"Such as?" I asked cautiously.

"My ships grow, day by day, taking shape under their

masters' hands. And again, I am denied what I most desire. I will not be allowed to sail on them. There is much common sense to that. Here, I am able to look out over all and direct all. Here, my life is not risked to the violence of the Red-Ship pirates. Here, I can coordinate the attacks of several vessels at once, and dispatch aid where it is most needed.'' He cleared his throat. ''On the other hand, I will not feel the wind or hear it snapping in the sail, and I will never be allowed to fight the Raiders as I long to, with a blade in my hand, killing swiftly and cleanly, taking blood for the blood they have taken.'' Cold fury rode his features as he spoke. After a moment's pause he went on more calmly. ''So. For those ships to function best, there must be someone aboard each one who can at least receive my information. Ideally, that one would also be able to relay to me detailed information as to what is going on aboard the ship. You have seen, this day, how I am limited. I can tell the thoughts of certain folk, yes, but I cannot direct them as to what they think about. Sometimes, I am able to find one more susceptible to my Skill, and influence his thoughts. But this is not the same thing as having a quick response to a direct question.

''Have you ever considered sailing, FitzChivalry?''

To say I was taken aback would be an understatement. ''I . . . you have just reminded me that my ability with the Skill is erratic, sir. And reminded me, yesterday, that in a fight, I am more a brawler than a swordsman, despite Hod's training—''

''And I now remind you that it is midwinter. There are not many months until spring. I have told you it is a possibility, no more than that. I will be able to give you only the barest help with what you need to master by then. I am afraid it is entirely up to you, FitzChivalry. Can you, by spring, learn to control both your Skill and your blade?''

''As you said to me, my prince. I cannot promise, but it will be my intention.''

''Fine.'' Verity looked at me steadily for a long moment. ''Will you begin today?''

''Today? Today I have to hunt. I dare not neglect that duty, even for this.''

"They need not exclude each other. Take me with you, today."

I stared at him blankly for a moment, then nodded assent. I had thought he would arise, to go and put on winter clothes and fetch a sword. Instead, he reached out toward me and took hold of my forearm.

As his presence flowed into me it was instinct to struggle against him. This was not like other times when he had shuffled through my thoughts as a man sorts scattered papers on a desk. This was a true occupation of my mind. I had not been so invaded since Galen had brutalized me. I tried to jerk free of his grip, but it was like iron on my wrist. Everything paused. *You have to trust me. Do you?* I stood sweating and shuddering like a horse with a snake in its stall.

I don't know.

Think about it, he bade me. He withdrew a trifle.

I could still sense him, waiting, but knew he was holding himself apart from my thoughts. My mind raced frantically. There were too many things to juggle. This was a thing I must do if I wished to win myself free from a life as an assassin. It was a chance to make all the secrets old secrets rather than an ongoing exclusion of Molly and her trust. I had to take it. But how could I do this, and keep secret from him Nighteyes and all that we shared? I quested toward Nighteyes. *Our bond is a secret. I must keep it so. Today, then, I must hunt alone. Do you understand?*

No. It is stupid and dangerous. I shall be there, but you may trust me to be unseen and unknowable.

"What did you do, just then?" It was Verity, speaking aloud. His hand was on my wrist. I looked down into his eyes. There was no harshness to his question. He asked it as I might ask it of a small child found carving on the woodwork. I stood frozen inside myself. I longed to unburden myself, to have one person in the world who knew all about me, everything that I was.

You already do, Nighteyes objected.

It was true. And I could not endanger him. "You must trust me, also," I found myself saying to my king-in-waiting.

And when he remained looking up at me consideringly, I asked, "My prince. Do you?"

"Yes."

With one word, he gave me his trust, and with it his confidence that whatever I had been doing would not bring him harm. It sounds a simple thing, but for a King-in-Waiting to permit his own assassin to keep secrets from him was a staggering act. Years ago, his father had bought my loyalty, with a promise of food and shelter and education and a silver pin thrust into my shirtfront. Verity's simple act of trust was suddenly more to me than any of these things. The love I had always felt for him suddenly knew no bounds. How could I not trust him?

He smiled sheepishly. "You can Skill, when you've heart to." With no more than that, he entered my mind again. As long as his hand was on my wrist, the joining of thoughts was effortless. I felt his curiosity and tinge of woe at looking down at his own face through my eyes. *A looking glass is kinder. I have aged.*

With him ensconced in my mind, it would have been useless to deny the truth of what he said. So, *it was a necessary sacrifice,* I agreed.

He lifted his hand from my wrist. For a moment I had dizzying double vision, looking at myself, looking at him, and then it settled. He turned carefully to set his own eyes once more on the horizon, and then sealed that vision from me. Without his touch, this clasping of minds was a different thing. I left the room slowly and went down the stairs as if I were balancing a wineglass full to the brim. *Exactly. And in both cases, it is easier to do if you do not look at it and think about it so heavily. Just carry.*

I went down to the kitchens, where I ate a solid breakfast and tried to behave normally. Verity was right. It was easier to maintain our contact if I didn't focus on it. While everyone there was busied at other tasks, I managed to slip a plateful of biscuits into my carry sack. "Going hunting?" Cook asked me as she turned about. I nodded.

"Well, be careful. What are you going after?"

"Wild boar," I improvised. "Just to locate one, not to

attempt a kill today. I thought it might be a fine amusemen
during Winterfest.''

''For who? Prince Verity? You won't budge him out of the
Keep, pet. Keeps too much to his rooms these days, he does
and poor old King Shrewd hasn't taken a real meal with us ir
weeks. I don't know why I keep cooking his favorites, wher
the tray comes back as full as I sent it. Now, Prince Regal, he
might go, long as it didn't muss his curls.'' There was a general clucking of laughter among the kitchen maids at that. My
cheeks burned at Cook's boldness. *Steady. They don't know
I'm here, boy. And naught of what is said to you shall be held
against them by me. Don't betray us now.* I sensed Verity's
amusement, and also his concern. So I permitted myself a grin,
thanked Cook for the pasty she insisted I take, and left the
Keep kitchen.

Sooty was restive in her stall, more than eager for ar
outing. Burrich passed by as I was saddling her. His dark eyes
took in my leathers and the tooled sheath and fine hilt of the
sword. He cleared his throat, but then stood silent. I had never
been able to decide exactly how much Burrich knew of my
work. At one time, in the Mountains, I had divulged my assassin's training to him. But that had been before he took a blow
on the head attempting to protect me. When he recovered from
it, he professed to have lost the memories of the day that
preceded it. But sometimes I wondered. Perhaps it was his sage
way of keeping a secret a secret; that it could not be discussed
even by those who shared it. ''Be careful,'' he said at last,
gruffly. ''Don't you let that mare come to harm.''

''We'll be careful,'' I promised him, and then led Sooty
out past him.

Despite my errands it was still early morning, with just
enough winter light to make it safe to canter. I let Sooty out,
allowing her to choose her pace and express her spirits, and
letting her warm herself without allowing her to break a sweat.
There was broken cloud cover, and the sun was slipping
through it to touch the trees and banked snow with glistening
fingers. I pulled Sooty in, pacing her. We would be taking a
roundabout way to get to the creek bed; I did not want to leave
the trodden paths until we must.

Verity was with me every second. It was not that we conversed, but he was privy to my internal dialogue. He enjoyed the fresh morning air, Sooty's responsiveness, and the youth of my own body. But the farther I went from the Keep, the more aware I became of keeping a grip on Verity. From a touch he had initially imposed on me, the sharing had changed to a mutual effort more like clasping hands. I wondered if I would be able to maintain it. *Don't think about it. Just do it. Even breathing becomes a task if you pay attention to every breath.* I blinked my eyes, suddenly aware that he was now in his study, carrying on his normal morning tasks. Like the humming of faraway bees, I was aware of Charim consulting with him about something.

I could detect no sign of Nighteyes. I was trying not to think about him, nor look for him, a strenuous mental denial that was fully as demanding as keeping Verity's consciousness with me. So quickly had I become accustomed to reaching out for my wolf and finding him awaiting my touch that I felt isolated, and as unbalanced as if my favorite knife were missing from my belt. The only image that could completely displace him from my mind was Molly's, and that, too, was one I did not wish to dwell on. Verity had not rebuked me for my actions of the night before, but I knew he regarded them as less than honorable. I had an uneasy feeling that if I allowed myself time to truly consider all that had happened, I would agree with him. Cowardly, I kept my mind reined away from that, too.

I realized I was putting most of my mental effort to not thinking. I gave my head a shake and opened myself up to the day. The road I was following was not well traveled. It wound through the rolling hills behind Buckkeep, and far more sheep and goats trod it than men. Several decades ago a lightning fire had cleared it of trees. The first growth of trees on it was mostly birch and cottonwood, now standing bare but for snow burden. This hilly country was ill-suited to farming, and served mostly as summer pasturage for grazing animals, but from time to time I would catch a whiff of wood smoke and see a trodden path leading from the road to a woodcutter's cottage, or a trapper's hut. It was an area of small, isolated homesteads occupied by folk of humbler persuasions.

The road became narrower, and the trees changed as I entered an older part of the forest. Here the dark evergreens still stood thick and crowded close to the road's edge. Their trunks were immense, and beneath their spreading branches snow lay in uneven hummocks on the forest floor. There was little underbrush. Most of the year's snowfall was still up above, resting on those thickly needled limbs. It was easy to turn Sooty aside from the trail here. We traveled under the snow-laden canopy through a grayish daylight. The day seemed hushed in the dimness of the great trees.

You are seeking a specific place. You have definite information as to where the Forged ones are?

They were seen on a certain creek bank, eating from a winter-killed deer. Just yesterday. I thought we could trail them from there.

Who saw them?

I hesitated. *A friend of mine. He is shy of most folk. But I have gained his confidence, and sometimes, when he sees odd things, he comes to me and tells me.*

Um. I could sense Verity's reservations as he considered my reticence. *Well. I shall ask no more. Some secrets are necessary, I suppose. I remember a little half-wit girl who used to come and sit at my mother's feet. My mother kept her clothed and fed and gave her trinkets and sweets. No one ever paid much attention to her. But once I came upon them unawares, and heard her telling my mother about a man in a tavern who had been selling pretty necklaces and armbands. Later that week the King's guard arrested Rife the highwayman in the very same tavern. Quiet folk often know much.*

Indeed.

We rode on in a companionable silence. Occasionally I had to remind myself that Verity was not here in the flesh. *But I begin to wish I were. It has been too long, boy, since I rode through these hills simply for the sake of riding. My life has become too heavy with purpose. I cannot remember the last time I did something simply because I wanted to do it.*

I was nodding to his thought when the scream shattered the forest quiet. It was the wordless cry of a young creature, cut off in midshriek, and before I could control myself, I quested toward it. My Wit found wordless panic, death fear, and sudden horror from Nighteyes. I sealed off my mind to it, but turned Sooty's head that way and urged her toward it. Clinging low to her neck, I nudged her along through the maze of banked snow and fallen limbs and clear ground that was the forest floor. I worked my way up a hill, never getting up to the speed I suddenly so desperately wanted. I crested the hill, and looked down on a scene I shall never be able to forget.

There were three of them, raggedy and bearded and smelly. They snarled and muttered at each other as they fought. They gave off no life sense to my Wit, but I recognized them as the Forged ones that Nighteyes had shown me the night before. She was small, three perhaps, and the woolly tunic she wore was bright yellow, the loving work of some mother's hands. They fought over her as if she were a snared rabbit, dragging on the limbs of her little body in an angry tug-of-war with no heed to the small life that still resided in her. I roared my fury at the sight and drew my sword just as one Forged one's determined jerk on her neck snapped her free of her body. At my cry, one of the men lifted his head and turned to me, his beard bright with blood. He had not waited for her death to begin feeding.

I kicked Sooty and rode down on them like vengeance on horseback. From the woods to my left, Nighteyes burst onto the scene. He was upon them before I was, leaping to the shoulders of one and opening his jaws wide to set his teeth into the back of the man's neck. One turned to me as I came down, and threw up a useless hand to shield himself from my sword. My blow was such that my fine new blade half severed his neck from his body before wedging in his spine. I pulled my belt knife and launched myself from Sooty's back to grapple with the man who was trying to plunge his knife into Nighteyes. The third Forged one snatched up the girl's body and raced off into the woods with it.

The man fought like a maddened bear, snapping and stabbing at us even after I had opened up his belly. His entrails hung over his belt, and still he came stumbling after us. I could not even take time for the horror I felt. Knowing he would die, I left him and we plunged off after the one who had fled.

Nighteyes was a befurred gray streak that undulated up the hillside, and I cursed my slow two legs as I sped after him. The trail was plain, trampled snow and blood and the foul stench of the creature. My mind was not working well. I swear that as I raced up that hillside I somehow thought I could be in time to undo her death and bring her back. To make it have never happened. It was an illogical drive that sped me on.

He had doubled back. From behind a great stump he leaped at us, flinging the girl's body at Nighteyes and then leaping bodily onto me. He was big and muscled like a smithy. Unlike other Forged ones I had encountered, this one's size and strength had kept him fed and well clothed. The boundless anger of a hunted animal was his. He seized me, lifting me clear off my feet, and then fell upon me with one knotty forearm crushing my throat. He landed atop me, barrel chest on my back, pinning my chest and one arm to the earth below him. I reached back, to sink my knife twice into a meaty thigh. He roared with anger and increased the pressure. He pressed my face into the frozen earth. Black dots spotted my vision, and Nighteyes was a sudden addition to the weight on my back. I thought my spine would snap. Nighteyes slashed at the man's back with his fangs, but the Forged one only drew his chin into his chest and hunched his shoulders against the attack. He knew he was killing me with his strangle. Time enough to deal with the wolf when I was dead.

The struggle opened up the wound on my neck and warm blood spilled out. The added pain was a tiny spur to my struggle. I shook my head wildly in his grip, and the slipperiness of my own blood was enough to let me turn my throat a tiny bit. I got in one desperate wheeze of air before the giant shifted his grip on me. He began to bend my head back. If he could not throttle me, he would simply break my neck. He had the muscle for it.

Nighteyes changed tactics. He could not open his jaws wide enough to get the man's head into them, but his scraping teeth found enough purchase to tear part of the man's scalp from his skull. He set his teeth in the flap of flesh and pulled. Blood rained down on me as the Forged one roared wordlessly and kneed me in the small of the back. He let go with one arm to flail at Nighteyes. I eeled around in his arms, to bring one knee up into his groin, and then to get a good knife thrust into his side. The pain must have been incredible, but he did not release me. Instead he cracked his head against mine in a flash of blackness, and then wrapped his huge arms around me, pinning me to him as he began to crush my chest.

That is as much of the struggle as I can remember coherently. I don't know what came over me next; perhaps it was the death fury some legends speak of. Teeth, nails, and knife I fought him, taking flesh from his body wherever I could reach it. Still, I know it would not have been enough had not Nighteyes also been attacking with the same boundless frenzy. Sometime later I crawled from under the man's body. There was a foul coppery taste in my mouth and I spat out dirty hair and blood. I wiped my hands down my pants and then rubbed them in clean snow, but nothing could ever cleanse them.

Are you all right? Nighteyes lay panting in the snow a yard or two way. His jaws were likewise bloodied. As I watched he snapped up a great mouthful of snow, then resumed his panting. I rose and stumbled a step or two toward him. Then I saw the girl's body and sank down beside it in the snow. I think that was when I realized I was too late, and had been too late from the instant I had spotted them.

She was tiny. Sleek black hair and dark eyes. Horribly, her little body was still warm and lax. I lifted her to my lap and smoothed the hair back from her face. A small face, even baby teeth. Round cheeks. Death had not yet clouded her gaze; the eyes that stared up into mine seemed fixed on a puzzle beyond understanding. Her little hands were fat and soft and streaked with the blood that had run down from the bites on her arms. I sat in the snow with the dead child on my lap. So this was how a child felt in one's arms. So small, and once so warm. So still. I bowed my head over her smooth hair and wept. Sudden shudders ran over me, uncontrollably. Nighteyes snuffed at my cheek and whined. He pawed roughly at my shoulder and I suddenly realized I had shut him out. I touched him with a quieting hand, but could not open my mind to him or anything else. He whined again, and I finally heard the hoofbeats. He gave my cheek an apologetic lick and then vanished into the woods.

I staggered to my feet, still holding my child. The riders crested the hill above me. Verity in the lead, on his black, with Burrich behind him, and Blade, and half a dozen others. Horribly, there was a woman, roughly dressed, riding behind Blade on his horse. She cried out aloud at the sight of me, and slid quickly from the horse's back, running toward me with hands reaching for the child. I could not bear the terrible light of hope and joy in her face. Her eyes seized on mine for an instant and I saw everything die in her face. She clawed her little girl from my arms, snatched at the cooling face on the lolling neck, and then began to scream. The desolation of her grief broke over me like a wave, sweeping my walls away and carrying me under with her. The screaming never stopped.

Hours later, sitting in Verity's study, I could still hear it. I vibrated to the sound, long shudders that ran over me uncontrollably. I was stripped to the waist, sitting on a stool before the fireplace. The healer was building the fire up while behind me a stonily silent Burrich was swabbing pine needles and dirt out of the gouge on my neck. "This, and this aren't fresh wounds," he observed at one point, pointing down to the other injury on my arm. I said nothing. All words had deserted me. In a basin of hot water beside him, dried iris flowers were uncurling with bits of bog myrtle floating beside them. He moistened a cloth in the water and sponged at the bruises on my throat. "The smith had big hands," he observed aloud.

"You knew him?" the healer asked as he turned to look at Burrich.

"Not to talk to. I'd seen him, a time or two, at Springfest when some of the outlying trade folk come to town with their goods. He used to bring fancy silverwork for harness."

They fell silent again. Burrich went back to work. The blood tingeing the warm water wasn't mine, for the most part. Other than a lot of bruises and sore muscles, I'd escaped with mostly scratches and scrapes and one huge lump on my forehead. I was somehow ashamed that I hadn't been hurt. The little girl had died; I should have at least been injured. I don't know why that thought made sense to me. I watched Burrich make a neat white bandage snug on my forearm. The healer brought me a mug of tea. Burrich took it from him, sniffed it thoughtfully, then gave it over to me. "I would have used less valerian," was all he said to the man. The healer stepped back and went to sit by the hearth.

Charim came in with a tray of food. He cleared a small table and began to set it out on it. A moment later Verity strode into the room. He took his cloak off and flung it over a chairback. "I found her husband in the market," he said. "He's with her now. She had left the child playing on the doorstep while she went to the stream for water. When she got back, the child was gone." He glanced toward me, but I couldn't meet his eyes. "We found her calling her little girl in the woods. I knew. . . ." He glanced abruptly at the healer. "Thank you, Dem. If you've finished with FitzChivalry, you may go."

"I haven't even looked at—"

"He's fine." Burrich had run a length of bandaging across my chest and under my opposite arm and up again in an effort to keep a dressing in place on my neck. It was useless. The bite was right atop the muscle between the tip of my shoulder and my neck. I tried to find something amusing in the irritated look the healer gave Burrich before he left. Burrich didn't even notice it.

Verity dragged up a chair to face me. I began to lift the mug to my lips, but Burrich casually reached over and took it from my hand. "After you've talked. There's enough valerian in here to drop you in your tracks." He took it and himself out of the way. Over by the hearth, I watched him dump out half of the tea and dilute what was left with more hot water. That done, he crossed his arms on his chest and leaned against the mantelpiece, watching us.

I shifted my gaze to Verity's eyes, and waited for him to speak.

He sighed. "I saw the child with you. Saw them fighting over her. Then you were suddenly gone. We lost our joining, and I couldn't find you again, not even with all my strength. I knew you were in trouble and set out to reach you as soon as I could. I'm sorry I wasn't faster."

I longed to open myself up and tell Verity everything. But it might be too revealing. To possess a Prince's secrets does not give one the right to divulge them. I glanced at Burrich. He was studying the wall. I spoke formally. "Thank you, my prince. You could not have come faster. And even if you had, it would have been too late. She died at almost the same instant I saw her."

Verity looked down at his hands. "I knew that. Knew it better than you did. My concern was for you." He looked up at me and tried for a smile. "The most distinctive part of your fighting style is the incredible way you have of surviving it."

From the corner of my eye, I saw Burrich shift, open his mouth to speak, then close it again. Cold dread uncoiled in me. He had seen the bodies of the Forged ones, seen the tracks. He knew I hadn't fought alone against them. It was the only thing that could have made the day worse. I felt as if my heart were suddenly caught in a cold stillness. That Burrich had not spoken of it yet, that he was reserving his accusations for a private time only made it worse.

"FitzChivalry?" Verity called my attention back to him.

I started. "I beg your pardon, my prince."

He laughed, almost, a brief snort. "Enough of 'my prince.' Rest assured that I do not expect it of you just now, and neither does Burrich. He and I know each other well enough; he did not 'my prince' my brother at moments like this. Recall that he was king's man to my brother. Chivalry drew on his strength, and oftentimes not gently. I am sure Burrich knows that I have used you likewise. And knows also that I rode with your eyes today, at least as far as the top of that ridge."

I looked to Burrich, who nodded slowly. Neither of us was certain why he was being included here.

"I lost touch with you when you went into a battle frenzy. If I am to use you as I wish, that cannot happen." Verity drummed his fingers lightly on his thighs for a moment, in thought. "The only way I can see for you to learn this thing is to practice it. Burrich. Chivalry once told me that in a tight spot, you were better with an ax than a sword."

Burrich looked startled. Plainly he had not expected Verity

to know this about him. He nodded again, slowly. "He used to mock me about it. Said it was a brawler's tool, not a gentleman's weapon."

Verity permitted himself a tight smile. "Appropriate for Fitz's style, then. You will teach him to use one. I don't believe it's something Hod teaches as a general rule. Though no doubt she could if I asked her. But I'd rather it was you. Because I want Fitz to practice keeping me with him while he learns it. If we can tie the two lessons together, perhaps he can master them both at once. And if you are teaching him, then he'll not be too distracted about keeping my presence a secret. Can you do it?"

Burrich could not completely disguise the dismay that crept over him. "I can, my prince."

"Then do so, please. Beginning tomorrow. Earlier is better for me. I know you have other duties as well, and few enough hours to yourself. Don't hesitate to pass some of your duties on to Hands while you are busy with this. He seems a very capable man."

"He is," Burrich agreed. Guardedly. Another tidbit of information that Verity had at his fingertips.

"Fine, then." Verity leaned back in his chair. He surveyed us both as if he were briefing a whole roomful of men. "Does anyone have any difficulties with any of this?"

I saw the question as a polite closing.

"Sir?" Burrich asked. His deep voice had gone very soft and uncertain. "If I may . . . I have . . . I do not intend to question my prince's judgment, but . . ."

I held my breath. Here it came. The Wit.

"Speak it out, Burrich. I thought I had made it clear that the 'my princing' was to be suspended here. What worries you?"

Burrich stood up straight, and met the King-in-Waiting's eyes. "Is this . . . fitting? Bastard or no, he is Chivalry's son. What I saw up there, today . . ." Once started, the words spilled out of Burrich. He was fighting to keep anger from his voice. "You sent him . . . He went into a slaughterhouse situation, alone. Most any other boy of his age would be dead now. I . . . try not to pry into what is not my area. I know there are many ways to serve my king, and that some are not as pretty as others. But up in the Mountains . . . and then what I saw today. Could not you find someone besides your brother's child for this?''

I glanced back to Verity. For the first time in my life I saw full anger on his face. Not expressed in a sneer or a frown, but simply as two hot sparks deep in his dark eyes. The line of his lips was flat. But he spoke evenly. ''Look again, Burrich. That's no child sitting there. And think again. I did not *send* him *alone*. I went with him, into a situation that we expected to be a stalk and a hunt, not a direct confrontation. It didn't turn out that way. But he survived it. As he has survived similar things before. And likely will again.'' Verity stood suddenly. The whole air of the room was abruptly charged to my senses, boiling with emotion. Even Burrich seemed to feel it, for he gave me a glance, then forced himself to stand still, like a soldier at attention while Verity stalked about the room.

''No. This isn't what I would choose for him. This isn't what I would choose for myself. Would that he had been born in better times! Would that he had been born in a marriage bed, and my brother still upon the throne! But I was not given that situation, nor was he. Nor you! And so he serves, as I do. Damn me, but Kettricken has had it right all along. The King is the sacrifice of the people. And so is his nephew. That was carnage up there today. I know of what you speak; I saw Blade go aside to puke after he saw that body, I saw him walk well clear of Fitz. I know not how the boy . . . this man survived it. By doing whatever he had to, I suppose. So what can I do, man? What can I do? I need him. I need him for this ugly, secret battling, for he is the only one equipped and trained to do it. Just as my father sets me in that tower, and bids me burn my mind out with sneaking, filthy killing. Whatever Fitz must do, whatever skills he must call upon—''

(My heart stood still, my breath was ice in my lungs.)

''—then let him use. Because that is what we are about now. Survival. Because—''

''They are my people.'' I did not realize I had spoken until they both swung to stare at me. Sudden silence in the room. I took a breath. ''A long time ago an old man told me that I would someday understand something. He said that the Six Duchies people were my people, that it was in my blood to care about them, to feel their hurts as my own.'' I blinked my eyes, to clear Chade and that day at Forge from my vision. ''He was right,'' I managed to say after a moment. ''They killed my child today, Burrich. And my smith, and two other men. Not the Forged ones. The Red-Ship Raiders. And I must have their blood in return, I must drive them from my coast. It is as simple now as eating or breathing. It is a thing I must do.''

Their eyes met over my head. ''Blood will tell,'' Verity observed quietly. But there was a fierceness in his voice, and a pride that stilled the day-long trembling of my body. A deep calm rose in me. I had done the right thing today. I suddenly knew it as a physical fact. Ugly, demeaning work, but it was mine, and I had done it well. For my people. I turned to Burrich, and he was looking at me with that considering gaze usually reserved for when the runt of a litter showed unusual promise.

''I'll teach him,'' he promised Verity. ''What few tricks I know with an ax. And a few other things. Shall we begin tomorrow, before first light?''

''Fine,'' Verity agreed before I could object. ''Now let us eat.''

I was suddenly famished. I rose to go to the table, but Burrich was suddenly beside me. ''Wash your face and hands, Fitz,'' he reminded me gently.

The scented water in Verity's basin was dark with the smith's blood when I was through.

14

Winterfest

WINTERFEST IS AS *much a celebration of the darkest part of the year as a festival of the returning light. For the first three days of Winterfest, we pay homage to the darkness. The tales told and puppet shows presented are those that tell of resting times and happy endings. The foods are salt fish and smoked flesh, harvested roots and fruit from last summer. Then, on the midday of the festival, there is a hunt. New blood is shed to celebrate the breaking point of the year, and new meat is brought fresh to the table, to be eaten with grain harvested from the year before. The next three days are days that look toward the coming summer. The looms are threaded with gayer thread, and the weavers take over an end of the Great Hall to vie among themselves for the brightest patterns and lightest weave. The tales told are ones that tell of beginnings of things, and of how things came to be.*

⊷⊜⊰

I tried to see the King that afternoon. Despite all that had transpired, I had not forgotten my promise to myself. Wallace turned me away, saying that King Shrewd felt poorly and was seeing no one. I longed to hammer on the door and shout for the Fool to make Wallace admit me. But I did not. I was not so sure of the Fool's friendship as I had once been. We'd had no contact since that last mocking song of his. Thinking of him put me in mind of his words, and when I went back to my room, I once more rooted through Verity's manuscripts.

· Reading made me sleepy. Even the diluted valerian had been a strong dose. Lethargy took over my limbs. I pushed the scrolls aside, no wiser than when I had begun. I pondered other avenues. Perhaps a public trumpeting at Winterfest that those trained in the Skill, no matter how old or how weak, were being sought? Would that make targets of any who responded? I thought again of the obvious candidates. Those who had trained alongside me. None of them had any fondness for me, but that did not mean they were not still faithful to Verity. Tainted perhaps by Galen's attitudes, but could not that be cured? I ruled August out immediately. His final experience of the Skill at Jhaampe had burned his abilities out of him. He had retired quietly to some town on the Vin River, old before his time, it was said. But there had been others. Eight of us had survived the training. Seven of us had come back from the testing. I had failed it, August had been burned clean of it. That left five.

Not much of a coterie. I wondered if they all hated me as much as Serene did. She blamed me for Galen's death and made no secret of it to me. Were the others as knowledgeable as to what had happened? I tried to recall them all. Justin. Very taken with himself and too proud of his Skilling. Carrod. He had once been a sleepy, likable boy. The few times I had seen him since he had become a coterie member, his eyes had seemed almost empty. As if nothing was left of who he had been. Burl had let his physical strength run to fat once he could Skill instead of carpenter for a living. Will had always been unremarkable. Skilling had not improved him. Still, they were all proven to have Skill ability. Could not Verity retrain them? Perhaps. But when? When did he have time for such an undertaking?

Someone comes.

I came awake. I was sprawled facedown on my bed, scrolls tumbled around me. I hadn't meant to sleep, and seldom slept so deeply. Had Nighteyes not been using my own senses to watch over me, I would have been taken completely unaware. I watched the door of my room ease open. The fire had burned low and there was little other light in the room. I had not latched the door; I had not expected to sleep. I lay very quiet, wondering who came so softly, hoping to take me unawares. Or was it someone hoping to find my room empty, someone after the scrolls perhaps? I eased my hand to my belt knife, gathered my muscles for a spring. A figure came slipping around the door, pushed it quietly shut. I eased the knife out of its sheath.

It's your female. Somewhere, Nighteyes yawned and stretched. His tail gave a lazy wag. I found myself taking a deep breath through my nose. *Molly,* I confirmed to myself with satisfaction as I took in her sweet scent, and then felt an amazing physical quickening. I lay still, eyes closed, and let her come to the bed. I heard her softly chiding exclamation, and then the rustling as she gathered up the scattered scrolls and set them safely atop the table. Hesitantly, she touched my cheek. "Newboy?"

I could not resist the temptation to feign sleep. She sat beside me and the bed gave sweetly with her warm weight. She leaned over me, and as I lay perfectly motionless she set her soft mouth atop mine. I reached out and drew her to me, marveling. Yesterday, I had been a man seldom touched: the clap of a friend on my shoulder, or the casual jostling of a crowd, or too often lately, hands seeking to throttle me. That had been the extent of my personal contact. Then, last night, and now this. She finished the kiss and then lay beside me, gently arranging herself against me. I took a deep breath of her scent and kept still, savoring the places where her body touched mine and made warmth. The sensation was like a soap bubble floating on the wind; I feared even to breathe lest it vanish.

Nice, agreed Nighteyes. *Not so much aloneness here. More like pack.*

I stiffened and pulled slightly away from Molly.

"Newboy? What's wrong?"

Mine. This is mine, and not a thing to share with you. Do you understand?

Selfish. This is not a thing like meat, made more or less by sharing.

"Just a moment, Molly. I've cramped a muscle."

Which one? Smirking.

No, it is not like meat. Meat I would always share with you, and shelter, and always I will come to fight beside you if you need me. Always I will let you join me in the hunt, and always I will help you hunt. But this, with my . . . female. This I must have to myself. Alone.

Nighteyes snorted, scratched at a flea. *You are always marking off lines that do not exist. The meat, the hunt, the defending of territory, and females . . . these are all pack. When she bears cubs, shall I not hunt to feed them? Shall I not defend them?*

Nighteyes . . . I cannot explain this to you just now. I should have spoken with you earlier. For now, will you withdraw? I promise we shall discuss it. Later.

I waited. Nothing. No sense of him at all. One down, one to go.

"Newboy? Are you all right?"

"I'm fine. I just . . . need a moment." I think it was the hardest thing I have ever done. Molly was beside me, suddenly hesitant, on the point of pulling away from me. I had to concentrate on finding my boundaries, on placing my mind in the middle of myself and setting limits to my thoughts. I took the breaths and let them out evenly. Adjusting harness. That was what it always reminded me of, and the image I always used. Not loose enough to slip, not tight enough to bind. Confining myself to my own body, lest I startle Verity awake.

"I heard the rumors," Molly began, then stopped. "I'm sorry. I should not have come. I thought perhaps you might need . . . but maybe what you need is to be alone."

"No, Molly, please, Molly, come back, come back," and I flung myself across the bed after her and managed to catch the hem of her skirt as she stood.

She turned back to me, still full of uncertainty.

"You are always exactly what I need. Always."

A smile ghosted across her lips and she sat on the edge of the bed. "You seemed so distant."

"I was. Sometimes I just need to clear my mind." I stopped, uncertain of what else I could say without lying to her.

I was determined to do that no longer. I reached and took her hand into mine.

"Oh," she said after a moment. There was an awkward little pause as I offered no further explanation. "Are you all right?" she asked carefully after a few more moments had slipped by.

"I'm fine. I didn't get in to see the King today. I tried, but he wasn't feeling well, and—"

"Your face is bruised. And scratched. There were rumors. . . ."

I took a silent breath. "Rumors?" Verity had enjoined the men to silence. Burrich wouldn't have spoken, nor Blade. Perhaps none of them had spoken to anyone who hadn't been there. But men will always discuss what they have witnessed together, and it wouldn't take much for anyone to overhear them.

"Don't play cat and mouse with me. If you don't want to tell me, then say so."

"The King-in-Waiting asked us not to speak of it. That isn't the same as not wanting to tell you about it."

Molly considered a moment. "I suppose not. And I shouldn't listen to gossip, I know. But the rumors were so strange . . . and they brought bodies back to the Keep, for burning. And there was a strange woman, weeping and weeping in the kitchen today. She said that Forged ones had stolen and killed her child. And someone said you had fought them to try and get the baby back, and another said, no, that you'd come upon them just as a bear attacked them. Or something. The rumors were so confusing. Someone said you had killed them all, and then someone who had helped burn the bodies said that at least two of them had been mauled by an animal of some kind." She fell silent and looked at me. I didn't want to think about any of it. I didn't want to lie to her, nor even to tell her the truth. I couldn't tell anyone the complete truth. So I just looked into her eyes and wished that things were simpler for us.

"FitzChivalry?"

I would never get used to hearing that name from her. I sighed. "The King asked us not to speak of it. But . . . yes, a child was killed by Forged ones. And I was there, too late. It was the ugliest, saddest thing I have ever witnessed.''

"I'm sorry. I didn't mean to pry. It's just so hard, not knowing.''

"I know.'' I reached out to touch her hair. She leaned her head against my hand. "I told you once that I had dreamed of you, at Siltbay. I journeyed from the Mountain Kingdom, all the way back to Buckkeep, not knowing if you had survived. Sometimes I thought the burning house had fallen on the cellar; other times, I thought the woman with the sword had finished you. . . .''

Molly looked at me levelly. "When the house fell, a great wind of sparks and smoke whooshed toward us. It blinded her, but my back was to it. I . . . I killed her with the ax.'' She suddenly started to tremble. "I told no one of it. No one. How did you know?''

"I dreamed it.'' I pulled gently at her hand and she came down on the bed beside me. I put my arms around her, and felt her trembling still. "I have true dreams, sometimes. Not often,'' I told her quietly.

She drew back a little from me. Her eyes searched my face. "You would not lie to me about this, Newboy?''

The question hurt, but I deserved it. "No. This is not a lie. I promise you that. And I promise that I shall never lie—''

Her fingers stopped my lips. "I hope to spend the rest of my life with you. Make me no promises that you cannot keep for the rest of your days.'' Her other hand went to the lacing of my shirt. It was my turn to tremble.

I kissed her fingers. And then her mouth. At some time Molly got up and latched and barred my door. I remember sending up a fervent prayer that this would not be the night that Chade finally returned from his journeying. It was not. Instead I journeyed afar that night, into a place that was becoming ever more familiar, but no less wondrous to me.

She left me in the deep of the night, shaking me awake to insist that I latch and bar the door after her. I wanted to dress and walk her back to her room, but she refused me indignantly, saying she was perfectly capable of going up some stairs, and that the less we were seen together, the better. I reluctantly conceded her logic. The sleep I fell into then was deeper than any the valerian had induced.

I awoke to thunder and shouting. I found myself on my feet, dazed and confused. After a moment the thunder turned to pounding on my door, and the shouting was Burrich's repetition of my name. "A moment!" I managed to call back. I ached everywhere. I dragged on some clothes and staggered to the door. It took a long time for my fingers to manage the catch. "What's wrong?" I demanded.

Burrich just stared at me. He was washed and dressed, hair and beard combed, and carrying two axes.

"Oh."

"Verity's tower room. Hurry up, we're already late. But wash first. What is that scent?"

"Perfumed candles," I extemporized. "They're supposed to bring restful dreams."

Burrich snorted. "That's not the kind of dreams that scent would bring me. It's full of musk, boy. Your whole room reeks of it. Meet me up in the tower."

And he was gone, striding purposefully down the hall. I went back into my room, groggily realizing that this was his idea of early morning. I washed myself thoroughly with cold water, not enjoying it, but lacking the time to warm any. I dug about for fresh clothes and was dragging them on when the pounding at my door began again. "I'm nearly there," I called out. The pounding went on. That meant Burrich was angry. Well, so was I. Surely he could understand how badly I ached this morning. I jerked the door open to confront him, and the Fool slipped in as smoothly as a waft of smoke. He wore a new motley of black and white. The sleeves of his shirt were all embroidered with black vines crawling up his arms like ivy. Above the black collar, his face was as pale as a winter moon. Winterfest, I thought dully. Tonight was the first night of Winterfest. The winter had already been as long as any five others I had known. But tonight we would begin to mark the midpoint of it.

"What do you want?" I demanded, in no mood for his silliness.

He took a deep appreciative sniff. "Some of what you had

would be lovely," he suggested, and then danced back gracefully at the look on my face. I was instantly angry. He leaped lightly to the center of my tousled bed, then to the other side, putting it between us. I lunged across it after him. "But not from you," he exclaimed coquettishly and fluttered his hands at me in girlish rebuke before retreating again.

"I've no time for you," I told him disgustedly. "Verity's expecting me and I cannot keep him waiting." I rolled off the bed and stood to adjust my clothing. "Out of my room."

"Ah, such a tone. Time was when the Fitz could handle a jest better than this." He pirouetted in the center of my room, then stopped abruptly. "Are you truly angry with me?" he demanded straightforwardly.

I gaped to hear him speak so bluntly. I considered the question. "I was," I said guardedly, wondering if he was deliberately drawing me out. "You made a fool of me that day, with that song, before all those people."

He shook his head. "Don't take titles to yourself. Only I am the Fool. And the Fool is always only what I am. Especially that day, with that song, before all those people."

"You made me doubt our friendship," I said bluntly.

"Ah, good. For doubt not that others must always doubt our friendship if we are to remain doughty friends."

"I see. Then it was your end to sow rumors of strife between us. I understand, then. But I still must go."

"Farewell, then. Have fun playing at axes with Burrich. Try not to be dumbstruck with all he teaches you today." He put two logs onto my failing fire and made a great show of settling himself before it.

"Fool," I began uncomfortably. "You are my friend, I know. But I like not to leave you here, in my room, while I am gone."

"I like it not when others enter my room when I am not there," he pointed out archly.

I flushed miserably. "That was long ago. And I apologized for my curiosity. I assure you, I have never done it again."

"Nor shall I, after this. And when you come back, I shall apologize to you. Shall that do?"

I was going to be late. Burrich was not going to be

amused. No help for it. I sat down on the edge of the rumpled bed. Molly and I had lain here. Suddenly it was a personal area. I tried to be casual as I tugged the quilts up over the feather beds. "Why do you want to stay in my room? Are you in danger?"

"I live in danger, Fitzy-fitz. As do you. We are all in danger. I should like to stay here for part of the day, and try to find a way out of that danger. Or at least a way to lessen it." He shrugged significantly toward the scatter of scrolls.

"Verity entrusted those to me," I said uneasily.

"Obviously because he feels you are a man whose judgment he trusts. So, perhaps you shall judge it safe to entrust them to me?"

It is one thing to trust a friend with one's own possessions. It is another to allow him those another has put in your safe-keeping. I found I had no doubt of my own trust of the Fool. But. "Perhaps it would be wiser to ask Verity first," I offered.

"The less connection between Verity and me, the better it is for both of us." The Fool spoke flatly.

"You do not care for Verity?" I was startled.

"I am the King's fool. He is the King-in-Waiting. Let him wait. When he is king, I shall be his. If he does not get us all killed before then."

"I will hear nothing spoken against Prince Verity," I told him softly.

"No? Then you must walk about with your ears closely stoppered these days."

I walked to the door, set my hand to the latch. "We must leave now, Fool. I am already late." I kept my voice steady. His sneer at Verity had cut me as deeply as if aimed at me.

"Do not be the Fool, Fitz. That is my role. Think. A man can serve only one master. No matter what your lips may say, Verity is your king. I fault you not for that. Do you fault me that Shrewd is mine?"

"I do not fault you. Nor do I make mock of him before you."

"Nor do you come to visit him, no matter how many times I have urged it."

"I was at his door just yesterday. I was turned away. They said he was not well."

"And if that were to happen at Verity's door, would you take it so meekly?"

That made me stop and think. "No. I don't suppose I would."

"Why do you give him up so easily?" The Fool spoke softly, like a man grieved. "Why does not Verity bestir himself for his father, instead of luring away Shrewd's men to his side?"

"I have not been lured away. Rather Shrewd has not seen fit to see me. As for Verity, well, I cannot speak for him. But all know it is Regal that Shrewd favors of his sons."

"Do all know that? Then do all know as well where Regal's heart is truly set?"

"Some do," I said briefly. This was dangerous talk.

"Reflect on this. Both of us serve the King we love best. Yet there is another that we love least. I do not think we have a conflict of loyalty, Fitz, while we are united in who we love least. Come. Confess to me that you have scarce had time to set your eyes upon the scrolls, and I shall remind you that the time you have not had has fled us all too swiftly. This is not a task that can wait upon your convenience."

I teetered on the decision. The Fool came suddenly closer. His eyes were always hard to meet and harder to read. But the set of his mouth showed me his desperation. "I will trade you. I offer you a bargain you will find nowhere else. A secret I hold, promised to you, after you have let me search the scrolls for a secret which may not even be there."

"What secret?" I asked reluctantly.

"My secret." He turned aside from me and stared at the wall. "The mystery of the Fool. Whence comes he and why?" He cast me a sidelong glance and said no more.

The curiosity of a dozen years leaped in me. "Freely given?" I asked.

"No. Offered as a bargain, as I said."

I considered. Then: "I'll see you later. Latch the door when you leave." And I slipped out.

There were serving folk moving about in the corridors. I

was grievously late. I forced myself into a creaking trot, and then to a run. I did not slow for the stairs to Verity's tower, but rushed up their full length, knocked once, and then entered.

Burrich turned to me, greeting me with a frown. The spartan furnishings of the room had already been pushed to one wall, save for Verity's window chair. Verity was already ensconced in it. He turned his head to me more slowly, with eyes still full of distance. There was a drugged look to his eyes and mouth, a laxness painful to see when one knew what it meant. The Skill hunger gnawed at him. I feared that what he wished to teach me would only feed it and increase it. Yet how could either of us say no? I had learned something yesterday. It had not been a pleasant lesson, but once learned, it could not be undone. I knew now that I would do whatever I must to drive the Red-Ships from my shore. I was not the King, I would never be the King, but the folk of the Six Duchies were mine, just as they were Chade's. I understood now why Verity spent himself so recklessly.

"I beg pardon that I am late. I was detained. But I am ready to begin now."

"How do you feel?" The question came from Burrich, asked with genuine curiosity. I turned to find him regarding me as sternly as before, but also with some puzzlement.

"Stiff, sir. A bit. The run up the stairs warmed me up some. Sore, from yesterday. But otherwise I am all right."

A bit of amusement quirked at his face. "No tremors, FitzChivalry? No darkening at the edge of your vision, no dizzy spells?"

I paused to think for a moment. "No."

"Be damned." Burrich gave a snort of amusement. "Evidently the cure has been to beat it out of you. I'll remember that the next time you need a healer."

Over the next hour he seemed intent on applying his new theory of healing. The heads of the axes were blunt ones, and he had bundled them both in rags for this first lesson, but that did not prevent bruises. To be honest, most of them I earned with my own clumsiness. Burrich was not trying to land any blows that day, but only to teach me to use the whole weapon, not just the head of it. To keep Verity with me was effortless, for he remained in the same room with us. He was silent within me that day, offering no counsels or observations or warnings, but merely riding with my eyes. Burrich told me that the ax was not a sophisticated weapon, but was a very satisfactory one if used correctly. At the end of the session, he pointed out to me that he had been gentle with me, in consideration of the wounds I already bore. Verity dismissed us, and we both went down the stairs rather more slowly than I had come up.

"Be on time tomorrow," Burrich charged me as we parted at the kitchen door, he going back to his stables, and I to find breakfast. I ate as I had not in days, with a wolf's appetite, and wondered at the source of my own sudden vitality. Unlike Burrich, I did not put it down to any beating I had received. Molly, I thought, had healed with a touch what all the herbs and rest in a year could never have put to rights. The day suddenly stretched long in front of me, full of unbearable minutes of unendurable hours before nightfall and the kindly dark allowed us to be together again.

I set her resolutely from my mind and resolved to fill the day with tasks. A dozen immediately leaped to mind. I had been neglecting Patience. I had promised my aid with Kettricken's garden. An explanation was owed to Brother Nighteyes. A visit was owed King Shrewd. I tried to order them in importance. Molly kept moving to the top of the list.

I resolutely set her to last. King Shrewd, I decided. I gathered my crockery from the table and took it back to the kitchen. The bustle was deafening. It puzzled me for a moment, until I recalled that tonight was the first night of Winterfest. Old Cook Sara looked up from the bread she was kneading and motioned me over. I went and stood beside her as I often had as a child, admiring the deft way her fingers shaped handfuls of dough into rolls and set them to rise. She was flour to her dimpled elbows, and flour smudged one cheek as well. The racket and rush of the kitchen created a strange sort of privacy. She spoke quietly through the clatter and chatter, and I had to strain to hear her.

"I just wanted you to know," she grunted as she folded and pushed a new batch of dough, "that I know when a rumor is nonsense. And I speak it so when anyone tries to tell it here in my kitchen. They can gossip all they like in the laundry court, and tattle tales as much as they wish while they spin, but I'll not have ill said of you here in my kitchen.'' She glanced up at me with snapping black eyes. My heart stood still with dread. Rumors? Of Molly and me?

''You've et at my tables, and often enough, stood aside me and stirred a pot while we chatted when you were small. I think that maybe I know you better than most. And them what says you fight like a beast because you're more than half beast are talking evil nonsense. Them bodies was tore up bad, but I've seen worse done by men in a rage. When Sal Flatfish's daughter was raped, she cut up that beast with her fish knife, chop, chop, chop, right there in the market, just like she was cutting bait to set her lines. What you done was no worse than that.''

I knew an instant of dizzying terror. More than half beast . . . It wasn't so long ago or far away that folk with the Wit were burned alive. ''Thank you,'' I said, fighting for a calm voice. I added a modicum of truth when I said, ''Not all of that was my doing. They were fighting over . . . their prey when I came on them.''

''Ginna's daughter. You need not hide words from me, Fitz. I've children of my own, growed now, but if any was to attack them, why, I'd pray there'd be one like to you to defend them, no matter how. Or avenge them, if that's all you could do.''

''I'm afraid it was, Cook.'' The shudder that ran over me was not feigned. I saw again the lines of blood trickled over a fat little fist. I blinked, but the image stayed. ''I've got to hurry off now. I'm to wait on King Shrewd this day.''

''Are ye? Well, there's a spot of good news, then. You just run these up with you, then.'' She trundled over to a cupboard to take out a covered tray of small pastries baked rich with soft cheese and currants. She set a pot of hot tea beside them and a clean cup. She arranged the pastries lovingly. ''And you see he eats them, Fitz. His favorites, they are, and if he tastes one, I know he'll eat them all. And do him good, too.''

Mine, too.

I jumped as if poked with a pin. I tried to cover it with a cough, as if I had suddenly choked, but Cook still looked at me oddly. I coughed again, and nodded at her. "I'm sure he'll love them," I said in a choked voice, and bore the tray out of the kitchen. Several sets of eyes followed me. I smiled pleasantly and tried to pretend I didn't know why.

I didn't realize you were still with me, I told Verity. A tiny part of me was reviewing every thought I'd had since I left his tower, and was thanking Eda that I had not decided to seek out Nighteyes first, even as I pushed such thoughts aside, unsure how private they were.

I know. I didn't intend to be spying on you. Only to show you that when you do not focus so tightly on this, you are able to do it.

I groped after his Skilling. *More your effort than mine,* I pointed out as I climbed the stairs.

You're annoyed with me. Beg pardon. From now on, I shall be sure you are aware of me whenever I am with you. Shall I leave you to your day?

My own surliness had left me feeling embarrassed. *No. Not yet. Ride with me a bit more while I visit King Shrewd. Let's see how far we can carry this.*

I sensed his assent. I paused before Shrewd's door and balanced the tray with one hand as I hastily smoothed my hair back and tugged my jerkin straight. My hair had begun to be a problem lately. Jonqui had cut it short during one of my fevers in the mountains. Now that it was growing out, I didn't know whether to tie it back in a tail as Burrich and the guardsmen did, or keep it at my shoulders as if I were a page still. I was much too old to wear it in the half braid of a child.

Tie it back, boy. I'd say you'd earned the right to wear it as a warrior, as much as any guardsman. Just don't start fussing about it and twining it into oiled curls as Regal does.

I fought the smirk off my face and knocked at the door.

I waited a bit, then knocked again, more loudly.

Announce yourself and open it, Verity suggested.

"It's FitzChivalry, sire. I've brought you something from Cook." I set my hand to the door. It was latched from within.

That's peculiar. It has never been my father's way to latch a door. Put a man on it, yes, but not latch it and ignore someone knocking. Can you slip it?

Probably. But let me try knocking again first. I all but pounded on the door.

"A moment! A moment!" someone whispered from inside. But it was considerably more than that before several latches were undone and the door opened a hand's width. Wallace peered out at me like a rat from under a cracked wall. "What do you want?" he demanded accusingly.

"Audience with the King."

"He's asleep. Or was before you came pounding and shouting. Be off with you."

"A moment." I shoved my booted foot into the closing door. With one free hand, I turned up the collar of my jerkin to expose the red-stoned pin I was seldom without. The door was closed firmly on my foot. I put a shoulder against it, leaned as much as I could without dropping the tray I still carried. "This was given to me by King Shrewd a number of years ago. With it he gave the promise that whenever I showed it, I would be admitted to see him."

"Even if he's asleep?" Wallace asked snidely.

"He placed no limitations on it. Do you?" I glared at him through the cracked door. He considered a moment, then stepped back from it.

"By all means, then, do come in. Come and see your king asleep, trying to get the rest he so badly needs in his condition. But do you disturb it, I as his healer shall tell him to take away that pretty pin and see that you do not bother him again."

"You may recommend that as you wish. And if my king desires it, I shall not dispute it."

He stood aside from me with an elaborate bow. I desperately wanted to knock that knowing sneer from his face, but I ignored it.

"Wonderful," he elaborated as I passed him. "Sweet pastries to upset his digestion and tax him all the more. Thoughtful lad, aren't you?"

I kept my temper. Shrewd was not in his sitting room. The bedchamber?

"Will you truly bother him there? Well, why not? You've shown no other manners, why should I expect consideration now?" Wallace's voice was full of snide condescension.

I gripped my temper.

Don't just accept that from him. Turn and face him down now. This was not advice from Verity, but a command. I set the tray down atop a small table carefully. I took a breath and turned to face Wallace. "Have you a dislike of me?" I asked directly.

He took a step back but tried to keep his sneer in place. "A dislike? Why should I, a healer, mind if someone comes to disturb an ill man when he is finally resting?"

"This room reeks of Smoke. Why?"

Smoke?

An herb they use in the Mountains. Seldom for medicine, save pains nothing else will halt. But more often the burning fumes are breathed for pleasure. Much as we use carris seed at Springfest. Your brother has a liking for it.

As did his mother. If it is the same herb. She called it mirthleaf.

Almost the same leaf, but the Mountain plant grows taller with fleshier leaves. And thicker smoke.

My exchange with Verity had taken less than a blink of an eye. One can Skill information as fast as one can think it. Wallace was still pursing his lips over my question. "Are you claiming to be a healer?" he demanded.

"No. But I've a working knowledge of herbs, one that suggests Smoke is not appropriate to a sick man's chambers."

Wallace was still a moment as he formulated an answer. "Well. A King's pleasures are not his healer's area of concern."

"Perhaps they are mine, then," I offered, and turned away from him. I picked up the tray and pushed open the door to the King's dimly lit bedchamber.

The reek of Smoke was heavier here, the air thick and cloying with it. Too hot a fire was burning, making the room close and stuffy. The air was still and stale as if no fresh wind had blown through the room for weeks. My own breath seemed heavy in my lungs. The King lay still, breathing stertorously beneath a mound of feather quilts. I looked about for a place to set down the tray of pastries. The small table close to his bed was littered. There was a censer for Smoke, the drifting ash

thick on its top, but the burner was out and cold. Beside it was
a goblet of lukewarm red wine, and a bowl with some nasty
gray gruel in it. I set the vessels on the floor and brushed the
table clean with my shirtsleeve before setting the tray down. As
I approached the King's bed there was a fusty, fetid smell that
became even stronger as I leaned over the King.

This is not like Shrewd at all.

Verity shared my dismay. *He has not summoned me much
of late. And I have been too busy to call upon him unless he
bids me to. The last time I saw him was in his sitting room, in
an evening. He complained of headaches, but this . . .*

The thought trailed away between us. I glanced up from
the King to find Wallace peering 'round the door at us. There
was something in his face; I know not whether to call it satisfaction or confidence, but it roused me to fury. In two steps I
had reached the door. I slammed it, and had the satisfaction of
hearing him yelp as he jerked his pinched fingers out. I
dropped into place an ancient bar that had probably never been
used in my lifetime.

I moved to the tall windows, jerked aside the tapestries
that covered it, and flung wide the wooden shutters. Clear
sunlight and fresh cold air spilled into the room.

Fitz, this is rash.

I made no reply. Instead, I moved about the room, dump-
ing censer after censer of ash and herb out the open window. I
brushed the clinging ash out with my hand to free the room
from its reek. From about the room I gathered half a dozen
sticky goblets of stale wine, and a trayful of bowls and plates of
untouched or half-eaten food. I stacked them by the door. Wallace was pounding on it and howling with fury. I leaned against
it and spoke through the crack. "Hush!" I told him sweetly.
"You'll waken the King."

*Have a boy sent with ewers of warm water. And tell Mis-
tress Hasty that the King's bed requires clean linens,* I requested of Verity.

Such orders cannot come from me. A pause. *Don't waste
time in anger. Think, and you'll see why it must be so.*

I understood, but knew also that I would not leave Shrewd
in this dingy, smelly room any more than I would abandon him

to a dungeon. There was half a ewer of water, stale, but mostly clean. I set it to warm by the hearth. I wiped his bed table clean of ash and set out the tea and pastry tray atop it. Rummaging boldly through the King's chest, I found a clean nightshirt, and then washing herbs. Leftover, no doubt, from Cheffers's time. I had never thought I would so miss a valet.

Wallace's pounding ceased. I did not miss it. I took the warmed water scented with the herbs and a washing cloth and set it by the King's bedside. "King Shrewd," I said gently. He stirred slightly. The rims of his eyes were red, the lashes gummed together. When he opened his lids, he blinked red-veined eyes at the light.

"Boy?" He squinted about the room. "Where is Wallace?"

"Away for the moment. I've brought you warm wash water and fresh pastries from the kitchen. And hot tea."

"I . . . I don't know. The window's open. Why is the window open? Wallace has warned me about taking a chill."

"I opened it to clear the air in the room. But I'll close it if you like."

"I smell the sea. It's a clear day, isn't it? Listen to those gulls cry a storm coming. . . . No. No, close the window, boy. I dare not take a chill, not as ill as I am already."

I moved slowly to close the wooden shutters. "Has Your Majesty been ill long? Not much has been said of it about the palace."

"Long enough. Oh, forever it seems. It is not so much that I am ill as that I am never well. I am sick, and then I get a bit better, but as soon as I try to do anything, I am sick again, and worse than ever. I am so weary of being sick, boy. So tired of always feeling tired."

"Come, sir. This will make you feel better." I damped the cloth and wiped his face gently. He recovered himself enough to motion me aside as he washed his own hands, and then wiped his face again more firmly. I was appalled at how the wash water had yellowed as it cleansed him.

"I've found a clean nightshirt for you. Shall I help you into it? Or would you rather that I sent for a boy to bring a tub and warm water? I would bring clean linens for the bed while you bathed.''

"I, oh, I haven't the energy, boy. Where is that Wallace? He knows I cannot manage alone. What possessed him to leave me?''

"A warm bath might help you to rest," I tried persua-sively. Up close, the old man smelled. Shrewd had always been a cleanly man; I think that his grubbiness distressed me more than anything else.

"But bathing can lead to chills. So Wallace says. A damp skin, a cool wind, and whisk, I'm gone. Or so he says.'' Had Shrewd really become this fretful old man? I could scarcely believe what I was hearing from him.

"Well, perhaps just a hot cup of tea, then. And a pastry. Cook Sara said these were your favorites." I poured the steam-ing tea into the cup and saw his nose twitch appreciatively. He had a sip or two, and then sat up to look at the carefully arranged pastries. He bade me join him, and I ate a pastry with him, licking the rich filling from my fingers. I understood why they were his favorites. He was well into a second when there were three solid thuds against the door.

"Unbar it, Bastard. Or the men with me will take it down. And if any harm has come to my father, you shall die where you stand." Regal did not sound at all pleased with me.

"What's this, boy? The door barred? What goes on here? Regal, what goes on here?'' It pained me to hear the King's voice crack querulously.

I crossed the room, I unbarred the door. It was flung open before I could touch it, and two of Regal's more muscular guards seized me. They wore his satin colors like bulldogs with ribbons about their necks. I offered no resistance, so they had no real excuse to throw me up against the wall, but they did. It awoke every pain I still bore from yesterday. They held me there while Wallace rushed in, tut-tutting about how cold the room was, and what was this, eating this, why, it was no less than poison to a man in King Shrewd's condition. Regal stood, hands on hips, very much the man in charge, and stared at me through narrowed eyes.

Rash, my boy. I very much fear that we have overplayed our hand.

"Well, Bastard? What have you to say for yourself? Exactly what were your intentions?" Regal demanded when Wallace's litany ran down. He actually added another log to the fire in the already stifling room, and took the half-eaten pastry from the King's hand.

"I came to report. And finding the King ill cared for, sought to remedy that situation first." I was sweating, more from pain than nervousness. I hated to see Regal smile at it.

"Ill cared for? What exactly are you saying?" he accused me.

I took a breath for courage. Truth. "I found his chamber untidy and musty. Dirty plates left about. The linens of his bed unchanged—"

"Dare you to say such things?" Regal hissed.

"I do. I speak the truth to my king, as I ever have. Let him look about with his own eyes and see if it is not so."

Something in the confrontation had stirred Shrewd to a shadow of his old self. He pushed himself up in bed and looked about himself. "The Fool has likewise made these complaints, in his own acid way—" he began.

Wallace dared to interrupt him. "My lord, the state of your health has been tender. Sometimes uninterrupted rest is more important than rolling you out of your bed to fuss with a change of blankets or linen. And a dish or two stacked about is less annoyance than the rattle and prattle of a page come in to tidy."

King Shrewd looked suddenly uncertain. My heart smote me. This was what the Fool had wished me to see, why he had so often urged me to visit the King. Why had not he spoken more plainly? But then, when did the Fool ever speak plainly? Shame rose in me. This was my king, the King I had sworn to. I loved Verity, and my loyalty to him was unquestioning. But I had abandoned my king at the very moment when he needed me most. Chade was gone, for how long I did not know. I had left King Shrewd with no more than the Fool to protect him. And yet when had King Shrewd ever needed anyone to shelter him before? Always that old man had been more than capable of guarding himself. I chided myself that I should have been more emphatic with Chade about the changes I noted when I first returned home. I should have been more watchful of my sovereign.

"How did he get in here?" Regal suddenly demanded with a savage glare at me.

"My prince, he had a token from the King himself, he claimed. He said the King had promised always to see him if he but showed that pin—"

"What rot! You believed such nonsense—"

"Prince Regal, you know it is true. You were witness when King Shrewd first gave it to me." I spoke quietly but clearly. Within me, Verity was silent, waiting and watching, and learning much. At my expense, I thought bitterly, and then strove to call back the thought.

Moving calmly and unthreateningly, I pulled one wrist free of a bulldog's grip. I turned back the collar of my jerkin and drew the pin out. I held it up for all to see.

"I recall no such thing," Regal snapped, but Shrewd sat up.

"Come closer, boy," he instructed me. Now I shrugged clear of my guards and tugged my clothing straight. Then I bore the pin up to the King's bedside. Deliberately, King Shrewd reached out. He took the pin away from me. My heart sank inside me.

"Father, this is—" Regal began annoyedly, but Shrewd interrupted him.

"Regal. You were there. You do recall it, or you should." The King's dark eyes were bright and alert as I remembered them, but also plain were the lines of pain about those eyes and the corner of his mouth. King Shrewd fought for this lucidity. He held the pin up and looked at Regal with a shadow of his old calculating glance. "I gave the boy this pin. And my word, in exchange for his."

"Then I suggest you take them back again, pin and word both. You will never get well with this type of disruption going on in your rooms." Again, that edge of command in Regal's voice. I waited, silent.

The King lifted a hand to shakily rub his face and eyes. "I

gave those things," he said, and the words were firm, but the strength was fading from his voice. "Once given, a man's word is no longer his to call back. Am I right about this, FitzChivalry? Do you agree that once a man has given his word, he may not take it back?" The old test was in that question.

"As ever I have, my king, I agree with you. Once a man has given his word, he may not call it back. He must abide by what he has promised."

"Good, then. That's settled. It's all settled." He proffered the pin to me. I took it from him, relief so immense it was like vertigo. He leaned back into his pillows. I had another dizzying moment. I knew those pillows, this bed. I had lain there, and looked with the Fool down on the sack of Siltbay. I had burned my fingers in that fireplace. . . .

The King heaved a heavy sigh. There was exhaustion in it. In another moment he would be asleep.

"Forbid him to come and disturb you again, unless you summon him," Regal commanded.

King Shrewd pried his eyes open one more time. "Fitz. Come here, boy."

Like a dog, I came closer to him. I knelt by his bed. He lifted a thinned hand, patted me awkwardly. "You and I, boy. We have an understanding, don't we?" A genuine question. I nodded. "Good lad. Good. I've kept my word. You see that you keep yours, now. But"—he glanced at Regal, and that pained me—"it were better if you came to see me in the afternoons. I am stronger in the afternoons." He was slipping away again.

"Shall I come back this afternoon, sire?" I asked quickly.

He lifted a hand and waved it in a vaguely denying gesture. "Tomorrow. Or the next day." His eyes closed and he sighed out as heavily as if he would never breathe in again.

"As you wish, my lord," I concurred. I bowed deeply, formally. As I straightened I carefully returned the pin to my jerkin lapel. I let them all spend a moment or two watching me do that. Then: "If you will excuse me, my prince?" I requested formally.

"Get out of here," Regal growled.

I bowed less formally to him, turned carefully, and left.

His guards' eyes watched me go. I was outside the room before I recalled that I had never brought up the subject of me marrying Molly. Now it seemed unlikely I would have an opportunity to for some time. I knew that afternoons would now find Regal or Wallace or some spy of theirs always at King Shrewd's side. I had no wish to broach that topic before anyone save my king.

Fitz?

I'd like to be alone for a while just now, my prince. If you do not mind?

He vanished from my mind like a bursting soap bubble. Slowly I made my way down the stairs.

15

Secrets

*P*RINCE VERITY CHOSE *to unveil his fleet of warships on the midday of Winterfest that decisive year. Tradition would have had him wait until the coming of better weather, to launch them on the first day of Springfest. That is considered a more auspicious time to launch a new ship. But Verity had pushed his shipwrights and their crews hard to have all four vessels ready for a midwinter launch. By choosing the midday of Winterfest, he ensured himself a large audience, both for the launch and for his words. Traditionally, a hunt is held that day, with the meat brought in seen as a harbinger of days to come. When he had the ships pushed out of the sheds on their rollers, he announced to the gathered folk that these were his hunters, and that the only prey that would slake them would be Red-Ships. The reaction to his announcement was muted, and clearly not what he had hoped for. It is my belief that the people wanted to put all thoughts of the Red-Ships from their minds, to hide themselves in winter and pretend that the spring would never come. But Verity refused to let them. The ships were launched that day, and the training of the crews begun.*

⇢═╞⇠

Nighteyes and I spent the early afternoon hunting. He grumbled about it, saying it was a ridiculous time of day to hunt, and why had I wasted the early dawn hours tussling with my litter mate? I told him that that was simply a thing that had to be, and would continue to be for several days, and possibly longer. He was not pleased. But neither was I. It rattled me not a little that he could be so clearly aware of how I spent my hours even if I had no conscious sense of being in touch with him. Had Verity been able to sense him?

He laughed at me. *Hard enough to make you hear me sometimes. Should I batter through to you and then shout for him as well?*

Our hunting success was small. Two rabbits, neither with much fat. I promised to bring him kitchen scraps on the morrow. I had even less success at conveying to him my demand for privacy at certain times. He could not grasp why I set mating apart from other pack activities such as hunting or howling. Mating suggested offspring in the near future, and offspring were the care of the pack. Words cannot convey the difficulties of that discussion. We conversed in images, in shared thoughts, and such do not allow for much discretion. His candor horrified me. He assured me he shared my delight in my mate and my mating. I begged him not to. Confusion. I finally left him eating his rabbits. He seemed piqued that I would not accept a share of the meat. The best I had been able to get from him was his understanding that I did not want to be aware of him sharing my awareness of Molly. That was scarcely what I wanted, but it was the best I could convey it to him. The idea that at times I would want to sever my bond to him completely was not a thought he could comprehend. It made no sense, he argued. It was not pack. I left him wondering if I would ever again really and truly have a moment to myself.

I returned to the Keep and sought the solitude of my own room. If only for a moment, I had to be where I could close the door behind me and be alone. Physically, anyway. As if to fuel my quest for quiet, the halls and stairways were full of hurrying folk. Servants were cleaning away old rushes and spreading new ones, fresh candles were being placed in holders, and boughs of evergreen were hung in festoons and swags everywhere. Winterfest. I didn't much feel like it.

I finally reached my own door and slipped inside. I shut it firmly behind me.

"Back so soon?" The Fool looked up from the hearth, where he crouched in a semicircle of scrolls. He seemed to be sorting them into groups.

I stared at him with unconcealed dismay. In an instant it flashed into anger. "Why didn't you tell me of the King's condition?"

He considered another scroll, after a moment set it in the pile to his right. "But I did. A question in exchange for yours: why didn't you already know of it?"

That set me back. "I admit I've been lax in calling upon him. But—"

"None of my words could have had the impact of seeing for yourself. Nor do you pause to think what it would have been like had I not been there every single day, emptying chamber pots, sweeping, dusting, carrying out dishes, combing his hair and his beard. . . ."

Again he had shocked me into silence. I crossed the room, sat down heavily atop my clothing chest. "He's not the King I remember," I said bluntly. "It frightens me that he could sink so far, so fast."

"Frightens you? Appalls me. At least you've another King when this one's been played." The Fool flipped another scroll onto the pile.

"We all do," I pointed out carefully.

"Some more than others," the Fool said shortly.

Without thinking, my hand rose to tuck the pin tighter in my jerkin. I'd almost lost it today. It had made me think of all it had symbolized all these years. The King's protection, for a bastard grandson that a more ruthless man would have done away with quietly. And now that he needed protection? What did it symbolize to me now?

"So. What do we do?"

"You and I? Precious little. I'm but a Fool, and you are a bastard."

I nodded grudgingly. "I wish Chade were here. I wish I knew when he was coming back." I looked to the Fool, wondering how much he knew.

"Shade? Shade returns when the sun does, I've heard."
Evasive as always. "Too late for the King, I imagine," he
added more quietly.

"So we are powerless?"

"You and I? Never. We've too much power to act here;
that is all. In this area, the powerless ones are always the most
powerful. Perhaps you are right; they are who we should consult in this. And now . . ." Here he rose and made a show of
shaking all his joints loose as if he were a marionette with
tangled strings. He set every bell he had to jingling. I could not
help but smile. "My king will be coming into his best time of
day. And I will be there, to do what little I can for him."

He stepped carefully out of his ring of sorted scrolls and
tablets. He yawned. "Farewell, Fitz."

"Farewell."

He halted, puzzled, by the door. "You have no objections
to my going?"

"I believe I objected first to your staying."

"Never bandy words with a Fool. But do you forget? I
offered you a bargain. A secret for a secret."

I had not forgotten. But I was not sure, suddenly, that I
wanted to know. "Whence comes the Fool, and why?" I asked
softly.

"Ah." He stood a moment, then asked gravely, "You are
certain you wish the answers to these questions?"

"Whence comes the Fool, and why?" I repeated slowly.

For an instant he was dumb. I saw him then. Saw him as I
had not in years, not as the Fool, glib-tongued and wits as
cutting as any barnacle, but as a small and slender person, all
so fragile, pale flesh, bird-boned, even his hair seemed less
substantial than that of other mortals. His motley of black and
white trimmed in silver bells, his ridiculous rat scepter were all
the armor and sword he had in this court of intrigues and
treachery. And his mystery. The invisible cloak of his mystery.
I wished for an instant he had not offered the bargain, and that
my curiosity had been less consuming.

He sighed. He glanced about my room, then walked over
to stand before the tapestry of King Wisdom greeting the
Elderling. He glanced up at it, then smiled sourly, finding some

humor there I had never seen. He assumed the stance of a poet about to recite. Then he halted, looked at me squarely once more. "You are certain you wish to know, Fitzy-fitz?"

Like a liturgy, I repeated the question. "Whence comes the Fool and why?"

"Whence? Ah, whence?" He went nose to nose with Ratsy for a moment, formulating a reply to his own question. Then he met my eyes. "Go south, Fitz. To lands past the edges of every map that Verity has ever seen. And past the edges of the maps made in those countries as well. Go south, and then east across a sea you have no name for. Eventually, you would come to a long peninsula, and on its snaking tip you would find the village where a Fool was born. You might even find, still, a mother who recalled her wormy-white babe, and how she cradled me against her warm breast and sang." He glanced up at my incredulous, enraptured face and gave a short laugh. "You cannot even picture it, can you? Let me make it harder for you. Her hair was long and dark and curling, and her eyes were green. Fancy that! Of such rich colors was this transparency made. And the fathers of the colorless child? Two cousins, for that was the custom of that land. One broad and swarthy and full of laughter, ruddy-lipped and brown-eyed, a farmer smelling of rich earth and open air. The other as narrow as the one was wide, and gold to his bronze, a poet and songster, blue-eyed. And, oh, how they loved me and rejoiced in me! All the three of them, and the village as well. I was so loved." His voice grew soft, and for a moment he fell silent. I knew with great certainty that I was hearing what no other had ever heard from him. I remembered the time I had ventured into his room, and the exquisite little doll in its cradle that I had found there. Cherished as the Fool had once been cherished. I waited.

"When I was . . . old enough, I bade them all farewell. I set off to find my place in history, and choose where I would thwart it. This was the place I selected; the time had been destined by the hour of my birth. I came here, and became Shrewd's. I gathered up whatever threads the fates put into my hands, and I began to twist them and color them as I could, in the hopes of affecting what was woven after me."

I shook my head. "I don't understand a thing you just said."

"Ah." He shook his head, setting his bells to jingling. "I offered to tell you my secret. I didn't promise to make you understand it."

"A message is not delivered until it is understood," I countered. This was a direct quote from Chade.

The Fool teetered on accepting it. "You do understand what I said," he compromised. "You simply do not accept it. Never before have I spoken so plainly to you. Perhaps that is what confuses you."

He was serious. I shook my head again. "You make no sense! You went somewhere to discover your place in history? How can that be? History is what is done and behind us."

He shook his head, slowly this time. "History is what we do in our lives. We create it as we go along." He smiled enigmatically. "The future is another kind of history."

"No man can know the future," I agreed.

His smile widened. "Cannot they?" he asked in a whisper. "Perhaps, Fitz, somewhere, there is written down all that is the future. Not written down by one person, know, but if the hints and visions and premonitions and foreseeings of an entire race were written down, and cross-referenced and related to one another, might not such a people create a loom to hold the weaving of the future?"

"Preposterous," I objected. "How would anyone know if any of it were true?"

"If such a loom were made, and such a tapestry of predictions woven, not for a few years, but for tens of hundreds of years, after a time it could be shown that it presented a surprisingly accurate foretelling. Bear in mind that those who keep these records are another race, an exceedingly long-lived one. A pale lovely race, that occasionally mingled its bloodlines with that of men. And then!" He spun in a circle, suddenly fey, pleased insufferably with himself. "And then, when certain ones were born, ones marked so clearly that history must recall them, they are called to step forward, to find their places in that future history. And they might further be exhorted to examine that place, that juncture of a hundred threads, and say, these threads, here, these are the ones I shall tweak, and in the tweaking, I shall change the tapestry, I shall warp the weft, alter the color of what is to come. I shall change the destiny of the world.''

He was mocking me. I was certain of it now. ''Once, in perhaps a thousand years, there may come a man capable of making such a great change in the world. A powerful King, perhaps, or a philosopher, shaping the thoughts of thousands. But you and I, Fool? We are pawns. Ciphers.''

He shook his head pityingly. ''This, more than anything else, is what I have never understood about your people. You can roll dice, and understand that the whole game may hinge on one turn of a die. You deal out cards, and say that all a man's fortune for the night may turn upon one hand. But a man's whole life, you sniff at, and say, what, this naught of a human, this fisherman, this carpenter, this thief, this cook, why, what can they do in the great wide world? And so you putter and sputter your lives away, like candles burning in a draft.''

''Not all men are destined for greatness,'' I reminded him.

''Are you sure, Fitz? Are you sure? What good is a life lived as if it made no difference at all to the great life of the world? A sadder thing I cannot imagine. Why should not a mother say to herself, if I raise this child aright, if I love and care for her, she shall live a life that brings joy to those about her, and thus I have changed the world? Why should not the farmer that plants a seed say to his neighbor, this seed I plant today will feed someone, and that is how I change the world today?''

''This is philosophy, Fool. I have never had time to study such things.''

''No, Fitz, this is life. And no one has time not to think of such things. Each creature in the world should consider this thing, every moment of the heart's beating. Otherwise, what is the point of arising each day?''

''Fool, this is beyond me,'' I declared uneasily. I had never seen him so impassioned, never heard him speak so plainly. It was as if I had stirred gray-coated embers and suddenly found the cherry-red coal that glowed in their depths. He burned too brightly.

"No, Fitz. I have come to believe it is through you." He reached out and tapped me lightly with Ratsy. "Keystone. Gate. Crossroads. Catalyst. All these you have been, and continue to be. Whenever I come to a crossroads, whenever the scent is uncertain, when I put my nose to the ground, and cast about and bay and snuffle, I find one scent. Yours. You create possibilities. While you exist, the future can be steered. I came here for you, Fitz. You are the thread I tweak. One of them, anyway."

I felt a sudden chill of foreboding. Whatever more he had to say, I did not wish to hear it. Somewhere, far away, a thin howl arose. A wolf baying in midday. A shiver ran up me, setting up every hair on my body. "You've had your joke," I said, laughing nervously. "I should have known better than to expect a real secret from you."

"You. Or not you. Linchpin, anchor, knot in the line. I have seen the end of the world, Fitz. Seen it woven as plainly as I've seen my birth. Oh, not in your lifetime, nor even mine. But shall we be happy, to say that we live in the dusk rather than in the full night? Shall we rejoice that we shall only suffer, while your offspring will be the ones to know the torments of the damned? Shall this be why we do not act?"

"Fool. I wish not to hear this."

"You had a chance to deny me. But thrice you demanded it, and hear it you shall." He lifted his staff as if leading a charge, and spoke as if he addressed the full Council of the Six Duchies. "The fall of the Kingdom of the Six Duchies was the pebble that started the landslide. The soulless ones moved on from there, spreading like a bloodstain down the world's best shirt. Darkness devours, and is never satiated until it feeds upon itself. And all because the line of House Farseer failed. That is the future as it is woven. But wait! Farseer?" He cocked his head and peered at me, considering as a gore-crow. "Why do they call you that, Fitz? What have your ancestors ever foreseen afar to gain such a name? Shall I tell you how it comes about? The very name of your house is the future reaching back in time to you, and naming you by the name that someday your house will deserve. The Farseers. That was the clue I took to my heart. That the future reached back to you, to your house, to where your bloodlines intersected with my lifetime, and named you so. I came here, and what did I discover? One Farseer, with no name at all. Unnamed in any history, past or future. But I have seen you take a name, FitzChivalry Farseer. And I shall see that you deserve it." He advanced on me, seized me by the shoulders. "We are here, Fitz, you and I, to change the future of the world. To reach out and hold in place the tiny pebble that could trigger the boulder's tumbling."

"No." A terrible cold was welling up inside me. I shook with it. My teeth began to chatter, and the bright motes of light to sparkle at the edges of my vision. A fit. I was going to have another fit. Right here, in front of the Fool. "Leave!" I cried out, unable to abide the thought. "Go away. Now! Quickly. Quickly!"

I had never seen the Fool astonished before. His jaw actually dropped open, revealing his tiny white teeth and pale tongue. A moment longer he gripped me, and then he let go. I did not stop to think of what he might feel at my abrupt dismissal. I snatched the door open and pointed out it, and he was gone. I shut it behind him, latched it, and then staggered to my bed as wave after wave of darkness surged through me. I fell facedown on the coverlets. "Molly!" I cried out. "Molly, save me!" But I knew she could not hear me, and I sank alone into my blackness.

⇢═┋

The brightness of a hundred candles, festoons of evergreen and swags of holly and bare black winter branches hung with sparkling sugar candies to delight the eye and tongue. The clacking of the puppets' wooden swords and the delighted exclamations of the children when the Piebald Prince's head actually came flying off and arced out over the crowd. Mellow's mouth wide in a bawdy song as his unattended fingers danced independently over his harp strings. A blast of cold as the great doors of the hall were thrown open and yet another group of merrymakers came into the Great Hall to join us. The slow knowledge stole over me that this was no longer a dream, this was Winterfest, and I was wandering benignly through the celebration, smiling blandly at everyone and seeing no one. I blinked my eyes slowly. I could do nothing quickly. I was wrapped in soft wool, I was drifting like an unmanned sailboat on a still day. A wonderful sleepiness filled me. Someone touched my arm. I turned. Burrich frowning and asking me something. His voice, always so deep, almost a color washing against me when he spoke. "It's all good," I told him calmly. "Don't worry, it's all good." I floated away from him, wafting through the room with the milling of the crowd.

King Shrewd sat on his throne, but I knew now that he was made of paper. The Fool sat on the step by his feet and clutched his rat scepter like an infant clutches a rattle. His tongue was a sword, and as the King's enemies drew closer to the throne, the Fool slew them, slashed them to bits, and turned them back from the paper man on the throne.

And here were Verity and Kettricken on another dais, pretty as the Fool's doll, each of them. I looked and saw they were both made of hungers, like containers made of emptiness. I felt so sad, I'd never be able to fill either of them, for they were both so terribly empty. Regal came to speak to them, and he was a big black bird, not a crow, no, not so merry as a crow, and not a raven, he hadn't the cheery cleverness of a raven, no, a miserable eye-pecker of a bird, circling, circling, dreaming of them as carrion for himself to feast on. He smelled of carrion, and I covered my mouth and nose with a hand and walked away from them.

I sat down on a hearth, next to a giggling girl, happy in her blue skirts. She chattered like a squirrel and I smiled at her, and soon she leaned against me and began to sing a funny little song about three milkmaids. There were others sitting and standing about the hearth, and they joined in the song. We all laughed at the end, but I wasn't sure why. And her hand was warm, resting so casually on my thigh.

Brother, are you mad? Have you eaten fishbones, are you burned by fever?

"Huh?"

Your mind is clouded. Your thoughts are bloodless and sickly. You move like prey.

"I feel fine."

"Do you, sir? Then I do, too." She smiled up at me. Chubby little face, dark eyes, curly hair peeking out from under her cap. Verity would like this one. She patted my leg companionably. A bit higher than she had touched me before.

"FitzChivalry!"

I looked up slowly. Patience was standing over me, with Lacey at her elbow. I smiled to see her there. She so seldom came out of her rooms to socialize. Especially in winter. Winter was a hard time for her. "I shall be so glad when summer returns, and we can walk in the gardens together," I told her.

She looked at me silently for a moment. "I have something heavy I wish carried up to my rooms. Will you bring it for me?"

"Certainly." I stood carefully. "I have to go," I told the little servant girl. "My mother needs me. I liked your song."

"Good-bye, sir!" she chirped at me, and Lacey glared at her. Patience's cheeks were very rosy. I followed her through the ebb and press of folk. We came to the foot of the stairs.

"I forget how to do these," I told her. "And where is the heavy thing you wish carried?"

"That was an excuse to get you away from there before you completely disgraced yourself!" she hissed at me. "What is the matter with you? How could you behave so badly? Are you drunk?"

I thought about it. "Nighteyes said I was poisoned by fishbones. But I feel fine."

Lacey and Patience looked at me very carefully. Then they each took an arm and guided me upstairs. Patience made tea. I talked to Lacey. I told her how much I loved Molly and that I was going to marry her as soon as the King said I could. She patted my hand and felt my forehead and asked what I'd eaten today and where. I couldn't remember. Patience gave me tea. Very soon I puked. Lacey gave me cold water. Patience gave me more tea. I puked again. I said I didn't want any more tea. Patience and Lacey argued. Lacey said she thought I'd be all right after I slept. She took me back to my room.

I woke up with no clear idea of what had been dream and what had been real, if anything. My entire recall of the evening's events had the same distance as events that had happened years ago. This was compounded by the open staircase with its beckoning yellow light and the draft from it chilling my room. I scrabbled out of bed, swayed for a moment as a wave of dizziness overtook me, and then slowly mounted the stairs, one hand always touching the cold stone wall to reassure myself that it was real. About midway up the steps, Chade came down to meet me. "Here, take my arm," he commanded, and I did.

He put his free arm around me and we went up the stairs together. "I've missed you," I told him. With my next breath, I told him, "King Shrewd is in danger."

"I know. King Shrewd is always in danger."

We gained the top of the stairwell. There was a fire in his hearth, and a meal set out next to it on a tray. He guided me toward both.

"I think I might have been poisoned today." A sudden shivering ran up me and I shuddered all over. When it passed, I felt more alert. "I seem to be waking up in stages. I keep thinking I'm awake, and then suddenly everything is clearer."

Chade nodded gravely. "I suspect it was the ash residue. You weren't thinking when you tidied King Shrewd's room for him. Many times the burned residue of an herb concentrates the potency of the herb. You got it all over your hands and then sat there eating pastries. There was little I could do. I thought you would sleep it off. What possessed you to go downstairs?"

"I don't know." Then: "How do you always know so much?" I asked peevishly as he pushed me down into his old chair. He took my usual perch on the hearthstones. Even in my fuddled state, I noticed how fluidly he moved, as if he had somewhere abandoned the cramps and aches of an old man's body. There was windburned color to his face and arms as well, the tan fading the pocks' stigma. I had once noticed his resemblance to Shrewd. Now I saw Verity in his face as well.

"I have my little ways of finding things out." He grinned at me wolfishly. "How much do you remember of Winterfest tonight?"

I winced as I considered it. "Enough to know that tomorrow is going to be a difficult day." The little servant girl suddenly popped up in my memory. Leaning on my shoulder, her hand on my thigh. Molly. I had to get to Molly tonight and somehow explain things to her. If she came to my room tonight, and I wasn't there to answer her knock . . . I started up in my chair, but then another shiver ran up over me. It felt almost like a skin being peeled off me.

"Here. Eat something. Puking your guts out wasn't the best thing for you, but I'm sure Patience meant well. And under other circumstances, it could have been a lifesaver. No, you idiot, wash your hands first. Haven't you heard a word I've said?"

I noticed then the vinegar water set out beside the food. I washed my hands carefully to remove every trace of whatever had clung to them, and then my face, amazed at how much more alert I suddenly felt. "It's been like an extended dream, all day . . . is this what Shrewd has been feeling?"

"I've no idea. Perhaps not all those burning herbs down there are what I think they are. It was one of the things I wanted to discuss with you tonight. How has Shrewd been? Has this come on him suddenly? How long has Wallace been calling himself a healer?"

"I don't know." I hung my head in shame. I forced myself to report to Chade just how lax I had been in his absence. And how stupid. When I was finished, he did not disagree with me.

"Well," he said heavily. "We can't undo, we can only salvage. Too much is happening here to sort at one sitting." He looked at me consideringly. "Much of what you tell me does not surprise me. Forged ones converging still on Buckkeep, the King's illness lingering. But King Shrewd's health has declined much more swiftly than I can account for, and the squalor in his rooms makes no sense to me. Unless . . ." He did not finish the thought. "Perhaps they believe that Lady Thyme was his only defender. Perhaps they think we no longer care; perhaps they believe him an isolated old man, an obstacle to be removed. Your carelessness has drawn them out, at least. And having drawn them out, perhaps we can cut them off." He sighed. "I thought I could use Wallace as a tool, lead him subtly through the advice of others. He has little knowledge of herbs of his own; the man is a dabbler. But the tool I left carelessly lying about, perhaps another employs now. We shall have to see. Still. There are ways to stop this.''

I bit my tongue before I could utter Regal's name. "How?" I asked instead.

Chade smiled. "How were you rendered ineffective as an assassin in the Mountain Kingdom?"

I winced at the memory. "Regal revealed my purpose to Kettricken."

"Exactly. We shall shine a bit of daylight on what goes on in the King's chambers. Eat while I talk.''

And so I did, listening to him as he outlined my assignments for the next day, but also noting what he chose to feed me. The flavor of garlic predominated, and I knew his confidence in its purifying abilities. I wondered just what I had ingested, and also how much it colored my recollection of my conversation with the Fool. I flinched as I recalled my brusque dismissal of him. He would be another I would have to seek out tomorrow. Chade noticed my preoccupation. "Sometimes," he observed obliquely, "you have to trust people to understand you are not perfect.''

I nodded, then suddenly yawned immensely. "Beg pardon," I muttered. My eyelids were suddenly so heavy I could barely keep my head up. "You were saying?"

"No, no. Go to bed. Rest. It's the real healer.''

"But I haven't even asked you where you've been. Or what you've been doing. You move and act as if you'd lost ten years of age.''

Chade puckered his mouth. "Is that a compliment? Never mind. Such questions would be useless anyway, so you may save them for another time, and be frustrated then when I refuse to answer them. As to my condition . . . well, the more one forces one's body to do, the more it can do. It was not an easy journey. Yet I believe it was worth the hardship.'' He held up a halting hand as I opened my mouth. "And that is all I am going to say. To bed, now, Fitz. To bed.''

I yawned again as I rose, and stretched until my joints popped. "You've grown again," Chade complained admiringly. "At this rate, you'll even top your father's height.''

"I've missed you," I mumbled as I headed toward the stair.

"And I you. But we shall have tomorrow night for catching up. For now, bed for you."

I went down his stairs with the sincere intention of following his suggestion. As it always did, the staircase sealed itself moments after I exited it, by a mechanism I had never been able to discover. I threw three more logs on my dying fire and then crossed to my bed. I sat down on it to pull my shirt off. I was exhausted. But not so tired that I could not catch a faint trace of Molly's scent on my own skin as I pulled my shirt off. I sat a moment longer, holding my shirt in my hands. Then I put it back on and rose. I went to my door and slipped out into the hallway.

It was late, by any other night's standard. Yet this was the first night of Winterfest. There were many below who would not think of their beds until dawn was on the horizon. Others who would not find their own beds at all this night. I smiled suddenly as I realized I intended to be part of the latter group.

There were others in the halls that night and on the staircases. Most were too inebriated, or too engrossed in themselves to notice me. As for the others, I resolved to let Winterfest be my excuse for any questions asked of me the next day. Still, I was discreet enough to be sure the corridor was clear before I tapped on her door. I heard no reply. But as I lifted my hand to tap again, the door swung silently open into darkness.

It terrified me. In an instant I was sure harm had come to her, that someone had been here and hurt her and left her there in the darkness. I sprang into the room, crying out her name. The door swung shut behind me and "Hush!" she commanded.

I turned to find her, but it took a moment for my eyes to adjust to the darkness. The light from the hearth fire was the only illumination in the room, and it was to my back. When my eyes did penetrate the darkness, I felt as if I could not breathe.

"Were you expecting me?" I asked at last.

In a little cat voice, she replied, "Only for hours."

"I thought you would be at the merrymaking in the Great Hall." Slowly it dawned on me that I had not seen her there.

"I knew I would not be missed there. Except by one. And I thought perhaps that one might come seeking me here."

I stood motionless and looked at her. She wore a wreath of holly atop the tumble of her hair. That was all. And she stood against the door, wanting me to look at her. How can I explain the line that had been crossed? Before we had ventured into this together, exploring and inquisitive. But this was different. This was a woman's frank invitation. Can there be anything so compelling as the knowledge that a woman desires you? It overwhelmed me and blessed me and somehow redeemed me from every stupid thing I had ever done.

Winterfest.

The heart of night's secret.

Yes.

She shook me awake before dawn, and put me out of her rooms. The farewell kiss that she gave me before shooing me out the door was such that I stood in the hall trying to persuade myself that dawn was not all that close. After a few moments I recalled that discretion was called for, and wiped the foolish smile off my face. I straightened my rumpled shirt and headed for the stairs.

Once inside my room, an almost dizzying weariness overtook me. How long had it been since I had had a full night's sleep? I sat down on my bed and dragged my shirt off. I dropped it to the floor. I fell back onto the bed and closed my eyes.

A soft tap at my door jerked me upright. I crossed the room swiftly, smiling to myself. I was still smiling as I swung the door wide.

"Good, you're up! And almost dressed. I was afraid from the way you looked last night that I'd be dragging you out of your bed by the scruff of your neck."

It was Burrich, freshly washed and brushed. The lines across his forehead were the only visible signs of the last night's revelry. From my years of sharing quarters with him, I knew that no matter how fierce a hangover he might have, he would still rise to face his duties. I sighed. No good asking quarter, for none would be given. Instead I went to my clothes chest and found a clean shirt. I put it on as I followed him to Verity's tower.

There is an odd threshold, physical as well as mental. There have been but a few times in my life that I have been pushed over it, but each time an extraordinary thing happened. That morning was one of those times. After an hour or so had passed, I stood in Verity's tower room, shirtless and sweating. The tower windows were open to the winter wind, but I felt no chill. The padded ax Burrich had given me was but a little lighter than the world itself, and the weight of Verity's presence in my mind felt as if it were forcing my brain out my eyes. I could no longer keep my ax up to guard myself. Burrich came at me again, and I made no more than a token defense. He batted it aside with ease, then came in swiftly, one, two blows, not hard, but not softly either. "And you're dead," he told me, and stood back. He let the head of his ax sag to the floor and stood leaning on it and breathing. I let my own ax thud head-first to the floor. Useless.

Within my mind, Verity was very still. I glanced over to where he sat staring out the window across the sea to the horizon. The morning light was harsh on the lines in his face and the gray in his hair. His shoulders were slumped forward. His posture mirrored what I felt. I closed my eyes a moment, too weary to do anything anymore. And suddenly we meshed. I saw to the horizons of our future. We were a country besieged by a ravenous enemy who came to us only to kill and maim. That was their sole goal. They had no fields to plant, no children to defend, no stock to tend to distract them from their raiding. But we strove to live our day-to-day lives at the same time we tried to protect ourselves from their destruction. For the Red-Ship Raiders, their ravages were their day-to-day lives. That singleness of purpose was all they needed to destroy us. We were not warriors; had not been warriors for generations. We did not think like warriors. Even those of us who were soldiers were soldiers who had trained to fight against a rational enemy. How could we stand against an onslaught of madmen? What weapons did we have? I looked around. Me. Myself as Verity.

One man. One man, making himself old as he strove to walk the line between defending his people and being swept away in the addictive ecstasy of the Skill. One man, trying to rouse us, trying to ignite us to defend ourselves. One man, with his eyes afar, as we squabbled and plotted and bickered in the rooms below him. It was useless. We were doomed to fail.

The tide of despair swept over me and threatened to pull me down. It swirled around me, but suddenly, in the middle of it, I found a place to stand. A place where the very uselessness of it was funny. Horribly funny. Four little warships, not quite finished, with untrained crews. Watchtowers and fire signals to call the inept defenders forth to the slaughter. Burrich with his ax, and me standing in the cold. Verity staring out the window, while below, Regal fed his own father drugs. In the hopes of stealing his mind, and inheriting the whole mess, I didn't doubt. It was all so totally useless. And so unthinkable to give it up. A laughter welled up from inside me, and I could not contain it. I stood leaning on my ax, and laughed as if the world were the funniest thing I'd ever seen, while Burrich and Verity both stared at me. A very faint answering smile crooked the corners of Verity's mouth; a light in his eyes shared my madness.

"Boy? Are you all right?" Burrich asked me.

"I'm fine. I'm absolutely fine," I told them both when my waves of laughter had subsided.

I pulled myself up to stand straight. I shook my head, and I swear I almost felt my brain settle. "Verity," I said, and embraced his consciousness to mine. It was easy; it had always been easy, but before, I had believed there was something to lose by doing it. We did not meld into one person, but instead fit together like bowls stacked in a cupboard. He rode me comfortably, like a well-loaded pack. I took a breath and lifted my ax. "Again," I said to Burrich.

As he came at me I no longer allowed him to be Burrich. He was a man with an ax, come to kill Verity, and before I could stop my momentum, I had laid him out on the floor. He rose, shaking his head, and I saw a touch of anger in his face. Again we came together, and again I made a telling touch. "Third time," he told me, and his battle smile lit up his weathered face. We came together again with a jolt in the joy of struggle, and I overmatched him cleanly.

Twice more we clashed before Burrich suddenly stepped back from one of my blows. He lowered his ax to the floor and stood, hunkered slightly forward until his breath came easy again. Then he straightened and looked at Verity. "He's got it," he said huskily. "He's caught the knack of it now. Not that he's fully honed yet. Drill will make him sharper, but you've made a wise choice for him. The ax is his weapon."

Verity nodded slowly. "And he is mine."

16

Verity's Ships

IN THE THIRD *summer of the Red-Ship War, the Six Duchies warships were blooded. Although they numbered only four, they represented an important change in tactics to defending our realm. Our encounters that spring with the Red-Ships swiftly taught us that we had forgotten much of being warriors. The Raiders were right; we had become a race of farmers. But we were farmers who had determined to take a stand and fight. We quickly found the Raiders to be resourceful and savage fighters. This was true to the extent that none of them ever surrendered or were taken alive. That, perhaps, should have been our first clue as to the nature of Forging and what we actually battled, but at the time it was too subtle a hint, and we were too busy surviving to wonder at it.*

⤞⊚⧽

The rest of that winter passed as swiftly as the first half had dragged. The separate parts of my life became like beads and I the string that ran through them all. I believe if I had ever paused to consider the intricacy of all I did to keep those parts separate, I would have found it impossible. But I was young then, much younger than I suspected, and somehow I found the energy and time to do and be it all.

My day began before dawn, with a session with Verity. At

least twice a week Burrich and his axes were included. But most often it was Verity and I alone. He worked on my Skill sense, but not as Galen had. He had specific tasks in mind for me, and these were what he trained me in. I learned to see through his eyes, and to give him the use of mine. I practiced being aware of the subtle way he would steer my attention, and in keeping up a constant mental commentary that kept him informed of all that was going on around us. This involved me leaving the tower, and carrying his presence about with me like a hawk on my wrist as I went about my other daily tasks. At first a few hours were as long as I could sustain the Skill bond, but as time went on I managed to share my mind with him for days at a time. The bond did weaken with the passing of time, however. It was not a true Skilling from me to Verity, but a touch-imposed bond that had to be renewed. It still gave me a sense of accomplishment to be able to do at least this much.

I put in a fair share of time in the Queen's Garden, moving and then shifting again benches and statuary and pots, until Kettricken was finally satisfied with the arrangements there. For those hours I always made sure Verity was with me. I hoped it would do him good to see his queen as others saw her, especially when she was caught up in the enthusiasm of her snowy garden spot. Glowing pink-cheeked and gold-haired, wind-kissed and lively: this was how I showed her to him. He heard her speak freely of the pleasure she hoped this garden would bring him. Was this a betrayal of Kettricken's confidences to me? I pushed such uneasiness firmly away. I took him with me when I paid my duties to Patience and Lacey.

I also tried to carry Verity out and among the folk more. Since he had begun his heavy Skill duties, he was seldom among the common folk he had once so enjoyed. I took him to the kitchen, and the watch room, to the stables, and down to the taverns in Buckkeep Town. For his part, he steered me to the boat sheds, where I watched the final work being done on his ships. Later I frequently visited the dock where the ships were tied, to talk to the crews as they got to know their vessels. I made him aware of the grumbling of the men who thought it treasonous that some Outislander refugees had been allowed to become crew members of our defense vessels. It was plain to any eye that these men were experienced in the handling of sleek raiding vessels and were making our ships more effective with their expertise. Plain, too, that many of the Six Duchies men resented and distrusted the handful of immigrants among them. I was not sure if Verity's decision to use them had been wise. However, I said nothing of my own doubts, but only showed him the mutterings of other men.

He was with me, too, the times when I called upon Shrewd. I learned to make my visits in late morning or early afternoon. Wallace seldom admitted me easily, and it always seemed there were others in the room, serving maids I did not know, a workman ostensibly repairing a door, when I went to visit. I hoped impatiently for a chance to talk with him privately about my marriage ambitions. The Fool was there always, and kept his word not to show friendship to me before other eyes. His mockery was sharp and stinging, and even though I knew its purpose, he still could manage to fluster or irritate me. The only satisfaction I could take was in the changes I saw in the room. Someone had tattled to Mistress Hasty about the state of the King's chamber.

In the midst of the Winterfest activities, such a troop of housemaids and serving boys flocked to the room that it brought the festivities to the King. Mistress Hasty, fists on hips, stood at the center of the room and oversaw it all, all the while berating Wallace for ever letting things reach such a state. Evidently he had been assuring her that he had been personally seeing to the tidying and laundering in an effort to keep the King from being disturbed. I spent one very merry afternoon there, for the activity awoke Shrewd, and soon he seemed almost his old self. He hushed Mistress Hasty when she berated her own folk for laxness, and instead exchanged banter with them as floors were scrubbed, fresh reeds strewn, and the furniture rubbed well with fragrant cleansing oil. Mistress Hasty bundled a veritable mountain of quilts atop the King while she ordered the windows opened and the room aired. She, too, sniffed at all the ashes and burn pots. I quietly suggested that Wallace might best see to their cleansing, as he was most familiar with the qualities of the herbs that had burned there. He was a much more docile and tractable man when he returned with the pots. I wondered if he himself knew just what effect his smokes had upon Shrewd. But if these smokes were not his doing, then whose? The Fool and I exchanged more than one secret significant glance.

Not only was the chamber scrubbed out, but made bright as well, with festive candles and wreaths, evergreens and bare branches of trees gilded and hung with painted nuts. It brought the color back into the King's cheeks. I sensed Verity's quiet approval. When that night the King descended from his chambers to join us in the Great Hall, and actually called out for his favorite musicians and songs, I took it as a personal victory.

Some moments were solely mine, of course, and not just my nights with Molly. As often as I could manage, I would creep off from the Keep to run and hunt with my wolf. Bonded as our minds were, I was never completely isolated from him, but a simple mind link did not have the deep satisfaction of sharing a hunt. It is hard to express the completeness of two beings moving as one, for a single purpose. Those times were really the fulfilling of our bond. But even when I went days without physically seeing him, he was with me. His presence was like a perfume, which one is aware of greatly when one first encounters it, but then becomes simply a part of the air one breathes. I knew he was there in small ways. My sense of smell seemed more acute, and I attributed this to his expertise in reading what the air brought me. I became more aware of others around me, as if his consciousness were guarding my back, and alerting me to small sensory clues I might otherwise have ignored. Food was more savory, perfumes more tangible. I tried not to extend this logic to my appetite for Molly's company. I knew he was there, but as he had promised, he did nothing overt to make me aware of him at such times.

A month after Winterfest, I found myself thrown into a new labor. Verity had told me he wished me aboard a ship. I found myself summoned one day to the deck of the *Rurisk* and assigned a spot at an oar. The master of the vessel openly wondered why he had been sent a twig when he asked for a log. I could not dispute the question. Most of the men around me were brawny fellows and seasoned ship hands. My only possible chance to prove myself was to throw myself into my tasks

with every bit of energy I could muster. At least I had the
satisfaction of knowing I was not alone in my inexperience.
While the other men aboard had all served in some fashion on
other vessels, all save the Outislanders among the crew were
new to this style of ship.

Verity had had to seek out our oldest shipwrights to come
up with men who knew how to build a fighting ship. The
Rurisk was the largest of the four vessels launched at
Winterfest. The lines of the boat were sleek and sinuous, and
her shallow draft meant that she could skim across a calm sea
like an insect on a pond, or ride out rough swell as handily as
any gull. In two of the other boats, the planking was pegged
edge to edge into the ribs, but the *Rurisk* and her smaller sister
ship *Constance* were clinker-built, with the planking over-
lapped. The *Rurisk* had been built by Mastfish, and the planking was well fitted, but still had the give to withstand any
battering the seas might offer. Only a minimum of caulking
with tarred rope had been needed, so lovingly had this ship
been crafted. Her mast of pine supported a sail of spun flax
reinforced with rope. Verity's buck graced the sail of the
Rurisk.

The new ships still smelled of wood shavings and tarred
rope. Her decks were scarcely scarred, and the oars were clean
their entire length. Soon the *Rurisk* would take on a character
of its own; a bit of marlinspike work to make it easier to grip an
oar, a splice in a line, all the nicks and dings of a well-used
ship. But for now, the *Rurisk* was as green as we were. When
we took the ship out, it reminded me of an inexperienced rider
on a green-broke horse. She sidled about, shied and curtsied
among the waves, and then, as we all found a rhythm, stepped
out and cut through the water like a greased knife.

It was Verity's will that I immerse myself in these new
skills. I was given a bunk in the warehouse with the rest of my
shipmates. I learned to be unobtrusive, but energetic in jumping to any order. The master was Six Duchies through and
through, but the mate was an Outislander, and he it was who
really taught us to handle the *Rurisk* and just what the ship
could do. There were two other Outislander immigrants
aboard, and when we weren't learning the ship or doing main-

tenance and sleeping, they congregated and spoke quietly among themselves. I wondered that they didn't see how this set the Six Duchies folk to muttering. My bunk was near to theirs, and oftentimes as I lay trying to fall asleep, I was aware of Verity urging me to pay attention to soft words spoken in a language I didn't understand. So I did, knowing that he made more sense of the sounds than I did. After a time I came to realize that it was not so very different from the Duchies' tongue, and that I could understand some of what was said for myself. I found no talk of betrayal or mutiny among them. Only soft, sad words of kin Forged away from them by their own countrymen, and harsh bitter vows of vengeance to be carried out against their own kind. They were not so different from the Six Duchies men and women of the crew. Almost everyone onboard had lost someone to Forging. Guiltily, I wondered how many of those lost souls I had sent into the oblivion of death. It made a small barrier between me and the other crew members.

Despite the fury of the winter storms, we took the ships out nearly every day. We fought mock battles against each other, practicing techniques for grappling or ramming another ship, and also gauging a leap so that one boarded the other vessel rather than ending up in the waters between them. Our master was at pains to explain all our advantages to us. The enemy we would encounter would be far from home, and already worn from weeks at sea. They would have been living aboard their vessels, cramped and punished by the weather, while we would be fresh each day and well fed. The rigors of their journey would demand that every oarsman must also be a Raider, while we could carry additional fighters who could use their bows or board another vessel while keeping our oars fully manned. Often I saw the mate shaking his head over these words. Privately, he confided to his fellows that the rigors of a raiding journey were what made a crew hard and fierce. How could soft, well-fed farmers hope to prevail against sea-honed Red-Ship Raiders?

One day out of ten I was allowed a day to myself, and those days I spent at the Keep. They were scarcely restful. I reported to King Shrewd, detailing to him my experiences aboard the *Rurisk,* and taking pleasure in the interest that awoke in his eyes at such times. He seemed better, but was still not the robust King I remembered from my youth. Patience and Lacey likewise demanded a visit, and I made a dutiful call on Kettricken as well. An hour or two for Nighteyes, a clandestine visit to Molly's chambers, and then the excuses to hurry back to my own chamber for the rest of the night so that I might be there when Chade would summon me for his quizzings. The following dawn, a brief report to Verity, where with a touch he renewed our Skill bond. Often it was a relief to return to the crew's quarters to get a solid night of sleep.

Finally, as winter drew to a close, chance afforded me an opportunity to speak privately with Shrewd. I had gone to his chambers on one of my days away from the boat, to report to him on our training progress. Shrewd was in better health than usual and was sitting up in his chair by the fire. Wallace was not about that day. Instead, there was a young woman, ostensibly tidying the chamber, but almost certainly spying for Regal. The Fool, too, was underfoot as always, and taking a keen pleasure in making her uncomfortable. I had grown up with the Fool, and had always accepted his white skin and colorless eyes as simply the way he was. The woman obviously felt differently. She began, it must be admitted, peering at the Fool whenever she thought he might not be paying attention. But as soon as he noted it, he began to peek back at her, and each time affected a more lascivious glance than the last. She became more and more nervous, and when finally she must pass by us with her bucket, and the Fool sent Ratsy on his scepter to peek up under her skirts, she leaped back with a shriek, dousing herself and the floor she had just scrubbed with dirty water. Shrewd rebuked the Fool, who groveled extravagantly and remorselessly, and then dismissed the woman to get dry clothes on. I sprang to my opportunity.

She was scarcely clear of the room before I spoke. "My liege, there is something I have been wishing to petition you about, for some time."

Some note in my voice must have alerted both fool and king, for I instantly had their undivided attention. I glared at the Fool, and he knew plainly I wished him to withdraw, but instead he leaned closer, actually resting his head against Shrewd's knee as he simpered at me infuriatingly. I refused to let it rattle me. I looked at the King beseechingly.

"You may speak, FitzChivalry," he said formally.

I drew a breath. "My liege, I would ask your permission to marry."

The Fool's eyes grew round with surprise. But my king smiled as indulgently as if I were a child begging a sweetmeat. "So. Finally, it has come. But surely you mean to court her first?"

My heart was thundering in my chest. My king looked entirely too knowing. But pleased, very pleased. I dared to hope. "May it please my king, I fear I have already begun to court her. Yet know I did not intend to do so presumptuously. It just . . . came about."

He laughed good-naturedly. "Yes. Some things do. Though when you did not speak out sooner, I wondered what your intentions were, and if the lady had deceived herself."

My mouth went dry. I could not breathe. How much did he know? He smiled at my terror.

"I have no objections. In fact, I am well pleased with your choice. . . ."

The smile that broke out on my face was amazingly echoed by one on the Fool's countenance. I drew a trembling breath, until Shrewd continued, "But her father has reservations. He has told me that he would like to delay this, at least until her older sisters are pledged."

"What?" I could barely utter the word. Confusion whirled in me. Shrewd smiled benignly.

"Your lady, it seems, is as good as her name. Celerity asked her father for permission to court you the very day you left for Buckkeep. I think you won her heart when you spoke so plainly to Virago. But Brawndy denied her, for the reason I have told you. I understand the lady raised quite a storm with her father, but Brawndy is a firm man. He did, however, send word to us, lest we take offense. He wishes us to know he has no opposition to the match itself, only to her preceding her sisters in marriage. I acceded in this. She is, I believe, but fourteen?"

I could not speak.

"Do not look so distressed, boy. You are both young, and there is plenty of time. While he does not choose to allow a formal courting to begin as yet, I am sure he does not intend that you shall not see each other." King Shrewd looked on me so tolerantly, with so much kindliness in his eyes. The Fool's eyes flickered back and forth between us. I could not read his face.

I was trembling, as I had not in months. I would not allow this to continue, to become any worse than it was already. I found my tongue, formed words in my dry throat. "My king, that is not the lady I was considering."

Silence descended. I met my king's eyes, and saw his look change. Had I not been so desperate, I know I would have looked aside from that displeasure. Instead I looked at him beseechingly, praying he might understand. When he did not speak further, I attempted to.

"My king, the woman I speak of is presently a lady's maid, but in her own right she is not a servant. She is—"

"Be silent."

It could not have been sharper if he had struck me. I was still.

Shrewd looked me up and down carefully. When he spoke, it was with the force of all his majesty. I thought I felt even the pressure of the Skill in his voice. "Be entirely certain of what I say to you, FitzChivalry. Brawndy is my friend, as well as my duke. Neither he, nor his daughter, shall be offended or slighted by you. At this time you shall court no one. No one. I suggest you consider well all you are offered when Brawndy considers you favorably as a match for Celerity. He makes no matter of your birth. Few others would do so. Celerity will have land and a title of her own. As will you, from me, if you have the wisdom to bide your time and do well by the lady. You will come to find that it is the wise choice. I will tell you when you may begin courting her."

I summoned the last of my courage. "My king, please, I—"

"Enough, Chivalry! You have heard my word on this subject. There is no more to say!"

A short time later he dismissed me, and I went shaking from his rooms. I do not know if fury or heartbreak were the force behind my trembling. I thought again of how he had called me by my father's name. Perhaps, I told myself spitefully, it was because in his heart he knew I would do as my father had done. I would wed for love. Even, I thought savagely, if I had to wait until King Shrewd was in his grave, for Verity to keep his word to me. I went back to my rooms. To have wept would have been a relief. I could not even find tears. Instead I lay on my bed and stared at the hangings. I could not imagine telling Molly what had just transpired between my king and me. Telling myself that not to speak was also a deception, I resolved to find a way to tell her. But not right away. A time would come, I promised myself, a time when I could explain and she would understand. I would wait for it. Until then, I would not think about it. Nor, I resolved coldly, would I go to my king unless I were summoned.

As spring drew closer Verity arranged his ships and men as carefully as tokens on a game board. The watchtowers on the coast were always manned, and their signal fires kept ever ready for a torch. Such signal fires were for the purpose of alerting local citizenry that Red-Ships had been sighted. He took the remaining members of the Skill coterie Galen had fashioned and distributed them in the towers and on the ships. Serene, my nemesis and heart of Galen's coterie, remained at Buckkeep. Privately I wondered why Verity used her there, as a center for the coterie, rather than having each member Skill individually to him. With Galen's death, and August's forced retirement from the coterie, Serene had taken on Galen's post, and seemed to consider herself the Skill Master. In some ways, she almost became him. It was not just that she stalked Buckkeep in austere silence and wore always a disapproving frown. She seemed to have acquired his testiness and foul humor as well. The serving folk now spoke of her with the same dread and distaste they had once reserved for Galen. I understood she had taken over Galen's personal quarters as well. I avoided her assiduously on the days I was home. I would have been more relieved if Verity had placed her elsewhere.

But it was not up to me to question my king-in-waiting's decisions.

Justin, a tall gangly young man with two years on me, was
assigned as coterie member to the *Rurisk*. He had despised me
since we had studied the Skill together and I had failed so
spectacularly at it. He snubbed me at every opportunity. I bit
my tongue and did my best not to encounter him. The close
quarters of the ship made that difficult. It was not a comfortable situation.

After great debate, with himself and me, Verity placed
Carrod aboard the *Constance,* Burl at the Neatbay Tower, and
sent Will far north, to the Red Tower up in Bearns that commanded such a wide view of the sea as well as the surrounding
countryside. Once he had arranged their tokens on his maps, it
made a reality of the pathetic thinness of our defenses. "It
reminds me of the old folktale of the beggar who had but a hat
to cover his nakedness," I told Verity. He smiled without humor.

"Would that I could move my ships as swiftly as he did his
hat," he wished grimly.

Two of the ships Verity set to duty as roving patrol vessels.
Two he kept in reserve, one docked at Buckkeep, and that was
the *Rurisk,* while the *Stag* anchored in South Cove. It was a
pitifully small fleet to protect the Six Duchies' straggling
coastline. A second set of ships was being constructed, but it
was not expected they would be finished soon. The best of the
seasoned wood had been used in the first four vessels, and his
shipwrights cautioned him he would be wiser to wait than to
attempt to use green wood. It chafed him, but he listened to
them.

Early spring saw us practicing drills. The coterie members,
Verity privately told me, functioned almost as well as carrier
pigeons at relaying simple messages. His situation with me was
a more frustrating one. For his own reasons, he had chosen not
to disclose to anyone his training of me in the Skill. I believe he
was enjoying the advantages of being able to go with me and
observe and listen undetected to the everyday life of Buckkeep
Town. I understood that the *Rurisk*'s master had been given
word that I was to be heeded if I requested a sudden change in

course or announced that we were required at a certain location immediately. I fear he saw this mostly as Verity's indulgence of his bastard nephew, but in this he followed his orders.

Then, one early spring morning, we reported to our ship for yet another practice. We functioned well as a crew now in maneuvering our ship. This exercise was to have us rendezvous with the *Constance* at an undisclosed location. It was a Skill exercise that so far we had not succeeded at. We were resigned to a frustrating day, save for Justin, who was stonily intent on succeeding. Arms crossed on his chest, dressed all in dark blue (I believe he thought the blue robe made him appear more Skilled), he stood on the dock and stared out into the thick fog that blanketed the ocean. I was forced to pass him as I put a keg of water aboard.

"To you, Bastard, it's an opaque blanket. But to me, all is as clear as a mirror."

"How unfortunate for you," I said kindly, ignoring his use of the word "bastard." I had all but forgotten how much sting could be put into a word. "I'd rather see the fog than your face of a morning." Petty, but satisfying. I had the additional satisfaction of watching his robe bind about his legs as he boarded. I was sensibly dressed, in snug leggings, an undershirt of soft cotton, and a leather jerkin over that. I had considered some sort of mail, but Burrich had shook his head over it. "Better to die cleanly from a weapon's wound than fall overboard and drown," he'd advised me.

Verity had quirked a smile at that. "Let's not burden him with too much overconfidence," he suggested wryly, and even Burrich had smiled. After a moment.

So I had abandoned any thought of mail or armor. At any rate, today would be a rowing day, and what I wore was comfortable for that. No shoulder seams to strain against, no sleeves to catch on my forearms. I was inordinately proud of the chest and shoulders I was developing. Even Molly had expressed an astonished approval. I settled into my seat and rolled my shoulders, smiling as I thought of her. I'd had far too little time with her lately. Well, only time would cure that. Summer brought the Raiders. As the long fair days came on I'd

have even less time with her. Autumn could not come too soon
for me.

We settled in, a full complement of rowers and warriors.
At some moment, as ropes were cast off and the steersman
took his post and the oars began their steady beat, we became
one animal. It was a phenomenon I had noted before. Perhaps I
was more sensitized to it, nerves abraded clean by my Skill
sharing with Verity. Perhaps it was that all the men and women
onboard shared a single purpose, and that for most of them it
was vengeance. Whatever it was, it lent a unity to us that I had
never sensed before in a group of folk. Perhaps, I thought, this
was a shadow of what it was to belong to a coterie. I felt a pang
of regret, of opportunities lost.

You are my coterie. Verity, like a whisper behind me. And
somewhere, from the distant hills, something less than a sigh.
Are we not pack?

I do have you, I thought back to them. Then I settled in
and paid attention to what I was doing. Oars and backs dipped
and rose in unison and the *Rurisk* went nosing boldly out into
the fog. Our sail hung limp. In a moment we were a world unto
ourselves. Sounds of water, of the rhythmic unity of our
breathing as we rowed. A few of the fighters spoke softly
among themselves, their words and thoughts muffled by the
mist. Up in the bow, Justin stood beside the master, staring out
into the fog. His brow was lined, his eyes distant, and I knew he
reached for Carrod aboard the *Constance.* Almost idly, I
reached out, too, to see if I could sense what he Skilled.

Stop that! warned Verity, and I drew back feeling as if he
slapped my hand. *I'm not ready for anyone to have suspicions
about you yet.*

There was a lot behind that warning, more than I could
devote myself to just now. As if what I had begun to do were
actually a very dangerous action. I wondered what he feared,
but I concentrated on the steady rhythm of my rowing, and let
my eyes stare into the infinite gray. Most of that morning
passed in a mist. Several times Justin asked the master to have
the steersman change his course. It made little difference that I
could see, save in the texture of the rowing. All of the inside of
a fog bank looks much the same. The steady physical effort,

the lack of anything to focus on put me into a waking dream about nothing.

The cries of the young watchman broke my trance. " 'Ware treachery!" he cried out, his shrill voice deepening as blood engulfed it. "We are attacked!"

I leaped up from my rowing bench, staring wildly all about. Fog. Only my oar dangling and skipping on the surface of the water, while my fellow oarsmen glared at me for breaking the rhythm. "You, Fitz! What ails you?" the master demanded. Justin stood at his side, clear-browed and self-righteous.

"I . . . my back cramped. Sorry." I stooped to my oar again.

"Kelpy, relieve him. Stretch and move about a bit, boy, then take your oar back," the mate directed in his thick accent.

"Aye, sir." I acknowledged his order and stood to let Kelpy have my bench and oar. It did feel good to pause. My shoulders cracked when I rolled them. But I was ashamed, too, to take a rest when the others did not. I rubbed my eyes and gave my head a rattle, wondering what nightmare had seized me so firmly. What watchman? Where?

Antler Island. They came in under the fog's cover. No town there, but the signal tower. I think they intend to slaughter the watchers, and then do their best to destroy the towers. A brilliant strategy. Antler Island is one of our first lines of defense. The outer tower watches the sea, the inner tower passes on the signals to both Buckkeep and Neatbay. Verity's thoughts, almost calm with the same steadiness that seizes one as a weapon is brought to the ready. Then, after a moment: *The single-minded slug is so intent on reaching Carrod, he won't let me through. Fitz. Go to the master. Tell him Antler Island. If you get into the channel, the current will practically fly you to the cove where the tower is. The Raiders are there already, but they'll have to beat against the current to get out again. Go now, and you may catch them on the beach. NOW!*

Easier to give orders than to obey them, I thought, and then hurried forward. "Sir?" I requested, and then stood an eternity waiting for the master to turn and speak to me, while the mate glared at me for going straight to the master rather than through him.

"Oarsman?" the master said at last.

"Antler Island. If we make for it now, and catch the current in the channel, we'll practically fly to the cove where the tower is."

"That's true. Do you read currents, then, boy? It's a useful skill. I thought I was the only man onboard with an idea of where we actually are."

"No, sir." I took a deep breath. Verity had ordered this. "We should go there, sir. Now."

The "now" drew his brows together in a frown.

"What is this nonsense!" Justin demanded angrily. "Are you trying to make me look a fool? You'd sensed that we were getting close to each other, didn't you? Why do you want me to fail? So you won't feel so alone?"

I wanted to kill him. Instead I drew myself straight and told the truth. "A secret order from the King-in-Waiting, sir. One I was to pass on to you at this time." I addressed only the master. He dismissed me with a nod and I returned to my bench and took my oar back from Kelpy. The master stared dispassionately into the mist.

"Jharck. Have the steersman swing her about and catch the current. Take her a bit deeper into the channel."

The mate nodded stiffly, and in an instant we had changed course. Our sail bellied slightly, and it was as Verity had said it would be. The current combined with our rowing sent us skating down the channel. Time passes oddly in a fog. All senses are distorted in it. I don't know how long I rowed, but soon Nighteyes whispered that there was a tinge of smoke in the air, and almost immediately we became aware of the cries of men in battle, carrying clear but ghostly through the fog. I saw Jharck the mate exchange glances with the master. "Put your backs into it!" he snarled suddenly. "We've got a Red-Ship attacking our tower."

Another moment and the stink of the smoke was distinguishable in the fog, as were the battle cries and screams of men. Sudden strength leaped in me, and about me I saw the same, the clenched jaws, the muscles that knotted and sprang as we rowed, even a different tang to the sweat of those who labored around me. If we had been one creature before, we were now part of the same enraged beast. I felt the leap of the heating anger igniting and spreading. It was a Wit thing, a surging of hearts on the animal level that flooded us with hate.

We drove the *Rurisk* forward, sending her skimming up finally into the shallows of the cove, and then we leaped out and ran her up the beach just as we had practiced. The fog was a treacherous ally, concealing us from the attackers that we would in turn attack, but concealing from us also the lay of the land and a view of exactly what was happening. Weapons were seized and we rushed toward the sounds of the fighting. Justin stayed with the *Rurisk,* standing and staring into the fog toward Buckkeep earnestly, as if that would help him Skill the news to Serene.

The Red-Ship was drawn up on the sand, just as the *Rurisk* was. Not far from her were the two small boats that served as ferries to the mainland. Both had been stove in. There had been Six Duchies men down here on the beach when the Red-Ships arrived. Some of them were still there. Carnage. We ran past crumpled bodies leaking blood into the sand. All of them seemed to be our own folk. Suddenly the Antler Island inner tower loomed gray above us. Atop it her signal fire burned a ghostly yellow in the fog. The tower was besieged. The Raiders were dark muscular men, wiry rather than massive. Most were heavily bearded and their hair hung black and wild to their shoulders. They wore body armor of plaited leather and carried heavy blades and axes. Some wore helms of metal. Their bared arms were marked in coils of scarlet, but whether this was tattoo or paint I could not tell. They were confident, swaggering, laughing, and talking like workmen completing a task. The guardians of the tower were cornered; the structure had been built as a basis for a signal light, not as a defensible rampart. It was a matter of time before all the cornered men were dead. The Outislanders did not look back toward us as we came pouring up the rocky incline. They believed they had nothing to fear from behind them. One tower gate hung on its hinges, a huddle of men inside barricaded behind a wall of bodies. As we advanced they sent a thin hail of arrows out toward the encircled Raiders. None of them hit.

I gave a cry between a whoop and a howl, terrible fear and vengeful joy merged into one sound. The emotions of those who ran beside me found vent in me, and spurred me on. The attackers turned to see us as we closed with them.

We caught the Raiders between us. Our ship's crew outnumbered them, and at sight of us, the beleaguered defenders of the tower took heart and poured forth themselves. Scattered bodies about the tower gate attested to several efforts before this one. The young watchman still lay where I had seen him fall in my dream. Blood had spilled from his mouth and soaked into his embroidered shirt. A dagger thrown from behind had taken him. An odd detail to note as we rushed forward to join in the melee.

There was no strategy, no formation, no plan of battle. Simply a group of men and women suddenly offered the opportunity for vengeance. It was more than enough.

If I thought I had been one with the crew before, I was now engulfed in them. Emotions battered and thrust me forward. I will never know how much or which feelings were my own. They overwhelmed me, and FitzChivalry was lost in them. I became the emotions of the crew. Ax raised, roaring, I led the way. I had no desire for the position I had seized. Instead I was thrust forward by the crew's extreme desire for someone to follow. I suddenly wanted to kill as many Raiders as I could, as fast as I could. I wanted my muscles to crack with each swing, I wanted to fling myself forward through a tide of dispossessed souls, to tread on the bodies of fallen Raiders. And I did.

I had heard legends of berserks. I had thought them animalistic brutes, powered by bloodlust, insensitive to the damage they wrought. Perhaps, instead, they were oversensitized, unable to defend their own minds from the emotions that rushed in to drive them, unable to heed the pain signals of their own bodies. I do not know.

I have heard tales of myself on that day. Even a song. I do not recall that I frothed and roared as I fought. But neither do I recall that I did not. Somewhere, within me, were both Verity and Nighteyes, but they, too, were drowned in the passions of those around me. I know I killed the first Raider that went down before our mad rush. I also know that I finished the last standing man, in a battle we fought ax to ax. The song says it was the master of the Red-Ship vessel. I suppose it could have been. His leather surcoat was well made, and spattered with the blood of other men. I don't recall another thing about him except how my ax crushed his helm deep into his skull, and how the blood gouted from beneath the metal as he sank to his knees.

So the battle ended, and defenders rushed forth to embrace our crew, to shout the victory and pound one another's backs. The change was too much for me. I stood, leaning on my ax, and wondered where my strength had fled. The anger had abandoned me as suddenly as carris seed leaves an addict. I felt drained and disoriented, as if I had wakened from one dream into another. I could have dropped and slept among the bodies, so totally exhausted was I. It was Nonge, one of the Outislanders in the crew, who brought me water, and then walked me clear of the bodies so I could sit down to drink it. Then he waded back in among the carnage to join in the looting. When he came back to me a while later, he held out to me a bloodied medallion. It was hammered gold, on a silver chain. A crescent moon. When I did not reach to take it from him, he looped it over the gory head of my ax. "It was Harek's," he said, finding the Six Duchies words slowly. "You fought him well. He died well. He'd want you to have it. He was a good man, before the Korriks took his heart." I did not even ask him which one had been Harek. I did not want any of them to have names.

After a time I began to be alive again. I helped to clear the bodies from the door of the tower, and then from the battlefield. The Raiders we burned, the Six Duchies men we laid out and covered, for kin to claim. I remember odd things about that long afternoon. How a dead man's heels leave a snaking trail in the sand when you drag him. How the young watchman with the dagger in him wasn't quite dead when we went to gather him up. Not that he lasted long afterward. He soon was just one more body to add to a row that was too long already.

We left our warriors with what was left of the tower guard

to help fill up the watches until more men could be sent out.
We admired the vessel we'd captured. Verity would be pleased,
I thought to myself. Another ship. A very well-made one. I
knew all these things, but felt nothing about any of them. We
returned to the *Rurisk,* where a pale Justin awaited us. In a
numbed silence, we launched the *Rurisk* and took our places at
the oars and headed back to Buckkeep.

We encountered other boats before we were halfway there.
A hastily organized flotilla of fishing vessels laden with
soldiers hailed us. The King-in-Waiting had sent them, at Justin's urgently Skilled behest. They seemed almost disappointed
to find that the fighting was over, but our master assured them
they would be welcomed at the tower. That, I think, was when I
realized I could no longer sense Verity. And hadn't for some
time. I groped after Nighteyes immediately, as another man
might grope after his purse. He was there. But distant. Exhausted, and awed. *Never have I smelled so much blood,* he
told me. I agreed. I still stank of it.

Verity had been busy. We were scarcely off the *Rurisk*
before there was another crew aboard to take her back to Antler
Island Tower. Watch soldiers and another crew of rowers set
her heavy in the water. Verity's prize would be tied up at his
home dock by this night. Another open boat followed them, to
bring our slain home. The master, the mate, and Justin departed on provided horses to report directly to Verity. I felt
only relief that I hadn't been summoned also. Instead, I went
with my crew mates. Faster than I would have thought possible,
word of the battle and our prize spread through Buckkeep
Town. There was not a tavern that was not anxious to pour us
full of ale and hear our exploits. It was almost like a second
battle frenzy, for wherever we went, folk ignited around us
with savage satisfaction in what we had done. I felt drunk on
the surging emotions of those around me long before the ale
overwhelmed me. Not that I held back from that. I told few
tales of what we had done, but my drinking more than made up
for it. I threw up twice, once in an alley, and later in the street. I
drank more to kill the taste of the vomit. Somewhere in the
back of my mind, Nighteyes was frantic. *Poison. That water is
poisoned.* I couldn't frame a thought to reassure him.

Sometime before morning, Burrich hauled me out of a tavern. He was stonily sober, and his eyes were anxious. In the street outside the tavern, he stopped by a dying torch in a street sconce. "There's still blood on your face," he told me, and stood me up straight. He took out his handkerchief, dipped it in a rain barrel, and wiped my face as he had not since I was a child. I swayed under his touch. I looked into his eyes and forced my gaze to focus.

"I've killed before," I said helplessly. "Why is this so different? Why does it sicken me like this, afterward?"

"Because it does," he said softly. He put an arm around my shoulders, and I was surprised we were of a height. The walk back to Buckkeep was steep. Very long. Very quiet. He sent me to the baths and told me to go to bed afterward.

I should have stayed in my own bed, but I had not the sense. Luckily the castle was abuzz, and one more drunk clambering up a staircase was not remarkable. Stupidly, I went to Molly's room. She let me in. But when I tried to touch her, she pulled away from me. "You're drunk," she told me, almost crying. "I told you, I promised myself to never kiss a drunk. Or be kissed by one."

"But I'm not drunk that way," I insisted.

"There's only one way to be drunk," she told me. And turned me out of her rooms, untouched.

By noon the next day, I knew how much I had hurt her by not coming straight to her to find comfort. I could understand what she felt. But I also knew that what I had carried that night was nothing to take home to someone you loved. I wanted to explain that to her. But a boy came running up to me to tell me I was needed on the *Rurisk,* and right now. I gave him a penny for his troubles and watched him dash off with it. Once, I had been the boy earning the penny. I thought of Kerry. I tried to remember him as the boy with the penny in his hand, running at my side, but forever now he was the Forged one dead on a table. No one, I told myself, had been taken for Forging yesterday.

Then I headed down to the docks. On the way I stopped at the stable. I gave the crescent moon over into Burrich's hands. "Keep this safe for me," I asked him. "And there will be a bit more, my crewshare from the raid. I want to have you hold it for me . . . what I make at doing this. It's for Molly. So if ever I don't come back, you be certain she gets it. She doesn't like being a servant.''

I hadn't spoken so plainly of her to Burrich in a long time. A line creased his brow, but he took the bloodied moon. ''What would your father say to me?'' he wondered aloud as I turned wearily away from him.

''I don't know,'' I told him bluntly. ''I never knew him. Only you.''

''FitzChivalry.''

I turned back to him. Burrich met my eyes as he spoke. ''I don't know what he'd say to me. But I know I can say this for him, to you. I'm proud of you. It's not the kind of work a man does that says he can be proud or not. It's how he does it. Be proud of yourself.''

''I will try,'' I told him quietly. I went back to my ship.

Our next encounter with a Red-Ship was a less decisive victory. We met them on the sea, and they were not surprised, for they had seen us coming. Our master stood the course, and I think they were surprised when we began the engagement by ramming them. We sheared off a number of their oars, but missed the steering oar we had targeted. There was little damage to the ship itself; the Red-Ships were as flexible as fish. Our grapples flew. We outnumbered them, and the master intended to use that advantage. Our warriors boarded them, and half our oarsmen lost their heads and jumped in, too. It became a chaos that spread briefly to our own decks. It took every bit of will I could muster to withstand the vortex of emotions that engulfed us, but I stayed with my oar as I had been ordered. Nonge, at his oar, watched me strangely. I gripped my oar and ground my teeth until I could find myself. I muttered a curse when I discovered that I'd lost Verity again.

I think our warriors let up a bit when they knew we had reduced our enemy's crew to where they could no longer manage their vessel. It was a mistake. One of the Raiders set fire to their own sail while a second one attempted to chop through their own planking. I guess they hoped the fire would spread and they could take us down with them. Certainly at the end they fought with no care for the damage they took to their ship or their own bodies. Our fighters finally finished them, and we got the fire put out, but the prize we towed back to Buckkeep was smoking and damaged, and man for man, we had lost more lives than they had. Still, it was a victory, we told ourselves. This time, when the others went out drinking, I had the sense to seek out Molly. And early the next morning, I found an hour or two for Nighteyes. We went hunting together, good clean hunting, and he tried to persuade me to run away with him. I made the mistake of telling him that he could leave if he wished, meaning only the best for him, and hurt his feelings. It took me another hour to convey to him what I had meant. I went back to my ship wondering if my ties were worth the effort it took to keep them intact. Nighteyes assured me they were.

That was the last clear victory for the *Rurisk*. It was far from the last battle of the summer. No, the clear pleasant weather stretched impossibly long before us, and every fine day was a day when I might kill someone. I tried not to count them as days on which I might be killed. We had many skirmishes, and gave pursuit many times, and it did seem there were fewer raids attempted in the area we regularly patrolled. Somehow that only made it all the more frustrating. And there were successful raids for the Red-Ships, times when we put into a town but an hour or so after they had left, and could do no more than help stack bodies or put out fires. Then Verity would roar and curse in my mind that he could not get messages more swiftly, that there were not enough ships and watches to be everywhere. I would rather have faced the fury of a battle than Verity's savage frustration racking through my brain. There was never any end in sight, save the respite that bad weather might bring us. We could not even put an accurate number to the Red-Ships that plagued us, for they were painted identically, and as like as peas in a pod. Or drops of blood on the sand.

While I was an oarsman on the *Rurisk* that summer, we had one other encounter with a Red-Ship that is worth telling for the strangeness of it. On a clear summer night, we had been tumbled from our beds in the crew shed and sent racing toward our ship. Verity had sensed a Red-Ship lurking off Buck Point. He wanted us to overtake it in the dark.

Justin stood in our prow, Skill-linked to Serene in Verity's tower. Verity was a wordless mumble in my mind as he felt our way through the dark toward the ship he sensed. And something else? I could feel him groping out, beyond the Red-Ship, like a man feeling forward in the darkness. I sensed his uneasiness. We were allowed no talk, and our oars were muffled as we came closer. Nighteyes whispered to me that he had scent of them, and then we spotted them. Long and low and dark, the Red-Ship was cutting through the water ahead of us. A sudden cry went up from their deck; they had seen us. Our master shouted to us to lay into our oars, but as we did, a sick wave of fear engulfed me. My heart began to hammer, my hands to tremble. The terror that swept through me was a child's nameless fear of things lurking in the dark, a helpless fear. I gripped my oar but could find no strength to ply it.

"Korrikska," I heard a man groan in a thick Outislander accent. I think it was Nonge. I became aware I was not the only one unmanned. There was no steady beat to our oars. Some sat on their sea chests, head bowed over their oars, while others rowed frantically, but out of rhythm, the blades of the oars skipping and slapping against the water. We skittered on the surface like a crippled skater bug while the Red-Ship forged purposefully toward us. I lifted up my eyes and watched my death coming for me. The blood hammered so in my ears that I could not hear the cries of the panic-stricken men and women about me. I could not even take a breath. I lifted up my eyes to the heavens.

Beyond the Red-Ship, almost glowing on the black water, was a white ship. This was no raiding vessel; this was a ship, easily three times the size of the Red-Ship, her two sails reefed, riding at anchor on the quiet water. Ghosts strode her deck, or Forged ones. I felt no hint of life from them, and yet they moved purposefully, readying a small boat to be lowered over the side. A man stood on the afterdeck. The moment I saw him, I could not look away.

He was cloaked in gray, yet I saw him limned against the dark sky as clearly as if a lantern illuminated him. I swear I could see his eyes, the jut of his nose, the dark curly beard that framed his mouth. He laughed at me. ''Here's one come to us!'' he called out to someone, and lifted a hand. He pointed it at me, and laughed aloud again, and I felt my heart squeeze in my chest. He looked at me with a terrible singleness, as if I alone of our crew were his prey. I looked back at him, and I saw him, but I could not sense him. *There! There!* I shrieked the word aloud, or perhaps the Skill I could never control sent it bounding off the insides of my skull. There was no response. No Verity, no Nighteyes, no one, nothing. I was alone. All the world had gone silent and still. Around me my crew fellows rattled with terror and cried out aloud, but I felt nothing. They were no longer there. No one was there. No gull, no fish in the sea, no life anywhere as far as any of my inner senses would reach. The cloaked figure on the ship leaned far out on the rail, the accusing finger pointing at me. He was laughing. I was alone. It was a loneliness too great to be endured. It wrapped me, coiled about me, blanketed me, and began to smother me.

I *repelled* at it.

In a reflex I did not know I had, I used the Wit to push away from it as hard as I could. Physically, I was the one that flew backward, landing in the bilge atop the thwarts, tangled in the feet of the other oarsmen. I saw the figure on the ship stumble, sag, and then tumble over the side. The splash was not large, but there was only one. If he rose to the surface at all, I did not see it.

Nor was there time to look for him. The Red-Ship hit us amidships, shattering oars and sending oarsmen flying. The Outislanders were shouting with their confidence, mocking us with their laughter as they leaped from their ship to ours. I scrabbled to my feet and lunged to my bench, reaching for my ax. Around me, the others were making the same sort of recovery. We were not battle ready, but neither were we paralyzed by fear anymore. Steel met our boarders and battle was joined.

There is no place so dark as the open water at night. Fellow and foe were indistinguishable in the dark. A man leaped onto me; I caught at the leather of his foreign harness, bore him down, and strangled him. After the numbness that had briefly clenched me, there was a savage relief in his terror beating against me. I think it happened quickly. When I straightened up, the other boat was pulling away from us. She had only about half her oarsmen, and there was still fighting on our decks, but she was leaving her men. Our master was shouting at us to finish them and be after the Red-Ship. It was a useless command. By the time we had killed them and thrown them off our decks, the other ship was lost in the darkness. Justin was down, throttled and battered, alive, but incapable of Skilling to Verity just then. In any case, one bank of our oars was a splintered mess. Our master cursed us all soundly as the oars were redistributed and shipped, but it was too late. He shouted us down to stillness, but we could hear nothing, and see nothing. I stood on my sea chest and turned slowly in a complete circle. Empty black water. Of the oared vessel, no sign. But even more strange to me was what I spoke aloud. "The white ship was at anchor. But she's gone, too!"

Around me, heads turned to stare at me. "White ship?"

"Are you all right, Fitz?"

"A Red-Ship, boy, it was a Red-Ship we fought."

"Speak not of a white ship. To see a white ship is to see your own death. Bad luck." This last was hissed to me by Nonge. I opened my mouth to object that I had seen an actual ship, not some vision of disaster. He shook his head at me and then turned away to stare out over the empty water. I closed my mouth and sat down slowly. No one else had seen it. Nor did any of the others speak of the terrible fear that had gripped us and changed our battle plans to panic. When we got back to town that night, the way it was told in the taverns was that we had come up on the ship, engaged battle, only to have the Red-Ship flee us. No evidence remained of that encounter but some shattered oars, some injuries, and some Outislander blood on our decks.

When I privately conferred with both Verity and Nighteyes, neither had seen anything. Verity told me that I had excluded him as soon as we sighted the other vessel. Nighteyes was miffed to admit that I had completely closed myself to him as well. Nonge would say nothing to me of white ships; he was not much for conversation on any topic. Later I found mention of the white ship in a scroll of old legends. There it was an accursed ship, where the souls of drowned sailors unworthy of the sea would work forever for a merciless master. I was forced to set aside all mention of it or be thought mad.

The rest of the summer, the Red-Ships evaded the *Rurisk*. We would catch sight of them, and give chase, but never managed to run one down. Once it was our good fortune to chase one that had just raided. She threw her captives overboard to lighten herself and fled us. Of twelve folk they threw in, we rescued nine, and returned them unForged to their village. The three who drowned before we reached them were mourned, but all agreed it was a better fate than Forging.

The other ships had much the same luck. The *Constance* came upon Raiders in the midst of attacking a village. They didn't manage a quick victory, but had the foresight to damage the beached Red-Ship so that the Raiders could not make a clean escape. It took days to hunt them all down, for they scattered into the woodlands when they saw what had been done to their ship. The other vessels had similar experiences: we gave chase, we drove off Raiders, the other ships even had some few successes at sinking raiding vessels, but we captured no more intact ships that summer.

So, the Forgings were reduced, and each time we sent a ship down, we told ourselves it was one less. But it never seemed to make a difference in how many remained. In one sense, we brought hope to the folk of Six Duchies. In another way, we gave them despair, for despite all we did, we could not drive the threat of Raiders from our shore.

For me, that long summer was a time of terrible isolation and incredible closeness. Verity was often with me, yet I found I could never seem to sustain the contact once any sort of fighting had begun. Verity himself was aware of the maelstrom of emotions that threatened to overwhelm me each time our crew engaged. He ventured the theory that in attempting to defend against the thoughts and feelings of others, I set up my boundaries so firmly that not even he could breach them. He also suggested that this might mean I was strong in the Skill, stronger than he was even, but so sensitized that to let down my barriers during a battle drowned me in the consciousnesses of everyone around me. It was an interesting theory, but one that offered no practical solutions to the problem. Still, in the days when I carried Verity about, I developed a feel for him that I had for no other man, save perhaps Burrich. With chilling familiarity, I knew how the Skill hunger gnawed at him.

When I was a boy, Kerry and I had one day climbed a tall cliff over the ocean. When we reached the top and looked out over it, he confessed to me an almost overwhelming impulse to fling himself off. I think this was akin to what Verity felt. The pleasure of the Skill enticed him, and he longed to fling all of himself, every ounce of his being, out into its web. His close contact with me only fed it. And yet we did too much good for the Six Duchies for him to give it up, even though the Skill was eating him hollow. Perforce I shared with him many of his hours at his lonely tower window, the hard chair where he sat, the weariness that destroyed his appetite for food, even the deep bone aches of inactivity. I witnessed how he wasted away.

I do not know that it is good to know someone so well. Nighteyes was jealous, and said so plainly. At least with him it was an open anger about being slighted, as he saw it. It was a more difficult thing with Molly.

She could see no real reason why I had to be away so much. Why did I, of all people, have to crew on one of the warships? The reason I was able to give her, that Verity wished me to, satisfied her not at all. Our brief times together began to have a predictable pattern. We would come together in a storm of passion, find peace in each other briefly, and then begin to wrangle about things. She was lonely, she hated being a servant, the little bit of money she could set aside for herself grew terribly slowly, she missed me, why did I have to be gone so much when I was the only thing that made her life bearable? I approached her once with the offer of what money I had earned aboard the ship, but she stiffened as if I had called her a whore. She would take nothing of mine until we were joined in marriage before all. And I could offer her no real hope as to when that might happen. I still had never found the moment in which to reveal Shrewd's plans for Celerity and me. We were apart so much, we lost the threads of one another's day-to-day lives, and when we did come together, we always rechewed the bitter rinds of the same arguments over and over.

One night, when I came to her, I found her with her hair bound back all in red ribbons and graceful silver earrings shaped like willow leaves dangling against her bare neck. Clad as she was in her simple white nightgown, the sight of her took my breath away. Later, during a quieter moment when we had breath for speaking, I complimented her on the earrings. Artlessly, she told me that when Prince Regal had last come to buy candles of her, he had gifted her with them, for he said he was so pleased with what she created that he scarcely felt he paid her what such finely scented candles were worth. She smiled proudly as she told me this, her fingers toying with my warrior's queue while her own hair and ribbons tangled wildly upon the pillows. I do not know what she saw in my face, but it widened her eyes and she drew back from me.

"You will take gifts from Regal?" I asked her coldly. "You will not accept from me coin that I have honestly earned, but you take jewelry from that . . ."

I teetered on the edge of treason, but could find no word to express what I thought of him.

Molly's eyes narrowed, and it was my turn to draw back. "What should I have said to him? 'No, sir, I cannot accept your largesse, until you marry me'? There is not between Regal and me what there is between us. This was a perquisite from a customer, such as is often given to a skilled craftsman. Why did you think he gave them to me? In exchange for my favors?"

We stared at one another, and after a time I managed to speak what she was almost willing to accept as an apology. But then I made the mistake of suggesting that perhaps he had given them to her solely because he knew it would vex me. And then she wanted to know how Regal might know what was between us, and did I think her work so poor that a largesse such as the earrings was not due her? Suffice to say that we mended our quarrels as well as we could in the short time we had left together. But a mended pot is never as sound as a whole one, and I returned to the ship as lonely as if I had had no time at all with her.

In the times when I leaned on my oar and kept perfect rhythm and tried to think of nothing at all, I often found myself

missing Patience and Lacey, Chade, Kettricken, or even Burrich. The few times I was able to call on our queen-in-waiting
that summer, I always found her on her tower-top garden. It
was a beautiful place, but despite her efforts, it was nothing
like the other Buckkeep gardens had ever been. There was too
much of the Mountains in her for her ever to convert entirely to
our ways. There was a honed simplicity to how she arranged
and trained the plants. Simple stones had been added, and bare
driftwood branches twisted and smoothed by the sea rested
against them in stark beauty. I could have meditated calmly
there, but it was not a place to loll in the warm wind of summer, and I suspected that was how Verity had recalled it. She
kept herself busy there, and enjoyed it, but it did not bond her
to Verity as she had once believed it would. She was as beautiful as ever, but always her blue eyes were clouded gray with a
preoccupation and a worry. Her brow was furrowed so often
that when she did relax her face, one saw the pale lines of the
skin the sun had never reached. In the times I spent with her
there, she often dismissed most of her ladies, and then quizzed
me about the *Rurisk*'s activities as thoroughly as if she were
Verity himself. When I had finished reporting to her, often she
folded her lips into a firm line and went to stare out over the top
of the tower wall and beyond to the sea touching the edge of
the sky. Toward the end of summer, as she was staring so one
afternoon, I ventured close to her to ask to be excused from her
presence to return to my ship. She scarcely seemed to hear
what I had asked. Instead, she said softly, "There has to be a
final solution. Nothing, no one can go on like this. There must
be a way to make an end of this."

"Autumn storms come soon, my lady queen. Already,
frost has touched some of your vines. Storms are never far
behind the first chilling, and with them comes peace for us."

"Peace? Ha." She snorted in disbelief. "Is it peace to lie
awake and wonder who will die next, where will they attack
next year? That is not peace. That is a torture. There must be a
way to put an end to the Red-Ships. And I intend to find it."

Her words sounded almost like a threat.

17

Interludes

OF STONE WERE *their bones made, of the sparkling veined stone of the Mountains. Their flesh was made of the shining salts of the earth. But their hearts were made of the hearts of wise men.*

They came from afar, those men, a long and trying way. They did not hesitate to lay down the lives that had become a weariness to them. They ended their days and began eternities, they put aside flesh and donned stone, they let fall their weapons and rose on new wings. Elderlings.

⎯⎯ ⧓ ⎯⎯

When the King finally summoned me, I went to him. True to my promise to myself, I had not voluntarily gone to his chambers since that afternoon. Bitterness still ate at me over his arrangements with Duke Brawndy concerning Celerity and me. But a summons from one's king was not a thing to be ignored, regardless of what anger churned inside me still.

He sent for me on an autumn morning. It had been at least two months since I had last stood before King Shrewd. I had ignored the wounded looks the Fool flung at me when I encountered him, and turned aside Verity's occasional query as to why I had not sought out Shrewd's chamber. It was easy enough. Wallace still guarded his door like a serpent on the hearth, and the King's poor health was no secret from anyone. No one was admitted to his rooms before noon anymore. So I told myself this morning summons betokened something important.

I had thought the morning would belong to me. An unseasonably early and vicious autumn storm had pounded us for two days. The driving wind was merciless, while drenching rain promised that anyone in an open boat would be fully occupied with bailing. I had spent the evening before in the tavern with the rest of the *Rurisk*'s crew, toasting the storm and wishing the Red-Ships the full kiss of it. I had come back to the Keep to tumble soddenly into my bed, certain that I could sleep as long as I wished the next morning. But a determined page had battered my door until sleep forsook me, and then delivered to me the King's formal summons.

I washed, shaved, smoothed my hair back into a tail, and donned clean clothes. I steeled myself to betray nothing of my smoldering resentment. When I was confident I was master of myself, I left my chamber. I presented myself at the King's door. I fully expected Wallace to sneer and turn me aside. But this morning he opened the door promptly to my knock. His glance was still disapproving, but he immediately ushered me into the King's presence.

Shrewd sat before his hearth in a cushioned chair. Despite myself, my heart sank at how wasted he had become. His skin was papery and translucent as parchment, his fingers gone to bone. His face sagged, skin drooping where flesh had once held it firm. His dark eyes were sunken into his face. He clasped his hands in his lap in a gesture I knew well. Thus did I hold my hands to conceal the trembling that occasionally overtook me still. A small table at his elbow supported a censer, and Smoke rose from it. The fumes already made a bluish haze about the rafters. The Fool sprawled disconsolately at his feet.

"FitzChivalry is here, Your Majesty," Wallace announced me.

The King started as if poked, then shifted his gaze to me. I moved to stand before him.

"FitzChivalry," the King acknowledged me.

There was no force behind the words, no presence at all.

My bitterness was still strong in me, but it could not drown the pain I felt to see him so. He was still my king.

"My king, I have come as you ordered," I said formally. I tried to cling to my coldness.

He looked at me wearily. He turned his head aside, coughed once into his shoulder. "So I see. Good." He stared at me for a moment. He took a deep breath that whispered into his lungs. "A messenger arrived from Duke Brawndy of Bearns last night. He brought the harvest reports and such, mostly news for Regal. But Brawndy's daughter Celerity also sent this scroll. For you."

He held it out to me. A small scroll, bound with a yellow ribbon and sealed with a blob of green wax. Reluctantly I stepped forward to take it.

"Brawndy's messenger will be returning to Bearns this afternoon. I am sure that by that time you will have created an appropriate reply." His tone did not make this a request. He coughed again. The roil of conflicting emotions I felt for him soured in my stomach.

"If I may," I requested, and when the King did not object, I broke the seal on the scroll and untied the ribbon. I unwound it to discover a second scroll coiled inside it. I glanced over the first one. Celerity wrote with a clear, firm hand. I unrolled the second one and considered it briefly. I looked up to find Shrewd's eyes on me. I met them without emotion. "She writes to wish me well, and to send me a copy of a scroll she found in the Ripplekeep libraries. Or, properly, a copy of what was still legible. From the wrapping, she believed it pertained to Elderlings. She had noted my interest in them during my visit to Ripplekeep. It looks to me as if the writing was actually philosophy, or perhaps poetry."

I offered the scrolls back to Shrewd. After a moment he took them. He unfurled the first one and held it out at arm's length. He furrowed his brow, glared at it briefly, then set it down in his lap. "My eyes are befogged, sometimes, of a morning," he said. He rerolled the two scrolls together, carefully, as if it were a difficult task. "You will write her a proper note of thanks."

"Yes, my king." My voice was carefully formal. I received once more the scrolls he proffered me. When I had stood before him for some moments longer while he stared through me, I ventured, "Am I dismissed, my king?"

"No." He coughed again, more heavily. He took another long sighing breath. "You are not dismissed. Had I dismissed you, it would have been years ago. I would have let you grow up in some backwater village. Or seen that you did not grow up at all. No, FitzChivalry, I have not *dismissed* you." Something of his old presence came back into his voice. "Some years ago I struck a bargain with you. You have kept your end of it. And kept it well. I know how I am served by you, even when you do not see fit to report to me personally. I know how you serve me, even when you are brimming with anger at me. I could ask little more than what you have given me." He coughed again, suddenly, a dry racking cough. When he could speak, it was not to me.

"Fool, a goblet of the warmed wine, please. And ask Wallace for the . . . spicing herbs to season it." The Fool rose immediately, but I saw no willingness on his face. Instead, as he passed behind the King's chair, he gave me a look that should have drawn blood. The King made a small gesture at me to wait. He rubbed his eyes, and then stilled his hands once more in his lap. "I but seek to keep my end of the bargain," he resumed. "I promised to see to your needs. I would do more than that. I would see you wed to a lady of quality. I would see you . . . ah. Thank you."

The Fool was back with the wine. I marked how he filled the goblet but halfway, and how the King picked it up with both hands. I caught a waft of unfamiliar herbs mingled with the rising scent of the wine. The rim of the goblet chattered twice against Shrewd's teeth before he stilled it with his mouth. He took a long deep draft of it. He swallowed, then sat still a moment longer, eyes closed as if listening. When he opened his eyes to look up at me once more, he seemed briefly puzzled. After a moment he recollected himself. "I would see you with a title, and land to steward." He lifted the goblet and drank again. He sat holding it, warming his thin hands around it while he considered me. "I should like to remind you it is no small thing that Brawndy deems you a fit match for his daughter. He does not hesitate over your birth. Celerity will come to you with a title and estates of her own. Your match gives me the opportunity to see that you have the same. I wish only the best for you. Is this so hard to understand?''

The question left me free to speak. I took a breath and tried to reach him. ''My king, I know you wish me well. I am well aware of the honor that Duke Brawndy does me. The Lady Celerity is as fair a woman as any man could wish. But the lady is not of my choosing.''

His look darkened. ''Now there you sound like Verity,'' he said crossly. ''Or your father. I think they suckled stubbornness from their mother's breasts.'' He lifted the goblet and drained it off. He leaned back in his chair and shook his head. ''Fool. More wine, please.''

''I have heard the rumors,'' he resumed heavily after the Fool had taken his cup. ''Regal brings them to me and whispers them like a kitchen maid. As if they were important. Chickens clucking. Dogs barking. Just as important.'' I watched the Fool obediently refill the goblet, his reluctance plain in every muscle of his slender body. Wallace appeared as if summoned by magic. He heaped more Smoke onto the censer, blew on a tiny coal with carefully pursed lips until the heap smoldered, and then drifted away. Shrewd leaned carefully so that the fumes curled past his face. He breathed in, gave a tiny cough, then drew in more of the Smoke. He leaned back in his chair. A silent Fool stood holding his wine.

''Regal claims you are enamored of a chambermaid. That you pursue her relentlessly. Well, all men are young once. As are all maids.'' He accepted his goblet and drank again. I stood before him, biting the inside of my cheek, willing my eyes to stoniness. My traitorous hands began the shaking that physical exertion no longer wrung from them. I longed to cross my arms on my chest to still them, but I kept my hands at my side. I concentrated on not crushing the small scroll I gripped.

King Shrewd lowered the goblet. He set it on the table at his elbow and sighed heavily. He let his lax hands uncurl quietly in his lap as he leaned his head back against the cushions of his chair. ''FitzChivalry,'' he said.

I stood numbly before him and waited. I watched as his

eyelids drooped, then closed. Then opened again a crack. His head wavered slightly as he spoke. "You have Constance's angry mouth," he said. His eyes drooped again. "I would like to do well by you," he muttered. After a moment a snore buzzed from his slack mouth. And still I stood before him and gazed at him. My king.

When finally I dropped my eyes from him, I saw the only thing that could have wrenched me into greater turmoil. The Fool huddled disconsolately at Shrewd's feet, his knees drawn up to his chest. He stared at me furiously, his mouth a flat line. Clear tears brimmed in his colorless eyes.

I fled.

Within my chamber, I paced a bit before my hearth. The feelings inside me seared me. I forced myself to calmness, sat down, and took out pen and paper. I penned a brief, correct note of thanks to Duke Brawndy's daughter, carefully rolled it up, and sealed it with wax. I stood up, tugged my shirt straight, smoothed my hair back, and then threw the scroll onto my hearth fire.

Then I sat down again with my writing tools. I wrote a letter to Celerity, the shy girl who had flirted with me at table, and stood with me on the cliffs in the wind and waited for a challenge that never came. I thanked her for the scroll. And then I wrote to her of my summer. Of pulling an oar on the *Rurisk,* day after day. Of my clumsiness with a sword that made the ax my weapon. I wrote of our first battle, in ruthless detail, and of how sickened I had been afterward. I told her of sitting frozen with terror at my oar while a Red-Ship attacked us. I neglected to mention the white ship I had seen. I finished by confiding that I was still troubled by tremors occasionally as the aftermath of my long illness in the Mountains. I read it over carefully. Satisfied that I had presented myself as a common oarsman, an oaf, a coward, and an invalid, I rolled the letter into a scroll and tied it with the same yellow ribbon she had used. I did not seal it. I did not care who read it. Secretly, I hoped that Duke Brawndy might peruse this letter to his daughter, and then forbid her ever to mention my name again.

When I knocked again at King Shrewd's door, Wallace answered it with his usual grim displeasure. He took the scroll from me as if it were dirtied with something, and shut the door firmly in my face. As I went back up to my room I thought of what three poisons I would use on him, were I given the opportunity. It was less complicated than thinking of my king.

Back in my room, I flung myself down on my bed. I wished it were night and safe to go to Molly. Then I thought of my secrets, and even that pleasant anticipation vanished. I bounced up from my bed to fling open the window shutters wide to the storm. But even the weather cheated me.

Blue had cracked the overcast wide, to admit a watery sunlight. A bank of black clouds boiling and mountaining over the sea promised that this respite would not last long. But for now the wind and the rain had ceased. There was even a hint of warmth in the air.

Nighteyes came to my mind immediately.

It's too wet to hunt. Water clings to every blade of grass. Besides, it's full daylight. Only men are stupid enough to hunt in full daylight.

Lazy hound, I rebuked him. I knew he was curled, nose to tail, in his den. I sensed the warm satiation of his full belly.

Perhaps tonight, he suggested, and drifted back to sleep.

I pulled back from him, then snatched up my cloak. My feelings were not conducive to a day within walls. I left the Keep and headed down toward Buckkeep Town. Anger at Shrewd's decision for me warred with dismay at how he had weakened. I walked briskly, trying to escape the King's trembling hands, his drugged sleep. Damn Wallace! He had stolen my king from me. My king had stolen my life from me. I refused to think anymore.

Dripping water and yellow-edged leaves fell from the trees as I passed. Birds sang clearly and joyously at the unexpected respite from the downpour. The sun grew stronger, making everything sparkle with the wet, and steaming rich scents up from the earth. Despite my turmoil, the beauty of the day touched me.

The recent downpours had washed Buckkeep Town clean. I found myself in the market, in the midst of an eager crowd. Everywhere folk hurried to make purchases and rush them home before the storm could drench us again. The amiable busyness and friendly clatter was at odds with my sour mood, and I glared about the market until a bright scarlet cloak and hood caught my eye. My heart turned over inside me. Molly might wear servant blue about the Keep, but when she came to market, she still wore her old cloak of red. No doubt Patience had sent her out on errands during this respite from the rain. I watched her, unnoticed, as she haggled stubbornly over packets of spiced tea from Chalced. I loved the jut of her chin as she shook her head at the merchant. A sudden inspiration lifted my heart.

I had coin in my pockets, my oarsman's pay. With it I bought four sweet apples, two currant buns, a bottle of wine, and some pepper meat. I bought, too, a string bag to carry it in and a thick wool blanket. Red. It took every bit of every skill Chade had ever taught me to make my purchases and still keep sight of Molly without being seen. Even more taxing was to follow her unobtrusively as she went to the milliner's to buy silk ribbon, and then to trail behind her as she started up toward Buckkeep.

At a certain bend in the path, overshadowed by trees, I caught up to her. She gasped as I light-footed up behind her, to lift and swing her suddenly in my arms. I landed her on her feet and kissed her soundly. Why it felt so different to kiss her out of doors and under the bright sun, I cannot say. I only know all my troubles suddenly fell from me.

I made a sweeping bow to her. "Will my lady join me for a brief repast?"

"Oh, we cannot," she replied, but her eyes sparkled. "We'll be seen."

I made a great show of glancing about us, then seized her arm and pulled her from the road. Beneath the trees there was not much underbrush. I hurried her through the dripping trees, over a fallen log, and past a patch of buckbrush that clutched wetly at our legs. When we came to the cliff's edge above the boom and susurrus of the ocean, we scrambled like children down the rock chimneys to get to a small sandy beach.

Driftwood was piled haphazardly in this nook in the bay. An overhang of the cliffs had kept a small patch of sand and shale almost dry, but did not block the reaching sunbeams. The sun shone now with surprising warmth. Molly took the food and blanket from me, and commanded that I assemble firewood. She was the one who finally got the damp wood to burn, however. The salt made it burn with greens and blues, and it gave enough heat that we both set aside our cloaks and hoods. It was so good to sit with her and look at her out under the open sky, with the bright sun bringing out glints on her hair and the wind rosying her cheeks. It was so good to laugh aloud, to mingle our voices with the cries of the gulls without fear of awakening anyone. We drank the wine from the bottle, and ate with our fingers, and then walked down to the waves' edge to wash the stickiness from our hands.

For a brief time we scrambled about on the rocks and driftwood, looking for treasures tossed up by the storm. I felt more like myself than I had since I had returned from the Mountains, and Molly looked very much the wild hoyden of my childhood. Her hair came unbraided and blew about her face. She slipped when I chased her, and stumbled into a tide pool. We went back to the blanket, where she took off her shoes and hose to let them dry by the fire. She leaned back on the blanket and stretched.

Taking things off suddenly seemed a very good idea.

Molly was not as sure of that as I. "There's fully as much stone as sand under this blanket. I've no wish to go back with bruises up my back!"

I leaned over her to kiss her. "Am not I worth it?" I asked persuasively.

"You? Of course not!" She gave me a sudden push that sent me sprawling on my back. Then she flung herself boldly atop me. "But I am."

The wild sparkle in her eyes as she looked down on me took my breath away. After she had claimed me ruthlessly, I discovered she had been right, both about the rocks, and her being well worth the bruises. I had never seen anything so spectacular as the blue sky glimpsed through the cascade of her hair over my face.

Afterward she lay more than half atop me and we dozed in the chill sweet air. Eventually she sat up, shivering, to pull her clothing back around herself. Reluctantly I watched her lace up her blouse again. Darkness and candlelight had always hidden too much from me. She looked down at my bemused look, stuck her tongue out at me, then paused. My hair had come loose from its tail. She pulled it forward to frame my face, then set a fold of her red cloak across my forehead. She shook her head. "You would have been a singularly homely girl."

I snorted. "I am not so much better as a man, either."

She looked offended. "You are not ill-favored." She traced a finger down the musculature of my chest speculatively. "The other day, in the washing courts, some were saying you were the best thing to come out of the stables since Burrich. I think it is your hair. It is not near as coarse as most Buck men." She twined strands of it through her fingers.

"Burrich!" I said with a snort. "You cannot tell me he is favored among the women!"

She quirked a brow at me. "And why not? He is a very well-made man, and clean and mannered besides. He has good teeth, and such eyes! His dark humors are daunting, but not a few would like to try their hands at lightening those. The washing maids agreed that day that were he to turn up in their sheets, they would not hurry to shake him out."

"But that is not likely to happen," I pointed out.

"No," she agreed pensively. "That was another thing they agreed on. Only one claimed to have ever had him, and she admitted he was very drunk at the time. At a Springfest, I believe she said." Molly glanced at me, then laughed aloud at the incredulous look on my face. "She said," Molly went on teasingly, " 'He has used his time well amongst the stallions to learn their ways. I carried the mark of his teeth on my shoulders for a week.' "

"That cannot be," I declared. My ears burned for Burrich's sake. "He would not mistreat a woman, no matter how drunk he was."

"Silly boy!" Molly shook her head over me as her nimble fingers set to braiding her hair up again. "No one said she was mistreated." She glanced at me coyly. "Or displeased."

"I still do not believe it," I declared. Burrich? And the woman had liked it?

"Has he really a small scar, here, shaped like a crescent

moon?'' She put her hand high on my hip and looked at me from under her lashes.

I opened my mouth, shut it again. ''I cannot believe that women chatter of such things,'' I said at last.

''In the washing courts, they talk of little else,'' Molly divulged calmly.

I bit my tongue until curiosity overwhelmed me. ''What do they say of Hands?'' When we had worked in the stables together, his tales of women had always astonished me.

''That he has pretty eyes and lashes, but that all the rest of him needs to be washed. Several times.''

I laughed joyously, and saved the words for when next he bragged to me. ''And Regal?'' I encouraged her.

''Regal. Umm.'' She smiled dreamily at me, then laughed at the scowl on my face. ''We do not speak of the Princes, my dear. Some propriety is kept.''

I pulled her back down beside me and kissed her. She fit her body to mine and we lay still under the arching blue sky. Peace that had eluded me for so long now filled me. I knew that nothing could ever part us, not the plans of kings nor the vagaries of fate. It seemed, finally, to be the right time to tell her of my problems with Shrewd and Celerity. She rested warm against me and listened silently as I spilled out to her the foolishness of the King's plan and my bitterness at the awkward position it brought me. It did not occur to me that I was an idiot until I felt a warm tear spill and then slide down the side of my neck.

''Molly?'' I asked in surprise as I sat up to look at her. ''What's wrong?''

''What's wrong?'' Her voice went high on the words. She took a shuddering breath. ''You lie beside me and tell me you are promised to another. And then you ask me what's wrong?''

''The only one I am promised to is you,'' I said firmly.

''It's not that simple, FitzChivalry.'' Her eyes were very wide and serious. ''What will you do when the King tells you that you must court her?''

''Stop bathing?'' I asked.

I had hoped she would laugh. Instead she pulled away

from me. She looked at me with a world of sorrow in her eyes. "We haven't got a chance. Not a hope."

As if to prove her words, the sky darkened suddenly above us and the squall winds rose. Molly leaped to her feet, snatching up her cloak and shaking sand from it. "I'm going to get soaked. I should have been back to Buckkeep hours ago." She spoke flatly, as if those two things were the only concerns that she had.

"Molly, they would have to kill me to keep me from you," I said angrily.

She gathered up her market purchases. "Fitz, you sound like a child," she said quietly. "A foolish, stubborn child." With a pattering like flung pebbles, the first raindrops began to hit. They made dimples in the sand and swept across the rain in sheets. Her words had left me speechless. I could not think of a worse thing for her to have said to me.

I gathered up the red blanket, shook sand from it. She pulled her cloak tight against the wind that whipped at it. "Best we don't go back together," she observed. She came close to me, stood on tiptoe to kiss the angle of my jaw. I could not decide who I was angrier at: King Shrewd for creating this mess, or Molly for believing in it. I did not turn to her kiss. She said nothing of that, but only hurried away, to scrabble lightly up the rock chimney and vanish from sight.

All joy had gone out of my afternoon. What had been as perfect as a gleaming seashell was now crushed bits under my feet. I walked disconsolately home through gusting winds and pelting rain. I had not rebound my hair and it whipped in lank strands across my face. The wet blanket stank as only wool can and bled red dye onto my hands. I went up to my room and dried off, then amused myself by carefully preparing the perfect poison for Wallace. One that would rack his bowels before he died. When the powder was mixed fine and put in a twist of paper, I set it down and looked at it. For a while I considered taking it myself. Instead, I took up needle and thread to devise a pocket inside my cuff where I could carry it. I wondered if I would ever use it. The wondering made me feel more a coward than ever.

I did not go down to dinner. I did not go up to Molly. I

opened my shutters and let the storm spill rain across my floor. I let the hearth fire go out and refused to light any candles. It seemed a time for gestures like those. When Chade opened his passage to me, I ignored it. I sat on the foot of my bed, staring out into the rain.

After a time I heard hesitant footsteps come down the stairs. Chade appeared in my darkened room like a wraith. He glared at me, then crossed to the shutters and slammed them shut. As he hooked them he asked me angrily, "Have you any idea of the kind of draft that creates in my rooms?" When I didn't reply, he lifted his head and snuffed, for all the world like a wolf. "Have you been working with baneleaf in here?" he asked suddenly. He came to stand before me. "Fitz, you've not done anything stupid, have you?"

"Stupid? Me?" I choked on a laugh.

Chade stooped to peer into my face. "Come up to my chamber," he said, in an almost kindly voice. He took my arm and I went with him.

The cheery room, the crackling fire, the autumn fruit ripe in a bowl; all of it clashed so badly with what I felt that I wanted to smash things. Instead I asked Chade, "Does anything feel worse than being angry with people you love?"

After a bit he spoke. "Watching someone you love die. And being angry, but not knowing where to direct it. I think that's worse."

I flung myself onto a side chair, kicked my feet out in front of me. "Shrewd has taken up Regal's habits. Smoke. Mirthweed. El only knows what else in his wine. This morning, without his drugs, he began to shake, and then he drank them mixed with his wine, took a chestful of Smoke, and went to sleep in my face. After telling me, again, that I must court and marry Celerity, for my own good." The words spilled from me. I had no doubt that Chade already knew of everything I told him.

I pinned Chade with my eyes. "I love Molly," I told him bluntly. "I have told Shrewd that I love another. Yet he insists that I will be paired with Celerity. He asks how I cannot understand he means the best for me. How cannot he understand that I wish to wed whom I love?"

Chade looked considering. "Have you discussed this with Verity?"

"What good would that do? He could not even save himself from being wed off to a woman he did not desire." I felt disloyal to Kettricken as I said this. But I knew it was true.

"Would you care for wine?" Chade asked me mildly. "It might calm you."

"No."

He raised his eyebrows at me.

"No. Thank you. After watching Shrewd 'calm' himself with wine this morning . . ." I let my complaint trail away. "Was that man never young?"

"Once, he was very young." Chade permitted himself a small smile. "Perhaps he remembers that Constance was a woman chosen for him by his parents. He did not court her willingly, nor wed her gladly. It took her death to make him know how deeply he had come to love her. Desire, on the other hand, he chose for himself, in a passion that fevered him." He paused. "I will not speak ill of the dead."

"This is different," I said.

"How?"

"I am not to be king. Who I wed affects no one but me."

"Would it were that simple," Chade said softly. "Can you believe you can refuse Celerity's courtship without offending Brawndy? At a time when the Six Duchies need every bond of unity?"

"I am convinced I can make her decide she does not want me."

"How? By being an oaf? And shaming Shrewd?"

I felt caged. I tried to think of solutions, but found only one answer in me. "I will marry no one except Molly." I felt better simply by saying it aloud. I met Chade's eyes.

He shook his head. "Then you will marry no one," he pointed out.

"Perhaps not," I acceded. "Perhaps we shall never be married in name. But we shall have a life together—"

"And little bastards of your own."

I stood convulsively, my fists knotting of their own accord.

"Don't say that," I warned Chade. I turned away from him to glare into his fire.

"I wouldn't. But everyone else will." He sighed. "Fitz, Fitz, Fitz." He came up behind me and put his hands on my shoulders. Very, very gently, he said, "It might be best to let her go."

The touch and the gentleness had disarmed me of my anger. I lifted my hands to cover my face. "I cannot," I said through my fingers. "I need her."

"What does Molly need?"

A little chandlery with beehives in the backyard of it. Children. A legitimate husband. "You are doing this for Shrewd. To make me do as he wishes," I accused Chade.

He lifted his hands from my shoulders. I listened to him walk away, to wine being poured into a single cup. He brought his wine with him to his chair and sat down before his fire.

"I'm sorry."

He looked at me. "Someday, FitzChivalry," he warned me, "those words will not be enough. Sometimes it is easier to pull a knife out of a man than to ask him to forget words you have uttered. Even words uttered in anger."

"I am sorry," I repeated.

"So am I," he said shortly.

After a time I asked humbly, "Why did you wish to see me tonight?"

He sighed. "Forged ones. Southwest of Buckkeep."

I felt ill. "I had thought I would not have to do that anymore," I said quietly. "When Verity put me on a ship to Skill for him, he said that perhaps—"

"This does not come from Verity. It was reported to Shrewd, and he wishes it taken care of. Verity is already . . . overtaxed. We do not wish to trouble him with anything else just now."

I put my head back into my hands. "Is there no one else who can do this?" I begged him.

"Only you and I are trained for this."

"I did not mean you," I said wearily. "I do not expect you to do that sort of work anymore."

"Don't you?" I looked up to find the anger back in his

eyes. "You arrogant pup! Who do you think kept them from Buckkeep all summer, Fitz, while you were out on the *Rurisk*? Did you think that because you wished to avoid a task, the need for such work ceased?"

I was as shamed then as I have ever been. I looked aside from his anger. "Oh, Chade. I am sorry."

"Sorry that you avoided it? Or sorry that you thought me incapable of doing it anymore?"

"Both. Everything." I conceded it all suddenly. "Please, Chade, if one more person I care about becomes angry with me, I don't think I shall be able to bear it." I lifted my head and looked at him steadily until he was forced to meet my eyes.

He lifted a hand to scratch at his beard. "It has been a long summer for both of us. Pray El for storms to drive the Red-Ships away forever."

We sat a time in silence.

"Sometimes," Chade observed, "it would be much easier to die for one's king than to give one's life to him."

I bowed my head in assent. The rest of the night we spent preparing the poisons I would need in order to begin killing for my king again.

18

Elderlings

THE AUTUMN OF *the third year of the Red-Ship War was a bitter one for King-in-Waiting Verity. His warships had* been his dream. He had founded all his hopes on them. He had believed he could rid his own coast of Raiders, and be so successful at it that he could send forth raiders against the hostile Outisland coasts even during the worst of the winter storms. Despite early victories, the ships never achieved the command of the coast that he had hoped they would. Early winter found him with a fleet of five ships, two of which had recently sustained severe damage. One intact was the captured Red-Ship vessel, which had been refitted and sent out with a crew to assist in patrols and escorting of merchant vessels. When the winds of autumn finally arrived, only one of his ships' masters expressed enough confidence in his crew's skills and his vessel to be willing to undertake a raid against the Outislander coasts. The other masters argued for at least one winter of practicing seamanship along our own rough coast, and another summer of practicing tactics, before undertaking such an ambitious goal.

Verity would not send unwilling men, but neither did he hide his disappointment. He expressed it well when he outfitted the one willing ship, for the Revenge, as the vessel had been renamed, was provisioned handsomely. The master's handpicked crew were outfitted as well, in whatever armor they chose for themselves, and were given new weapons of the best craftsmanship available. There was quite a ceremony at her send-off, with even King Shrewd in attendance despite his failing health. The Queen herself hung the gull's feathers from the ship's mast that are said to bring a vessel swiftly and safely back to her home port. A great cheer arose as the Revenge set out, and the health of the captain and crew were drunk many times over that evening.

A month later, to Verity's chagrin, we would receive word that a vessel matching the Revenge's description was pirating in the calmer waters to the south of the Six Duchies and bringing much misery to the merchants of Bingtown and the Chalced States. That was as much news of the captain and crew and ship as ever came back to Buckkeep. Some blamed it on the Outislanders among the crew, but there were as many good Six Duchies hands aboard as Outislanders, and the captain had been raised right in Buckkeep Town. This was a crushing blow to Verity's pride and to his leadership of his people. Some believe it was then that he decided to sacrifice himself in the hopes of finding a final solution.

⊷◌⊱

I think the Fool put her up to it. Certainly he had spent a great many hours in the tower-top garden with Kettricken, and his admiration for what she had accomplished there was unfeigned. Much goodwill can be won with a sincere compliment. By the end of the summer, not only was she laughing at his jests when he came up to entertain her and her ladies, but he had persuaded her to be a frequent caller in the King's chambers. As queen-in-waiting, she was immune to Wallace's humors. Kettricken herself undertook to mix King Shrewd strengthening tonics, and for a time the King did seem to rally under her care and attention. I think the Fool decided that he would accomplish through her what he had been unable to nag Verity and me into doing.

It was a wintry fall evening when she first broached the subject to me. I was up on the tower top with her, helping her to tie bundles of straw about the more tender of the plants there, that they might better withstand the winter snows. This was something Patience had decreed must be done, and she and Lacey were performing the same task on a bed of windbower plants behind me. She had become a frequent adviser to Queen Kettricken in matters of growing things, albeit a very timid one. Little Rosemary was at my elbow, handing me twine as we needed it. Two or three of Kettricken's other ladies, well bundled, had stayed, but they were at the other end of the garden, talking quietly together. The others she had dismissed back to their hearths when she had noted them shivering and blowing on their fingers. My bare hands were near numb, as were my ears, but Kettricken seemed perfectly comfortable. As was Verity, tucked away somewhere inside my skull. He had insisted that I start carrying him again after he had discovered that once more I was going out after Forged ones alone. I scarcely noticed his presence in the back of my mind anymore. Yet I believe that I felt him startle when Kettricken asked me, as she knotted a string about a bundled plant I was supporting, what I knew of the Elderlings.

"Little enough, my lady queen," I replied honestly, and once more made a promise to myself to go through the long-neglected manuscripts and scrolls.

"Why not?" she demanded.

"Well, little was actually written about them. I believe at one time a knowledge of them was so common as not to need writing down. And the bits that are written about them are scattered here and there, not gathered in one place. It would take a scholar to track down all the remnants. . . ."

"A scholar like the Fool?" she asked tartly. "He seems to know more of them than anyone else I have asked."

"Well. He is fond of reading, you know, and—"

"Enough of the Fool. I wish to speak to you of the Elderlings," she said abruptly.

I startled at her tone, but found her staring, gray-eyed, out over the sea once more. She had not intended either a rebuke or a rudeness. She was simply intent upon her objective. I reflected that in my months away she had become more certain of herself. More queenly.

"I know a little bit," I offered hesitantly.

"As do I. Let us see if what each of us knows agrees. I shall begin."

"As you wish, my queen."

She cleared her throat. "Long ago, King Wisdom was bitterly besieged by raiders from the sea. When all else had failed him, and he feared that the next summer of kind weather would bring the end of the Six Duchies and House Farseer, he resolved to spend the winter searching for a legendary folk. The Elderlings. Do we agree so far?"

"Mostly. As I have heard it, the legends called them not a folk, but near gods. And the folk of the Six Duchies had always believed Wisdom something of a religious fanatic, almost a madman where such things were concerned."

"Men of passion and vision are often seen as mad," she calmly informed me. "I shall continue. He left his castle one fall, with no more information than that the Elderlings resided in the Rain Wilds beyond the tallest mountains of the Mountain Kingdom. Somehow, he found them, and he won their alliance. He returned to Buckkeep, and together they drove the raiders and invaders away from the coasts of the Six Duchies. Peace and trade were reestablished. And the Elderlings swore to him that if they were ever needed again, they would return. Do we still agree?"

"As before, mostly. I have heard many minstrels say that the ending is a standard one in tales of heroes and quests. Always, they promise that if ever they are needed again, they will return. Some even pledge to return from beyond the grave if they must."

"Actually," Patience suddenly observed, rocking back on her heels, "Wisdom himself never returned to Buckkeep. The Elderlings came to his daughter, Princess Mindful, and it was to her they offered allegiance."

"Whence do you have that knowledge?" Kettricken demanded.

Patience shrugged. "An old minstrel my father used to have always sang it that way." Unconcerned, she went back to knotting twine about a straw-bundled plant.

Kettricken considered a moment. The wind teased loose a long lock of her hair and blew it across her face like a net. She looked at me through the pale web. "It doesn't matter what the tales say about their returning. If a King once sought them, and they gave aid, do you not think they might do so again, if a King again beseeched them? Or a Queen?"

"Perhaps," I said grudgingly. Privately I wondered if the Queen longed for her homeland and would make any excuse for a visit there. Folk were beginning to talk about her lack of pregnancy. While many ladies attended her now, she really had no favorites that were genuinely her friends. Lonely, I suspected. "I think . . ." I began gently, pausing to consider how to frame a discouraging reply.

Tell her she should come to me and speak of it. I wish to know more of what she has gleaned. Verity's thought quivered with excitement. It unsettled me.

"I think you should take your idea to the King-in-Waiting and discuss it with him," I dutifully suggested to her.

She was silent a long time. When she spoke, her voice was pitched very low, for my ears alone. "I think not. He will consider it another one of my foolishnesses. He will listen for a bit, and then begin to look at the maps on the wall, or move things about on his table as he waits for me to finish so he can smile and nod and send me on my way. Again." Her voice hoarsened on the last word. She brushed the hair back from her face, then brushed at her eyes again. She turned from me to look out over the sea again, as distant as Verity when he Skilled.

She's crying?

I could not conceal from Verity my annoyance that this surprised him.

Bring her to me. Now, at once!

"My queen?"

"A moment." Kettricken looked aside from me. With her face away from me, she pretended to be scratching her nose. I knew she brushed at tears.

"Kettricken?" I ventured the familiarity as I had not for months. "Let us go to him now with this idea. At once. I will go with you."

She spoke hesitantly, not turning to look at me. "You do not think it is foolish?"

I would not lie, I reminded myself. "I think that as things stand, we must consider any possible sources of aid." As I spoke the words I found I believed them. Had not both Chade and the Fool hinted, no, pleaded for this very idea? Perhaps Verity and I were the ones who were shortsighted.

She took a shuddering breath. "We shall do it, then. But . . . you must wait for me outside my chamber. I wish to fetch several scrolls to show him. I will be but a short time." She turned to Patience, spoke more loudly. "Lady Patience, might I ask you to finish these plants for me as well? I have something else I wish to attend to."

"Of course, my queen. I should be pleased to."

We left the garden, and I followed her to her chambers. I waited for more than a short time. When she emerged, her little maid Rosemary was behind her, insisting on carrying the scrolls for her. Kettricken had washed the soil from her hands. And changed her gown, and added scent and dressed her hair and was wearing the jewelry Verity had sent to her when she was pledged to him. She smiled at me cautiously as I looked at her. "My lady queen, I am dazzled," I ventured.

"You flatter me as wildly as Regal does," she proclaimed, and hastened away down the hall, but a blush warmed her cheeks.

She dresses so just to come to speak to me?

She dresses so to . . . attract you. How could a man so astute at reading men be so ignorant of women?

Perhaps he has had little time ever to learn much of their ways.

I clamped my mind shut on my thoughts and hastened after my queen. We arrived at Verity's study just in time to see Charim leaving. He was carrying an armful of laundry. It seemed odd until we were admitted. Verity was wearing a soft shirt of pale blue linen, and the mingled scents of lavender and cedar were lively in the air. It reminded me of a clothes chest. His hair and beard were freshly smoothed; well I knew that his hair never stayed that way for more than a few minutes. As Kettricken advanced shyly to curtsy to her lord, I saw Verity as I had not for months. The summer of Skilling had wasted him again. The fine shirt belled about his shoulders, and the smoothed hair was as much gray as black now. There were lines, too, about his eyes and mouth that I had never noticed before.

Do I look so poorly, then?

Not to her, I reminded him.

As Verity took her hand and drew her to sit down beside him on a bench near the fire, she looked at him with a hunger as deep as his Skill drive. Her fingers clung to his hand, and I looked aside as he lifted her hand to kiss it. Perhaps Verity was right about a Skill sensitivity. What Kettricken felt battered at me as roughly as the fury of my crew mates during battle.

I felt a flutter of astonishment from Verity. Then: *Shield yourself,* he commanded me brusquely, and I was suddenly alone inside my skull. I stood still a moment, dizzied by the abruptness of his departure. *He really had no idea,* I found myself thinking, and felt glad the thought remained private.

"My lord, I have come to ask a moment or two of your time for . . . an idea I have." Kettricken's eyes searched his face as she spoke quietly.

"Certainly," Verity agreed. He glanced up at me. "FitzChivalry, will you join us?"

"If you will, my lord." I took a seat on a stool on the opposite side of the hearth. Rosemary came and stood at my elbow with her armload of scrolls. Probably filched from my room by the Fool, I suspected. But as Kettricken began to talk to Verity she took up the scrolls one by one, in each case to illustrate her argument. Without exception, they were scrolls that dealt, not with the Elderlings, but with the Mountain Kingdom. "King Wisdom, you may recall, was the first of Six Duchies nobility to come to our land . . . to the land of the Mountain Kingdom, for anything other than the making of war upon us. So he is well remembered in our histories. These scrolls, copied from ones made in his time, deal with his doings and travels in the Mountain Kingdom. And thus, indirectly, with the Elderlings." She unrolled the last scroll. Verity and I both leaned forward in amazement. A map. Faded with time, poorly copied probably, but a map. Of the Mountain Kingdom, with passes and trails marked on it. And a few straggling lines leading into the lands beyond.

"One of these paths, marked here, must lead to the Elderlings. For I know the trails of the Mountains, and these are not trade routes, nor do they go to any village I know. Nor do they lie in conjunction with the trails as I know them now to be. These are older roads and paths. And why else would they be marked here, save that they go where King Wisdom went?"

"Can it be that simple?" Verity rose quickly, to return with a branch of candles to light the map better. He smoothed the vellum lovingly with his hands and leaned close over it.

"There are several paths marked that go off into the Rain Wilds. If that is what all this green represents. None seem to have anything marked at the end. How would we know which one?" I objected.

"Perhaps they all go to the Elderlings," Kettricken ventured. "Why should they reside in but one place?"

"No!" Verity straightened up. "Two at least have something marked at the end. Or had something. The damned ink has faded. But there was something there. I intend to find out what."

Even Kettricken looked astonished at the enthusiasm in his voice. I was shocked. I had expected him to hear her out politely, not to endorse her plan wholeheartedly.

He rose suddenly, paced a quick turn around the room. The Skill energy radiated off him like heat from a hearth. "The full storms of winter are upon the coast now. Or will be, any day now. If I leave quickly, in the next few days, I can be to the Mountain Kingdom while the passes can still be used. I can force my way through to . . . whatever is there. And return by spring. Perhaps with the help we need."

I was speechless. Kettricken made it worse.

"My lord, I had not intended that you should go. You should remain here. I must go. I know the Mountains; I was born to their ways. You might not survive there. In this, I should be Sacrifice."

It was a relief to see Verity as dumbfounded as I was. Perhaps, having heard it from her lips, he would now realize how impossible it was. He shook his head-slowly. He took both her hands in his and looked solemnly at her. "My queen-in-waiting." He sighed. "I must do this. I. In so many other ways

I have failed the Six Duchies. And you. When first you came here to be queen, I had no patience with your talk of Sacrifice. I thought it a girl's idealistic notion. But it is not. We do not speak it here, but it is what is felt. It is what I learned from my parents. To put the Six Duchies always ahead of myself. I have tried to do that. But now I see that always I have sent others in my place. I sat and Skilled, it is true, and you have an inkling what it has cost me. But it has been sailors and soldiers who I have sent out to put down their lives for the Six Duchies. My own nephew, even, doing the crude and bloody work for me. And despite those I have sent to be sacrificed, our coast is still not safe. Now it comes to this last chance, to this hard thing. Shall I send my queen to do it for me?''

"Perhaps . . ." Kettricken's voice had gone husky with uncertainty. She looked down at the fire as she suggested, "Perhaps we might go together?"

Verity considered. He actually earnestly considered it, and I saw Kettricken realize he had taken her request seriously. She began to smile, but it faded as he slowly shook his head. "I dare not," he said quietly. "Someone must remain here. Someone I trust. King Shrewd is . . . my father is not well. I fear for him. For his health. With myself away, and my father ill, there must be someone to stand in my stead."

She looked aside. "I would rather go with you," she said fiercely.

I averted my eyes as he reached and took her chin in his fingers and lifted her face so he might see her eyes. "I know," he said evenly. "That is the sacrifice I must ask you to make. To stay here, when you would rather go. To be alone, yet again. For the sake of the Six Duchies."

Something went out of her. Her shoulders sagged as she bowed her head to his will. As Verity gathered her to him I rose silently. I took Rosemary with me and we left them alone.

I was in my room, poring belatedly over the scrolls and tablets there, when the page came to my door that afternoon. "You are summoned to the King's chambers, in the hour after dinner," was the only message he gave me. Dismay rolled over me. It had been two weeks since my last visit to his chamber. I did not wish to confront the King again. If he were summoning me to say that he expected me to begin courting Celerity, I did not know what I would do or say. I feared I would lose control of myself. Resolutely I unrolled one of the Elderling scrolls and tried to study it. It was hopeless. I saw only Molly.

In the brief nights we had shared since our day on the beach, Molly had refused to discuss Celerity with me any further. In some ways it was a relief. But she had also stopped teasing me about all she would demand from me when I was truly her husband and all the future children we would have. She had quietly given up hope that we would ever be wed. If I stopped to think of it, it grieved me to the edge of madness. She did not rebuke me with it, as she knew it was not of my choosing. She did not even ask what was to become of us. Like Nighteyes, she seemed to live only in the present now. Each night of closeness we shared, she accepted as a thing complete, and did not question if there would be another. What I sensed from her was not despair, but containment: a fierce resolve that we would not lose what we had now to what we could not have tomorrow. I did not deserve the devotion of such a faithful heart.

When I dozed beside her in her bed, safe and warm amid the perfume of her body and her herbs, it was her strength that protected us. She did not Skill, she had no Wit. Her magic was a stronger kind, and she worked it by her will alone. When she closed and bolted her door behind me late at night, she created within her chamber a world and a time that belonged to us. If she had blindly placed her life and happiness in my hands, it would have been intolerable. But this was even worse. She believed there would eventually be a terrible price to pay for her devotion to me. Still she refused to forsake me. And I was not man enough to turn away from her and bid her seek a happier life. In my most lonely hours, when I rode the trails around Buckkeep with my saddlebags full of poisoned bread, I knew myself for a coward, and worse than a thief. I had once told Verity I could not draw off another man's strength to feed my own, that I would not. Yet every day, that was what I did to Molly. The Elderling scroll fell from my lax fingers. My room was suddenly suffocating. I pushed aside the tablets and scrolls

I had been attempting to study. In the hour before dinner, I sought out Patience's chamber.

It had been some time since I had last called upon her. But her sitting chamber never seemed to change, save in the uppermost layer of litter that reflected her current passion. This day was no exception. Fall-gathered herbs, bundled for drying, were suspended everywhere, filling the room with their scents. I felt I was strolling through an inverted meadow as I ducked to avoid the dangling foliage.

"You've hung these a bit low," I complained as Patience entered.

"No. You've managed to grow a bit too tall. Stand up straight and let me look at you now."

I obeyed, even though it left me with a bundle of catmint resting on my head.

"Well. At least rowing about killing people all summer has left you in good health. Much better than the sickly boy who came home to me last winter. I told you those tonics would work. As long as you've gotten that tall, you may as well help me hang up these lot."

Without more ado, I was put to work stringing lines from sconces to bedposts to anything else that a string could be tied to, and then to fastening bundles of herbs to them. She had me treed, up on a chair and tying bundles of balsam, when she demanded, "Why do you no longer whine to me about how much you miss Molly?"

"Would it do me any good?" I asked her quietly after a moment. I did my best to sound resigned.

"No." She paused a moment as if thinking. She handed me yet another bouquet of leaves. "Those," she informed me as I fastened them up, "are stipple-leaf. Very bitter. Some say they will prevent a woman conceiving. They don't. At least, not dependably. But if a woman eats them for too long, she can become ill from them." She paused as if considering. "Perhaps, if a woman is sick, she does not conceive as easily. But I would not recommend them to anyone, least of all anyone I cared about."

I found my tongue, sought a casual air. "Why do you dry them, then?"

"An infusion of them, gargled, will help a sore throat. So Molly Chandler told me, when I found her gathering them in the women's garden."

"I see." I fastened the leaves to the line, dangling them like a body from a noose. Even their odor was bitter. Had I wondered, earlier, how Verity could be so unaware of what was right before him? Why had I never thought of this? How must it be for her, to dread what a rightfully married woman would long for? What Patience had longed for in vain?

". . . seaweed, FitzChivalry?"

I started. "Beg pardon?"

"I said, when you have an afternoon free, would you gather seaweed for me? The black, crinkly sort? It has the most flavor this time of year."

"I will try," I replied absently. For how many years would Molly have to worry? How much bitterness must she swallow?

"What are you looking at?" Patience demanded.

"Nothing. Why?"

"Because I've asked you twice to get down so we can move the chair. We've all these other packets to hang, you know."

"Beg pardon. I didn't get much sleep last night; it's left me dull-witted today."

"I agree. You should start sleeping more at night." These words were uttered a bit heavily. "Now come down and move the chair so we can hang these mints."

I didn't eat much at dinner. Regal was alone on the high dais, looking sullen. His usual circle of fawners clustered at a table just below him. I did not understand why he chose to dine separately. Certainly, he had the rank to, but why choose this isolation? He summoned one of the more flattering of the minstrels he had recently imported to Buckkeep. Most of them were from Farrow. All of them affected the nasal intonations of that region and favored the long, chanting styles of epics. This one sang a long telling of some adventure of Regal's maternal grandfather. I listened as little as I was able; it seemed to have to do with riding a horse to death in order to be the one to shoot a great stag that had eluded a generation of hunters. It praised endlessly the greathearted horse who had gone to his death at his master's bidding. It said nothing of the master's stupidity in wasting such an animal to gain some tough meat and a rack of antlers.

"You look half-sick," Burrich observed as he paused beside me. I rose to leave table and walked through the hall with him.

"Too much on my mind. Too many directions to think in all at once. I sometimes feel that if I had time to focus my mind on just one problem, I could solve it. And then go on to solve the others."

"Every man believes that. It isn't so. Slay the ones you can as they come to hand, and after a while you get used to the ones you can do nothing about."

"Such as?"

He shrugged and gestured downward. "Such as having a game leg. Or being a bastard. We all get used to things we once swore we could never live with. But what's eating your liver this time?"

"Nothing I can tell you about just yet. Not here, anyway."

"Oh. More of those, huh." He shook his head. "I don't envy you, Fitz. Sometimes all a man needs is to growl about his problems to another man. They've denied you even that. But take heart. I have faith you can handle them even if you think you can't."

He clapped me on the shoulders, and then left in a blast of cold air from the outer doors. Verity was right. The winter storms were rising, if tonight's wind was any indicator. I was halfway up the stairs before I reflected that Burrich now spoke to me straight across. He finally believed I was a man grown. Well, maybe I would do better if I believed that about myself. I squared my shoulders and went up to my room.

I put more effort into dressing than I had in a long time. As I did I thought of Verity hastily changing his shirt for Kettricken. How had he ever managed to be so blind to her? And I to Molly? What other things did Molly do for our sake that I had never realized? My misery returned, stronger than ever. Tonight. Tonight after Shrewd was done with me. I could not let her continue her sacrifices. For now, I could do nothing save put it out of my mind. I pulled my hair back into the warrior's tail that I felt fully earned now, and tugged the front of my blue jerkin straight. It was a bit snug across the shoulders, but so was everything I owned lately. I left my room.

In the hallway outside King Shrewd's apartments, I encountered Verity with Kettricken on his arm. Never had I seen them as they presented themselves now. Here, suddenly, was the King-in-Waiting and his queen. Verity was dressed in a long formal robe of deep forest green. An embroidered band of stylized bucks graced the sleeves and hem. He wore on his brow the silver circlet with the blue gem that was the mark of the King-in-Waiting. I had not seen him wear it in some time. Kettricken was dressed in the purple and white that she so often chose. Her gown of purple was very simple, the sleeves cut short and wide to reveal narrower and longer sleeves of white beneath them. She wore the jewelry that Verity had gifted her with, and her long blond hair had been intricately dressed with a net of silver chain junctured with amethysts. I halted at the sight of them. Their faces were grave. They could be going nowhere except to see King Shrewd.

I presented myself formally, and carefully let Verity know that King Shrewd had summoned me.

"No," he told me gently. "I summoned you to present yourself to King Shrewd. Along with Kettricken and me. I wished you witness for this."

Relief flooded me. This was not about Celerity, then. "Witness for what, my prince?" I managed to ask.

He looked at me as if I were daft. "I ask the King's permission to leave on a quest. To seek out the Elderlings and bring back the aid we so desperately need."

"Oh." I should have noticed the quiet page, all in black, bearing an armful of scrolls and tablets. The boy's face was white and stiff. I would wager he had never before done anything more formal for Verity than wax his boots. Rosemary, freshly washed and clothed in Kettricken's colors, reminded me of a scrubbed purple-and-white turnip. I smiled at the chubby child, but she returned my look gravely.

Without preamble, Verity rapped once on King Shrewd's door. "A moment!" called a voice. Wallace's. He opened the door a crack, glared out, then realized that this was Verity he was keeping out. He had a moment of too obvious hesitation before he swung the door wide.

"Sir," he quavered. "I did not expect you. That is, I was not informed that the King was to have—"

"You are not needed for this. You may go, now." Usually Verity did not dismiss even a page so coldly.

"But . . . the King may have need of me. . . ." The man's eyes shifted wildly about. He feared something.

Verity's eyes narrowed. "If he does, I will see you are summoned. In fact, you may wait. Just outside the door. Be there if I call for you."

After an instant's pause Wallace stepped outside the door and stood beside it. We entered the King's chambers. Verity himself set hand to the door and shut it. "I do not like that man," he observed, more than loudly enough to be heard through the door. "He is officiously subservient, and greasily obsequious. A very poor combination."

The King was not in his sitting room. As Verity crossed it the Fool suddenly appeared in Shrewd's bedroom doorway. He goggled at us, grinned in a sudden lift of joy, and then made a floor-sweeping bow to all of us. "Sire! Awaken! It is as I have foretold, the minstrels have arrived!"

"Fool," Verity growled, but it was good-natured. He brushed past him, fending off the Fool's mocking attempts to kiss the hem of his robe. Kettricken lifted a hand to smother a smile and followed Verity. The Fool all but succeeded in tripping me with a suddenly stretched-forth foot. I avoided it, but made a clumsy entrance, nearly colliding with Kettricken. The Fool grinned and simpered at me, then capered over to Shrewd's bedside. He lifted the old man's hand, patted it with true gentleness. "Your Majesty? Your Majesty? You have callers."

In the bed, Shrewd stirred and took a sudden deep breath. "What's this? Who's here? Verity? Pull back the curtains, Fool, I can scarcely see who's here. Queen Kettricken? What's all this? The Fitz! What is this about?" His voice was not strong, and there was a querulous note to it, but for all that, he was better than I had expected. As the Fool drew back the bed curtains and propped pillows behind him, I found myself facing a man who looked older than Chade. The resemblance between the two seemed to become more marked as Shrewd aged. The flesh of the King's face had fallen, to reveal the same browline and cheekbones as his bastard brother. The eyes beneath those brows were alert, but weary. He seemed better than the last time I had seen him. He pushed himself more upright to confront us. "Well, what is this about?" he demanded, his eyes scanning our circle.

Verity bowed deeply, formally, and Kettricken echoed it with her curtsy. I did as I knew was required: went down on one knee and stayed there, head bowed. I still managed to peek up when Verity spoke. "King Shrewd. My father. I come to ask your permission for an undertaking."

"Which is?" the King asked testily.

Verity lifted his eyes to meet his father's. "I wish to leave Buckkeep with a picked band of men, to attempt to follow the same path King Wisdom took so long ago. I wish to journey this winter to the Rain Wilds beyond the Mountain Kingdom, to find the Elderlings and ask them to keep the pledge they made to our ancestor."

An incredulous look passed briefly over Shrewd's face. He pushed himself upright in bed, swung his thin legs over the side. "Fool. Bring wine. Fitz, get up and help him. Kettricken, dear, your arm if you will to help me to that chair by the fire. Verity, fetch the small table by the window. Please."

With this handful of requests, Shrewd popped the bubble of formality. Kettricken helped him with a familiarity that showed me she had a genuine bond with the old man. The Fool pranced off to the cupboard in the sitting room for wineglasses, leaving me to select a bottle of wine from the small store that Shrewd kept in his rooms. The bottles were covered in dust, as if he had not tasted these wines for a long time. I wondered suspiciously what was the source for what Wallace gave him. At least the rest of the room, I noted, was in good order. Much better than it had been before Winterfest. The Smoke censers that had so distressed me stood cold in the corner. And tonight the King seemed to have his wits still.

The Fool helped the King into a thick woolen robe and knelt to slipper his feet. Shrewd settled into his chair by the fire and set his wineglass on the table at his elbow. Older. Much older. But the King I had reported to so often in my youth once more held council before me. Suddenly I wished I could be the one speaking to him tonight. This sharp-eyed old man might actually hear out my reasons for wishing to wed Molly. I felt a new roiling of anger at Wallace for the habits he had led my king into.

But this was not my time. Despite the King's informality, Verity and Kettricken were strung tight as bowstrings. The Fool and I brought chairs that they might be seated to either side of Shrewd. I stood behind Verity and waited.

"Tell it simply," Shrewd requested of Verity, and he did. Kettricken's scrolls were unfurled one at a time, and Verity read aloud the pertinent passages. The old map was studied at length. Shrewd did nothing but ask questions at first, making no comments or judgments until he was sure he had from them every scrap of information. The Fool stood at his elbow, alternately beaming at me and making terrible faces at Verity's page in an attempt to make the petrified boy at least smile. I think it more likely he frightened the lad. Rosemary forgot entirely where she was and wandered off to toy with the tassels on the bed curtains.

When Verity had finished speaking, and Kettricken had added her comments, the King leaned back in his chair. He drained the bit of wine that was still in his glass, then held it out to the Fool to refill. He took a sip, sighed, then shook his head. "No. There is too much of pecksies and nursery tales to this for you to undertake it right now, Verity. You have shown me enough to make me believe it worth our while to send an emissary there. A man of your choosing, with a fitting entourage, gifts, and letters from you and me to confirm he is there at our behest. But yourself, the King-in-Waiting? No. We have not the resources to spare just now. Regal was at me earlier today, going over the costs of the new ships being built, and the fortifying of the towers on Antler Island. Money is becoming scarce. And it might not make the folk feel safe to have you leave the city."

"I do not flee, I leave on a quest. A quest with their benefit as my goal. And I leave behind my queen-in-waiting, to represent me to them while I am gone. I did not have in mind a caravan with minstrels and cooks and embroidered tents, sir. We would be traveling on snowy roads, going into the heart of winter itself. I would take a military contingent, and travel as soldiers do. As I always have.''

"And you think this would impress the Elderlings? If you find them? If they ever existed at all?''

"Legend has it that King Wisdom went on his own. I believe the Elderlings existed, and that he found them. If I fail, I will return, to take up again with my Skilling and my warships. What will we have lost? If I succeed, I bring back a powerful ally.''

"And if you die in the seeking?'' Shrewd asked heavily.

Verity opened his mouth to reply. But before he could speak, the sitting-room door was flung open and Regal boiled into the room. His face was flushed. ''What goes on here? Why was I not informed of this council?'' He shot me a venomous look. Behind him, Wallace peeked in at the door.

Verity permitted himself a small smile. ''If you were not informed by your spies, why are you here now? Rebuke them that you did not know sooner, not me.'' Wallace's head jerked back out of sight.

"Father, I demand to know what goes on here!'' Regal very nearly stomped his foot. Behind Shrewd, the Fool mimicked Regal's facial expression. At this, Verity's page finally smiled, but then his eyes widened and he straightened his face.

King Shrewd addressed Verity instead. ''Is there a reason that you wished Prince Regal excluded from this discussion?''

"I did not see that it concerned him.'' He paused. ''And I wished to be sure the decision reached was exclusively your own.'' Verity, faithful to his name.

Regal hackled, his nostrils pinching white, but Shrewd held up a hand to quell him. Again he spoke only to Verity. ''Does not concern him? But on whom would fall the mantle of authority while you were gone?''

Verity's eyes went icy. ''My queen-in-waiting would represent my reign, of course. You wear the mantle of authority still, my king.''

"But if you did not return . . . ?''

"I am sure my brother could adapt to that situation at a moment's notice." Verity did not bother to mask the dislike in his voice. I knew then how deep the poison of Regal's treacheries had worked into him. Whatever bond they had ever shared as brothers was eaten away by it. Solely rivals, now. Shrewd heard it, too, I did not doubt. I wondered if he was surprised at all by it. If he was, he covered it well.

As for Regal, his ears had pricked up at the mention of Verity leaving. He now stood as avariciously alert as a dog begging at table. He spoke just a moment too soon to have any ring of sincerity to his voice. "If someone would explain to me where Verity is going, perhaps I could speak for myself as to what I might be ready to assume."

Verity kept his tongue. Clear-browed and silent, he looked at his father.

"Your brother"—the phrase sounded a bit heavy to my ears—"wishes me to grant him leave for a quest. He wishes to go, and soon, to the Rain Wilds beyond the Mountain Kingdom. To seek out the Elderlings and obtain from them the help once promised us."

Regal's eyes went owly. I don't know if he could not believe in the notion of Elderlings, or if he could not believe the quantity of good fortune he had suddenly been dealt. He licked his lips.

"I, of course, have forbidden it." Shrewd watched Regal as he said it.

"But why?" Regal demanded. "Surely all courses must be considered. . . ."

"The expense is prohibitive. Did not you report to me, just a short time ago, that the building of the warships and the manning and provisioning of them have all but drained our reserves?"

Regal's eyes flickered as swiftly as a snake's tongue. "But I have had the rest of the harvest reports since then, Father. I had not known they would be so good. Funds could be found. Provided he was willing to travel simply."

Verity breathed out through his nose. "I thank you for your consideration, Regal. I had not realized such decisions were your province."

"I but advise the King, just as you do," Regal pointed out hastily.

"You do not think sending an emissary would be the more sensible thing to do?" Shrewd probed. "What would the people think of their king-in-waiting leaving Buckkeep at such a time, and on such an errand?"

"An emissary?" Regal appeared to consider it. "I think not. Not for all we must ask. Do not the legends say that King Wisdom went himself? What do we know of these Elderlings? Do we dare take a chance of sending an underling to offend them? In this, no, I believe the son of the King at least is called for. As for his leaving Buckkeep . . . well, you are the King, and you are still here. As would his wife be."

"My queen," Verity growled, but Regal continued speaking.

"And I. Buckkeep would hardly be abandoned. And the errand itself? It might capture the people's imagination. Or, if you choose, the reason for his going might be kept quiet. It could be seen as a simple visit to our allies the Mountain folk. Especially if his wife went along."

"My queen remains here." Verity used her title pointedly. "To represent my reign. And to protect my interests."

"Do not you trust our father to do that?" Regal asked blandly.

Verity held his tongue, and looked at the old man in his chair by the fire. The question in his look was plain to anyone with eyes. Can I trust you? it asked him. But Shrewd, true to his name, replied only with a question of his own.

"You have heard Prince Regal's thoughts on this undertaking. And mine. You know your own. Given these counsels, what do you now wish to do?"

I blessed Verity then, for he now turned and looked only at Kettricken. No nod, no whisper passed between them. But he turned back to his father with their accord. "I wish to go to the Rain Wilds beyond the Mountain Kingdom. And I wish to leave as soon as possible."

As King Shrewd slowly nodded, my heart fell into the pit of my belly. But behind his chair, the Fool turned back flips across the room, and then cartwheeled back, to stand as attentively behind him as if he had never moved. Regal was unsettled by this. But as Verity knelt to kiss King Shrewd's hand and thank him for his permission, the smile that spread across Regal's face was wide enough to engulf a shark.

There was little more to the council. Verity wished to leave in seven days. Shrewd accepted it. He wished to choose his own entourage. Shrewd accepted that, though Regal looked thoughtful. I was not pleased, when the King finally dismissed all of us, to note how Regal dawdled behind, to converse with Wallace in the sitting room as we filed out. I found myself wondering if Chade would allow me to kill Wallace. He had already forbidden my solving Regal that way, and I had since promised to my king I would not. But Wallace had no such immunity.

In the hallway, Verity briefly thanked me. I dared to ask him why he had wanted me present.

"To witness," he said heavily. "Witnessing something is much more than hearing about it afterward. To keep in your memory all the words that were said . . . so they may not be forgotten."

I knew then to expect a summons from Chade that night.

But I could not resist going to Molly. Seeing the King as a King again had fanned my failing hope. I promised myself my visit would be brief, just to talk to her, to let her know I appreciated all she did. I would be in my chambers before the small hours Chade favored for our conversations.

I knocked on her door furtively; she let me in quickly. She must have seen how driven I was, for she came immediately into my arms, without questions or qualms. I stroked her shining hair, I looked down into her eyes. The passion that came over me suddenly was like a spring flood that bursts suddenly down a creek, flinging all winter's debris out of its way. My intentions of quietly talking were swept away. Molly gasped as I held her to me fiercely, then surrendered herself to me.

It seemed months rather than days since we had last been together. When she kissed me hungrily, I felt suddenly awkward, uncertain as to why she would desire me. She was so young and so beautiful. It seemed vanity to believe she could want someone as battered and worn down as I. She did not allow me to keep my doubts, but drew me down atop her without hesitation. Deep in that sharing, I finally recognized the reality of the love in her blue eyes. I gloried in the passionate way she pulled me to her and clasped me in her strong pale arms. Later I would recall glimpses of golden hair spread across a pillow, the scents of honeywood and mountainsweet on her skin, even the way she threw back her head and gave soft voice to her fervor.

Afterward, Molly whispered in amazement that my intensity made me seem a different man. Her head was pillowed on my chest. I kept silent, and stroked the dark hair that smelled always of her herbs. Thyme and lavender. I closed my eyes. I knew I had warded well my thoughts. It had long ago become a habit when I was with Molly.

Verity, then, had not.

I had not willed what had happened. I doubted that anyone had. Perhaps, I hoped, I was the only one who had sensed it fully. Then there might be no real harm done, as long as I never spoke of it. As long as I could blot forever from my mind the sweetness of Kettricken's mouth, and the softness of her white, white skin.

19

Messages

KING-IN-WAITING *Verity departed Buckkeep at the beginning of the third winter of the Red-Ship Wars. He took with him a small group of handpicked followers who would accompany him on his quest, as well as his personal guard, who would travel with him as far as the Mountain Kingdom and remain there to await his return. His reasoning was that a smaller expedition needed a smaller baggage train, and traveling through the Mountains in winter demanded that all food supplies be carried with him. He had also decided that he did not wish to convey a martial aspect to the Elderlings. His real mission was disclosed to few except his companions. Ostensibly he went to the Mountain Kingdom to treat with his queen's father, King Eyod, about possible military support against the Red-Ships.*

Of those he asked to accompany him, there are several worth noting. Hod, arms master for Buckkeep, was one of the first he selected. Her grasp of tactics was not exceeded by any within the realm and her prowess with weapons was still remarkable despite her years. Charim, Verity's body servant, had been with him so long and accompanied him on so many campaigns, it was unthinkable to either of them that he be left behind. Chestnut, brown as his name, had been a member of Verity's military guard for over a decade of years. He was missing an eye and most of an ear, but despite that seemed twice as alert as any other man. Keef and Kef, born twins, and like Chestnut, members of Verity's honor guard for years, went also. One other, Burrich, the master of stables at Buckkeep, joined the party of his own accord. When his leaving Buckkeep was protested, he pointed out that he left an able man in charge of Buckkeep's stables, and that the party would need a man who was knowledgeable of animals in order to get the beasts alive through the Mountains in midwinter. His abilities as a healer and his experience as a King's Man to Prince Chivalry were also qualifications he pointed out, but this last one was known to but a few.

⊷═▷

The night before Verity was to leave, he summoned me to his study. "You don't approve of this, do you? You think it's a fool's errand," he greeted me.

I had to smile. Inadvertently, he had exactly stated what I thought. "I am afraid I have serious doubts," I agreed cautiously.

"As do I. But what else is left to me? This, at least, is a chance for me to actually do something myself. Other than sit in that bedamned tower and Skill myself to death."

He had painstakingly recopied Kettricken's map over the last few days. As I watched he rolled it carefully and slid it into a leather case. The difference the last week had made in the man amazed me. He was still gray, his body still worn and sadly dwindled from too many months of sitting. But he moved with energy, and both he and Kettricken had graced the Great Hall every evening since the decision had been made. It had been a pleasure to watch him eat with an appetite, and once more linger over a glass of wine while Mellow or another of the minstrels entertained us all. The renewed warmth between Kettricken and him was another appetite he had recovered. Her eyes seldom left her lord's countenance when they were at table. While the minstrels entertained, her fingers were always resting on the back of his forearm. She glowed in his presence like a burning candle. Shield myself as I might, I was all too aware of how much they enjoyed their nights. I had attempted to hide from their passions by immersing myself in Molly. I ended up feeling guilty that Molly was so pleased with my renewed ardor. How would she feel if she knew my appetites were not entirely my own?

The Skill. I had been warned of its powers and pitfalls, of how it might call to a man and drain him of everything except a hunger for its use. This was one trap I had never been warned about. In some ways, I was looking forward to Verity leaving so I could call my soul my own again.

"What you do in that tower is not a lesser task. If folk could but understand how you burn yourself for them . . ."

"As you understand only too well. We've grown close this summer, boy. Closer than I'd ever have thought possible. Closer than any man has been to me since your father died."

Closer even than you might suspect, my prince. But I did not utter those words. "We have."

"I've a favor to ask you. Two, actually."

"You know that I won't refuse you."

"Never say that so easily. The first is that you look after my lady. She has grown wiser in Buckkeep ways, but she is still far too trusting. Keep her safe until I return."

"That is always yours without asking, my prince."

"And the other." He took a breath, sighed it out. "I wish to try to stay here as well. In your mind. For as long as I can."

"My prince." I hesitated. He was right. This was not a thing I wished to grant him. But I had already said I would. I knew that for the sake of the kingdom, it was a wise thing to do. But for myself? Already I had felt the boundaries of my self eroding before Verity's strong presence. We were not talking about a contact of hours now, or days, but of weeks and likely months. I wondered if this was what happened to coterie members, if eventually they ceased having separate lives. "What of your coterie?" I asked quietly.

"What of them?" he retorted. "I leave them in place, in the watchtowers and on my ships for now. Whatever messages they must send, they can send to Serene. In my absence, she will take them to Shrewd. If there is anything they feel I must know, they can Skill me." He paused. "There will be other sorts of information that I would seek through you. Things I would prefer kept private.''

Tidings of his queen, I thought to myself. How Regal would employ his powers in his brother's absence. Gossip and intrigues. In one sense, trifling things. In another, the detail that secured Verity's position. I wished for the thousandth time that I could Skill reliably of my own accord. If I had had that ability, Verity would not have needed to ask this of me. I would have been able to reach out to him at any time. But as matters stood, the touch-imposed Skill bond we had used over the summer was our only resource. Through it, he could be aware of what went on at Buckkeep when he chose to, and I could receive instructions from him. I hesitated, but already knew that I would accede. From loyalty to him and to the Six Duchies, I told myself. Not from any Skill hunger in myself. I looked up at him. ''I will do it.''

''Knowing well that this is how it begins,'' he said. It was not a question. Already, this was how accurately we could read one another. He did not wait for my answer. ''I will be as inconspicuous as I can,'' he promised. I walked to him. He lifted a hand and touched my shoulder. Verity was with me again, as he had not consciously been since the day in his study when he had bid me to shield myself.

The day of the departure was fine, crisply cold, but the skies were clear blue. Verity, true to his word, had kept his expedition to a minimum. Riders had been dispatched the morning after the council to precede him on his route and arrange supplies and lodgings in the towns where he would pass. This would allow him to travel swiftly and lightly through much of the Six Duchies.

As his expedition set off that chill morning I alone of the crowd did not bid Verity farewell. He nestled inside my mind, small and silent as a seed waiting for spring. As unnoticed, almost, as Nighteyes. Kettricken had chosen to watch the departure from the frosty walls of the Queen's Garden. She had said her farewells to him earlier, and chosen this spot so that if she wept, none would take it amiss. I stood at her side and endured the resonance of what she and Verity had come to share in the last week. I was both glad for her and heartsick that what she had so recently found must so quickly be taken from her. Horses and men, pack animals and banners finally passed behind a shoulder of hills and out of our sight. Then I felt that which sent a chill up my spine. She Wit-quested after him. Very faintly, it was true, but enough that somewhere in my heart, Nighteyes sat up, eyes aflame, and asked, *What's this?*

Nothing. Nothing to do with us, anyway. I added, *We hunt together soon, my brother, as we have not for too long.*

For a few days after the cavalcade's departure, I almost had my own life again. I had dreaded Burrich's leaving with Verity. I understood what drove him to follow his king-in-waiting, but felt uncomfortably exposed with them both gone. That told me much about myself that I really did not want to know. But the other side of that coin was that with Burrich gone and Verity's presence inside me coiled tight, Nighteyes and I were finally free to use the Wit as openly as we wished. Almost every dawn I was with him, miles from the Keep. On the days when we sought Forged ones, I rode Sooty, but she did not ever feel completely comfortable around the wolf. After a time there seemed far fewer of them, and no more coming into the area. We began to be able to hunt game for ourselves. For that, I went afoot, for we hunted more companionably that way. Nighteyes approved of my physical improvement over the summer. That winter, for the first time since Regal had poisoned me, I felt I had the full use of my body and strength again. The vigorous mornings of hunting and the deep hours of the night with Molly would have been enough life for any man. There is something completely satisfying about simple things such as these.

I suppose I wanted my life to be always this simple and complete. I tried to ignore things I knew were dangerous. The continued fine weather, I told myself, would assure Verity a fine start to his journey. I put from my mind whether there would be any end-of-season raids from the Red-Ships while we were so unprotected. I avoided, too, Regal and the sudden round of social occasions that filled Buckkeep with his followers and kept the torches burning late every night in the Great Hall. Serene and Justin were also much more in evidence about Buckkeep. I never entered a room where they were but that I felt the arrows of their dislike. I began to avoid the common rooms in the evenings, where I must either encounter them, or Regal's guests who had come to swell our winter court.

Verity had not been gone more than two days before I heard rumors that the true purpose of his quest was to seek the Elderlings. I could not blame these on Regal. Those Verity had hand-chosen had known of their true mission. Burrich had ferreted it out for himself. If he could, so could another, and noise it about. But when I overheard two pantry boys laughing about "King Wisdom's folly, and Prince Verity's myth," I suspected the ridicule was Regal's doing. Verity's Skilling had made him too much the recluse. Folk wondered what he did so long alone in his tower. That is, they knew he Skilled, but that was too tame a topic for gossip. His preoccupied stare, his odd hours for eating and rest, his silent ghosting through the castle while other folks were abed were all grist for this mill. Had he lost his mind, and set out on a madman's errand? Speculation began to grow, and Regal gave it fertile ground. He found excuses and reasons for all sorts of banquets and gatherings of his nobles. King Shrewd was seldom well enough to be present and Kettricken did not enjoy the company of the witty knaves that Regal cultivated. I knew enough to stay away. I had only myself and Chade to grumble to about the cost of these parties when Regal had insisted that there were scarcely funds for Verity's expedition. Chade only shook his head.

The old man had become more closemouthed of late, even with me. I had the uncomfortable feeling that Chade kept a secret from me. Secrets in themselves were nothing new. The old assassin was stuffed full of secrets. I simply could not be rid of the feeling that this secret somehow touched on me directly. I could not ask him outright, but I watched him. His worktable showed signs of heavy use when I was not about. Even stranger, all messes associated with that work had been cleaned meticulously away whenever he summoned me. This was bizarre. For years I had tidied after him and his "cooking." Now for him to straighten up after himself seemed either a sharp rebuke to me or a concealment of whatever he had been doing.

Unable to resist, I watched him whenever I could. I

learned nothing of his secret, but saw much that I had previously missed. Chade was getting old. The stiffness cold weather brought to his joints no longer yielded to the cozy evenings before his hearth. He was Shrewd's elder half brother, bastard as I was, and despite his stiffness, he still seemed the younger of the two. But he held scrolls farther from his nose when he read now and avoided reaching for anything over his head. To watch these changes in him was as painful as to know he kept a secret from me.

Twenty-three days after Verity left, I came back from a dawn hunt with Nighteyes to find the Keep abuzz. The feeling was that of a stirred ant nest, but with none of their purposefulness. I went straight to Cook Sara and asked her what had happened. The kitchen of any keep is the heart of the rumor mill, second only to the guardroom. At Buckkeep, the kitchen gossip was usually more accurate.

"A rider come in, his horse near to dead. Said there's been a raid up at Ferry. The whole city near gone from the fires they set. Seventy folk Forged. How many dead, there's not telling yet. And more will die, made homeless in this cold. Three shiploads of Raiders, the boy said. He went straight to Prince Regal, he did, and reported. Prince Regal sent him here to be fed; he's in the guardroom now, asleep." She lowered her voice. "That boy came all this way on his own. Got fresh horses in towns he went through, coming down the coast road, but wouldn't let no one else carry his message for him. He told me that every leg of the way, he kept expecting to find help coming, to hear from someone that they already knew and that ships had been sent out. But there was nothing."

"From Ferry? Then it's been at least five days since it happened. Why weren't the signal tower fires lit?" I demanded. "Or the message birds sent to Gull and Sealbay? King-in-Waiting Verity left a patrol ship in that area. The patrol ship should have been able to see the light from Gull or Ferry. And there's a coterie member, Will, at Red Tower. He should have seen the signal fires. He should have sent word back here, to Serene. How could it be that no word was received here; how could we know nothing at all of this?"

Cook lowered her voice even more, gave the dough she

was kneading a meaningful thump. "Boy said the signal fires were lit, at Ferry and at Ice Town. He says the birds were sent to Gull. The ship never came."

"Then why didn't we know?" I took a deep shuddering breath, set aside my useless anger. Within me, I felt a faint stirring of concern from Verity. Too faint. The Skill bond was fading, just when I wished it strong. "Well, I suppose it's no good asking that just now. What has Regal done? Sent out the *Rurisk*? I wish I'd been here to go with them."

Cook snorted and paused to throttle the dough a bit. "Go now, then, for you won't be late. Nothing's been done, no one sent that I've heard. No one sent, no one is being sent. No one.

"You know I've no tongue for gossip, Fitz, but what was whispered was that Prince Regal did know of it. When the boy came in, oh, the Prince was so kind, so full of sympathy as to make the ladies' hearts melt. A meal, a new coat, a small purse for his troubles. But he told the boy it was too late now. The Raiders would be long gone. No sense to send a ship out now, or soldiers."

"Too late to fight Raiders, perhaps. But what of those burned out in Ferry? A contingent of workers to help repair houses, some wagons of food . . ."

"Says there's no coin for it." Cook bit each word off separately. She began to break her dough into rolls and to slap each one down to rise. "Says the treasury was drained to build ships and man them. Said Verity took what little was left for this expedition to find Elderlings." A world of disdain on that last word. Cook paused to wipe her hands on her apron. "Then he said he was very sorry. Very truly sorry."

A cold fury uncoiled inside me. I patted Cook's shoulder and assured her that everything would be all right. Like a man in a daze, I left the kitchen and went to Verity's study. Outside the study, I paused, groping. One clear glimpse of Verity's intent. In the back of a drawer, I would find an antique emerald necklace, the stones set in gold. It had been his mother's mother's. It would be enough to hire men, and buy grain to send with them. I pushed open the study door, and halted.

Verity was an untidy man, and he had packed hastily. Charim had gone with him; he had not been here to clean up after him. But this was no act of either of them. To another man's eyes, probably little would have seemed amiss. But I saw the room both as myself and as Verity. It had been gone through. Whoever had done it had either not cared if it was detected, or had not known Verity well. Every drawer was neatly shut, every cupboard closed. The chair was pushed up close to the table. It was all too tidy. Without much hope, I went to the drawer and opened it. I pulled it completely open and peered into the back corner. Perhaps Verity's own untidiness had saved it. I would not have looked for an emerald necklace under a jumble that included an old spur, a broken belt buckle, and a piece of antler partly worked into a knife haft. But it was there, wrapped up in a scrap of homespun. There were several other small but valuable items to be removed from the room. As I gathered them I was puzzled. If these had not been taken, what had been the goal of the search? If not minor valuables, then what?

Methodically, I sorted out a dozen vellum maps, and then began to remove several others from the wall. As I was carefully rolling one of them Kettricken entered silently. My Wit had made me aware of her before she had even touched the door, so I glanced up to meet her eyes without surprise. I stood firm before the surge of Verity's emotion that rushed through me. The sight of her seemed to strengthen him within me. She was lovely, pale and slender in a robe of soft blue wool. I caught my breath and looked aside. She looked at me quizzically.

"Verity wanted these put away while he was gone. Damp can harm them, and this room is seldom heated when he is not here," I explained as I finished rolling the map.

She nodded. "It seems so empty and cold in here without him. Not just the cold hearth. There is no scent of him, none of his clutter. . . ."

"Then you tidied in here?" I tried to ask it casually.

"No!" She laughed. "My tidying only destroys what little order he keeps here. No, I will leave it as he left it, until he returns. I want him to come home to his own things in their places." Her face grew grave. "But this room is the least of it.

I sent a page to find you this morning, but you were out. Have
you heard the news about Ferry?"

"Only the gossip," I replied.

"Then you have heard as much as I. I was not summoned," she said coldly. Then she turned to me, and there was
pain in her eyes. "I heard the most of it from Lady Modesty,
who heard Regal's serving man talking to her maid. The
guardsmen went to Regal, to tell him of the messenger's arrival. Surely, they should have sent to me? Do not they think of
me as a Queen at all?"

"My lady queen," I reminded her gently. "By all rights,
the message should have been taken directly to King Shrewd. I
suspect it was, and Regal's men, who mind the King's door,
sent for him instead of you."

Her head came up. "There is a thing that must be remedied, then. Two can play at that silly game."

"I wonder if other messages have similarly gone astray," I
speculated aloud.

Her blue eyes turned gray with chill. "What do you
mean?"

"The message birds, the signal fires. A Skill message,
from Will in Red Tower to Serene. Surely at least one of these
things should have brought us word that Ferry was attacked.
One might go astray, but all three?"

Her face paled, her mind made the leap. "The Duke of
Bearns will believe his call for aid went unheeded." She lifted
a hand to cover her mouth. She whispered through it, "This is
treachery to defame Verity!" Her eyes grew very round and
she hissed at me suddenly, "It shall not be tolerated!"

She turned and rushed for the door, anger in her every
motion. I was barely able to leap in front of her. I put my back
to it, held it closed. "Lady, my lady queen, I beg you, wait!
Wait and consider!"

"Consider what? How best to reveal the depth of his per-
fidy?"

"We are not in the best position of power in this. Please,
wait. Think with me. You think, as I do, that Regal must have
known something of this and kept silent. But we have no proof.
None at all. And perhaps we are wrong. We must go a step at a

time, lest we bring dissension when we want it least. The first person to speak to must be King Shrewd. To see if he has been aware of this at all, to see if he has sanctioned Regal to speak on his behalf.''

"He would not!" she declared angrily.

"He is often not himself," I reminded her. "But he, not you, must be the one to rebuke Regal publicly, if it is to be public. If you speak out against him, and the King later supports him, the nobles will see the Farseers as a house divided. Already, there has been too much doubt and discord sown amongst them. This is not a time to set Inland Duchies against Coastal ones, with Verity not here."

She halted. I could see that she still quivered with anger, but at least she was hearing me. She took a breath. I sensed her calming herself.

"This was why he left you here, Fitz. To see these things for me."

"What?" It was my turn to be jolted.

"I thought you had known. You must have wondered why he did not ask you to accompany him. It was because I asked him who I should trust, as an adviser. He said to rely on you."

Had he forgotten Chade's existence? I wondered, and then realized that Kettricken knew nothing of Chade. He must have known I would function as a go-between. Inside myself, I felt Verity's agreement. Chade. In the shadows as always.

"Think with me again," she bade me. "What will happen next?"

She was right. This was not an isolated instance.

"We will have visitors. The Duke of Bearns and his lesser nobles. Duke Brawndy is not a man to send emissaries on a mission like that. He will come himself and he will demand answers. And all the Coastal Dukes will be listening to what is said to him. His coast is the most exposed of all, save that of Buck itself."

"Then we must have answers worth hearing," Kettricken declared. She closed her eyes. She set her hands to her forehead for a moment, then pressed her own cheeks. I realized how great a control she was keeping. Dignity, she was telling herself, calm and rationality. She took a breath and looked at me again. "I go to see King Shrewd," she announced. "I shall ask him about everything. This whole situation. I shall ask him what he intends to do. He is the King. His position must be affirmed to him."

"I think that is a wise decision," I told her.

"I must go alone. If you go with me, if you are always at my side, it will make me appear weak. It may give rise to rumors of a schism in the reign. You understand this?"

"I do." Though I longed to hear for myself what Shrewd might say to her.

She gestured at the maps and items I had sorted onto a table. "You have a safe place for those?"

Chade's chambers. "I do."

"Good." She gestured with a hand, and I realized I was still blocking her from the door. I stepped aside. As she swept past me her mountainsweet scent engulfed me for a moment. My knees went weak, and I cursed the fate that sent emeralds to rebuild houses when they should have girdled that graceful throat. But I knew, too, with a fierce pride, that if I set them in her hands this moment, she would insist they be spent for Ferry. I slipped them into a pocket. Perhaps she would be able to rouse King Shrewd's wrath, and he would rattle the coin loose from Regal's pocket. Perhaps, when I returned, these emeralds could still clasp that warm skin.

If Kettricken had looked back, she would have seen the Fitz blushing with her husband's thoughts.

I went down to the stables. It had always been a soothing place for me, and with Burrich gone I felt a certain obligation to look in on it from time to time. Not that Hands had shown any signs of needing my help. But this time as I approached the stable doors, there was a knot of men outside them, and voices raised in anger. A young stable boy hung on to the headstall of an immense draft horse. An older boy was tugging at a lead attached to the horse's halter, attempting to take the horse from the boy, as a man in Tilth colors looked on. The usually placid animal was becoming distressed at the tugging. In a moment someone was going to get hurt.

I stepped boldly into the midst of it, plucking the lead from the startled boy's hand even as I quested soothingly toward the horse. He did not know me as well as he once had, but he calmed at the touch. "What goes on here?" I asked the stable boy.

"They came and took Cliff out of his stall. Without even asking. He's my horse to take care of each day. But they didn't even tell me what they were doing."

"I have orders—" began the man who had been standing by.

"I am speaking to someone," I informed him, and turned back to the boy. "Has Hands left orders with you about this horse?"

"Only the usual ones." The boy had been close to tears when I first came on the struggle. Now that he had a potential ally, his voice was firming. He stood up straighter and met my eyes.

"Then it's simple. We take the horse back to his stall until we have other orders from Hands. No horse moves from the Buckkeep stable without the knowledge of the acting stablemaster." The boy had never let go his grip on Cliff's headstall. Now I placed the lead rope in his hands.

"Exactly what I thought, sir," he told me chippily. He turned on his heel. "Thank you, sir. Come on, Cliffie." The boy marched off with the big horse lumbering placidly after him.

"I have orders to take that animal. Duke Ram of Tilth wishes him sent up the river immediately." The man in Tilth colors was breathing through his nose at me.

"He does, does he? And has he cleared that with our stablemaster?" I was sure he had not.

"What goes on here?" This was Hands come running, very pink about the ears and cheeks. On another man it might have looked funny. I knew it meant he was angry.

The Tilth man drew himself up straight. "This man, and one of your stable hands, interfered when we came to get our stock from the stables!" he declared haughtily.

"Cliff isn't Tilth stock. He was foaled right here at Buckkeep. Six years ago. I was present at the time," I pointed out.

The man gave me a condescending look. "I was not

speaking to you. I was speaking to him." He jerked a thumb at Hands.

"I have a name, *sir,*" Hands pointed out coldly. "Hands. I'm acting as stablemaster while Burrich is gone with king-in-waiting Verity. He has a name, too. FitzChivalry. He assists me from time to time. He belongs in my stable. As does my stable boy, and my horse. As to you, if you have a name, I haven't been told it. I know of no reason why you should be in my stable."

Burrich had taught Hands well. We exchanged a glance. In accord, we turned our backs and began to go back into the stables.

"I am Lance, a stable man for Duke Ram. That horse was sold to my duke. And not just him. Two spotted mares, and a gelding as well. I have the papers here."

As we turned back slowly the Tilth man proffered a scroll. My heart lurched at the sight of a blob of red wax with the buck sign mashed into it. It looked real. Hands took it slowly. He gave me a sideways glance, and I moved to stand beside him. He had some letters, but reading was usually a lengthy business for him. Burrich had been working on it with him, but letters did not come easily to him. I looked over his shoulder as he unrolled the scroll and began to study it.

"It's quite clear," said the Tilth man. He reached for the scroll. "Shall I read it to you?"

"Don't bother," I told him as Hands rerolled the scroll. "What's written there is as plain as what's not. Prince Regal has signed it. But Cliff is not his horse. He, and the mares and gelding, are Buckkeep horses. Only the King may sell them."

"King-in-Waiting Verity is away. Prince Regal acts in his stead now."

I put a restraining hand on Hands's shoulder. "King-in-Waiting Verity is indeed away. But King Shrewd is not. Nor is Queen-in-Waiting Kettricken. One of those must sign to sell a horse from Buckkeep stable."

Lance snatched his scroll back, examined the signature for himself. "Well, Prince Regal's mark should be good enough for you, with Verity away. After all, everyone knows the old King is not in his right mind most of the time. And Kettricken is, well . . . not of the family. Really. So, with Verity gone, Regal is—''

"Prince." I spoke the word crisply. "To say less of him would be treason. As it would be to say he were king. Or queen. When he is not."

I let the implied threat settle into his mind. I would not directly accuse him of treason, for then he would have to die for it. Not even a pompous ass like Lance deserved to die just for parroting what his master had no doubt spoken aloud. I watched his eyes grow wide.

"I meant nothing. . . ."

"And no harm is done," I filled in. "As long as you remember one cannot buy a horse from a man who doesn't own it. And these are Buckkeep horses, owned by the King."

"Of course," Lance dithered. "Perhaps this is the wrong paper. I am sure there is a mistake of some kind. I will go back to my master."

"A wise choice." Hands spoke softly beside me, taking authority back.

"Well, come along, then," Lance snapped at his boy and gave the lad a shove. The boy glowered at us as he trailed off after his master. I scarcely blamed him. Lance was the sort who must vent his ill temper somewhere.

"Will they be back, do you think?" Hands asked me quietly.

"Either that, or Regal must give Ram his coin back."

We silently considered the likelihood of that.

"So. What must I do when they come back?"

"If it's only Regal's mark, nothing. If the King or Queen-in-Waiting's mark is upon it, then you must give him the horses."

"One of those mares is pregnant!" Hands protested. "Burrich has big plans for the foal. What will he say to me if he comes back and those horses are gone?"

"We have always had to remember that these horses belong to the King. He will not fault you for obeying a proper command."

"I don't like this." He looked up at me with anxious eyes.

"I don't think this would be happening if Burrich were still here."

"I think it would, Hands. Don't take any blame to yourself. I doubt that this is the worst that we'll see before the winter is over. But, send me word if they do come back."

He nodded gravely and I left him, my visit to the stables soured. I did not want to walk down the rows of stalls and wonder how many horses would still remain by the end of winter.

I walked slowly across the courtyard and then inside and up the stairs to my room. I paused on the landing. *Verity?* Nothing. I could sense his presence inside myself, he could convey his will to me and sometimes even his thoughts. But still, whenever I tried to reach out to him, there was nothing. It frustrated me. If only I had been able to Skill reliably, none of this would be happening. I paused to carefully curse Galen and all he had done to me. I had had the Skill, and he had burned it out of me, and left me with but this unpredictable form of it.

But what about Serene? Or Justin, or any of the others of the coterie? Why was not Verity using them to keep in touch with what was happening, and to let his will be known?

A creeping dread filled me. The messenger birds from Bearns. The signal lights, the Skilled ones in the towers. All the lines of communications within the kingdom and with the King seemed not to be working very well. They were what stitched the Six Duchies into one and made of us a kingdom rather than an alliance of Dukes. Now, in these troubled times, more than ever we needed them. Why were they failing?

I saved the question to ask Chade, and prayed that he would summon me soon. He called me less often than he had once, and I felt I was not as privy to his councils as I once had been. Well, and had not I excluded him from much of my life as well? Perhaps what I felt was only a reflection of all the secrets I kept from him. Perhaps it was the natural distance that grew between assassins.

I arrived at the door of my room just as Rosemary had given up knocking.

"Did you need me?" I asked her.

She dropped a grave curtsy. "Our lady, the Queen-in-

Waiting Kettricken, wishes you to attend her at your earliest convenience.''

''That's right now, isn't it?'' I tried to get a smile out of her.

''No.'' She frowned up at me. ''I said 'at your earliest convenience, sir.' Isn't that right?''

''Absolutely. Who has you practicing your manners so assiduously?''

She heaved a great sigh. ''Fedwren.''

''Fedwren is back from his summer travels already?''

''He's been back for two weeks, sir!''

''Well, see how little I know! I shall be sure to tell him of how well you spoke when next I see him.''

''Thank you, sir.'' Forgetting her careful decorum, she was skipping by the time she reached the top of the stairs, and I heard her light footsteps go cascading down them like a tumble of pebbles. A likely child. I doubted not that Fedwren was grooming her to be a messenger. It was one of his duties as scribe. I went into my room briefly to put on a fresh shirt, and then took myself down to Kettricken's chambers. I knocked on the door and Rosemary opened it.

''It is now my earliest convenience,'' I told her, and this time was rewarded with a dimpled smile.

''Enter, sir. I shall tell my mistress you are here,'' she informed me. She gestured me to a chair and vanished into the inner chamber. From within, I could hear a quiet muttering of ladies' voices. Through the open door I glimpsed them at their needlework and chatter. Queen Kettricken tilted her head to Rosemary, and then excused herself to come to me.

In a moment Kettricken stood before me. For an instant I just looked at her. The blue of the robe picked up the blue of her eyes. The late-fall light finding its way through the whorled glass of the windows glinted off the gold of her hair. I stared, I realized, and lowered my eyes. I rose immediately and bowed. She didn't wait for me to straighten up. ''Have you been recently to visit the King?'' she asked me without preamble.

''Not in the last few days, my lady queen.''

''Then I suggest you do so this evening. I am concerned for him.''

"As you wish, my queen." I waited. Surely that was not what she had called me here to say.

After a moment she sighed. "Fitz. I am alone here as I have never been before. Cannot you call me Kettricken and treat me as a person for a bit?"

The sudden change in tone took me off balance. "Certainly," I replied, but my voice was too formal. *Danger,* Nighteyes whispered.

Danger? How?

This is not your mate. This is the leader's mate.

It was like finding an aching tooth with your tongue. The knowledge jarred through me. There was a danger here, one to guard against. This was my queen, but I was not Verity and she was not my love, no matter how my heart set to beating at the sight of her.

But she was my friend. She had proven that in the Mountain Kingdom. I owed her the comfort that friends owe one another.

"I went to see the King," she told me. She gestured me to sit and took a chair of her own across the hearth from me. Rosemary fetched her little stool to sit at Kettricken's feet. Despite our being alone in the room, the Queen lowered her voice and leaned toward me as she spoke. "I asked him directly why I had not been summoned when the rider came in. He seemed puzzled by my question. But before he could even begin an answer, Regal came in. He had come in haste, I could tell. As if someone had run to tell him I was there, and he had immediately dropped everything to come."

I nodded gravely.

"He made it impossible for me to speak to the King. Instead, he insisted on explaining it all to me. He claimed that the rider had been brought directly to the King's chamber, and that he had encountered the messenger as he came to visit his father. He had sent the boy to rest while he talked with the King. And that together they had decided that nothing could be done now. Then Shrewd had sent him to announce that to the boy and the gathered nobles, and to explain to them the state of the treasury. According to Regal, we are very near on the brink of ruin, and every penny must be watched. Bearn must look out for Bearn's own, he told me. And when I asked if Bearn's own were not Six Duchies folk, he told me that Bearn had always stood more or less on its own. It was not rational, he said, to expect that Buck could guard a coast so far to the north of us, and so long. Fitz, did you know that the Near Islands had already been ceded to the Raiders?''

I shot to my feet. ''I know that no such thing is true!'' I blurted in outrage.

''Regal claims it is so,'' Kettricken continued implacably. ''He says that Verity had decided before he left that there was no real hope of keeping them safe from the Raiders. And that is why he called back our ship *Constance*. He says Verity Skilled to Carrod, the coterie member on the ship, to order the ship back home for repairs.''

''That ship was refitted just after harvest. Then she was sent out, to keep the coast between Sealbay and Gulls, and to be ready should the Near Islands call for her. It is what her master asked for; more time to practice seamanship in winter waters. Verity would not leave that stretch of coast unwatched. If the Raiders establish a stronghold on the Near Islands, we shall never be free of them. They can raid winter and summer alike from there.''

''Regal claims that is what they have done already. He says our only hope now is to treat with them.'' Her blue eyes searched my face.

I sank down slowly, near stunned. Could any of this be true? How could it have been kept from me? My sense of Verity within me mirrored my confusion. He knew nothing of this either. ''I do not think the King-in-Waiting would ever treat with the Raiders. Save with the sharp of his sword.''

''This is not, then, a secret kept from me lest it distress me? Regal implied as much, that Verity would keep these things secret from me, as beyond my understanding.'' There was a trembling in her voice. It went beyond her anger that the Near Islands might have been abandoned to the Raiders, to a more personal pain that her lord might have found her unworthy of his confidences. I longed so badly to take her in my arms and comfort her that I ached inside.

''My lady,'' I said hoarsely. ''Take this truth from my lips as surely as it came from Verity's own. All this is as false as you are true. I shall find the bottom of this net of lies and slash it wide open. We shall see what sort of fish falls out.''

''I can trust you to pursue this quietly, Fitz?''

''My lady, you are one of the few who knows the extent of my training in quiet undertakings.''

She nodded gravely. ''The King, you understand, denied none of this. But neither did he seem to follow all that Regal said. He was . . . like a child, listening to his elders converse, nodding, but understanding little. . . .'' She glanced down fondly at Rosemary at her feet.

''I shall go to see the King as well. I promise, I shall have answers for you, and soon.''

''Before Duke Bearns arrives,'' she cautioned me. ''I must have the truth by then. I owe him at least that.''

''We shall have more than just the truth for him, my lady queen,'' I promised her. The emeralds weighed heavy still in my pouch. I knew she would not begrudge them.

20

Mishaps

URING THE YEARS *of the Red-Ship raids, the Six Duchies suffered significantly from their atrocities. The folk of the Six Duchies at that time learned a greater hatred of the Outislanders than ever they had felt before.*

In their grandfathers' and fathers' times, Outislanders had been both traders and pirates. Raids were carried out by solitary ships. We had not had a raiding "war" such as this since the days of King Wisdom. Although pirate attacks were not rare occurrences, they were still far more infrequent than the Outisland ships that came to our shores to trade. The blood ties among the noble families to Outisland kin were openly acknowledged, and many a family owned to a "cousin" in the Outislands.

But after the savage raiding that preceded Forge, and the atrocities at Forge, all friendly talk of the Outislands ceased. Their ships had always been more wont to visit our shores than our traders to seek out their ice-plagued harbors and swift-tided channels. Now trade ceased entirely. Thus our folk knew nothing of their Outisland kin during the days when we suffered the Red-Ships. "Outislander" became synonymous with "Raider," and in our minds, all Outisland vessels had red hulls.

But one, Chade Fallstar, a personal adviser to King

Shrewd, took it upon himself to travel to the Outislands in those perilous days. From his journals we have this:

Kebal Rawbread was not even a name known in the Six Duchies. It was a name not breathed in the Outislands. The independent folk of the scattered and isolated villages of the Outislands had never owed allegiance to any one King. Nor was Kebal Rawbread thought of as a King there. Rather he was a malevolent force, like a freezing wind that so coats a ship's rigging with ice that in a hour she turns belly-up on the sea.

The few folk I encountered that did not fear to talk said Kebal had founded his power by subduing the individual pirates and raiding ships to his control. With those in hand, he turned his efforts to "recruiting" the best navigators, the most capable captains, and the most skillful fighters the scattered villages had to offer. Those who refused his offers saw their families escralled, or Forged, as we have come to call it. Then they were left alive to cope with the shattered remnants of their lives. Most were forced to put family members to death with their own hands; Outislander customs are strict regarding a householder's duty to maintain order amongst family members. As word of these incidents spread, fewer resisted the offers of Kebal Rawbread. Some few fled: their extended families still paid the price of escral. Others chose suicide, but again, the families were not spared. Such examples left few daring to defy Rawbread or his ships.

Even to speak against him invited escral. Sparse as was the knowledge I gained on this visit, it was gained with great difficulty. Rumors I gathered as well, though they were as sparse as black lambs in a white flock. I list them here. A "white ship" is spoken of, a ship that comes to separate souls. Not to take them, or destroy them: to separate them. They whisper, too, of a pale woman whom even Kebal Rawbread fears and reveres. Many related the torments of their land to the unprecedented advances of the "ice whales" or glaciers. Always present in the upper reaches of their narrow valleys, they now advanced more swiftly than in the memory of any living man. They were rapidly covering what little arable soil the Outislands possessed and, in a way no one could or would explain to me, bringing a "change of water."

I went to see the King that evening. It was not without trepidation on my part. He would not have forgotten our last talk about Celerity, any more than I had. I reminded myself firmly that this visit was not for my personal reasons but for Kettricken and Verity. Then I knocked and Wallace grudgingly admitted me. The King was sitting up in his chair by the hearth. The Fool was at his feet, staring pensively into the fire. King Shrewd looked up as I entered. I presented myself and he greeted me warmly, then bade me be seated and tell him how my day had gone. At this, I shot the Fool a brief puzzled glance. He returned me a bitter smile. I took a stool opposite the Fool and waited.

King Shrewd looked down on me benignly. "Well, lad? Did you have a good day? Tell me about it."

"I have had a . . . worrisome day, my king."

"Have you, now? Well, have a cup of tea. It does wonders to soothe the nerves. Fool, pour my boy a cup of tea."

"Willingly, my king. I do so at your command even more willingly than I do it for yourself." With a surprising alacrity, the Fool leaped to his feet. There was a fat clay pot of tea warming in the embers at the edges of the fire. From this the Fool poured me a mug and then handed it to me, with the wish, "Drink as deeply as our king does, and you shall share his serenity."

I took the mug from his hand and lifted it to my lips. I inhaled the vapors, then let the liquid lap lightly against my tongue. It smelled warm and spicy, and tingled pleasantly against my tongue. I did not drink, but lowered the cup with a smile. "A pleasant brew, but is not merrybud addictive?" I asked the King directly.

He smiled down on me. "Not in such a small quantity. Wallace has assured me it is good for my nerves, and for my appetite as well."

"Yes, it does wonders for the appetite," the Fool chimed in. "For the more you have, the more you shall want. Drink yours quickly, Fitz, for no doubt you will have company soon. The more you drink, the less you shall have to share." With a gesture like a petal unfurling, the Fool waved toward the door at the precise instant that it opened to admit Regal.

"Ah, more visitors." King Shrewd chuckled pleasantly. "This shall be a merry evening indeed. Sit down, my boy, sit down. The Fitz was just telling us he'd had a vexatious day. So I offered him a mug of my tea to soothe him."

"No doubt it will do him well," Regal agreed pleasantly. He turned his smile on me. "A vexatious day, Fitz?"

"A troubling one. First, there was the small matter down at the stables. One of Duke Ram's men was down there, claiming that the Duke had purchased four horses. One of them Cliff, the stud horse we use for the cart mares. I persuaded him there must be some mistake, for the papers were not signed by the King."

"Oh, those!" The King chuckled again. "Regal had to bring them back to me; I'd forgotten to sign them at all. But it is all taken care of now, and I am sure the horses will be on their way to Tilth by the morrow. Good horses, too, Duke Ram will find them. He made a wise bargain."

"I had never thought to see us sell our best stock away from Buckkeep." I spoke quietly, looking to Regal.

"And neither did I. But with the treasury as depleted as it is, we have had to take hard measures." He regarded me coolly a moment. "Sheep and cattle are to be sold as well. We have not the grain to winter them over anyway. Better to sell them now than to see them starve this winter."

I was outraged. "Why have not we heard of these shortages before? I have heard nothing of a failed harvest. Times are hard, it is true, but—"

"You have heard nothing because you have not been listening. While you and my brother have immersed yourselves in the glories of war, I have been dealing with the purse to pay for it. And it is well nigh empty. Tomorrow, I will have to tell the men working on the new ships that they must either labor for the love of it or leave off their work. There is no longer coin to pay them, nor to buy the materials that would be needed to finish the ships." He finished his speech and leaned back, considering me.

Within me, Verity roiled. I looked to King Shrewd. "This is true, my king?" I asked.

King Shrewd started. He looked over at me and blinked his eyes a few times. "I did sign those papers, did I not?" He seemed puzzled, and I think his mind had gone back to a previous conversation. He had not followed our talk at all. At his feet, the Fool was strangely silent. "I thought I had signed the papers. Well, bring them to me now, then. Let us get this done, and then get on with a pleasant evening."

"What is to be done about the situation in Bearns? Is it true that the Raiders have taken parts of the Near Islands?"

"The situation in Bearns," he said. He paused, considering. He took another sip of his tea.

"Nothing can be done about the situation in Bearns," Regal said sadly. Smoothly he added, "It is time Bearns took care of Bearns's troubles. We cannot beggar all Six Duchies to protect a barren stretch of coastline. So the Raiders have helped themselves to a few frozen rocks. I wish them joy of them. We have folk of our own to care for, villages of our own to rebuild."

I waited in vain for Shrewd to rouse, to say something in defense of Bearns. When he was silent, I asked quietly, "The town of Ferry is scarcely a frozen rock. At least, it wasn't until the Red-Ships called. And when did Bearns cease to be part of the Six Duchies?" I looked to Shrewd, tried to make him meet my eyes. "My king, I beg you, order Serene to come. Have her Skill to Verity, that you may counsel together about this."

Regal grew suddenly weary of our cat and mouse. "When did the dog boy come to be so concerned with politics?" he asked me savagely. "Why cannot you understand that the King can make decisions without the permission of the King-in-Waiting? Do you quiz your king on his decisions, *Fitz*? Have you so far forgotten your place? I knew Verity had made something of a pet of you, and perhaps your adventures with your ax have given you large ideas of yourself. But Prince Verity has seen fit to go gallivanting off after a chimera, and I am left to keep the Six Duchies rattling along as best I may."

"I was present when you endorsed King-in-Waiting Verity's proposal to seek the Elderlings," I pointed out. King

Shrewd seemed to have gone off into another waking dream. He stared into the fire.

"And why that was so, I have no idea," Regal rejoined smoothly. "As I observed, you have come to have large ideas of yourself. You eat at the high table, and are clothed by the King's largesse, and somehow you have come to believe this gives you privileges rather than duties. Let me tell you who you really are, Fitz." Regal paused. To me it seemed he looked at the King, as if gauging how safe it was for him to speak.

"You," he continued in a lowered voice, tone as sweet as a minstrel's. "You are the misbegotten bastard of a princeling who had not even the courage to continue as King-in-Waiting. You are the grandson of a dead Queen whose common breeding showed in the common woman her eldest son bedded to conceive you. You who take the name to yourself of FitzChivalry Farseer need do no more than scratch yourself to find Nameless the dog boy. Be grateful I do not send you back to the stables, but suffer to let you abide in the Keep."

I do not know what I felt. Nighteyes was snarling to the venom in Regal's words, while Verity was capable of fratricide at that moment. I glanced at King Shrewd. He cupped his mug of sweet tea in both hands and dreamed into the fire. From the corner of my eyes, I had a glimpse of the Fool. There was fear in his colorless eyes, fear as I had never seen there before. And he was looking, not at Regal, but at me.

I abruptly realized that I had arisen and was standing over Regal. He was looking up at me. Waiting. There was a glint of fear in his eyes, but also the shine of triumph. All I would have to do was strike at him, and he could call the guards. It would be treason. He would hang me for it. I felt how the fabric of my shirt was binding on my shoulders and chest, so swollen with rage was I. I tried to exhale, willed the balled fists of my hands to loosen. It took a moment. *Hush,* I told them. *Hush, or you'll get me killed.* When I had my voice under control, I spoke.

"Many things have been made clear to me this night," I said quietly. I turned to King Shrewd. "My lord king, I bid you good evening, and ask to be excused from your presence."

"Eh? So you . . . had an anxious day, lad?"

"I did, my lord king," I said softly. His deep eyes looked

up into mine as I stood before him, waiting to be released. I looked deep into their depths. He was not there. Not as he once had been. He looked at me puzzledly, blinked a few times.

"Well. Perhaps you had best get some rest, then. As should I. Fool? Fool, is my bed prepared? Warm it with the warming pan. I grow so cold at night these days. Ha! At night these days! There's a bit of nonsense for you, Fool. How would you say it, to get it aright?"

The Fool sprang to his feet, bowed deeply before the King. "I would say there's the chill of death about the days these nights as well, Your Majesty. A cold fair to curl the bones, it is. A man could take his death of it. 'T would warm me more to hide in your shade than to stand before your sun's heat."

King Shrewd chuckled. "You don't make a bit of sense, Fool. But then you never did. Good night to all, and off to bed, lads, both of you. Good night, good night."

I slipped out while Regal was saying a more formal good night to his father. It was all I could do to walk past Wallace's simpering smile without smashing it from his face. Once in the hall outside, I swiftly sought my own room. I would take the Fool's advice, I thought, and hide myself in Chade rather than stand before the heat of the King's son.

I spent the rest of that evening in my room alone. I knew that as night deepened, Molly would wonder when I did not come tapping at her door. But I had no heart for it tonight. I could not summon the energy to slip out of my room and go creeping up the stairs and slinking down the corridors, always worrying that someone might step out abruptly and find me where I had no right to be. At one time I would have sought out Molly's warmth and affection and found a measure of peace there. That was no longer the case. Now I dreaded the stealth and anxiety of our meetings, and a guardedness that did not even end when her door closed behind me. For Verity rode within me, and ever I must guard that what I felt and thought with Molly did not spill over into the link I shared with Verity.

I gave up on the scroll I had been trying to read. What use now to learn of Elderlings, anyway? Verity would find whatever Verity found. I flung myself back on my bed and stared up at the ceiling. Even still and silent, there was no peace in me.

My link to Verity was like a hook in my flesh; so must a snagged fish feel when it fights the line. My ties to Nighteyes were on a deeper, more subtle level, but ever he was there as well, green eyes lambent in a dark corner of myself. These parts of me never slept, never rested, were never quiescent at all. And that constant strain was beginning to tell on me.

Hours later the candles were guttering and the fire burned low. A change in the air of my room let me know that Chade had opened his soundless door to me. I arose and went to him. But with every step I took up that drafty staircase, my anger grew. It was not the kind of anger that led to ranting and blows between men. This was an anger born as much from weariness and frustration as from any hurt. This was the sort of anger that led a man to stop everything, to say simply, ''I cannot bear this anymore.''

''Cannot bear what?'' Chade asked me. He looked up from where he hunched over some concoction he was grinding on his stained stone table. There was genuine concern in his voice. It made me really stop and look at the man I addressed. A tall, skinny old assassin. Pox-scarred. Hair gone almost entirely white now. Wearing the familiar gray wool robe, always with stains or the tiny burns he inflicted on his clothes while he worked. I wondered how many men he had killed for his king, killed simply at a word or nod from Shrewd. Killed without question, true to his oath. For all those deaths, he was a gentle man. Suddenly I had a question, a question more pressing than answering his question.

''Chade,'' I asked, ''have you ever killed a man for your own sake?''

He looked startled. ''For my own sake?''

''Yes.''

''To protect my own life?''

''Yes. I don't mean when on the King's business. I mean killed a man to . . . make your life simpler.''

He snorted. ''Of course not.'' He looked at me strangely.

''Why not?'' I pressed.

He looked incredulous. ''One simply does not go about killing people for convenience. It's wrong. It's called murder, boy.''

"Unless you do it for your king."

"Unless you do it for your king," he agreed easily.

"Chade. What's the difference? If you do it for yourself, or if you do it for Shrewd?"

He sighed and gave up on the mixture he was making. He moved around the end of the table, sat on a tall stool there. "I remember asking these questions. But of myself, as my mentor was gone by the time I was your age." He met my eyes firmly. "It comes down to faith, boy. Do you believe in your king? And your king has to be more to you than your half brother, or your grandfather. He has to be more than good old Shrewd, or fine honest Verity. He has to be the King. The heart of the kingdom, the center of the wheel. If he is that, and if you have faith that the Six Duchies are worth preserving, that the good of all our people are furthered by dispensing the King's justice, then, well."

"Then you can kill for him."

"Exactly."

"Have you ever killed against your own judgment?"

"You have many questions this night," he warned me quietly.

"Perhaps you have left me alone too long to think of them all. When we met near nightly, and talked often and I was busy all the time, I did not think so much. But now I do."

He nodded slowly. "Thinking is not always . . . comforting. It is always good, but not always comforting. Yes. I've killed against my own judgment. Again, it came down to faith. I had to believe that the folk who gave the order knew more than I did, and were wiser in the ways of the wider world."

I was silent for a long moment. Chade started to relax. "Come in. Don't stand there in the draft. Let's have a glass of wine together, and then I need to talk to you about—"

"Have you ever killed solely on the basis of your own judgment? For the good of the kingdom?"

For a time Chade looked at me, troubled. I did not look away. He did, finally, staring down at his old hands, rubbing their papery-white skin against each other as he fingered the brilliant red pocks. "I do not make those judgments." He looked up at me suddenly. "I never accepted that burden, nor wished to. It is not our place, boy. Those decisions are for the King."

"I am not 'boy,' " I pointed out, surprising myself. "I am FitzChivalry."

"With an emphasis on the Fitz," Chade pointed out harshly. "You are the illegitimate get of a man who did not step up to become king. He abdicated. And in that abdication, he set aside from himself the making of judgments. You are not king, Fitz, nor even the son of a true King. We are assassins."

"Why do we stand by while the true King is poisoned?" I asked bluntly then. "I see it, you see it. He is lured into using herbs that steal his mind and, while he cannot think well, lured to use ones that make him even more foolish. We know its immediate source, and I suspect its true source. And yet we watch him dwindle and grow feeble. Why? Where is the faith in that?"

His words cut me like knives. "I do not know where your faith is. I had thought perhaps it would be in me. That I knew more about it than you did, and that I was loyal to my king."

It was my turn to drop my eyes. After a moment I crossed the room slowly, to the cabinet where Chade kept the wine and the glasses. I took down a tray and poured two careful glasses from the glass-stoppered bottle. I took the tray to the small table by the hearth. As I had for so many years, I seated myself on the hearthstones. After a moment my master came and took his place in his well-cushioned chair. He lifted his wineglass from the tray and sipped.

"This last year has not been an easy time for either of us."

"You have so seldom called me. And when you do, you are full of secrets." I tried to keep the accusation from my voice, but couldn't quite.

Chade gave a short bark of laughter. "And you being such an open spontaneous fellow, that annoys you?" He laughed again, ignoring my offended look. When he had done, he wet his mouth with wine again, then looked at me. Amusement still danced in his dark eyes.

"Do not glower at me, *boy*," he told me. "I have not expected anything from you that you have not demanded from ιe twofold. And more. For I have it in my mind that a master as some right to expect faith and trust from his student."

"You do," I said after some moments. "And you are ight. I have my secrets as well, and I have expected you to rust that they are honorable ones. But my secrets do not contrain you as yours do mine. Every time I visit the King's hambers, I see what Wallace's Smokes and potions are doing o him. I want to kill Wallace, and restore my king to his wits. And after that, I want to . . . finish the task. I want to elimiate the source of the poisons."

"You wish to kill me, then?"

It was like being doused with cold water. "You are the ource of the poisons Wallace gives to the King?" I was sure I ιad misunderstood.

He nodded slowly. "Some of them. Probably the ones you nost object to."

My heart was cold and still inside me. "But, Chade, vhy?"

He looked at me, his lips folded tight. After a moment he ɔpened his mouth and spoke softly. "A King's secrets belong ɔ a King only. They are not mine to give away, no matter if I hink the receiver would keep them safe or not. But if you would only use your mind as I have trained you, you would ɟnow my secrets. For I have not hidden them from you. And from my secret, you could deduce much on your own."

I turned to poke at the fire behind me. "Chade. I am so weary. Too weary to play at games. Cannot you simply tell me?"

"Of course I could. But it would compromise my promise ɟo my king. What I do is bad enough."

"You are splitting hairs over this!" I exclaimed angrily.

"Perhaps, but they are mine to split," he replied with equanimity.

His very calmness infuriated me. I shook my head violently, put the whole puzzle away from myself for a bit. "Why did you summon me tonight?" I asked flatly.

There was a shadow of hurt behind the calm in his eyes now. "Perhaps just to see you. Perhaps to forestall your doing something foolish and permanent. I know that much of what is

going on right now distresses you greatly. I assure you, I share
your fears. But for now, we must continue on our allotted
paths. With faith. Surely you believe that Verity will return
before spring, and put all to rights.''

"I don't know," I admitted grudgingly. "It shocked me
when he set off on this ridiculous quest. He should have stayed
here and continued with his original plan. By the time he
returns, half his kingdom will be beggared or given away, the
way Regal is going at things.''

Chade looked at me levelly. " 'His' kingdom is still King
Shrewd's kingdom. Remember? Perhaps he has faith in his
father to keep it intact.''

"I do not think King Shrewd can even keep himself intact,
Chade. Have you seen him of late?''

Chade's mouth went to a flat line. "Yes." He bit the word
off. "I see him when no one else does. I tell you that he is not
the feeble idiot you seem to believe he is.''

I shook my head slowly. "If you had seen him tonight,
Chade, you would share my anxiety.''

"What makes you so sure I did not?" Chade was nettled
now. I had no wish to anger the old man. But it seemed to be
going all wrong, no matter how I spoke. I forced myself to
keep silent now. Instead of speaking, I took another sip of my
wine. I stared into the fire.

"Are the rumors about the Near Islands true?" I asked at
last. My voice was my own again.

Chade sighed and rubbed at his eyes with his knuckly
hands. "As in all rumors, there is a germ of truth. It may be
true that the Raiders have established a base there. We are not
certain. We have certainly not ceded the Near Islands to them.
As you observed, once they had the Near Islands, they would
raid our coast winter and summer.''

"Prince Regal seemed to believe that they could be bought
off. That perhaps those islands and a bit of Bearns's coast were
what they were truly after." It was an effort, but I kept my
voice respectful as I spoke of Regal.

"Many men hope that by saying a thing they can make it
so," Chade said neutrally. "Even when they must know better," he added as a darker afterthought.

"What do you think the Raiders want?" I asked.

He stared past me into the fire. "Now, there is a puzzle. What do the Raiders want? It is how our minds work, Fitz. We think they attack us because they want something from us. But surely, if they wanted something, by now they would have demanded it. They know the damage they do to us. They must know that we would at least consider their demands. But they ask for nothing. They simply go on raiding."

"They make no sense." I finished the thought for him.

"Not the way we see sense," he corrected me. "But what if our basic assumption is wrong?"

I just stared at him.

"What if they don't want anything, except what they already have? A nation of victims. Towns to raid, villages to torch, people to torture. What if that is their entire aim?"

"That's insane," I said slowly.

"Perhaps. But what if it is so?"

"Then nothing will stop them. Except destroying them."

He nodded slowly. "Follow that thought."

"We don't have enough ships to even slow them down." I considered a moment. "We had best all hope the myths about the Elderlings are true. Because it seems to me they, or something like them, is our only hope."

Chade nodded slowly. "Exactly. So you see why I approve of Verity's course."

"Because it's our only hope of survival."

We sat for a long time together, staring into the fire silently. When I finally returned to my bed that night, I was assailed by nightmares of Verity attacked and battling for his life while I stood by and watched. I could not kill any of his attackers, for my king had not said I could.

⇥═╠

Twelve days later, Duke Brawndy of Bearns arrived. He came down the coast road, at the head of enough men to be impressive without being an open threat. He had mustered as much pomp and panoply as his dukedom could afford. His daughters rode at his side, save for the eldest, who had remained behind to do all that could be done for Ferry. I spent most of the early afternoon in the stables, and then in the guardroom, listening to the talk of the lesser members of his entourage. Hands acquitted himself well at seeing that there was space and care for their beasts, and as always, our kitchens and barracks made themselves hospitable places. Still, there was plenty of hard talk among the folk from Bearns. They spoke bluntly of what they had seen at Ferry, and how their summons for help had gone unheeded. It shamed our soldiers that there was little they could say to defend what King Shrewd had apparently done. And when a soldier cannot defend what his leader has done, he must either agree with the criticism or find another area in which to disagree. So there were fistfights between Bearns men and Buckkeep troops, isolated incidents for the most part, and over trivial differences. But such things did not usually happen under the discipline at Buckkeep, and so they were all the more unsettling. It underscored to me the confusion among our own troops.

I dressed carefully for dinner that evening, unsure as to who I might encounter or what might be expected of me. I had glimpsed Celerity twice that day, and each time slipped away before I could be noticed. I expected she would be my dinner partner, and dreaded it. Now was no time to give anyone from Bearns any sort of affront, but I did not wish to encourage her. I could have saved my worrying. I found myself seated far down the table, among the lesser nobility, and the younger ones at that. I spent an uncomfortable evening as a minor novelty. Several of the girls at the table attempted to be flirtatious. This was a new experience for me and not one I relished. It made me realize just how great an influx of folk had swollen the Buckkeep court that winter. Most of them were from the Inland Duchies, sniffing after scraps from Regal's plate, but as these young women plainly indicated, they would be happy to court political influence wherever they could. The effort to follow their attempts at witty banter and respond on a level of at least moderate politeness made it nearly impossible for me to give any attention to what was going on at the High Table. King Shrewd was there, seated between Queen-in-Waiting Kettricken and Prince Regal. Duke Brawndy and his daughters Celerity and Faith were seated closest to them. The rest of the

able was filled with Regal's pets. Duke Ram of Tilth and his
Lady Placid, and their two sons were the most noteworthy.
Regal's cousin Lord Bright was there as well; the young heir to
he Duke of Farrow was new to court.

From where I sat, I could see little, and hear even less. I
elt Verity's churning frustration at the situation, but there was
nothing I could do about it. The King looked more weary than
dazed that evening, which I took to be positive. Kettricken,
seated beside him, was near colorless save for two spots of pink
on her cheeks. She did not seem to be eating much, and seemed
graver and more silent than usual. Prince Regal, in contrast,
was both social and merry. With Duke Ram and Lady Placid
and their boys. He did not quite ignore Brawndy and his daughters, but his merriment clearly grated on the visitors' mood.

Duke Brawndy was a large man, and well muscled even in
his old age. Shocks of white hair in his black warrior's tail
attested to old battle injuries, as did a hand missing a few
fingers. His daughters sat just downtable from him, indigo-
eyed women whose high cheekbones told of his late queen's
Near Island ancestry. Faith and Celerity wore their hair cut
short and sleek in the northern style. The quick ways they
turned their heads to observe everyone at the table reminded
me of hawks on a wrist. These were not the gentled nobility of
the Inland Duchies that Regal was used to dealing with. Of all
the Six Duchies, the folk of Bearns came closest to being
warriors still.

Regal was courting disaster to make light of their griev-
ances. I knew they would not expect to discuss Raiders at the
table, but his festive tone was completely at odds with their
mission here. I wondered if he knew how badly he offended
them. Kettricken obviously did. More than once I saw her
clench her jaw, or cast her eyes downward at one of Regal's
witticisms. He was drinking too heavily as well, and it began to
show in his extravagant hand gestures, and the loudness of his
laughter. I wished desperately I could hear what he was finding
so humorous in his own words.

Dinner seemed interminable. Celerity rapidly located me
at table. After that, I was hard put to avoid the measuring looks
she sent my way. I nodded affably to her the first time our eyes

locked; I could tell she was puzzled by where I had been
seated. I dared not ignore every look she sent my way. Regal
was offensive enough without my appearing to snub Bearns's
daughter as well. I felt I teetered on a fence. I was grateful
when King Shrewd rose and Queen Kettricken insisted on taking his arm to help him from the room. Regal frowned a trifle
drunkenly to see the party disperse so soon, but made no effort
to persuade Duke Brawndy and his daughters to stay at table.
They excused themselves rather stiffly as soon as Shrewd had
departed. I likewise made excuse of a headache and left my
giggling companions for the solitude of my room. As I opened
my door and went into my bedchamber, I felt myself the most
powerless person in the Keep. Nameless the dog boy indeed.

"I see dinner was absolutely fascinating for you," the
Fool observed. I sighed. I didn't ask how he had gotten in. No
point to asking questions that would not be answered. He was
sitting on my hearth, silhouetted against the dancing flames of
a small fire he had kindled there. There was a peculiar stillness
to him, no jingling of bells, no tumbling mocking words.

"Dinner was insufferable," I told him. I did not bother
with candles. My headache had not been entirely a fiction. I
sat, then lay back on my bed with a sigh. "I do not know what
Buckkeep is coming to, nor what I can do about it."

"Perhaps what you have already done is enough?" the
Fool ventured.

"I've done nothing noteworthy lately," I informed him.
"Unless you count knowing when to stop talking back to Regal."

"Ah. That's a skill we're all learning, then," he agreed
morosely. He drew his knees up to his chin, rested his arms
atop them. He took a breath. "Have you no news, then, that
you'd care to share with a Fool? A very discreet Fool?"

"I've no news to share with you that you would not already know, and probably sooner than I did." The darkness of
the room was restful. My headache was easing.

"Ah." He paused delicately. "Shall I, perhaps, ask a
question? To be answered or not as you see fit?"

"Save your breath and ask it. You know you shall, whether
I give you permission or no."

"Indeed, there you are right. Well then. The question. Ah, I surprise myself, I blush, I do. FitzChivalry, have you made a fitz of your own?"

I sat up slowly on my bed and stared at him. He did not move nor flinch. "What did you ask me?" I demanded quietly.

He spoke softly, almost apologetically now. "I must know. Is Molly carrying your child?"

I sprang at him from the bed, caught him by the throat, and dragged him up to his feet. I drew back my fist, and then stopped, shocked by what the firelight revealed on his face.

"Batter away," he suggested quietly. "New bruises will not show much atop the old ones. I can creep about unseen for a few more days."

I snatched my hand back from him. Strange, how the act I had been about to commit now seemed so monstrous when I discovered someone else had already done it. As soon as I released him, he turned away from me, as if his discolored and swollen face shamed him. Perhaps the pallor of his skin and his delicate bone structure made it all the more horrifying to me. It was as if someone had done this to a child. I knelt by the fire and began to build it up.

"Didn't get a good enough look?" the Fool asked acidly. "I'll warn you, it gets no better by giving more light to it."

"Sit on my clothes chest and take your shirt off," I told him brusquely. He didn't move. I ignored that. I had a small kettle for tea water. This I set to heat. I lit a branch of candles and set them atop the table, and then took out my small store of herbs. I did not keep that many in my room; I wished now I had Burrich's full store to draw on, but I was sure that if I left to go to the stables, the Fool would be gone when I returned. Still, those I kept in my room were mostly for bruises and cuts and the types of injuries my other profession exposed me to most often. They would do.

When the water was warm, I poured some into my washbasin and added a generous handful of herbs, crushing them as I did so. I found an outgrown shirt in my clothing chest and tore it into rags. "Come into the light." This I phrased as a request. After a moment he did so, but moving hesitantly and shyly. I looked at him briefly, then took him by the shoulders and sat him down atop my clothing chest. "What happened to you?" I asked, awed by the damage to his face. His lips were cut and swollen, and one eye swollen near closed.

"I've been going about Buckkeep, asking bad-tempered individuals if they've fathered bastards lately." His one good eye met my glare straight on. Red webbed the white of it. I found I could neither be angry with him, nor laugh.

"You should know enough medicine to take better care of something like this. Sit still now." I made the rag into a compress, held it gently but firmly to his face. After a moment he relaxed. I sponged away some dried blood. There wasn't much; he had obviously cleaned himself up after this beating, but some of the cuts had continued to ooze blood. I ran my fingers lightly down the lines of his jaw, and around his eye sockets. At least no bone seemed damaged. "Who did this to you?" I asked him.

"I walked into a series of doors. Or the same one several times. It depends on which door you ask." He spoke glibly for someone with mashed lips.

"That was a serious question," I told him.

"As was mine."

I glared at him again and he dropped his eyes. For a moment neither of us spoke as I searched out a pot of salve Burrich had given me for cuts and scrapes. "I'd really like to know the answer," I reminded him as I took the lid off the pot. The familiar biting scent rose to my nostrils, and I suddenly missed Burrich with an amazing intensity.

"As would I." He flinched slightly under my touch as I applied the salve. I knew it stung. I also knew it worked.

"Why do you ask such a question of me?" I finally demanded.

He considered a moment. "Because it is easier to ask of you than to ask Kettricken if she carries Verity's child. As far as I can determine, Regal has shared his favors only with himself of late, so that dismisses him. You or Verity, then, must be the father."

I looked at him blankly. He shook his head sadly for me. "Cannot you feel it?" he asked in a near whisper. He stared off in the distance dramatically. "Forces shift. Shadows flutter.

Suddenly there is a rippling in the possibilities. A reordering of the futures, as destinies multiply. All paths diverge, and diverge again.'' He looked back to me. I smiled at him, thinking he jested, but his mouth was sober. ''There is an heir to the Farseer line,'' he said quietly. ''I am certain of it.''

Have you ever missed a step in the dark? There is that sudden feeling of teetering on the edge, and no knowledge of how far you may fall. I said, far too firmly, ''I have fathered no child.''

The Fool regarded me with a skeptical eye. ''Ah,'' he said with false heartiness. ''Of course not. Then it must be Kettricken who is carrying.''

''It must,'' I agreed, but my heart sank. If Kettricken were pregnant, she would have no reason to conceal it. Whereas Molly would. And I had not been to see Molly in several nights. Perhaps she had news for me. I felt suddenly dizzied, but I forced myself to take a long calming breath. ''Take your shirt off,'' I told the Fool. ''Let's see your chest.''

''I've seen it, thank you, and I assure you it's fine. When they popped the bag over my head, I presume it was to provide a target. They were most conscientious about striking nowhere else.''

The brutality of what they had done to him sickened me into silence. ''Who?'' I finally managed to ask.

''With a bag over my head? Come now. Can you see through a bag?''

''No. But you must have suspicions.''

He canted his head at me in disbelief. ''If you do not know what those suspicions are already, then you are the one with your head in a bag. Let me cut a bit of a hole for you. 'We know you are false to the King, that you spy for Verity the pretender. Send him no more messages, for if you do, we shall know of it.' '' He turned to stare into the fire, swung his heels briefly, *thunk, thunk, thunk,* against my clothing chest.

''Verity the pretender?'' I asked in outrage.

''Not my words. Theirs,'' he pointed out.

I forced my anger down, tried to think. ''Why would they suspect you spy for Verity? Have you sent him messages?''

''I have a King,'' he said softly. ''Although he does not

always remember he is my king. You must look out for your king. As I am sure you do.''

"What will you do?"

''What I have always done. What else can I do? I cannot stop doing what they command me to stop, for I have never begun it.''

A creeping certainty shivered up my spine. ''And if they act again?''

He gave a lifeless laugh. ''There is no point to my worrying about it, for I cannot prevent it. That is not to say I look forward to it. This,'' he said, with a half gesture toward his face. ''This will heal. What they did to my room will not. I shall be weeks picking up that mess.''

The words trivialized it. A terrible hollow feeling welled up in me. I had been in the Fool's tower chamber once. It had been a long climb up a disused staircase, past the dust and litter of years, to a chamber that looked out over the parapets and contained a garden of wonder. I thought of the bright fish swimming in the fat pots, the moss gardens in their containers, the tiny ceramic child, so meticulously cared for, in its cradle. I closed my eyes as he added to the flames, ''They were most thorough. Silly me. To think there was such a thing as a safe place in the world.''

I could not look at him. Save for his tongue, he was a defenseless person whose only drive was to serve his king. And save the world. Yet someone had smashed his world. Worse, I suspected the beating he had taken was in revenge for something I had done.

''I could help you set it to rights,'' I offered quietly.

He shook his head tightly, quickly twice. ''I think not,'' he said. Then he added in a more normal voice, ''No offense intended.''

''None taken.''

I bundled the cleansing herbs with the pot of salve and the leftover rags from my shirt. He hopped off my clothes chest. When I offered them to him, he took them gravely. He walked to the door, stiffly despite his claims that they had only damaged his face. At the door he turned. ''When you know for certain, you will tell me?'' He paused significantly. His voice dropped. "After all, if this is what they do to a King's fool, what might they do to a woman carrying a King-in-Waiting's heir?"

"They wouldn't dare," I said fiercely.

He snorted disdain. "Wouldn't they? I no longer know what they would or would not dare, FitzChivalry. Neither do you. I'd find a sounder way to latch my door, if I were you. Unless you wish to find your head in a bag as well." He gave a smile that wasn't even a shadow of his usual mocking grin, and slipped out again. I walked to the door after he had left it, and dropped the bar into place. I leaned my back against it and sighed.

"It's all very well for the rest of them, Verity," I said aloud to the silent room. "But for myself, I think you should turn yourself about right now and ride home. There's more afoot than Red-Ships, and somehow I misdoubt that Elderlings would be much help against the other threats we face."

I waited, hoping to feel some sort of acknowledgment or agreement from him. There was nothing. My frustrations whirled in me. I was seldom certain of when Verity was aware with me, and never sure if he sensed the thoughts I wished to send him. I wondered again at why he did not direct Serene as to the actions he wished taken. He had Skilled to her all summer about Red-Ships; why was he so silent now? Had he Skilled to her already, and she concealed it? Or revealed it, perhaps, to Regal only. I considered it. Perhaps the bruises on the Fool's face reflected Regal's frustration at finding Verity aware of what was going on in his absence. Why he had chosen the Fool as the culprit was anyone's guess. Perhaps he had simply chosen him as a vent for his rage. The Fool had never avoided offending Regal. Or anyone else.

Later that night, I went to Molly. It was a dangerous time to go, for the Keep was abuzz with extra folk and extra servants taking care of them. But my suspicions would not let me stay away. When I tapped on the door that night, Molly asked through the wood, "Who is it?"

"It's me," I replied incredulously. She had never asked before.

"Oh," she replied, and opened the door. I slipped inside

and bolted it behind me as she crossed to the hearth. She knelt before it, adding wood it didn't need and not looking at me. She was dressed in her blue servant's dress, and her hair was still bundled up. Every line of her body warned me. I was in trouble again.

"I'm sorry I haven't been here much lately."

"So am I," Molly said shortly.

She wasn't leaving me much in the way of openings. "A lot has been going on, and they've been keeping me pretty busy."

"With what?"

I sighed. I already knew where this conversation was going. "With things I can't talk to you about."

"Of course." For all the calmness and coolness in her voice, I knew her fury was raging just beneath the surface. The slightest wrong word would set it off. So would not saying anything. So my question might as well be tackled head-on.

"Molly, the reason I came tonight—"

"Oh, I knew there had to be some special reason for you to finally drop by. The only thing that really surprises me is myself. Why am I here? Why do I come straight to my room after my duties each day and wait, on the off chance that you might show up? There are other things I could be doing. There are minstrels and puppet shows aplenty lately. Prince Regal sees to that. I could be at one of the lesser hearths with the other servants, enjoying their company. Instead of up here alone. Or I could be getting some work done. Cook lets me use the kitchen when it's not a busy time. I have wicking and herbs and tallow; I should be using them while the herbs still have their full potency. But no, I am up here, on the off chance that you'll remember me and want to spend a few moments with me."

I stood like a rock in the battering waves of her words. There was nothing else I could do. Everything she said was true. I looked at my feet while she caught her breath. When she spoke again, the anger had faded from her voice, to be replaced with something worse. Misery and discouragement.

"Fitz, it's just so hard. Every time I think I have accepted it, I turn a corner and catch myself hoping again. But there's never going to be anything for us, is there? Never going to be a time that belongs just to us, never going to be a place that is just ours.'' She paused. She looked down, biting on her lower lip. When she spoke, her voice trembled. ''I've seen Celerity. She's beautiful. I even made an excuse to speak to her. . . . I asked if they needed more candles for their rooms. . . . She spoke back, shyly, but courteously. She even thanked me for being concerned, as few here thank servants. She's . . . she's nice. A Lady. Oh, they'll never give you permission to marry me. Why would you want to marry a servant?''

''You are not a servant to me,'' I said quietly. ''I never think of you that way.''

''Then what am I? I am not a wife,'' she pointed out quietly.

''In my heart, you are,'' I said miserably. It was a pitiful comfort to offer her. It shamed me that she accepted it, and came to rest her forehead on my shoulder. I held her gently for a few moments, then pulled her into a warmer embrace. As she nestled against me I said softly into her hair, ''There's something I have to ask you.''

''What?''

''Are you . . . with child?''

''What?'' She pulled back from me, to look up into my face.

''Are you carrying my child?''

''I . . . no. No, I'm not.'' A pause. ''What makes you ask such a thing all of a sudden?''

''It just occurred to me to wonder. That's all. I mean—''

''I know what you mean. If we were married, and I weren't pregnant by now, the neighbors would be shaking their heads over us.''

''Really?'' Such a thing had never occurred to me before. I knew that some folk wondered if Kettricken were barren, as she had not conceived in over a year of marriage, but a concern over her childlessness was a public issue. I had never thought of neighbors watching newlyweds expectantly.

''Of course. By now, someone would have offered me a tea recipe from their mother's telling. Or powdered boar's tusk to slip into your ale at night.''

"Oh really?" I gathered her closer to me, grinning fool-ishly.

"Um." She smiled back up at me. The smile faded slowly. "As it is," she said quietly, "there are other herbs I take. To be sure that I do not conceive."

I had all but forgotten Patience scolding me that day. "Some herbs like that, I've heard, can make a woman ill, if she takes them for long."

"I know what I'm doing," she said flatly. "Besides, what is the alternative?" she added with less heart.

"Disaster," I conceded.

She nodded her head against me. "Fitz. If I had said yes tonight. If I were pregnant . . . what would you have done?"

"I don't know. I haven't thought about it."

"Think about it now," she begged me.

I spoke slowly. "I suppose I'd . . . get a place for you, somehow, somewhere." (I'd go to Chade, I'd go to Burrich, and I'd beg for help. Inwardly I blanched to think of it.) "A safe place. Away from Buckkeep. Upriver, maybe. I'd come to see you when I could. Somehow, I'd take care of you."

"You'd set me aside is what you're saying. Me, and our . . . my child."

"No! I'd keep you safe, put you where no one would point shame at you or mock you for having a child alone. And when I could, I'd come to you and *our* child."

"Have you ever considered that you could come with us? That we could leave Buckkeep, you and I, and go upriver now?"

"I can't leave Buckkeep. I've explained that to you every way I know how."

"I know you have. I've tried to understand it. But I don't see why."

"The work I do for the King is such that—"

"Stop doing it. Let someone else do it. Go away with me, to a life of our own."

"I can't. It's not that simple. I wouldn't be allowed to just leave like that." Somehow, we had come uncoupled. Now she folded her arms across her chest.

"Verity's gone. Almost no one believes he's coming back.

King Shrewd grows more feeble each day, and Regal prepares himself to inherit. If half of Regal's feelings for you are what you say they are, why on earth would you wish to stay here with him as king? Why would he want to keep you here? Fitz, can't you see that it's all tumbling apart? The Near Islands and Ferry are just the beginning. The Raiders won't stop there."

"All the more reason for me to stay here. To work and, if need be, fight for our people."

"One man can't stop them," Molly pointed out. "Not even a man as stubborn as you. Why not take all that stubbornness and fight for us instead? Why don't we run away, up the river and inland, away from the Raiders, to a life of our own? Why should we have to give up everything for a hopeless cause?"

I couldn't believe what I was hearing from her. If I had said it, it would have been treason. But she said it as if it were the commonest sense. As if she and I and a child that didn't exist yet were more important than the King and the Six Duchies combined. I said as much.

"Well," she asked me, looking at me levelly. "It's true. To me. If you were my husband and I had our child, that's how important it would be to me. More important than the whole rest of the world."

And what was I to say to that? I reached for the truth, knowing it wouldn't satisfy her. "You would be that important to me. You are that important to me. But it's also why I have to stay here. Because something that important isn't something you run away and hide with. It's something that you stand and defend."

"Defend?" Her voice went up a notch. "When will you learn we aren't strong enough to defend ourselves? I know. I've stood between Raiders and children of my own blood, and just barely survived. When you've done that, talk to me about defending!"

I was silent. Not just that her words cut me. They did, and deeply. But she brought back to me a memory of holding a child, studying the blood that had trickled down her cooling arm. I couldn't abide the thought of ever doing it again. But it could not be fled. "There is no running away, Molly. We either

stand and fight here, or are slaughtered when the fighting over-
takes us.''

"Really?'' she asked me coldly. "It isn't just your putting
your loyalty to a King ahead of what we have?'' I could not
meet her eyes. She snorted. "You're just like Burrich. You
don't even know how much you're like him!''

"Like Burrich?'' I was left floundering. I was startled that
she said it at all, let alone that she said it as if it were a fault.

"Yes.'' She was decisive.

"Because I am true to my king?'' I was still grasping at
straws.

"No! Because you put your king before your woman . . .
or your love, or your own life.''

"I don't know what you're talking about!''

"There! You see! .You really don't. And you go about,
acting like you know all these great things and secrets and
every important thing that ever happened. So answer me this.
Why does Patience hate Burrich?''

I was completely at a loss now. I had no idea how this
figured into what was wrong with me. But I knew somehow
Molly would make a connection. Gingerly I tried: "She blames
him for me. She thinks Burrich led Chivalry into bad
ways . . . and hence into conceiving me.''

"There. You see. That's how stupid you are. It's nothing
of the kind. Lacey told me one night. A bit too much elderberry wine, and I was talking of you and she of Burrich and
Patience. Patience loved Burrich first, you idiot. But he
wouldn't have her. He said he loved her, but he couldn't marry
her, even if her father would give consent for her to wed beneath her station. Because he was already sworn, life and
sword, to a lord of his own. And he didn't think he could do
justice to both of them. Oh, he said he wished he were free to
marry her, and that he wished he hadn't sworn before he'd met
her. But all the same, he said he wasn't free to marry her just
then. He said something stupid to her, about no matter how
willing the horse, it can only wear one saddle. So she told him,
well, go off, then, go follow this lord who's more important to
you than I am. And he did. Just as you would, if I told you that

you had to choose.'' There were two spots of high color on her cheeks. She tossed her head as she turned her back on me.

So there was the connection to my fault. But my mind was reeling as bits and pieces of stories and comments suddenly fell into place. Burrich's tale of first meeting Patience. She'd been sitting in an apple tree, and she'd demanded that he take a splinter out of her foot. Scarcely something a woman would ask of her lord's man. But something a direct young maid might ask of a young man who had caught her eye. And his reaction the night I had spoken to him about Molly and Patience, and repeated Patience's words about horses and saddles.

''Did Chivalry know anything of all this?'' I asked.

Molly spun about to consider me. It was obviously not the question she had expected me to ask. But she couldn't resist finishing the story either. ''No. Not at first. When Patience first came to know him, she had no idea he was Burrich's master. Burrich had never told her what lord he was sworn to. At first Patience would have nothing to do with Chivalry. Burrich still held her heart, you see. But Chivalry was stubborn. From what Lacey says, he loved her to distraction. He won her heart. It wasn't until after she had said yes, she'd marry him, that she found out he was Burrich's master. And only because Chivalry sent Burrich to deliver a special horse to her.''

I suddenly remembered Burrich in the stable, looking at Patience's mount and saying, ''I trained that horse.'' I wondered if he'd trained Silk, knowing she was to go to a woman he'd loved, as a gift from the man she'd marry. I'd bet it was so. I had always thought that Patience's disdain for Burrich was a sort of jealousy that Chivalry could care so much for him. Now the triangle was an even stranger one. And infinitely more painful. I closed my eyes and shook my head at the unfairness of the world. ''Nothing is ever simple and good,'' I said to myself. ''There is always a bitter peel, a sour pip somewhere.''

''Yes.'' Molly's anger seemed suddenly spent. She sat down on the bedside, and when I went and sat beside her, she didn't push me away. I took her hand and held it. A thousand thoughts cluttered my mind. How Patience hated Burrich's drinking. How Burrich had recalled her lapdog, and how she

always carried it about in a basket. The care he always took
with his own appearance and behavior. ''Just because you cannot see a woman does not mean she does not see you.'' Oh,
Burrich. The extra time he still took, grooming a horse that she
seldom rode anymore. At least Patience had had a marriage to
a man she loved, and some years of happiness, complicated as
they were by political intrigues. But some years of happiness,
anyway. What would Molly and I ever have? Only what Burrich had now?

She leaned against me and I held her for a long time. That
was all. But somehow in that melancholy holding that night,
we were closer than we had been for a very long time.

21

Dark Days

*K*ING EYOD OF *the Mountains held the Mountain throne during the years of the Red-Ships. The death of his elder son, Rurisk, had left his daughter, Kettricken, sole heir to the Mountain throne. By their customs, she would become queen of the Mountains, or "Sacrifice," as that people call it, upon the demise of her father. Thus her marriage to Verity ensured not only that we had an ally at our back during those unstable years, but also promised the eventual joining of a "seventh duchy" to the Kingdom of the Six Duchies. That the Mountain Kingdom bordered only on the two Inland Duchies of Tilth and Farrow made the prospect of any civil sundering of the Six Duchies of especial concern to Kettricken. She had been raised to be "Sacrifice." Her duty to her folk was of supreme importance in her life. When she became Verity's queen-in-waiting, the Six Duchies folk became her own. But it could never have been far from her heart that on her father's death, her Mountain folk would once more claim her as "Sacrifice" as well. How could she fulfill that obligation if Farrow and Tilth stood between her and her folk, not as part of the Six Duchies, but as a hostile nation?*

A thick storm set in the next day. It was a mixed blessing. No one need fear Raiders anywhere along the coast on a day like that, but it also kept a restless and disparate group of soldiers penned up together. Up in the Keep itself, Bearns was as visible as Regal was not. Whenever I ventured into the Great Hall, Duke Brawndy was there, pacing restlessly or staring coldly into one of the blazing hearths. His daughters flanked him like guardian snowcats. Celerity and Faith were young yet, and their impatience and anger showed more plainly on their faces. Brawndy had requested an official audience with the King. The longer he was kept waiting, the greater the implied insult. It denied the importance of what had brought him here. And the Duke's continued presence in our Great Hall was a plain announcement to his followers that, as yet, the King had not consented to see him. I watched that kettle coming to a slow boil and wondered who would be scalded worst when it spilled over.

I was making my fourth cautious survey of the room when Kettricken appeared. She was dressed simply, a long straight robe of purple with an overwrap of soft white with voluminous sleeves that overhung her hands. Her hair was long and loose on her shoulders. She came in with her usual lack of ceremony, preceded only by Rosemary, her little maid, and accompanied only by Lady Modesty and Lady Hopeful. Even now that she had become a bit more popular with the ladies, she did not forget that these two had followed her first, when she was alone, and she often honored them by making them her companions. I do not believe Duke Brawndy recognized his queen-in-waiting as the simply clad woman who approached him directly.

She smiled and took his hand in greeting. It was a simple Mountain way of recognizing one's friends. I doubt she realized how she honored him, or how much that simple gesture did to assuage his hours of waiting. Only I saw the weariness in her face, I am sure, or the new circles under her eyes. Faith and Celerity were immediately charmed by this attention to their father. Kettricken's clear voice carried throughout the Great

Hall, so those at any hearth who wished to hear undoubtedly did. As she had intended.

"I have called on our king twice this morning. I regret that he has been . . . ill both times. I hope you have not found this waiting fretful. I know you will want to speak directly to the King about your tragedy and all that must be done to help our folk. But, for now, while he rests, I thought perhaps you might wish to join me for some refreshment."

"That would be welcome, lady queen," Bearns replied cautiously. Already she had done much to soothe his rumpled feathers. But Brawndy was not one to be too easily charmed.

"I am pleased," Kettricken replied. She turned and stooped slightly to whisper to Rosemary. The little maid gave a quick nod and turned and fled like a rabbit. All marked her exit. In but moments she was back, this time at the head of a procession of serving folk. A table was claimed and moved down before the Great Hearth. A snowy cloth was spread, and then one of Kettricken's bowl gardens set to grace the center of it. A parade of kitchen folk trooped past, each to deposit platters, or cups of wine or sweetmeats or late-fall apples in a wooden bowl. So wonderfully was it orchestrated that it seemed almost magical. In moments the table was set, the guests were seated, and Mellow appeared with his lute, already singing as he entered the Great Hall. Kettricken beckoned her ladies to join them, and then espying me as well, summoned me with a nod. She chose others from the other hearths at random; not by their nobility or wealth, but folk I knew she considered interesting. Fletch with his hunting stories, and Shells, a friendly girl of an age with Brawndy's daughters were among those summoned. Kettricken seated herself at Brawndy's right hand, and again I do not think she realized all the honor she did him to arrange it so.

When some bit of food and talk had been enjoyed, she signaled Mellow to soften his strumming. She turned to Brawndy and said simply, "We have heard only the bare bones of your news. Will you share with us what has befallen Ferry?"

He hesitated briefly. He had brought his complaint for the King to hear and act on. But how could he refuse a Queen-in-

Waiting who had treated him so graciously? He lowered his
eyes a moment, and when he spoke, his voice was husky with
unfeigned emotion. "My lady queen, we have taken grievous
hurt," he began. Every voice at the table was quickly stilled.
All eyes turned to him. I perceived that all of those chosen by
the Queen were attentive listeners as well. From the time he
launched into his tale, there was not a sound at the table, save
soft exclamations of sympathy or mutters of anger at what the
Raiders had done. He paused once in his tale, then visibly
made a decision, and went on to tell how they had sent forth
their summons for aid, and waited in vain for any response.
The Queen heard him out, with no objections or denials. When
his tale of woe was done, his burden had visibly lifted simply
in the telling of it. For a few long moments all were silent.

"Much of what you tell me is new to my ears," Kettricken
said quietly at last. "And none of it is good. I do not know
what our king will say of all this. You will have to wait for him
to hear his words. But for myself, for now, I will say that my
heart is full of grief for my people. And anger. I promise you
that, for myself, these wrongs shall not go unredressed. Nor
shall my folk be left shelterless in winter's bite."

Duke Brawndy of Bearns looked down at his plate and
toyed with the edge of the tablecloth. He looked up, and there
was fire in his eyes, but also regret. When he spoke, his voice
was firm. "Words. These are but words, my lady queen. The
folk of Ferry cannot eat words, nor shelter beneath them at
nightfall."

Kettricken met his eyes squarely. Something seemed to
tighten inside her. "Well do I know the truth of what you say.
But words are all I have to offer you just now. When the King
is well enough to see you, we shall see what can be done for
Ferry."

Brawndy leaned toward her. "I have questions, my queen.
My need for answers is almost as great as my need for money
and men. Why did our summons for help go unheeded? Why
did the ship that should have come to our aid instead set sail for
home port?"

Kettricken's voice trembled very slightly. "To these questions, I have no answers, sir. And that is a shameful thing for

me to admit. No word of your situation reached my ears until your young messenger arrived on horseback.''

Strong misgivings arose in me as she spoke. Should the Queen have admitted these things to Brawndy? Perhaps not, for the sake of political wisdom. But Kettricken, I knew, served truth before politics. Brawndy looked long into her face, and the lines around his mouth deepened. Boldly, he asked, but softly, ''Are not you queen-in-waiting?''

Kettricken's eyes went sword gray as she met his gaze. ''I am. Do you ask me if I lie to you?''

It was Brawndy's turn to look aside. ''No. No, my queen, that thought was never in my mind.''

The silence stretched overlong. I do not know if there was some subtle signal from Kettricken, or if it was simply Mellow's instincts that swept his fingers more vigorously across the strings. In a moment his voice took up a winter song, full of blowing notes and skirling choruses.

More than three days passed before Brawndy was finally summoned to the King's chambers. Kettricken tried to provide amusements, but it is hard to entertain a man whose mind is on his dukedom's vulnerability. He was courteous, but distracted. Faith, his second daughter, quickly formed a friendship with Shells, and seemed to forget some of her sorrows in her company. Celerity, however, clung to her father's side, and when her dark blue eyes did meet mine, they were like wounds. I experienced a strange variety of emotions from that gaze. I was relieved that she did not seek me out as an individual to pay attention to. At the same time I knew her coolness to me was a reflection of her father's present feelings toward all of Buckkeep. I welcomed her slighting of me; at the same time it rankled, as I did not feel I deserved it. When the summons came at last, and Brawndy hastened to the King, I hoped that the awkwardness would be over.

I am sure I was not the only one who noticed that Queen Kettricken was not invited to the council. Neither was I present, being also uninvited. But it is not often that a Queen is relegated to the same social standing as a bastard nephew. Kettricken kept her equanimity, and went on showing Brawndy's daughters and Shells a Mountain technique for weaving beads into embroidery work. I hovered near the table, but doubted that their minds were on their craft any more than mine was.

We had not long to wait. In less than an hour, Duke Brawndy reappeared in the Great Hall with all the bluster and chill of a storm wind. To Faith, he said, "Pack our things." To Celerity: "Tell our guard to be ready to depart within the hour." He gave Queen Kettricken a very stiff bow. "My queen, I excuse myself to depart. As House Farseer will offer no aid, Bearns must now tend to its own."

"Indeed. I see your need for haste," Kettricken replied gravely. "But I shall require that you attend me for but one more meal. It is not good to depart on a journey on an empty stomach. Tell me. Do you enjoy gardens?" Her question was addressed to his daughters as much as to Bearns. They looked to their father. After a moment he gave a curt nod.

Both the daughters admitted cautiously to Kettricken that they enjoyed gardens. But their puzzlement was plain. A garden? In winter, during a howling storm? I shared their misgivings, especially as at that moment Kettricken gestured to me.

"FitzChivalry. Attend to my wish. Rosemary, go with Lord FitzChivalry to the kitchens. Prepare food as he directs you and bring it to the Queen's Garden. I shall escort our guests there."

I widened my eyes at Kettricken desperately. No. Not there. The climb to the tower alone was taxing to many, let alone taking a cup of tea on a storm-lashed tower top. I could not fathom what she thought she was about. The smile she returned my anxious look was as open and serene as any I had seen. Taking Duke Brawndy's arm, she steered him out of the Great Hall, while the daughters trailed behind with the Queen's ladies. I turned to Rosemary and changed her orders.

"Go find warm wraps for them, and catch up with them. I'll take care of the food."

The child scampered merrily off while I hastened to the kitchen. I tersely informed Sara of our sudden need, and she quickly created a platter of warmed pastries and hot mulled wine for me. "Take these yourself, and I'll send more with a boy in a bit." I smiled to myself as I took the tray and hurried off toward the Queen's Gardens. The Queen herself might refer to me as Lord FitzChivalry, but Sara the cook would never think twice of ordering me off with a tray of food. It was oddly comforting.

I took the stairs as quickly as I could, then paused to breathe at the top landing. I braced myself for the rain and wind, and pushed the door open. The tower top was as miserable as I had expected it to be. The Queen's ladies and Brawndy's daughters and Shells were huddled in a bit of shelter offered by two adjoining walls and a stretch of canvas that had been set up as a shady spot last summer. It broke most of the wind, and diverted a great deal of the freezing rain as well. There was a small table within its pathetic shelter and here I set the tray of warm food. Rosemary, snugly bundled, smiled smugly as she snitched a pastry from the edge of the tray. Lady Modesty presided over serving the food.

As quickly as I could, I secured mugs of warmed wine for the Queen and Duke Brawndy and, on pretext of serving them, joined them. They were at the very edge of the parapet, looking out over the crenated wall at the open sea below. The wind had lashed it to white froth, and was flinging seagulls about with a fine disregard for the birds' attempts to fly. As I approached I could see they were speaking softly, but the roar of the wind frustrated my attempt to eavesdrop. I wished I had thought to get a cloak for myself. I was soaked through almost instantly and the wind blew off what heat my body generated by shivering. I tried to smile past my chattering teeth as I presented them with the wine.

"Lord FitzChivalry is known to you?" she asked Brawndy as they took the wine from me.

"Indeed, I have had the pleasure of having him at my own table," Brawndy assured her. Rain dripped off his bushy eyebrows while the wind had set his warrior's tail to flapping.

"You would not mind, then, if I asked him to join us in our conversation?" Despite the rain that soaked her, the Queen spoke calmly, as if we basked in spring sunshine.

I wondered if Kettricken knew that Brawndy would see her request as a veiled command.

"I would welcome his counsels, if you consider he has wisdom to offer, my queen," Brawndy acquiesced.

"I had hoped you would. FitzChivalry. Fetch yourself some wine, and rejoin us here, please."

"As my queen wishes." I bowed low and hurried off to obey. My contact with Verity had grown more tenuous with each passing day that he journeyed farther away, but at that moment I could sense his nudging, eager curiosity. I hastened back to my queen's side.

"There is no undoing what has been done," the Queen was saying as I returned to them. "I grieve that we were not able to protect our folk. Yet if I cannot undo what the Raiders from the sea have done already, at least, perhaps, I can help to shelter them from the storms to come. This, I bid you take them, from their queen's hand and heart."

I noticed in passing that she made no mention of King Shrewd's evident refusal to act. I watched her. She moved leisurely and purposefully at once. The loose white sleeve that she drew back from her arm was already dripping with cold rain. She ignored it as she bared her pale arm, to reveal a snaking of gold wire up her arm, with the dark opals of her Mountains caught here and there in its web. I had seen the dark flash of Mountain opals before, but never ones of this size. Yet she held out her arm for me to unfasten the catch, and with no hesitation at all, she unwound the treasure from her arm. From her other sleeve, she drew a small velvet bag. I held its mouth open as she slid the bracelets into it. She smiled warmly at Duke Brawndy as she pressed it into his hand. "From your king-in-waiting Verity and me," she said quietly. I barely resisted Verity's impulse in me to fling himself on his knees at the feet of this woman and declare her far too royal for his insignificant love. Brawndy was left stuttering his amazed thanks and vowing to her that not a penny of its worth would go to waste. Stout houses would rise once more in Ferry, and the folk there would bless the Queen for the warmth of them.

I suddenly saw the reason for the Queen's Garden as a site. This was a Queen's gift, not contingent on anything Shrewd or Regal might have to say. Kettricken's choice of place, and her manner of presenting it to Brawndy, made that clear to him. She did not tell him to keep it secret; she did not need to.

I thought of the emeralds hidden in a corner of my clothes chest, but within me Verity was quiet. I made no move to get them. I hoped to see Verity himself fasten them about his queen's neck one day. Nor did I wish to lessen the significance of her gift to Brawndy by adding another from a bastard. For that was how I would have had to present it. No, I decided. Let the Queen's gift and her presentation of it stand alone in his memory.

Brawndy turned from his queen to consider me. "My queen, you seem to hold this young man in considerable esteem, to make him privy to your counsels."

"I do," Kettricken replied gravely. "He has never betrayed my trust in him."

Brawndy nodded, as if confirming something to himself. He permitted himself a small smile. "My youngest daughter, Celerity, was somewhat troubled by a missive from Lord FitzChivalry. Especially as her older sisters had opened it for her, and found much there to tease her with. But when she brought her misgivings to me, I told her that it is a rare man who so candidly admits to what might be seen as shortcomings. Only a braggart would claim to go fearless into battle. Nor would I wish to give my trust to a man who could kill and not feel heart-lost afterward. As to your physical health"—he clapped me suddenly on the shoulder—"I would say a summer of pulling oars and wielding an ax had done you good." His hawk's eyes pierced mine. "I have not changed my assessment of you, FitzChivalry. Nor has Celerity. I wish you to be sure of that."

I said the words I knew I must. "Thank you, sir."

He turned to look over his shoulder. I followed his gaze through the blowing rain to where Celerity gazed at us. Her father gave her a tiny nod, and her smile broke like the sun from behind a cloud. Faith, watching her, said something, and Celerity turned blushing to give her sister a push. My guts turned to ice when Brawndy told me, "You may bid my daughter farewell, if you wish."

There were few things I wished less to do. But I would not

undo what Kettricken had so laboriously wrought. I could not.
So I bowed and excused myself, and forced myself to cross the
rain-pelted garden to present myself to Celerity. Faith and
Shells immediately withdrew to a not-quite-discreet distance to
watch us.

I bowed to her with absolute correctness. "Lady Celerity,
I must thank you again for the scroll you sent me," I said
awkwardly. My heart was pounding. As was hers, I am sure,
for a completely different reason.

She smiled at me through the falling rain. "I was glad to
send it, and gladder of your reply. My father explained it to me.
I hope you do not take it amiss that I showed it to him. I did not
understand why you would belittle yourself so. He said, 'The
man who must brag for himself knows that no one else will.'
Then he told me there is no better way to learn the sea than at
the oar of a boat. And that, in his younger years, the ax was
always his weapon, too. He has promised my sisters and me a
dory of our own, next summer, that we can take out on the sea
on fine days. . . ." She faltered suddenly. "I chatter, do I
not?"

"Not at all, my lady," I assured her quietly. I much preferred that she do the talking.

"My lady," she repeated softly, and then blushed as furiously as if I had kissed her right there.

I looked aside from her, only to find Faith's wide eyes on
us, her mouth an O of scandalized delight. Imagining what she
imagined I had said to her sister brought the color and heat to
my face as well. As I went scarlet she and Shells burst out
giggling.

It seemed an eternity before we left the storm-battered
Queen's Garden. Our guests sought their rooms, both to
change from sodden clothing and to prepare for their journey. I
did likewise, dressing hastily lest I miss anything of their departure. I was at the outer courtyard to see Brawndy and his
guard mount. So was Queen Kettricken, in her now familiar
purple and white, and her honor guard had been turned out as
well. She stood beside Brawndy's horse to bid him farewell,
and before he mounted, he went down on one knee and kissed
her hand. Some brief words were spoken, I know not what, but

the Queen smiled as the winds lashed her hair about her face. Brawndy and his troops set off into the teeth of the storm. There was anger yet in the set of Brawndy's shoulders, but his obeisance to the Queen showed me that as of yet not all was lost.

Celerity and Faith both looked back to me as they rode off, and Celerity dared to lift a hand in farewell. I returned the gesture. I stood watching them go, chilled by more than the rain. I had supported Verity and Kettricken this day, but at what cost to myself? What was I doing to Celerity? Was Molly, perhaps, right about all this?

Later that evening, I went to pay my respects to my king. He had not summoned me. I did not intend to discuss Celerity with him. I went, wondering if Verity willed it in me or if it was my own heart cautioning me not to abandon him. Wallace grudgingly admitted me, with a stern warning that the King was still not feeling completely himself, and I must not weary him.

King Shrewd was sitting up before his fireplace. The air of the room was cloying with Smoke. The Fool, his face still an interesting landscape of purples and blues, sat at the King's feet. He had the good fortune to be below the most pungent level of the haze. I had no such luck as I took the low backless stool that Wallace so thoughtfully provided for me.

A few moments after I had presented myself and sat down, the King turned to me. He regarded me blearily for a few moments as his head swayed on his neck. "Ah, Fitz," the King greeted me belatedly. "How have your lessons been? Is Master Fedwren pleased with your progress?"

I glanced at the Fool, who did not meet my eyes, but poked morosely at the fire.

"Yes," I said quietly. "He has said my lettering is good."

"That's fine. A clear hand is a thing any man may be proud of. And what of our bargain? Have I kept my word to you?"

It was our old litany. Once more I considered the terms he had offered me. He would feed me, clothe me, and educate me, and in return he would have my complete loyalty. I smiled at the familiar words, but my throat closed at how the man who

said them had wasted away, and what they had come to cost
me.

"Yes, my king. You have," I answered softly.

"Good. Then see you keep your word to me as well." He
leaned back heavily in his chair.

"I shall, Your Majesty," I promised, and the Fool's eyes
met mine as he witnessed again that promise.

For a few moments the room was still, save for the crackling of the fire. Then the King sat up as if startled by a sound.
He looked about confusedly. "Verity? Where's Verity?"

"He's gone on a quest, my king. To seek the help of the
Elderlings to drive the Red-Ships from our shores."

"Ah, yes. Of course. Of course he has. But just for a
moment, I thought . . ." He leaned back in his chair. Then all
the hair on my skin prickled up. I could feel him vaguely
Skilling, in an unfocused fumbling way. His mind tugged at
mine like old hands seeking for a grip. I had believed him
incapable of Skilling anymore, I had thought that he had
burned out his talent years ago. Verity had told me once that
Shrewd used his talent but seldom anymore. I had set those
words aside as his loyalty to his father. But the ghostly Skill
plucked at my thoughts like unschooled fingers at harp strings.
I sensed Nighteyes hackling at this new invasion. *Silence,* I
cautioned him.

My breath snagged suddenly on an idea. Fostered by Verity within me? I set aside all cautions, reminded myself that
this was what I had promised this man so long ago. Loyalty in
all things. "My king?" I asked his permission as I moved my
stool closer to his chair. I took his withered hand in mine.

It was like plunging myself into a rushing river. "Ah,
Verity, my boy, there you are!" Just for a moment I glimpsed
Verity as King Shrewd still saw him. A chubby boy of eight or
nine, more friendly than smart, not so tall as his big brother,
Chivalry. But a sound and likable Prince, an excellent second
son, not too ambitious, not too questioning. Then, just as if I
had stepped off a riverbank, I tumbled into a black, rushing
roar of Skill. It was disorienting to see suddenly through
Shrewd's eyes. The edges of his vision were filmy with haze.
For a moment I glimpsed Verity forging wearily through snow.

What's this? Fitz? Then I was whirled away, carried into the heart of King Shrewd's pain. Skilled deep inside him, beyond where the herbs and smoke deadened him, I was scorched with the agony. It was a slow-growing pain, along his spine and in his skull, a pushing crowding thing that would not be ignored. His choices were to be consumed by the agony that would not let him think, or to deaden his body and mind with herbs and Smokes to hide from it. But deep inside his fogged mind, a King still lived and raged at his confinement. The spirit was still there, battling the body that no longer obeyed him and the pain that devoured the last years of his life. I swear I saw him, a young man, perhaps a year or so older than myself. His hair had been as bushy and unruly as Verity's, his eyes were wide and lively, and once his face's only lines had been from a wide grin. This was who he still was, in his soul, this young man, trapped and desperate. He seized on me, asking wildly, "Is there a way out?" I felt myself sinking with his grip.

Then, like two rivers merging, another force crashed against me, sent me spinning with its current. *Boy! Contain yourself.* It was as if strong hands steadied me and established me as a separate strand in the twisting rope we were forming. *Father. I am here. Are you in need?*

No. No. All is as it has been for some time. But Verity . . .

Yes. I am here.

Bearns is no longer true to us. Brawndy harbors Red-Ships there, in exchange for protection for his own villages. He has turned on us. When you come home, you must . . .

The thought wandered, lost strength.

Father. Whence come these tidings? I sensed Verity's sudden desperation. If what Shrewd spoke was true, there was no hope for Buckkeep to stand the winter.

Regal has spies. They bring word to him, and he comes to me. This must remain a secret, for a time, until we have the strength to strike back at Brawndy. Or until we decide to abandon him to his Red-Ship friends. Yes. That is Regal's plan. To hold the Red-Ships off from Buck, and then they will turn on Brawndy and punish him for us. Brawndy even sent a false call for help, in the hopes of luring our warships to their destruction.

Can this be so?

All Regal's spies confirm it. And I fear we can no longer trust your foreign wife. While Brawndy was here, Regal marked how she dallied with him, and made many excuses for private talk. He fears that she plots with our enemies to overthrow the throne.

THIS IS NOT SO! The force of this denial went through me like a sword's point. For an instant I was drowning again, lost, selfless, in the flood of Skill passing through me. Verity sensed it, steadied me again. *We must be careful of the boy. He has not the strength to be used like this. Father, I beg you. Trust my queen. I know she is not false. And be wary of what Regal's spies report to you. Put spies upon the spies, before you act on any of their reports. Consult with Chade. Promise me this.*

I am not a fool, Verity. I know how to hold my throne.

Good. Good then. Make sure the boy is tended to. He is not trained for this.

Someone snatched my hand back then, as if from a burning stove. I sagged forward, put my head down between my knees while the world spun around me. Next to me, I could hear King Shrewd panting for his breath as if he had run a race. The Fool pushed a glass of wine into my hand, then went back to urging small sips of wine into the King. And over all, suddenly, Wallace's voice, demanding, "What have you done to the King?"

"It is both of them!" There was a sharp edge of fear to the Fool's voice. "They were talking together, quite calmly, then suddenly this! Take the damned Smoke censers away! I fear you have killed them both!"

"Silence, Fool! Do not accuse my healing of this!" But I heard the hurry in Wallace's step as he made the rounds of the room, pinching out the burning twists in each censer or capping them with brass cups. In a moment the windows were thrown wide to the icy winter night. The cool air steadied me. I managed to sit up and take a sip of the wine. Gradually my senses came back to me. Even so, I was still sitting there when Regal came bustling into the room, demanding to know what had happened. He addressed the question to me, as the Fool was helping Wallace put the King to bed.

I shook my head at him dumbly, and the giddiness was not all pretended.

"How is the King? Will he recover?" he called to Wallace.

Wallace immediately came hurrying to Regal's side. "He seems to be steadying, Prince Regal. I do not know what overcame him. There was no sign of a struggle, but he is as wearied as if he had run a race. His health will not stand this sort of excitement, my prince."

Regal turned an appraising glance on me. "What did you do to my father?" he growled.

"I? Nothing." That at least was truthful. Whatever had happened, it had been the King's doing and Verity's. "We were talking quietly. Suddenly I felt overwhelmed. Dizzy. Weak. As if I were losing consciousness." I turned my gaze to Wallace. "Could it have been the Smoke?"

"Perhaps," he conceded unhappily. He looked nervously at Regal's darkening stare. "Well, it seems every day I must make it stronger, for it to have any effect at all. And still he complains that—"

"SILENCE!" Regal cut him off with a roar. He gestured at me as if I were offal. "Get him out of here. Then get back here to tend the King."

At that moment Shrewd moaned in his sleep, and I felt again the feather-soft brushing of the Skill against my senses. My hair hackled.

"No. Go to the King now, Wallace. Fool. You get the Bastard out of here. And see that this is not spoken of amongst the servants. I shall know if I am disobeyed. Hurry up, now. My father is not well."

I had thought I could rise on my own and depart, but found that I did need the Fool's assistance, at least to stand. Once I was up on my feet, I teetered along precariously, feeling as if I tottered on stilts. Walls loomed near and then far, the floor heaved gently beneath me like the deck of a ship when she rides a slow swell.

"I can manage from here," I told the Fool once we were outside the door. He shook his head.

"You are too vulnerable to be left alone just now," he told me quietly, and then linked arms with me, and began some nonsensical discourse. He put a fine front of camaraderie on helping me up the stairs and to my door. He waited, chattering on, while I unlatched it and then followed me in.

"I told you, I am all right," I said with some annoyance. All I wanted to do was lie down.

"Are you? And how is my king? What did you do to him, back there?"

"I did nothing!" I gritted out as I sat down on the foot of my bed. My head was beginning to pound. Elfbark tea. That was what I needed just now. I had none.

"You did! You asked his permission, and then you took his hand. And in the next instant you were both gasping like fish."

"Just an instant?" It had felt like hours to me. I had thought the whole evening spent.

"No more than three heartbeats."

"Ooh." I put my hands to my temples, tried to push my skull back into one piece. Why did Burrich have to be gone just now? I knew he would have elfbark. The pain demanded I take a chance. "Do you have any elfbark? For tea?"

"With me? No. But I could go beg some of Lacey. She keeps a horde of all sorts of herbs."

"Would you?"

"What did you do to the King?" The trade he offered was plain.

The pressure in my head built, pushing out on my eyes. "Nothing," I gasped. "And what he did to me is for him to tell. If he chooses. Is that plain enough for you?"

A silence. "Perhaps. Are you really in that much pain?"

I lay back very slowly on my bed. Even putting my head down hurt.

"I'll be back shortly," he offered. I heard the door of my room open and shut. I lay still, eyes closed. Gradually the sense of what I had eavesdropped on formed itself in my mind. Despite my pain, I sorted information. Regal had spies. Or claimed to. Brawndy was a traitor. Or so Regal claimed his supposed spies had informed him. I suspected Brawndy was as much a traitor as Kettricken was. Oh, the spreading poison. And the pain. Suddenly I remembered the pain. Had not Chade bid me simply to observe as I had been taught to find an answer to my question? It had been plain before me all the time, if only I had not been so blinded with fears of traitors and plots and poisons.

A disease was eating King Shrewd, gnawing him away from the inside. He drugged himself against the pain. In an effort to have some corner of his mind to himself, a place where the pain could not come and rob him. If someone had just told me of that a few hours ago, I would have scoffed. Now, lying on my bed, trying to breathe softly because the slightest movement triggered another wave of agony, I could understand. Pain. I'd only been enduring this for a few minutes, and I'd already sent the Fool running for elfbark. Another consideration pushed itself into my mind. I expected this pain to pass, that by tomorrow I would rise up free from it. What if I had to face it every moment for the rest of my life, with the certainty that it was devouring what hours were left to me? No wonder Shrewd kept himself drugged.

I heard my door open and close quietly. When I did not hear the Fool begin to make tea, I forced my eyes open. Justin and Serene stood inside the doors of my room. They stood frozen, as if in the lair of a savage beast. When I shifted my head slightly to look at them, Serene's lips actually drew back as if she snarled. Within me, Nighteyes snarled back. The tempo of my heart suddenly increased. Danger here. I tried to loosen my muscles, to be ready to take any action. But the pain bludgeoning my head bade me only be still, be still. "I didn't hear your knock," I managed to say. Each word was edged in red as my voice echoed in my skull.

"I didn't knock," Serene said harshly. Her clearly spoken words were as painful to me as a clubbing. I prayed she didn't know how much power she had over me just then. I prayed for the Fool to come back. I tried to appear nonchalant, as if I kept to my bed only because I considered Serene's visit so unimportant.

"Did you need something from me?" I sounded brusque. In reality, each word cost too much effort to waste even one.

"Need? Never," Serene scoffed.

Skill nudged me. Clumsily. Justin, prodding at me. I could not repress the shudder that went through me. My king's use of me had left my mind as raw as a bleeding wound. Justin's awkward Skilling was like having cat's claws rake my brain.

Shield yourself. Verity was a whisper. I made an effort to set my guards, but could not find enough of myself to do it. Serene was smiling.

Justin was pushing into my mind like a hand shoving into a pudding. My senses jumbled suddenly. He smelled foul in my head, he was a terrible rotten greenish yellow and sounded like spurs jingling. *Shield,* Verity pleaded. He sounded desperate, weak, and I knew he was trying very hard to hold the tattered pieces of myself together for me. *He's going to kill you with sheer stupidity. He doesn't even know what he's doing.*

Help me!

From Verity, nothing. Our link was fading like perfume in the wind as my strength dwindled.

WE ARE PACK!

Justin slammed back against the door of my room so hard his head bounced. It was more than *repelling.* I had no word for what Nighteyes did from within Justin's own mind. It was a hybrid magic, Nighteyes using the Wit through a bridge the Skill had created. He attacked Justin's body from within Justin's mind. Justin's hands flew to his throat, fighting jaws he could not seize. Claws shredded skin and raised red welts on the skin beneath Justin's fine tunic. Serene screamed, a sword of a sound slashing through me, and flung herself on Justin, trying to help him.

Don't kill. Don't kill! DON'T KILL!

Nighteyes finally heard me. He dropped Justin, flinging him aside like a rat. He came and stood astraddle me, guarding me. Almost I could hear his panting breath, feel the warmth of his hide. I had no energy to question what had happened. I curled myself into a puppy, sheltered beneath him. I knew no one could get through Nighteyes' defense of me.

"What was that? What was that? What was that?" Serene

was screaming hysterically. She had Justin by the shirtfront and had dragged him to his feet. There were livid marks on his throat and chest, but through barely opened eyes, I could see them fading rapidly. Soon there was no sign of Nighteyes' attack save the wet stain spreading down the front of Justin's trousers. His eyes sagged closed. Serene shook him like a doll. "Justin! Open your eyes. Justin!"

"What are you doing to that man?" The Fool's stage voice, expressing outrage and surprise, filled my room. Behind him, my door stood open wide. A passing maid, arms full of shirts, peeped in, startled, then stopped to stare. The little page girl carrying a basket behind her came hurrying to peek around the door's edge. The Fool set the tray he was carrying down on the floor and came into my room. "What is the meaning of this?"

"He attacked Justin," Serene sobbed.

Disbelief flooded the Fool's face. "Him? He looks like he could not attack a pillow. You were the one I saw worrying that boy."

Serene let go of Justin's collar, and he dropped like a rag at her feet. The Fool looked down at him pityingly.

"Poor fellow! Was she trying to force herself on you?"

"Don't be ridiculous!" Serene was outraged. "It was him!" She pointed at me.

The Fool looked at me consideringly. "This is a grave accusation. Answer me truthfully, Bastard. Was she really trying to force herself on you?"

"No." My voice came out like I felt. Sick, exhausted and groggy. "I was sleeping. They came quietly into my room. Then . . ." I knit my brows, and let my voice trail off. "I think I have had too much Smoke this night."

"And I agree!" There was fine disdain in the Fool's voice. "Such an unseemly show of lust I have seldom seen!" The Fool spun suddenly on the peeping page and maid. "This shames all of Buckkeep! To find our own Skilled ones behaving so. I charge you to speak of this to no one. Let no gossip about this begin." He turned back suddenly on Serene and Justin. Serene's face was flooded scarlet, her mouth open in outrage. Justin pulled himself to a sitting position at her feet

and sat, swaying. He clutched at her skirts like a toddler trying
to stand.

"I do not lust after this man," she said coldly and clearly.
"Nor did I attack him."

"Well, whatever it is you are doing, it were better done in
your own chambers!" The Fool cut across her words sternly.
Without another glance at her, he turned, picked up his tray,
and bore it off down the hallway. At the sight of the elfbark tea
departing, I could not contain a groan of despair. Serene spun
back to me, lips drawn back in a grimace.

"I will get to the bottom of this!" she snarled at me.

I took a breath. "But in your own chambers, please." I
managed to lift a hand and point at the open door. She stormed
out, with Justin staggering along in her wake. The maid and
page drew back in distaste from them as they passed. My
chamber door was left standing ajar. It took a vast effort to rise
and go close it. I felt as if my head were something I balanced
on my shoulders. Once the door was closed, I didn't even try to
return to bed, but just slid down the wall to sit with my back to
the door. I felt raw.

My brother. Are you dying?

No. But it hurts.

Rest. I will stand watch.

I cannot explain what happened next. I let go of something, something I had clutched all my life without being aware
of gripping it. I sank down into soft warm darkness, into a safe
place, while a wolf kept watch through my eyes.

22

Burrich

*L*ADY PATIENCE, SHE *who was queen-in-waiting to Chivalry's king-in-waiting, came originally of inland stock. Her parents, Lord Oakdell and Lady Averia, were of very minor nobility. For their daughter to rise in rank to marry a Prince of the realm had to have been a shock to them, especially given their daughter's wayward and, some might say, obtuse nature. Chivalry's avowed ambition to wed Lady Patience was the cause of his first difference with his father, King Shrewd. By this marriage, he gained no valuable alliances or political advantages; only a highly eccentric woman whose great love for her husband did not preclude her forthright declaring of unpopular opinions. Nor did it dissuade her from the single-minded pursuit of any avocation that caught her fleeting fancy. Her parents preceded her in death, dying in the year of the Blood Plague, and she was childless and presumed barren when her husband, Chivalry, fell to his death from a horse.*

⊶⊰⊱⊷

I awoke. Or, at least, I came back to myself. I was in my bed, surrounded by warmth and gentleness. I didn't move, but cautiously searched myself for pain. My head no longer pounded, but I felt tired and achy, stiff as one sometimes is after pain passes. A shiver went up my back. Molly was naked beside me, breathing gently against my shoulder. The fire had burned low, nearly out. I listened. It was either very very late, or very early. The Keep was near silent.

I didn't remember getting here.

I shivered again. Beside me, Molly stirred. She pulled closer to me, smiled sleepily. "You are so strange sometimes," she breathed. "But I love you." She closed her eyes again.

Nighteyes!

I am here. He was always there.

Suddenly I couldn't ask, I didn't want to know. I just lay still, feeling sick and sad and sorry for myself.

I tried to rouse you, but you were not ready to come back. That Other One had drained you.

That "Other One" is our king.

Your king. Wolves have no kings.

What did . . . I let the thought trail off. *Thank you for guarding me.*

He sensed my reservations. *What should I have done? Turned her away? She was grieving.*

I don't know. Let us not talk of it. Molly was sad, and he had comforted her? I didn't even know why she was sad. Had been sad, I amended, looking at the soft smile on her sleeping face. I sighed. Better face it sooner than later. Besides, I had to send her back to her own room. It would not do for her to be here when the Keep awoke.

"Molly?" I said gently.

She stirred and opened her eyes. "Fitz," she agreed sleepily.

"For safety's sake, you have to go back to your own room."

"I know. I shouldn't have come in the first place." She stopped. "All those things I said to you a few days ago. I didn't—"

I put a finger across her lips. She smiled past it. "You make these new silences . . . very interesting." She pushed my hand aside, kissed me warmly. Then she slid from my bed and began to dress briskly. I arose, moving more slowly. She glanced over at me, her face full of love. "I'll go alone. It's safer. We should not be seen together."

"Someday, that will—" I began. This time she silenced me, small hand on my lips.

"We will talk of nothing like that now. Let us leave tonight as it is. Perfect." She kissed me again, quickly, and slipped from my arms and then out the door. She shut it silently behind her. Perfect?

I finished dressing and built up my fire. I sat down in my chair by the hearth and waited. It was not long before I was rewarded. The entrance to Chade's domain opened. I went up the stairs as quickly as I could manage. Chade was sitting before his hearth. "You have to listen to me," I greeted him. His eyebrows rose in alarm at the intensity in my voice. He gestured at the chair opposite him, and I took it. I opened my mouth to speak. What Chade did then put every hair on my body on end. He glanced all around himself, as if we stood in the midst of a great crowd. Then he touched his own lips, and made a gesture for softness. He leaned toward me until our heads were nearly touching. "Softly, softly. Sit down. What is it?"

I sat, in my old place on the hearth. My heart was hammering in my chest. Of all places in Buckkeep, I had never expected to have to use caution in what I said here.

"All right," he breathed out to me. "Report."

I took a breath and began. I left out nothing, revealing my link with Verity so that the entire story would make sense. I put in every detail: the Fool's beating, and Kettricken's offering to Bearns, as well as my service to the King that evening. Serene and Justin in my room. When I whispered of Regal's spies, he pursed his mouth, but did not seem overly surprised. When I was finished, he regarded me calmly.

A whisper again. "And what do you conclude from all this?" he asked me, as if it were a puzzle he had set me as a lesson.

"May I speak frankly of my suspicions?" I asked quietly.

A nod.

I sighed in relief. As I spoke of the picture that had emerged for me over the past weeks, I felt a great burden lifting. Chade would know what to do. And so I spoke, quickly, tersely. Regal knew that the King was dying of disease. Wallace was his tool, to keep the King sedated and open to Regal's whisperings. He would discredit Verity, he would strip Buckkeep of every bit of wealth that he could. He would abandon Bearns to the Red-Ships, to keep them busy while Regal acted on his own ambitions. Paint Kettricken as a foreigner with ambitions to the throne. A devious, disloyal wife. Gather power to himself. His eventual aim, as ever, was the throne. Or at least as much of the Six Duchies as he could gather to himself. Hence his lavish entertainments for the Inland Dukes and their nobles.

Chade nodded unwillingly as I spoke. When I paused, he injected softly, "There are many holes in this web you say Regal is weaving."

"I can fill in a few," I whispered. "Suppose the coterie that Galen created is loyal to Regal? Suppose all messages go to him first, and only those he approves continue to their intended destination?"

Chade's face grew still and grave.

My whisper grew more desperate. "What if messages are delayed just enough to make our efforts to defend ourselves pathetic? He makes Verity look a fool, he undermines confidence in the man."

"Wouldn't Verity be able to tell?"

I shook my head slowly. "He is powerfully Skilled. But he cannot be listening everywhere at once. The strength of his talent is his ability to focus it so tightly. To spy on his own coterie, he would have had to give off watching the coast waters for Red-Ships."

"Does he . . . is Verity aware of this discussion right now?"

I shrugged ashamedly. "I don't know. That is the curse of my flaws. My link with him is erratic. Sometimes I know his mind as clearly as if he stood beside me and spoke it aloud. At other times I am scarcely aware of him at all. Last night, when they spoke through me, I heard every word. Right now . . ." I felt about inside myself, a pocket-patting sort of thinking. "I feel nothing more than that we are still linked.'' I leaned forward and put my head in my hands. I felt drained.

''Tea?'' Chade asked me gently.

''Please. And if I could just sit for a bit longer, quietly. I don't know when my head has throbbed this badly.''

Chade set the kettle over the fire. I watched with distaste as he mixed brewing herbs for it. Some elfbark, but not near as much as I would have required earlier. Peppermint and catmint leaves. A bit of precious ginger root. I recognized much of what he used to give Verity for his Skill exhaustion. Then he came back to sit close beside me again. ''It could not be. What you suggest would require blind loyalty from the coterie to Regal.''

''It can be created by one strongly Skilled. My flaw is a result of what Galen did to me. Do you remember Galen's fanatical admiration of Chivalry? That was a created loyalty. Galen could have done it to them, before he died, when he was finishing their training.''

Chade shook his head slowly. ''Do you think Regal could be so stupid as to think the Red-Ships would stop at Bearns? Eventually they will want Buck, they will want Rippon and Shoaks. Where does that leave him?''

''With the Inland Duchies. The only ones he cares about, the only ones with which he has a mutual loyalty. It would give him a vast perimeter of land as an insulation against anything the Red-Ships might do. And like you, perhaps, he may believe they are not after territory, but only a raiding grounds. They are sea folk. They will not come that far inland to trouble him. And the Coastal Duchies will be too busy fighting the Red-Ships to turn on Regal.''

''If the Six Duchies loses her seacoast, she loses her trade, her shipping. How pleased will his Inland Dukes be with that?''

I shrugged. ''I do not know. I have not all the answers, Chade. But this is the only theory I've been able to put together in which almost all the pieces fit.''

He rose, to pour steaming water from the kettle into a fat brown pot. He rinsed it well with the boiling water, then dumped in the paper of herbs he had compounded. I watched him pour the boiling water over the herbs. The scent of a garden filled his chambers. I took the image of the old man putting the lid on the pot, wrapped up the homey simple moment of him setting the pot on the tray with some cups, and stowed it carefully somewhere in my heart. Age was creeping up on Chade, just as surely as disease devoured Shrewd. His deft movements were no longer quite so sure, his bird alertness not as quick as it once had been. My heart ached suddenly with my glimpse of the inevitable. As he set a warm cup of steaming tea in my hand, he frowned at my expression.

"What's wrong?" he whispered. "Do you want some honey in that?"

I shook my head to his questions, took a sip of tea, and near scalded my tongue. A pleasant taste overlay the bite of the elfbark. After a few moments I felt my mind clear and a pain I had scarcely been aware of went back to sleep. "That's much better." I sighed, and Chade sketched a bow at me, pleased with himself.

He leaned close again. "It is still a weak theory. Perhaps we simply have a self-indulgent Prince, who pleases himself with entertainments for his flatterers while the heir is away. He neglects protecting his coastline because he is shortsighted, and because he expects his brother will come home and tidy up his mess. He raids the treasury and sells off horses and cattle to amass wealth to himself while there is no one to stop him."

"Then why paint Bearns as a traitor? And set up Kettricken as an outsider? Why spread rumors of ridicule about Verity and his quest?"

"Jealousy. Regal has always been his father's spoiled pet. I do not think he would turn on Shrewd." Something in Chade's voice made me realize this was what he desperately wished to believe. "I supply the herbs that Wallace administers to Shrewd for his pain."

"I do not doubt your herbs. But I think others are added to them."

"What would be the point? Even if Shrewd dies, Verity is still the heir."

"Unless Verity dies first." I held up my hand as Chade opened his mouth to protest. "It need not really happen. If

Regal controls the coterie, he can supply word of Verity's death at any time. Regal becomes king-in-waiting. Then . . ." I let my words trail off.

Chade let out a long sigh. "Enough. You have given me enough to ponder. I will look into these ideas, with my own resources. For now, you must watch over yourself. And Kettricken. And the Fool. If there is even a drop of truth in your theories, you all become obstacles to Regal's goal."

"And what of you?" I asked quietly. "What is this caution we now must suffer?"

"There is a chamber, whose wall adjoins this one. Always before, it was left empty. But one of Regal's guests is now ensconced in it. Bright, Regal's cousin, and heir to Farrow Duchy. The man is a very light sleeper. He has complained to the servants of rats squeaking in the walls. Then, last night, Slink overset a kettle, with quite a clatter. It awoke him. The man is overly curious as well. He asks servants now if spirits have ever been known to walk in Buckkeep. And I have heard him tapping at the walls. I think he suspects this chamber. It need not concern us all that much; soon he will be leaving, I'm sure. But a bit more caution is called for."

I felt there was more, but whatever he did not wish to say would not be gained by questions. I asked one more, however. "Chade. Are you still able to see the King once a day?"

He glanced down at his hands and shook his head slowly. "Regal seems to suspect my existence. I will admit that to you. At least, he suspects something, and seems always to have some of his folk lurking about. It makes life difficult. But enough of our worries. Let us try to think of how things may go right."

And then Chade began a long discussion of Elderlings, based on what little we knew of them. We chatted of how it would be if Verity succeeded, and speculated what form the Elderlings' aid would take. Chade seemed to speak with great hope and sincerity, even enthusiasm. I tried to share it, but my belief was that the salvation of the Six Duchies depended on eliminating the viper in our midst. It was not long before he sent me back to my own room. I lay down on the bed, intending to rest for just a few minutes before facing the day, but instead fell into a deep sleep.

We were blessed with storms for a time. Each day that I woke to driving wind and rain against my shutters was a day to be treasured. I tried to be unobtrusive about the Keep, avoiding Regal even if it meant taking all my meals in the watch room, drifting out of any room that Justin and Serene might enter. Will, too, had returned from his Skill post at the Red Tower in Bearns. On rare occasions I saw him in company with Serene and Justin. More often he dawdled in the hall at table, his half-lidded eyes always seeming on the verge of closing. His dislike of me was not the focused hatred that Serene and Justin shared for me, but all the same I avoided him as well. I told myself I was wise, but feared myself a coward. I attended my king as often as I was allowed to. It was not often enough.

Came a morning when I was jolted awake to someone pounding on my door and yelling my name. I stumbled from my bed and jerked the door open. A white-faced stable boy stood shaking on my doorstep. "Hands says come to the stables. Right now!"

He gave me no time to reply to his urgent message, but raced off as if seven kinds of demons were after him.

I pulled on yesterday's clothes. I thought of splashing my face with water, or smoothing my hair back into its tail afresh, but those thoughts occurred to me halfway down the stairs. As I raced across the courtyard I could already hear the raised voices of a quarrel in the stable. I knew Hands would not have called me for a simple squabble among stable hands. I could not imagine what he would call me for. I pushed open the stable doors, then shoved my way past a gaggle of stable boys and grooms to get to the center of the commotion.

It was Burrich. He was no longer shouting. Travel worn and weary, he now stood silent. Hands was beside him, white-faced but standing firm. "I had no choice," he said quietly in answer to something Burrich had said. "You would have had to do the same."

Burrich's face looked ravaged. His eyes were unbelieving, empty with shock. "I know," he said after a moment. "I know." He turned to look at me. "Fitz. My horses are gone." He swayed slightly on his feet.

"It wasn't Hands's doing," I said quietly. Then I asked, "Where is Prince Verity?"

His brows knit and he looked at me oddly. "You did not expect me?" He paused, said more loudly, "Messages were sent ahead of me. Didn't you get them?"

"We've heard nothing. What happened? Why are you back?"

He looked around at the gaping stable boys, and something of the Burrich I knew came into his eyes again. "If you have not heard yet, then it is not for gossip and common talk. I must go straight to the King." He drew himself up straight, looked around again at the boys and grooms. The old whiplash was back in his voice as he demanded, "Have you no work to do? I shall be looking over how you have cared for things in my absence as soon as I return from the Keep."

Like fog in the sunlight, the workers dissipated. Burrich turned to Hands. "Would you care for my horse? Poor Ruddy's been poorly treated these last days. Treat him well, now that he's home."

Hands nodded. "Of course. Shall I send for the healer? I could have him waiting here for you when you come back."

Burrich shook his head. "What can be done for this, I can do for myself. Come, Fitz. Give me your arm."

In disbelief, I offered my arm and Burrich took it, leaning on me heavily. For the first time I glanced down. What I had taken to be heavy winter leggings at first glance was actually a thick wrap of bandaging on his bad leg. He favored it, putting most of his weight on me as he limped along. I could feel the exhaustion thrumming through him. Up close, I could smell the sweat of pain on him. His clothing was stained and torn, his hands and face begrimed. This was as unlike the man I knew as anything I could imagine. "Please," I said quietly as I helped him toward the castle. "Is Verity all right?"

He gave me a ghost of a smile. "You think our prince could be dead, and I still be alive? You insult me. Besides, use your wits. You'd know if he was dead. Or injured." He paused and studied me carefully. "Wouldn't you?"

It was plain what he spoke of. Ashamedly, I admitted, "Our link is not reliable. Some things are clear. Some are not. Of this, I knew nothing. What's happened?"

He looked thoughtful. "Verity said he would try to send word through you. If you've relayed no tidings to Shrewd, then this information should first go to the King."

I asked no more questions.

I had forgotten how long it had been since Burrich had seen King Shrewd. Mornings were not the King's best times, but when I mentioned this to Burrich, he said he would rather report immediately at a bad time than delay information. So we knocked and, to my surprise, were admitted. Once within, I realized this was because Wallace was nowhere about.

Instead, as I entered, the Fool asked me graciously, "Back for more Smoke?" Then, as he caught sight of Burrich, the mocking grin faded from his face. His eyes met mine. "The Prince?"

"Burrich has come to report to the King."

"I shall try to rouse him. Though the way he has been of late, one might as well report to him sleeping as awake. He takes as much notice either way."

Accustomed as I was to the Fool's mockery, this still jarred me. The sarcasm bit wrong, for there was too much resignation in his voice. Burrich looked at me worriedly. He whispered, "What is wrong with my king?"

I shook my head at him for quiet and tried to get him to take a seat.

"I stand before my king, until he bids me be seated," he said stiffly.

"You are injured. He would understand."

"He is my king. That is what I understand."

So I gave off urging him. We waited for a time, and more than a time. At last the Fool came out of the King's bedchamber. "He is not well," he cautioned us. "It has taken me a time to make him understand who is here. But he says he will hear your report. In his chambers."

So Burrich leaned on me as we went into the dimness and smoke of the King's bedchamber. I saw Burrich wrinkle his nose in distaste. Acrid fumes of Smoke hung heavy here, and several small censers burned. The Fool had drawn back the bed curtains, and as we stood he patted and poked cushions and pillows behind the King's back until Shrewd waved him aside with a small gesture.

I looked at our monarch and wondered how I had not seen the signs of his disease. They were plainly there when one looked. The general wasting of his body, the sour edge of his sweat, the yellow in the whites of his eyes: these were the least things I should have seen. The shock on Burrich's face told me plainly that the change since Burrich had last seen him was immense. But he covered it well and drew himself up straight.

"My king, I have come to report," he said formally.

Shrewd blinked slowly. "Report," he said vaguely, and I was not sure if he gave Burrich an order, or simply repeated the word. Burrich took it as a command. He was as thorough and exact as he had always insisted I be. I stood, and he supported his weight on my shoulder as he told of journeying with Prince Verity through the winter snows, traveling always toward the Mountain Kingdom. He did not mince words, but spoke plainly. The journey had been full of hardships. Despite messengers sent ahead of Verity's expedition, hospitality and aid along the way had been poor. Those nobles whose homes lay along their route professed to have known nothing of Verity's coming. In many cases, they found only servants to greet them, and the hospitality no more than what would have been offered to any ordinary traveler. Supplies and extra horses that should have been waiting for them at assigned locations were not. The horses had suffered more grievously than the men. The weather had been savage.

As Burrich reported I felt a tremor run through him from time to time. The man was at the edge of complete exhaustion. But each time he shook, I felt him take a deep breath, steady himself, and go on.

His voice quavered only slightly as he told how they had been ambushed on the plains of Farrow, before they came in sight of Blue Lake. He drew no conclusions himself, but only observed that these highwaymen fought in a military style. While they wore no Duke's colors, they seemed well dressed and well armed for brigands. And Verity was obviously their intended target. When two of the baggage animals broke loose and fled, none of their attackers broke away to follow them. Bandits usually would have preferred chasing laden pack beasts to fighting armed men. Verity's men had finally found a place to take a stand and had successfully stood them off. Their attackers had finally given up when they realized that Verity's guard would die to the last man before surrendering or giving way. They had ridden off, leaving their fallen dead in the snow.

"They had not defeated us, but we were not unscathed. We lost a good portion of our supplies. Seven men and nine horses were killed outright. Two of us were injured seriously. Three others took minor injuries. It was Prince Verity's decision to send the injured back to Buckkeep. With us he sent two sound men. His plan was to continue his quest, to take his guard with him as far as the Mountain Kingdom, and to have them stay there to await his return. Keen was placed in charge of those of us returning. To him, Verity entrusted written information. I do not know what that information packet contained. Keen and the others were killed five days ago. We were ambushed just outside the border of Buck, as we were traveling by the Buck River. Archers. It was very . . . quick. Four of us went down right away. My horse was struck in the flank. Ruddy's a young beast. He panicked. He plunged over an embankment into the river, and I with him. The river is deep there, and the current strong. I clung to Ruddy, but we were both swept downriver. I heard Keen shouting to the others to ride, that some must make it back to Buckkeep. But none of them did. When Ruddy and I managed to clamber out of the Buck, we went back. I found the bodies. The papers Keen had carried were gone."

He stood straight as he reported, and his voice was clear. His words were simple. His report was a simple description of what had happened. He mentioned nothing of what he had felt at being sent back, or at being the sole survivor to return. He would drink himself sodden tonight, I suspected. I wondered if he would want company for that. But for now, he stood, silent, awaiting his king's questions. The silence stretched overlong. "My king?" he ventured.

King Shrewd shifted in the shadows of his bed. "It reminds me of my younger days," he said hoarsely. "Once I

could sit a horse and hold a sword. When a man loses that—
well, once that is gone, he has actually lost far more than that.
But your horse was all right?''

Burrich furrowed his brow. ''I did what I could for him,
my king. He will take no permanent harm from it.''

''Well. At least there is that, then. At least there is that.''
King Shrewd paused. For a moment we listened to his breathing. He seemed to be working at it. ''Go and get some rest,
man,'' he said at last, gruffly. ''You look terrible. I may . . .''
He paused and took two breaths. ''I will call you back later.
When you are rested. I am sure there are things to ask. . . .''
His voice trailed off, and again he simply breathed. The deep
breaths a man takes when the pain is almost too much to bear. I
remembered what I had felt that night. I tried to imagine listening to Burrich report while enduring such pain. And struggling
not to show it. The Fool leaned in over the King to look into his
face. Then he looked at us and gave a tiny shake to his head.

''Come,'' I said softly to Burrich. ''Your king has given
you an order.''

He seemed to lean on me more heavily as we left the
King's bedchamber.

''He did not seem to care,'' Burrich said quietly, carefully
to me as we moved laboriously down the corridor.

''He does. Trust me. He cares deeply.'' We had come to
the staircase. I hesitated. A flight down, through the hall, the
kitchen, across the court, and into the stables. Then up the
steep stairs to Burrich's loft. Or up two flight of steps and
down the hall to my room. ''I'm taking you up to my room,'' I
told him.

''No. I want to be in my own place.'' He sounded fretful
as a sick child.

''In a while. After you've rested a bit,'' I told him firmly.
He did not resist as I eased him up the steps. I don't think he
had the strength. He leaned against the wall while I unlatched
my door. Once the door was open, I helped him in. I tried to get
him to lie down on my bed, but he insisted on the chair by the
hearth. Once ensconced there, he leaned his head back and
closed his eyes. When he relaxed, all the privations of his

journey showed in his face. Too much bone showed beneath his flesh, and his color was terrible.

He lifted his head and looked around the room as if he'd never seen it before. "Fitz? Have you anything to drink up here?"

I knew he didn't mean tea. "Brandy?"

"The cheap blackberry stuff you drink? I'd sooner drink horse liniment."

I turned back to him, smiling. "I might have some of that up here."

He didn't react. It was as if he hadn't heard me.

I built up my fire. I quickly sorted through the small supply of herbs I kept in my room. There wasn't much there. I had given most of them to the Fool. "Burrich, I'm going to go get you some food, and a few things. All right?"

There was no reply. He was already deeply asleep sitting there. I went to stand by him. I did not even need to touch the skin of his face to feel the fever burning there. I wondered what had happened to his leg this time. An injury atop an old injury, and then traveled on. It would not be soon healed, that was plain to me. I hurried out of my room.

In the kitchens, I interrupted Sara at pudding making, to tell her that Burrich was injured and sick and in my room. I lied and said he was ravenously hungry, and to please send a boy up with food, and some buckets of clean hot water. She immediately put someone else to stirring the pudding and began to clatter trays and teapots and cutlery. I would have enough food to supply a small banquet very quickly.

I ran out to the stables to let Hands know that Burrich was up in my room and would be for a while. Then I climbed the steps to Burrich's room. I had it in my mind to get the herbs and roots I would need there. I opened the door. The chamber was cold. The damp had got into it, and mustiness. I made a mental note to have someone come up and make a fire, and bring in a supply of wood, water, and candles. Burrich had expected to be gone all winter. Characteristically, he had tidied his room to the point of severity. I found a few pots of herbal salve, but no stores of freshly dried herbs. Either he had taken them with him, or given them away before he left.

I stood in the center of the room and looked around me. It had been months since I'd been here. Childhood memories came crowding back into my head. Hours spent before that hearth, mending or oiling harness. I'd used to sleep on a mat before the fire. Nosy, the first dog I'd ever bonded to. Burrich had taken him away, to try to break me of using the Wit. I shook my head at the flood of conflicting emotions, and quickly left the room.

The next door I knocked on was Patience's. Lacey opened it and, at the look on my face, demanded immediately, "What's wrong?"

"Burrich's come back. He's up in my room. He's badly hurt. I don't have much in the way of healing herbs—"

"Did you send for the healer?"

I hesitated. "Burrich has always liked to do things his own way."

"Indeed he has." It was Patience, entering the sitting room. "What's that madman done to himself now? Is Prince Verity all right?"

"The Prince and his guard were attacked. The Prince was not harmed and has continued to the Mountains. He sent back those who were injured, with two sound men as an escort. Burrich was the only one to survive and get home."

"Was the journey back so difficult?" Patience asked. Lacey was already moving about the room, gathering herbs and roots and materials for bandaging.

"It was cold and treacherous. Little hospitality was offered them along the way. But the men died when they were ambushed by archers, just across the Buck border. Burrich's horse carried him off into a river. They were swept downstream quite a ways; it was probably the only thing that saved him."

"How is he hurt?" Now Patience was moving, too. She opened a little cupboard and began to take out prepared salves and tinctures.

"His leg. The same one. I don't know exactly, I haven't looked at it yet. But it won't take his weight; he can't walk by himself. And he has a fever."

Patience took down a basket and began loading the medicines into it. "Well, what are you standing about for?" she

snapped at me as I waited. "Go back to your room and see
what you can do for him. We'll be up in a moment with these."

I spoke bluntly. "I don't think he'll let you help."

"We'll see," Patience said calmly. "Now go see that there
is hot water."

The buckets of water I had asked for were outside my
door. By the time the water in my kettle was boiling, people
had begun to converge on my room. Cook sent up two trays of
food, and warmed milk as well as hot tea. Patience arrived and
began to set out her herbs on my clothing chest. She quickly
sent Lacey to fetch a table for her, and two more chairs. Burrich slept on in my chair, deeply asleep despite occasional
bouts of shivering.

With a familiarity that astounded me, Patience felt his
forehead, then searched under the angle of his jaw for swelling.
She crouched slightly to look into his sleeping face. "Burr?"
she queried quietly. He did not even twitch. Very gently, she
stroked his face. "You are so thin, so worn," she grieved
softly. She damped a cloth in warm water and gently wiped his
face and hands as if he were a child. Then she swept a blanket
off my bed and tucked it carefully about his shoulders. She
caught me staring at her, and glared at me. "I need a basin of
warmed water," she snapped. As I went to fill one she
crouched before him and calmly took out her silver shears and
snipped up the side of the bandaging wrapping his leg. The
stained wrappings did not look as if they had been changed
since his dunk in the river. It went up past his knee. As Lacey
took the basin of warmed water and knelt next to her, Patience
opened the soiled bandaging as if it were a shell.

Burrich came awake with a groan, dropping his head forward onto his chest as his eyes opened. For a moment he was
disoriented. He looked at me standing over him, and then at the
two women crouched by his leg. "What?" was all he managed.

"This is a mess," Patience told him. She rocked back on
her heels and confronted him as if he'd tracked muck on a
clean floor. "Why haven't you at least kept it clean?"

Burrich glanced down at his leg. Old blood and river silt
were caked together over the swollen fissure down his knee. He
recoiled visibly from it. When he replied to Patience, his voice

was low and harsh. "When Ruddy took me into the river, we lost everything. I had no clean bandaging, no food, nothing. I could have bared it and washed it, and then frozen it. Do you think that would have improved it?"

"Here is food," I said abruptly. It seemed the only way to prevent their quarreling was to prevent them from talking to each other. I moved the small table laden with one of Cook's trays over beside him. Patience stood to be out of his way. I poured him a mug of the warmed milk and put it into his hands. They began to shake slightly as he raised it to his mouth. I had not realized how hungry he was.

"Don't gulp that!" Patience objected. Both Lacey and I shot her warning looks. But the food seemed to take Burrich's attention completely. He set down the mug and took a warm roll that I had slathered butter onto. He ate most of it in the space of time it took me to refill his mug. It was odd to see him begin to shake once he had the food in his hands. I wondered how he had managed to hold himself together before that.

"What happened to your leg?" Lacey asked him gently. Then: "Brace yourself," she warned him, and placed a warm, dripping cloth onto his knee. He gave a shudder and went paler, but refrained from making a sound. He drank some more milk.

"An arrow," he said at last. "It was just damnably bad luck that it struck where it did. Right where that boar ripped me, so many years ago. And it lodged against the bone. Verity cut it out for me." He leaned back suddenly in the chair, as if the memory sickened him. "Right on top of the old scar," he said faintly. "And every time I bent my knee, it pulled open and bled some more."

"You should have kept the leg still," Patience observed sagely. All three of us stared at her. "Oh, I suppose you couldn't, really," she amended.

"Let's take a look at it now," Lacey suggested, and reached for the wet cloth.

Burrich fended her off with a gesture. "Leave it. I'll see to it myself, after I've eaten."

"After you've eaten, you'll rest," Patience informed him. "Lacey, please move aside."

To my amazement, Burrich said nothing more. Lacey

stepped back, out of the way, and Lady Patience knelt before
the stablemaster. He watched her, a strange expression on his
face, as she lifted the cloth away. She damped the corner of the
cloth in clean water, wrung it out, and deftly sponged the
wound. The warm wet cloth had loosened the crusted blood.
Cleaned, it did not look as evil as it had at first. It was still a
nasty injury, and the hardships that Burrich had endured would
complicate its healing. The parted flesh gaped and proud flesh
had formed where it should have closed. But everyone visibly
relaxed as Patience cleaned it. There was redness, and swelling,
and infection at one end. But there was no putrefaction, no
darkening of the flesh around it. Patience studied it a moment.
"What do you think?" she asked aloud, of no one in particular. "Devil's-club root? Hot, mashed in a poultice? Do we have
any, Lacey?"

"Some, my lady," and Lacey turned to the basket they
had brought and began to sort through it.

Burrich turned to me. "Are those pots from my room?"

At my nod, he nodded in return. "I thought so. That fat
little brown one. Bring it here."

He took it from my hands and lifted the stopper from its
mouth. "This. I had some of this, when I set out from
Buckkeep, but it was lost with the pack animals, during the
first ambush."

"What is it?" Patience asked. She came, devil's-club root
in hand, to gaze curiously.

"Chickweed and plantain leaves. Simmered in oil, then
worked with beeswax into a salve."

"That should work well," she conceded. "After the root
poultice."

I braced myself for his argument, but he only nodded. He
suddenly looked very tired. He leaned back and pulled the
blanket more closely about himself. His eyes sagged shut.

There was a knock at my door. I went to answer it, and
found Kettricken standing there, with Rosemary at her elbow.
"One of my ladies told me there was a rumor Burrich had
returned," she began. Then she looked past me into the room.
"It's true, then. And he's hurt? What of my lord, oh, what of
Verity?" She went suddenly paler than I thought she could be.

"He's fine," I reassured her. "Come in." I cursed myself for my thoughtlessness. I should have sent word to her immediately of Burrich's return and of the tidings he carried. I should have known that otherwise she would not be told. As she entered, Patience and Lacey looked up from the devil's-club root they were steaming to welcome her with quick curtsies and murmurs of greeting.

"What's happened to him?" Kettricken demanded. And so I told her, reporting all that Burrich had told King Shrewd, for I thought she had as much right to word of her husband as Shrewd had to word of his son. She blanched again at mention of the attack on Verity, but kept silent until my telling was done. "Thank all our gods that he draws closer to my Mountains. There he will be safe, from men at least." That said, she drew closer to where Patience and Lacey were preparing the root. It had been steamed soft enough to crush into a pliable mass, and they were letting it cool before applying it to the infection.

"Mountain ash berry makes an excellent wash for such an injury," she suggested aloud.

Patience looked up at her shyly. "I have heard of that. But this warmed root will do much to draw the infection from the wound. Another good wash for proud flesh such as this is raspberry leaf and slippery elm. Or as a poultice."

"We have no raspberry leaf," Lacey reminded Patience. "The damp got into it somehow and it molded."

"I have raspberry leaf if you are in need of it," Kettricken said softly. "I had prepared it for a morning tea. It was a remedy my aunt taught me." She looked down and smiled oddly.

"Oh?" Lacey asked in sudden interest.

"Oh my dear," Patience suddenly exclaimed. She reached to take Kettricken's hand with a sudden, strange familiarity. "Are you sure?"

"I am. At first I thought it was just . . . But then I began to have the other signs. Some mornings, even the smell of the sea can make me so miserable. And all I want to do is sleep."

"But you should," Lacey exclaimed with a laugh. "As for the queasiness, it passes, after the first few months."

I stood very still, foreign, excluded, forgotten. All three women suddenly laughed together. "No wonder you were so anxious to have word of him. Did he know, before he left?"

"I did not even suspect it then. I so long to tell him, to watch his face."

"You're with child," I said stupidly. They all turned to look at me, and then burst out laughing anew.

"It's a secret, still," Kettricken cautioned me. "I want no rumors before the King has been told. I want to be the one to tell him."

"Of course not," I assured her. I did not tell her that the Fool already knew, and had known for days. Verity's child, I thought to myself. A sudden strange shivering raced over me. The branching of the path that the Fool had seen, the sudden multiplying of possibilities. One factor emerged above all others: the sudden removal of Regal, pushed one more step away from the throne. One more small life standing between him and the power he craved. How little he would care for that.

"Of course not," I repeated more heartily. "This news is best kept an absolute secret." For once it was out, I had no doubt that Kettricken would be in as much danger as her husband.

23

Threats

*T*HAT WINTER SAW *Bearns devoured slowly, as a cliff is eaten by storm tides. At first, Duke Brawndy sent tidings to Kettricken on a regular basis. Word came to her by liveried messengers coming on horseback directly from the Duke. At first the tidings they brought were optimistic. Her opals rebuilt Ferry. The folk there sent her not only their thanks, but a small chest of the very tiny pearls so prized by them. Odd. What had been too treasured to be sacrificed even to rebuild their own village was freely offered in thanks to a Queen who had surrendered her jewels that they might have shelter. I doubt that the significance of their sacrifice would have meant as much to any other. Kettricken wept over the tiny chest.*

Later messengers brought grimmer tidings. Between storms, the Red-Ships struck again and again. The messengers reported to Kettricken that Duke Brawndy wondered why the coterie member had left the Red Tower. When Kettricken boldly questioned Serene as to whether this was so, she said it had become too dangerous to keep Will there, for his Skill was too precious to be risked to the Red-Ships. The irony was lost on few folk. With each arriving messenger, the news worsened. The Outislanders had established footholds on Hook and Besham islands. Duke Brawndy assembled fishing vessels and warriors and boldly attacked on his own, but found the Red-

Ships too well entrenched there. Ships and warriors perished, and Bearns reported gravely that there were no funds for another expedition. At that juncture, Verity's emeralds were turned over to Kettricken. She sent them off without a qualm. If they did any good, we did not hear of it. We were not even certain they were ever received. Messages from Bearns became more erratic, and it was soon obvious that there had been tidings sent that we had not received. Communication with Brawndy broke down entirely. After two of her own messengers had been sent forth from Buckkeep, never to return, Kettricken vowed she would risk no more lives. By then, the Raiders from Hook and Besham had begun to harry farther down the coast, avoiding the immediate vicinity of Buckkeep, but making feints and challenges to both the north and south of us. To all these raids, Regal remained staunchly indifferent. He claimed he was conserving resources until Verity could return with the Elderlings to drive the Raiders away once and for all. But the merriment and entertainments at Buckkeep became ever more lavish and frequent, and his gifts to his Inland dukes and nobles ever more generous.

⤙═◦═⤚

By midafternoon, Burrich was back in his own chambers. I had wanted to keep him where I could watch over him, but he had scoffed at the idea. Lacey herself had seen to getting his chamber ready, and Burrich had grumbled enough about that. All she had done was to build up the fire, see water brought fresh, the bedding aired and shaken, and the floors swept and fresh rushes strewn. One of Molly's candles burned in the center of his table, putting a fresh piney scent into the musty room. But Burrich had growled that it scarcely felt like his own room. I had left him there, well propped up in bed and with a bottle of brandy close to hand.

I had understood the bottle only too well. As I had helped him through the stables and up to his loft, we had passed one empty stall after another. Not only horses were missing; prime hunting dogs were gone. I had no heart to go look in the mews; I was sure I would find them likewise plundered. Hands had walked beside us, silent but stricken. His efforts were plain.

The stables themselves were immaculate, the remaining horses groomed until they shone. Even the empty stalls were scrubbed and whitewashed. But an empty cupboard, no matter how clean, is no comfort to a starving man. I understood that the stables were Burrich's treasure and home. He had come back to find both looted.

After I left Burrich, I took a walk down to the barns and pens. Here the best of the breeding stock were wintered over. I found them as depleted as the stables. Prize bulls were gone. Of the curly-backed black sheep that used to fill one pen, there were only six ewes and one runty ram left. I was not as aware of what other stock had once been there, but too many pens and stalls were empty at a time of year when all were usually full.

From the barns, I wandered through the storage houses and outbuildings. Outside of one, some men were loading sacks of grain into a wagon. Two other wagons, already loaded, stood nearby. I stood a bit, watching them, and then offered to help as the wagon's load grew higher and the sacks harder to load. They accepted my help readily, and we talked as we worked. I waved them a cheery good-bye when the work was done, and walked slowly back to the Keep, wondering why a full warehouse of grain was being loaded onto a barge and sent upriver to Turlake.

I decided I would check on Burrich before going back to my own chambers. I climbed the steps to his chambers and was unsettled to find the door ajar. Fearing some sort of treachery, I pushed in, startling Molly, who was setting out dishes on a small table beside Burrich's chair. The sight of her there rattled me, and I stared at her. When I turned to Burrich, I found him watching me.

"I thought you were alone," I said lamely.

Burrich regarded me owlishly. He had made inroads on his bottle of brandy. "I thought I would be," he said gravely. As ever, he held his spirits well, but Molly was not deceived. Her lips were set in a thin line. She continued with her duties, ignoring me. Instead she spoke to Burrich.

"I shall not disturb you long. Lady Patience sent me to see that you had hot food, for you ate little this morning. I shall be leaving as soon as I have set out his meal."

"And taking my thanks with you," Burrich added. His eyes went from me to Molly, sensing the awkwardness, and also her displeasure with him. He attempted an apology. "I have had a harsh journey, mistress, and my injury gives me some pain. I hope I have not given offense."

"It is not my place to take offense at anything you wish to do, sir," she replied. She finished setting out the food she had brought. "Is there anything else I can do for you to make you comfortable?" she asked. There was courtesy in her voice, no more than that. She did not look at me at all.

"You could accept my thanks. Not just for the food, but also for the candles that freshened my chamber. I understand they are your handiwork."

I saw her thaw slightly. "Lady Patience asked me to bring them here. I was happy to oblige her."

"I see." The next words he spoke cost him more. "Then please extend my thanks to her. And to Lacey as well, I am sure."

"I shall. There is nothing more that you need, then? I have errands in Buckkeep Town for Lady Patience. She told me that if there was anything you required from town, I should fetch it for you."

"Nothing. But it was kind of her to think of it. Thank you."

"You are welcome, sir." And Molly, empty basket on her arm, marched out past me as if I were not even there.

Burrich and I were left regarding one another. I glanced after Molly, then tried to put her out of my mind. "It's not just the stables," I told him, and briefly reported what I had seen in the barns and warehouses.

"I could have told you a bit of that," he said gruffly. He looked at the food Molly had brought, then poured himself more brandy. "As we came down the Buck River road there were rumors and tidings. Some said Regal sold the beasts and grain off to fund the defense of the coasts. Others that he sent the breeding stock inland to safer pastures in Tilth." He drank his brandy down. "The best of the horses are gone. I saw that at a glance when I came back. In ten years, I might breed stock up again to the quality of what we had. But I doubt it." He poured again. "There's my life's work gone, Fitz. A man likes to think he'll leave his touch on the world somewhere. The horses I had brought together here, the bloodlines I was establishing—gone now, scattered throughout the Six Duchies. Oh, not that they won't improve anything they're bred to. But I'll never see what would have come if I'd been allowed to continue. Steady will be studding rangy Tilth mares, no doubt. And when Ember drops her next foal, whoever rubs it off will think it just another horse. For six generations, I've been waiting for just that foal. They'll take the finest coursing horse that's ever been foaled and hook it to a plow."

There was nothing to say about that. I feared it was all true. "Eat something," I suggested. "How's your leg now?"

He lifted the blanket to inspect it casually. "Still there, anyway. I suppose I should be grateful for that. And better than it was this morning. The devil's-club did draw out the infection. Chicken-brained as she is, the woman still knows her herbs."

I did not need to ask to whom he referred. "Are you going to eat?" I prodded.

He set down his cup and took up a spoon. He tasted the soup Molly had set out, grudgingly nodded his approval. "So," he observed between bites, "that was the girl. Molly."

I nodded.

"Seemed a bit cool with you today."

"A bit," I said dryly.

Burrich grinned. "You're as testy as she was. I imagine Patience did not speak well of me to her."

"She doesn't like drunks," I told him bluntly. "Her father drank himself to death. But before he finished the job, he managed to make her life unpleasant for years. Beating her when she was smaller. Railing and berating her when she got too big to beat."

"Oh." Burrich carefully refilled his cup. "I'm sorry to hear that."

"She was sorry to live it."

He looked at me levelly. "I did not do it, Fitz. Nor was I rude to her when she was here. I'm not even drunk. Not yet. So stuff your disapproval, and tell me what's been going on at Buckkeep while I was away.''

So I stood and reported to Burrich, just as if he had a right to demand it. In a way, I suppose he did. He ate as I spoke. When I was finished, he poured himself more brandy and leaned back in his chair, holding it. He swirled the brandy in the cup, looked down at it, then up at me. ''And Kettricken is with child, but neither the King nor Regal know of it yet.''

''I thought you were asleep.''

''I was. I half thought I'd dreamed that conversation. Well.'' He downed the brandy. He sat up, swept the blanket off his leg. As I watched he deliberately bent his knee until the pulling flesh began to gap the wound open. I winced at the sight of it, but Burrich only looked thoughtful. He poured more brandy, drank it off. The bottle was half-gone. ''So. I'm going to have to splint the leg straight, if I'm going to keep that closed.'' He glanced up at me. ''You know what I'll need. Will you fetch it for me?''

''I think you should stay off it for a day or so. Give it a chance to rest. You don't need a splint if you're in bed.''

He gave me a long look. ''Who guards Kettricken's door?''

''I don't think . . . I assume she has women who sleep in the outer chamber of her apartments.''

''You know he'll try to kill her and the unborn child, as soon as he finds out.''

''It's a secret still. If you start guarding her door, all will know.''

''By my count, five of us know. That's no secret, Fitz.''

''Six,'' I admitted ruefully. ''The Fool surmised it some days ago.''

''Oh!'' I had the satisfaction of seeing Burrich look shocked. ''Well, at least that's one tongue that won't go wagging. Still, as you see, it won't be secret long. Rumors will fly before the day's out, mark my words. I guard her door this night.''

''Must it be you? Can't you rest, and I will—''

''A man can die of failure, Fitz. Do you know that? Once, I told you, the fight isn't over until you've won. This''—and he

stured at his leg in disgust—"this will not be my excuse for
ving up. Shame enough for me that my prince went on with-
it me. I shall not fail him here. Besides"—he gave a bark of
ur laughter—"there's not enough in the stables now to keep
th Hands and me busy. And the heart for it has gone out of
e. Now. Will you go get the splint works?"

So I did, and took them back to him, and helped him
near the wound with his salve before we wrapped it well and
linted it. He cut a pair of old trousers to go over the splint,
d I helped him down the stairs. Then, despite his words, he
ent to Ruddy's stall to see if his horse's arrow wound had
en cleaned and doctored. I left him there and went back up to
e Keep. I wanted to speak to Kettricken, to let her know there
ould be a man on guard on her door that night, and why.

I knocked at her chamber door and was admitted by Rose-
ary. The Queen was indeed there, and a selection of her
dies. Most were working embroidery or small lap looms as
ey talked. The Queen herself had her window opened to the
ild winter day and was looking out over the calm sea with a
own. She reminded me of Verity when he Skilled, and I
uspected that much the same worries plagued her. I followed
er gaze, and wondered, like her, where the Red-Ships would
trike today, and what was going on up in Bearns. Useless to
vonder. Officially, there was no word at all from Bearns. The
umors were that the coasts ran red with blood.

"Rosemary. I wish a quiet word with Her Majesty."

Rosemary nodded gravely and went over to curtsy to her
queen. In a moment the Queen looked up, and with a nod and a
gesture invited me to join her in her window seat. I greeted her
quietly and gestured smilingly out over the water as if we
chatted of the fine weather. But softly I said, "Burrich wishes
o guard your door, beginning this night. He fears that when
others discover you are with child, your life will be in danger."

Another woman might have blanched or at least seemed
surprised. Instead, Kettricken lightly touched the very service-
able knife she always wore beside her keys. "Almost, I would
welcome so direct an attack." She considered. "I suppose it is
wise. What harm can come of letting them know we suspect.
Nay, that we know. Why should I be circumspect and tactful?

Burrich has already received their greetings, in the form of a
arrow through the leg.'' The bitterness in her voice, and th
ferocity beneath it, shocked me. ''He may take the guard pos
and with it my thanks. I could choose a sounder man, but
would not have the trust in him that I have in Burrich. Will h
leg injury permit him to do this duty?''

''I do not think his pride would permit any other to do it.''

''Fine, then.'' She paused. ''I will have a chair placed fc
him.''

''I doubt he will use it.''

She sighed. ''We all have our own ways of offering sacr
fice. It shall be there, nonetheless.''

I bowed my head in acceptance and she dismissed me.
went back up to my room intending to tidy away all that ha
been dragged out for Burrich's use. But as I walked softl
down the hall I was startled to see the door of my room ope
slowly. I eased to another doorway and flattened myself insid
it. After a moment Justin and Serene emerged from my room.
stepped out to confront them.

''Still looking for a spot for your tryst?'' I asked acidly.

They both froze. Justin stepped back, stood almost behin
Serene. Serene glared at him, then stood firm before me. ''W
don't have to answer to you for anything.''

''Not even for being in my room? Did you find anythin
interesting there?''

Justin was breathing as if he'd just run a race. I deliber
ately met his eyes. He was speechless. I smiled at him.

''We need not speak to you at all,'' Serene announced
''We know what you are. Come, Justin.''

''You know what I am? Interesting. Rest assured that
know what you are. And that I am not the only one whc
knows.''

''Beast man!'' Justin hissed. ''You wallow in the filthies
of magics. Did you think you could go undetected amongst us?
No wonder Galen found you unfit to Skill!''

His arrow had struck home and quivered in my most secre
fear. I tried not to let it show. ''I am loyal to King Shrewd.''
Face composed, I gazed at them steadily. I said no more thar
that. Not in words. But I looked them up and down, measuring

em against what they should be, and found them lacking. In
ne minute shifting of their feet, in their quick glances at one
nother, I decided that they knew they were traitors. They
eported to Regal; they knew they should report to the King.
They were not deceived as to what they were; they understood.
erhaps Galen had burned a loyalty to Regal into their minds;
erhaps they could not conceive of turning against him. But
arts of them still knew that Shrewd was king, and that they
vere disloyal to a King they had sworn to. I tucked away that
it of knowledge; it was a crack that might someday hold a
vedge.

I stepped forward, and enjoyed watching Serene shrink
way from me while Justin cowered between her and the wall.
But I made no attack. I turned my back to them and opened my
loor. As I entered my room I felt a sneaky little wisp of Skill
grope at the edges of my mind. Without thinking, I blocked as
Verity had taught me to. "Keep your thoughts to yourself," I
varned them, and did not dignify them by looking back at
hem. I shut the door.

For a moment I stood breathing. Calm. Calm. I did not
elax my mind guards. Then quietly, carefully, I worked my
atches. Once the door was secured, I moved cautiously
hrough my room. Chade had once told me that assassins must
always believe the other person has more skill than they do. It
s the only way to remain alive and keep sharp. So I touched
nothing lest it had been coated with poison. Instead, I stood in
he center of my room, closed my eyes, and tried to recall
exactly how it had looked when I last left it. Then I opened my
eyes and looked for changes in the room.

The small tray of herbs was squarely atop my clothing
chest. I had left it to one end, within easy reach of Burrich. So
they had been through my clothing chest. The tapestry of King
Wisdom, that had been slightly askew for months, now hung
straight. That was all I could see. It puzzled me. I had no idea
what they had been looking for. That they had dug through my
clothing chest seemed to suggest it was a small enough item to
fit in there. But why lift a tapestry and look behind it? I stood
still, thinking a moment. This had not been a random search. I
was not sure what they had been hoping to find. But I sus-

pected they had been told to look for a secret passageway in m
room. That meant that Regal had concluded that killing Lad
Thyme had not been enough. His suspicions were stronger tha
Chade had led me to believe. I was almost grateful I had neve
been able to discover how to work the entry to Chade's apar
ments. It gave me more confidence in its secrecy.

I inspected every item in my room before I handled it.
saw that every scrap of food that had remained on Cook's tray
was disposed of where no one and nothing would taste it.
discarded the water in the buckets as well as that in my ewer.
inspected my supply of firewood and candles for powders o
resins, checked my bedding for powder, and reluctantly dis
carded my complete supply of herbs. I would take no chances.
could discover no possessions missing, nor that anything had
been added to my room. Sometime later I sat down on my bed
feeling exhausted and unnerved. I would have to be more on
my guard, I concluded. I recalled the Fool's experience and
pondered it. I did not want to encounter a bag and a beating the
next time I entered my room.

My room suddenly seemed confining, a trap that I must
return to each day. I left it, not bothering to lock it as I went.
Locks were useless. Let them see I did not fear their intrusion.
Even though I did.

Outside, it was a mild, clear late afternoon. The unseasonably kind weather ate at me, even as I enjoyed my walk through
the inner circle of the Keep. I decided I would walk down to
town, to pay a visit to the *Rurisk* and my shipmates there, and
then perhaps go into a tavern for a beer. It had been too long
since I'd walked to town, and far too long since I'd listened to
the gossip of town folk. It would be a relief to get away from
Buckkeep intrigues for a while.

I was going out the gate when a young guardsman stepped
into my path. "Stand!" he commanded me, then: "Please,
sir," he added as he recognized me.

I halted obediently. "Yes?"

He cleared his throat, then suddenly went scarlet all the
way to his hairline. He took a breath, then stood silent.

"Did you need something from me?" I asked.

"Please to wait a moment, sir," the boy blurted.

The lad disappeared back into the guardhouse, and a moment later an older watch officer emerged. She regarded me gravely, took a breath as if to steel herself, then said quietly, "You are denied passage out of the Keep."

"What?" I could not believe my ears.

She drew herself up. When she spoke, her voice was firmer. "You are denied passage out of the Keep."

A surge of anger heated me. I forced it down. "By whose command?"

She stood firm before me. "My commands come from the captain of the watch, sir. That is all I know of it."

"I would speak to that captain." I kept my voice courteous.

"He is not in the guardroom. Sir."

"I see." But I did not, quite. I could perceive all the nooses tightening about me, but could not understand why just now. The other obvious question to ask, however, was "why not?" With Shrewd's enfeeblement, Verity had become my protector. But he was away. I could turn to Kettricken, but only if I were willing to bring her into open conflict with Regal. I was not. Chade was, as always, a shadow power. All of this passed through my mind quickly. I was turning away from the gate when I heard my name called. I turned back.

Coming up the hill from town was Molly. Her servant's blue dress flapped around her calves as she ran. And she ran heavily, unevenly, unlike her usual graceful stride. She was exhausted, or nearly so. "Fitz!" she cried out again, and there was fear in her voice.

I started to go to her, but the guard stepped suddenly into my path. Fear was on her face, too, but also determination. "I cannot let you go out of the gate. I have my orders."

I wanted to smash her from my path. I forced my rage down. A struggle with her would not help Molly. "Then you go to her, damn you! Can't you see the woman is in trouble of some kind?"

She stood eye to eye with me, unmoving. "Miles!" she called, and the boy leaped out. "Go see what is wrong with that woman. Quickly now!"

The boy took off like a shot. I stood, with the guard stand-

ing squarely before me, and watched helplessly over her shoul
der as Miles raced to Molly. When he reached her, he put an
arm around her and took her basket on his other arm. Leaning
heavily on him, gasping and near weeping, Molly came toward
the gate. It seemed to take forever before she was through the
gate and in my arms. "Fitz, oh Fitz," she sobbed.

"Come," I told her. I turned her away from the guard
walked her away from the gate. I knew I had done the sensible
thing, the calm thing, but I felt shamed and small from it.

"Why didn't you . . . come to me?" Molly panted.

"The guard would not let me. They have orders I am not
to leave Buckkeep," I said quietly. I could feel her trembling
as she leaned against me. I took her around the corner of a
warehouse, out of sight of the guards standing gaping in the
gate. I held her in my arms until she quieted. "What's wrong?
What happened?" I tried to make my voice soothing. I brushed
back the hair that hung about her face. After a few moments
she quieted in my arms. Her breathing steadied, but she still
trembled.

"I had gone into town. Lady Patience had given me the
afternoon. And I needed to get a few things . . . for my candles." As she spoke, her trembling lessened. I tilted her chin
up so that she looked into my eyes.

"And then?"

"I was . . . coming back. I was on the steep bit, just
outside of town. Where the alders grow?"

I nodded. I knew the spot.

"I heard horses coming. In a hurry. So I stepped off the
road to make way for them." She started to tremble again. "I
kept walking, thinking they would pass me. But suddenly they
were right behind me, and when I looked back, they were
coming right at me. Not on the road, but right at me. I jumped
back into the brush, and still they rode right at me. I turned and
ran, but they kept coming. . . ." Her voice was getting higher
and higher.

"Hush! Wait a bit. Calm down. Think. How many of
them? Did you know them?"

She shook her head wildly. "Two. I couldn't see their
faces. I was running away, and they were wearing the kind of

helm that comes down over your eyes and nose. They chased me. It's steep there, you know, and brushy. I tried to get away, but they just rode their horses right through the brush after me. Herding me, like dogs herd sheep. I ran, and ran, but I couldn't get away from them. Then I fell, I caught my foot on a log and I fell. And they jumped from their horses. One pinned me down while the other snatched up my basket. He dumped it all out, like he was looking for something, but they were laughing and laughing. I thought . . ."

My heart was hammering as hard as Molly's now. "Did they hurt you?" I asked fiercely.

She paused, as if she could not decide, then shook her head wildly. "Not like you fear. He just . . . held me down. And laughed. The other one, he said . . . he said, I was pretty stupid, letting myself be used by a bastard. They said . . ."

Again she paused a moment. Whatever they had said to her, called her was ugly enough that she could not repeat it to me. It was like a sword through me, that they had been able to hurt her so badly she would not even share the pain. "They warned me," she went on at last. "They said stay away from the bastard. Don't do his dirty work for him. They said . . . things I didn't understand, about messages and spies and treason. They said they could make sure that everyone knew I was the Bastard's whore." She tried just to say the word, but it came out with greater force. She defied me to flinch from it. "Then they said . . . I would be hanged . . . if I didn't pay attention. That to run errands for a traitor was to be a traitor." Her voice grew strangely calmer. "Then they spit on me. And they left me. I heard them ride away, but for a long time I was afraid to get up. I have never been so scared." She looked at me and her eyes were like open wounds. "Not even my father ever scared me that bad."

I held her close to me. "It's all my fault." I did not even know I had spoken aloud until she drew back from me, to look up in puzzlement.

"Your fault? Did you do something wrong?"

"No. I am no traitor. But I am a bastard. And I've let that spill over onto you. Everything Patience warned me of, everything Ch—everyone warned me about, it's all coming true I've got you caught up in it.''

"What is happening?'' she asked softly, eyes wide. Her breath suddenly caught. "You said . . . the guard wouldn't let you out the gate. That you can't leave Buckkeep? Why?''

"I don't know, exactly. There's a lot I don't understand. But one thing I do know. I have to keep you safe. That means staying away from you, for a time. And you from me. Do you understand?''

A glint of anger came into her eyes. "I understand you're leaving me alone in this!''

"No. That's not it. We have to make them believe that they've scared you, that you're obeying them. Then you'll be safe. They'll have no reason to come after you again.''

"They have scared me, you idiot!'' she hissed at me. "One thing I know. Once someone knows you're afraid of him, you're never safe from that person. If I obey them now, they will come after me again. To tell me to do other things, to see how far I'll obey them in my fear.''

These were the scars her father had left on her life. Scars that were a kind of strength, but also a vulnerability. "Now is not the time to stand up to them,'' I whispered. I kept looking over her shoulder, expecting that at any moment the guard would come to see where we had vanished. "Come,'' I said, and led her deeper into the maze of warehouses and outbuildings. She walked silently beside me for a ways, then suddenly jerked her hand from mine.

"It is time to stand up to them,'' she declared. "Because once you start putting it off, you never do it. Why should not this be the time?''

"Because I don't want you caught up in this. I don't want you hurt. I don't want people saying you are the Bastard's whore.'' I could barely force the words from my mouth.

Molly's head came up. "I have done nothing I'm ashamed of,'' she said evenly. "Have you?''

"No. But—''

" 'But.' Your favorite word,'' she said bitterly. She walked away from me.

"Molly!'' I sprang after her, seized her by the shoulders.

She spun and hit me. Not a slap. A solid punch in the mouth that rocked me back and put blood in my mouth. She stood glaring, daring me to touch her again. I didn't. "I didn't say I wouldn't fight back. Only that I didn't want you caught up in it. Give me a chance to fight this my way," I said. I knew blood was running over my chin. I let her look at it. "Trust that given time, I can find them and make them pay. My way. Now. Tell me about the men. What they wore, how they rode. What did the horses look like? Did they speak like Buck folk, or Inlanders? Did they have beards? Could you tell the color of their hair, their eyes?"

I saw her trying to think, saw her mind veer away from thinking about it. "Brown," she said at last. "Brown horses, with black manes and tails. And the men talked like anybody else. One had a dark beard. I think. It's hard to see face down in the dirt."

"Good. That's good," I told her, though she had told me nothing at all. She looked down, away from the blood on my face. "Molly," I said more quietly. "I won't be coming . . . to your room. Not for a while. Because—"

"You're afraid."

"Yes!" I hissed. "Yes, I'm afraid. Afraid they'll hurt you, afraid they'll kill you. To hurt me. I won't endanger you by coming to you."

She stood still. I could not tell if she was listening to me or not. She folded her arms across her chest, hugged herself.

"I love you too much to see that happen." My words sounded weak, even to myself.

She turned and walked away from me. She still hugged herself, as if to keep herself from flying apart. She looked very alone, in her draggled blue skirts with her proud head bowed. "Molly Redskirts," I whispered after her, but I could no longer see that Molly. Only what I had made of her.

24

Neatbay

*T*HE POCKED MAN *is the legendary harbinger of disaster for the folk of the Six Duchies. To see him, striding down the road, is to know that disease and pestilence will soon come to call. To dream of him is said to be a warning of a death to come. Often the tales of him show him appearing to those deserving of punishment, but sometimes he is used, most often in puppet shows, as a general omen of disaster to come. A marionette of the Pocked Man, hung dangling across the scenery, is a warning to all in the audience that soon they will witness a tragedy.*

⊷═╣←

The days of winter dragged agonizingly slow. With every passing hour, I was braced for something to happen. I never walked into a room without surveying it first, ate no food I had not seen prepared, drank only the water I drew from the well myself. I slept poorly. The constant watchfulness told on me in a hundred ways. I was snappish to those who spoke to me casually, moody when I checked on Burrich, reticent with the Queen. Chade, the only one to whom I could have unburdened myself, did not summon me. I was miserably alone. I dared not go to Molly. I kept my visits to Burrich as brief as possible for fear of bringing my troubles down on him. I could not openly leave Buckkeep to spend time with Nighteyes, and I feared to leave by our secret way lest I be watched. I waited and I watched, but that nothing further happened to me became a sophisticated torture of suspense.

I did call on King Shrewd daily. I watched him dwindle before my eyes, saw the Fool become daily more morose, his humor more acid. I longed for savage winter weather to match my mood, but the skies continued blue and the winds calm. Within Buckkeep, the evenings were noisy with gaiety and revel. There were masked balls, and summonings of minstrels to compete for fat purses. The Inland Dukes and nobles ate well at Regal's table, and drank well with him late into the night.

"Like ticks on a dying dog," I said savagely to Burrich one day as I was changing the dressing on his leg for him. He had made comment that it was no trick to stay awake on his night guard duty at Kettricken's door, for the noise of the revelry would have made it difficult to sleep.

"Who's dying?" he asked.

"All of us. One day at a time, we're all dying. Did no one ever tell you that? But this is healing, and surprisingly well for all you've done to it."

He looked down at his bared leg and cautiously flexed it. The tissue pulled unevenly, but held. "Maybe the gash is closed up, but it doesn't feel healed inside," he observed. It was not a complaint. He lifted his brandy cup and drained it off. I eyed it narrowly. His days had a pattern now. Once he left Kettricken's door in the morning, he went to the kitchen and ate. Then he came back to his room and began drinking. After I appeared and helped him change the bandaging on his leg, he would drink until it was time for him to sleep. And wake up in the evening, just in time to eat and then go guard Kettricken's door. He no longer did anything in the stables. He had given them over to Hands, who went about looking as if the job were a punishment he hadn't deserved.

Every other day or so, Patience sent Molly up to tidy Burrich's room for him. I knew little of these visits other than that they happened, and that Burrich, surprisingly, tolerated them. I had mixed feelings about them. No matter how much

Burrich drank, he always treated women graciously; yet the emptied brandy bottles in a row could not but remind Molly of her father. Still, I wished them to know one another. One day I told Burrich that Molly had been threatened because of her association with me. "Association?" he had asked sharply.

"Some few know that I care for her," I admitted gingerly.

"A man does not bring his problems down on a woman he cares for," he told me severely.

I had no reply to that. Instead I gave him the few details Molly had recalled about her attackers, but they suggested nothing to him. For a time he had stared off, right through the walls of his room. After a time he picked up his cup and drained it. He spoke carefully. "I am going to tell her that you are worried about her. I am going to tell her that if she fears danger, she must come to me. I am more in a position to deal with it." He looked up and met my eyes. "I am going to tell her that you are wise to stay away from her, for her sake." As he poured himself another drink he had added quietly to the tabletop, "Patience was right. And she was wise to send her to me."

I blanched to consider the full implications of that statement. For once, I was smart enough to know when to be quiet. He drank his brandy down, then looked at the bottle. Slowly, he slid it across the table toward me. "Put that back on the shelf for me, will you?" he requested.

❧

Animals and winter stores continued to be drained from Buckkeep. Some were sold off cheaply to Inland Duchies. The very finest of the hunting and riding horses were barged up the Buck, to an area near Turlake. Regal announced this as a plan to preserve our best breeding stock far from the ravages of the Red-Ships. The mutter of the folk in Buckkeep Town, so Hands told me, was that if the King could not hold his own castle, what hope was there for them? When a shipment of fine old tapestries and furniture were sent upriver as well, the murmur became that soon the Farseers would abandon Buckkeep entirely, without even a fight, without even waiting for an assault. I had the uncomfortable suspicion the rumor was correct.

Confined as I was to Buckkeep, I had little direct access to the talk of the common folk. A silence greeted my entry to the watchroom now. With my restriction to the Keep had come gossip and speculation. The talk that had flown about me on the day I had failed to save the little girl from the Forged ones found new life. Few of the guard spoke to me of anything other than the weather or other pleasantries. While they did not make me a total pariah, I was banished from the easy conversations and rambling arguments that usually filled the watchroom. To talk to me had become bad luck. I wouldn't inflict that on men and women I cared about.

I was still welcome about the stables, but I strove not to talk to any one person too much, or appear too close to any of the beasts. The stable workers were a morose lot these days. There was not enough work to busy them, so quarrels were more frequent. The stable hands were my major source of news and rumors. None of it was cheery. There were garbled stories of raids on Bearns towns, gossip about brawls in the taverns and on the docks of Buckkeep Town, and accounts of folk moving south or inland as their means allowed. What talk there was of Verity and his quest was demeaning or ridiculing. Hope had perished. Like me, the folk of Buckkeep were waiting in suspense for disaster to come to their doorsteps.

We had a month of stormy weather, and the relief and rejoicing in Buckkeep were more destructive than the preceding period of tension had been. A waterfront tavern caught fire during an especially wild evening of revelry. The fire spread, and only the drenching rain that followed the gusting winds saved it from spreading to the dock warehouses. That would have been a disaster in more than one way, for as Regal drained the Keep warehouses of grain and supplies, folk in the town saw little reason to conserve what was left. Even if the Raiders never came to Buckkeep itself, I was resigned to short rations before the winter was out.

I woke one night to stark stillness. The howl of the storm winds and the rattling of rain had stilled. My heart sank. A terrible premonition filled me, and when I rose to a clear blue morning, my dread increased. Despite the sunny day, the atmosphere in the Keep was oppressive. Several times I felt the tickling of the Skill against my senses. It nearly drove me mad, for I did not know if it was Verity attempting better contact, or Justin and Serene prying. A late-afternoon visit to King Shrewd and the Fool disheartened me further. The King, wasted to little more than bones, was sitting up and smiling vaguely. He Skilled feebly toward me as I came in the door, and then greeted me with, "Ah, Verity, my lad. How did your sword lesson go today?" The rest of his conversation made as much sense. Regal appeared almost immediately after I arrived. He sat on a straight-backed chair, arms crossed on his chest, and looked at me. No words were exchanged between us. I could not decide if my silence were cowardice or self-restraint. I escaped him as soon as I decently could, despite a rebuking look from the Fool.

The Fool himself looked little better than the King. On so colorless a creature as the Fool, the dark circles under his eyes looked painted on. His tongue had grown as still as the clappers in his bells. When King Shrewd died, nothing would stand between the Fool and Regal. I wondered if there was any way I could aid him.

As if I could aid myself, I reflected sourly.

In the solitude of my room that evening, I drank more than I should of the cheap blackberry brandy that Burrich despised. I knew I would be sick from it tomorrow. I didn't care. Then I lay on my bed, listening to the distant sounds of merriment from the Great Hall. I wished Molly were there to scold me for being drunk. The bed was too large, the linens glacier white and cold. I closed my eyes and sought comfort in the company of a wolf. Confined as I was to the Keep, I had begun to seek his dream company on a nightly basis, just to have an illusion of freedom.

I came awake just before Chade seized me and shook me. It was good I had recognized him in that split instant, for otherwise I am sure I would have tried to kill him. "Up!" he whispered hoarsely. "Get up, you sodden fool, you idiot! Neatbay is under siege. Five Red-Ships. I wager they'll leave nothing standing if we delay. Get up, damn you!"

I staggered to my feet, the muzziness of drink giving way before the shock of his words.

"What can we do?" I asked stupidly.

"Tell the King. Tell Kettricken, tell Regal. Surely not even Regal can ignore this, it is at our very doorstep. If the Red-Ships take and hold Neatbay, they will have us bracketed. No ships will get out of Buck Harbor. Even Regal will see that. Now go! Go!"

I dragged on trousers and a tunic, ran for the door barefoot with my hair draggling about my face. I halted there. "How do I know this? Whence do I say this warning comes?"

Chade hopped up and down in frustration. "Damn and damn! Tell them anything! Tell Shrewd you had a dream of the Pocked Man scrying it in a pool of water! He at least should understand that! Tell them an Elderling brought you the news! Say anything, but get them to act and now!"

"Right!" I raced off down the hallway, skidded down the steps, and raced down the corridor to King Shrewd's chambers. I hammered on Shrewd's door. At the far end of the hall, Burrich stood beside his chair outside Kettricken's door. He looked at me, drew his short sword, and took a ready stance, eyes darting everywhere. "Raiders!" I called down the hall to him, not caring who overheard or how they reacted. "Five Red-Ships in Neatbay! Rouse Her Majesty, tell her they need our aid now!"

Burrich turned without a question to tap on Kettricken's door and be immediately admitted. It did not go so easily for me. Wallace finally opened the door a grudging crack, but would not budge until I suggested he should be the one to race down the stairs and inform Regal of my tidings. I believe it was the prospect of making a dramatic entrance and conferring with the Prince before all the merrymakers that decided him. He left the door unguarded as he hurried to his small ante-chamber to make himself presentable.

The King's bedchamber was in total darkness and heavy with the reek of Smoke. I took a candle from his sitting room, kindled it at the dwindling fire, and hastened in. In the darkness, I nearly trod upon the Fool, who was curled up like a cur at the King's bedside. I gaped in astonishment. He had not so much as a blanket or cushion for comfort, but huddled on the rug beside the King's bed. He uncurled stiffly, coming awake, and then alarmed in an instant. "What is it? What's happened?" he demanded.

"Raiders in Neatbay. Five Red-Ships. I have to rouse the King. What are you doing, sleeping here? Are you afraid to go back to your own room anymore?"

He laughed bitterly. "More like I fear to leave this one, lest I never be allowed in again. The last time Wallace locked me out, it took me an hour of yammering and hammering before the King realized I was missing and demanded to know where I was. The time before that, I slipped in with the breakfast things. The time before that—"

"They seek to separate you from the King?"

He nodded. "With honey or a whip. This night, Regal offered me a purse with five bits of gold in it, if I would make myself presentable and come down to entertain them. Oh, how he did go on after you had left, over how badly I was missed at the court below, and what a shame it was for me to waste my youth shut away up here. And when I said I found King Shrewd's company more congenial than that of other fools, he flung the teapot at me. Put Wallace in a fair bit of a huff, for he had just brewed up as nasty a mess of herb tea as would make one long for the perfume of farts."

The Fool had been kindling candles and poking up the fire on the King's hearth as we spoke. Now he drew back one of the heavy bed curtains. "My liege?" he said as gently as one might speak to a sleeping child. "FitzChivalry is here with important tidings for you. Will you awaken and hear him?"

At first the King made no response. "Your Majesty?" the Fool called to him again. He damped a cloth in a bit of cool water and patted the King's face with it. "King Shrewd?"

"My king, your folk have need of you." The words tumbled from me in desperation. "Neatbay is besieged by Red-Ships. Five of them. We must send aid now, or all is lost. Once they have a toehold there—"

"They could close Buck Harbor." The King's eyes opened as he spoke. He did not move from his prone position, but he squeezed his eyes more tightly shut as if clenching them against pain. "Fool. A bit of the red wine. Please." His voice was soft, scarce more than a breath, but it was the voice of my king. My heart surged as if I were an old dog hearing the voice of a returning master.

"What must we do?" I begged of him.

"Every ship we have, down the coast to them. Not just the warships. Roust out the fishing fleet. We fight for our lives now. How dare they come this close, how came they to such boldness! Send horse overland. On their way tonight, within the hour, I say. They may not get there until day after tomorrow, but send them all the same. Put Keen in charge of it."

My heart flip-flopped in my chest. "Your Majesty," I broke in gently. "Keen is dead. Coming back from the mountains, with Burrich. They were attacked by highwaymen."

The Fool glared at me, and I instantly regretted my interruption. The command faded from King Shrewd's voice. Uncertainly, he said, "Keen is dead?"

I took a breath. "Yes, Your Majesty. But there is Red. Kerf is also a good man."

The King took the wine the Fool proffered. He sipped, and seemed to draw strength with it. "Kerf. Give it to Kerf, then." A shade of the confidence came back. I bit my tongue against saying that what horse we had left was not worth sending. Doubtless the folk of Neatbay would welcome whoever came to reinforce them.

King Shrewd considered. "What is the word from South Cove? Have they sent out warriors and ships?"

"Your Majesty, there is no word from there as yet." This was not a lie.

"What goes on here?" The shouting began before he even reached the bedchamber. It was Regal, puffy with drink and fury. "Wallace!" He pointed an accusing finger at me. "Get him out of here. Get help to do it if you need it. You needn't be gentle!"

Wallace had not far to look. Two of Regal's brawny inland guardsmen had followed him up from the feasting. I was lifted off my feet; Regal had chosen burly men for this duty. I looked about for the Fool, for any ally, but the Fool had vanished. I caught a glimpse of a pale hand vanishing under the bed and resolutely looked away. I did not blame him. There was nothing he could do for me by staying except be thrown out with me.

"My father, has he disturbed your rest with his wild tales? And you so ill?" Regal bent solicitously over the bed.

They had me almost to the door when the King spoke. His voice was not loud, but command was in it. "Stand where you are," King Shrewd ordered the guards. He still was prone in his bed, but he turned his eyes to Regal. "Neatbay is besieged," King Shrewd said firmly. "We must send aid."

Regal shook his head sadly. "It is just another of the Bastard's ploys, to upset you and steal rest from you. There has been no call for help, no message of any kind."

One of the guards was very professional in his grip. The other seemed intent on dislocating my shoulder even if I refused to struggle against him. I carefully memorized his face while trying not to show the pain.

"You need not have troubled yourself, Regal. I will discover the truth or the lie here." Queen Kettricken had paused to dress. Short white fur jacket, purple trousers and boots. Her long Mountain sword was at her side and Burrich stood in the door, holding a heavy-hooded riding cloak and gloves. She spoke as one would to a spoiled child. "Go back to your guests. I will ride to Neatbay."

"I forbid it!" Regal's voice rang out strangely shrill. Stillness suddenly flooded the room.

Queen Kettricken pointed out quietly what everyone in the room already knew. "A Prince does not forbid the Queen-in-Waiting. I ride tonight."

Regal's face purpled. "This is a hoax, a plot of the Bastard's to throw Buckkeep into an uproar, and instill fear in the folk. There has been no word of an attack on Neatbay."

"Silence!" The King spat out the word. Everyone in the room froze. "FitzChivalry? Damn it, release that man. FitzChivalry, stand before me. Report. Whence came your news?"

I tugged my jerkin square again and smoothed my hair back. As I went to stand before my king I was painfully aware of my bare feet and tousled hair. I took a breath and threw it all away. "In my sleep I had a vision, sire. Of the Pocked Man, scrying in a pool of water. He showed me the Red-Ships at Neatbay.''

I dared emphasize no word. I stood firm before them. One of the guardsmen snorted in disbelief. Burrich's jaw dropped open and his eyes widened. Kettricken merely looked confused. On the bed, King Shrewd closed his eyes and breathed out slowly.

''He's drunk,'' Regal declared. ''Get him out of here.'' I had never heard so much satisfaction in Regal's voice. His guards reacted swiftly to seize me again.

''As . . .''—the King drew a deep breath in, obviously fighting pain—''I commanded.'' He found a bit of strength. ''As I commanded. Go now. NOW!''

I jerked my arms free from the astonished guards. ''Yes, Your Majesty,'' I said into the silence. I spoke clearly for the benefit of all. ''That is, all warships dispatched to Neatbay, and as many of the fishing fleet as can be rallied. And all available horse to be sent overland, under Kerf's command.''

''Yes.'' The King sighed the word. He swallowed, took a breath, opened his eyes. ''Yes, I order it so. Now go.''

''Some wine, my liege?'' The Fool had materialized on the other side of the bed. I was the only one who startled. The Fool smiled a secret smile over that. Then he bent over the King, helping him to raise his head and sip at the wine. I bowed deeply, deeply, to my king. I straightened and turned to leave the room.

''You may ride with my guard, if you wish,'' Queen Kettricken told me.

Regal's face was scarlet. ''The King did not tell you to go!'' he sputtered at her.

''Nor did he 'forbid' it.'' The Queen looked at him flatly.

''My queen!'' One of her guard announced herself at the door. ''We are ready to ride.'' I looked at her in astonishment. Kettricken merely nodded.

She glanced at me. ''You'd best make haste, Fitz. Unless you plan to ride like that.''

Burrich shook out the Queen's cloak for her. ''Is my horse ready?'' Kettricken asked her guard.

"Hands promised it at the door by the time you descended."

"I will need but a moment or two to ready myself," Burrich said quietly. I noticed he did not phrase it as a request.

"Go then. Both of you. Plan on catching up with us as quickly as you can."

Burrich nodded. He followed me to my room, where he helped himself to winter garb from my clothing chest while I got dressed. "Brush your hair back and wash your face," he ordered me tersely. "Warriors have more confidence in a man who looks like he expected to be awake at this hour."

I did as he advised and then we hastened down the stairs. His lame leg seemed forgotten tonight. Once we were in the courtyard, he started bellowing for stable boys to bring up Sooty and Rud. He sent another boy scrambling to find Kerf and pass on the orders, and another to ready every available horse in the stables. Four men he dispatched to town, one to the warships, three others to make the rounds of the taverns and rally the fleet. I envied his efficiency. He did not realize he had taken command away from me until we were mounting. He looked suddenly uncomfortable. I smiled at him. "Experience counts," I told him.

We rode for the gates. "We should be able to catch up with Queen Kettricken before she reaches the coast road," Burrich was saying just as a guardsman stepped out to bar our way.

"Hold!" he commanded, his voice breaking on the word.

Our horses reared back in alarm. We reined in. "What's this?" Burrich demanded.

The man stood firm. "You may pass, sir," he told Burrich respectfully. "But I have orders that the Bastard is not allowed out of Buckkeep."

"The Bastard?" I had never heard such outrage in Burrich's voice. "Say 'FitzChivalry, son of Prince Chivalry.' "

The man gaped at him in astonishment.

"Say it now!" Burrich bellowed, and pulled steel. He suddenly seemed twice as large as he had. Anger radiated from him in waves I could feel.

"FitzChivalry, son of Prince Chivalry," the man babbled.

He took a breath and swallowed. "But however I call him, I have my orders. He is not allowed out."

"Not an hour ago I heard our queen command us to ride with her, or to catch up as swiftly as we might. Do you say your order is superior to hers?"

The man looked uncertain. "One moment, sir." He stepped back into the guardhouse.

Burrich snorted. "Whoever trained him ought to be ashamed. He relies entirely on our honor to keep us from riding through."

"Maybe he just knows you," I suggested.

Burrich glared at me. After a moment the captain of the watch came out. He grinned at us. "Ride well, and best of luck at Neatbay."

Burrich flung him something between a salute and a fare-well, and we urged our horses through. I let Burrich choose the pace. It was dark, but once we were down the hill, the road was straight and good and there was a bit of a moon. Burrich was as reckless as I had ever seen him, for he put the horses to a canter and kept up the pace until we saw the Queen's guard ahead of us. He slowed us just short of joining them. I saw them turn to recognize us, and one soldier raised a hand in greeting.

"A pregnant mare, in early pregnancy, does well to be exercised." He looked over at me through the darkness. "I don't know that much about women," he said hesitantly.

I grinned at him. "And you think I do?" I shook my head and grew sober. "I don't know. Some women don't ride at all when they are carrying. Some do. I think Kettricken would not put Verity's child at risk. Besides. She is safer with us here than left behind with Regal."

Burrich said nothing, but I sensed his assent. It was not all I sensed.

We hunt together again at last!

Quietly! I warned him with a sideways glance at Burrich. I kept my thoughts tiny and private. *We go far. Will you be able to keep pace with the horses?*

Over a short distance they can outspeed me. But nothing outdistances the trotting wolf.

Burrich stiffened slightly in his saddle. I knew Nighteyes

was off to the side of the road, trotting through the shadows. It
did feel good to be out and alongside him again. It felt good to
be out and doing things. It was not that I rejoiced at Neatbay
being attacked; it was that at last I would have a chance to do
something about it, even if it was only to clean up whatever
was left standing. I glanced over at Burrich. Anger radiated
from him.

"Burrich?" I ventured.

"It's a wolf, isn't it?" Burrich spoke grudgingly into the
darkness. He looked straight ahead as we rode. I knew the set
of his mouth.

You know I am. A grinning, tongue-lolling reply.

Burrich flinched as if poked.

"Nighteyes," I admitted quietly, rendering the image of
his name into human words. Dread sat me. Burrich had sensed
him. He knew. No point in denying anything anymore. But
there was a tiny edge of relief in it as well. I was deathly tired
of all the lies I lived. Burrich rode on silently, not looking at
me. "I did not intend for it to happen. It just did." An explanation. Not an apology.

I gave him no choice. Nighteyes was being very jocular
about Burrich's silence.

I put my hand on Sooty's neck, took comfort in the
warmth and life there. I waited. Burrich still said nothing. "I
know you will never approve," I said quietly. "But it is not
something I can choose. It is what I am."

It is what we all are. Nighteyes smirked. *Come, Heart of
the Pack, speak to me. Will not we hunt well together?*

Heart of the Pack? I wondered.

*He knows it is his name. It is what they called him, all
those dogs that worshiped him, when they all gave tongue in
the chase. It was what they taunted one another with. "Heart
of the Pack, here, here, the game is here, and I have found it for
you, for you!" So they all yelped and tried to be first to yelp it
to him. But now they are all gone, taken far away. They did not
like to leave him. They knew he heard, even if he would not
reply. Had you never heard them?*

I suppose I tried not to.

A waste. Why choose to be deaf? Or mute?

"Must you do this in my presence?" Burrich's voice was stiff.

"Beg pardon," I said, gravely aware that he was truly offended. Nighteyes snickered again. I ignored him. Burrich would not look at me. After a bit he nudged Ruddy and cantered forward to overtake Kettricken's guard. I hesitated, then kept pace with him. He formally reported to Kettricken of all he had done before leaving Buckkeep, and she nodded gravely as if accustomed to taking such reports. At a signal from her, we were honored to fall back and ride to her left, while her captain of the guard, one Foxglove, rode to her right. Before dawn found us, the rest of the mounted soldiers from Buckkeep had caught up with us. When they joined us, Foxglove slowed the pace for a time, to allow their winded horses to breathe. But after we had come to a stream and let all the beasts water, we pushed on determinedly. Burrich did not speak to me.

Years earlier, I had made a trip to Neatbay as part of Verity's entourage. Then it had taken us five days, but we had traveled with wagons and litters, jugglers and musicians and valets. This time we traveled by horse, with seasoned warriors, and we need not keep to the wide coast road. The only thing that did not favor us was the weather. By midmorning of our first day out, a winter storm swept in. It was miserable riding, not just for the physical discomfort but in the unsettling knowledge that the driving winds would slow our companion ships. Whenever our path took us overlooking the water, I watched for sails, but never saw any.

The pace Foxglove set was demanding but not destructive to horse or rider. While stops were not frequent, she varied the pace and saw that no animal wanted for water. At such stops, there was grain for the horses and hard bread and dried fish for their riders. If anyone ever noticed a wolf shadowing us, no one spoke of it. Two full days later, as dawn and a gap in the weather found us, we were looking out over the wide river valley that opened onto Neatbay.

Bayguard was the Keep of Neatbay. And Bayguard was the home Keep of Duke Kelvar and Lady Grace, the heart of Rippon Duchy. The watchtower was on a sandy cliff above the town. The Keep itself had been built on fairly level land, but fortified with a series of earthen walls and ditches. Once I had been told that no enemy had ever made it past the second wall. It was no longer true. We halted and looked out over the destruction.

The five Red-Ships were still drawn up on the beach. The boats of Neatbay, mostly small fishing vessels, were a burned and scuttled wreckage spread along the beach. The tides had played with them since the Raiders had destroyed them. Blackened buildings and smoldering wreckage fanned out from where they had landed, marking their path like a spreading contagion. Foxglove stood in her stirrups and pointed out over Neatbay, combining her observations with what she knew of the town and Keep. "It's a shallow, sandy bay, all the way out. So when the tide goes out, it goes way out. They've drawn their boats up too high. If we can force them to retreat, we want to do it on a low tide, when their ships are sitting high and dry. They've cut through the town like a hot knife through butter; I doubt there was much of an effort to defend it, it's not really defensible. Probably everyone headed for the Keep at the first sight of a red keel. It looks to me like the Outislanders have battered their way in past the third circle. But Kelvar should be able to hold them off almost indefinitely now. The fourth wall is worked stone. It took years to build. Bayguard has a good well, and her warehouses should still be fat with grain, this early in winter. She won't fall unless she falls to treachery." Foxglove stopped gesturing and settled in her saddle again. "It makes no sense, this attack," she said more softly. "How can the Red-Ships expect to sustain a long siege? Especially if they are, in turn, attacked by our forces?"

"The answer could be that they did not expect anyone to come to Bayguard's aid," Kettricken said succinctly. "They have the town to pillage for supplies, and perhaps other ships are expected." She turned to Kerf, motioned him alongside Foxglove. "I have no battle experience," she said simply. "You two will have to plan this. I listen now, as a soldier. What should we do next?"

I saw Burrich wince. Such honesty is admirable, but not always good leadership. I saw Foxglove and Kerf exchange measuring glances. "My queen, Kerf has more battle experience than I. I would accept his command,'' Foxglove offered quietly.

Kerf looked down, as if mildly ashamed. ''Burrich was Chivalry's man. He has seen far more battles than I have,'' he observed to his mare's neck. He looked up suddenly. ''I commend him to you, my queen.''

Burrich's face was a struggle of conflicting emotions. For a moment his eyes lit. Then I saw a hesitation build.

Heart of the Pack, they will hunt well for you, Nighteyes urged him.

''Burrich, take command. They will fight with heart for you.''

My skin prickled to hear Queen Kettricken virtually echo Nighteyes' thought. From where I sat, I could actually see a shiver run over Burrich. He straightened in his saddle. ''We have no hope of surprising them in this flat country. And the three circles they have already gained can become defenses for them. We are not a vast force. What we have most of, my queen, is time. We can pen them. They have no access to fresh water. If Bayguard stands, and we keep the Outislanders trapped where they are, between the third earthwork and the wall, we can simply wait for our ships to arrive. At that time we can judge if we wish to join an attack on them, or simply starve them out.''

''This seems wise to me,'' the Queen approved.

''They are fools if they have not left at least a small force with their ships. Those we will have to contend with immediately. Then we must set our own guards to the ships, with orders to destroy them if it looks like any of the Outislanders have gotten past us and are trying to escape. If not, you will have ships to add to King-in-Waiting Verity's fleet.''

''This, too, seems sensible.'' The idea clearly pleased Kettricken.

''It is tidy, but only if we act swiftly. They will soon be aware of us, if they are not already. Certainly they will see the situation as clearly as we have. We need to get down there, and contain those besieging the Keep and destroy those guarding the ships.''

Kerf and Foxglove were both nodding. Burrich looked at

them. "I want your archers for our circle around the Keep. We want to contain them there, not get into any close fighting Simply pin them down where they are. Wherever they breached the walls is where they will try to trickle out again. Guard most heavily there, but watch all along the outer wall. And for now, do not try to go within the outer wall at all. Let them scuttle about like crabs in a pot."

Terse nods from both captains. Burrich continued.

"I want swords for the ships. Expect the fighting to be nasty. They'll be defending their only escape routes. Send a few lesser archers, and have them prepare fire arrows. If all else fails, burn the ships where they're beached. But try to take them first."

"The *Rurisk*!" Someone in the back ranks gave a cry. All heads turned to the water. There was the *Rurisk,* rounding the north tooth of Neatbay. In a moment a second sail appeared. Behind us, the mounted warriors raised a shout. But out beyond our ships, anchored in deep water, white as a dead man's belly and her sails as bloated, floated the white ship. The moment I saw it, an icicle of terror sliced my guts.

"The white ship!" I choked. Fear sent a shudder through me that was almost like pain.

"What?" Burrich asked, startled. It was the first word he had spoken to me that day.

"The white ship!" I repeated, and pointed a hand.

"What? Where? That? That's a fog bank. Our ships are coming into the harbor over there."

I looked. He was right. A fog bank, melting in the morning sun even as I watched. My terror receded like the ghost of mocking laughter. But the day seemed suddenly chillier, and the sun that had briefly parted the storm clouds a weak and watery thing. An evil cast lingered on the day, like a bad smell.

"Split your forces and deploy them now," Burrich said quietly. "We don't want our ships to meet any resistance as they come into shore. Quickly, now. Fitz. You're to go with the force that attacks the Red-Ships. Be there when the *Rurisk* beaches, and let those on board know what we've decided. As quickly as those Red-Ships are cleaned out, we shall want all fighters to join us in containing the Outislanders. I wish there was a way to get word to Duke Kelvar of what we're doing. I suppose he'll see, soon enough. Well, let's get going.''

There was some milling about, some conferring between Kerf and Foxglove, but in a surprisingly short time I found myself riding behind Foxglove with a contingent of warriors. I had my sword, but what I really missed was the ax I had become so comfortable with over the summer.

Nothing was as tidy as was planned. We encountered Outislanders in the wreckage of the town, long before we reached the beach. They were moving back toward their ships and were hampered with a coffle of prisoners. We attacked the Raiders. Some stood and fought, and some abandoned their prisoners and ran before our horses. Our troops were soon scattered throughout the still-smoldering buildings and debris-scattered streets of Neatbay. Some of our force stayed to cut the ropes on the prisoners and help them as best they could. Foxglove swore at the delay, for the Raiders that had fled would warn the ship guards. Swiftly she split our force, leaving a handful of soldiers to help the battered townsfolk. The smells of dead bodies and rain on charred timbers brought back my memories of Forge with a vividness that almost unmanned me. There were bodies everywhere, far more than we had expected to find. Somewhere I sensed a wolf prowling through the ruins, and took comfort from him.

Foxglove cursed us all with surprising skill, and then organized those she kept with her into a wedge. We swept down on the Red-Ships in time to see one being launched into the retreating tide. There was little we could do about that, but we were in time to prevent a second ship from getting off. We killed those ones with surprising alacrity. There were not many, only a skeleton rowing crew. We even managed to kill them before they could slay most of their captives who lay bound on the thwarts of the ships. We suspected that the ship that got off had been similarly laden. And hence, I surmised to myself, not initially planning to engage the *Rurisk* or any of the ships that now converged on the one that had eluded us.

But the Red-Ships had been outward bound with hostages. To where? To a ghost ship that only I had glimpsed? Even to think of the white ship brought a shudder over me and a pressure in my head like the beginning of pain. Perhaps they had intended to drown their hostages, or to Forge them, however that was done. I was not in a position to give it great thought then, but I saved the knowledge for Chade. Each of the three remaining beached ships had a contingent of warriors, and they fought as desperately as Burrich had predicted they would. One ship was set afire by an overzealous archer, but the others were taken intact.

We had secured all the ships by the time the *Rurisk* was beached. There was time now to lift my head and to look out over Neatbay. No sign of the white ship. Perhaps it had been only a cloud bank. Behind the *Rurisk* came the *Constance,* and behind them a flotilla of fishing vessels and even a couple of merchant ships. Most of them had to anchor out in the shallow harbor, but the men aboard them were ferried swiftly ashore. The warship crews waited for their captains to hear word of what went on, but those from the fishing vessels and merchant ships swept past us and headed directly for the besieged Keep.

The trained crews from the warships soon over took them, and by the time we reached the outer walls of the Keep, there was an attitude of cooperation, if not any real organization. The prisoners we had freed were weak from lack of food and water, but recovered quickly and were indispensable in giving us intimate knowledge of the outer earthworks. By afternoon, our siege of the besiegers was in place. With difficulty, Burrich persuaded all involved that at least one of our warships should remain fully manned and on alert, in the water. His premonition was proven correct the next morning, when two more Red-Ships sailed around the northern point of the bay. The *Rurisk* ran them off, but they fled too easily for us to take any satisfaction in it. All knew they would simply find an undefended village to raid farther up the coast. Several of the fishing vessels belatedly gave chase, though there was little chance of them catching the oared vessels of the Raiders.

By the second day of waiting, we were beginning to be bored and uncomfortable. The weather had turned foul again. The hard bread was starting to taste of mold, the dried fish was no longer completely dry. To cheer us, Duke Kelvar had added the Buck flag of the Six Duchies to his own pennon flying over

Bayguard to acknowledge us. But like us, he had chosen a waiting strategy. The Outislanders were penned. They had not attempted to break out past us, nor to advance closer to the Keep. All was still and waiting.

"You don't listen to warnings. You never have." Burrich spoke quietly to me.

Night had fallen. It was the first time since our arrival that we had had more than a few moments together. He sat on a log, his injured leg stretched straight in front of him. I crouched by the fire, trying to warm my hands. We were outside a temporary shelter set up for the Queen, tending a very smoky fire. Burrich had wanted her to settle in one of the few intact buildings left in Neatbay, but she had refused, insisting on staying close to her warriors. Her guard came and went freely, in her shelter and at her fire. Burrich frowned over their familiarity, but also approved her loyalty. "Your father, too, was like that," he observed suddenly as two of Kettricken's guard emerged from her shelter and went to relieve others still on watch.

"Didn't take warnings?" I asked in surprise.

Burrich shook his head. "No. Always his soldiers, coming and going, at all hours. I've always wondered when he found the privacy to create you."

I must have looked shocked, for Burrich suddenly flushed as well. "Sorry. I'm tired and my leg is . . . uncomfortable. I wasn't thinking what I was saying."

I found a smile unexpectedly. "It's all right," I said, and it was. When he had found out about Nighteyes, I was afraid he was going to banish me again. A jest, even a rough jest, was welcome. "You were saying about warnings?" I asked humbly.

He sighed. "You said it. We are as we are. And *he* said it. Sometimes they don't give you a choice. They just bond to you."

Somewhere off in the darkness, a dog howled. It was not really a dog. Burrich glared at me. "I can't control him at all," I admitted.

Nor I, you. Why should there be control, one of the other?

"Nor does he stay out of personal conversations," I observed.

"Nor personal anything," Burrich said flatly. He spoke in the voice of a man who knew.

"I thought you said you never used . . . it." Even out here, I would not say "the Wit" aloud.

"I don't. No good comes of it. I will tell you plainly now what I've told you before. It . . . changes you. If you give in to it. If you live it. If you can't shut it out, at least don't seek after it. Don't become—"

"Burrich?"

We both jumped. It was Foxglove, come quietly out of the darkness to stand on the other side of the fire. How much had she heard?

"Yes? Is there a problem?"

She hunkered down in the darkness, lifted her red hands to the fire. She sighed. "I don't know. How do I ask this? Are you aware she's pregnant?"

Burrich and I exchanged glances. "Who?" he asked levelly.

"I've got two children of my own, you know. And most of her guard is women. She pukes every morning, and lives off raspberry-leaf tea. She can't even look at the salt fish without retching. She shouldn't be here, living like this." Foxglove nodded toward the tent.

Oh. The Vixen.

Shut up.

"She did not ask our advice," Burrich said carefully.

"The situation here is under control. There is no reason she should not be sent back to Buckkeep," Foxglove said calmly.

"I can't imagine 'sending her back' to anywhere," Burrich observed. "I think it would have to be a decision she reached on her own."

"You might suggest it to her," Foxglove ventured.

"So might you," Burrich countered. "You are captain of her guard. The concern is rightly yours."

"I haven't been keeping watch outside her door each night," Foxglove objected.

"Perhaps you should have," Burrich said, then tempered it with a "Now that you know."

Foxglove looked into the fire. "Perhaps I should. So. The question is, who escorts her back to Buckkeep?"

"All of her personal guard, of course. A Queen should travel with no less."

Somewhere off in the darkness there was a sudden outcry. I sprang to my feet.

"Stand fast!" Burrich snapped at me. "Wait for word. Don't rush off until you know what is happening!"

In a moment Whistle of the Queen's guard reached our fire. She stood before Foxglove to report. "Two-pronged attack. At the breach just below the south tower, they tried to break out. And some got through at—"

An arrow swept through her and carried off forever whatever she had begun to tell us. Outislanders were suddenly upon us, more of them than my mind could grasp, and all converging on the Queen's tent. "To the Queen!" I shouted, and had the slim comfort of hearing my cry taken up farther down the line. Three guards rushed out of the tent to put their backs to its flimsy walls while Burrich and I stood our ground in front of it. I found my sword in my hand, and from the corner of my eye saw firelight run red up the edge of Burrich's. The Queen appeared suddenly in the door of the tent.

"Don't guard me!" she rebuked us. "Get to where the fighting is."

"It's here, my lady," Burrich grunted and stepped forward suddenly to take off the arm of a man who had ventured too close.

I remember those words clearly and I remember seeing Burrich take that stride. It is the last coherent memory I have of that night. After that, all was shouting and blood, metal and fire. Waves of emotions pounded against me as all around me soldiers and Raiders fought to the death. Early on, someone set fire to the tent. Its towering blaze lit the battle scene like a stage. I remember seeing Kettricken, robe looped up and knotted, fighting bare-legged and barefoot on the frozen ground. She held her ridiculously long Mountain sword in a two-handed grip. Her grace made a deadly dance of the battle that would have distracted me at any other time.

Outislanders continued to appear. At one point I was sure I heard Verity shouting commands, but could not make sense of any of them. Nighteyes appeared from time to time, fighting always at the edge of the light, a low sudden weight of fur and teeth, hamstringing with a slash, adding his weight to change a Raider's charge to a stumble. Burrich and Foxglove fought back-to-back at one point when things were going poorly for us. I was part of the circle that protected the Queen. At least, I thought I was, until I realized she was actually fighting beside me.

At some time I dropped my sword to snatch up a fallen Raider's ax. I picked my blade up the next day from the frozen ground, crusted with mud and blood. But at the moment I did not even hesitate to discard Verity's gift for a more savagely effective weapon. While we were fighting there was only the now to consider. When at last the tide of the battle turned, I did not consider the wisdom of it, but pursued and hunted scattered enemy through the night-black fire-stinking wreckage of Neatbay village.

Here, indeed, Nighteyes and I hunted very well together. I stood toe to toe with my final kill, ax against ax, while Nighteyes snarled and savaged his way past a smaller man's sword. He finished his but seconds before I dropped my man.

That final slaughtering held for me a wild and savage joy. I did not know where Nighteyes left off and I began; only that we had won and we both still lived. Afterward we went to find water together. We drank deep from a communal well's bucket, and I laved the blood from my hands and face. Then we sank down and put our backs to the brick well to watch the sun rise beyond the thick ground mist. Nighteyes leaned warm against me, and we did not even think.

I suppose I dozed a bit, for I was jostled alert as he quickly left me. I looked up to see what had startled him, only to discover a frightened Neatbay girl staring at me. The early sun struck glints off her red hair. A bucket was in her hand. I stood and grinned, lifting my ax in greeting, but she sheered off like a frightened rabbit among the ruined buildings. I stretched, then made my way back through the trailing fog to where the Queen's tent had been. As I walked, images of last night's wolf hunting came back to me. The memories were too sharp, too red and black, and I pushed them down deep in my mind. Was this what Burrich had meant by his warning?

Even by the light of day, it was still difficult to understand all that had happened. The earth around the blackened remains of the Queen's shelter was trampled into mud. Here the fighting had been heaviest. Here was where most of the enemy had fallen. Some bodies had been dragged aside and tumbled into a heap. Others still lay where they had fallen. I avoided looking at them. It is one thing to kill in fear and anger. It is another thing to consider one's handiwork by the chill gray light of morning.

That the Outislanders had tried to break through our siege was understandable. They had, perhaps, had a chance of making it as far as their ships and reclaiming one or two of them. That the attack seemed to focus on the Queen's tent was least comprehensible. Once clear of the earthworks, why had not they seized their chance for survival and headed for the beach?

"Perhaps," observed Burrich, gritting his teeth as I probed the angry swelling on his leg, "they did not hope to escape at all. It is their Outislander way, to decide to die, and then to attempt to do as much damage before doing so. So they attacked here, hoping to kill our queen."

I had discovered Burrich, limping about the battleground. He did not say he had been looking for my body. His relief at seeing me was evidence enough of that.

"How did they know it was the Queen in that tent?" I pondered. "We flew no banners, we issued no challenges. How did they know she was here? There. Is that any better?" I checked the bandage for snugness.

"It's dry and it's clean and the wrapping seems to help the pain. I don't suppose we can do much more than that. I suspect that whenever I work that leg hard, I'm going to have the swelling and heat in it." He spoke as dispassionately as if he discussed a horse's bad leg. "At least it stayed closed. They did seem to make straight for the Queen's tent, didn't they?"

"Like bees to honey," I observed tiredly. "The Queen is in Bayguard?"

"Of course. Everyone is. You should have heard the cheer when they opened the gates to us. Queen Kettricken walked in, her skirts still bundled to one side, her drawn blade still dripping. Duke Kelvar went down on his knees to kiss her hand. But Lady Grace looked at her, and said, 'Oh, my dear, I shall have a bath drawn for you at once.' "

"Now there is the stuff they make songs of," I said, and we laughed. "But not all are up at the Keep. I saw a girl just now, coming for water, down in the ruins."

"Well, up at the Keep they are rejoicing. There will be some who will have small heart for that. Foxglove was wrong. The folk of Neatbay did not yield easily before the Red-Ships. Many, many died before the Neatbay folk retreated to the Keep."

"Does anything strike you as odd about that?"

"That folk should defend themselves? No. It is—"

"Does not it seem to you that there were too many Outislanders here? More than five ships' worth?"

Burrich halted. He looked back to the scattered bodies. "Perhaps those other ships had left them here, and then gone out on patrol. . . ."

"That is not their way. I suspect a larger ship, transporting a sizable force of men."

"Where?"

"Gone now. I think I glimpsed it, going into that fog bank."

We fell silent. Burrich showed me to where he had tethered Ruddy and Sooty and we rode together up to Bayguard. The great doors of the Keep stood wide open, and a combination of Buckkeep soldiers and Bayguard folk mingled there. We were greeted with a shout of welcome, and offered brimming cups of mead before we were even dismounted. Boys begged to take our horses for us, and to my surprise, Burrich let them. Within the hall was genuine rejoicing that would have put any of Regal's revels to shame. All of Bayguard had been thrown open for us. Ewers and basins of warm scented water had been set out in the Great Hall for us to refresh ourselves, and tables were heavy with food, none of it hard bread or salt fish.

We remained three days at Neatbay. During this time our dead were buried, and the bodies of the Outislanders burned. Buckkeep soldiers and Queen's guard fell in alongside the people of Neatbay to assist in the repairs to Bayguard's fortifications and in salvaging what was left of Neatbay Town. I made a few quiet inquiries. I found that the watchtower signal had been lit as soon as the ships were sighted, but that the Red-Ships had made extinguishing it one of their first goals. What of their coterie member? I asked. Kelvar looked at me in surprise. Burl had been recalled weeks ago, for some essential duty inland. He had gone to Tradeford, Kelvar believed.

The day after the battle, reinforcements arrived from South Cove. They had not seen the signal fire, but the messengers sent out on horse had gotten through to them. I was present when Kettricken commended Duke Kelvar for his foresight in setting up a relay of horse for such messages, and sent her thanks also to Duke Shemshy of Shoaks for his response. She suggested they divide the captured ships, that they need no longer wait for warships to arrive, but could dispatch their own, for mutual defense. This was a sumptuous gift, and it was received in an awed silence. When Duke Kelvar recovered himself, he rose to offer a toast to his queen and to the unborn Farseer heir. So swiftly had the rumor become general knowledge. Queen Kettricken colored prettily, but managed her thanks well.

Those brief days of victory were a healing balm to us all. We had fought, and fought well. Neatbay would rebuild, and the Outislanders had no hold in Bayguard. For a brief time it seemed possible that we could win free of them entirely.

Before we had left Neatbay, the songs were already being sung, about a Queen with her skirts bundled up standing bold against the Red-Ships, and of the child in her womb who was a warrior before birth. That the Queen would risk not only herself but the heir to the throne for Rippon Duchy was not lost upon any of them. First Duke Brawndy of Bearns, and now Kelvar of Rippon, I thought to myself. Kettricken was doing well at winning the Duchies' loyalty.

I had my moments at Neatbay, both warming and chilling. For Lady Grace, on seeing me in the Great Hall, recognized me and came to speak to me. "So," she had said after greeting me quietly, "my kitchen dog boy has the blood of kings in him. No wonder you advised me so well, those years ago." She had grown well into being a lady and a Duchess. Her feist dog still went everywhere with her, but now he ran about at her heels, and this change pleased me almost as much as her easy carriage of her title and her obvious affection for her duke.

"We have both changed much, Lady Grace," I replied, and she accepted the compliment I intended. The last time I had seen her had been when I had traveled here with Verity. She had not then been so comfortable being a Duchess. I had met her in the kitchens, when her dog had been choking on a bone. I had persuaded her then that her duke's coin was better spent on watchtowers than jewelry for her. Back then, she had been very new to being a Duchess. Now she seemed never to have been anything else.

"Not a dog boy anymore?" she asked with a wry smile.

"Dog boy? Man wolf!" observed someone. I turned to see who had spoken, but the hall was crowded and no face seemed turned to watch us. I shrugged as if the remark were of no consequence, and Lady Grace appeared not to have even heard it. She presented me with a token of her favor before I left. It still makes me smile to think on it: a tiny pin in the shape of a fish's bones. "I had this made, to remind me . . . I should like you to have it now." She herself seldom wore jewelry anymore, she told me. She handed it to me on a balcony, on a dark evening when the lights of Duke Kelvar's watchtowers glittered like diamonds against the black sky.

25

Buckkeep

*T*RADEFORD CASTLE ON *the Vin River was one of the traditional residences of the ruling family of Farrow. This was the place where Queen Desire had spent her childhood, and here she returned with her son Regal during the summers of his childhood. The town of Tradeford is a lively place, a center for commerce in the heart of orchard-and-grain country. The Vin River is a sleepily navigable water, making travel easy and pleasant. Queen Desire had always insisted it was superior to Buckkeep in every regard and would have served much better as a seat for the royal family.*

—◦═▷—

The trip back to Buckkeep was eventful only in small ways. Kettricken was worn and tired by the time we were to return. Although she tried not to show it, it was evident in the circles under her eyes and the set of her mouth. Duke Kelvar furnished her with a litter for the trip home, but a brief ride in it showed her that its swaying only made her more nauseated. She returned it with thanks and rode home astride her mare.

Our second night on the road home, Foxglove came to our fire and told Burrich she thought she had seen a wolf, several times that day. Burrich shrugged indifferently and assured her it was probably just curious, and was no threat to us. After she left, Burrich turned to me and said, "That's going to happen once too often."

"What?"

"A wolf, seen in your vicinity. Fitz, have a care. There were rumors, back when you killed those Forged ones. There were tracks all about, and the marks on those men were never made by any blade. Someone told me they saw a wolf prowling Neatbay the night of the battle. I even heard a wild tale about a wolf who changed into a man when the battle was over. There were tracks in the mud outside the Queen's very tent from that night; as well for you that everyone was so tired and in so much of a hurry to dispose of the dead. There were a few there that did not die at a man's hand."

A few? Fa!

Burrich's face contorted in anger. "That will cease. Now."

You are strong, Heart of the Pack, but—

The thought was broken and I heard a sudden yelp of surprise from off in the brush. Several of the horses startled and looked in that direction. I myself was staring at Burrich. He had *repelled* at Nighteyes, fiercely and from a distance.

Luckily for you, from a distance, for the strength of that . . . I began to warn Nighteyes.

Burrich's gaze swung to me. "I said, that will cease! Now!" He looked aside from me in disgust. "I'd rather you rode with your hand in your pants than that you did that constantly in my presence. It offends me."

I could think of nothing to say. Years of living together had taught me that he would not be argued out of his feelings about the Wit. He knew I was bonded to Nighteyes. That he would still tolerate my presence was as far as he could unbend. I need not constantly remind him that the wolf and I shared minds. I bowed my head in assent. That night, for the first time in a long time, my dreams were my own.

I dreamed of Molly. She wore red skirts again, and crouched on the beach, cutting sheel from the stones with her belt knife and eating them raw. She looked up at me and smiled. I came closer. She leaped up and ran barefoot down the beach in front of me. I chased her, but she was as fleet as she had ever been. Her hair blew back off her shoulders, and she only laughed when I called out to her to wait, wait. I awoke feeling strangely glad that she had outrun me, and with the dream scent of lavender still in my mind.

We expected to be well greeted at Buckkeep. The ships, given the kinder weather, should have made land before us, to give tidings of our success. So we were not surprised to see a contingent of Regal's guard coming forth to meet us. What did seem strange was that after they sighted us, they continued to walk their horses. Not a man yelled, or waved a greeting. Instead they came toward us silent and sober as ghosts. I think Burrich and I saw at the same time the baton the lead man carried, the small polished stick that betokened serious tidings.

He turned to me as we watched them approach. Dread was written large on his face. "King Shrewd has died?" he suggested softly.

I felt no surprise, only a gaping loss in me. A frightened boy inside me gasped that now no one and nothing could stand between me and Regal. In another part, I wondered what it would have been like to call him "Grandfather" instead of "my king." But those selfish parts were small compared with what it meant to this King's Man. Shrewd had shaped me, made me what I was, for good or ill. He had picked up my life one day, a boy playing under a table in the Great Hall, and set his stamp upon it. His decision that I must read and write, must be able to wield a sword or disperse a poison. It seemed to me that with his passing, I must take responsibility for my own acts now. It was a strangely frightening thought.

All had become aware of the lead man's burden. We halted on the road. Like a curtain parting, Kettricken's guard opened to allow him to approach her. A terrible silence held as he handed her the baton, and then the small scroll. The red sealing wax flaked away from her nail. I watched it fall to the muddy road. Slowly she opened the scroll and read it. Something went out of her in that reading. Her hand fell to her side. She let the scroll follow the wax to the mud, a thing done with, a thing she never wished to peruse again. She did not faint, nor cry out. Her eyes looked afar, and she set her hand gently atop her belly. And in that motion, I knew it was not Shrewd who was dead, but Verity.

I reached for him. Somewhere, surely somewhere, coiled small inside me, a spark of a link, the tiniest thread of a connection . . . no. I did not even know when it had vanished. I recalled that whenever I fought, I was likely to break my link with him. It did not help. I recalled now what had seemed just an oddity on the night of the battle. I had thought I had heard Verity's voice, crying out, issuing orders that made no sense. I could not recall one individual word of what he might have shouted. But now it seemed to me that they had been battle orders, orders to scatter, to seek cover perhaps, or . . . but I could not recall anything with certainty. I looked over at Burrich, to find the question in his eyes. I had to shrug. ''I don't know,'' I said quietly. His brow furrowed as he considered this.

Queen-in-Waiting Kettricken sat very still on her horse. No one moved to touch her, no one spoke a word. I glanced at Burrich, met his eyes. I saw fatalistic resignation there. This was the second time he had seen a King-in-Waiting fall before ascending the throne. After a long silence, Kettricken turned in her saddle. She surveyed her guard, and the mounted soldiers who followed her. ''Prince Regal has had tidings that King-in-Waiting Verity is dead.'' She did not raise her voice, but her clear words carried. Merriment faded, and the triumph went out of many an eye. She gave it a few moments to settle in. Then she nudged her horse to a walk, and we followed her back to Buckkeep.

We approached the gate unchallenged. The soldiers on watch looked up at us as we passed. One made a sketchy salute to the Queen. She did not notice it. Burrich's scowl deepened, but he said nothing.

Within the castle courtyard, it seemed an ordinary day. Stable help came to take the horses while other servants and folk moved about on the ordinary business of the Keep. Somehow the very familiarity of it rattled against my nerves like stones. Verity was dead. It did not seem right that life should go on in such a workaday fashion.

Burrich had helped Kettricken to dismount into a cluster of her ladies. A part of me noted the look on Foxglove's face as

Kettricken was hustled away by court ladies who were exclaiming over how worn she looked, was she well, amid exclamations of sympathy, regret, and sorrow. A twinge of jealousy passed over the face of the captain of the Queen's guard. Foxglove was but a soldier, sworn to protect her queen. She could not, at this time, follow her into the Keep, no matter how much she cared about her queen. Kettricken was in the care of her court ladies now. But I knew Burrich would not stand guard alone before Kettricken's door tonight.

The solicitous murmuring of her ladies on Kettricken's behalf was enough to let me know that the rumor of her pregnancy had been spread. I wonder if it had yet been shared with Regal. I was well aware that some gossip circulated almost entirely through the women before becoming common knowledge. I suddenly wanted very badly to know if Regal knew that Kettricken carried the heir to the throne. I handed Sooty's reins to Hands, thanked him, and promised to tell him all later. But as I headed for the Keep Burrich's hand fell on my shoulder.

"A word with you. Now."

Sometimes he treated me almost as if I were a Prince, sometimes as less than a stable boy. These words now were no request. Hands gave me Sooty's reins back with a wry smile and vanished to see to other animals. I followed Burrich as he led Ruddy into the stables. He had no problem finding an empty stall for Ruddy near Sooty's regular stall. There were only too many stalls available. We both began matter-of-factly to work on the horses. The old familiarity of that routine, seeing to a horse while Burrich worked nearby, was comforting. Our end of the stable was relatively quiet, but he waited until no one was about before asking, "Is it true?"

"I don't know, exactly. My link with him is gone. It had been faint before we went to Neatbay, and I always have a problem maintaining my link to Verity when I get into a fight. He says I put my guard up so strongly against those around me that I wall him out."

"I don't understand any of that, but I knew of that problem. Are you sure that is when you lost him?"

So I told him, about a vague sense of Verity during the

battle, and the possibility that he had been under attack at the same time. Burrich nodded impatiently.

"But can't you Skill out to him, now that things are calm? Renew the link?"

I took an instant, pushed down my own seething frustration. "No. I can't. I don't have the Skill that way."

Burrich frowned. "Look. We know that messages have gone awry lately. How do we know that this one hasn't been invented?"

"We don't, I suppose. Though it is hard to believe that even Regal would be so bold as to say Verity was dead if he was not."

"There is nothing I believe him incapable of," Burrich said quietly.

I straightened up from cleaning the mud out of Sooty's hooves. Burrich was leaning on the door of Ruddy's stall, staring off into distance. The white streak in his hair was a vivid reminder of just how ruthless Regal could be. He had ordered Burrich killed as casually as one might swat an annoying fly. It had never seemed to give Regal a moment's concern that he had not stayed dead. He had no fear of retribution from a stablemaster or a bastard.

"So. What would he say when Verity came back?" I asked quietly.

"Once he was king, he could see that Verity never came back. The man who sits on the throne of the Six Duchies can do away with people who are inconvenient." Burrich did not look directly at me as he said this, and I tried to let the barb go by me. It was true. Once Regal was in power, I had no doubt there would be assassins ready to do his bidding. Perhaps there already were some. That thought put a queer chill up me.

"If we want definite word that Verity is still alive, our only choice is to send someone to find him, and to come back with tidings of him." I considered Burrich.

"Assuming the messenger managed to survive, it would still take too long. Once Regal is in power, the word of a messenger is nothing to him. The bearer of such tidings would not dare speak them aloud. We need proof that Verity is alive, proof that King Shrewd will accept, and we need it before

Regal comes into power. That one would not be king-in-waiting long.''

"King Shrewd and Kettricken's child still stand between him and the throne," I protested.

"That location has proven unhealthy for full-grown, strong men. I doubt an ailing old man or an unborn child will find it any luckier a place to be." Burrich shook his head and set that thought aside. "So. You cannot Skill to him. Who can?"

"Any of the coterie."

"Pah. I have faith in none of them."

"King Shrewd might be able to," I suggested hesitantly. "If he took strength from me."

"Even if your link with Verity is broken?" Burrich asked intently.

I shrugged and shook my head. "I don't know. That is why I said 'might.' "

He ran a final hand down Ruddy's newly sleek coat. "It will have to be tried," he said decisively. "And the sooner the better. Kettricken must not be left to fret and grieve if there is no cause for it. She might lose the child of it." He sighed and looked at me. "Go get some rest. Plan on visiting the King tonight. Once I see you go in, I will see that there are witnesses to whatever King Shrewd finds out."

"Burrich," I protested, "there are too many uncertainties. I do not even know that the King will be awake tonight, or able to Skill, or that he will if I ask it. If we do this, Regal, and all else, will know that I am a King's Man in the Skill sense. And—"

"Sorry, boy." Burrich spoke abruptly, almost callously. "There is more at stake here than your well-being. Not that I do not care about you. But I think you will be safer if Regal thinks you can Skill, and all know Verity is alive, than if all believe Verity is dead and Regal thinks it timely to be rid of you. We must try tonight. Perhaps we shall not succeed. But we must try."

"I hope you can get some elfbark somewhere," I grumbled to him.

"Are you developing a fondness for that? Be wary." But then he grinned. "I am sure I can get some."

I returned the grin, and then was shocked at myself. I didn't believe Verity was dead. That was what I admitted to myself with that grin. I did not believe my king-in-waiting was dead, and I was about to stand toe to toe with Prince Regal and prove it was so. The only way that could have been more satisfying would be if I could do it with an ax in my hands. Yet.

"Do me one favor?" I asked of Burrich.

"What?" he asked guardedly.

"Be very very careful of yourself."

"Always. See that you do the same."

I nodded, then stood silent, feeling awkward.

After a moment Burrich sighed and said, "Out with it. If I happen to see Molly, you'd like me to tell her . . . what?"

I shook my head at myself. "Only that I miss her. What else can I say to her? I've nothing to offer her but that."

He glanced at me: an odd look. Sympathy, but no false comfort. "I'll let her know," he promised.

I left the stables feeling that somehow I had grown. I wondered if I would ever stop measuring myself by how Burrich treated me.

I went directly to the kitchen, intending to get something to eat, then go rest as Burrich had suggested. The watch room was packed with the returning soldiers, telling stories to the ones who had stayed home while devouring stew and bread. I had expected that, and intended to find my own provisions and carry them off to my room. But within the kitchen, everywhere, kettles were bubbling, bread was rising, and meat was turning on spits. Kitchen servants were chopping, stirring, and going to and fro hurriedly.

"There is a feast tonight?" I asked stupidly.

Cook Sara turned to face me. "Oh, Fitz, so you're back and alive and in one piece for a change." She smiled as if she had complimented me. "Yes, of course, there's a feast to celebrate the victory at Neatbay. We would not neglect you."

"With Verity dead, we still sit down to feast?"

Cook looked at me levelly. "Were Prince Verity here, what would he wish?"

I sighed. "He would probably say to celebrate the victory. That folk need hope more than mourning."

"So exactly Prince Regal explained it to me this morning," Cook said with satisfaction. She turned back to rubbing spices into a leg of venison. "We'll mourn him, of course. But you have to understand, Fitz. He left us. Regal is the one who stayed here. He stayed here to look after the King, and mind the coasts as best as he could. Verity is gone, but Regal is still here with us. And Neatbay is not fallen to the Raiders."

I bit my tongue and waited for the fit to pass. "Neatbay did not fall because Regal stayed here to protect us." I wanted to make certain that Cook was connecting those two events, not merely mentioning them both in the same lecture.

She nodded as she kept rubbing the meat. Pounded sage, my nose told me. And rosemary. "It's what's been needed all along. Soldiers sent right away. Skilling is fine, but what's the good of knowing what's happening if no one does anything about it?"

"Verity always sent out the warships."

"And they always seemed to get there too late." She turned to me, wiping her hands down the front of her apron. "Oh, I know you worshiped him, lad. Our Prince Verity was a goodhearted man, who wore himself to death trying to protect us. I'm not speaking against the dead. I'm only saying that Skilling and chasing down Elderlings are not the way to fight these Red-Ships. What Prince Regal done, sending the soldiers and ships out the minute he heard, that's what was needed all along. Maybe with Prince Regal in charge, we'll survive here."

"What about King Shrewd?" I asked softly.

She misunderstood my question. In doing so, she showed me what she really thought. "Oh, he's as good as can be expected. He'll even be down to the feast tonight, at least for a bit. Poor man. He's suffering so much. Poor, poor man."

Dead man. She as much as said it. King no longer, Shrewd was just a poor, poor man to her. Regal had it. "Do you think our queen will be at the feast?" I asked. "After all, she has just heard of the death of her husband and king."

"Oh, I think she'll be there." Sara nodded to herself. She turned the leg over with a thud, to begin pricking the other side full of herbs. "I've heard it said she's saying she's with child now." The cook sounded skeptical. "She'll want to announce it tonight."

"Do you doubt she's with child?" I asked bluntly. Cook was not offended by it.

"Oh, I don't doubt she's pregnant, if she says she is. It just seems a bit odd, is all, her telling it after word of Verity's death came in instead of before."

"How's that?"

"Well, some of us are bound to wonder."

"Wonder what?" I asked coldly.

Cook darted a glance at me and I cursed my impatience. Shutting her up was not what I wanted to do. I needed to hear the rumors, all of them.

"Well . . ." She hesitated, but could not deny my listening ears. "What's always wondered, when a woman doesn't conceive, and then when her husband's away, suddenly she announces she's pregnant by him." She glanced about to see who else might be listening. All seemed busy at their work, but I didn't doubt a few ears were tilted our way. "Why now? All of a sudden. And if she knew she was pregnant, what was she thinking of, racing off in the middle of the night, right into battle? That's strange behavior for a Queen carrying the throne's heir."

"Well"—I tried to make my voice mild—"I suppose when the child is born will show when it was conceived. Those who want to count moons on their fingers may do so then. Besides"—and I leaned in conspiratorially—"I heard that some of her ladies knew of it before she left. Lady Patience, for instance, and her maid Lacey." I would have to make sure that Patience bragged of her early knowledge, and that Lacey noised it about among the servants.

"Oh. That one." Cook Sara's dismissal quashed my hopes of an easy victory. "Well, not to offend, Fitz, but she can be a bit daft on occasion. Lacey, though, Lacey is solid. But she don't say much, and don't want to listen to what others have to say either."

"Well"—I smiled and tipped her a wink—"that was where I heard it from. And I heard it well before we left for

Neatbay.'' I leaned in closer. ''Ask about. I bet you'll find Queen Kettricken's been drinking raspberry-leaf tea for her morning sickness. You check, and see if I'm right. I'll wager a silver bit I am.''

''A silver bit? Ohe. As if I've such to spare. But I'll ask, Fitz, that I will. And shame on you for not sharing such a rich bit of gossip with me before. And all I tell you!''

''Well, here's something for you, then. Queen Kettricken's not the only one with child!''

''Oh? Who else?''

I smiled. ''Can't tell you just yet. But you'll be among the first to know, from what I've heard.'' I had no idea who might be pregnant, but it was safe to say that someone in the Keep was, or would be, in time to substantiate my rumor. I needed to keep Cook pleased with me if I were to count on her for court talk. She nodded sagely at me, and I winked.

She finished her venison leg. ''Here, Dod, come take this and put it on the meat hooks over the big fire. Highest hooks, I want it cooked, not scorched. Go on with you, now. Kettle? Where's that milk I asked you to fetch?''

I snagged bread and apples before I left for my room. Plain fare, but welcome to one as hungry as I. I went straight to my room, washed up, ate, and lay down to rest. I might have small chance at the King tonight, but I still wanted to be as alert as possible during the feast. I thought of going to Kettricken to ask her not to mourn Verity just yet. But I knew I would never get past her ladies for a quiet word with her. And what if I were wrong? No. When I could prove Verity was still alive would be soon enough to tell her.

I awoke later to a tap on my door. I lay still for a moment, not sure if I had heard anything, then rose to undo my latches and open the door a crack. The Fool stood outside my door. I do not know if I was more surprised that he had knocked instead of slipping the latches, or at the way he was attired. I stood gaping at him. He bowed genteelly, then pushed his way into my room, closing the door behind him. He fastened a couple of latches, then stepped to the center of the room and extended his arms. He turned in a slow circle for me to admire him. ''Well?''

"You don't look like you," I said bluntly.

"I am not intended to." He tugged his overjerkin straight, then plucked at his sleeves to display better not only the embroidery on them, but the slashes that showed off the rich fabric of the sleeves beneath them. He fluffed his plumed hat, set it once more atop his colorless hair. From deepest indigo to palest azure went the colors, and the Fool's white face, like a peeled egg, peeping out of them. "Fools are no longer in fashion."

I sat down slowly on my bed. "Regal has dressed you like this," I said faintly.

"Hardly. He supplied the clothing, of course, but I dressed myself. If Fools are no longer in fashion, consider how lowly would be the valet of a Fool."

"How about King Shrewd? Is he no longer in fashion?" I asked acidly.

"It is no longer in fashion to be overly concerned with King Shrewd," he replied. He cut a caper, then stopped, drew himself up with dignity as befitted his new clothes, and took a turn about the room. "I am to sit at the Prince's table tonight, and be full of merriment and wit. Do you think I shall do well at it?"

"Better far than I," I said sourly. "Care you not at all that Verity is dead?"

"Care you not at all that the flowers are blooming beneath the summer sun?"

"Fool, it is winter outside."

"The one is as true as the other. Believe me." The Fool stood suddenly still. "I have come to ask a favor of you, if you can believe that."

"The second as easily as the first. What is it?"

"Do not slay my king with your ambitions for your own."

I looked at him in horror. "I would never slay my king! How dare you say it!"

"Oh, I dare much, these days." He put his hands behind him and paced about the room. With his elegant clothes and unaccustomed postures, he frightened me. It was as if another being inhabited his body, one I knew not at all.

"Not even if the King had killed your mother?"

A terrible sick feeling rose in me. "What are you trying to tell me?" I whispered.

The Fool whirled at the pain in my voice. "No. No! You mistake me entirely!" There was sincerity in his voice, and for an instant I could see my friend again. "But," he continued in a softer, almost sly tone, "if you believed the King had killed your mother, your much-cherished, loving, indulgent mother, had killed her and snatched her forever away from you. Do you think you might then kill him?"

I had been blind for so long that it took me a moment to understand him. I knew Regal believed his mother had been poisoned. I knew it was one source of his hatred for me, and for "Lady Thyme." He believed we had carried out the killing. At the behest of the King. I knew it all to be false. Queen Desire had poisoned herself. Regal's mother had been overly fond of both drink and those herbs that bring surcease from worry. When she had not been able to rise to the power she believed was her right, she had taken refuge in those pleasures. Shrewd had tried several times to stop her, had even applied to Chade for herbs and potions that would end her cravings. Nothing had worked. Queen Desire had been poisoned, it was true, but it was her own self-indulgent hand that had administered it. I had always known that. And knowing it, I had discounted the hate that would breed in the heart of a coddled son, suddenly bereft of his mother.

Could Regal kill over such a thing? Of course he could. Would he be willing to bring the Six Duchies to the teetering edge of ruin as an act of vengeance? Why not? He had never cared for the Coastal Duchies. The Inland Duchies, always more loyal to his inland mother, were where his heart was. If Queen Desire had not wed King Shrewd, she would have remained Duchess of Farrow. Sometimes, when in her cups and heady with herbal intoxicants, she would ruthlessly suggest that if she had remained as Duchess, she would have been able to wield more power, enough to persuade Farrow and Tilth to unite under her as queen and shrug off their allegiance to the Six Duchies. Galen, the Skill Master, Queen Desire's own bastard son, had nurtured Regal's hatred along with his own. Had he hated enough to subvert his coterie to Regal's revenge?

To me it seemed a staggering treason, but I found myself accepting it. He would. Hundreds of folk slain, scores Forged, women raped, children orphaned, entire villages destroyed for the sake of a Princeling's vengeance over an imagined wrong. It staggered me. But it fit. It fit as snug as a coffin lid.

"I think perhaps the present Duke of Farrow should have a care for his health," I mused.

"He shares his older sister's fondness for fine wine and intoxicants. Well supplied with these, and careless of all else, I suspect he will live a long life."

"As perhaps King Shrewd might?" I ventured carefully.

A spasm of pain twitched across the Fool's face. "I doubt that a long life is left to him," he said quietly. "But what is left might be an easy one, rather than one of bloodshed and violence."

"You think it will come to that?"

"Who knows what will swirl up from the bottom of a stirred kettle?" He went suddenly to my door, and set his hand to the latch. "That is what I ask you," he said quietly. "To forgo your twirling, Sir Spoon. To let things settle."

"I cannot."

He pressed his forehead to the door, a most un-Fool-like gesture. "Then you shall be the death of kings." Grieved words in a low voice. "You know . . . what I am. I have told you. I have told you why I am here. This is one thing of which I am sure. The end of the Farseer line was one of the turning points. Kettricken carries an heir. The line will continue. That is what was needed. Cannot an old man be left to die in peace?"

"Regal will not let that heir be born," I said bluntly. Even the Fool widened his eyes to hear me speak so plain. "That child will not come to power without a King's hand to shelter under. Shrewd, or Verity. You do not believe Verity is dead. You have as much as said so. Can you let Kettricken endure the torment of believing it is so? Can you let the Six Duchies go down in blood and ruin? What good is an heir to the Farseer throne, if the throne is but a broken chair in a burned-out hall?"

The Fool's shoulders slumped. "There are a thousand

crossroads," he said quietly. "Some clear and bold, some shadows within shadows. Some are nigh onto certainties; it would take a great army or a vast plague to change those paths. Others are shrouded in fog, and I do not know what roads lead out of them, or to where. You fog me, bastard. You multiply the futures a thousandfold, just by your existing. Catalyst. From some of those fogs go the blackest, twisted threads of damnation, and from others shining twines of gold. To the depths or the heights, it seems, are your paths. I long for a middle path. I long for a simple death for a master who was kind to a freakish, jeering servant."

He made no more rebuke than that. He lifted the latches and undid the bolts and left quietly. The rich clothing and careful walk made him appear deformed to me, as his motley and capers never had. I closed the door softly behind him and then stood leaning against it as if I could hold the future out.

I prepared myself most carefully for dinner that evening. When I was finally dressed in Mistress Hasty's latest set of clothes for me, I looked almost as fine as the Fool. I had decided that as yet I would not mourn Verity, nor even give the appearance of mourning. As I descended the stairs it seemed to me that most of the Keep was converging on the Great Hall this evening. Evidently all had been summoned to attend, grand folk and humble.

I found myself seated at a table with Burrich and Hands and other of the stable folk. It was as humble a spot as I had ever been given since King Shrewd had taken me under his wing, and yet the company was more to my liking than that of the higher tables. For the honored tables of the Great Hall were packed with folk little known to me, the Dukes and visiting nobility of Tilth and Farrow for the most part. There were a scattering of faces I knew, of course. Patience was seated as almost befit her rank, and Lacey was actually seated at a table above me. I saw no sign of Molly anywhere. There were a scattering of folk from Buckkeep Town, most of them the well-to-do, and most of them seated more favorably than I would have expected. The King was ushered in, leaning on the newly elegant Fool, followed by Kettricken.

Her appearance shocked me. She wore a simple robe of

drab brown, and she had cut her hair for mourning. She had left
herself less than a hand's width of hair, and bereft of its rich
weight, it stuck out about her head like a dandelion gone to
seed. Its color seemed to have been cut away with its length,
leaving it as pale as the Fool's. So accustomed had I been to
seeing the heavy gold braids of her hair that her head now
appeared oddly small atop her wide shoulders. Her pale blue
eyes were made strange by eyelids reddened by weeping. She
did not look like a mourning Queen. Rather she appeared bizarre, a new kind of fool for the court. I could see nothing of
my queen, nothing of Kettricken in her garden, nothing of the
barefoot warrior dancing with her blade; only a foreign
woman, newly alone here. Regal, in contrast, was as lavishly
clothed as if to go a-courting, and moved as surely as a hunting
cat.

What I witnessed that evening was as cleverly paced and
carefully led as a puppet play. There was old King Shrewd,
doddering and thin, nodding off over his dinner, or making
vague and smiling conversation to no one in particular. There
was the Queen-in-Waiting, unsmiling, barely eating, silent and
mourning. Presiding over it all was Regal, the dutiful son
seated next to the failing father, and beside him the Fool,
magnificently clad and punctuating Regal's conversation with
witticisms to make the Prince's conversation more sparkling
than it truly was. The rest of the High Table was the Duke and
Duchess of Farrow, and the Duke and Duchess of Tilth, and
their current favorites among the lesser nobility of those duchies. Bearns, Rippon, and Shoaks Duchies were not represented
at all.

Following the meat, two toasts were offered to Regal. The
first came from Duke Holder of Farrow. He toasted the Prince
lavishly, declaring him the defender of the realm, praising his
swift action on behalf of Neatbay, and lauding also his courage
in taking the measures necessary for the best interests of the
Six Duchies. That made me prick up my ears. But it was all a
bit vague, congratulating and praising, but never quite laying
out exactly what Regal had decided to do. Had it gone on any
longer, it would have been suitable as a eulogy.

Early into the speech, Kettricken had sat up straighter and

looked incredulously at Regal, obviously unable to believe that he would quietly nod and smile to praises not his due. If anyone besides myself noticed the Queen's expression, none commented on it. The second toast, predictably, came from Duke Ram of Tilth. He offered a toast to the memory of King-in-Waiting Verity. This was a eulogy, but a condescending one, speaking of all that Verity had attempted and intended and dreamed of and wished for. His achievements already having been heaped on Regal's plate, there was little left to add. Kettricken grew, if anything, whiter and more pinched about the mouth.

I believe that when Duke Ram finished, she was on the verge of rising to speak herself. But Regal arose, almost hastily, holding up his newly filled glass. He motioned all to silence, then extended that glass toward the Queen.

"Too much has been said of me this night, and too little of our most fair Queen-in-Waiting, Kettricken. She has returned home to find herself most sadly bereaved. Yet I do not think my late brother Verity would wish sorrow for his death to overshadow all that is due his lady by her own effort. Despite her condition"—and the knowing smile of Regal's face was perilously close to a sneer—"she deemed it in the best interests of her adopted kingdom to venture forth to confront the Red-Ships herself. Doubtless many Raiders fell to her valiant sword. No one can doubt that our soldiers were inspired by the sight of their queen, determined to do battle on their behalf, regardless of what she risked."

Two spots of high color began to glow on Kettricken's cheeks. Regal continued, shading his account of Kettricken's deeds with condescension and flattery. The insincerity of his courtier's phrases somehow diminished her deed to something done for show.

I looked in vain for someone at the High Table to champion her. For me to rise from my common place and pit my voice against Regal's would have seemed almost more mocking. Kettricken, never sure of her place in her husband's court, and now without him to sustain her, seemed to shrink in on herself. Regal's retelling of her exploits made them seem questionable and reckless rather than daring and decisive. I saw her dwindle before herself, and knew she would not speak up for herself now. The meal resumed with a very subdued Queen attending to the addled King Shrewd beside her, grave and silent to the King's vague efforts at conversation.

But worse was to come. At the end of the meal, Regal once more called for silence. He promised the assembled folk that there would be minstrels and puppeteers to follow the meal, but asked them to endure while he announced but one more thing. After much grave consideration and great consultation, and with great reluctance, he had realized what the attack at Neatbay had justly proven. Buckkeep itself was no longer the safe and secure place it was once. It was certainly no place for anyone of delicate health. And so, a decision had been reached that King Shrewd (and the King lifted up his head and blinked about at the mention of his name) would be journeying inland, to reside in safety at Tradeford on the Vin River in Farrow until his health had improved. Here he paused to lavishly thank Duke Holder of Farrow for making the Tradeford Castle available to the royal family. He added, too, that he was greatly pleased it was so accessible to both the main castles of Farrow and Tilth, for he wished to remain in good contact with these most loyal Dukes, who had so often of late journeyed so far to assist him in these troubled, troubled times. It would please Regal to bring the life of the royal court to the ones who had previously had to travel far to enjoy it. Here he paused to accept their nodded thanks and murmurs of continued support: They subsided in immediate obedience when he next raised his hand.

He invited, nay, he entreated, he begged the Queen-in-Waiting to join King Shrewd there. She would be more safe, she would find it more comfortable, for Tradeford Castle had been built as a home, not a fortress. It would put the minds of her subjects at rest to know that the coming heir and his mother were well cared for and well away from the dangerous coast. He promised that every effort would be made to make her feel at home. He promised her a merry court would re-form there. Many many of the furnishings and treasures of Buckkeep were to be moved there when the King went, to make the move less upsetting for him. Regal smiled all the while that he relegated his father to a position of elderly idiot and Kettricken to brood-mare. He dared to pause to hear her acceptance of her fate.

"I cannot," she said with great dignity. "Buckkeep is where my lord Verity left me, and before he did so, he commended it to my care. Here I shall stay. This is where my child will be born."

Regal turned his head, ostensibly to hide a smile from her, but actually to display it better to the assemblage. "Buckkeep shall be well guarded, my lady queen. My own cousin, Lord Bright, heir to Farrow, has expressed an interest in assuming the defense of it. The full militia will be left in place here, for we have no need of them at Tradeford. I doubt that they shall need the assistance of one more woman hampered by her skirts and a burgeoning belly."

The laughter that erupted shocked me. It was a crude remark, a witticism more worthy of a tavern brawny than a Prince in his own Keep. It reminded me of nothing so much as of Queen Desire when she was at her worst, inflamed with wine and herbs. Yet they laughed, at the High Table, and not a few at the lower tables joined them. Regal's charms and entertainments had served him well. No matter what insult or buffoonery he served up tonight, these fawners would sit and accept it with the meat and wine they gobbled at his table. Kettricken seemed incapable of speech. She actually rose and would have left the table, had not the King reached out a trembling hand. "Please, my dear," he said, and his faltering voice carried all too clearly. "Do not leave me. I wish you at my side."

"You see, it is the wish of your king," Regal hastily admonished her, and I doubt that even he could fully token the good luck that had led the King to make such a request of her at such a time. Kettricken sank back unwillingly in her seat. Her lower lip trembled and her face flushed. For one terrifying instant I thought she would burst into tears. It would have been the final triumph for Regal, a betrayal of her emotional weakness as a breeding female. Instead, she took a deep breath. She turned to the King and spoke low but audibly as she took his hand. "You are my king, to whom I am sworn. My liege, it shall be as you wish. I shall not leave your side."

She bowed her head, and Regal nodded affably, and a general outbreak of conversation congratulated itself on her agreement. Regal nattered on a bit longer when the din died down, but he had already achieved his goal. He spoke mostly of the wisdom of his decision, and how Buckkeep would be better able to defend itself without fearing for its monarch. He even had the audacity to suggest that by removing himself and the King and Queen-in-Waiting, he would be making Buckkeep a lesser target for the Raiders, as they would have less to gain by capturing it. It was all a nothing, a winding down for show. Not long after, the King was taken away, carted off back to his chamber, his display duty done. Queen Kettricken excused herself to accompany him. The feast broke down into a general cacophony of entertainments. Kegs of beer were brought out, along with casks of the lesser wines. Various inland minstrels held forth at opposite corners of the Great Hall, while the Prince and his cohorts chose the amusement of a puppet show, a bawdy piece entitled *The Seduction of the Innkeeper's Son*. I pushed back my plate and looked to Burrich. Our eyes met, and we rose as one.

26

Skilling

THE FORGED ONES *appeared to be incapable of any emotion. They were not evil, they did not take joy in their wickedness or crimes. When they lost their capacity to feel anything for fellow humans, or any other creatures of the world, they lost their ability to be part of society. An unsympathetic man, a harsh man, an insensitive man still retains enough sensibilities to know that he cannot always express how little he cares for others, and still be accepted into the kinship of a family or a village. The Forged ones had lost even the ability to dissemble that they felt for their fellows. Their emotions did not simply stop; they were forgotten, lost to them so entirely that they could not even predict the behavior of other humans based on emotional reaction.*

A Skilled one might be seen as the other end of this spectrum. Such a man can reach forth and tell from afar what others are thinking and feeling. He can, if strongly Skilled, impose his thoughts and feelings on others. In this increased sensitivity to the emotions and thoughts of others, he has a surfeit of what Forged ones lack entirely.

King-in-Waiting Verity confided that the Forged

*ones seemed immune to his Skilling abilities. That is,
he could not feel what they felt, nor discover their
thoughts. This does not, however, mean that they were
insensible to the Skill. Could Verity's Skilling have
been what drew them to Buckkeep? Did his reaching
out awaken in them a hunger, a remembrance perhaps
of what they had lost? Drawn as they were, through
ice and flood, to travel always toward Buckkeep, the
motivation must have been intense. And when Verity
departed Buckkeep on his quest, the movement of
Forged ones toward Buckkeep seemed to abate.*

—Chade Fallstar

⊷≡⊱

We arrived at King Shrewd's door and knocked. The Fool
opened it. I had marked well that Wallace was one of the
feasters below, and had remained when the King had departed.
"Let me in," I said quietly while the Fool glared at me.

"No," he said flatly. He started to close the door.

I put my shoulder to it, and Burrich assisted. It was the
first and last time I would ever use force against the Fool. I took
no joy in proving that I was physically stronger than he was.
The look in his eyes as I forced him aside was something no
one should ever see in a friend's face.

The King was sitting before his hearth, vapidly mumbling.
The Queen-in-Waiting sat desolately beside him, while Rosemary dozed at her feet. Kettricken rose from her seat to regard
us with surprise. "FitzChivalry?" she asked quietly.

I went swiftly to her side. "I have much to explain, and a
very little time in which to do it. For what I need to do must be
done now, tonight." I paused, tried to decide how best to
explain it to her. "Do you remember when you pledged yourself to Verity?"

"Of course!" She looked at me as if I were crazy.

"He used August, then, a coterie member, to come and
stand with you in your mind, to show you his heart. Do you
remember that?"

She colored. "Of course I do. But I did not think anyone else knew exactly what had happened then."

"Few did." I looked around, to find Burrich and the Fool following the conversation wide-eyed.

"Verity Skilled to you, through August. He is strong in the Skill. You know that, you know how he guards our coasts with it. It is an ancestral magic, a talent of the Farseer line. Verity inherited it from his father. And I inherited a measure of it from mine."

"Why are you telling me this?"

"Because I do not believe Verity is dead. King Shrewd used to be strong in the Skill, I am told. That is no longer the case. His illness has stolen it away, as it has stolen so many other things. But if we can persuade him to try, if we can rouse him to the effort, I can offer him my strength to sustain him. He may be able to reach Verity."

"It will kill him." The Fool spoke his challenge flatly. "I have heard of what the Skill takes out of a man. My king has not that left to give."

"I don't think it will. If we reach Verity, Verity will break it off before it hurts his father. More than once he has drawn back from draining my strength, to be sure of not injuring me."

"Even a Fool can see the failure of your logic." The Fool tugged at the cuffs of his fine new shirt. "If you reach Verity, how will we know it is true, and not a show?"

I opened my mouth in an angry protest, but the Fool held up a forbidding hand. "Of course, my dear, dear Fitz, we should all believe you, as you are our friend, who has only our very best interests at heart. But there may be a few others prone to doubt your word, or regard you as so selfless." His sarcasm bit at me like acid, but I managed to stand silent. "And if you don't reach Verity, what do we have? An exhausted and drained King to be further flaunted about as incapable. A grieving Queen, who must wonder, in addition to all her other pains, if perhaps she grieves for a man who is not dead yet. That is the worst type of grieving there is. No. We gain nothing, even if you succeed, for our belief in you would not be enough to stop the wheels that are already turning. And we have much to lose if you fail. Too much.''

Their eyes were on me. There was question even in Burrich's dark eyes, as if he debated the wisdom of what he had urged me to do. Kettricken stood very still, trying not to pounce on the bare bone of hope that I had thrown at her feet. I wished that I had waited, to talk first with Chade. I suspected I would never have another chance after this night, to have these people in this room, Wallace out of the way, and Regal busy below. It had to be now or it would not be.

I looked at the only one who was not watching me. King Shrewd idly watched the leap and play of the flames in his hearth. ''He is still the King,'' I said quietly. ''Let us ask him, and let him decide.''

''Not fair! He is not himself!'' The Fool flung himself between us. He stood high on his feet to try to look me in the eye. ''On the herbs fed him, he is as tractable as a plow horse. Ask him to cut his own throat, and he'll wait for you to hand him the knife.''

''No.'' The voice quavered. It had lost its timbre and resonance. ''No, my fool, I am not so far gone as that.''

We waited, breathless, but King Shrewd spoke no more. At last I slowly crossed the room. I crouched down beside him, tried to make his eyes meet mine. ''King Shrewd?'' I begged.

His eyes came to mine, darted away, came back unwillingly. At last he looked at me.

''Have you heard all we have said? My king, do you believe Verity is dead?''

He parted his lips. His tongue was grayish behind them. He took a long breath. ''Regal told me Verity is dead. He had word. . . .''

''From where?'' I asked gently.

He shook his head slowly. ''A messenger . . . I think.''

I turned to the others. ''It would have to have come by messenger. From the Mountains, for Verity must be there by now. He was nearly to the Mountains when Burrich was sent back. I do not believe a messenger would come all the way from the Mountains, and not stay to convey such news to Kettricken herself.''

"It might have come by relay," Burrich said unwillingly. "For one man and one horse, it is too exhausting a trip. A rider would have to exchange horses. Or pass on the word to another rider, who would go on, on a swift horse. The last is most likely."

"Perhaps. But how long would such word take to come to us all the way from the Mountains? I know Verity was alive on the day Bearns departed here. Because that was when King Shrewd used me to speak to him. That night when I all but fainted on this hearth. That was what had happened, Fool." I paused. "I believe I felt him with me during the battle at Neatbay."

I saw Burrich count back the days in his mind. He shrugged unwillingly. "It is still possible. If Verity were killed that day, and word were sent out immediately, and the riders and horses were both good . . . it could be so. Barely."

"I don't believe it." I turned to the rest of them, tried to force my hope into them. "I don't believe Verity is dead." I turned my eyes up to King Shrewd once more. "Do you? Do you believe your son could have died, and you not feel anything?"

"Chivalry . . . went like that. Like a fading whisper. 'Father,' he said, I think. Father."

A silence seeped into the room. I waited, crouched on my heels, for my king's decision. Slowly his hand lifted, as if it had a life of its own. It crossed the small space to me, rested on my shoulder. For a moment; that was all. Just the weight of my king's hand on my shoulder. King Shrewd shifted slightly in his chair. He took a breath through his nostrils.

I closed my eyes and we plunged into the black river again. Once more I faced the desperate young man trapped in King Shrewd's dying body. We tumbled together in the sweeping current of the world. "There's no one here. No one here but us anymore." Shrewd sounded lonely.

I couldn't find myself. I had no body, no tongue here. He held me under with him in the rush and the roar. I could hardly think at all, let alone remember what little of the Skill lessons I had retained from Galen's harsh instruction. It was like trying to recite a memorized speech while being throttled. I gave up. I gave it all up. Then from somewhere, like a feather floating in a breeze, or a mote dancing in a sunbeam, came Verity's voice telling me, "Being open is simply not being closed."

The whole world was a spaceless place, all things inside of all other things. I did not say his name aloud or think of his face. Verity was there, had always been right there, and joining him was effortless. *You live!*

Of course. But you won't, spilling all over like this. You're pouring out everything you have in one gush. Regulate your strength. Be precise. He steadied me, shaped me back into myself, then gasped in recognition.

Father!

Verity pushed at me roughly. *Get back! Let go of him, he hasn't the strength for this. You're draining him, you idiot! Let go!*

It was like being *repelled,* but rougher. When I found myself and opened my eyes, I was sprawled on my side before the fireplace. My face was uncomfortably close to it. I rolled over, groaning, and saw the King. His lips were puffing in and out with each breath, and there was a bluish cast to his skin. Burrich and Kettricken and the Fool were a helpless circle standing about him. "Do . . . something!" I gasped up at them.

"What?" demanded the Fool, believing I knew.

I floundered about in my mind, came up with the only remedy I could recall. "Elfbark," I croaked. The edges of the room kept turning black. I shut my eyes and listened to them panicking about. Slowly I understood what I had done. I had Skilled.

I had tapped my king's strength to do it.

"You will be the death of kings," the Fool had told me. A prophecy or a shrewd guess? A Shrewd guess. Tears came to my eyes.

I smelled elfbark tea. Plain strong elfbark, no ginger or mint to disguise it. I prised my eyes open a crack.

"It's too hot!" hissed the Fool.

"It cools quickly in the spoon," Burrich insisted, and ladled some into the King's mouth. He took it in, but I did not see him swallow. With the casual expertise of years in the stables, Burrich tugged gently at the King's lower jaw and then stroked his throat. He ladled another spoonful into his slack mouth. Not much was happening.

Kettricken came to crouch by me. She lifted my head to her knee, put a hot cup to my mouth. I sucked at it, too hot, I didn't care, I sucked in air with it, noisily. I swallowed it, fought choking against its bitterness. The darkness receded. The cup came back, I sipped again. It was strong enough to near numb my tongue. I looked up at Kettricken, found her eyes. I managed a tiny nod.

"He lives?" she asked softly.

"Yes." It was all I could manage.

"He lives!" She cried it out aloud to the others, joy in her voice.

"My father!" Regal shouted the words. He stood swaying in the door, face red with drink and anger. Behind him I glimpsed his guard, and little Rosemary peeping around the corner, wide-eyed. Somehow she managed to slip past the men, to race to Kettricken and clutch at her skirts. For an instant our tableau held.

Then Regal swept into the room, ranting, demanding, questioning, but giving no one a chance to speak. Kettricken kept a protective crouch beside me, or I swear Regal's guards would have had me again. Above me, in his chair, the King had a bit of color again in his face. Burrich put another spoonful of tea to his lips, and I was relieved to see him sip at it.

Regal was not. "What are you giving him? Stop that! I won't have my father poisoned by a stable hand!"

"The King had another attack, my prince," the Fool said suddenly. His voice cut through the chaos in the room, made a hole that became a silence. "Elfbark tea is a common restorative. I am sure that even Wallace has heard of it."

The Prince was drunk. He was not sure if he was being mocked or conciliated. He glared at the Fool, who smiled benignly back.

"Oh." He said it grudgingly, not really wishing to be mollified. "Well, what, then, of him?" He gestured at me in anger.

"Drunk." Kettricken stood up, letting my head drop to the

floor with a convincing thump. Flashes of light marred my vision. There was only disgust in her voice. "Stablemaster. Get him out of here. You should have stopped him before he got this far. Next time, see that you use your judgment when he has none of his own."

"Our stablemaster is well-known for having his own taste for the cup, lady queen. I suspect they have been at it together." Regal sneered.

"The news of Verity's death hit him hard," Burrich said simply. He was true to himself, offering an explanation, but no excuse. He took hold of my shirtfront, jerked me from the floor. With no effort at playacting, I swayed on my feet until he gripped me more firmly. I caught a passing glimpse of the Fool hastily spooning another dose of elfbark into the King. I prayed no one would interrupt him. As Burrich ushered me roughly out of the room, I heard Queen Kettricken rebuking Regal, saying he should be below with his guests, and promising that she and the Fool could get the King to bed. As we were going up the stairs I heard Regal and his guard going down. He was still muttering and then ranting, complaining that he was not stupid, he could tell a plot when he saw one. It worried me, but I was fairly certain he had no real idea of what had been going on.

At my door, I was well enough to work my latches. Burrich followed me in. "If I had a dog that was sick as often as you are, I'd put it down," he observed kindly. "Do you need more elfbark?"

"It wouldn't hurt me any. But in a gentler dose. Do you have any ginger or mint or rose hips?"

He gave me a look. I sat on my chair while he poked at the pathetic embers in my fireplace until he got them to glow. He built up a fire, put water in the kettle, and set it to heat. He found a pot and put in the flaked elfbark, then found a mug and wiped the dust out of it. He set the things out ready, then looked about himself. Something like disgust was on his face. "Why do you live like this?" he demanded.

"Like what?"

"In so bare a room, with so little care for it? I've seen winter-quarter tents that were homier than this room. It's as if

ou've never expected to stay here more than a night or two
onger."

I shrugged. "I've never given it much thought."

There was a silence for a bit. "You should," he said un-
villingly. "And you should think about how often you're hurt,
r sick."

"This, what happened tonight, this couldn't be helped."

"You knew what it would do to you, but you went ahead
vith it anyway," he pointed out.

"I had to." I watched him pour steaming water over the
lfbark in the pot.

"Did you? It seemed to me the Fool had a pretty convinc-
ng argument against it. Yet you went ahead. You and King
hrewd, both of you."

"So?"

"I know a bit about the Skill," Burrich said quietly. "I
vas king's man to Chivalry. Not often, and it did not leave me
s bad as you are now, save for once or twice. But I've felt the
xcitement of it, the—" He groped for words, sighed. "The
ompletion of it. The oneness with the world. Chivalry once
poke to me about it. A man can get addicted, he said. So that
le looks for excuses to Skill, and then finally he is absorbed
nto it." He added after a moment, "It is not unlike the rush of
battle, in some ways. The sense of moving unhampered by
ime, of being a force more powerful than life itself."

"As I cannot Skill alone, I daresay it is not a danger to
ne."

"You offer yourself very often to those who can." Bluntly
poken. "As often as you willingly plunge yourself into dan-
erous situations that offer that same kind of excitement. In a
battle, you go into a frenzy. Is that what happens to you when
ou Skill?"

I had never considered the two together in such a light.
Something like fear nibbled at me. I pushed it aside.

"To be a King's Man is my duty. Besides, was not this
vening your suggestion?"

"It was. But I would have let the Fool's words dissuade us
rom it. You were determined. You put no value at all on what it
vould do to you. Perhaps you should have a care for yourself."

"I know what I'm doing." I spoke more sharply than intended, and Burrich did not reply. He poured the tea he had made, and handed it to me with a "see what I mean" look on his face. I took the mug and stared into the fire. He sat down on my clothing chest.

"Verity is alive," I said quietly.

"So I heard the Queen say. I had never believed he was dead." He accepted it very calmly. As calmly as he added, "But we have no proof."

"Proof? I spoke to him. The King spoke to him. Isn't that enough?"

"For me, more than enough. For most other folks, well . . ."

"When the King recovers, he will bear me out. Verity lives."

"I doubt it will be enough to prevent Regal from proclaiming himself King-in-Waiting. The ceremony is scheduled for next week. I think he would have done it tonight, save that every Duke must be present to witness it."

Elfbark battling with exhaustion, or simply the unrelenting march of events, suddenly made the room tilt around me. I felt I had thrown myself in front of a wagon to stop it, and instead it had rolled over me. The Fool had been right. What I had done tonight counted for little, save the peace of mind it brought Kettricken. A sudden welling of despair filled me. I set down my empty cup. The Six Duchies kingdom was falling apart. My king-in-waiting, Verity, would return to a mockery of what he had left: a sundered country, a ravaged coastline, a plundered and empty Keep. Perhaps if I had believed in Elderlings I could have found some way to believe it would all come out right. All I could see now was my failure.

Burrich was looking at me oddly. "Go to bed," he suggested. "A bleak spirit is sometimes what follows an overindulgence in elfbark. Or so I have heard."

I nodded. To myself, I wondered if that might account for Verity's often dour moods.

"Get some real rest. In the morning, things may look better." He gave a bark of laughter and smiled wolfishly. "Then again, they may not. But the rest will at least leave you etter prepared to face them.'' He paused, sobering. ''Molly came to my room, earlier.''

''Is she all right?'' I demanded to know.

''Bringing candles she knew I did not need,'' Burrich went on as if I had not spoken. ''Almost as if she wanted an excuse to speak to me . . .''

''What did she say?'' I rose from my chair.

''Not very much. She is always very correct with me. I am very direct with her. I simply told her you missed her.''

''And she said?''

''Nothing.'' He grinned. ''But she blushes very prettily.'' He sighed, suddenly serious. ''And, as directly, I asked her if anyone had given her any further cause to fear. She squared her little shoulders and tucked in her chin like I was trying to force a bit in her teeth. She said she thanked me kindly for my concern, as she had before, but that she was capable of seeing to herself.'' In a quieter voice, he asked, ''Will she ask for help if she needs it?''

''I don't know,'' I confessed. ''She has her own store of courage. Her own way of fighting. She turns and confronts things. Me, I slink about and try to hamstring them when they aren't looking. Sometimes, she makes me feel a coward.''

Burrich stood up, stretching so that his shoulders cracked. ''You're no coward, Fitz. I'll vouch for you there. Perhaps you just understand odds better than she does. I wish I could put your mind at rest about her. I can't. I'll watch over her as well as I can. As much as she'll let me.'' He gave me a sideways glance. ''Hands asked me today who the pretty lady is who calls on me so often.''

, ''What did you tell him?''

''Nothing. I just looked at him.''

I knew the look. There would be no more questions from Hands.

Burrich left and I sprawled on my bed, trying to rest. I could not. I made my body be still, reasoning that at least my flesh would take some rest, even if my mind persisted in rattling on. A better man's thoughts would have been solely of his king's plight. I am afraid a good share of mine went to Molly,

alone in her room. When I could stand it no more, I rose from
my bed and ghosted out into the Keep.

Sounds of dying revelry still drifted up from the Great
Hall below. The corridor was empty. I ventured silently toward
the stairs. I told myself I would be very, very careful, that all I
would do was tap at her door, perhaps go in for a few moments
just to see she was all right. No more than that. Just the briefest
of visits . . .

You are followed. Nighteyes' new caution of Burrich made
his voice but the tiniest whisper in my head.

I did not halt. That would have let my follower know I was
suspicious. Instead I scratched my shoulder, making it an excuse to swivel my head about and glance behind me. I saw no
one.

Snuff.

I did, a short breath followed by a deeper intake. A bare
scent on the air. Sweat and garlic. I quested gently and my
blood went cold. There, at the far end of the hall, concealed in
a doorway. Will. Dark, slender Will, with his eyes always half-
lidded. The coterie member who had been recalled from
Bearns. Very cautiously I touched the Skill shield that hid him
from me, a subtle bidding that I not notice him, a quiet scent of
self-confidence sent my way to bolster me in doing whatever I
wished to do. Very guileful. Very artful, much more delicate a
touch than either Serene or Justin had ever shown me.

A much more dangerous man.

I went to the landing of the stairs and took candles from
the extra ones stored there, then returned to my room as if that
had been my sole errand.

When I closed my door behind me, my mouth was dry. I
sighed out a shuddering breath. I forced myself to examine the
guards that warded my mind. He had not been in me, that I
could tell. He was not sniffing out my thoughts, then, but only
imposing his on me to make it easier for him to shadow me.
Had it not been for Nighteyes, he would have followed me right
to Molly's door tonight. I forced myself to lie down on my bed
again, to try to recall all of my actions since Will had returned
to Buckkeep. I had been dismissing him as an enemy simply
because he did not radiate the hatred for me that Serene and

Justin did. He had always been a quiet and unimposing youth. He had grown to be an unremarkable man, scarce worth anyone's attention.

I had been a fool.

I do not think he has followed you before. But I cannot be sure either.

Nighteyes, my brother. How do I thank you?

Stay alive. A pause. *And bring me ginger cake.*

You shall have it, I promised fervently.

Burrich's fire had burned low and I still had not slept when I felt Chade's draft sweep through my room. It was almost a relief to rise and go to him.

I found him awaiting me impatiently, pacing about his small room. He pounced on me as I came out of the stairwell.

"An assassin is a tool," he informed me in a hiss. "Somehow, I never got that across to you. We are tools. We do not do anything of our own volition."

I stopped still, shocked at the anger in his voice. "I haven't killed anyone!" I said indignantly.

"Shush! Speak softly. I would not be too sure of that, were I you," he replied. "How many times have I done my job, not by putting the knife in myself, but simply by giving someone else sufficient reason and opportunity to do it for me?"

I said nothing.

He looked at me and sighed, the anger and strength going out of him. Softly he said, "Sometimes, the best you can do is just salvage work. Sometimes we have to resign ourselves to that. We are not the ones to set the wheels in motion, boy. What you did tonight was ill-considered."

"So the Fool and Burrich have both told me. I don't think Kettricken would agree."

"Kettricken and her child could both have lived with her grief. As could King Shrewd. Look at what they were. A foreign woman, widow of a dead King-in-Waiting, mother of a child that isn't visible yet, and who will be unable to wield power for years to come. Regal judged Shrewd to be but a doddering helpless old man, useful as a puppet perhaps, but harmless enough. Regal had no immediate reason to put them aside. Oh, I agree Kettricken's position was not as secure as it could be, but she was not in direct opposition to Regal. That is where she is now.''

"She did not tell him what we had discovered," I said unwillingly.

"She did not have to. It will show, in her bearing and in her will to resist him. He had reduced her to a widow. You have restored her to a Queen-in-Waiting. But it is for Shrewd that I worry. Shrewd is the one who holds the key, who can stand up and say, even in a whisper, 'Verity still lives, Regal has no right to be king-in-waiting.' He is the one Regal must fear.''

"I have seen Shrewd, Chade. Really seen him. I do not think he will betray what he knows. Beneath that faltering body, beneath the numbing drugs and the savage pain, there is a shrewd man still.''

"Perhaps. But he is buried deep. Drugs, and pain even more so, will drive a sagacious man to foolish acts. A man dying of his wounds will leap to his horse to lead a last charge. Pain can make a man take risks, or assert himself in strange ways.''

What he was saying made all too much sense. "Cannot you counsel him against letting Regal know that he knows Verity is alive?''

"I could try, perhaps. Were not that damnable Wallace always in my way. It was not so bad at first; at first, he was tractable and useful, easy to manipulate from afar. He never knew I was behind the herbs the peddlers brought him; never even suspected I existed. But now he clings to the King like a limpet, and not even the Fool can drive him away for long. I seldom have more than a few minutes with Shrewd at a time anymore. And I am lucky if my brother is lucid for half of them.''

There was something in his voice. I lowered my head, shamed. "I am sorry," I said quietly. "Sometimes I forget that he is more to you than just your king.''

"Well. We were never really that close, that way. But we are two old men, who have grown old together. Sometimes that is a greater closeness. We have come through time to your day and age. We can talk together, quietly, and share memories of a time that exists no more. I can tell you how it was, but it is not the same. It is like being two foreigners, trapped in a land we have come to, unable to return to our own, and having only each other to confirm the reality of the place we once lived. At least, once we could.''

I thought of two children running wild on the beaches of Buckkeep, plucking sheel off the rocks and eating them raw. Molly and I. It was possible to be homesick for a time, and to be lonely for the only other person who could recall it. I nodded.

''Ah. Well. Tonight we contemplate salvage. Now. Listen to me. On this I must have your word. You will not take actions of major consequence without conferring with me first. Agreed?''

I looked down. ''I want to say yes. I am willing to agree to it. But lately even small actions of mine seem to take on consequences like a pebble in a landslide. And events pile up to where I have to make a choice suddenly, with no chance to consult anyone else. So I cannot promise. But I will promise to try. Is that enough?''

''I suppose. Catalyst,'' he muttered.

''So the Fool calls me, too,'' I complained.

Chade stopped abruptly in the midst of starting to say something. ''Does he really?'' he asked intently.

''He clubs me with the word every chance he gets.'' I walked down to Chade's hearth and sat down before his fire. The heat felt good. ''Burrich says that too strong a dose of elfbark can lead to bleak spirits afterward.''

''Do you find it so?''

''Yes. But it could be the circumstances. Yet Verity seemed often depressed, and he used it frequently. Again, it could be the circumstances.''

''It may be we shall never know.''

''You speak very freely tonight. Naming names, ascribing motives.''

''All is gaiety in the Great Hall tonight. Regal was certain he had bagged his game. All his watches were relaxed, all his spies given a night's liberty.'' He looked at me sourly. ''I am sure it will not be the same again for a while.''

''So you think what we say here can be listened to.''

"Anywhere I can listen and peep, from there it is possible I could be overheard and spied upon. Only just possible. But one does not get to be as old as I am by taking chances."

An old memory suddenly made sense. "You once told me that in the Queen's Garden, you are blind."

"Exactly."

"So you did not know—"

"I did not know what Galen was putting you through, at the time he was doing it. I was privy to gossip, much of it unreliable and all of it far after the fact. But on the night he beat you and left you to die . . . No." He looked at me strangely. "Had you believed I could know of such a thing and take no action?"

"You had promised not to interfere with my instruction," I said stiffly.

Chade took his chair, leaned back with a sigh. "I don't think you will ever completely trust anyone. Or believe that someone cares about you."

Silence filled me. I didn't know the answer. First Burrich and now Chade, forcing me to look at myself in uncomfortable ways.

"Ah, well," Chade conceded to my silence. "As I began to say earlier. Salvage."

"What do you want me to do?"

He breathed out through his nose. "Nothing."

"But . . ."

"Absolutely nothing. Remember this at all times. King-in-Waiting Verity is dead. Live that belief. Believe that Regal has the right to claim his spot, believe he has the right to do all the things he does. Placate him for now, give him nothing to fear. We must make him believe he has won."

I thought for a moment. Then I stood and drew my belt knife.

"What are you doing?" Chade demanded.

"What Regal would expect me to do, did I truly believe Verity was dead." I reached in back of my head, to where a leather thong bound my hair back in a warrior's tail.

"I have shears," Chade pointed out in annoyance. He went and got them and stood behind me. "How much?"

I considered. "As extreme as I can be, short of mourning him as a crowned King."

"Are you sure?"

"It's what Regal would expect of me."

"That's true, I suppose." With a single clip, Chade took off my hair at the knot. It felt strange to have it suddenly fall forward, short, not even to my jaw. As if I were a page again. I reached up and felt its shortness as I asked him, "What will you be doing?"

"Trying to find a safe place for Kettricken and the King. I must make all things ready for their flight. When they go, they must vanish like shadows when the light comes."

"Are you sure this is necessary?"

"What else is left for us? They are no more than hostages now. Powerless. The Inland Dukes have turned to Regal, the Coastal Dukes have lost faith in King Shrewd. Kettricken has made herself allies amongst them, however. I must tug at the strings she has spun and see what I can arrange. At least we can see them placed where their safety cannot be used against Verity when he comes back to reclaim his crown."

"If he returns," I said gloomily.

"When. The Elderlings will be with him." Chade looked at me sourly. "Try to believe in something, boy. For my sake."

Without a doubt, the time that I spent under Galen's tutelage was the worst period of my life at Buckkeep. But the week that followed that night with Chade runs a close second. We were an anthill, kicked apart. No matter where I went in the Keep, there were constant reminders that the foundations of my life had been shattered. Nothing would ever be as it was before.

There was a great influx of folk from the Inland Duchies, come to witness Regal becoming king-in-waiting. Had not our stables been so depleted already, it would have taxed Burrich and Hands to keep up with them. As it was, it seemed like Inlanders were everywhere, tall, towheaded Farrow men, and brawny Tilth farmers and cattlemen. They were a bright contrast to the glum Buckkeep soldiers with their mourning-cropped hair. Not a few clashes occurred. The grumble from Buckkeep Town took the form of jests comparing the invasion of the Inlanders with the raids of the Outislanders. The humor had always a bitter edge.

For the counterpoint to this influx of folk and business in Buckkeep Town was the outflow of goods from Buckkeep. Rooms were stripped shamelessly. Tapestries and rugs, furniture and tools, supplies of all kinds were drained out of the Keep, to be loaded on barges and taken upriver to Tradeford, always to be "kept safe" or "for the comfort of the King." Mistress Hasty was at her wit's end to house so many guests when half the furniture was being hauled off to barges. Some days it seemed that Regal was attempting to see that all he could not carry off with him was devoured before he left.

At the same time he was sparing no expense to be sure that his crowning as king-in-waiting would be as full of pomp and ceremony as possible. I truly did not know why he bothered with it at all. To me, at least, it seemed plain he planned on abandoning four of the Six Duchies to their own devices. But as the Fool had once warned me, there was no point to trying to measure Regal's wheat with my bushels. We had no common standard. Perhaps to insist the Dukes and nobles of Bearns and Rippon and Shoaks come to witness him assume Verity's crown was some subtle form of revenge I could not understand. Little enough did he care what hardship it worked upon them to come to Buckkeep at a time when their shores were so beleaguered. I was not surprised that they were slow to arrive, and that when they did, they were shocked at the sacking of Buckkeep. Word of Regal's plan to remove himself and the King and Kettricken had not been spread to the Coastal Duchies by any means other than rumor.

But long before the Coastal Dukes arrived, while I still endured the greater general chaos, the rest of my life began to rattle into pieces. Serene and Justin began to haunt me. I was aware of them, often physically following me, but just as often Skilling at the edges of my consciousness. They were like pecking birds come after any loose thoughts I might have, snatching at casual daydreams or any unguarded moment of my life. That was bad enough. But I saw them now as only the distraction, the diversion created to keep me from being aware of Will's more subtle haunting. So I set my guards most strongly about my mind, knowing I probably shielded out Verity as well. I feared this was their actual intent, but dared reveal that fear to no one. I watched constantly behind myself, using every sense Nighteyes and I possessed. I vowed I would be more wary, and set myself the task of discovering what the other coterie members worked at. Burl was at Tradeford, ostensibly helping prepare the place for King Shrewd's comfort. I had no idea where Carrod was, and there was no one I could discreetly ask. The only thing I could discover for certain was that he was no longer on the *Constance*. So I worried. And became almost mad with worry that I did not detect Will shadowing after me anymore. Did he know I had become aware of him? Or was he so good I could not detect him? I began to live my life as if every move I made were watched.

Horses and breeding stock were not all that was taken from the stables. Burrich told me one morning that Hands was gone. He had not had time to bid anyone good-bye. "They took the last of the good stock yesterday. The best is long gone, but these were good horses, and they were taking them overland to Tradeford. Hands was simply told he was to go along. He came to me, protesting, but I told him to go. At least the horses will have well-trained hands taking care of them in their new home. Besides, there is nothing for him here. There is no stable left for anyone to be stablemaster over."

I followed him silently on what had once been our morning rounds. The mews held only ancient or injured birds. The clamor of dogs had been reduced to a sparse baying and a few yips. The horses that remained were the unsound, the almost promising, the past their prime, the injured that had been kept in the hopes of breeding something from them. When I came to Sooty's empty stall, my heart stood still. I could not speak. I leaned on her manger, my face in my hands. Burrich put a hand on my shoulder. When I looked up at him, he smiled oddly. He shook his cropped head. "They came for her and Ruddy yesterday. I told them they were fools, they had taken them last week. And truly they were fools, for they believed me. They did get your saddle."

"Where?" I managed to ask.

"Better you don't know," Burrich said darkly. "One of us

dangling as a horse thief would be quite enough.'' No more would he say of it to me.

A late-afternoon visit to Patience and Lacey was not the quiet interlude I had hoped for. I knocked, and there was an uncharacteristic pause before the door was opened. I found the sitting room in a shambles, worse than I had ever seen it, and Lacey dispiritedly trying to put things to rights. A great many more things were on the floor than usual.

''A new project?'' I hazarded, attempting a bit of levity.

Lacey looked at me glumly. ''They came this morning to take my lady's table away. And my bed. They claimed they were needed for guests. Well, I shouldn't be surprised, with so much of the rest of the things gone upriver. But I greatly doubt that we'll see either item again.''

''Well, perhaps they'll be waiting for you when you get to Tradeford,'' I suggested inanely. I had not realized the whole extent of the liberties Regal was taking.

There was a very long silence before Lacey spoke. ''Then they'll wait a long time, FitzChivalry. We are not among those to be taken to Tradeford.''

''No. We're among the odd folk to be left here, with the oddments of furniture.'' This from Patience as she abruptly reentered the room. Her eyes were red and her cheeks pale, and I suddenly knew she had hidden herself when I first knocked until she had her tears under control.

''Then surely you shall return to Withywoods,'' I suggested. My mind was working very swiftly. I had assumed that Regal was moving the entire household to Tradeford. Now I wondered who else was to be abandoned here. I put myself at the head of the list. I added Burrich and Chade. The Fool? Perhaps that was why he seemed lately to be Regal's creature. That he might be allowed to follow the King to Tradeford.

Odd, how I had not even considered that the King and Kettricken were to be whisked not only out of Chade's reach, but mine. Regal had renewed his orders confining me to Buckkeep itself. I had not wanted to trouble Kettricken to override them. I had, after all, promised Chade not to make waves.

''I cannot return to Withywoods. August rules there, the

King's nephew. He who was head of Galen's coterie, before his accident. He has no fondness for me, and I have no right to demand to be there. No. We shall be staying here, and making the best we can of it.''

I floundered for whatever comfort I could offer. ''I have a bed still. I shall have it brought down here for Lacey. Burrich will help me bring it.''

Lacey shook her head. ''I've made up a pallet, and I'll be comfortable enough. Keep it where it is. Perhaps they daren't take it from you. Were it down here, no doubt it would just be carried off tomorrow.''

''Has King Shrewd no care for what is happening?'' Lady Patience asked of me sadly.

''I do not know. All are turned away from his door these days. Regal has said he is too ill to see anyone.''

''I thought perhaps it was just me he would not see. Ah, well. Poor man. To lose two sons, and see his kingdom come to this. Tell me, how is Queen Kettricken? I have not had a chance to go see her.''

''Well enough, last I saw her. Grieved by her husband's death, of course, but—''

''Then she was not injured in her fall? I feared she would miscarry.'' Patience turned aside from me, to gaze at a wall bereft of a familiar tapestry. ''I was too cowardly to go and see her myself, if you would know the truth. I know too well the pain of losing a child before you have held it in your arms.''

''Her fall?'' I said stupidly.

''Had not you heard? On those awful steps coming down from the Queen's Garden. There was talk that some statuary had been removed from the gardens, and she had gone up to see what, and on her way back down she fell. Not a great tumbling fall, but heavily. On her back on those stone steps.''

I could not keep my mind on Patience's conversation after that. Much of it centered on the depletion of the libraries, a thing I did not wish to think of anyway. As soon as I graciously could, I excused myself, on the flimsy promise that I would bring them direct word of the Queen.

I was turned away from Kettricken's door. Several ladies told me at once not to fret, not to worry, she was fine, she but needed to rest, oh, but it was terrible. . . . I endured enough to be sure that she had not miscarried, then fled.

But I did not go back to Patience. Not yet. Instead, I slowly climbed the stairs to the Queen's Garden. I carried a lamp with me, and went most carefully. On the tower top, I found it was as I had feared. The smaller and more valuable of the statuary had been removed. Only the sheer weight had saved the larger pieces, I was sure. The missing bits took away the careful balance of Kettricken's creation and added to the desolation of the garden in winter. I shut the door carefully behind me and went down the steps. Ever so slowly. Ever so carefully. On the ninth step down, I found it. I nearly discovered it as Kettricken had. But I caught my balance and then crouched low to study the step. Lampblack had been mixed with the grease, to take the sheen off it and blend it with the well-used steps. It was right where the foot would most naturally fall, especially if one were hastening down the stairs in a temper. Close enough to the tower top that a slip could be blamed on slush or mud from the gardens still on a shoe. I rubbed at the black on the step that came off on my fingers, then sniffed at it.

"A fine bit of pork fat," observed the Fool. I leaped to my feet and nearly fell down the steps. A wild pinwheeling of my arms brought my balance back.

"Interesting. Do you think you could teach me to do that?"

"Not funny, Fool. I have been followed of late, and my nerves are a-jangle." I peered down the stairwell into the darkness. If the Fool had crept up on me, could not Will? "How's the King?" I demanded quietly. If this attempt had been made on Kettricken, I had no faith in Shrewd's safety.

"You tell me." The Fool stepped out of the shadows. Gone were his fine clothes, replaced with an old motley of blue and red. It went well with the new bruises that mottled one side of his face. On his right cheek, the flesh had been split. One arm carried the other close to his chest. I suspected a dislocated shoulder.

"Not again," I gasped.

"Exactly what I said to them. They paid small attention. Some folk just have not the knack of conversation."

"What happened? I thought you and Regal—"

"Yes, well, not even a Fool can seem stupid enough to please Regal. I did not wish to leave King Shrewd's side today. They were questioning him relentlessly about what had happened the night of the feast. I became perhaps a trifle too witty in suggesting other ways they might amuse themselves. They threw me out."

My heart sank in me. I was sure I knew exactly which guard had assisted him out the door. It was as Burrich had always warned me. One could never know what Regal might dare. "What did the King tell them?"

"Ah! Not, was the King all right, or was the King recovering? No. Only what did the King tell them? Do you fear your precious hide is in danger, Princeling?"

"No." I could feel no resentment at his question, or even how he phrased it. I deserved it. I had not taken good care of our friendship lately. Despite that, when he needed help, he had come to me. "No. But as long as the King says nothing of Verity being alive, then Regal has no reason to—"

"My king was being . . . taciturn. It had started out as a pleasant conversation between father and son, with Regal telling him how pleased he should be to have him finally as king-in-waiting. King Shrewd was rather vague, as he often is these days. Something about it irritated Regal, and he began to accuse him of not being pleased, of even being opposed. Finally he began to insist there was a plot, a conspiracy to see that he never came to the throne. No man is so dangerous as the man who cannot decide what he fears. Regal is that man. Even Wallace was put ajar by his rantings. He had brought the King one of his brews, to deaden his mind along with his pain, but as he brought it near, Regal dashed it from his hands. He then spun on the poor trembling Wall's Ass and accused him of being part of the conspiracy. He claimed Wallace had intended to drug our king to keep him from speaking what he knew. He ordered Wallace from the room, saying the King would have no need of him until he had seen fit to speak plainly to his son. He ordered me out as well, then. My reluctance to leave was overcome by a couple of his hulking inland plowmen."

A creeping dread rose in me. I remembered my moment of

sharing the King's pain. Regal would remorselessly watch while that pain crept past the numbing herbs to overwhelm his father. I could not imagine a man being capable of this. Yet I knew Regal would do it. "When did this happen?"

"Just an hour or so ago. You are not an easy person to find."

I looked more closely at the Fool. "Go down to the stables, to Burrich. See what he can do for you." The healer, I knew, would not touch the Fool. Like many around the Keep, he feared his strange appearance.

"What will you be doing?" the Fool asked quietly.

"I don't know," I replied honestly. This was exactly one of the situations I had warned Chade about. I knew whether I acted or not, the consequences would be grave. I needed to distract Regal from what he was doing. Chade, I was sure, was aware of what was going on. If Regal and all others could be lured away for a time . . . I could think of only one piece of news that might be important enough to Regal to make him leave Shrewd.

"You'll be all right?"

The Fool had sunk down to sit on the cold stone steps. He leaned his head against the wall. "I suppose so. Go."

I started down the steps.

"Wait!" he called suddenly.

I halted.

"When you take my king away, I go with him."

I just stared up at him.

"I mean it. I wore Regal's collar for the sake of that promise from him. It means nothing now to him."

"I can make no promises," I said quietly.

"I can. I promise that if my king is taken, and I do not go with him, I will betray every one of your secrets. Every one." The Fool's voice was shaking. He put his head back against the wall.

I turned away hastily. The tears on his cheeks were tinged pink from the cuts on his face. I could not bear to see them. I ran down the stairs.

27

Conspiracy

The Pocked Man at your window
The Pocked Man at your door
The Pocked Man brings the plague days
To stretch you on the floor.

When blue flames at your candles suck
You know a witch has got your luck.

Don't suffer a snake upon your hearthstone
Or plague will whittle your children to bone.

Your bread not to rise, your milk to stand sour,
Your butter not to churn.
Your arrow shafts to twist as they dry,
Your own knife to turn and cut you,
Your roosters to crow by moonlight—
By these may a householder know himself cursed.

⊷═▷

"We will need blood from somewhere." Kettricken had heard me out, and now made this request as calmly as if asking for a cup of wine. She looked from Patience to Lacey seeking for ideas.

"I'll go fetch a chicken," Lacey said unwillingly at last. "I'll need a sack to put it in to keep it quiet—"

"Go then," Patience told her. "Go quickly. Bring it back to my room. I shall fetch a knife and a basin, and we shall do it there, and bring but a cup of the blood back here. The less we do here, the less we must conceal."

I had gone first to Patience and Lacey, knowing I would never get past the Queen's attendants on my own. While I made a quick visit to my room, they had gone before me to the Queen, ostensibly taking her a special herbal tea but really to quietly beg a private audience for me. She had dismissed all her ladies, telling them she would be fine with just Patience and Lacey, and then sent Rosemary to fetch me. Rosemary played by the hearth now, absorbed in dressing a doll.

As Lacey and Patience left the room Kettricken looked to me. "I will splatter my gown and my bedding with the blood, and I will send for Wallace, telling him I fear a miscarriage from my fall. But that is as far as I will go, Fitz. I will not allow that man to lay a hand on me, nor be so foolish as to drink or eat anything of his concocting. I do this only for the sake of distracting him from my king. Nor will I say I have lost the child. Only that I fear it." She spoke fiercely. It chilled me that she accepted so easily what Regal had done and was doing, and what I said she must do as a countermove. I wished desperately I was sure her trust in me was well placed. She did not speak of treachery or evil. She only discussed strategy as coldly as a general planning a battle.

"It will be enough," I promised her. "I know Prince Regal. Wallace will run to him with the tale, and he will follow Wallace here, no matter how inappropriate. He will not be able to resist, he will long to see exactly how well he has succeeded."

"It is tedious enough to have all my women always commiserating with me over Verity's death. It will be all I can bear to have them speak as if my child were gone as well. But I can bear it, if I must. What if they leave a guard with the King?" Kettricken asked.

"As soon as they leave to visit you, I intend to knock on the door and create a diversion. I will deal with any guard they have left."

"But if you are drawing off the guard, how can you hope to accomplish anything?"

"I have a . . . another who will be assisting me." I hoped. I cursed again that Chade had never let me establish some way of reaching him in situations such as this. "Trust me," he had always told me. "I watch, I listen where I should. I summon you when it is safe to do so. A secret is only a secret as long as only one man knows it." I would not confide to anyone that I had already divulged my plans to my fireplace, in the hopes Chade was somehow listening. I hoped that in the brief time I would be able to buy, Chade would find a way to the King, to bring him respite from his pain, that he might withstand Regal's badgering.

"It amounts to torture," Kettricken said quietly, as if able to read my thoughts. "To abandon an old man like that to his pain." She looked at me directly. "You do not trust your queen enough to tell me who your assistant is?"

"It is not my secret to share, but my king's," I told her gently. "Soon, I believe, it will have to be revealed to you. Until then—"

"Go," she dismissed me. She shifted uncomfortably on her couch. "As bruised as I am, at least I shall not have to feign misery. Only tolerance of a man who would seek to kill his unborn kin and torment his aged father."

"I go," I said quickly, sensing her rage building and not desiring to feed it. All must be convincing for this masquerade. She must not reveal that she now knew her fall had not been any clumsiness of her own. I went out, brushing past Lacey, who was carrying a tray with a teapot. Patience was on her heels. There would not be tea in that pot. As I went past the Queen's ladies in her antechamber, I took care to look concerned. Their reactions to the Queen's request that King Shrewd's personal healer be sent for would be genuine enough. I hoped it would be enough to draw Regal out of his lair.

I slipped into Patience's rooms and left the door just barely ajar. I waited. As I waited I thought of an old man, the herbs fading from his body and his pain reawakening in him. I had visited that pain. Given that, and a man relentlessly questioning me, how long could I remain silent and vague? Days seemed to pass. Finally there was a flurry of skirts and pattering footsteps down the hall, and a frenzied knocking at King Shrewd's door. I did not need to hear words, it was all in the tone, the frightened pleading of the women with someone at the door, then Regal's angry questions, turning suddenly to feigned concern. I heard him call Wallace from whatever corner he had been banished to, heard the excitement in his voice as he ordered the man to attend the Queen immediately, she was suffering a miscarriage.

The ladies clattered past my door again. I stood still, holding my breath. That trot, that mutter, that would be Wallace, laden no doubt with all sorts of remedies. I waited, taking slow quiet breaths, trying to be patient, waited until I was sure my ploy had failed. Then I heard the more deliberate strides of Regal, and then the running strides of a man overtaking him. "That's good wine, you idiot, don't jostle it," Regal rebuked him, and then they were out of my hearing. I waited again. Long after I was sure he had been admitted to the Queen's apartments, I forced myself to wait for another hundred count. And then I eased out of the door and went to the King's.

I tapped. I did not knock loudly, but my tapping was insistent and unending. After a moment or two a voice demanded to know who was there.

"FitzChivalry," I said boldly. "I demand to see the King."

A silence. Then: "No one is to be admitted."

"By whose order?"

"Prince Regal."

"I bear a token from the King, one on which he gave me his word that I would always be admitted to see him whenever I so wished."

"Prince Regal said specifically that you were not to be admitted."

"But that was before . . ." And I let my voice drop lower as I muttered a few meaningless syllables.

"What did you say?"

I muttered again.

"Speak up."

"This is not for all the Keep to hear!" I retorted indignantly. "This is no time to spread a panic."

That did it. The door opened a tiny crack. "What is it?" the man hissed.

I leaned in close to the door, looked up and down the

corridor. I peered past him through the crack. "Are you alone?" I asked suspiciously.

"Yes!" Impatiently. "Now what is it? It had better be good!"

I lifted my hands to my mouth as I leaned toward the door, unwilling to let the slightest breath of my secret escape. The guard leaned closer to the crack. I gave a quick puff of my lips and a white powder misted his face. He staggered back, clawing at his eyes and strangling. In an instant he was down. Nightmist: it was quick, it was effective. It was also often deadly. I could not find it in myself to care. It was not so much that this was my shoulder-wrenching friend. This guard could not have stood in the antechamber of Shrewd's room and been totally unaware of what went on within.

I had reached in through the crack and was struggling to undo the chains that secured the door when I heard a familiar hiss. "Get out of here. Leave the door alone, just go away. Don't unlatch it, you fool!" I had a brief glimpse of a pocked visage and then the door was shut firmly in my face. Chade was right. It would be best for Regal to encounter a fully latched door, and to spend his time having his men chop through it. Every moment Regal was shut out was another moment that Chade had with the King.

What followed was harder to do than what I had already done. I went down the stairs to the kitchen, made friendly talk with the cook, and then asked her what the commotion upstairs had been. Had the Queen lost her baby? She banished me quickly to find folk to talk to who would know more. I made my way into the watch room off the kitchen to consume a small beer and force myself to eat as if I wanted to. The food lay in my stomach like so much gravel. No one spoke to me much, but I was a presence. The gossip about the Queen's fall ebbed and flowed around me. There were Tilth and Farrow guards here now, big, slow-moving men, part of their dukes' retinues, hobnobbing with the Buckkeep counterparts. It was more bitter than bile to hear them speak avidly of what the loss of the child would mean to Regal's chances for the throne. It was as if they bet on a horse race.

The only other gossip that could compete with it was a

rumor that a boy had seen the Pocked Man by the castle well in the courtyard. It was supposed to have been nearly midnight when the lad saw him. Not one had the sense to wonder what the boy was doing out there, or what light his eyes had used to see this vision of ill omen. Instead they were vowing to stay well away from water, for surely this omen meant the well had gone bad. At the rate at which they were drinking beer, I decided they had little to worry about. I stayed until word was sent down that Regal wanted three strong men with axes sent immediately to the King's chambers. That excited a fresh round of talk, and during it, I quietly left the room and went to the stables.

I had intended to seek out Burrich and see if the Fool had found him yet. Instead I encountered Molly coming down his steep stairs just as I had begun to climb them. She looked down at the astounded look on my face and laughed. But it was a short laugh, and it never reached her eyes.

"Why did you go to see Burrich?" I demanded, and instantly realized how rude my question was. I had feared she had gone seeking help.

"He is my friend," she said succinctly. She started to push past me. Without thinking, I stood firm. "Let me past!" she hissed savagely.

Instead I put my arms around her. "Molly, Molly, please," I said hoarsely as she pushed at me without heart. "Let us find a place to talk, if only for a moment. I cannot bear to have you look at me that way, when I swear I have done you no wrong. You act as if I have cast you off, but you are in my heart always. If I cannot be with you, it is not because I do not wish to."

She stopped struggling suddenly.

"Please?" I begged her.

She glanced about the dim barn. "We will stand and we will talk. Briefly. Right here."

"Why are you so angry with me?"

She nearly answered me. I saw her bite back words, then turn suddenly cold. "Why do you think that what I feel about you is the centermost pillar of my life?" she retorted. "Why do you think I have no other concerns but you?"

I gaped at her. "Perhaps because it is how I feel about you," I said gravely.

"It is not." She was exasperated, correcting me the way she would correct a child who insisted the sky was green.

"It is," I insisted. I tried to gather her to me, but she was wooden in my arms.

"Your king-in-waiting Verity was more important. King Shrewd is more important. Queen Kettricken and her unborn child are more important." She ticked them off on her fingers as if she were numbering my faults.

"I know my duty," I said quietly.

"I know where your heart is," she said flatly. "And it is not first with me."

"Verity is . . . is no longer here to protect his queen, his child, or his father," I said reasonably. "So, for this time, I must put them ahead of my own life. Ahead of everything I hold dear. Not because I love them more but . . ." I floundered uselessly after words. "I am a King's Man," I said helplessly.

"I am my own woman." Molly made it the loneliest statement in the world. "I will take care of myself."

"Not forever," I protested. "Someday we will be free. Free to wed, to do—"

"Whatever your king asks you to do," she finished for me. "No, Fitz." There was finality in her voice. Pain. She pushed away from me, stepped past me on the staircase. When she was two steps away and all of winter seemed to be blowing between us, she spoke.

"I have to tell you something," she said, almost gently. "There is another in my life now. One who is for me what your king is for you. One who comes before my own life, who comes ahead of all else I hold dear. By your own words, you cannot fault me." She looked back up at me.

I do not know what I looked like, only that she looked aside as if she could not bear it.

"For the sake of that one, I am going away," she told me. "To a safer place than this."

"Molly, please, he cannot love you as I do," I begged.

She did not look at me. "Nor can your king love you as

I . . . used to. But. It is not a matter of what he feels for me,"
she said slowly. "It is what I feel for him. He must be first in
my life. He needs that from me. Understand this. It is not that I
no longer care for you. It is that I cannot put that feeling ahead
of what is best for him." She went down two more steps.
"Good-bye, Newboy." She no more than breathed those final
words, but they sank into my heart as if branded there.

I stood on the steps, watching her go. And suddenly that
feeling was too familiar, the pain too well-known. I flung myself down the steps after her, I seized her arm, I pulled her
under the loft stairs into the darkness there. "Molly," I said,
"please."

She said nothing. She did not even resist my grip on her
arm.

"What can I give you, what can I tell you to make you
understand what you are to me? I can't just let you go!"

"No more can you make me stay," she pointed out in a
low voice. I felt something go out of her. Some anger, some
spirit, some will. I have no word for it. "Please," she said, and
the word hurt me, because she begged. "Just let me go. Don't
make it hard. Don't make me cry."

I let go of her arm, but she did not leave.

"A long time ago," she said carefully, "I told you that
you were like Burrich."

I nodded in the darkness, not caring that she could not see
me.

"In some ways you are. In others you are not. I decide for
us, now, as he once decided for Patience and himself. There is
no future for us. Someone already fills your heart. And the gap
between our stations is too great for any love to bridge. I know
that you love me. But your love is . . . different from mine. I
wanted us to share all our lives. You wish to keep me in a box,
separate from your life. I cannot be someone you come to
when you have nothing more important to do. I don't even
know what it is that you do when you are not with me. You
have never even shared that much with me."

"You wouldn't like it," I told her. "You don't really want
to know."

"Don't tell me that," she whispered angrily. "Don't you

ee that that is what I cannot live with, that you do not let me
ven decide that for myself? You cannot make that decision for
1e. You have no right! If you cannot even tell me that, how can
believe you love me?''

''I kill people,'' I heard myself say. ''For my king. I'm an
ssassin, Molly.''

''I don't believe you!'' she whispered. She spoke too
uickly. The horror in her voice was as great as the contempt.
\ part of her knew I had spoken the truth to her. Finally. A
errible silence, brief but so cold, grew between us as she
vaited for me to admit a lie. A lie she knew was truth. At last
he denied it for me. ''You, a killer? You couldn't even run past
he guard that day to see why I was crying! You didn't have the
ourage to defy them for me! But you want me to believe you
ill people for the King.'' She made a choking sound, of anger
nd despair. ''Why do you say such things now? Why now, of
ll times? To impress me?''

''If I had thought it would impress you, I probably would
1ave told you a long time ago,'' I confessed. And it was true.
Vly ability to keep my secrets had been soundly based on my
ear that telling Molly would mean losing her. I was right.

''Lies,'' she said, more to herself than me. ''Lies, all lies.
rom the very beginning. I was so stupid. If a man hits you
once, he'll hit you again, they say. And the same is true for
ying. But I stayed, and I listened and I believed. What a fool
've been!'' This last, so savagely that I recoiled from it as
rom a blow. She stood clear of me. ''Thank you,
itzChivalry,'' she said coldly, formally. ''You've made this so
nuch easier for me.'' She turned away from me.

''Molly,'' I begged. I reached to take her arm, but she
pun about, her hand raised to slap me.

''Don't touch me,'' she warned in a low voice. ''Don't
ou ever dare to touch me again!''

She left.

After a time I remembered I was standing under Burrich's
tairs in the dark. I shivered with cold and something more.
No. Something less. My lips drew back from my teeth in some-
hing neither a smile nor a snarl. I had always feared that my
ies would make me lose Molly. But the truth had severed in an

instant what my lies had held together for a year. What must
learn from that? I wondered. Very slowly I climbed up the
steps. I knocked on the door.

"Who is it?" Burrich's voice.

"Me." He unlatched the door and I came into the room
"What was Molly doing here?" I asked him, not caring how i
might sound, not caring that the bandaged Fool sat still a
Burrich's table. "Did she need help?"

Burrich cleared his throat. "She came for herbs," he said
uneasily. "I could not help her, I did not have what she wanted
Then the Fool came, and she stayed to help me with him."

"Patience and Lacey have herbs. Lots of them," I pointed
out.

"That is what I told her." He turned away from me, and
began clearing away the things he had used to work on the
Fool. "She did not wish to go to them." There was something
in his voice, almost prodding, pushing me to the next question

"She's going away," I said in a small voice. "She's going
away." I sat down on a chair before Burrich's fire and
clenched my hands between my knees. I became aware I was
rocking back and forth, tried to stop.

"Did you succeed?" the Fool asked quietly.

I stopped rocking. I swear that for an instant I had no idea
what he was talking about. "Yes," I said quietly. "Yes, I think
I did." I had succeeded at losing Molly, too. Succeeded a
wearing away her loyalty and her love, taking her for granted
succeeded at being so logical and practical and loyal to my
king that I had just lost any chance of ever having a life of my
own. I looked at Burrich. "Did you love Patience?" I asked
suddenly. "When you decided to leave?"

The Fool started, then visibly goggled. So there were some
secrets even he did not know. Burrich's face went as dark as I
had ever seen it. He crossed his arms on his chest, as if to
restrain himself. He might kill me, I thought. Or maybe he
sought only to hold some pain inside himself. "Please," I
added, "I have to know."

He glared at me, then spoke carefully. "I am not a change-
able man," he told me. "If I had loved her, I would love her
still."

So. It would never go away. "But, still, you decided—"

"Someone had to decide. Patience would not see it could not be. Someone had to end the torment for us both."

As Molly had decided for us. I tried to think just what I should do next. Nothing came to me. I looked at the Fool. "Are you all right?" I asked him.

"I'm better off than you are," he replied sincerely.

"I meant, your shoulder. I had thought . . ."

"Wrenched, but not broken. Much better than your heart."

A quick bantering of witty words. I had not known he could weight a jest with so much sympathy. The kindness pushed me to the edge of breaking. "I don't know what to do," I said brokenly. "How can I live with this?"

The brandy bottle made a very small thud as Burrich set it in the center of the table. He put out three cups around it. "We will have a drink," he said. "To Molly finding happiness somewhere. We will wish it for her with all our hearts."

We drank a round and Burrich refilled the cups.

The Fool swirled the brandy in his cup. "Is this wise, just now?" he asked.

"Just now, I am done with being wise," I told him. "I would rather be a fool."

"You do not know of what you speak," he told me. All the same, he raised his glass alongside mine. To fools of all kinds. And a third time, to our king.

We made a sincere effort, but fate did not allow us sufficient time. A determined rapping at Burrich's door proved to be Lacey with a basket on her arm. She came in quickly, shutting the door fast behind her. "Get rid of this for me, will you?" she asked, and tumbled the slain chicken out on the table before us.

"Dinner!" announced the Fool enthusiastically.

It took Lacey a moment to realize the state we were in. It took her less than that to be furious. "While we gamble our lives and reputations, you get drunk!" She rounded on Burrich. "In twenty years, you have not learned that it solves nothing!"

Burrich flinched not at all. "Some things cannot be

solved,'' he pointed out philosophically. "Drink makes those things much more tolerable.'' He came to his feet easily, stood rock steady before her. Years of drinking seemed to have taught him the knack of handling it well. "What did you need?''

Lacey bit her lip a moment. She decided to follow where he had pointed the conversation. "I need that disposed of. And I need an ointment for bruises.''

"Does no one around here ever use the healer?'' the Fool asked of no one in particular. Lacey ignored him.

"That is what I supposedly came here for, so I had best return with it, in case someone asks to see it. My real mission is to find the Fitz, and ask him if he knows there are guards chopping down King Shrewd's door with axes.''

I nodded gravely. I wasn't going to attempt Burrich's graceful stance. The Fool leaped to his feet instead, crying, "What?'' He rounded on me. "I thought you said you had succeeded! What success is this?''

"The best I could manage on very short notice,'' I retorted. "It will either be all right, or it won't. We've done all we can just now. Besides, think on it. That's a good stout oaken door. It will take them a while to get through it. And when they do, I fancy they will find the inner door to the King's bedchamber is likewise bolted and barred.''

"How did you manage that?'' Burrich asked quietly.

"I didn't,'' I said brusquely. I looked at the Fool. "I have said enough, for now. It is time to have a bit of trust.'' I turned to Lacey. "How are the Queen and Patience? How went our masquerade?''

"Well enough. The Queen is sore bruised from her fall, and for myself, I am not all that sure that the babe is out of danger of being lost. A miscarriage from a fall does not always happen immediately. But let us not borrow trouble. Wallace was concerned but ineffectual. For a man who claims to be a healer, he knows remarkably little of the true lore of herbs. As for the Prince . . .'' Lacey snorted, but said no more.

"Does no one beside myself think there is a danger to letting a rumor of a miscarriage circulate?'' the Fool asked airily.

"I had no time to devise anything else," I retorted. "In a day or so, the Queen will deny the rumor, saying that all seems to be well with the child."

"So. For the moment we are as secured as we may be," Burrich observed. "But what comes next? Are we to see the King and Queen Kettricken carried off to Tradeford?"

"Trust. I ask for one day of trust," I said carefully. I hoped it would be enough. "And now we must disperse and go about our lives as normally as we can."

"A stablemaster with no horses and a Fool with no king," the Fool observed. "Burrich and I can continue to drink. I believe that is a normal life under these circumstances. As for you, Fitz, I have no idea what title you give yourself these days, let alone what you normally do all day. Hence—"

"No one is going to sit about and drink," Lacey intoned ominously. "Put the bottle aside and keep your wits sharp. And disperse, as Fitz here said. Enough has been said and done in this room to put us all swinging from a tree for treason. Save you, of course, FitzChivalry. It would have to be poison for you. Those of the royal blood are not allowed to swing."

Her words had a chilling effect. Burrich picked up the cork and restoppered the bottle. Lacey left first, a pot of Burrich's ointment in her basket. The Fool followed her a short time later. When I left Burrich, he had finished cleaning the fowl and was plucking the last stubborn feathers from it. The man wasted nothing.

I went out and wandered about a bit. I watched behind me for shadows. Kettricken would be resting, and I did not think I could withstand Patience's nattering, or her insights just then. If the Fool was in his chamber, it was because he did not want company. And if he was elsewhere, I had no idea where that might be. The whole of Buckkeep was as plagued with Inlanders as a sick dog with fleas. I strolled through the kitchen, purloining gingerbread. Then I wandered about disconsolately, trying not to think, trying to appear without purpose as I headed back to the hut where once I had hidden Nighteyes. The hut was empty now, as cold within as without. It had been some time since Nighteyes had laired here. He preferred the forested hills behind Buckkeep. But I did not wait long before his shadow crossed the threshold of the open door.

Perhaps the greatest comfort of the Wit bond is never having to explain. I did not need to recount the last day's events to him, did not have to find words to describe how it felt to watch Molly walk away from me. Nor did he ask questions or make sympathetic talk. The human events would have made small sense to him. He acted on the strength of what I felt, not why. He simply came to me and sat beside me on the dirty floor. I could put an arm around him and lean my face against his ruff and sit.

Such packs men make, he observed to me after a while. *How can you hunt together when you cannot all run in the same direction?*

I made no reply to this. I knew no answer and he did not expect one.

He leaned down to nibble an itch on his foreleg. Then he sat up, shook himself all over, and asked, *What will you do for a mate now?*

Not all wolves take mates.

The leader always does. How else would the pack multiply?

My leader has a mate, and she is with child. Perhaps wolves have it aright, and men should pay attention. Perhaps only the leader should mate. That was the decision that Heart of the Pack made long ago. That he could not have both a mate, and a leader he followed with all of his heart.

That one is more wolf than he cares to admit. To anyone. A pause. *Gingerbread?*

I gave it to him. He gobbled it greedily while I watched.

I've missed your dreams at night.

They are not my dreams. They are my life. You are welcome to them, so long as Heart of the Pack does not get angry with us. Life shared is better. A pause. *You would rather have shared the female's life.*

It is my weakness to want too much.

He blinked his deep eyes. *You love too many. My life is much simpler.*

He loved only me.

That is true. The only real difficulty I have is knowing that you will never trust that is so.

I sighed heavily. Nighteyes sneezed suddenly, then shook himself all over. *I mislike this mouse dust. But before I go, use your so clever hands to scratch inside my ears. It is hard for me to do well without leaving welts.*

And so I scratched his ears, and under his throat and the back of his neck, until he fell over on his side like a puppy.

"Hound," I told him affectionately.

For that insult, you pay! He flipped himself up onto his feet, bit me hard through my sleeve, and then darted out the door and was gone. I pulled back my sleeve to survey the deep white dents in my flesh that were not quite bleeding. Wolf humor.

The brief winter day had ended. I went back to the Keep and forced myself to go through the kitchens, to allow Cook to tell me all the gossip. She stuffed me full of plum cake and mutton as she told me of the Queen's possible miscarriage, and then how the men had chopped through the outer door of the King's room after his guard had suddenly perished of apoplexy. "And the second door, too, all the time Prince Regal worriting and urging them on, for fear something had befallen the King himself. But when they got through, despite all that chopping, the King was sleeping like a babe, sir. And so deep a sleep they could not rouse him at all, to tell him why they'd chopped his doors away."

"Amazing," I agreed, and she went on to the lesser gossip of the Keep. I found that centered these days mostly on who was and was not included in the flight to Tradeford. Cook was to go, for the sake of her gooseberry tarts and bundle cakes. She did not know who was to take over the cooking here, but no doubt it would be one of the guards. Regal had told her she might take all her best pots, for which she was grateful, but what she would really miss was the west hearth, for she had never cooked on a better, for the draft being just right and the meat hooks at all the right heights. I listened to her, and tried to think only of her words, to be fully intrigued by the small details of what she considered important in her life. The Queen's guard, I found, was to stay at Buckkeep, as would those few who still wore the colors of King Shrewd's personal guard. Since they had lost the privilege of his rooms, they had become a dispirited lot. But Regal insisted it was necessary those groups stay, to maintain a royal presence in Buckkeep. Rosemary would go, and her mother, but that was hardly surprising, seeing as who they served. Fedwren would not, nor Mellow. Now, there was a voice she would miss, but she'd probably get used to that inland warbling after a while.

She never thought to ask me if I was going.

As I climbed the stairs to my room I tried to visualize Buckkeep as it would be. The High Table would be empty at every meal, the food served would be the simple campaign food the military cooks were most familiar with. For as long as the food supplies lasted. I expected we would eat a lot of wild game and seaweed before spring. I worried more for Patience and Lacey than I did for myself. Rough quarters and coarse food did not bother me, but it was not what they were used to. At least there would be Mellow still to sing, if his melancholy nature did not overtake him at his abandonment. And Fedwren. With few children to teach, perhaps he and Patience could finally study out their paper making. So putting a brave face on it all, I tried to find a future for us.

"Where have you been, Bastard?"

Serene, stepping out suddenly from a doorway. She had expected me to startle. I had known by the Wit someone was there. I did not flinch. "Out."

"You smell like a dog."

"At least I have the excuse of having been with dogs. What few are left in the stable."

It took her an instant to discover the insult in my polite reply.

"You smell like a dog because you are more than half a dog yourself. Beast-magicker."

I nearly responded with some remark about her mother. Instead, I suddenly and truly recalled her mother. "When we were first learning to scribe, remember how your mother always made you wear a dark smock, for you splattered your ink so?"

She stared at me sullenly, turning the remark every which

way in her mind, trying to discover some insult or slight or trick in it.

"What of it?" she asked at last, unable to leave it hanging.

"Nothing. I but remembered it. Was a time when I helped you getting the tails right on your letters."

"That has nothing to do with now!" she declared angrily.

"No, it does not. This is my door. Were you expecting to come in with me?"

She spat, not quite at me, but it landed on the floor at my feet. For some reason, I decided she would not have done it had not she been leaving Buckkeep with Regal. It was no longer her home, and she felt free to soil it before leaving it. It told me much. She never expected to come back here.

Inside my room, I reset every latch and bolt meticulously, then added the heavy bar to the door. I went and checked my window and found it well shuttered still. I looked under my bed. Finally, I sat down in a chair by my hearth to doze until Chade summoned me.

I came out of a light doze to a tapping at my door. "Who is it?" I called.

"Rosemary. The Queen wishes to see you."

By the time I had undone the latches and catches, the child was gone. She was only a girl, but it still unnerved me to have such a message vocalized through a door. I groomed myself hastily and then hurried down to the Queen's chambers. I noted in passing the wreckage that had once been the oak door to Shrewd's room. A bulky guard stood in the gap; an Inlander, not a man I knew.

Queen Kettricken was reclining on a couch near her hearth. Several knots of her ladies gossiped in different corners of the room, but the Queen herself was alone. Her eyes were closed. She looked so utterly worn that I wondered if Rosemary's message had been an error. But Lady Hopeful ushered me to the Queen's side and fetched me a low stool to perch upon. She offered me a cup of tea and I accepted. As soon as Lady Hopeful departed to brew it, Kettricken opened her eyes. "What next?" she asked in so low a voice that I had to lean closer to hear it.

I looked askance at her.

"Shrewd sleeps now. He cannot sleep forever. Whatever was given him will wear off, and when it does, we are back to where we were."

"The King-in-Waiting ceremony approaches. Perhaps the Prince will be busied with that. No doubt there are new clothes to be sewn and tried upon him, and all the other details he glories in. It may keep him from the King."

"After that?"

Lady Hopeful was back with my cup of tea. I took it with murmured thanks, and as she pulled up a chair beside us, Queen Kettricken smiled weakly and asked if she might have one also. I was almost shamed by how swiftly Lady Hopeful leaped to do her bidding.

"I do not know," I murmured in reply to her earlier question.

"I do. The King would be safe in my Mountains. He would be honored and protected, and perhaps Jonqui would know of—oh, thank you, Hopeful." Queen Kettricken took the proffered cup and sipped at it as Lady Hopeful settled herself.

I smiled at Kettricken, and chose my words carefully, trusting her to read my meaning. "But it is so far to the Mountains, my queen, and the weather so hard this time of year. By the time a courier got through to seek your mother's remedy, it would be nigh on to spring. There are other places that might offer the same cure for your troubles. Bearns or Rippon, perhaps, might offer if we asked. The worthy Dukes of those provinces can deny you nothing, you know."

"I know," Kettricken smiled wearily. "But they have such problems of their own just now, I hesitate to ask anything more of them. Besides, the root we call livelong grows only in the Mountains. A determined courier could travel there, I think." She sipped again at her tea.

"Who to send with such a request; ah, that would be the hardest question," I pointed out. Surely she could see the difficulties of sending a sick old man off on a journey to the Mountains in winter. He could not go alone. "The man that went would have to be very trustworthy and strong of will."

"Such a man sounds like a woman to me," Kettricken quipped, and Hopeful laughed merrily, more to see the

Queen's mood lightened than at the witticism. Kettricken paused with her cup at her lips. "Perhaps I should have to go myself, to see the thing done right," she added, and smiled when my eyes widened. But the look she gave me was serious.

There followed some light talk, and a recipe of mostly fictitious herbs from Kettricken that I promised to do my best to find for her. I believed I took her meaning. When I excused myself and went back to my room, I wondered how I would keep her from acting before Chade could. It was a pretty puzzle.

I had scarcely refastened all my door catches and bars before I felt a draft up my back. I turned to find the entry to Chade's realm standing ajar. I climbed the stairs wearily. I longed to sleep, but knew that once I lay down, I would be unable to close my eyes.

The smell of food enticed me as I entered Chade's chamber, and I was suddenly aware I was hungry. Chade was already at the small table he had set out. "Sit down and eat," he told me tersely. "We must plot together."

I was two bites into a meat pie when he asked me softly, "How long do you think we might keep King Shrewd here, in these chambers, undetected?"

I chewed and swallowed. "I've never been able to find a way into this chamber," I pointed out quietly.

"Oh, but they do exist. And as food and other necessities must go in and out of them, there are some few who are aware of them, without knowing exactly what they know. My warren connects to rooms in the Keep which are regularly stocked with supplies for me. But my life was much simpler when food and linens were supplied for Lady Thyme."

"How will you fare after Regal is gone to Tradeford?" I asked.

"Likely not as well as I have. Some tasks will be done out of habit, if those with the habits remain, no doubt. But as food becomes scarcer some will wonder why they store supplies of it in a disused part of the Keep. But we were speaking of Shrewd's comfort, not mine."

"It depends on how Shrewd disappeared. If Regal thought he had left the Keep by ordinary means, you might keep him hidden here for some time. But if Regal knows he is within Buckkeep still, he will stop at nothing. I suspect his first order would be to put men with hammers to work on the walls of the King's bedchamber.''

"Direct, but effective,'' Chade concurred.

"Have you found a safe place for him, at Bearns or Rippon?''

"As swift as that? Of course not. We would have to hide him here, for days or perhaps weeks before a place was made ready. And then he must be smuggled out of the Keep. It would mean finding men who can be bribed, and knowing when they are on the gate. Unfortunately, men that can be bribed to do a thing can be bribed to speak of it later. Unless they had accidents.'' He looked at me.

"Let that not be a concern. There is another way out of Buckkeep,'' I told him, thinking of my wolf's way. "We have another problem also, and that is Kettricken. She will act on her own if she does not soon know we have a plan. Her own thoughts have taken her in the same direction as yours. Tonight she proposed herself taking Shrewd to the Mountains for safety.''

"A pregnant woman and a sick old man in midwinter? Ridiculous.'' Chade paused. "But. It would never be expected. They would never look for them on that road. And with all the flow of folk that Regal has created going up the Buck River, one more woman and her ailing father would scarcely be marked.''

"It's still ridiculous,'' I protested. I did not like the sparks of interest I had seen kindle in Chade's eyes. "Who could go with them?''

"Burrich. It would save him from drinking himself to death from boredom, and he could manage their animals for them. And likely much else they would need. Would he go?''

"You know he would,'' I said unwillingly. "But Shrewd would never survive such a trip.''

"He is more likely to survive such a trip than to survive going with Regal. That which eats at him will continue to devour his life, wherever he is.'' He frowned more darkly.

''But why it eats at him so much more swiftly these days is beyond me to say.''

''The cold. The privation. It will not help him.''

''There are inns for part of the way. I can find some coin for them yet. Shrewd looks so little like he used to, we almost need not fear him being recognized. The Queen would be trickier. There are few women with her coloring and height. Still, clothed heavily, we could increase her girth. Hood her hair, and—''

''You cannot be serious.''

''Tomorrow night,'' he replied. ''We must do something by tomorrow night. For that is when the sleeping potion I gave Shrewd will wear off. Another attempt will probably not be made on the Queen until she is on her way to Tradeford. But once Regal has her in his power, well, so many accidents can happen on a journey. A slip from a barge into a freezing river, a runaway horse, a meal of bad meat. If his assassin is half as good as we are, he'll succeed.''

''Regal's assassin?''

Chade gave me a pitying look. ''You don't suppose our prince is up to spreading grease and lampblack on steps himself, do you? Who do you think it is?''

''Serene.'' The name popped to my lips.

''Then most obviously it is not her. No, we will find it to be some mouse of a man with a pleasant demeanor and a settled life. If we ever find him out at all. Ah, well, set it aside for now. Though there's nothing quite as challenging as stalking another assassin.''

''Will,'' I said quietly.

''Will what?'' he asked.

I told him of Will, quickly and quietly. As he listened his eyes widened.

''It would be brilliant,'' he said admiringly. ''A Skilled assassin. It's a wonder no one thought of it before.''

''Perhaps Shrewd did,'' I said quietly. ''But perhaps his assassin failed to learn. . . .''

Chade leaned back in his chair. ''I wonder,'' he said speculatively. ''Shrewd is closemouthed enough to have such an idea, and keep it even from me. But I doubt, myself, that

Will is any more than a spy, just now. A formidable one, and no mistaking that. You must be especially vigilant. But I do not think we need fear him as an assassin.'' He cleared his throat. ''Ah, well. The urgency for speed becomes ever plainer. The escape must be made from the King's room. You must find a way to draw the watchers all off again.''

''During the King-in-Waiting ceremony—''

''No. We dare not wait that long. Tomorrow night. No later than that. You need not keep them occupied long. Just a few minutes will be all I will need.''

''We must wait! Otherwise, the whole plot is impossible. By tomorrow night, you wish me to have the Queen and Burrich prepared, which means telling them you exist. And Burrich will have to see to horses and supplies—''

''Plug horses. Nothing fine. They would be noticed too quickly. And a litter for the King.''

''Plug horses we have in plenty, for they are all that is left. But it will stick in Burrich's craw for his king and queen to ride them.''

''And a mule for himself. They are to be humble folk, with scarce the coin to journey inland. We have no wish to attract highwaymen.''

I snorted to think of Burrich astride a mule. ''It cannot be done,'' I said quietly. ''The time is too short. It must be done the night of the King-in-Waiting ceremony. All will be down at the feasting.''

''Anything that must be done, can be done,'' Chade asserted. He sat thoughtfully a moment. ''Perhaps you have a point. Regal cannot have the King incapacitated for the ceremony. If he is not there, not one of the Coastal Dukes will give it any credence. Regal will have to allow Shrewd his pain herbs, to keep him tractable, if nothing else. Very well, then. The night after tomorrow. And if you absolutely must speak to me tomorrow, put some bitterbark on your hearthfire. Not a lot, I have no wish to be smoked out. But a generous handful. I will open the way.''

''The Fool will want to go with the King.'' I reminded myself slowly.

''He cannot,'' Chade said decisively. ''There is no disguising him. He would only increase the danger. Besides, it is necessary he stay. We will need his help to prepare for this disappearance.''

''I do not think that will change his mind.''

''Leave the Fool to me. I can show him that his King's life depends on his getting away from here cleanly. An 'atmosphere' must be created, in which the King and Queen's disappearance is not seen as . . . ah, well. Leave that part to me. I will discourage them from smashing walls. The Queen's role is easy. All she need do is retire early from the ceremony, and declare that she wishes to sleep long, and send her attendants away. She should leave word she does not wish to be disturbed until she summons them. If all goes well, we should be able to give Shrewd and Kettricken most of the night hours to gain some distance.'' He smiled at me kindly. ''Well. I think that is as much planning as we can do. No, no, I know nothing is fixed. It is better this way. We are more flexible. Now go get what sleep you can, boy. You've a busy day tomorrow. And I've much to do right now. I must mix enough medicines to take King Shrewd all the way to the Mountains. And package them clearly. Burrich reads, does he not?''

''Very well,'' I assured him. I paused. ''Were you at the Keep well last night, about midnight? Supposedly the Pocked Man was seen. Some are saying it means the well will go bad. Others are seeing it as a bad omen for Regal's ceremony.''

''Oh? Well, and perhaps it is.'' Chade chuckled to himself. ''Omens and portents they shall have, boy, until a vanishing King and a missing Queen seem but a natural thing in the midst of it.'' He grinned like a boy, and the years dropped from his face. Something like their old spark of mischief came into his green eyes. ''Go get some rest. And let Burrich and the Queen know of our plans. I shall speak to Shrewd and the Fool. No others are to know even a whisper. For some of it, we must trust to luck. But for the rest, trust to me!''

His laughter was not a wholly reassuring sound as it followed me down the stairs.

28

Treasons and Traitors

PRINCE REGAL WAS *the only child of King Shrewd and Queen Desire to survive birth. Some say the midwives never cared for the Queen and did not do overmuch to see her babes lived. Others that the midwives, in their anxiety to spare the Queen her birth pangs, gave her too much of those herbs that dull pain. But as only two of her stillborn children had been carried more than seven months in her womb, most midwives say the Queen's use of intoxicants was at fault, as well as her evil habit of carrying her belt knife with the blade toward her belly, as all know this is bad luck for a woman of childbearing years.*

⚜

I did not sleep. Whenever I pushed my worries about King Shrewd from my mind, Molly stood there instead, beside someone else. My mind shuttled between them, weaving me a coat of misery and worry. I promised myself that as soon as King Shrewd and Kettricken were safe, I would find a way to win Molly back from whoever had stolen her from me. That decided, I turned over and stared into the dark some more.

Night's reign was still solid when I rolled from my bed. I ghosted past empty stalls and sleeping animals to go silently up

Burrich's stairs. He heard me out, then asked gently, "Are you sure you've not had a bad dream?"

"If I have, it's lasted most of my life," I pointed out quietly.

"I begin to feel that way myself," he agreed. We were talking in the dark. He was still in bed and I was sitting on the floor beside it, whispering. I would not suffer Burrich to build up his fire, or even light a candle, for I did not desire anyone to wonder about a sudden departure from his routine. "For us to accomplish all he is asking in two days means that every task must be done perfectly the first time. I have come to you first. Can you do it?"

He was silent and in the darkness I could not see his face. "Three sturdy horses, a mule, a litter, and supplies for three. All without anyone noticing it." Another silence. "I can't very well just load up the King and Queen and ride out through the gates of Buckkeep, either."

"You know that copse of alder where the big dog fox used to den? Have the horses waiting there. The King and Kettricken will meet you there." Reluctantly I added, "The wolf will guide them to you."

"Must they know, as well as I, what you do?" He was aghast at the thought.

"I use what tools I have. And I do not perceive it as you do."

"How long can you share minds with one who scratches and licks himself, who will roll in carrion, who goes mad when a female is in season, who thinks no further than his next meal, before you accept his values as your own? Then what will you be?"

"A guardsman?" I hazarded.

Despite himself, Burrich gave a snort of laughter. "I was serious," he said after a moment.

"So am I, about the King and Queen. We must put our minds to how we will accomplish this. I no longer care what I sacrifice to accomplish it."

He was quiet a moment. "So somehow I'm to get four animals and a litter out of Buckkeep without exciting any interest?"

I nodded in the dark, then: "Can it be done?"

Grudgingly he said, "There's a stable hand or two left that I trust. It's not a favor I like to ask of anyone. I don't want a lad swinging over something I asked him to do. But I suppose it could be made to look as if they were part of a coffle being taken upriver. But my lads are not stupid; I won't have a stupid hand in the stable. Once the news is out that the King is missing, they'll figure it out quickly."

"Choose one who loves the King."

Burrich sighed. "Food supplies. It won't be sumptuous rations. More like marching fare. Am I to supply winter clothing as well?"

"No. Only for yourself. Kettricken can wear and carry what she'll need. And Chade can see to the King's needs."

"Chade. The name is almost familiar, as if I heard it before, long ago."

"He is supposed to have died, long ago. Before that, he was seen about the Keep."

"To live all these years as a shadow." He marveled.

"And he plans to go on living as a shadow."

"You need not fear I'll betray him." Burrich sounded hurt.

"I know. I am just so—"

"I know. Go on, then. You've told me enough for me to do my part. I'll be there with the horses and supplies. What time?"

"Sometime in the night, when the feasting is still lively. I don't know. I'll get word to you somehow."

He shrugged. "As soon as it gets dark, I'll go out there and wait."

"Burrich. Thank you."

"He is my king. She is my queen. I need no thanks from you to do my duty."

I left Burrich to creep down his staircase. I kept to the shadows and extended every sense I had to try to be sure no one was spying on me. Once I was clear of the stables, I flitted from warehouse to sty to pen, from shadow to shadow until I came to the old hut. Nighteyes came panting to meet me. *What is it? Why am I called back from my hunting?*

Tomorrow night, when it gets dark. I may need you. Will you stay here, within the Keep, to come quickly if I send for you?

Of course. But why summon me here for this? You need not be this close to me to ask such a simple favor.

I crouched down in the snow and he came to me, to rest his throat on my shoulder. I hugged him hard.

Foolishness, he told me gruffly. *Go on, now. I will be here in case you need me.*

My thanks.

My brother.

Stealth and haste battled as I made my way back to the Keep and up to my room. I fastened my door shut and lay down on my bed. Excitement thundered through me. I would know no real rest until all had been accomplished.

At midmorning I was admitted to the Queen's chamber. I brought with me a number of scrolls on herbs. Kettricken was reclining on a couch before the hearth, playing the part of both bereaved wife and anxious mother-to-be. I could see that it wore on her, and that her fall had caused her more pain in truth than she cared to admit. She looked little better than she had the night before, but I greeted her warmly and proceeded to work my way through every herb listed, one after the other, with much discussion as to the benefits of each. I succeeded in boring most of her ladies away, and she finally dismissed the last three to bring tea, find her more pillows, and look for another scroll on herbs that Kettricken said was in Verity's study. Little Rosemary had long since dozed off in a warm corner by the hearth. As soon as the rustle of their skirts had faded, I spoke quickly, knowing I had little time.

"You will be leaving tomorrow night, after the King-in-Waiting ceremony," I told her, and spoke on although she had parted her lips to ask a question. "Dress warmly and take winter things. Not many. Go to your bedchamber alone, as early as you decently can. Plead that the ceremony and your grief have exhausted you. Send your attendants away, say you must sleep, and tell them not to come back until you summon them. Bar your door. No. Only listen. There is little time. Ready yourself to leave, and then stay in your room. One will come for you. Trust the Pocked Man. The King is going with you. Trust me,'' I told her desperately as we heard returning footsteps. "All else will be arranged. Trust me.''

Trust. I did not trust that any of it would come to pass. Daffodil was back with the pillows, and shortly after that, the tea arrived. We chatted amiably, and one of Kettricken's younger ladies even flirted with me. Queen Kettricken asked me to leave the herbal scrolls with her, as her back still pained her. She had decided she would retire early this evening, and perhaps the scrolls would help her while away the time before she slept. I made my gracious farewells and escaped.

Chade had said he would handle the Fool. I had made my pathetic attempts at planning the escape. Now all that remained was for me somehow to arrange for the King to be alone after the ceremony. A few minutes were all Chade had asked for. I wondered if I would have to give my life for them. I put the notion aside. Just a few minutes. The two broken doors would be a hindrance or a help. I wasn't sure which. I considered all the obvious ploys. I could feign drunkenness and bait the guards out to fight. Unless I had an ax, it wouldn't take them more than a few minutes to deal with me. Plain fisticuffs had never worked very well for me. No. I wanted to remain functional. I considered and rejected a dozen schemes. Too much depended on factors I couldn't control. How many guards would be there, would they be ones I knew, would Wallace be there, would Regal have dropped by for a chat?

On my earlier foray to Kettricken's room, I had noticed that makeshift curtains had been tacked up over the splintered door frames of the King's chambers. Most of the wreckage had been carried off, but bits of oaken door still littered the corridor. No workmen had been called in to do repairs. Another sign that Regal had no intention of ever returning to Buckkeep.

I tried to find some excuse to introduce myself into that room. The Keep downstairs was busier than ever, for today the Dukes of Bearns, Rippon, and Shoaks Duchies were expected to arrive with their retinues to witness the King-in-Waiting ceremony for Regal. They were being put in the lesser guest rooms, across the Keep. I wondered how they would react to the sudden disappearance of the King and Queen. Would it be seen as treachery, or would Regal find some way to conceal it from them? What would it auger for his new reign to begin so? I put it from my mind; it wasn't helping me get the King alone in his chamber.

I left my room and went pacing through Buckkeep, hoping for inspiration. Instead I found only confusion. Noble folk of every degree were arriving for Regal's ceremony, and the influx of guests and their households and servants swept and eddied about the outflow of goods and folk that Regal was sending inland. My feet carried me unplanned to Verity's study. The door was ajar and I went in. The hearth was cold, the room musty with disuse. There was a distinct odor of mouse in the air. I hoped whatever scrolls they were nesting in weren't irreplaceable. I was fairly certain I had removed the ones Verity treasured to Chade's rooms. I walked about the room, touching his things. I suddenly missed him acutely. His unyielding steadiness, his calmness, his strength; he would never have let things come to such a situation. I sat down in his work chair at his map table. Scuffs and scribbles of ink where he had tried colors on it marred the tabletop. Here were two badly cut quills, discarded with a brush worn hairless. In a box on the table were several little pots of color, cracked and dried now. They smelled like Verity to me, in the same way that leather and harness oil always smelled like Burrich. I leaned forward on the table and put my head in my hands. "Verity, we need you now."

I cannot come.

I leaped to my feet, my legs tangling in the chair's, and fell on the rug. Frantically I scrabbled to my feet, and even more frantically scrabbled after the contact. *Verity!*

I hear you. What is it, boy? A pause. *You've reached me on your own, have you? Well done!*

We need you to come home right now!

Why?

Thoughts tumbled so much faster than words, and in far greater detail than he could have wished to know. I felt him grow sad with the information, and wearier. *Come home. If you were here, you could put it all to rights. Regal could not claim to be King-in-Waiting, he could not strip Buckkeep like this, or take away the King.*

I cannot. Be calm now. Think this through. I could not come home in time to prevent any of this. It grieves me. But I am too close now to give up my goal. And if I am to be a father —his thoughts were warm with this new feeling—*it becomes even more important that I succeed. My goal must be to retain the Six Duchies intact, and with a coast freed of sea wolves. This, for the child to inherit.*

What am I to do?

Just as you have planned. My father, my wife, and my child; it is a weighty burden I have put upon you. He sounded suddenly uncertain.

I will do what I can do, I told him, fearing to promise any more than that.

I have faith in you. He paused. *Did you feel that?*

What?

Another is here, trying to break in, to listen on our Skilling. One of Galen's spying brood of vipers.

I did not think that possible!

Galen found a way, and schooled his poisonous offspring in it. Skill no more to me now.

I felt something similar to when he had broken our Skill contact the last time to save Shrewd's strength, but much rougher. A surging outward of Verity's Skill that pushed someone away from us. I thought I felt the effort it cost him. Our Skill contact broke.

He was gone, as abruptly as I had found him. I groped tentatively after our contact, found nothing. What he had said about another listening in on us rattled me. Fear warred with triumph in me. I had Skilled. We had been spied upon. But I had Skilled, alone and unaided! But how much had they overheard? I pushed back the chair from the table, sat a moment longer in the storm of my thoughts. Skilling had been easy. I still didn't know quite how I had initiated it, but it had been easy. I felt like a child who had worked a puzzle box, but was unable to recall the exact sequence of moves. The knowledge that it could be done made me want instantly to attempt it again. I set the temptation aside firmly. I had other tasks to accomplish, ones of far more weight.

I sprang up and rushed out of the study, almost tripping over Justin. He sat, legs outstretched, with his back against the wall. He looked drunk. I knew better. He was half-stunned by the push Verity had given him. I brought myself up short and stared down at him. I knew I should kill him. The poison I had composed for Wallace so long ago still rode in a pocket in my cuff. I could force it down his throat. But it was not designed to act quickly. As if he could guess my thoughts, he cowered away from me, scrabbling along the wall.

For a moment longer I stared at him, striving to think calmly. I had promised Chade to take no more actions on my own without consulting him. Verity had not bid me find and kill the spy. He could have, in less than an instant of thought. This decision did not belong to me. One of the hardest things I have ever done was to force myself to walk away from Justin. Half a dozen strides down the hall, I suddenly heard him blurt, "I know what you've been doing!"

I rounded to confront him. "What are you talking about?" I asked in a low voice. My heart began to thunder. I hoped he'd make me kill him. Frightening to know suddenly how badly I wanted to.

He blanched but did not back down. He reminded me of a braggart child. "You walk like you are the King himself, you sneer down at me, and make mock of me behind my back. Don't think I don't know it!" He clawed his way up the wall, staggered to his feet. "But you are not so great. You Skill once, and think you are a master, but your Skilling stinks of your dog magic! Do not think you will walk so proud always. You will be brought down! And soon!"

A wolf clamored in me for instant vengeance. I leashed my temper. "Do you dare to spy upon my Skilling to Prince Verity, Justin? I did not think you had the courage."

"You know I did, Bastard. I do not fear you so that I must hide from you. I dare much, Bastard! Much more than you would suppose." His stance showed him growing braver by the minute.

"Not if I suppose treachery and treason, though. Has not

King-in-Waiting Verity been declared dead, oh loyally sworn coterie member? Yet you spy upon me Skilling to him, and you express no surprise?''

For a moment Justin stood stock-still. Then he grew bold. ''Say what you like, Bastard. No one will believe you if we deny it.''

''Have the sense to be silent at least,'' Serene declared. She came down the hallway like a ship under full sail. I did not step aside, but forced her to brush past me. She seized Justin's arm, claiming him like a dropped basket.

''Silence is but another form of lying, Serene.'' She had turned Justin about and was walking him away from me. ''You know that King Verity still lives!'' I shouted after them. ''Do you think he will never return? Do you think you will never have to answer for the lie you live?''

They turned a corner and were gone, leaving me to seethe silently, and curse myself for shouting so blatantly aloud what as yet we must conceal. But the incident had pushed me into an aggressive frame of mind. I left Verity's study and prowled the Keep. The kitchens were abustle and Cook had no time for me, other than to ask if I had heard that a serpent had been found lying before the fire on the main hearth. I said doubtless it had crawled into the firewood to shelter for the winter and come in with a log. The warmth would have brought it to life. She just shook her head and said she had never heard of the like, but that it boded evil. She told me again of the Pocked Man by the well, but in her story, he had been drinking from the bucket, and when he lowered it from his spotted face, the water that ran down his chin was red as blood. She was making the kitchen boys bring water from the well in the washing courts for all the cooking. She'd have no one dropping dead at her table.

On that cheerful note, I left the kitchen, with a couple of sweet cakes I had light-fingered from a tray. I had not gotten far before a page stood before me. ''FitzChivalry, son of Chivalry?'' he addressed me cautiously.

His wider cheekbones marked him as probably being Bearns stock, and when I looked for it, I found the yellow flower that was the Bearns sigil sewn to his patched jerkin. For a boy of his height, he was wretchedly thin. I nodded gravely.

"My master, Duke Brawndy of Bearns, desires that you wait upon him as soon as you handily may." He spoke the words carefully. I doubted he had been a page long.

"That would be now."

"Then shall I show you to him?"

"I can find my way. Here. I should not take these up there with me." I handed him the sweet cakes, and he received them doubtfully.

"Shall I save them for you, sir?" he asked seriously, and it smote me to see a boy put such a high value on food.

"Perhaps you would eat them for me, and if they suit you, you might go in the kitchens and tell our cook Sara what you think of her work."

No matter how busy it was in there, I knew a compliment from a skinny boy would win him at least a bowl of stew.

"Yes, sir!" His face lit at my orders and he hastened away from me, half of one cake already in his mouth.

The lesser guest rooms were those on the opposite side of the Great Hall from the King's rooms. They were considered lesser, I suppose, mostly because their windows faced onto the mountains rather than the sea, and hence the rooms were gloomier. But the chambers were no smaller, nor less handsome in any other way.

Save that the last time I had been admitted to one, it had been decently furnished. Bearns guards admitted me to a sitting room that offered only three chairs in which to sit and a bare rickety table in the middle. Faith greeted me, neutrally formal, and then went to let Duke Brawndy know I was there. The tapestries and hangings that had once warmed the walls and given color to the stone chamber were gone. It was as cheery as a dungeon, save that a warm fire on the hearth brightened it. I remained standing in the center of the room until Duke Brawndy emerged from his bedchamber to greet me. He invited me to be seated, and awkwardly we drew two of the chairs closer to the hearth. There should have been breads and pastries upon the table, there should have been kettles and mugs and brewing herbs for tea, and bottles of wine in these rooms to welcome Buckkeep's guests. It pained me that there were not. Faith hovered in the background like a hunting hawk. I could not help but wonder where Celerity was.

We exchanged a few minor pleasantries, and then Brawndy plunged into his topic like a draft horse into a snowdrift. "I understand King Shrewd is ill, too ill to see any of his dukes. Regal, of course, is much too busy with preparations for tomorrow." The sarcasm was heavy as thick cream. "So I wished to visit Her Majesty Queen Kettricken," he announced ponderously. "For as you know, she has been most courteous to me in the past. But at her door, her ladies told me she was not well and should not have visitors. I have heard a rumor that she was with child, and that now, in her grief and her foolishness at riding to Rippon's defense, she has lost it. Is this so?"

I took a breath, studied fair words for my response. "Our king is, as you say, very ill. I do not think you shall see him, save at the ceremony. Our queen is likewise indisposed, but I am sure that if she had been told you were at her door yourself, you would have been admitted. She has not lost the child. She rode to the defense of Neatbay for the same reasons she has gifted you with opals; for fear that if she did not act, no other would. Nor was it her actions at Neatbay that threatened her child, but a fall down a tower stair here at Buckkeep. And the child was only threatened, not lost, though our queen was sorely bruised."

"I see." He sat back in his chair and pondered for a bit. The silence took root between us and grew while I waited. At last he leaned forward and motioned me to do the same. When our heads were close together, he asked quietly, "FitzChivalry, have you any ambitions?"

This was the moment. King Shrewd had predicted it years ago, and Chade more recently. When I made no immediate answer, Brawndy went on as if each word were a stone he shaped before handing it to me. "The heir to the Farseer throne is a babe as yet unborn. Once Regal has declared himself King-in-Waiting, do you think he will wait long to claim the throne? We do not. For although these words come from my lips, I speak for Rippon and Shoaks Duchies as well. Shrewd has become old, and feeble. A King in name only. We have had a taste of what kind of king Regal would be. What should we suffer while Regal holds title until Verity's child comes of age? Not that I expect the child will manage to be born, let alone mount the throne.'' He paused, cleared his throat, and looked at me earnestly. Faith stood by the door as if guarding our talk. I kept my silence.

''You're a man we know, a son of a man we knew. You bear his looks and almost his name. You've as much a right to call yourself royal as many who have worn the crown.'' He paused again. Waiting.

Again I kept silent. It was not, I told myself, a temptation. I would simply hear him out. That was all. He had said nothing, as yet, that suggested I would betray my king.

He floundered for words, then looked up and met my eyes. ''Times are difficult.''

''They are,'' I agreed quietly.

He looked down at his hands. They were worn hands, hands that bore the small scars and roughness of a man who did things with them. His shirt was freshly washed and mended, but it was not a new garment made especially for this occasion. Times might be hard in Buckkeep, but they were harder in Bearns. Quietly he said it. ''If you saw fit to oppose Regal, to declare yourself king-in-waiting in his stead, Bearns and Rippon and Shoaks would support you. It is my belief that Queen Kettricken would support you as well, and that Buck would follow her.'' He looked up at me again. ''We have talked much of this. We believe Verity's child would stand a better chance of gaining the throne with you as regent than with Regal.''

So. They had dismissed Shrewd already. ''Why not follow Kettricken?'' I asked carefully.

He looked into the flames. ''It's a hard thing to say, after she has shown herself so true. But she is foreign-born, and in some ways untried. It is not that we doubt her; we do not. Nor would we be setting her aside. Queen she is, and would remain, and her child to reign after her. But in these times, we need both king-in-waiting and queen.''

A question bubbled in me. A demon wanted me to ask, ''And if, when the child comes of age, I do not wish to relinquish power, what then?'' They had to have asked themselves, they had to have agreed on some answer to have ready for me. For a moment longer I sat still and silent. Almost I could feel the eddies of possibility swirling about me; was this what the Fool was always prattling about, was this one of his misty crossroads where I always stood in the center? "Catalyst," I taunted myself quietly.

"Beg pardon?" Brawndy leaned closer to me.

"Chivalry," I said. "As you have said, I bear his name. Almost. Duke Bearns. You are a man hard-pressed. I know what you have risked in speaking to me, and I will be as blunt with you. I am a man with ambitions. But I do not desire the crown of my king." I took a breath and looked into the fire. For the first time I really considered what it would do to Bearns, Rippon, and Shoaks for both Shrewd and Kettricken suddenly to disappear. The Coastal Duchies would become like a rudderless ship with decks awash. Brawndy had as much as said they would not follow Regal. Yet I had nothing else I could offer them at this time. To whisper to him that Verity lived would demand that they rise tomorrow, to deny Regal's right to declare himself king-in-waiting. To warn them that both Shrewd and Kettricken would suddenly vanish would be no assurance at all to them, but would certainly mean that too many folk would not be surprised when it happened. Once they were safely in the Mountain Kingdom, then, perhaps, the Coastal Dukes could be told all. But that could be weeks away. I tried to think what I could offer him now, what assurances, what hopes.

"For what it is worth, I, as a man, am with you." I said the words carefully, wondering if I spoke treason. "To King Shrewd I am pledged. To Queen Kettricken, and the heir she carries, I am loyal. I foresee dark days ahead of us, and the Coastal Duchies must act as one against the Raiders. We have no time to worry what Prince Regal does inland. Let him go to Tradeford. Our lives are here, and here we must stand and fight."

With my own words, I felt a sea change in me. Like the shedding of a cloak, or an insect crawling from its cocoon, I felt myself emerge. Regal was leaving me here at Buckkeep, abandoning me as he thought, to hardship and danger, along

with those I most cared about. Well let him. With the King and
Queen Kettricken safely stashed in the Mountains, I would no
longer fear Regal. Molly was gone, lost to me. What had Burrich said, a time ago? That I might not see her, but perhaps she
might see me. Let her see, then, that I could act, that one man
standing could make a difference. Patience and Lacey would be
safer in my keeping than inland as Regal's hostages. My mind
was racing. Could I make Buckkeep my own, and hold it for
Verity until he returned? Who would follow me? Burrich
would be gone. I could not count on using his influence. But
those swilling inland soldiers would be gone as well. What
would be left would be Buckkeep warriors, with a vested interest in keeping this cold rock of a castle from falling. Some had
watched me grow up, some had learned how to spar and swing
a sword at the same time I had. Kettricken's guard I knew, and
the old soldiers who still wore the colors of King Shrewd's
guard knew me. I had belonged to them before I had belonged
to King Shrewd. Would they remember that?

Despite the warmth of the fire, a shiver went up me, and if
I had been a wolf, my hackles would have stood on end. The
spark in me quickened. "I am no king. I am no prince. I am but
a bastard, but one who loves Buck. I want no bloodshed with
Regal, no confrontation. We have no time to waste, and I have
no heart for the killing of Six Duchies folk. Let Regal flee
inland. When he and the dogs that sniff after him are gone, I
am yours. And as much of Buck as I can rally to follow me."

The words were spoken, the commitment made. Treason,
traitor, whispered a small voice inside me. But in my heart I
knew the rightness of what I did. Chade might not see it my
way. But I felt in that moment that the only way to declare
myself for Shrewd and Verity and Kettricken's child was to
declare myself with those who would not follow Regal. Yet I
wanted to be sure they understood that loyalty clearly. I looked
deep into Brawndy's weary eyes. "This is my goal, Duke
Brawndy of Bearns. I speak it plainly, and I will back no other.
I will see a united Six Duchies, with her coastline freed of
Raiders, place a crown upon the head of Kettricken's and Verity's child. I must hear you say that you share that goal."

"I swear that I do, FitzChivalry, son of Chivalry." To my

horror, the war-scarred old man took my hands in his and
placed them on his forehead in the ancient sign of one who
gives fealty. It was all I could do not to snatch them away.
Loyalty to Verity, I told myself. This is how I have begun this,
and I must see that this is how I go on.

"I will speak to the others," Brawndy was going on quietly. "I will tell them that this is how you wish it. In truth, we
have no wish for bloodshed. It is as you say. Let the whelp run
inland with his tail between his legs. Here is where the wolves
shall stand and fight."

My scalp prickled at his choice of words.

"We will attend his ceremony. We will even stand before
him, and swear once more to be loyal to a King of the Farseer
line. But he is not that King. Nor ever shall be. I understand he
departs the very day after the ceremony. We shall let him go,
though by tradition a new King-in-Waiting is bound to stand
before his dukes and hear their counsels. It may be that we
shall linger close, a day or so longer, after Regal has departed.
Buckkeep at least shall be yours, ere we depart. We shall see to
that. And there will be much to discuss. The placement of our
ships. There are other ships, half-finished in the boat sheds, are
there not?"

At my short nod, Brawndy grinned in wolfish satisfaction.
"We shall see them launched, you and I. Regal has plundered
Buckkeep of supplies; this is known to all. We will have to look
into replenishing your warehouses. The farmers and shepherds
of Buck will have to understand that they must find more, must
give of what they held back, if their soldiers are to keep their
coast free. It will be a hard winter for all of us, but lean wolves
fight fiercest, or so they say."

And we are lean, my brother; oh, we are lean.

A terrible foreboding rose in me. I wondered what I had
done. I would have to find a way to speak to Kettricken before
she departed, to somehow assure her I had not turned on her.
And I must Skill to Verity, as soon as I possibly could. Would
he understand? He must. He had always been able to see into
the depths of my heart. Surely he would see what my intentions
were. And King Shrewd? Once, long ago, when he had first
bought my loyalty, he had said to me, "If ever any man or

woman seeks to turn you against me by offering you more than I do, then come to me, and tell me of the offer, and I shall meet it." Would you give Buckkeep into my hands, old King? I wondered.

I realized that Brawndy had fallen silent. "Do not fear, FitzChivalry," he said quietly. "Do not doubt the rightness of what we do, or we are all undone. If yours was not the hand that reached forth to claim Buckkeep, another would have. We could not leave Buck with no one at the helm. Be glad it is yourself, as we are. Regal has gone where none of us may follow, fled inland to hide beneath his mother's bed. We must stand on our own. All the omens and portents point us that way. They say the Pocked Man was seen drinking blood from a Buckkeep well, and that a serpent coiled on the main hearth in the Great Hall and dared to strike at a child. I myself, riding south to be here, witnessed a young eagle bedeviled by crows. But just as I thought she must plunge into the sea to avoid them, she turned and, in midair, seized a crow that had sought to dive on her from above. She clenched him and dropped him bloody to the water, and all the other crows fled squawking and flapping. These are signs, FitzChivalry. We'd be fools to ignore them."

Despite my skepticism for such signs, a shiver ran up me, setting the hair on my arms upright. Brawndy glanced away from me to the inner door of the chamber. I followed his eyes. Celerity stood there. The short dark hair framed her proud face and her eyes gleamed fierce blue. "Daughter, you have chosen well," the old man told her. "I wondered, once, what you saw in a scriber. Perhaps now I see it as well."

He beckoned her into the room, and she came in a rustle of skirts. She stood by her father, looking boldly at me. For the first time I glimpsed the steel will that hid inside the shy child. It was unnerving.

"I bade you wait, and you have," Duke Brawndy said to me. "You have shown yourself a man of honor in this. I have given you my loyalty this day. Will you take my daughter's pledge to be your wife as well?"

What a precipice I teetered on. I met Celerity's eyes. She had no doubts. If I had never known Molly, I would have found her beautiful. But when I looked at her, all I could see was who she was not. I had no heart left to give to any woman, let alone at a time like this. I turned my eyes back to her father, determined to speak firmly.

"You do me more honor than I deserve, sir. But, Duke Brawndy, it is as you have said. These are evil times, and uncertain. With you, your daughter is safe. At my side, she could know only greater uncertainty. What we have discussed here, today, some would call treason. I will not have it said that I took your daughter to bind you to me in a questionable endeavor, nor that you gave your daughter for such a reason." I forced myself to look back at Celerity, to meet her eyes. "Brawndy's daughter is safer than FitzChivalry's wife. Until my position is more certain, I pledge no one to me in any way. My regard for you is great, Lady Celerity. I am not a Duke, nor even a lord. I am as I am named, an illegitimate son of a Prince. Until I can say I am more than that, I will seek no wife, nor court any woman."

Celerity was clearly displeased. But her father nodded slowly to my words. "I see the wisdom of your words. My daughter, I fear, sees only the delay." He looked at Celerity's pout, smiled fondly. "Someday she will understand that the people who seek to protect her are the people who care for her." He ran his eyes over me as if I were a horse. "I believe," he said quietly, "that Buck will stand. And that Verity's child shall inherit the throne."

I left him with those words echoing in my mind. Again and again, I told myself I had done nothing wrong. If I had not reached forth to claim Buckkeep, another would have.

⟶═◎═⟵

"Who?" Chade demanded angrily of me some hours later.

I sat looking down at my feet. "I don't know. But they would have found someone. And that person would have been far more likely to cause bloodshed. To act at the King-in-Waiting ceremony, and jeopardize our efforts to get Kettricken and Shrewd clear of this mess."

"If the Coastal Dukes are as close to rebellion as your report indicates, then perhaps we should reconsider that plan."

I sneezed. The room still smelled of bitterbark. I had used too much. "Brawndy did not come to me speaking of rebellion, but of loyalty to the true and rightful King. And that was the spirit in which I responded. I have no wish to overthrow the throne, Chade, only to secure it for its lawful heir."

"I know that," he said briefly. "Otherwise I would go straight to King Shrewd with this . . . madness. I know not what to call it. It is not treason, quite, and yet . . ."

"I am no traitor to my king." I spoke with quiet vehemence.

"No? Let me ask you this, then. If, despite, or save us all, because of our efforts to save Shrewd and Kettricken, they both perish with the child unborn, and Verity never returns. What then? Will you still be so eager to cede the throne to the rightful King?"

"Regal?"

"By the line of succession, yes."

"He is no king, Chade. He's an indulged Princeling, and always will be. I've as much Farseer blood as he does."

"And so you might say of Kettricken's child, when the time came. Do you see what a dangerous path we set ourselves on when we set ourselves above our places? You and I, we swore to the Farseer line, of which we are but random shoots. Not to King Shrewd alone, or to a wise King alone, but to uphold the rightful King of the Farseer line. Even if he is Regal."

"You would serve Regal?"

"I have seen more foolish Princes than he become wise as they aged. What you contemplate will bring us civil war. Farrow and Tilth—"

"Have no interest in any kind of a war. They will say good riddance to us and let the Coastal Duchies go. Regal has always said as much."

"And he probably thinks he believes it. But when he finds that he cannot buy fine silk, and that the wines of Bingtown and beyond no longer flow up the Buck River to his palate, he will think better. He needs his port cities, and he will come back for them.''

"So what are we to do? What should I have done?"

Chade sat down across from me, clasped his mottled hands between his bony old knees. "I do not know. Brawndy is desperate indeed. If you had loftily refused him and rebuked him with treason, well . . . I don't say he'd have done away with you. But remember he had no hesitation about dealing quickly with Virago when she represented a threat to him. This is all too much for one old assassin. We need a King."

"Aye."

"Could you Skill again to Verity?"

"I fear to try. I do not know how to guard against Justin and Serene. Or Will." I sighed. "Still, I will try. Surely Verity will know if they ride with my Skilling." Another thought intruded. "Chade, tomorrow night, when you lead Kettricken to escape, you must find a moment or two, to tell her of what has transpired, and assure her of my loyalty."

"Oh, those will be reassuring tidings to give her as she flees back to the Mountains. No. Not tomorrow night. I will see that word reaches her, when she is safe. And you must continue to try to reach Verity, but beware of having your Skilling spied upon. Are you sure our plans are unknown to them?"

I had to shake my head. "But I believe they are safe. I had told all to Verity when first I Skilled him. It was not until the end that he said someone tried to spy upon us."

"You probably should have killed Justin," Chade grumbled to himself. Then he laughed at my outraged look. "No, no, calm yourself. I will not rebuke you that you refrained from it. Would that you had been so circumspect with the scheme that Brawndy brought you. Even a breath of this would be sufficient for Regal to have your neck stretched. And were he ruthless and foolish, he could try to hang his dukes as well. No. Let us not even think of that! The halls of Buckkeep would run blood before that was done. Would you had found a way to turn the conversation, before ever he made you such an offer. Save, as you say, that they might have found another. Ah, well. We cannot put old heads on young shoulders. Unfortunately, Regal could remove your young head from your young shoulders all too easily." He knelt and put another piece of wood on the fire. He took a breath and sighed it out. "Have you got all other things in readiness?" he asked abruptly.

I was only too glad to change the topic. "As much as I could. Burrich will be in place and waiting, in the alder copse where the dog fox used to den."

Chade rolled his eyes. "How do I find that? Ask a passing dog fox?"

I smiled inadvertently. "Close. Where will you emerge from Buck Castle?"

He was stubbornly silent for a moment. Still, that old fox hated to reveal his back door. Finally he said, "We will come out of the grain shed, the one third back from the stables."

I nodded slowly. "A gray wolf will meet you. Follow him silently, and he will show you a way out of the walls of Buck that does not take you through the gates."

For a long moment Chade just looked at me. I waited. For condemnation, for a look of disgust, even for curiosity. But the old assassin had studied too long how to mask his feelings. He said at last, "We are fools if we do not use every weapon that comes to hand. Is he any . . . danger to us?"

"No more than I am. You need not wear wolfsbane, nor offer him mutton to be allowed to pass." I was as familiar with the old folklore as Chade was. "Simply show yourself, and he will appear to guide you. He will take you through the walls, and out to the copse where Burrich waits with the horses."

"Is it a long walk?"

I knew he was thinking of the King. "It is not overly long, but it is not short, and the snow is deep and unpacked. It will not be easy to scrabble through the gap in the wall, but it can be done. I could ask Burrich to meet you at the wall instead, but I do not wish to draw attention to it. Perhaps the Fool could help you manage?"

"He will have to, from the sound of things. I am not willing to bring any others in on this plot. Our position seems only to become more and more untenable."

I bowed my head to the truth of that. "And you?" I ventured to ask.

"My tasks are done as completely as they could be, ahead

of time. The Fool has assisted me. He has spirited away both clothing and coin for his king's journey. Shrewd has reluctantly agreed to our plan. He knows it is wise, but every part of it chafes him. Despite all, Fitz, Regal is his son, his favored youngest. Even having felt Regal's ruthlessness, it is still hard for him to say the Prince threatens his life. You see how he is bound: to admit that Regal would turn on him is to admit he was wrong about his son. To flee Buckkeep is even worse, for that is admitting not only that Regal would turn on him, but that flight is his only option. Our king has never been a coward. It galls him now to run from one who should be most loyal of all to him. Yet he must. Of that I have convinced him; mostly, I'll admit, by saying that without his acknowledgment, Kettricken's child will have a poor claim on the throne." Chade sighed. "All is as ready as I can make it. I have prepared the medicines, and all is well packed."

"The Fool understands he cannot go with his king?"

Chade rubbed his forehead. "He intends to follow, a few days behind. He would not be dissuaded entirely. The best I could do was to get him to travel separately."

"Then it but depends on me to find a way to empty the King's room of witnesses, and for you to spirit him away."

"Ah, yes," Chade observed mirthlessly. "All is well planned and ready to carry out, save for the actual deed."

We stared together into the fire.

29

Escapes and Captures

*T*HE OUTBREAK OF *strife between the coastal and In-land Duchies at the end of King Shrewd's reign was not a new sundering, but rather a resumption of old differences. The four Coastal Duchies, Bearns, Buck, Rippon, and Shoaks, were a kingdom long before the Six Duchies came to be. When the unified battle tactics of the Chalced States convinced King Wielder that their conquest would be unprofitable, he turned his ambitions inland. The Farrow region, with its scattered nomadic tribal populations, fell easily to the organized armies he led. The more populous and settled Tilth grudgingly surren-dered to him when the erstwhile King of that region found his territory surrounded and his trade routes severed.*

Both the old kingdom of Tilth and the region that would come to be known as Farrow were held as conquered territory for over a generation. The wealth of their granaries, orchards, and herds were exploited lavishly for the benefit of the Coastal Duchies. Queen Munificence, granddaughter of Wielder, was wise enough to see that this was breeding discontent in the inland areas. She showed great tolerance and wisdom in ele-vating the tribal elders of the Farrow folk and the former ruling

families of Tilth to nobles. She used marriages and grants of
land to forge alliances between coastal and inland folk. She
first referred to her kingdom as the Six Duchies. But all of her
political maneuvers could not change the geographic and eco-
nomic interests of the different areas. Climate, folk, and liveli-
hoods of the Inland Duchies remained vastly different from that
of the coastal peoples.

During Shrewd's reign, the differing interests of the two
regions were exacerbated by the offspring of his two queens.
His elder sons, Verity and Chivalry, were the sons of Queen
Constance, a noblewoman of Shoaks with relatives among the
nobility of Bearns as well. She was very much of the coastal
folk. Shrewd's second queen, Desire, was from Farrow, but
traced her family lineage back to the long-foundered royalty of
Tilth as well as to distant Farseer connections. Hence came her
oft-repeated claim that her son Regal was more royal than
either of his half brothers, and hence had more right to the
throne.

With the disappearance of King-in-Waiting Verity and rumors of his death, and the obvious failing of King Shrewd, it
appeared to the Coastal Dukes that power and title would be
passed on to Prince Regal, born of inland lineage. They preferred to align with the unborn child of Verity, a coastal Prince,
and predictably did all they could to retain and consolidate
power in the coastal bloodlines. Threatened as the Coastal
Duchies were by Raiders and Forgings, it was really the only
rational choice they could make.

⊷═◐═⊷

The King-in-Waiting ceremony was too long. Folk were
assembled well ahead of time, to allow Regal to make a stately
entrance through our ranks and ascend to the high seat, where a
drowsing King Shrewd awaited him. Queen Kettricken, pale as
a wax taper, stood behind Shrewd at his left shoulder. Shrewd
was bedecked in robes and fur collars and the full regalia of the
royal jewels, but Kettricken had resisted Regal's suggestions
and enticements. She stood very tall and straight in a plain robe
of purple, belted above her rounding belly. A simple circlet of
gold confined the cropped remnants of her hair. Other than that

band of metal at her temples, she might have been a servant standing ready to attend Shrewd. I knew she saw herself still as Sacrifice rather than queen. She could not see that the starkness of her attire made her look dramatically foreign to the court.

The Fool was there as well, in a well-worn motley of black and white, and with Ratsy once more atop his scepter. He had striped his face in black and white as well, and I wondered if this was to camouflage his bruises, or simply to complement his motley. He had appeared sometime before Regal had, and had very obviously enjoyed the spectacle he created by sauntering up the aisle, waving Ratsy about in airy benediction, before he curtsied to the assemblage and then plopped gracefully at the King's feet. Guards had begun to move to intercept him, but were blocked by grinning, craning people. When he arrived at the dais and seated himself, the King had reached down to absently tousle the Fool's sparse locks, and so he had been suffered to remain where he was. Scowls or grins were exchanged over the Fool's performance, depending largely on how deeply one had pledged his allegiance to Regal. I myself feared that it would be the Fool's last prank.

The atmosphere in the Keep all day had been like to that of a seething pot. My trust that Bearns was a tight-lipped man had been misplaced. Entirely too many minor nobles were suddenly nodding to me, or catching my eye for an exchanged look. I feared it could not be missed by any of Regal's minions, and so had kept myself to my room or, for a good part of the early afternoon, in Verity's tower, where I had vainly attempted to Skill forth to him. I had chosen that spot in the hopes of invoking his memory cleanly to my mind, but I failed. Instead I found myself straining for a hint of Will's footstep on the tower stairs, or a brush of Justin's or Serene's presence against my Skill sense.

After I gave up on Skilling, I sat long, pondering the unsolvable riddle of how I would empty the King's room of guards. Outside, I could hear the pounding of the sea and the wind, and when I opened the windows briefly the gusting storm fair blew me across the room. Most saw this as a fair day for the ceremony; the rising storm might keep Raiders berthed wherever they were at present and assure us no new raids. I

watched the freezing rain putting a crust on the banked snow
while making the roads treacherously slick, and imagined Burrich traveling through it by night with the Queen and King
Shrewd in his litter. It was not a task I would enjoy.

The tone for something of great portent to happen had
been well set. Now, in addition to stories of the Pocked Man
and snakes on the hearth, there was despair in the kitchens. The
day's bake of bread had failed to rise, and the milk had curdled
in the casks before even the cream could be skimmed from it.
Poor Cook Sara had been shaken to her core and declared that
never before had such a thing dared to happen in her kitchens.
The pig men would not even let the soured milk be given to the
swine, so sure were all that it was cursed. The failure of the
bread had meant twice the catch-up work for the kitchen servants, who were already overburdened with feeding all the
guests who had come for the ceremony. I could now vouch that
the tempers of an entire Keep could be disturbed by an un-
happy kitchen crew.

There had been short rations for the watch room, and the
stew had been overly salted, while somehow the beer had gone
flat. The Duke of Tilth complained of vinegar instead of wine
in his rooms, which led the Duke of Bearns to comment to
those of Shoaks and Rippon that even a bit of vinegar would
have been welcome as a sign of hospitality in their rooms. The
unfortunate remark was conveyed somehow to Mistress Hasty,
who soundly scolded all the chamberlains and serving folk
who had not somehow managed to spread the thin cheer left at
Buckkeep to include the lesser guest rooms. There was a complaint among the lesser servants that an order had come down
to keep expenses for those guests to a minimum, but no one
could be found who would admit to giving such an order, or
even to passing it down. And so the day had gone, so that I had
been altogether relieved to isolate myself in Verity's tower.

But I dared not miss the King-in-Waiting ceremony, for
too much would have been inferred from that. And so I stood,
an uncomfortable victim of a shirt with overfull sleeves and
some very itchy leggings, patiently awaiting Regal's entrance.
My mind was not on his pomp and ceremony; rather it whirled
with questions and worries of my own. I fretted over whether

Burrich had been able to smuggle out the horses and litter. It was dark now. He was probably sitting outside in this storm, in the pathetic shelter of the alder copse. He would have blanketed the horses, no doubt, but that would do little against the sleet that now fell steadily. He had given me the name of the smithy where Sooty and Ruddy had been taken. Somehow I must find a way to keep up the man's weekly bribes, and to check on them often to be sure they were well cared for. This he had made me promise to entrust to no one else. Would the Queen be able to retire alone to her room? And again and again, how was I to empty King Shrewd's room that Chade might spirit him away?

A mutter of wonder broke me from my reverie. I glanced toward the dais where everyone seemed to be staring. There was a brief flickering, and for an instant one of the white tapers burning there flickered blue. Then another spat a spark, and burned blue for an instant. There was another mutter, but the wayward candles settled after that to burning evenly and well. Neither Kettricken nor King Shrewd appeared to notice anything amiss, but the Fool sat up and shook Ratsy at the errant candles in rebuke.

At length Regal did appear, resplendent in red velvet and white silk. A little maid walked before him, swinging a censer of sandalwood incense. Regal smiled upon all as he advanced leisurely toward the throne, meeting many an eye and nodding many an acknowledgment on his way to that high seat. I am sure it did not go off so finely as Regal had planned. King Shrewd faltered and then looked puzzled over the scroll that had been given him to read. At length Kettricken took it from his shaky hands, and he smiled up at her as she read aloud the words that must have cut her to the heart. It was a careful listing of the children that King Shrewd had sired, including a daughter who had died in infancy, by the order of their births, and then by order of their deaths, all leading up to Regal as sole survivor and legitimate heir. She did not hesitate at Verity's name, but read aloud the brief statement—"Lost to misfortune while on a quest to the Mountain Kingdom"—as if it were an ingredient list. Of the child she carried, no mention was made. A child as yet unborn was an heir, but not a King-in-Waiting.

The child could not step forward to claim that title until he or she was at least sixteen.

Kettricken had taken from Verity's chest the simple silver circlet with the blue gem that was crown for a King-in-Waiting, and the pendant of gold and emerald in the shape of a leaping buck. These she passed first to King Shrewd, who looked down at them as if bewildered. He made no move to bestow them upon Regal. At length Regal reached for them, and Shrewd allowed him to take them out of his hands. And so Regal set the crown upon his own head, and slipped the pendant about his own neck, and stood before us all, the new King-in-Waiting of the Six Duchies.

Chade's timing was slightly off. The candles did not seriously begin to flicker blue until the Dukes were wending their ways forward to pledge once more to House Farseer. Regal tried to ignore this phenomenon, until the muttering of the folk threatened to drown out Duke Ram of Tilth's oath. Then Regal turned and casually pinched out the offending candle. I admired his aplomb, especially when a second candle almost immediately went blue, and he repeated the gesture. I myself thought it was a bit too much of a portent when a torch set in a sconce by the main door suddenly whooshed out a blue flame and a foul stench before it guttered dark. All eyes had turned to watch it. Regal waited it out, but I saw the clench of his jaw and the tiny vein that throbbed on his temple.

I do not know how he had planned to end his ceremony, but he brought it to a rather abrupt close after that. At his curt signal, minstrels struck up abruptly, while at another nod the doors opened and men bore in table boards already laden, while boys hastened after them with the trestles to set them upon. At least for this feast he had spared nothing, and the well-prepared meats and pastries were welcomed by all. If there seemed to be something of a shortage of bread, no one thought to complain of it. Cloths and tables had been set in the Lesser Hall for the grand folk, and thither I saw Kettricken slowly escorting King Shrewd while the Fool and Rosemary trailed after them. For those of us with lesser rank, there were simpler but plentiful foods to hand and a cleared floor for dancing.

I had planned to make myself a hearty meal at the feasting, but again and again I was accosted by men who clapped my shoulder too firmly or women who met my eyes too knowingly. The Coastal Dukes were at table with the other high nobles, ostensibly breaking bread with Regal and cementing their new relationship to him. I had been told that all three Coastal Dukes would know I concurred with their plan. It was unnerving to find evidence that this was known among the lesser nobility as well. Celerity made no overt claim upon me as escort, but made me nervously aware of myself by following me about as mutely as a hound. I could not turn but I found her a half-dozen steps away. Plainly she wished me to speak to her, but I did not trust my wits to find suitable words. I almost broke when a lesser noble from Shoaks casually asked me if I thought any of the warships would be harbored as far south as False Bay.

With a sinking heart, I suddenly realized my error. None of them feared Regal. They saw no danger, only a spoiled popinjay of a boy who wished to wear fine clothes and a circlet and claim a title to himself. They believed he would go away and they could ignore him. I knew better.

I knew what Regal was capable of, in search of power, or on a whim, or simply because he believed he could get away with it. He would leave Buckkeep. He did not want it. But if he thought I did, he would do everything within his power to see that I did not get it. I was supposed to be dumped here, like a stray, left to starve or be raided. Not ascend to power on the wreckage he had left.

If I were not very careful, they would get me killed. Or worse, if there was anything Regal could devise that he saw as worse.

Twice I tried to slip away, and each time was cornered by someone who wanted a quiet moment of talk with me. I finally pleaded a headache and openly announced I was seeking my bed. Then I must be resigned to at least a dozen folk hastening to wish me good night before I retired. Just as I thought I was free Celerity touched a shy hand to mine and wished me good night in such a dispirited voice that I knew that I had hurt her feelings. That, I think, rattled me more than anything else that evening. I thanked her and, in my most cowardly act of that

night, dared to kiss her fingertips. The resurgence of light in
her eyes shamed me. I fled up the stairs. As I climbed them I
wondered how Verity had ever stood this sort of thing, or my
father. If I had ever thought or dreamed of being a real Prince
instead of a bastard, I abandoned the dream that night. It was
entirely too public a profession. With a sinking heart, I realized
that this was how life would be for me until Verity returned.
The illusion of power clung to me now, and too many would be
dazzled by it.

I went to my own chamber and, with great relief, changed
into sensible clothes. As I tugged on my shirt I felt the tiny
bulge of Wallace's poison, still sewn into my cuff. Perhaps, I
reflected bitterly, it would bring me luck. I left my room and
then committed possibly my most foolish act of the evening. I
went up to Molly's chamber. The servants' hall was empty, the
corridor but dimly lit with two wavering torches. I tapped at
her door. There was no reply. I tried the latch softly, but it was
not fastened. The door swung open at my touch.

Darkness. Emptiness. The small hearth held no fire. I
found a bit of a candle and kindled it at a torch. Then I went
back in her room and shut the door. I stood there while the
devastation finally became real. It was all too Molly. The
stripped bed, the hearth swept clean, but with a small stack of
wood set ready for a fire for the next resident. Those were the
touches that told me she had tidied herself out of the room. Not
a ribbon, not a taper, not even a scrap of wicking remained of
the woman who had lived a servant's life here. The ewer set
upside down in the basin to keep the dust out. I sat in her chair
before the cold hearth, I opened her clothing chest and peered
within. But it was not her chair, or hearth, or chest. These were
just objects she had touched in the brief time she had been
here.

Molly was gone.

She wasn't coming back.

I had held myself together by refusing to think of her. This
empty room jerked the blindfold from my eyes. I looked into
myself and despised what I saw. I wished I could call back the
kiss I had placed on Celerity's fingertips. Balm for a girl's
wounded pride, or the lure to bind her and her father to me? I

10 longer knew which it had been. Neither could be justified. Both were wrong, if I believed at all in the love I had pledged to Molly. That one act was proof I was guilty of all she had charged me with. I would always put the Farseers ahead of her. I had dangled marriage before Molly like bait, left her with no pride in herself nor belief in me. She had hurt me by leaving me. What she could not leave behind was what I had done to her belief in herself. That she must carry with her forever, a belief that she had been tricked and used by a selfish lying boy who lacked even the courage to fight for her.

Can desolation be a source of courage? Or was it merely recklessness and a desire for self-destruction? I went boldly back downstairs and went directly to the King's chambers. The torches in the wall sconces outside his door annoyed me by spitting blue sparks as I passed. A little too dramatic, Chade. I wondered if he had treated every candle and torch in the Keep. I pushed the hanging curtain aside and entered. No one was there. Not in the sitting room, not even in the King's bedchamber. The place had a threadbare look to it, with all the best things taken away and carted off upriver. It reminded me of a room in a mediocre inn. Nothing left here was worth stealing, or Regal would have left a guard on the door. In a strange way, it reminded me of Molly's room. Here there were objects left— bedding, garments, and the like. But this was no longer my king's room. I went and stood by a table, in the exact spot where I had stood as a young boy. Here, while Shrewd breakfasted, he had quizzed me astutely on my lessons each week, and made me aware, every time he spoke to me, that if I was his subject, he was also my king. That man was gone, stripped from this room. The clutter of an active man, the boot trees, the blades, the scatter of scrolls had been replaced with censers for burning herbs and sticky cups of drug tea. King Shrewd had left this room a long time ago. Tonight I would take away a sick old man.

I heard footsteps and cursed myself for my clumsiness. I slipped behind a hanging and stood motionless. I heard the murmur of voices from the sitting room. Wallace. That mocking reply would be the Fool. I ghosted from my hiding place to stand just inside the bedchamber and peer through the makeshift curtain. Kettricken sat on the couch beside the King talking with him softly. She looked weary. Dark circle smudged beneath her eyes, but she smiled for the King. I wa pleased to hear him murmur a reply to whatever she had aske him. Wallace crouched on the hearth, adding sticks of wood t the fire with excessive care. On the other side of the hearth Rosemary had collapsed in a heap, her new dress bunched u about her. As I watched she yawned sleepily, then heaved sigh and straightened herself up. I pitied her. The long cere mony had left me feeling exactly the same way. The Fool stoo behind the King's chair. He suddenly turned and stared directl at me, as if the curtain were no barrier at all. I could see no on else in the room.

The Fool turned abruptly back to Wallace. "Yes, blow, Si Wallace, blow well and hot. Perchance we shall not need th fire at all, with the warmth of your breath to drive the chil from the room."

Wallace did not rise from his crouch, but turned to glare a the Fool over his shoulder. "Bring me some wood, would you? Not a stick of this will catch. The flame runs along it well, bu the wood does not burn. I need hot water if I am to make th King his sleeping tea."

"Would I bring wood? Wood? Would I? Wooden am I not fair Wallace. Nor would I burn, no matter how closely you huffed and puffed upon me. Guards! Ho, guards! Enter, anc bring with you wood, if you would!" The Fool leaped up from his place behind the King and capered to the door, where he made a great show of attempting to treat the curtain as if it were a proper door. At last he thrust his head out into the hall and called loudly again for the guards. He drew his head back in after a moment and returned to the room with a dejected air. "No guards, no wood. Poor Wallace." He gravely studied the man. Wallace was on his hands and knees, poking angrily at the fire. "Perhaps were you to turn, bow to stern, and blow thus upon the fire, the flames might dance more merrily for you. Fore to aft, to create a draft, brave Wallace."

One of the candles that lit the room suddenly spat blue sparks. All, even the Fool, flinched to its hissing, while Wallace lumbered to his feet. I would not have thought him a superstitious man, but there was a brief wildness in his eyes that spoke well of how little he liked this omen. "The fire simply will not burn," he announced, and then as if realizing the significance of what he said, he paused, mouth agape.

"We are witched," said the Fool benignly. On the hearth, little Rosemary drew her knees up under her chin and looked about with round eyes. All trace of sleepiness was gone from her.

"Why are there no guards?" Wallace demanded angrily. He strode to the door of the room and peered out into the hallway. "The torches burn blue, every one of them!" he gasped. He drew his head back in, looked about wildly. "Rosemary. Run and fetch the guards. They said they would follow us shortly."

Rosemary shook her head and refused to budge. She hugged her knees tightly.

"Guards would follow us? Wood follow us? Followed by wood? Now that's a knotty subject! Would wooden guards burn?"

"Stop your nattering!" Wallace snapped at the Fool. "Go fetch the guards."

"Go fetch? First he thinks I am wood, now that I am his little pet dog. Ah! Go fetch the wood; the stick you mean. Where's the stick?" And the Fool began to bark like a feist and frolic about the room as if in search of a thrown stick.

"Go fetch the guards!" Wallace all but howled.

The Queen spoke firmly. "Fool. Wallace. Enough. You weary us with your antics, and Wallace, you are frightening Rosemary. Go and fetch the guards yourself, if you are so set on having them here. As for me, I would have a little peace. I am weary. Soon I must retire."

"My queen, there is something ill afoot this night," Wallace insisted. He glanced about him warily. "I am not a man swayed by chance omens, but of late there have been too many to ignore. I shall go fetch the guards, since the Fool here lacks the courage—"

"He clamors and weeps for the guards to come guard him from wood that will not burn, but I, I am the one who lacks courage? Ah, me!"

"Fool, peace, please!" The Queen's plea seemed genuine "Wallace. Go bring, not guards, but simply different wood Our king wishes not this commotion, but simply rest. Go now. Go."

Wallace hovered at the door, plainly reluctant to brave the blue light of the corridor alone.

The Fool simpered at him. "Shall I come with, to hold your hand, brave Wallace?"

That at last sent him striding from the room. As his foot steps faded, the Fool once more looked toward my hiding place, his invitation plain. "My queen," I said softly, and a quickly indrawn breath was the only sign that I startled her as I stepped out of the King's bedchamber. "If you wished to re tire, the Fool and I could see the King to his bed. I know you are weary and that you wished to rest early this night." From the hearth, Rosemary regarded me with round eyes.

"Perhaps I shall," said Kettricken, rising with surprising alacrity. "Come, Rosemary. Good night, my king."

She swept from the room, with Rosemary practically trot ting at her heels. The child gave us many a backward glance. As soon as the door curtain fell behind them, I was at the King's side. "My king, it is time," I told him gently. "I shall keep watch here as you go. Is there anything special you wished to take with you?"

He swallowed, then focused his eyes on me. "No. No, there is nothing here for me. Nothing to leave behind, and nothing to stay for." He closed his eyes, spoke softly. "I have changed my mind, Fitz. I think I shall stay here, and die in my own bed this night."

The Fool and I were both struck dumb for an instant.

"Ah, no!" the Fool cried softly, while I said, "My king, you are but tired."

"And the only thing I shall get is more tired." There was a strange lucidity in his eyes. The boy King I had touched briefly when we Skilled together looked out at me from that pain-racked body. "My body fails me. My son has become a ser pent. Regal knows his brother lives. He knows the crown he wears is not rightfully his. I did not think he would . . . I thought at the last, he would think better. . . ." Tears welled in his ancient eyes. I had thought to save my king from a disloyal Prince. I should have known there was no saving a father from the betrayal of a son. He reached a hand toward me, a hand gone from a muscled sword holder to a gaunt and yellowed claw. "I would say farewell to Verity. I would have him know, from me, that I did not countenance any of this. Let me at least keep that much faith with the son who kept faith with me." He pointed to a spot by his feet. "Come, Fitz. Take me to him."

There was no refusing that command. I did not hesitate. I came and knelt before him. The Fool stood behind him, tears cutting gray paths through the black-and-white paint on his face. "No," he whispered urgently. "My king, rise, let us go into hiding. There you may think this through. You need not decide this now."

Shrewd paid him no mind. I felt Shrewd's hand settle on my shoulder. I opened my strength to him, sorrowfully surprised that I had at last learned how to do that at will. We plunged together into the black Skill river. We turned in that current as I waited for him to give us direction. Instead, he suddenly embraced me. *Son of my son, blood of my blood. In my own way, I have loved you.*

My king.

My young assassin. What have I made of you? How have I twisted my own flesh? You do not know how young you still are. Chivalry's son, it is not too late to grow straight again. Lift up your head. See beyond all this.

I had spent my life becoming what he wished me to be. These words now filled me with confusion and questions there was no time to answer. I could feel his strength fading.

Verity, I whispered to remind him.

I felt him reach out, and steadied that reaching for him. I felt the brush of Verity's presence, and then a sudden dwindling of the King. I groped after him as one would dive after a drowning man in deep water. I seized his consciousness, held it to me, but it was like gripping a shadow. He was a boy in my arms, frightened and struggling against he knew not what.

Then he was gone.

Like a bubble popping.

I had thought I had glimpsed the frailty of life when I held the dead child in my arms. Now I knew it. Here, and then not here. Even a snuffed candle may leave a trailing wisp of smoke. My king was simply gone.

But I was not alone.

I think every child has flipped over the dead bird found in the woods, only to be shocked and terrified by the busy workings of the maggots on the underside. Fleas cluster thickest and ticks grow fattest on a dying dog. Justin and Serene, like sucking leeches forsaking a dying fish, rose and tried to fasten to me. Here, the source of their increased strength and the King's slow failing. Here the mist that had clouded his mind and filled his days with weariness. Galen, their master, had made Verity his target. But he had missed his kill, and instead met his own death. How long these had been fastened to the King, how long they had sucked Skill strength from him, I would never know. They would have been privy to all he Skilled through me to Verity. Much was suddenly made clear to me, but it was all too late. They closed on me, and I had no concept of how to evade them. I felt them fasten to me, knew they were drawing off my strength now, and that with no reason to refrain from it, they would kill me in moments.

Verity, I cried out, but I was already too weakened. I would never reach him.

Off him, curs! A familiar snarl, and then Nighteyes *repelled* through me. I did not think it would work, but as before, he forced the Wit weapon upon them through the channel the Skill had opened. The Wit and the Skill were two different things, as unlike as reading and singing, or swimming and riding a horse. Yet when they were linked to me by the Skill, they must have been vulnerable to this other magic. I felt them repulsed from me, but there were two of them to withstand the impact of Nighteyes' attack. It would not defeat them both.

Up and run! Flee those you cannot fight!

I found it a wise suggestion. Fear drove me back into my own body and I slammed the guards of my mind closed to their Skill touch. When I could, I opened my eyes. I lay on the floor of the King's study, gasping, while above me the Fool had thrown his body across the King's and was wildly weeping. I felt the creeping tendrils of the Skill sense groping after me. I withdrew deep into myself, shielded frantically in the way Verity had taught me. And still I felt their presence, like ghostly fingers plucking at my clothes, trailing down my skin. It filled me with revulsion.

"You've killed him, you've killed him! You've killed my king, you rotten traitor!" the Fool shrieked at me.

"No! It was not I!" I could barely gasp out the words.

To my horror Wallace stood in the door, taking in the whole scene with wild eyes. Then he lifted his glance and screamed aloud in horror. He dropped the armful of wood he had brought. Both the Fool and I turned our heads.

Standing in the door of the King's bedchamber was the Pocked Man. Even knowing it was Chade, I still knew one moment of hair-raising terror. He was dressed in tattered grave clothes, smeared with earth and mildew. His long gray hair hung in filthy locks about his face, and he had smeared his skin with ash that the livid scars might stand out the better. He lifted a slow hand to point at Wallace. The man screamed, and then fled shrieking down the halls. His yammering for the guards echoed through the Keep.

"What goes on here?" Chade demanded as soon as Wallace had fled. He crossed to his brother in a single stride, laid long thin fingers across the King's throat. I knew what he would find. I clambered painfully to my feet.

"He's dead. I DID NOT KILL HIM!" My shout cut across the Fool's rising wail. The Skill fingers plucked at me insistently. "I go to kill those who did. Take the Fool to safety. Have you the Queen?"

Chade's eyes were very wide. He stared at me as if he had never seen me before. All the candles in the room went suddenly to sputtering blue. It seemed only fitting. "Get her to safety," I ordered my master. "And see the Fool goes with her. If he stays here, he's dead. Regal will let no one live who has been in this room tonight."

"No! I will not leave him!" The Fool's eyes were wide and empty as a mad thing.

"Take him however you can, Chade! His life depends on it!" I grabbed the Fool by the shoulders and shook him savagely. His head whipped back and forth on his thin neck. "Go with Chade and be silent. Be silent, if you want your king's death avenged. For that is what I go to do." A sudden tremor ran over me and the world rocked, black at the edges. "Elfbark!" I gasped. "I need elfbark from you. Then flee!" I thrust the Fool into Chade's arms, and the old man took him in his ropy grasp. It was like watching him taken into the arms of death. They left the room, Chade propelling the weeping Fool along. After a moment I heard the barest grating of stone on stone. I knew they were gone.

I sank to my knees, then could not keep from toppling. I fetched up against my dead king's lap. His cooling hand fell from the chair arm to rest atop my head.

"A stupid time for tears," I said aloud to the empty room. But that did not stop them. Blackness swirled at the edge of my vision. The ghostly Skill fingers plucked at my walls, scraping at the mortar, trying every stone. I pushed at them, but they came right back. The way Chade had looked at me, I suddenly doubted that he would be back. Still. I took a breath.

Nighteyes. Guide them to the fox's den. I showed him the shed they would emerge from and where they must go. It was all I could manage.

My brother?

Guide them, my heart! I pushed him feebly away, and felt him go. Still the foolish tears tracked down my face. I reached to steady myself. My hand fell at the King's waist. I opened my eyes, forced my vision to clear. His knife. Not some jeweled dagger, but the simple knife that every man carries at his waist, for the simple day-to-day tasks he does. I took a breath, then pulled it from its sheath. I held it in my lap and looked at it. An honest blade, honed thin from years of use. A handle of antler, probably carved once, but worn smooth with the grip of his hand. I ran my fingers lightly over it, and they found what my eyes could no longer read. Hod's sign. The weaponsmaster had made this for her king. And he had used it well.

A memory tickled at the back of my mind. "We are tools," Chade had told me. I was the tool he had forged for the King. The King had looked at me, and wondered, *What have I made of you?* I did not need to wonder. I was the King's assassin. In more ways than one. But I would see that I served him as I had been intended, one last time.

Someone crouched beside me. Chade. I turned my head slowly to look at him. "Carris seed," he told me. "No time to prepare elfbark. Come. Let me take you into hiding as well."

"No." I took the small cake of carris seed compressed with honey. I put the whole thing in my mouth and chewed, grinding the seed between my back teeth to release the full strength. I swallowed. "Go," I bid him. "I have a task, and so have you. Burrich is waiting. The alarm will be raised soon. Get the Queen away quickly, while you have a chance of getting ahead of the hunt. I will keep them busy."

He released me. "Good-bye, boy," he said gruffly, and stooped to kiss me on the forehead. It was farewell. He didn't expect to see me alive again.

That made two of us.

He left me there, and before even I heard the grate of stone on stone, I felt the working of the carris seed. I had had the seed before, at Springfest when everyone does. A tiny pinch of it sprinkled across the top of a sugar cake brings a merry giddiness to the heart. Burrich had warned me that some dishonest horse traders fed their charges carris oil on their grain, for the purpose of winning a race, or to make a sick horse show well at an auction. He had also warned me that a horse so treated was often never the same beast again. If he survived. I knew Chade had used it, on occasion, and I had seen him drop like a stone when the effects wore off. Yet I did not hesitate. Perhaps, I conceded briefly, perhaps Burrich was right about me. The ecstasy of the Skill, or the frantic flush and heat of the hunt. Did I taunt self-destruction, or did I desire it? I did not worry about it for long. The carris seed took me. My strength was as the strength of ten, and my heart soared like an eagle. I sprang to my feet. I started for the door, then turned back.

I knelt before my dead king. I lifted his knife, held it before my brow as I swore to him, "This blade shall take your vengeance." I kissed his hand and left him there before the fire.

If I had thought the candles spitting blue sparks were unnerving, then the blue glow of the torches in the hall were otherworldly. It was like looking down through still deep water. I sprinted down the hall, giggling to myself. Below, I could hear a clamor, with Wallace's voice raised shrill above the rest. Blue flames and the Pocked Man, he was yammering. Not as much time had passed as I had thought, and now time waited for me. Light as the wind I darted down the hall. I found a door that would open and slipped within. I waited. They took forever to come up the stairs, even longer to go past my door. I let them reach the King's chamber, and when I heard the shouts of alarm begin, I sprang from my hiding place and dashed down the stairs.

Someone shouted after me as I fled, but no one gave chase. I was to the bottom of the stairs before I heard someone finally give the order to catch me. I laughed aloud. As if they could! Buckkeep Castle was a warren of back ways and servants' passages for a boy who had grown up there. I knew where I was going, but I didn't go there directly. Like a fox I ran, appearing briefly in the Great Hall, dashing across the cobbles of the washing courts, terrifying Cook with my frantic dash through her kitchens. And always, always, the pale Skill fingers plucked and fingered me, not knowing at all that I was coming, coming, my dears, coming to find you.

Galen, born and raised in Farrow, had always hated the sea. He feared it, I think, and so his chamber had been on the side of the Keep that faced the mountains. After he had died, I had heard it had become a shrine to him. Serene had taken over his bedchamber, but kept his sitting room as a gathering place for the coterie. I had never visited his rooms, but I knew the way. I took the steps up like an arrow in flight, whisked down the hall past a couple in a heated embrace and stopped at a heavy door banded with iron. But a thick door that is not properly barred is no barrier at all, and in moments this one swung open to my touch.

There was a semicircle of chairs set up around a tall table. A fat candle burned in the center of it. For focus, I imagined. Only two of the chairs were occupied. Justin and Serene sat side by side, hands clasped, eyes closed, heads lolled back in the throes of Skilling. No Will. I had hoped to find him here as well.

For the barest instant I looked at their faces. Perspiration gleamed on them, and I was flattered that they put so much effort to breaking down my walls. Their mouths twitched in small smiles, resisting the ecstasy of the Skill user, focusing on the object rather than on the pleasure of the pursuit. I did not hesitate. "Surprise!" I said softly. I jerked Serene's head back and pulled the King's blade across her exposed throat. She jerked once, and I let her fall to the floor. There was a remarkable amount of blood.

Justin leaped to his feet with a shriek and I braced myself for his onslaught. He fooled me, though. He fled squealing down the hall and I followed, knife in hand. He sounded just like a pig, and he was incredibly fast. No fox tricks for Justin, he favored the most direct route to the Great Hall, shrieking all the way. I laughed as I ran. Even now it seems to me incredible to recall that, but I cannot deny it. Did he suppose Regal would draw sword to defend him? Did he think, having killed my king, that anything in the world could stand between me and him?

In the Great Hall, musicians had been playing and folk dancing, but Justin's entrance put an end to that. I had gained on him, so that there were scarce a score of steps between us when he caromed into one of the laden tables. Folk were still standing shocked at his entrance when I leaped on him and pulled him down. I punched the knife in and out of him half a dozen times before anyone thought they should interfere. As Regal's Farrow-bred guards reached for me I flung his twitching body into them, found a table at my back, and leaped onto it. I held up my dripping blade. "The King's knife!" I told them, and showed it 'round. "Taking blood in vengeance for the King's death. That is all!"

"He's mad!" someone cried. "Verity's death has driven him mad!"

"Shrewd!" I cried in fury. "King Shrewd has fallen to treachery this night!"

Regal's Inlander guards hit my table in a wave. I had not thought there were that many of them. We all went down in a wave of food and crockery. Folk were screaming, but as many surged forward to witness as retreated in horror. Hod would

have been proud of me. With the king's belt knife, I held o
three men with short swords. I danced, I leaped, I pirouetted.
was much too fast for them and the cuts they did inflict on m
caused me no pain. I scored two good slashes on two of then
simply because they did not think I would dare lunge clos
enough to inflict them.

· Somewhere back in the crowd, someone raised a cry
"Arms! To the Bastard! They are killing FitzChivalry!" /
struggle began, but I could not see who was involved, nor giv
it any attention at all. I stabbed one of the guards in the han
and he dropped his blade. "Shrewd!" someone cried above th
din. "King Shrewd is slain!" By the sounds of the other strug
gle, more folk were becoming involved. I could not look to see
I heard another table crash to the floor, and a scream across th
room. Then Buckkeep's own guard came pouring into th
room. I heard Kerf's voice raised above the general din. "Sep
arate them! Quell it! Try not to spill blood in the King's ow
hall!" I saw my attackers ringed, saw Blade's look of conster
nation as he saw me and then cried out over his shoulder, "It'
FitzChivalry! They're trying to take down the Fitz!"

"Separate them! Disarm them!" Kerf butted heads wit
one of Regal's guards, dropping him. Beyond him I saw knot
of struggling break out as Buck guards fell on Regal's persona
guard, battering blades down and demanding that swords b
sheathed. I had space for a breath, and could lift my eyes from
my own struggle to see that, indeed, a great many folk ha
become involved, and not just guards. Fistfights had broken ou
among the guests as well. It looked to become both brawl an
riot when suddenly Blade, one of our own guardsmen, shoul
dered between two of my attackers, sending them sprawling t
the floor. He leaped forward and confronted me.

"Blade!" I greeted him with delight, thinking him an ally
Then, as I noticed his defensive stance, I told him, "You know
I would not draw blade against you!"

"I know that well, lad," he told me sadly, and the ol
soldier flung himself forward to trap me in a bear hug. I do no
know who hit me on the back of the head, or with what.

30

Dungeons

*I*F A HOUNDSMAN *suspects that a dog boy is using the Wit to defile and divert the hounds to his own ends, he should be watchful for these signs. If the boy speaks not overmuch to his fellows, be wary. If the hounds perk up before the boy is in sight, or whine before he has left, be watchful. If a hound will leave off his snuffing for a bitch in season, or turn aside from a blood trail and lie quiet at the boy's word, be certain. Let the boy be hanged, over water if possible, well away from the stables, and his body burned. Let every hound he has trained be drowned, as well as all sired by defiled hounds. A hound who has known the Wit use will neither fear nor respect any other master, but is sure to turn vicious when deprived of the Witted one. A Witted boy cannot be trusted to beat an unruly hound, nor will he suffer his Wit hound to be sold away, or used as bear bait, no matter how old the dog. A Wit boy will turn his master's hounds to his own purposes, and never has any true loyalty to his master, but only to his Wit hound.*

❦

I woke up sometime. Of all the cruel jests fate had recently played on me, I decided that awakening was the cruelest. I lay still and cataloged my various discomforts. The exhaustion

from my carris-seed frenzy combined well with the exhaustion
from my Skill battle with Justin and Serene. I had taken some
nasty sword cuts to my right forearm, and one to my left thigh
that I recalled not at all. None of them had been dressed; my
sleeve and trousers were matted to my skin with dried blood.
Whoever had knocked me unconscious had made sure of his
work with several more blows. Other than that, I was fine. I
told myself this a number of times, ignoring the trembling in
my left leg and arm. I opened my eyes.

The room I was in was small and stone. There was a pot in
the corner. When I finally decided I could move, I craned my
head enough to see that there was a door, with a small barred
window in it. This was the light source, fed by a torch somewhere down a hallway outside. Oh. Yes. The dungeons. My
curiosity satisfied, I closed my eyes again and slept. Nose to
tail, I rested safe in a deep den covered over by the blowing
snow. The illusion of safety was as much as Nighteyes could
offer me. So weak I was that even his thoughts to me seemed
misty. *Safe.* That was as much as he could convey.

I awoke again. I could tell time had passed by how much
thirstier I was. Other than that, everything was remarkably the
same. This time I determined that the bench I was lying on was
also made of stone. There was nothing between me and the
stone save the clothes I wore. "Hey!" I called. "Guards!"
There was no answer. Everything seemed a bit vague. After a
time I could not recall if I had already cried out, or if I was
summoning the strength to do so. After a bit more time I
decided I did not have the strength. I went back to sleep. I
couldn't imagine doing anything else.

I awoke to Patience's voice arguing. Whoever she was
arguing with wasn't answering much, and wasn't giving in.
"It's ridiculous. What are you afraid I'll do?" A silence. "I've
known him since he was a child." Another silence. "He's hurt.
What possible damage can it do for me to at least look at his
injuries? You can hang him whole as easily as you can
wounded, can't you?" Another silence.

After a time I decided I might be able to move. I had a lot
of bruises and scrapes I couldn't account for, probably gained
on the journey between the Great Hall and here. The worst part

of moving was that it tugged my clothing against the scabbed-
over cuts. I decided I could stand it. For such a small room, it
was a very long way from the bed to the door. When I got
there, I discovered I could just see out the little barred window.
What I could see was the stone wall on the opposite side of the
narrow corridor. I gripped the bars with my good left hand.

"Patience?" I croaked.

"Fitz? Oh, Fitz, are you all right?"

Such a question. I started to laugh and coughed instead,
finishing with the taste of blood in my mouth. I didn't know
what to say. I wasn't fine, but it wasn't healthy for her to be too
interested in me. Even as fuddled as I was, I knew that. "I'm
all right," I croaked at last.

"Oh, Fitz, the King is dead!" she called to me from down
the hall. The words tumbled from her in her haste to tell me all.
"And Queen Kettricken is missing, and King-in-Waiting Regal
says you are at the bottom of all of it. They say—"

"Lady Patience, you'll have to leave now," the guard
attempted to break in. She ignored him.

"—you went crazy in grief over Verity's death, and killed
the King and Serene and Justin, and they don't know what
you've done with the Queen, and no one can—"

"You cannot speak to the prisoner, madam!" He spoke
with conviction, but she paid no mind.

"—find the Fool. Wallace, he's the one, he said he saw
you and the Fool quarreling over the King's body, and then he
saw the Pocked Man, come to carry his spirit away. The man is
crazy! And Regal accuses you, too, of the low magic, of having
the soul of a beast! That's how he said you killed the King.
And—"

"Madam! You have to leave now, or I will have to have
you taken away."

"Then do that," Patience spat at him. "I just dare you to
try. Lacey, this man is bothering me. Ah! You dare to think of
touching me! I, who was Chivalry's queen-in-waiting! Now,
Lacey, do not hurt him, he's only a boy. A mannerless boy, but
a boy nonetheless."

"Lady Patience, I beg you. . . ." A change in tone from
the guard.

"You can't very well drag me away from here without leaving your post. Do you think I'm so stupid I can't see that? What will you do? Attack two old women with your sword?"

"Chester! Chester, where are you?" the guard on duty bellowed. "Damn you, Chester!" I could hear the frustration in his voice as he yelled for his partner, who had taken a break. He was probably up in the watch room off the kitchen. Drinking cold beer. Eating hot stew. A wave of dizziness passed over me.

"Chester?" The guard's voice was fading. He had actually been fool enough to leave Lady Patience by his post and go looking for his comrade. In a moment I heard the light patter of her slippers outside my door. I felt the touch of her fingers on my hand that gripped the bar. She was not tall enough to look in, and the corridor was so narrow she could not step back where I could see her. But the touch of her hand was as welcome as sunlight.

"Keep watch for him coming back, Lacey," she directed, then spoke to me. "How are you, really?" She spoke low, pitching her voice for my ears alone.

"Thirsty. Hungry. Cold. In pain." I saw no point in lying to her. "What is happening in the Keep?"

"Complete disorder. The Buckkeep guards broke up the riot in the Great Hall, but then, outside, there was a brawl between some of the Inlanders that Regal brought in and the Buckkeep guard. Queen Kettricken's guard drove a wedge between them, and their officers beat their troops back into line. Still, it's tense. The fighters weren't all soldiers. Many a guest has a black eye or walks with a limp still. Luckily, no one amongst the guests took serious harm. Blade took about the worst injuries, they say. He went down keeping the Farrow men off you. Cracked his ribs and blacked his eyes, did something to one of his arms. But Burrich says he will be all right. The lines have been drawn, however, and the Dukes walk about bristling at one another like dogs."

"Burrich?" I asked hoarsely.

"Did not get involved at all," she said reassuringly. "He's fine. If being ill-tempered and surly to all is fine. Which, for him, I suppose is normal."

My heart thundered inside me. Burrich. Why wasn't he gone? I dared ask no more about him. One question too many, and Patience would get curious. So. "And Regal?" I asked.

She snorted. "One gets the feeling that what really irritates Regal is that he no longer has an excuse to abandon Buckkeep. Before, you know, he was taking King Shrewd and Kettricken inland so they would be safe, and gutting the castle so they might have familiar things about them. He has no such excuse now, and the Coastal Dukes have demanded he stay and defend the Keep, or at least put in that place a man of their choosing. He has offered his cousin Lord Bright of Farrow, but the Coastal Dukes do not like him. Now that Regal finds himself suddenly a King, I do not think he is enjoying it as much as he expected to."

"Has he crowned himself, then?" A roaring threatened my ears. I stood by gripping the bars. Must not faint, I told myself. The guard would be back soon. I had only this time to hear what was going on.

"We have all been much too busy burying the King, and then searching for the Queen. When the King was found dead, we were sent to wake her, but found her doors locked and no answer to our knocking. Finally Regal resorted to his men and axes again. The inner-chamber door was closed and locked as well. But the Queen was gone. It is a great mystery to all of us."

"What does Regal say of it?" My head was clearing of cobwebs. Oh, how I hurt.

"Little, save that she and her child are surely dead, and you have brought it about somehow. He speaks wild charges of Beast magic, saying you have slain the King with your Wit. All demand proof for his claims, and he keeps saying, soon, soon."

No mention of searching the roads and byways for Kettricken, then. I had gambled that his Skill spies had not found out the whole of our plot. But, I cautioned myself, if he had sent out searchers, I doubted they were ordered to bring her back alive and safe.

"What does Will do?" I asked.

"Will?"

"Will, Hostler's son. A member of the coterie."

"Oh. Him. I have not seen him about, that I recall."

"Ah." Another wave of dizziness threatened me. Suddenly logic eluded me. I knew I should ask more questions, but I could not think of what they should be. Burrich was still here, but the Queen and the Fool were gone. What had gone wrong? There was no safe way to ask Patience. "Does anyone else know you are here?" I managed to ask. Surely, if Burrich had known she were coming, he would have sent a message.

"Of course not! This was not an easy thing to plan, Fitz. Lacey had to get an emetic into the one guard's food so he would leave only one on watch. Then we had to watch for him to leave—oh. Lacey said to bring you these. She is wise, that one." Her hand went away, and then came back, to fumble one, and then two small apples through the bars. They hit the floor before I could catch them. I resisted the urge to pounce on them immediately.

"What do they say of me?" I asked quietly.

She was silent a moment. "Mostly, folk say that you are crazy. Some, that you were witched by the Pocked Man to bring death amongst us that night. There is some gossip that you had planned to lead a rebellion, and killed Serene and Justin because they found out about it. Others, not many, agree with Regal, saying you have the Beast magic. Wallace, mostly, says such things. He declares the candles did not burn blue in the King's chamber until you entered it. And he says the Fool was shouting that you had killed the King. But the Fool is gone, too. There have been so many omens of evil, and so many fear now. . . ." Her voice dwindled away.

"I did not kill the King," I said quietly. "Justin and Serene did. That was why I killed them, with the King's own knife."

"The guards are coming back!" A hiss from Lacey. Patience ignored it.

"But Justin and Serene weren't even—"

"I don't have time to explain. It was done with Skill. But they did, Patience. I swear it." I paused. "What do they plan to do with me?"

"It isn't decided, really."

"We've no time for polite lies."

I actually heard her swallow. "Regal wants to hang you. He'd have had you killed right there that night, in the Great Hall, save that Blade held off his guards until the riot was quelled. Then the Coastal Dukes stood up for you. Lady Grace of Rippon reminded Regal that no carrier of the Farseer blood can be put to death by sword or hanging. He did not wish to concede you were of royal blood, but too many raised a shout when he denied it. Now he swears he can show you have the Wit, and hanging is what must be done for one that uses Beast magic."

"Lady Patience! You must leave now, you must, or I'm the one that will be hanging!" The guard was back, with Chester evidently, for there was more than one set of footsteps. They were hurrying down to the cell. Patience let go of my fingers.

"I will do what I can for you," she whispered. She had tried so hard not to let any fear come into her voice, but now it broke on those words.

And then she was gone, scolding at the guard like a jaybird all the way as Chester or whoever escorted her from the cells. The moment she was gone, I laboriously stooped down to gather up my apples. They were not large, and they were withered from being winter-stored, but I found them delicious. I ate even the stems. The little moisture they contained did nothing to quench my thirst. I sat on my bench for a bit, holding my head in my hands, forcing myself to stay alert. I knew I had to think, but it was terribly hard. My mind would not focus. I was tempted to pick my shirt free of the cuts on my arm, but forced myself to leave it alone. As long as they were not festering, I would not bother them. I could not afford to bleed. It took all my strength to hobble back to my door. "Guards!" I croaked.

They ignored me.

"I want water. And food."

Where are you? Another answered my request.

Beyond your reach, my friend. How are you?

Fine. But I have missed you. You slept so deep, almost I thought you dead.

Almost I thought myself dead. That night. Did you guide them to the horses?

I did. And they left. Heart of the Pack told them I was a half-breed you had tamed. Like I was a cur, doing tricks.

He sought to protect me, not to insult you. Why did not Heart of the Pack go with them?

I do not know. What shall we do now?

Wait.

"Guards!" I called again, as loudly as I was able. It wasn't very loud.

"Get back from the door." The man's voice was right outside my cell. I had been so occupied with Nighteyes I had not heard him approach. I was not myself at all.

A small panel at the bottom of the door slid open. A pot of water and a half a loaf were set inside. The panel closed again.

"Thank you."

There was no reply. I picked them up, examined both carefully. The water smelled as if it had been standing for some time, but neither smell nor a cautious sip revealed any trace of poison. I broke the loaf into smaller pieces, looking for flecks in the dough or any discoloration. It was not fresh, but it was not poisoned in any way I could detect. And someone had eaten the other half of it. In a very short time they were gone. I went and lay on my stone bench again, and tried to find the least uncomfortable position.

The cell was dry, but cold, in the way that any unused chamber in Buckkeep was cold during the winter. I knew exactly where I was. The cells were not far from the wine cellars. I knew I could scream my lungs bloody and no one but my guards would hear. I had explored down here as a boy. I had seldom found occupants in the cells, and even more rarely guards upon them. The swiftness of justice at Buckkeep meant there was seldom a reason to hold a prisoner for more than a few hours. Transgressions of the law usually demanded you pay with your life, or with the work of your hands. I suspected these cells would see a deal more use, now that Regal claimed to be king.

I tried to sleep, but insensibility had deserted me. Instead, I shifted about on the cold hard stone and thought. I tried for a while to convince myself that if the Queen had gotten away, I had won. After all, winning was getting what you wanted, wasn't it? Instead, I found myself thinking of how quickly King Shrewd had gone. Like a bubble popping. If they hanged me, would it be that swift for me? Or would I strangle and dangle a long time? To divert myself from those pleasant thoughts, I wondered how long a civil war Verity would have to fight with Regal before he could put the Six Duchies on a map once more as the Six Duchies. Assuming, of course, that Verity returned and was able to rid the coast of Red-Ships. When Regal abandoned Buckkeep, as I was sure he would, I wondered who would step forward to take it. Patience had said the Coastal Dukes wanted nothing of Lord Bright. Buck had a few lesser nobles, but none of them so bold as to claim Buckkeep, I thought. Perhaps one of the three Coastal Dukes would reach out a hand and claim it. No. None of them had the might right now to care for anything beyond their own borders. It would be each for his own now. Unless Regal stayed at Buckkeep. With the Queen missing and Shrewd dead, he was, after all, the rightful King. Unless one knew that Verity was alive. But few did. Would the Coastal Duchies accept Regal as king now? Would the Coastal Duchies accept Verity as their king when he returned? Or would they scorn the man who had left them for a foolish quest?

Time passed slowly in that unchanging place. I was not given food nor water unless I asked for them, and sometimes not then, so meals were no measure of the day. Awake, I was a prisoner of my thoughts and worries. Once I tried to Skill to Verity, but the effort brought on a darkening of my vision and a long period of pounding headache. I had not the strength for a second effort. Hunger became a constant, as unrelenting as the cold of the cell. I heard the guards twice turn Patience away, heard them refuse to give me the food and bandages she had brought. I did not call to her. I wanted her to give up, to disassociate herself from me. My only respite came when I slept and dream-hunted with Nighteyes. I tried to use his senses to explore what went on at Buckkeep, but he attached only a wolf's importance to things, and when I was with him, I shared his values. Time was not divided by days and nights, but from kill to kill. The meat I devoured with him could not sustain my human body, and yet there was satisfaction in the gorging. With his senses I found the weather changing, and awoke one morning knowing that a clear winter day had dawned. Raider weather. The Coastal Dukes could not linger much longer in Buckkeep, if they had lingered at all.

As if to bear me out, there were voices at the guard station and the rasp of boots against the stone floor. I heard Regal's voice, strained with anger, and the guard's conciliatory greeting, and then they came down the corridor. For the first time since I had awakened there, I heard a key in the lock of my cell, and the door was swung open. I sat up slowly. Three Dukes and a traitor Prince peered in at me. I managed to come to my feet. Behind my lords stood a row of soldiers armed with pikes, as if ready to hold a maddened beast at bay. A guard with a drawn sword stood beside the open door, between Regal and me. He did not underestimate my hatred.

"You see him," Regal declared flatly. "He is alive and well. I have not done away with him. But know also that I have the right to. He killed a man, my servant, right in my hall. And a woman upstairs in her chamber. I have a right to his life, for those crimes alone."

"King-in-Waiting Regal. You charge FitzChivalry killed King Shrewd using the Wit," Brawndy stated. With ponderous logic he added, "I have never heard of such a thing being possible. But if this is so, then the council has first right to his life, for he would have killed the King first. It would take a convening of the council, to decide his guilt or innocence, and to set his sentence."

Regal sighed in exasperation. "Then I will convene the council. Let us get it done and have it over with. It is ridiculous to delay my coronation for a murderer's execution."

"My lord, a King's death is never ridiculous," Duke Shemshy of Shoaks pointed out quietly. "And we will have done with one King before we have another, Regal, King-in-Waiting."

"My father is dead and buried. How much more done with him can you be?" Regal was becoming reckless. There was nothing of grief or respect in his retort.

''We will know how he died, and at whose hand,'' Brawndy of Bearns told him. ''Your man Wallace said FitzChivalry killed the King. You, King-in-Waiting Regal, agreed, saying he used the Wit to do it. Many of us believe that FitzChivalry was singularly devoted to his king and would not do such a thing. And FitzChivalry said the Skill users did.'' For the first time Duke Brawndy looked directly at me. I met his eyes and spoke to him as if we were alone.

''Justin and Serene killed him,'' I said quietly. ''By treachery, they killed my king.''

''Silence!'' Regal bawled. He lifted his hand as if to strike me. I did not flinch.

''And so I killed them,'' I continued, looking only at Brawndy. ''With the King's knife. Why else would I have chosen such a weapon?''

''Crazy men do strange things.'' This from Duke Kelvar of Rippon, while Regal strangled, livid with fury. I met Kelvar's eyes calmly. Last I had spoken with him had been at his own table, at Neatbay.

''I am not crazy,'' I asserted quietly. ''I was no more crazy that night than I was the night I wielded an ax outside the walls of Bayguard.''

''That may be so,'' Kelvar affirmed thoughtfully. ''It is common talk that he goes berserk when he fights.''

A glint came into Regal's eyes. ''It is common talk, too, that he has been seen with blood on his mouth after he has fought. That he becomes one of the animals that he was raised with. He is Witted.''

Silence greeted this remark. The Dukes exchanged glances, and when Shemshy glanced back at me, there was distaste in the look. Brawndy finally answered Regal. ''This is a grave charge you level. Have you a witness?''

''To blood on his mouth? Several.''

Brawndy shook his head. ''Any man may finish a battle with a bloody face. An ax is not a tidy weapon. I can attest to that. No. It would take more than that.''

''Then let us convene the council,'' Regal repeated impatiently. ''Hear what Wallace has to say about how my father died and at whose hand.''

The three Dukes exchanged glances. Their eyes came back to me, considering. Duke Brawndy led the coast now. I was certain of it when he was the one who spoke. "King-in-Waiting Regal. Let us speak plainly. You have accused FitzChivalry, son of Chivalry, of using the Wit, the Beast magic, to slay King Shrewd. This is indeed a grave charge. To satisfy us of it, we ask that you prove to us that not only is he Witted, but that he can use it to do injury to another. All of us were witness that there were no marks on King Shrewd's body, no sign of a death struggle at all. Had not you raised this cry of treachery, we might have accepted that he had died of his years. Some, even, have whispered that you but seek an excuse to be rid of FitzChivalry. I know you have heard these rumors; I speak them aloud that we may confront them." Brawndy paused, as if debating with himself. He glanced once more at his peers. When neither Kelvar nor Shemshy gave sign of dissension, he cleared his throat and continued.

"We have a proposal, King-in-Waiting Regal. Prove to us, sir, that FitzChivalry is Witted, and that he used that Wit to kill King Shrewd, and we will let you put him to death as you see fit. We will witness your coronation as king of the Six Duchies. Further, we will accept Lord Bright as your presence in Buckkeep and allow you to retire your court to Tradeford."

Triumph gleamed briefly on Regal's face. Then suspicion masked it. "And if, Duke Brawndy, I do not prove this to your satisfaction?"

"Then FitzChivalry lives," Brawndy calmly decreed. "And you give him stewardship of Buckkeep and the forces of Buck in your absence." All three Coastal Dukes lifted their eyes to meet Regal's.

"This is treason and treachery!" Regal hissed.

Shemshy's hand almost went to his sword. Kelvar reddened but said nothing. The tension in the line of men behind them tightened a notch. Only Brawndy remained unmoved. "My lord, do you bring more charges?" he asked calmly. "Again, we will demand them proved. It could further delay your coronation."

After a moment of their stony eyes and silence, Regal said quietly, "I spoke in haste, my dukes. These are trying times for me. Bereft of my father's guidance so suddenly, bereaved of my brother, our lady queen and the child she carries gone missing . . . These surely are enough cause to drive any man to hasty statements. I . . . very well. I will acquiesce to this . . . bargain you set before me. I will prove FitzChivalry Witted, or I will set him free. Does that satisfy you?''

''No, my king-in-waiting,'' Brawndy said quietly. ''Such were not the terms we set. If innocent, FitzChivalry will be set in command of Buckkeep. If you prove him guilty, we shall accept Bright. Those were our terms.''

''And the deaths of Justin and Serene, valuable servants and coterie members? Those deaths at least we know we may put at his door. He has admitted as much.'' The look Regal turned on me should have killed me right there. How deeply he must have regretted charging me with murdering Shrewd. But for Wallace's wild accusations and Regal's backing of them, he could have demanded me drowned for Justin's death. That, as everyone had witnessed, was my doing. Ironically, his own desire to vilify me was what was staving off my execution.

''You will have every chance to prove him Witted and the killer of your father. For those crimes, only, will we let you hang him. As to the others . . . he claims they were the killers of the King. If he is not the guilty one, we are willing to accept that those he killed died justly.''

''This is intolerable!'' Regal spat.

''My lord, those are our terms,'' Brawndy returned calmly.

''And if I refuse them?'' Regal flared angrily.

Brawndy shrugged. ''The skies are clear, my lord. Raider weather, for those of us with coasts. We must disperse to our own Keeps, to guard our coasts as well we may. Without the convening of the full council, you cannot crown yourself king, nor lawfully appoint a man to hold Buck in your stead. You must winter at Buckkeep, my lord, and confront the sea pirates even as we do.''

''You ring me 'round with traditions and petty laws, all to force me to your will. Am I your king or am I not?'' Regal demanded bluntly.

''You are not our king.'' Brawndy pointed it out quietly

but firmly. "You are our king-in-waiting. And likely to continue waiting until these charges and this issue is resolved."

The blackness of Regal's glare plainly showed how little this was to his liking. "Very well," he said flatly, all too quickly. "I suppose I must submit to this . . . bargaining. Remember that you have decreed it must be this way, not I." He turned and looked at me. I knew then that he would not keep his word; I knew I would die in this cell. That sick and sudden knowledge of my own death blackened the edges of my vision, set me swaying on my feet. I felt I had taken two steps back from life. A coldness crept up inside me.

"Then we are agreed," Brawndy said smoothly. He turned his eyes back to me, and frowned. Something of what I was feeling must have showed on my face, for he asked quickly, "FitzChivalry. Are you fairly treated here? Do they feed you?" As he asked this he unfastened the brooch at his shoulder. His cloak was much worn, but of wool, and when he threw it to me, the weight of it knocked me back against the wall.

I clutched the cloak, warm still with his body heat, gratefully. "Water. Bread," I said briefly. I looked down at the heavy wool garment. "Thank you," I said more quietly.

"It's better than many have!" Regal retorted angrily. "Times are hard," he added lamely. As if those he spoke to did not know that better than he did.

Brawndy regarded me for a few moments. I said nothing. Finally he swung a cold look to Regal. "Too hard to at least give him some straw to sleep on, instead of a slab of stone?"

Regal returned his glare. Brawndy did not quail. "We will need proof of his guilt, King-in-Waiting Regal, before we will countenance his execution. In the meantime we expect you to keep him alive."

"At least give him marching rations," Kelvar advised. "No one will say you have pampered him with those, and we shall have a live man, either for you to hang or to command at Buck for us."

Regal crossed his arms on his chest and made no reply. I knew I would get but water and half a loaf. I think he would have tried to take Brawndy's cloak away from me, save that he knew I would have fought for it. With a jerk of his chin, Regal indicated to the guard that he could close my door. As it slammed shut I flung myself forward, to grip the bars and stare after them. I thought of calling out, of telling them all that Regal would not let me live, that he would find a way to kill me here. But I did not. They would not have believed me. They still did not fear Regal as they needed to. If they had known him as I did, they would have known that no promise could bind him to their bargain. He would kill me. I was too deeply within his power for him to resist ending me.

I let go of the door and walked woodenly back to my bench. I sat down. Reflex more than thought made me drape Brawndy's cloak about my shoulders. The cold I felt now would not be warmed away by wool. As the wave of a rising tide rushes into a sea cavern, so the knowledge of my death once more filled me. Once again, I thought I might faint. I pushed at it, vaguely *repelling* at my own thoughts of how Regal might choose to kill me. There were so many ways. I suspected he would try to wring a confession from me. Given enough time, he might be successful. The thought made me sick. I tried to pull myself back from the brink, not to realize so thoroughly that I was going to die painfully.

With a peculiar lightening of heart, I reflected that I could cheat him. Within my blood-matted sleeve cuff was the tiny pocket that still held the poison I had so long ago prepared for Wallace. Had it offered a less horrendous death, I would have taken it right then. But I had not formulated that poison for a quick and painless sleep, but for cramps and flux and fever. Later, I thought, it might become preferable to whatever Regal offered. There was no comfort in that thought. I lay back on my slab and rolled myself up well in Brawndy's ample cloak. I hoped he would not miss it too much. It was probably the last kind thing anyone would ever do for me. I did not fall asleep. I fled, willfully submerging myself into my wolf's world.

I awoke later from a human dream in which Chade had been lecturing me for not paying attention. I drew myself smaller in Brawndy's cloak. Torchlight trickling into my cell. Day or night, I could not tell, but I thought it was deep night. I

tried to find sleep again. Chade's urgent voice had been pleading with me. . . .

I sat up slowly. The cadence and tone of the muffled voice
was definitely Chade's. It seemed fainter when I sat up. I lay
down again. Now it was louder, but I still couldn't pick out the
words. I pressed my ear to the stone bench. No. I got up slowly
and moved about my small cell, from wall to corner and back
again. There was one corner in which the voice was loudest,
but I still could not make out the words. "I can't understand
you," I said to my empty cell.

The muffled voice paused. Then it spoke again, a questioning inflection.

"I can't understand you!" I said more loudly.

Chade's voice resumed, more excitedly, but no louder.

"I can't understand you!" I shouted in frustration.

Footsteps outside my cell. "FitzChivalry!"

The guard was short. She couldn't see in. "What?" I
asked sleepily.

"What were you shouting?"

"What? Oh. Bad dream."

The footsteps went away. I heard her laugh to the other
guard and say, "Hard to imagine what dream could be worse
than waking up for him." She had an inland accent.

I went back to my bench and lay down. Chade's voice had
stopped. I tended to agree with the guard. I would not sleep
again for a while, but would wonder what Chade had been so
desperately trying to tell me. I doubted it would be good news,
and I did not want to imagine bad. I was going to have to die
here. At least let it be because I had aided the Queen's escape.
I wondered how far she was on her journey. I thought of the
Fool, and wondered how well he would withstand the rigors of
a winter journey. I forbade myself to wonder why Burrich was
not with them. Instead, I thought of Molly.

I must have drowsed, for I saw her. She was toiling up a
path, a yoke of water buckets on her shoulders. She looked pale
and sick and worn. On top of the hill was a tumbledown cottage, snow banked against its walls. She stopped and set her
water buckets down at the door and stood looking out, over the
sea. She frowned at the fair weather and the light wind that

only tipped the waves with white. The wind lifted her thick hair just as I used to and slid its hand along the curve of her warm neck and jaw. Her eyes went suddenly wide. Then tears brimmed them. "No," she said aloud. "No. I won't think of you anymore. No." She stooped and lifted the heavy buckets and went into the cottage. She shut the door firmly behind her. The wind blew past it. The roof was poorly thatched. The wind blew harder and I let it carry me away.

I tumbled on it, dove through it, and let it flow my pains away. I thought of diving deeper, down into the main flow of it, where it could sweep me entirely away, right out of myself and all my petty worries. I trailed my hands in that deeper current, swift and heavy as a moving river. It tugged at me.

I'd stand back from that if I were you.

Would you? I let Verity consider my situation for a moment.

Perhaps not, he replied grimly. Something like a sigh. *I should have guessed at how bad it was. It seems it takes great pain, or illness, or extreme duress of some kind to break down your walls so you can Skill.* He paused long and we were both silent, thinking of nothing and everything all at once. *So. My father is dead. Justin and Serene. I should have guessed somehow. His weariness and dwindling strength; those are the hallmarks of a King's Man, drained too low too often. I suspect it had been going on long, probably since before Galen . . . died. Only he could have conceived such a thing, let alone devised a way to do it. What a loathsome way to use the Skill. And they spied upon us?*

Yes. I do not know how much they learned. And there is another to fear. Will.

Damn me thrice for a fool. Look at it, Fitz. We should have known. The ships worked so well for us at first, and then, as soon as they knew what we were up to, you and I, they found ways to block us. The coterie has been in Regal's pocket since they were formed. Thus we have delayed messages, or messages not delivered. Help always sent too late, or never sent at all. He is as full of hate as a tick is full of blood. And he has won.

Not quite, my king. I reined my mind back from thinking

of Kettricken safely on her way to the Mountains. Instead, I repeated, *There is still Will. And Burl and Carrod. We must be circumspect, my prince.*

A shade of warmth. *I shall. But you know the depths of my thanks. Perhaps we paid highly, but what we bought was worth it. To me, at least.*

To me, also. I sensed the weariness in him, and the resignation. *Are you giving up?*

Not yet. But like yours, my future does not seem promising. The others are all dead or fled. I will go on. But I don't know how much farther I must go. Or what I must do when I get there. And I am so very tired. To give in would be so easy.

Verity read me with ease, I knew. But I had to reach for him and for all he was not conveying to me. I sensed the great cold that surrounded him, and an injury that made it painful to breathe. His aloneness, and the pain of knowing that those who had died had died so far from home, and for him. *Hod,* I thought, my own grief echoing his. *Charim.* Gone forever. And something else, something he could not quite convey. A temptation, a teetering at the brink. A pressure, a plucking, very similar to the Skillish plucking I had felt from Serene and Justin. I tried to push past him, to look at it more closely, but he held me back.

Some dangers become more dangerous when confronted, he warned me. *This is one of them. But I am sure it is the path I must follow, if I am to find the Elderlings.*

"Prisoner!"

I jolted out of my trance. A key turned in the lock of my door and it swung open. A girl stood in the doorway. Regal was beside her, one hand comfortingly on her shoulder. Two guards, Inlanders both by the cut of their clothes, flanked them. One leaned forward to thrust a torch into my cell. I cowered back inadvertently, then sat blinking in the unaccustomed light. "Is that him?" Regal asked the girl gently. She peered at me fearfully. I peered back, trying to decide why she looked familiar.

"Yes, sir, Lord Prince, King, sir. That's him. I went to the well that morning, had to, had to have water, or the baby would die, just as sure as if the Raiders killed him. And it had been quiet awhile, all Neatbay as quiet as the dead. So I went to the well in the early morning, creeping like through the mist, sir. Then there was this wolf there, right by the well, and he starts up and stares at me. And the wind moves the mist, and the wolf is gone, he's a man now. That man, sir. Your Majesty King.'' She continued to stare at me wide-eyed.

I recalled her now. The morning after the battle for Neatbay and Bayguard. Nighteyes and I had paused to rest by the well. I recalled how he had jostled me awake as he fled at the girl's approach.

"You're a brave girl,'' Regal praised her, and patted her shoulder again. "Here, guard, take her back above to the kitchens, and see she gets a good meal and a bed somewhere. No, leave me the torch.'' They backed out of the door, and the guard shut it firmly behind him. I heard departing footsteps, but the light outside the door stayed. After the footsteps had dwindled, Regal spoke again.

"Well, Bastard, it looks as if this game is played out. Your champions will abandon you fairly quickly, I suspect, once they understand what you are. There are other witnesses, of course. Ones who will speak of how there were wolf tracks and men dead of bites everywhere you fought at Neatbay. There are even some of our own Buckkeep guard who, when put to oath, must admit that when you have fought Forged ones, some of the bodies have borne the marks of teeth and claws.'' He heaved a great sigh of satisfaction. I heard the sounds of him setting the torch into a wall sconce. He came back to the door. He was just tall enough to peer in at me. Childishly I stood, and approached the door to look down at him. He stepped back. I felt petty satisfaction.

It had tweaked his temper. "You were so gullible. Such a fool. You came limping home from the Mountains with your tail between your legs, and thought that Verity's favor would be all you needed to survive. You and all your foolish plottings. I knew of them all. All of them, Bastard. All your little chats with our queen, the tower-garden bribes to turn Brawndy against me. Even her plans to leave Buckkeep. Take warm things, you told her. The King will go with you.'' He stood on tiptoe to be sure I could see his smile. "She left with neither,

Bastard. Not the King, nor the warm things she had packed.''
He paused. ''Not even a horse.'' His voice caressed the last
words as if he had been saving them for a long time. He
watched my face avidly.

I suddenly knew myself for nine kinds of a fool. Rosemary. Sweet, sleepy child, always nodding off in a corner. So
bright one could trust her with any errand. So young one forgot
she was even there. Yet I should have known. I was no older
when Chade had first begun to teach me my trade. I felt ill, and
it must have shown on my face. I could not recall what I had or
had not said in front of her. I had no way of knowing what
secrets Kettricken had confided over that little dark curly head.
What talks with Verity had she witnessed, what chats with
Patience? The Queen and the Fool were missing. That only I
knew for certain. Had they ever gotten out of Buckkeep alive?
Regal was grinning, well satisfied with himself. The barred
door between us was the only thing that kept my promise to
Shrewd intact.

He left, still grinning.

Regal had his proof that I had the Wit. The Neatbay girl
was the binding knot for that. All that remained now was for
him to torture from me a confession that I had killed Shrewd.
He had plenty of time for that. However much time as it would
take, he had.

I sank down onto the floor. Verity had been right. Regal
had won.

31

Torture

BUT NOTHING WOULD *satisfy the Willful Princess but that she rode the Piebald Stallion to the hunt. All her ladies warned her, but she turned aside her head and would not hear them. All the lords warned her, but she scoffed at their fears. Even the stablemaster sought to say her nay, telling her, "Lady Princess, the stallion should be put down in blood and fire, for he was trained by Sly o' the Wit, and only to him is he true!" Then the Willful Princess grew wroth and said, "Are these not my stables and my horses, and may I not choose which of my beasts I shall ride?" Then all grew silent before her temper, and she ordered the Piebald Stallion saddled for the hunt.*

Forth they went, with a great baying of hounds and fluttering of colors. And the Piebald Stallion bore her well, and carried her far ahead of the field, and at last out of sight of the other hunters entirely. Then, when the Willful Princess was far and away, over the hill and beneath the green trees, the Piebald Stallion bore her this way and that, until she was lost and the crying of the hounds but an echo in the hills. At last she stopped by a stream to sip the cool water, but lo, when she turned, the Piebald Stallion was gone, and

*in his place stood Sly o' the Wit, as mottled as his Wit
beast. Then he was with her as a stallion is with a
mare, so that ere the year had turned, she went heavy
with child. And when those who attended her birth
saw the babe, all mottled on the face and shoulders,
they cried aloud with fear. When the Willful Princess
saw him, she screamed, and gave up her spirit in
blood and shame, that she had borne Sly's Wit child.
So the Piebald Prince was born in fear and shame,
and that was what he brought into the world with him.*

— *"Legend of the Piebald Prince"*

The torch Regal had left set the shadows of the bars to
dancing. I watched them for a time, thoughtless, hopeless.
Knowledge of my own death numbed me. Gradually my mind
began to work again, but without order. Was this what Chade
had been trying to tell me? Without her horse; how much had
Regal known about the horses? Had he known the destination?
How had Burrich escaped detection? Or had he? Might not I
meet him in the torturer's chamber? Did Regal think Patience
was connected to the escape plan? If he did, would he still be
content simply to abandon her, or would he take more direct
vengeance? When they came for me, should I fight?

No. I would go with dignity. No. I would kill as many of
his inland-bred curs as I could with my bare hands. No. I would
go quietly, and wait for a chance at Regal. I knew he would be
there, to watch me die. My promise to Shrewd, not to kill one
of his own? It no longer bound me. Did it? No one could save
me. Don't even wonder if Chade would act, if Patience could
do anything at all. After Regal had tortured a confession from
me . . . would he keep me alive to hang and quarter before
all? Of course he would. Why deny himself that pleasure?
Would Patience come to watch me die? I hoped not. Maybe
Lacey could keep her away. I had thrown my life away, sacrificed all for nothing. At least, I had killed Serene and Justin.
Had it been worth it? Had my queen escaped at all, or was she
still hidden somewhere within the castle walls? Was that what

Chade had been trying to tell me? No. My mind paddled and scrabbled through thoughts like a rat fallen into a rain barrel. I longed to talk to someone, anyone. I forced myself to calmness, to rationality, and finally found a grip. Nighteyes. Nighteyes had said that he had taken them, had guided them to Burrich.

My brother? I reached for Nighteyes.

I am here. I am always here.

Tell me of that night.

What night?

The night you guided the people from the Keep to Heart of the Pack.

Ah. I sensed him struggling. His ways were a wolf's ways. A thing done was a thing done. He planned no further ahead than the next kill, recalled almost nothing of events that happened a month or a year ago, unless they touched most directly on his own survival. Thus he recalled the cage I had taken him from, but where he had hunted four nights ago was lost to him. General things he recalled: a well-used rabbit trail, a spring that did not freeze over, but specific details of how many rabbits he had killed three days ago were lost forever. I held my breath, hoping he could give me hope.

I took them all to Heart of the Pack. I wish you were here. I've a porcupine quill in my lip. I can't paw it loose. It hurts.

And how did you get that? In the midst of all else, I still had to smile. He knew better but had not been able to resist the fat waddling creature.

It isn't funny.

I know. Truly, it was not funny. A quill was a nasty barbed thing that would only work deeper, festering all the way. It could get bad enough to keep him from hunting. I turned my attention to his problem. Until I had solved it for him, he would be able to focus on nothing else. *Heart of the Pack would get it out for you, if you asked him nicely. You can trust him.*

He pushed me when I spoke to him. But then he spoke to me.

Did he?

A slow working through of thought. *That night. When I*

guided them to him. He said to me, "Bring them here to me,
not to the dog-fox place."

Picture me the place you went.

This was harder for him. But as he tried he recalled the
roadside, empty in the blowing snow, save for Burrich astride
Ruddy and leading Sooty. I glimpsed the Female and the
Scentless One, as he thought of them. Chade he remembered
well, chiefly for a fat beef bone bestowed on Nighteyes at their
parting.

Did they speak to one another?

Overly much. I left them yipping to one another.

Try as I might, that was really all he had for me. It was
enough that I knew the plans had changed drastically and at the
last minute. Odd. I had been willing to lay down my life for
Kettricken, but at the last accounting, I was not sure how I felt
about giving up my horse. Then I recalled I would probably
never ride a horse again, save the one that carried me to the
hanging tree. At least Sooty had gone with someone I cared
about. And Ruddy. Why those two horses? And only those
two? Had Burrich been unable to get others out of the stable?
Was that why he had not gone?

The quill hurts, Nighteyes reminded me. *I cannot eat for*
the pain.

I wish I could come to help you, but I cannot. You must ask
Heart of the Pack.

Cannot you ask him to do it? He does not push you.

I smiled to myself. *He did once. It was enough; I learned*
from it. But if you go to him, asking for help, he will not repel
you.

Cannot you ask him to help me?

I cannot speak to him as we speak. And he is too far away
for me to yip at him.

I will try, then, Nighteyes said doubtfully.

I let him go. I thought of trying to make him understand
my situation. I decided against it. There was nothing he could
do; it would only distress him. Nighteyes would tell Burrich I
had sent him; Burrich would know I was still alive. There was
little else to convey that he would not already know.

A long slow time passed then. I measured it in the small

ways I could. The torch Regal had left burned out. The guard changed. Someone came and put food and water through my door. I had not asked for it. I wondered if that meant a very long time had passed since I had last eaten. The guard changed again. These were a chatty pair, a man and a woman. But they spoke in low voices, and all I heard were the murmurs, and the laughter. Some sort of a ribald flirtation between the two, I surmised. Interrupted by someone's arrival.

The friendly chatter suddenly ceased. Low murmurs, in a very respectful tone. My stomach roiled cold inside me. Quietly I came to my feet, crept to my door. I peered through the doors toward the guards' station.

He came like a shadow down the hall. Silently. Not furtive. He was so unobtrusive, he did not need to worry about being furtive. This was Skill as I had never seen it used before. I felt the hairs on the back of my neck hackle when Will stopped outside the door and looked in at me. He did not speak and I dared not. Even looking at him was giving him too much of an opening to myself. Yet I feared to look away. The Skill shimmered around him like an aura of awareness. I coiled deep inside myself, tighter and tighter, pulling back everything I felt or thought, slamming my walls up as swiftly as I could, but knowing, somehow, that even those walls told him much about me. Even my defenses were a way for this one to read me. Even as my mouth and throat went dry with fear, a question hovered. Where had he been? What had been so important to Regal that he had set Will upon it rather than using him to secure the crown?

White ship.

The answer came to me from deep within me, founded on a connection so deep I could not unearth it. But I did not doubt it. I looked at him, considering him in conjunction with the white ship. He frowned. I felt an increase in the tension between us, a pressing of the Skill against my boundaries. He did not scrabble or pluck at me like Serene and Justin had. More I could compare it to an engagement of blades, where one tests the strength of his opponent's attack. I balanced myself against him, knowing that if I wavered, if for one instant I did not hold him out, he would slip past my guard and skewer my soul. His eyes widened and surprised me with a brief look of uncertainty. But he followed it with a smile as welcoming as a shark's maw.

"Ah," he sighed out. He seemed pleased. He stepped back from my door, stretched like a lazy cat. "They have underestimated you. I shall not make that mistake. Well I know the advantages one gains when your rival undervalues you." Then he left, neither abruptly nor slowly, but like smoke drifts away on a breeze. Here, and then gone.

After he was gone, I went back to my slab and sat. I took a deep breath and sighed it out to still the quivering inside me. I felt I had passed through a trial, and that this time, at least, I had held my own. I leaned back against the cold stone wall and glanced once more at my door.

Will's half-lidded eyes bored into me.

I leaped up so suddenly the scabbed-over injury on my leg tore open afresh. I glared at my window. Nothing. He was gone. Heart hammering, I forced myself to go to the tiny window and peer out it. No one was there, that I could see. He was gone. But I could not make myself believe he was gone.

I limped back to my seat and sat down again, gathering Brawndy's cloak about me. I stared at my window, looking for motion, for some change in the shadowy light from the guard's torch, for anything to indicate that Will lurked outside my door. There was nothing. I longed to quest out, Wit and Skill, to see if I could feel him out there. I dared not. I could not venture out of myself without leaving a way for another to push in.

I set my guards about my thoughts and, a few moments later, reset them. The harder I tried to calm myself, the fiercer my panic became when it rose. I had been fearing physical torture. Now the sour fear sweat trickled down my ribs and the sides of my face as I considered all that Will could do to me if he got past my walls. Once he got inside my head, I would stand before all the Dukes and tell in detail how I had killed King Shrewd. Regal had invented for me something worse than merely dying. I could go to my death a self-proclaimed coward and traitor as well. I would cower at Regal's feet and beg his forgiveness before all.

I think the time that passed was a night. I slept for none of it, save to doze off and then wake with a start from a dream of eyes at my window. I dared not even reach out to Nighteyes for comfort, and I hoped he would not try to reach me with thoughts. I came out of such a doze with a start, thinking I had heard footsteps down the hall. My eyes were sandy, my head ached with my vigilance, and my muscles were knotted from tension. I stayed where I was on the bench, conserving every bit of strength that I had.

The door was flung open. A guard thrust a torch into my cell, then cautiously followed it. Two other guards followed. "You. On your feet!" barked the one with the torch. Farrow was in his accent.

I saw no point in refusing to obey. I stood up, letting Brawndy's cloak fall back on the bench. Their leader made a curt gesture, and I fell in between the two guards. There were four others outside my cell, waiting. Regal was taking no chances. None of them were men I knew. They all wore the colors of Regal's guard. I could tell their orders by the looks on their faces. I gave them no excuses. They took me down the hall a short ways, past the deserted guard post, to the larger chamber that served once as a guardroom. It had been cleared of furniture, save for a comfortable chair. Every sconce boasted a torch, making the room painfully bright to my light-deprived eyes. The guards left me standing in the middle of the room and joined others lining the walls. Habit more than hope made me assess my situation. I counted fourteen guards. Surely that was an excess, even for me. Both doors to the chamber were closed. We waited.

Waiting, standing, in a brightly lit room surrounded by hostile men can be underestimated as a form of torture. I tried to stand quietly, to shift my weight unobtrusively. I rapidly grew tired. It was frightening to discover how quickly starvation and inactivity had weakened me. I felt almost a sense of relief when the door finally opened. Regal entered, followed by Will. Will was quietly remonstrating with him.

". . . unnecessary. Another night or so would be all I required."

"I prefer this," Regal said acidly.

Will bowed his head in silent assent. Regal was seated, and

Will took a position behind his left shoulder. Regal considered me for a moment, then leaned back negligently in his chair. He cocked his head to one side and breathed out through his nose. He lifted a finger, indicated a man. "Bolt. You. I want nothing broken. When we have what we want, I'll want to make him presentable once more. You understand."

Bolt nodded briefly. He stripped off his winter cloak and let it fall, pulled off his shirt as well. The other men watched stony-eyed. From some long-ago discussion with Chade, a small bit of advice came to mind. "You can hold out longer under torture if you focus on what you will say rather than what you won't. I've heard men repeating the same phrase, over and over, long past the point where they could hear the questions anymore. By focusing on what you will say, you make it less likely you'll say that which you don't wish to."

But his theoretical advice might not do much for me. Regal did not seem to have any questions to ask.

Bolt was taller than I was, heavier than I was. He looked as if his diet included a lot more than bread and water. He limbered and stretched as if we were going to wrestle for a Winterfest purse. I stood watching him. He met my look and smiled at me liplessly. I watched him pull on a pair of fingerless leather gloves. He'd come prepared for this. Then he bowed to Regal, and Regal nodded.

What's this?

Be silent! I ordered Nighteyes. But as Bolt stepped purposefully toward me I felt a snarl twitch at my upper lip. I dodged his first punch, stepped in to land one of my own, and then moved back as he swung again. Desperation lent me agility. I had not expected a chance to defend myself, I had expected to be bound and tormented. Of course, there was plenty of time for that. Regal had all the time he needed. Don't think of that. I had never been good in this kind of a fight. Don't think of that either. Bolt's fist grazed my cheek stingingly. Be wary. I was luring him to open up, taking his measure, when the Skill wrapped me. I reeled in Will's onslaught, and Bolt landed his next three blows effortlessly. Jaw, chest, and high on my cheek. All quick and solid. The style of a man who did this a lot. The smile of a man who enjoyed it.

There followed a timeless period for me. I could not both shield myself from Will and defend myself from Bolt battering me. I reasoned, if the thinking one does in such a state can be called reasoning, that my body had its own defenses against physical pain. I'd pass out, or die. Dying might be the only victory I could hope for here. So I chose to defend my mind rather than body.

I veer away from recalling that beating. My token defense was to move away from his blows and force him to pursue me, to keep my eyes on him, to block where I could as long as it did not distract me from my vigil against Will's Skill pressure. I heard the guards jeer at my supposed lack of spirit as I scarcely fought back. When one of his blows sent me staggering back against the soldiers who ringed us, their shoves and kicks drove me back toward Bolt again.

I could not devote my thoughts to strategy. When I swung, I swung wildly, and the few times my fists landed, it was with small impact. I longed to release myself, to tap my fury and just fling myself at Bolt and hammer at him any way I could. But that would have left me wide open to Will's intentions. No. I had to remain cool and endure. As Will increased his pressure on me, Bolt had a leisurely time of it. Eventually, I was reduced to two choices. I could use my arms to shelter either my head or my body. He merely shifted targets. The horror was that I knew the man was holding back, striking only to inflict pain and minor damage. I dropped my hands once and met Will's gaze face-on. I had the very brief satisfaction of seeing the sweat that streamed down his face. At that moment, Bolt's fist connected solidly with my nose.

Blade had once described to me the sound that he heard as his nose broke in a brawl. Words did not do it justice. A sickening sound combined with incredible pain. Pain so intense it was suddenly the only pain I was aware of. I blacked out.

I don't know how long I was out. I fluttered to the edge of consciousness, hovered there. Someone had flipped me over onto my back. Whoever it was straightened from inspecting me. "Nose is broke," he announced.

"Bolt, I said, nothing broken!" Regal remonstrated with

him angrily. "I have to be able to show him intact. Bring me some wine," he added irritably in an aside to someone else.

"Not a problem, King Regal," someone assured him. That person bent over me, took a firm grip on the bridge of my nose, and dragged it straight again. That crude setting of it hurt worse than the breaking, and once more I dipped down into unconsciousness. I lingered there, hearing the voices discuss me for some time before they resolved into words and the words into sense.

Regal's voice. "So what is he supposed to be able to do? Why hasn't he done it yet?"

"I know only what Serene and Justin told me, Your Majesty." Will's voice was tired. "They claimed he was weary from Skilling, and Justin was able to force his way into him. Then the Bastard . . . fought back in some way. Justin said he believed himself attacked by a great wolf. Serene said she actually saw the marks of claws on Justin, but that they faded shortly afterward."

I heard the creak of wood as Regal flung himself back in his chair. "Well, make him do it. I wish to see this Wit for myself." A pause. "Or are not you strong enough? Perhaps Justin was the one I should have held in reserve."

"I am stronger than Justin was, Your Majesty," Will asserted calmly. "But Fitz is aware of my intent. He was not expecting Justin's attack." More quietly he added, "He is stronger far than I was led to believe."

"Just do it!" Regal commanded in disgust.

So Regal wanted to see the Wit? I drew a breath, gathered what little strength was inside me. I tried to focus my anger at Regal, to *repel* at him hard enough to drive him through the wall. But I could not. I was too riddled with pain to concentrate. My own walls defeated me. All Regal did was start, and then look at me more closely.

"He's awake," he observed. Again his finger lifted lazily. "Verde. You may have him. But have a care to his nose. Leave his face alone. The rest of him is easily covered."

Verde devoted some little time to hauling me to my feet so he could knock me down again. I wearied of that repetition long before he did. The floor did as much damage as his fists. I could not seem to keep my feet under me, nor lift my arms to shield myself. I retreated inside myself, smaller and smaller, huddling there until sheer physical pain would force me to alertness and make me struggle again. Usually just before I passed out again. I became aware of another thing. Regal's enjoyment. He did not want to bind me and cause me pain. He wanted to watch me struggle, to see me attempt to fight back and fail. He watched his guard, too, noting, no doubt, which ones turned their eyes away from this sport. He used me to take their measure. I forced myself not to care that he took pleasure from my pain. All that truly mattered was keeping my walls up and keeping Will out of my head. That was the battle I had to win.

The fourth time I awoke, I was on the floor of my cell. A terrible snuffling, wheezing sound was what had wakened me. It was the sound of my breathing. I remained where they had dumped me. After a time I lifted a hand and pawed Brawndy's cloak down from the bench. It fell partially atop me. I lay a time longer. Regal's guards had listened to him. Nothing was broken. Everything hurt, but no bones were broken. All they had given me was pain. Nothing I could die from.

I crawled over to my water. I will not enumerate the pains it cost for me to lift it and drink. My initial attempts to defend myself had left my hands swollen and sore. I tried vainly to keep the edge of the water pot from bumping against my mouth. Finally, I managed to drink. The water strengthened me, to make me all the more aware of everywhere I hurt. My half loaf of bread was there as well. I stuck the end of it in what was left of my water, and then sucked the soaked bread from the loaf as it softened. It tasted like blood. Bolt's initial battering of my head had loosened teeth and cut my mouth. I was aware of my nose as an immense area of throbbing pain. I could not bring myself to touch it with my fingers. There was no pleasure in eating, only a partial relief from the hunger that clawed at me alongside my pain.

After a time I sat up. I dragged the cloak around me and considered what I knew. Regal would batter at me physically until I either manifested the Wit in an attack his guards could witness, or until I dropped my walls enough that Will could get

in my mind and inspire me to confess. I wondered which way
he would rather win. I did not doubt he would win. My sole
way out of this cell was by dying. Options. To try to make them
beat me to death before I either used the Wit or dropped my
Skill barrier to Will. Or, to take the poison I had made for
Wallace. I would die from it. That was definite. In my weakened state, it would probably be faster than I had planned it for
him. Still painful, though. Wretchedly painful.

One kind of pain seemed as good as another. Laboriously I
folded back my bloodied right cuff. The hidden pocket was
secured by a thread that should have come loose at a slight tug.
But blood had matted it closed. I picked at it carefully. Mustn't
spill it. I'd need to wait until they gave me more water to get it
down. Otherwise I'd just gag and retch on the bitter powder. I
was still working at it when I heard voices down the hallway.

It did not seem fair they would come back at me so soon. I
listened. It wasn't Regal. But anyone coming down here meant
something to do with me. A deep voice, rumbling along in a
rambling way. The guards replying briefly, in hostile tones.
Another voice, interceding, reasoning. The rumbling again,
getting louder, and the belligerence plain. Suddenly a shout.

"You're going to die, Fitz! Hanged over water, and your
body burned!"

Burrich's voice. A strange mix of anger and threat and
pain.

"Get him out of here." One of the guards, speaking loud
and plain now. She was obviously an Inlander.

"I will, I will." I knew that voice. Blade. "He's just had a
bit too much to drink, that's all. It's always been a problem
with him. And he had the boy as his apprentice down there in
the stables for years. Everyone's saying he should have known
about it, did know about it and didn't do anything, maybe."

"Yesssss." Burrich drew out the angry affirmation. "And
I'm out of a job now, bastard! No more buck's crest for me!
Well, by El's ass, it hardly matters. Horses are gone. Best damn
horses I ever trained, gone inland now, given over to fools!
Dogs are gone, hawks are gone! All that're left are the scrubs
and a couple mules. Don't have one horse I'd admit to own-
ing!" His voice was growing closer. There was madness in it.

I scrabbled up the door, clung to the bars to see. I couldn't see the guard post, but their shadows were on the wall. Burrich's shadow was attempting to come down the hall while the guards and Blade tried to drag him back.

"Wait. Now, just wait a minute," Burrich remonstrated drunkenly. "Wait. Look. I only want to talk to him. That's all." The cluster of people surged down the hall, halted again. The guards were between Burrich and my door. Blade was clinging to Burrich's arm. He still showed the marks from the brawl, and one of his arms was in a sling. He could do little to stop Burrich.

"Just get mine in before Regal gets his. That's all. That's all." Burrich's voice was deep and slurry with drink. "Come on. Just for a minute. What's it going to matter anyway? He's good as dead." Another pause. "Look. I'll make it worth your while. Look here."

The guards were exchanging glances.

"Uh, Blade, you got any coin left?" Burrich was digging through his pouch, then snorted with disgust and upended it over his hand. Coins fell in a shower, spilling past his fingers. "Here, here." There was the chink and rattle of coins dropped and rolling on the stone floor of the passageway and he flung his arms wide in a gesture of largesse.

"Hey, he doesn't mean it, Burrich, you don't bribe guards like that, you're going to get yourself tossed in a cell, too." Blade stooped hastily, making apologies as he hurried to gather up the spilled coins. The guards stooped alongside him and I saw a hand make a furtive trip from floor to pocket.

Suddenly Burrich's face peered in my window. For a moment we stood eye to eye at the barred window. Grief and outrage battled in his face. His eyes were webbed red from his drinking, and his breath was strong with it. The fabric of his shirt showed ragged where the buck crest had been torn from it. He glared at me, then, as he looked at me, his eyes widened in shock. For a moment our gaze held, and I thought something of understanding and farewell passed between us. Then he leaned back and spat full in my face.

"That, for you," he snarled. "That for my life, which you took from me. All the hours, all the days I spent upon you.

Better that you had lain down and died amongst the beasts before you let this come to pass. They're going to hang you, boy. Regal's having the gallows built, over water, like the old wisdom says. They'll hang you, then cut you up and burn you down to bones. Nothing left to bury. He's probably afraid the dogs would dig you up again. You'd like that, hey, boy? Buried like a bone, for some dog to dig up later? Better to just lie down and die right where you are.''

I had recoiled from him when he spat at me. Now I stood back from my door, swaying on my feet while he gripped the bars and stared in at me, his eyes wide and bright with madness and drink.

"You're so good with the Wit, they say. Why don't you change into a rat and scuttle out of there? Huh?'' He leaned his forehead against the bars and peered in at me. Almost pensively, he said, "Better that than to hang, whelp. Change into a beast and run off with your tail between your legs. If you can . . . I heard you can . . . they say you can turn into a wolf. Well, unless you can, you're going to hang. Hang by your neck, choking and kicking . . .'' His voice trailed off. His dark eyes locked with mine. They were teary with drink. "Better to lie down and die right there than hang.'' Suddenly he seemed full of fury. "Maybe I'll help you lie down and die!'' he threatened through gritted teeth. "Better you die my way than Regal's!'' He began to wrest at the bars, shaking the door back and forth against its locks.

The guards were instantly on him, one to an arm, tugging and cursing while he ignored them. Old Blade jigged up and down behind them, saying, "Give it up, come on, Burrich, you had your say, come on, man, before there's real trouble.''

They did not pry him loose, but he gave it up suddenly, just dropping his arms to his sides. It caught the guards by surprise and they both stumbled back. I clutched at the barred window.

"Burrich.'' It was hard to make my mouth form words. "I never meant to hurt you. I'm sorry.'' I took a breath, tried to find some words to end some of the torment in his eyes. "No one should blame you. You did the best with me you could.''

He shook his head at me, his face contorting with grief

and anger. "Lie down and die, boy. Just lie down and die." He turned and walked away from me. Blade was walking backward, apologizing a hundred times over to the two flustered guards who followed him up the corridor. I watched them go, and then watched Burrich's shadow go lurching off, while Blade's stayed a bit to mollify the guards.

I swiped at the spittle on my swollen face and went slowly back to my stone bench. I sat a long time, remembering. From the beginning he had warned me off the Wit. The first dog that I had ever bonded to, he had mercilessly taken from me. I had fought him for that dog, *repelled* at him with every bit of strength I had, and he had just deflected it back at me. So hard I had not even attempted to *repel* anyone for years after that. And when he had relented, ignoring if not accepting my bond with the wolf, it had rebounded onto him. The Wit. All those times he had warned me, and all those times I had been so sure I knew what I was doing.

You did.

Nighteyes. I acknowledged him. I had no spirit to do more than that.

Come with me. Come with me and we will hunt. I can take you far from all of this.

In a while, perhaps, I put him off. I did not have the strength to deal with him.

I sat a long time, actually. My encounter with Burrich hurt as badly as the beating had. I tried to think of one person in my life that I had not failed, had not disappointed. I could think of no one.

I glanced down at Brawndy's cloak. I was cold enough to want it, but too sore to pick it up. A pebble on the floor beside it caught my eye. It puzzled me. I had looked at this floor long enough to know there were no loose dark pebbles in my cell.

Curiosity is a disturbingly strong force. Finally, I leaned way over and picked up the cloak, and the pebble next to it. It took some time to get the cloak around me. Then I examined my pebble. It wasn't a pebble. It was dark and wet. A wad of something? Leaves. A pellet of wadded leaves. A pellet that had stung my chin when Burrich spat at me? Cautiously I held it up to the fickle light that wandered in the barred window.

Something white secured the outer leaf. I picked it loose. What had caught my eye was the white end of a porcupine quill, while the black barbed tip had secured the leaf wrapping. Unfolded, the leaf revealed a sticky brown wad. I lifted it to my nose and sniffed it cautiously. A mixture of herbs, but one dominated. I recognized the scent queasily. Carryme. A Mountain herb. A powerful painkiller and sedative, sometimes used to mercifully extinguish life. Kettricken had used it when she had tried to kill me in the Mountains.

Come with me.

Not just now.

This was Burrich's parting gift to me? A merciful end? I thought over what he had said. Better to just lie down and die. This, from the man who had taught me the fight wasn't over until you had won it? The contradiction was too sharp.

Heart of the Pack says you should come with me. Now. Tonight. Lie down, he says. Be a bone for the dogs to dig up later, he says. I could feel the effort Nighteyes was putting into relaying this message.

I was silent, thinking.

He took the quill from my lip, Brother. I think we can trust him. Come with me, now, tonight.

I considered the three things that lay in my hand. The leaf, the quill, the pellet. I rewrapped the pellet in the leaf, secured it with the quill again.

I don't understand what he wants me to do, I complained.

Lie down and be still. Still yourself, and go with me, as myself. A long pause as Nighteyes worked something through in his head. *Eat what he gave you only if you must. Only if you cannot come to me on your own.*

I have no idea what he is up to. But, like you, I think we can trust him. In the dimness, past all weariness, I sat picking at the stitching in my sleeve. When it finally came loose, I coaxed the tiny paper packet of powder out and then pushed the leaf-wrapped pellet in. I managed to force the quill to hold it there. I looked at the paper packet in my hand. A tiny idea came to me, but I refused to dwell on it. I gripped it in my hand. Then I wrapped myself in Brawndy's cloak and slowly lay myself down on the bench. I knew I should keep vigil, lest Will come back. I was too hopeless and too weary. *I am with you, Nighteyes.*

We sped away together, over crusted white snow, into a wolf world.

32

Execution

STABLEMASTER BURRICH WAS *renowned during his years at Buckkeep as an extraordinary horse handler as well as a houndsman and falconer. His skill with beasts was near legendary even in his own lifetime.*

He began his years of service as a common soldier. It is said he came from folk who had settled in Shoaks. Some say his grandmother was of slave stock, who bought herself free from a Bingtown master by an extraordinary service.

As a soldier, his fierceness in battle brought him to the attention of a young Prince Chivalry. It is rumored that he first appeared before his prince on a disciplinary matter regarding a tavern brawl. He served Chivalry for a time as a weapons partner, but Chivalry discovered his gift for animals and put him in charge of his guards' horses. He was soon caring for Chivalry's hounds and hawks as well, and eventually came to oversee the entire stables of Buckkeep. His sage doctoring of beasts and knowledge of their internal workings extended to cattle, sheep, and swine and the occasional treatment of fowl. No one exceeded him in his understanding of beasts.

Severely injured in a boar-hunting accident, Burrich acquired a limp he was to suffer the rest of his life. It seems to have mitigated the quick and savage temper that was his repu-

tation as a young man. However, it is also true he remained a man that few willingly crossed to the end of his days.

His herbal remedy was responsible for halting the outbreak of scallers that afflicted the lambs in Bearns Duchy following the Blood Plague years. He saved the flocks from total decimation, as well as kept the disease from spreading into Buck Duchy.

⇥

A clear night under shining stars. A sound healthy body, surging down a snowy hillside in a series of exuberant leaps. Our passage left snow cascading from bushes in our wake. We had killed, we had eaten. All hungers were satisfied. The night was fresh and open, cracking cold. No cage held us, no men beat us. Together, we knew the fullness of our freedom. We went to where the spring welled up so strongly it almost never froze, and lapped the icy water. Nighteyes shook ourselves all over, then took a deep snuff of the air.

Morning comes.

I know. I do not wish to think of it. Morning, when dreams must end and reality be endured.

You must come with me.

Nighteyes, I am already with you.

No. You must come with me, all the way. You must let go.

So he had told me, at least twenty times already. I could not mistake the urgency of his thoughts. His insistence was plain, and his single-mindedness amazed me. It was not like Nighteyes to cling so firmly to an idea that had nothing to do with food. This was a thing he and Burrich had decided. I must go with him.

I could not fathom what he wanted me to do.

Over and over, I had explained to him that I was trapped, my body in a cage, just as he had once been trapped in a cage. My mind could go with him, for a time at least, but I could not go with him as he urged me to. Each time he told me that he understood that, but I was not understanding him. And now we were back to it again.

I sensed him attempting patience. *You must come with me, now. All the way. Before they come to wake you.*

I cannot. My body is locked in a cage.

Leave it! he said savagely. *Let go!*

What?

Leave it, let go of it, come with me.

You mean, die? Eat the poison?

Only if you have to. But do it now, quickly, before they can hurt you more. Leave it and come with me. Let go of it. You did it once before. Remember?

The effort of making sense of his words was making me aware of our bond. The pain of my own racked body broke through to haunt me. Somewhere I was stiff with the cold, and aching with pain. Somewhere, every breath brought an answering twinge from my ribs. I scrabbled away from that, back to the wolf's strong sound body.

That's right, that's right. Just leave it. Now. Let go of it. Just let go.

I knew abruptly what he wanted me to do. I did not know quite how to do it, and I was not sure that I could. Once, yes, I remembered that I had let go of my body and left it in his care. Only to awaken hours later beside Molly. But I was not sure how I had done it. And it had been different. I had left the wolf to guard me, when I had gone wherever I had gone. This time he wanted me to just break my consciousness free from my body. To willingly let go the tie that bound mind to flesh. Even if I could discover how to do it, I did not know if I had the will to do it.

Just lie down and die, Burrich had told me.

Yes. That's right. Die if you must, but come with me.

I made an abrupt decision. Trust. Trust Burrich, trust the wolf. What did I have to lose?

I drew a deep breath, poised inside myself as for a dive into cold water.

No. No, just let go.

I am. I am. I groped about inside myself, looking for whatever bound me to my body. I slowed my breathing, I willed my heart to beat more slowly. I refused the sensations of pain, of cold, of stiffness. I sank away from all of it, deep into myself.

No! No! Nighteyes howled in desperation. *To me! Come to me, let go of that, come to me!*

But there was the scuff of footsteps, and the mutter of voices. A shudder of fear went through me, and despite myself, I cowered deeper into Brawndy's cloak. One eye would open a bit. It showed me the same dimly lit cell, the same tiny barred window. There was a deep cold pain inside me, something more insidious than hunger. They had broken no bones, but inside me, something was torn. I knew it.

You are back in the cage! Nighteyes cried. *Leave it! Leave your body and come to me!*

It's too late, I whispered. *Run away, run away. Don't share this.*

Are we not pack? Desperation as throbbing as a wolf's drawn-out howl.

They were at my door, it was swinging open. Fear seized me in its jaws and shook me. Almost I lifted my cuff to my mouth and chewed the pellet from my sleeve right then. Instead, I gripped the tiny paper packet in my fist and made a determined resolution to forget about it.

The same man with the torch, the same two guards. The same command. "You. On your feet."

I pushed Brawndy's cloak aside. One of the guards was still human enough to pale at what he saw. The other two were stolid. And when I could not move swiftly enough to suit them, one seized me by the arm and jerked me to my feet. I cried out wordlessly with pain; I could not help it. And that response set me to trembling with fear. If I could not keep from crying out, how could I hold my defenses against Will?

They took me from my cell and down the hall. I do not say I walked. All my bruises had stiffened in the night. The beating had reopened the sword cuts on my right forearm and on my thigh. Those pains, too, had been renewed. Pain was like air now; I moved through it, I breathed it in and out of myself. In the center of the guardroom, one shoved me and I fell. I lay on the floor on my side. I saw no point to struggling to sit up; I had no dignity to save. Better that they thought I could not stand. While I could, I would be still and marshall whatever strength I could still call my own. Slowly, laboriously, I cleared myself and began to set the guards on my mind. Over and over, through the pain haze, I went over the Skill walls I had erected, strengthening them, sealing myself away behind them. The walls of my mind were what I must guard, not the flesh of my body. Around me in the room, men lined the walls. They shuffled, and spoke quietly among themselves, waiting. I scarcely noticed them. My world was my walls and my pain.

There was the creak and draft of an opened door. Regal came in. Will walked behind him, carelessly radiating Skill strength. I was aware of him as I had never before been aware of a man. Even without sight, I could sense him, the shape of him, the heat of the Skill that burned inside him. He was dangerous. Regal supposed he was only a tool. I dared a tiny satisfaction in knowing Regal did not know the perils of such a tool as Will.

Regal took his chair. Someone brought a small table for him. I heard a bottle opened, then smelled wine as it was poured. The pain had tuned my senses to an unbearable keenness. I listened to Regal drink. I refused to acknowledge how much I longed for it.

"Dear me. Look at him. Do you suppose we have gone too far, Will?" Something in the arch amusement in Regal's voice informed me that he had taken more than wine today. Smoke, perhaps? So early? The wolf had said dawn. Regal would never be up at dawn . . . something was wrong with my time sense.

Will walked slowly toward me, stood over me. I did not try to move to see his face. I gripped my tiny store of strength firmly. He nudged me sharply with his foot and I gasped despite myself. At almost the same instant he slammed his Skill strength against me. There, at least, I held firm. Will took a short breath through his nose, snorted it out. He walked back to Regal.

"Your Majesty. You've done almost as much as you can to his body, without risking damage that would plainly show even a month hence. But within, he still resists. Pain can distract him from warding his mind, but it does not inherently weaken his Skill strength. I do not think you will break him this way."

"I did not ask you that, Will!" Regal rebuked him sharply. I listened to him shift himself to a more comfortable position. "Ah, this takes too long. My dukes grow impatient. He must be broken today." Almost pensively, he asked Will, "Almost as much as I can, you say, to his body? What then would you suggest as the next step?"

"Leave him alone with me. I can get what you wish from him."

"No." Regal's refusal was flat. "I know what *you* want from him, Will. You see him as a fat wineskin, full of Skill strength, which you would like to drain. Well, perhaps, at the end, there will be a way for you to have him. But not just yet. I want him to stand before the Dukes and confess himself a traitor. More, I want him to grovel before the throne and beg for mercy. I will have him denounce all those who have defied me. He, himself, shall accuse them. No one will doubt it when he says they are traitors. Let Duke Brawndy see his own daughter accused, let all the court hear that the Lady Patience who cries so loudly for justice has herself betrayed the crown. And for him . . . that candlemaker girl, that Molly."

My heart lurched sideways inside me.

"I have not yet found her, my lord," Will ventured.

"Silence!" Regal thundered. Almost, he sounded like King Shrewd. "Do not hearten him with that. She need not be found to be declared a traitor by his own lips. We can find her at our leisure. He can go to his death, knowing she will follow him, betrayed by his words. I will cleanse Buckkeep from dung heap to tower top of all who have sought to betray me and defy me!" He lifted his cup in a toast to himself and drank deeply.

He sounded, I thought to myself, very like Queen Desire had in her cups. One part braggart to one part sniveling coward. He would fear everyone he did not control. And the next day he would fear those he controlled even more.

Regal set his wine cup down with a thud. He leaned back in his chair. "Well. Let's continue, shall we? Kelfry, stand him up for us."

Kelfry was a competent man who took no joy in his work. He was not gentle, but neither was he rougher than he needed to be. He stood behind me, gripping me by the upper arms to keep me upright. Hod had not trained him. I knew if I snapped my head back swiftly, I could break his nose and possibly take out some of his front teeth. Snapping my head back swiftly struck me as only slightly simpler than picking up the floor under my own feet would be. I stood, hands curled defensively over my belly, pushing the pain aside, gathering my strength. After a moment I lifted my head and regarded Regal.

I ran my tongue about the inside of my mouth to free my lips from my teeth, then spoke. "You killed your own father."

Regal stiffened in his chair. The man holding me tensed. I leaned in his arms, forcing him to support my weight.

"Serene and Justin did it, but you ordered it," I said quietly. Regal came to his feet.

"But not before we had Skilled to Verity." I made my voice louder. The effort broke sweat on me. "Verity's alive, and he knows everything." Regal was coming at me, with Will right behind him. I swung my gaze to Will, put threat in my voice. "He knows about you, too, Will. He knows it all."

The guard held me as Regal backhanded me. Once. Another slap, and I felt the swollen skin of my face split under the impact. Regal drew his fist back. I set myself to take it, pushed away all pain, centered myself, got ready.

"Look out!" Will yelled, and sprang to knock Regal aside.

I had wanted it too badly, he had Skilled what I intended to do. As Regal swung I jerked free of my guard, slipped aside from Regal's blow, then stepped in. With one hand I seized the back of Regal's neck, to pull his face toward my other hand that gripped the now crushed paper of powder. My intent had been to rub it into his nose and mouth, to hope against hope he'd get enough of it to kill him.

Will spoiled it all. My swollen fingers would not close on Regal's neck. Will snatched Regal from my wooden grasp, swung him sideways away from me. As Will's shoulder collided with my chest I reached for his face instead, ground the torn paper and fine white powder into his nose and mouth and eyes. Most of it floated up in a fine cloud between us. I saw him gasp at the bitterness and then we were down, both of us, under a wave of Regal's guards.

I dove for unconsciousness, but it eluded me. I was struck, kicked, and throttled before Regal's frenzied cries of "Don't

kill him! Don't kill him!'' seemed to matter to anyone save me.
I felt them get off me, felt them drag Will from under me, but I
could not see. Blood was sheeting down over my face. My tears
mingled with it. My last chance, and I had failed. I had not
even gotten Will. Oh, he would be sick for a few days, but I
doubted he would die of it. Even now I heard them muttering
over him.

"Take him to a healer, then." I heard Regal finally give
the command. "See if he can figure out what's wrong with
him. Did one of you kick him in the head?''

I thought that he spoke of me, until I heard the sounds of
Will being carried out. So either I had gotten more into him
than I had thought, or someone had kicked him in the head.
Perhaps his gasp had pulled it into his lungs. I had no idea what
it would do there. As I felt his Skill presence fading it was
relief almost as blessed as surcease from pain. Cautiously I
relaxed my vigilance against him. It was like setting down a
terribly heavy weight. Another thought blessed me. They didn't
know. No one had seen the paper and powder, it had happened
too quickly for them. They might not even think of poison until
it was too late for him.

"Is the Bastard dead?" Regal demanded angrily. "If he
is, I swear, every man of you will hang!''

Someone stooped hastily beside me, to lay fingers at the
pulse in my throat. "He's alive," a soldier said gruffly, almost
sullenly. Someday Regal would learn not to threaten his own
guard. I hoped he'd be taught it by an arrow through his back.

A moment later someone dashed a bucket of cold water
over me. The shock of it jarred every pain I had to new frenzy.
I pulled my one eye open. The first thing I saw was the water
and blood on the floor in front of me. If all that blood was all
mine, I was in trouble. Dazedly, I tried to think of whose else it
could be. My mind did not seem to be working very well. Time
seemed to be flowing in jumps. Regal was standing over me,
angry and disheveled, and then suddenly he was sitting in his
chair. In and out. Light and dark and light again.

Someone knelt beside me, ran competent hands over me.
Burrich? No. That was a dream from long ago. This man had

blue eyes and the nasal twang of a Farrow man. "He's bleeding a lot, King Regal. But we can stop that." Someone put pressure on my brow. A cup of watered wine, held against my cracked lips, splashed into my mouth. I choked on it. "You see, he's alive. I'd leave off, for today, Your Majesty. I doubt if he'll be able to answer any more questions before tomorrow. He'll just faint on you." A calm professional opinion. Whoever it was stretched me out on the floor again and left.

A spasm rattled through me. Seizure coming soon. Good thing Will was gone. Didn't think I could keep my walls up through a seizure.

"Oh, take him away." Regal, disgusted and disappointed. "This has been nothing but a waste of my time today." His chair's legs scraped on the floor as he left it. I heard the sounds of his boots on the stone floor as he strode from the room.

Someone grabbed me by the shirtfront, jerked me to my feet. I could not even scream for the pain. "Stupid piece of dung," he snarled at me. "You'd better not die. I'm not going to take lashes over the likes of you dying."

"Great threat, Verde," someone mocked him. "What are you going to do to him after he's dead?"

"Shut up. It'll be your back flayed to the bone as much as mine. Let's get him out of here and clean this up."

⇒◦⇐

The cell. The blank wall of it. They had left me on the floor, facing away from the door. Somehow that seemed unfair of them. I'd have to do all the work of rolling over just to see if they'd left me any water.

No. It was too much trouble.

Are you coming now?

I really want to, Nighteyes. But I just don't know how.

Changer. Changer! My brother! Changer.

What is it?

You have been silent for so long. Are you coming now?

I have been . . . silent?

Yes. I thought you had died, without coming to me first. I could not reach you.

Probably a seizure. I didn't know it had happened. But now I am right here, Nighteyes. Right here.

Then come to me. Hurry, before you die.

A moment. Let us be sure of this.

I tried to think of a reason not to. I knew there had been some, but I could no longer recall them. Changer, he had called me. My own wolf, calling me that, just as the Fool or Chade called me a catalyst. Well. Time to change things for Regal. The last thing I could do was make sure I died before Regal broke me. If I had to go down, I would do it alone. No words of mine would implicate anyone else. I hoped the Dukes would demand to see my body.

It took a long time to get my arm from the floor to my chest. My lips were cracked and swollen, my teeth aching in my gums. But I put my shirt cuff to my mouth and found the tiny lump of the leaf pellet inside the fabric. I bit down at it as hard as I could, then sucked on it. After a moment the taste of carryme flooded my mouth. It was not unpleasant. Pungent. As the herb deadened the pain in my mouth, I could chew at my sleeve more strongly. Stupidly, I tried to be careful of the porcupine quill. Didn't want to get a quill in my lip.

It really hurts when that happens.

I know, Nighteyes.

Come to me.

I'm trying. Give me a moment.

How does one leave one's body behind? I tried to ignore it, to be aware of myself only as Nighteyes. Keen nose. Lying on my side, chewing diligently at a lump of snow wadded up in the space between my toes. I tasted snow and my own paw as I nibbled and licked it away. I looked up. Evening coming on. It would soon be a good time to hunt. I stood up, shook myself all over.

That's right, Nighteyes encouraged me.

But there was still that thread, that tiny awareness of a stiff and aching body on a cold stone floor. Just to think of it made it more real. A tremor ran through it, rattling its bones and teeth. Seizure coming. Big one this time.

Suddenly it was all so easy. Such an easy choice. Leave that body for this one. It didn't work very well anymore anyway. Stuck in a cage. No point to keeping it. No point to being a man at all.

I'm here.

I know. Let us hunt.

And we did.

33

Wolf Days

*T*HE EXERCISE FOR *centering oneself is a simple one. Stop thinking of what you intend to do. Stop thinking of what you have just done. Then, stop thinking that you have stopped thinking of those things. Then you will find the Now, the time that stretches eternal, and is really the only time there is. Then, in that place, you will finally have time to be yourself.*

—❦—

There is a cleanness to life that can be had when you but hunt and eat and sleep. In the end, no more than this is really needed by anyone. We ran alone, we the Wolf, and we lacked for nothing. We did not long for venison when a rabbit presented itself nor begrudge the ravens that came to pick through our leavings. Sometimes we remembered a different time and a different way. When we did, we wondered what had been so important about any of it. We did not kill what we could not eat, and we did not eat what we could not kill. Dusks and dawns were the best times for hunting, and other times were good for sleeping. Other than this, time had no meaning.

For wolves, as for dogs, life is a briefer thing than for men, if you measure it by counting days and how many turns of a season one sees. But in two years, a cub wolf does all a man does in a score. He comes to the full of his strength and size, he learns all that is needful for him to be a hunter or a mate or a leader. The candle of his life burns briefer and brighter than a man's. In a decade of years, he does all that a man does in five or six times that many. A year passes for a wolf as a decade does for a man. Time is no miser when one lives always in the now.

So we knew the nights and the days, the hunger and the filling. Savage joys and surprises. Snatch up a mouse, fling it up, eat it down with a snap. So good. To start a rabbit, to pursue it as it dodges and circles, then suddenly, to stretch your stride and seize it in a flurry of snow and fur. The shake that snaps its neck, and then the leisurely eating, the tearing open of its belly and nosing through the hot entrails, and then the thick meat of the haunches, the easy crunching of its backbone. Surfeit and sleep. And waken to hunt again.

Chase a doe over pond ice, knowing we cannot make such a kill, but rejoicing in the hunt. When through the ice she goes, and we circle, circle, circle endlessly as she battles her hooves against the ice and finally clambers out, too weary to evade the teeth that slash her hamstrings, the fangs that close in her throat. Eating to satiation, not once, but twice from the carcass. A storm comes full of sleet to drive us to the den. Sleeping snug, nose to tail, while the wind flings icy rain and then snow about outside the den. Awake to pale light glistening in through a layer of snow. Dig out to snuff the clear cold day that is just fading. There is meat still on the doe, frozen red and sweet, ready to be dug from the snow. What can be more satisfying than to know of meat that is waiting for you?

Come.

We pause. No, the meat is waiting. We trot on.

Come now. Come to me. I've meat for you.

We've meat already. And closer.

Nighteyes. Changer. Heart of the Pack summons you.

We pause again. Shake all over. This is not comfortable. And what is Heart of the Pack to us? He is not pack. He pushes us. There is meat closer. It is decided. We go to the pond's edge. Here. Somewhere here. Ah. Dig down to her through the snow. The crows come to watch us, waiting for us to be finished.

Nighteyes. Changer. Come. Come now. Soon it will be too late.

The meat is frozen, crisp and red. Turn our head to use our back teeth to scissor it from the bones. A crow flies down, lands on the snow nearby. Hop, hop. He cocks his head. For sport, we lunge at him, put him to flight again. Our meat, all of . Days and nights of meat.

Come. Please. Come. Please. Come soon, come now. Come back to us. You are needed. Come. Come.

He does not go away. We put back our ears, but still we hear him, *come, come, come.* He steals the pleasure from the meat with his whining. Enough. We have eaten enough for now. We will go, just to still him.

Good. That's good. Come to me, come to me.

We go, trotting through the gathering darkness. A rabbit sits up suddenly, scampers away across the snow. Shall we? No. Belly is full. Trot on. Cross a man's path, an open empty strip under the night sky. We fade across it swiftly, trot on through the woods that border it.

Come to me. Come. Nighteyes, Changer, I summon you. Come to me.

The forest ends. There is a cleared hillside below us, and beyond that a flat bare place, shelterless under the night sky. Too open. The crusted snow is untracked, but at the bottom of the hill, there are humans. Two. Heart of the Pack digs while another watches. Heart of the Pack digs fast and hard. His breath smokes in the night. The other has a light, a too bright light that shrinks the eye to behold. Heart of the Pack stops his digging. He looks up at us.

Come, he says. *Come.*

He jumps into the hole he has dug. There is black earth, frozen chunks of it, atop the clean snow. He lands with a thud like deer antlers on a tree. He crouches and there is a tearing sound. He uses a tool that thuds and tears. We settle down to watch him, wrapping tail around to warm front feet. What has this to do with us? We are full, we could go to sleep now. He looks up at us suddenly through the night.

Wait. A moment longer. Wait.

He growls to the other, and that one holds the light to the

hole. Heart of the Pack bends his back and the other reaches to
help him. They drag something from the hole. The smell of it
sets our hackles ajar. We turn, we leap to run, we circle, we
cannot leave. There is a fear here, there is a danger, a threat of
pain, of loneliness, of endings.

*Come. Come down to us here, come down. We need you
now. It is time.*

This is not time. Time is always, is everywhere. You need
us, but perhaps we do not want to be needed. We have meat
and a warm place to sleep, and even more meat for another
time. With a full belly and a warm den, what else is to be
needed? Yet. We will go closer. We will snuff it, we will see
what it is that threatens and beckons. Belly to snow, tail low,
we slink down the hill.

Heart of the Pack sits in the snow holding it. He motions
the other away, and that one steps back, back, back taking his
painful light with him. Closer. The hill is behind us now, bare,
shelterless. It is a far run back to hiding if we are threatened.
But nothing moves. There is only Heart of the Pack and that
which he holds. It smells of old blood. He shakes it, as if to
worry off a piece of meat. Then he rubs at it, moving his hands
like a bitch's teeth go over a cub to rid it of fleas. We know the
smell of it. Closer we come. Closer. It is but a leap away.

What do you want? We demand of him.

Come back.

We have come.

Come back here. Changer. He is insistent. *Come back to
this.* He lifts an arm, holds up a hand. He shows us a head
lolling on his shoulder. He turns its head to show us its face.
We do not know it.

That?

This. This is yours, Changer.

*It smells bad. It is spoiled meat, we do not want it. There is
better meat by the pond than that.*

Come here. Come closer.

This is not a good idea. We will come no closer. He looks
at us and grips us with his eyes. He edges closer to us, bringing
it with him. It flops in his arms.

Easy. Easy. This is yours, Changer. Come closer.

We snarl, but he does not look away. We cower, tail to belly, wanting to leave, but he is strong. He takes its hand and puts it on our head. He holds the scruff of our neck to still us.

Come back. You must come back. He is so insistent.

We cower down, digging claws into the snowy earth. Humping our back, we try to pull away, struggle to take one step backward. He still holds on to the scruff of our neck. We gather strength to wheel and break away.

Let him go, Nighteyes. He is not yours. A hint of teeth in those words, his eyes stare at us too hard.

He is not yours, either, Nighteyes says.

Whose am I, then?

A moment of teetering, of balancing between two worlds, two realities, two fleshes. Then a wolf wheels and flees, tail tucked, over the snow, running away alone, fleeing from too much strangeness. Atop a hill he stops, to point his nose at the sky and howl. Howl for the unfairness of it all.

→=►

I do not have a memory of that frozen graveyard that is my own. I have a sort of dream. I was wretchedly cold, stiff, and the raw taste of brandy burned, not just in my mouth, but all through me. Burrich and Chade would not leave me alone. They didn't care how much they were hurting me, they just kept on rubbing my hands and feet, careless of the old bruises, the scabs on my arms. And every time I closed my eyes, Burrich would seize me and shake me like a rag. "Stay with me, Fitz," he kept saying. "Stay with me, stay with me. Come on, boy. You're not dead. You're not dead." Then suddenly he hugged me to him, his bearded face bristling against mine and his hot tears falling on my face. He rocked me back and forth, sitting in the snow at the edge of my grave. "You're not dead, son. You're not dead."

EPILOGUE

I T WAS A thing Burrich had heard of, in a tale told by his grandmother. A tale of a Witted one who could leave her body, for a day or so, and then come back to it. And Burrich had told it to Chade, and Chade had mixed the poisons that would take me to the brink of death. They told me I had not died, that my body had but slowed to an appearance of death.

I do not believe that.

And so I lived once more in man's body. Though it took me some days and time to remember that I had been a man. And sometimes, still, I doubt it.

I did not resume my life. My life as FitzChivalry lay in smoking ruins behind me. In all the world, only Burrich and Chade knew I had not died. Of those who had known me, few remembered me with smiles. Regal had killed me, in every way that mattered to me as a man. To present myself to any of those who had loved me, to stand before them in my human flesh would have only been to give them proof of the magic I had tainted myself with.

I had died in my cell, a day or two after that final beating. The Dukes had been wroth about my death, but Regal had had enough evidence and witnesses to my Wit magic to save face with them. I believe that his guards saved themselves from the lash by testifying that I had attacked Will with the Wit, and that was why he lay ill so long. They said they had had to beat me to break my Wit hold on him. In the face of so many witnesses, the Dukes not only abandoned me, but witnessed Regal's coronation, and the appointment of Lord Bright as castellan for Buckkeep and all of Buck's coast. Patience had begged that my

ody not be burned, but be buried whole. The Lady Grace had
lso sent word on my behalf, much to her husband's disgust.
Only those two stood by me, in the face of Regal's proof of my
Vit taint. But I do not think it was out of any consideration for
hem that he gave me up, but only that by dying ahead of time, I
ad spoiled the spectacle that hanging and burning would have
fforded. Cheated of his full vengeance, Regal simply lost in-
erest. He left Buckkeep to go inland to Tradeford. Patience
laimed my body to bury me.

To this life did Burrich awaken me, to a life in which there
vas nothing left for me. Nothing save my king. The Six Duchies
vould crumble in the months to come, the Raiders would pos-
ess our good harbors almost at will, our folk were driven from
heir homes, or brought to slavery while the Outislanders
quatted there. Forgings flourished. But as my prince Verity
ad done, I turned my back on all of it, and went inland. But he
vent to be a King, and I went, following my queen, seeking my
ing. Hard days followed.

Yet even now, when the pain presses most heavily and
one of the herbs can turn its deep ache, when I consider the
ody that entraps my spirit, I recall my days as a Wolf, and
now them not as a few but as a season of living. There is a
omfort in their recalling, as well as a temptation. Come, hunt
vith me, the invitation whispers in my heart. Leave the pain
ehind and let your life be your own again. There is a place
vhere all time is now, and the choices are simple and always
our own.

Wolves have no Kings.

**And be sure not to miss the epic conclusion of
Robin Hobb's**
The Farseer Saga

ASSASSIN'S QUEST

available from Bantam Spectra Books

*With the help of his guardian, Burrich, and his tutor, Chade, Fitz
reluctantly emerges from the grave, only to find a kingdom rent by
disaster. Old King Shrewd is dead at the hands of his youngest son,
the ruthless Prince Regal. Prince Verity, the rightful heir, is lost
pursuing an antique dream, seeking the aid of the elusive Elderlings.
Buckkeep has been abandoned, leaving the people torn between the
predations of the Red-Ship Raiders and Regal's own rapacious
guards.*

*And Fitz, scarred and embittered—torn by the loss of his beloved
Molly—sees but one solution to the problem. After all, he is an assassin trained. So, he sets himself the ultimate quest: to eliminate the man
who has stolen the throne, and corrupted all he once held dear.*

*With Nighteyes at his side and the echoes of Verity in his mind, Fitz
sets out for the new capital at Tradeford to kill Regal . . .*

I was in a small sitting room. The furniture was shabby and ill-matched, so I surmised it was for servants or visiting craftsmen. I could not count on being alone there for long. There were, however, several large cupboards along the wall. I chose one that was not in direct view of the door should it open suddenly, and quickly re-arranged its contents in order to sit inside it. I ensconced myself with the door slightly ajar for some light and went to work. I inspected and organized my vials and packets of poisons. I treated both my belt knife and my sword's edge with poison, then resheathed them carefully. I arranged my sword to hang outside my trousers. Then I made myself comfortable and settled down to wait.

Days seemed to pass before dusk gave way to full dark. Twice folk briefly entered the room, but from their gossip I gathered that every servant was busy preparing for the gathering tonight. I passed the time by imagining how Regal would kill me if he caught me. Several times I almost lost my courage. Each time I reminded myself that if I walked away from this, I would have to live with the fear forever. Instead, I tried to prepare myself. If Regal were here, then his coterie would surely be close by. I put myself carefully through the exercises Verity had taught me to shield my mind from other Skilled ones. I was horribly tempted to venture out with a tiny touch of the Skill, to see if I could sense them. I refrained. I doubted I could sense them without betraying myself. And even if I could so detect them, what would it tell me that I did not already know? Better to concentrate on guarding myself from them. I refused to allow myself to think specifically of what I would do, lest they pick up traces of my thoughts. When finally the sky outside the window was full black and pricked with stars, I slipped out from my hiding place and ventured out into the hallway.

Music drifted on the night. Regal and his guests were at their festivities. I listened for a moment to the faint notes of a familiar song about two sisters, one of whom drowned the other. To me, the wonder of the song was not a harp that would play by itself, but a minstrel who would find a woman's body, and be inspired to make a harp of her breastbone. Then I put it out of my mind and concentrated on business.

I was in a simple corridor, stone-floored and paneled with wood, lit with torches set at wide intervals. Servants' area, I surmised; it was not fine enough for Regal or his friends. That did not make it safe for me, however. I needed to find a servants' stair and get myself to the second floor. I crept along the hall. I went from door to door, pausing to listen outside each one. Twice I heard folk within, women talking together in one, the clack of a weaving frame being used in another. The quiet doors that were not locked, I opened briefly. They were workrooms for the most part, with several given over to weaving and sewing. In one, a suit of fine blue fabric was pieced out on a table, ready for sewing. Regal apparently still indulged his fondness for fine clothing.

I came to the end of the corridor and peered around the corner. Another hallway, much finer and wider. The plastered ceiling overhead had been imprinted with fern shapes. Again I crept down a corridor, listening outside doors, cautiously peeping into some of them. Getting closer, I told myself. I found a library, with more vellum books and scrolls than I had ever known existed. I paused in one room where brightly plumed birds in extravagant cages dozed on their perches. Slabs of white marble had been set to hold ponds of darting fishes and water lilies. There were benches and cushioned chairs set about gaming tables there. Small cherrywood tables scattered about held Smoke censers. I had never even imagined such a room.

I eventually came to a proper hall with framed portraits along the walls and a floor of gleaming black slate. I drew back when I spotted the guard and stood silent in an alcove until his bored pacing carried him past me. Then I slipped out to flit past all those mounted nobles and simpering ladies in their sumptuous frames.

I blundered out into an antechamber. There were hangings on the wall and small tables supporting statuary and vases of flowers. Even the torch sconces here were more ornate. There were small portraits in gilt frames to either side of a fireplace with an elaborate mantle. Chairs were set close together for intimate talk. The music was louder here, and I could hear laughter and voices as well. Despite the lateness of the hour, the merriment went on. On the opposite wall were two tall carved doors. They led to the gathering hall where Regal and his nobles danced and laughed. I pulled myself back around the corner as I saw two servants in livery enter from a door to my far left. They bore trays carrying an assortment of incense pots. I surmised they were to replace ones that had burned out. I stood frozen, listening to their footsteps and conversation. They opened the tall doors and the music of harps spilled out more loudly and the narcotic scent of Smoke. Both were quenched by the closing doors. I ventured to peep out again. All was clear before me, but behind me—

"What do you here?"

My heart fell into my boots, but I forced a sheepish smile to my face as I turned to face the guard who had entered the room behind me. "Sir, I've lost my way in this great maze of a house," I said guilelessly.

"Have you? That doesn't explain why you wear a sword within the King's walls. All know weapons are forbidden save to the King's own guard. I saw you sneaking about just then. Did you think with the merrymaking going on, you could just slip about and fill your pockets with whatever you found, thief?"

I stood frozen with terror, watching the man approach me. I am sure he believed he had discovered my purpose from the stricken look on my face. Verde would never have smiled so if he thought he advanced on a man he had helped beat to death in a dungeon. His hand rested carelessly on the hilt of his own blade and he grinned confidently. He was a handsome man, very tall and fair as many of the Farrow folk were. The badge he wore was Mountwell of Farrow's golden oak, with the Farseer buck overleaping it. So Regal had modified his coat of arms as well. I but wished he'd left the buck off it.

A part of me noticed all these things as another part relived the nightmare of being dragged to my feet by my shirtfront and stood up, so that this man could strike me and drive me once more to the floor. He was not Bolt, the one who had broken my nose. No, Verde had followed him, beating me insensible a second time, after Bolt had left me too battered to stand on my own. He had towered over me then and I had cowered and flinched away from him, tried vainly to scrabble away from him over the cold stone floor that was already spattered with my blood. I remembered the oaths he had laughingly uttered each time he had to haul me to my feet so he could hit me again. "By Eda's tits," I muttered to myself, and with the words, fear died in me.

"Let's see what you have in that pouch," he demanded, and came closer.

I could not show him the poisons in my pouch. No way to explain those away. No amount of smooth lying would let me escape this man. I would have to kill him.

Suddenly it was all so simple.

We were much too close to the gathering hall. I wished no sound to alarm or alert anyone. So I retreated from him, a slow step at a time, backing in a wide circle that took me into the chamber I had just left. The portraits looked down on us as I backed hesitantly away from the tall guardsman.

"Stand still!" he ordered, but I shook my head wildly in what I hoped was a convincing display of terror. "I said, stand still, you scrawny little thief!" I glanced quickly over my shoulder, then back at him, desperate, as if I were trying to find the courage to turn and run from him. The third time I did so, he leaped for me.

I'd been hoping for that.

I sidestepped him and drove my elbow savagely into the small of his back, adding just enough momentum to his charge that he went to his nees. I heard them smack bonily against the stone floor. He gave a word-ess roar of both anger and pain. I could see how suddenly furious it made im for the scrawny thief to dare strike him. I silenced him sharply when I icked him under the chin, clacking his mouth shut. I was grateful that I'd witched back to my boots. Before he could make another sound I had my nife out and across his throat. He gurgled his amazement and lifted both ands in a vain attempt to contain that warm gushing of blood. I stood over him, looking down into his eyes. "FitzChivalry," I told him quietly. FitzChivalry." His eyes widened in sudden understanding and terror, hen lost all expression as life left him. Abruptly he was stillness and noth-ngness, as devoid of life as a stone. To my Wit-sense, he had disappeared.

So quickly it was done. Vengeance. I stood looking down at him, waiting to feel triumph or relief, or satisfaction. Instead I felt nothing, elt as lost to all life as he was. He was not even meat I could eat. I won-dered belatedly if there was somewhere a woman who had loved this andsome man, blond children who depended on his wages for food. It s not good for an assassin to have such thoughts; they had never plagued me when I had carried out the King's Justice for King Shrewd. I shook hem from my head.

He was making a very large puddle of blood on the floor. I had si-enced him quickly but this was just the sort of mess I hadn't wished to nake. He was a large man, and he'd had a lot of blood in him. My mind aced as I debated whether to take time to conceal the body, or to accept hat he would be quickly missed by his fellow guards and use that dis-covery as a diversion.

In the end I took off my shirt and sopped up as much of the blood as I could with it. Then I dumped it on his chest and wiped my bloody ands on his shirt. I seized him by the shoulders and dragged him out of he portrait hall, all the time almost shuddering with the effort of strain-ng my senses to be aware of anyone coming. My boots kept slipping on he polished floors and the sound of my panting breath was a roar to my ears. Despite my efforts at mopping up the blood, we left a sheen of red on the floors behind us. At the door to the room of birds and fish, I orced myself to listen well before entering. I held my breath and tried to gnore the pounding of my heart in my ears. The room was clear of hu-nans, however. I shouldered the door open and dragged Verde in. Then caught him up and tumbled him into one of the stone fish pools. The ish darted frantically as his blood trailed and swirled out into the clear water. I hastily rinsed my hands and chest clean of blood in another pond, and then left by a different door. They'd follow the blood trail nere. I hoped they'd take some time puzzling as to why the killer had dragged him here and dumped him in a pond.

I found myself in an unfamiliar room. I glanced quickly about at the vaulted ceiling and paneled walls. There was a grandiose chair on a dais at the far end. Some kind of an audience chamber then. I glanced about to get my bearings, then froze where I was. The carved doors to my far right swung suddenly open. I heard laughter, a muttered question, and giggling response. There was no time to hide and nothing to shelter behind. I flattened myself against a wall hanging and was still. The group entered on a wave of laughter. There was a note of helplessness in the laughter that told me they were either drunk or giddy with Smoke. They walked right past me, two men vying for the attention of a woman who simpered and tittered behind a tasseled fan. All three of them were dressed entirely in shades of red, and one of the men had tinkling silver charms not just at the lace of his cuffs, but all along his loose sleeves to his elbows. The other man carried a small censer of Smoke on an ornamented rod, almost like a scepter. He swung it back and forth before them as they walked so that they were always wreathed in the sweetish fumes. I doubted that they would have noticed me even if I had leaped out before them turning a cartwheels. Regal seemed to have inherited his mother's fondness for intoxicants, and to be turning it into a court fashion. I stood motionless until they passed. They went into the fish-and-bird room. I wondered if they would notice Verde in the pond. I doubted it.

I flitted to the doorway from which the courtiers had entered, and slipped through it. I found myself suddenly in a great entry hall. It was floored with marble and my mind boggled at the expense of hauling such an expanse of stone to Tradeford. The ceiling was high and plastered white, with designs of immense flowers and leaves pressed into the plaster. There were arched windows of stained glass, dark now against the night, but between them hung tapestries glowing with such rich colors as to seem windows on some other world and time. All was illuminated with ornate candelabra hung with sparkling crystals and suspended from gilded chains. Hundreds of candles burned in them. Statues were displayed on pedestals at intervals about the room and from the look of them, most were of Regal's Mountwell ancestors from his mother's side. Despite the danger I was in, the grandness of the room captured me for a moment. Then I lifted my eyes and saw the wide staircase ascending. This was the main staircase, not the back servants' stairs I had sought. Ten men abreast could have gone up it easily. The woodwork of the balustrades was dark and full of twirling knots, but shone with a deep luster. A thick rug spilled down the center of the steps like a blue cascade.

The hall was empty, as was the staircase. I did not give myself time to hesitate, but slipped silently across the room and up the stairs. I was halfway up when I heard the scream. Evidently they *had* noticed Verde.

At the top of the first landing, I heard voices and running footsteps coming from the right. I fled to the left. I came to a door, pressed my ear against it, heard nothing, and slipped inside, all in less time than it takes to tell it. I stood in darkness, heart thundering, thanking Eda and El and any other gods that might exist that the door had not been fastened.

I stood in the darkness, my ear pressed to the thick door, trying to hear more than my own pounding heart. I heard shouts from below, and boots running down the staircase. A moment or so passed, then I heard an authoritative voice shouting orders. I slipped to where the opening door would at least temporarily conceal me, and waited, breath stilled, hands trembling. Fear welled up in me like a sudden blackness, threatening to overwhelm me. I felt the floor rock under me and I crouched down quickly to keep from falling in a faint. The world spun about me. I made myself small, hugging myself tight and squeezing my eyes shut, as if somehow that would better conceal me. A second wave of fear washed over me. I sank the rest of the way to the floor and fell over on my side, all but whimpering. I curled in a ball, enduring a terrible squeezing pain in my chest. I was going to die. I was going to die and I'd never see them again, not Molly, not Burrich, not my king. I should have gone to Verity. I knew that now. I should have gone to Verity. I wanted to scream and weep, for I was suddenly certain I could never escape, that I would be found and tortured. They would find me and kill me very, very slowly. I experienced an almost overwhelming drive simply to leap up and run out of the room, to draw sword against the guards and force them to end me quickly.

Steady now. They try to trick you into betraying yourself. Verity's Skilling was finer than a cobweb. I caught my breath, but had the wisdom to keep still.

After what seemed a long time, my blind terror lifted. I took a long shuddering breath and seemed to come to myself again. When I heard the footsteps and voices outside the door, my fear surged up again, but I forced myself to lie still and listen.

"I was sure of it," said a man.

"No. He's long gone. If they find him at all, they'll find him out on the grounds. No one could have stood up to both of us. If he were still in the house, we would have flushed him out."

"I tell you, there was something."

"Nothing," insisted the other voice with some annoyance. "I sensed nothing."

"Check again," insisted the other.

"No. It's a waste of time. I think you were mistaken." The first man's anger was becoming obvious despite their subdued voices.

"I hope I was, but I fear I am not. If I am correct, we've given Will the excuse he's been looking for." There was anger in the second man's voice too, but also a whining self-pity.

"Looking for an excuse? Not that one. He speaks ill of us to the King at every turn. To hear him talk, you would think he was the only one who had made any sacrifices in King Regal's service. A maidservant told me yesterday that he makes no niceties at all about it anymore. You, he says, are fat, and me he accuses of every weakness of the flesh a man can have."

"If I am not as lean as a soldier, it is because I am not a soldier. It is not my body that serves the King, but my mind. As well look to him-self before he faults us, him with his one good eye." The whine was un-mistakable now. Burl, I suddenly realized. Burl speaking to Carrod.

"Well. I am satisfied that tonight at least he cannot fault us. There is nothing amiss here that I can find. He has you jumping at shadows and seeing danger in every corner. Calm yourself. This is a matter for the guards now, not us. They'll probably find it was done by a jealous hus-band or another guardsman. I've heard it said that Verde won a little too often at dice. Perhaps that is why he was left in the gaming room. So if you will excuse me, I will return to the fairer company from which you distracted me."

"Go, then, if that is all you can think of," the whiner said sulkily. "But when you've a moment to spare, I think we might be wise to take counsel together." After a moment, Burl added, "I've more than half a mind to go to him right now. Make it his problem."

"You'd only end up looking like a fool. When you worry so much, you are but giving into his influence. Let him mouth his warnings and dire predictions and spend every moment of his life on guard. To hear him tell it, his watchfulness is all the King needs. He seeks to instill that fear in us. Your quaking probably gives him much satisfaction. Guard such thoughts carefully."

I heard one set of footsteps walking briskly away. The roaring in my ears softened a little. After a time, I heard the other man leave, walking more ponderously and muttering to himself. When I could no longer hear his footfalls, I felt as if a great weight had been lifted off me. I swallowed dryly and debated my next move.

Dim light filtered in through tall windows. I could make out a bedstead, with the blankets turned back to expose the white linens. It was unoccupied. There was the dark shape of a wardrobe in the cor-ner, and by the bed a stand held a bowl and ewer.

I forced myself to calmness. I took long steadying breaths, then rose silently to my feet. I needed to find Regal's bedchamber, I reminded myself. I suspected it would be on this floor, with servants' quarters in the higher levels of the house. Stealth had got me this far, but perhaps now it was time to be bolder. I crossed to the wardrobe in the corner and opened it quietly. Luck had favored me again; this was a man's chamber. I went through the garments by touch, feeling for a fabric that felt servicable. I had to work hastily, for I assumed the rightful owner was at the festivities below and might return at any time. I found a light-colored shirt, much more fussy about the sleeves and collar than I could wish, but almost long enough in the arms. I managed to get into it, and a darker-colored pair of leggings that felt too loose on me. I belted them up and hoped they did not hang too strangely. There was a pot of scented pomade. I finger-brushed my hair back from my face with it and secured it afresh in a tail, discarding the tradesman's kerchief. Most of the courtiers I had seen earlier wore theirs in oiled curls much as Regal did, but a few of the younger ones kept their hair tied back. I felt about in several drawers. I found some sort of medallion on a chain and put it on. There was a ring, too large for my finger, but that scarcely mattered. I would pass a casual glance and hoped to attract no more than that. They would be looking for a shirtless man in coarse trousers to match the bloodied shirt I had left. I dared to hope they would be seeking him outside. At the threshold I paused, took a deep breath, and then slowly opened the door. The hall was empty and I stepped out.

Once out in the light, I was not pleased to find the leggings were a dark green and the shirt a buttery yellow. It was no more garish than what I had seen folk wearing earlier, though I could scarcely blend with the guests at his Scarlet Ball. I resolutely set the worry aside and struck off down the hall, walking casually yet purposefully to seek for a door that was larger and more ornate than the others.

I boldly tried the first one I came to, and found it unlocked. I entered, only to find myself in a room with an immense harp and several other musical instruments set out as if awaiting minstrels. A variety of cushioned chairs and couches filled the rest of the room. The paintings were all of songbirds. I shook my head, baffled at the endless riches of this one house. I continued my search.

My nervousness made the hall stretch out endlessly before me. I forced myself to walk in an unhurried and confident manner. I passed door after door, cautiously sampling a few. Those on my left seemed to be bedchambers, while those on my right were larger rooms, libraries and dining rooms and the like. Instead of wall sconces, the hall was lit with shielded candles. The wall hangings were richly colored, and at intervals niches held vases of flowers or small statuary. I could not help but contrast it to the stark stone walls of Buckkeep. I wondered how many warships would have been built and manned with the coin that instead went to ornament this finely feathered nest. My anger fed my competence. I would find Regal's chamber.

I passed three more doors, then came to one that looked promising. It was a double door, of golden oak, and the oak tree that was the symbol of Farrow was inlaid upon it. I set my ear briefly to the door and heard nothing. Cautiously I tried the burnished handle; the door was latched. My sheath knife was a crude tool for this type of work. Sweat soaked the yellow shirt to my back before the catch yielded to my efforts. I eased the door open and slipped inside, quickly locking it behind me.

This was certainly Regal's chamber. Not his bedchamber, no, but his nonetheless. I went through it swiftly. There were no less than four tall wardrobes, two on each side wall with a tall looking glass between each set. The ornately carved door of one wardrobe was ajar; or possibly the press of the clothing from within would not allow it to be fully closed. Other garments hung on hooks and racks about the room or were draped on chairs. A set of locked drawers in a small chest probably held jewelry. The looking glass between the wardrobes was framed by two branches of candles, now burned low in their holders. Two small censers for Smoke were set to either side of one chair that faced yet another mirror. Behind and to one side of the chair, a table held brushes, combs, pots of pomade, and vials of perfume. A narrow twining of gray fumes still rose from one of the censers. I wrinkled my nose against the sweet odor of it, and went to work.

Fitz. What do you do? The faintest query from Verity.

Justice. I put no more than a breath of Skill onto the thought. I was not sure if it was my own or Verity's apprehension that I suddenly felt. I brushed it aside and turned to my task.

It was frustrating. There was little here that was a sure vehicle for my poisons. I could treat the pomade, but I was more likely to kill whoever dressed his hair for him than Regal. The censers held mostly ash. Anything I placed there would probably be dumped with the ash. The corner hearth was swept clean for the summer and there was no supply of wood. Patience, I told myself. His bedchamber could not be far, and opportunities would be better there. For now, I treated the bristles of his hairbrush with one of my more potent concoctions and used what was left to dip as many of his earrings as I could. The last drops I added to his vials of scent but with small hope that he would apply enough to kill himself. For the scented handkerchiefs folded in his drawer, I had the white spore of the death angel mushroom to beguile his hours until death with hallucinations. I took greater pleasure in dusting the insides of four sets of gloves with deadroot powder.

This was the poison Regal had used on me in the Mountains, and the most likely source of the seizures that had plagued me intermittently since then. I hoped he would find his own falling fits as amusing as he had mine. I selected three of his shirts that I thought he would favor, and treated their collars and cuffs as well. There was no wood in the hearth, but I had a poison that blended well with the traces of ash and soot left on the brick. I sprinkled it generously and hoped that when they set a fire upon it, the burning fumes might reach Regal's nose. I had just returned my poison to my pouch when I heard a key turn the door latch.

I stepped silently around the corner of a wardrobe and stood there. My knife was already in my hand, waiting. A deadly calm had settled on me. I breathed silently, waiting, hoping fortune had brought Regal to me. Instead, it was another guardsman in Regal's colors. The man pushed into the room and cast a quick glance about. His irritation showed in his face as he impatiently said, "It was locked. There's no one in here." I waited for his partner to reply, but he was alone. He stood still a moment, then sighed and walked over to the open wardrobe. "Foolishness. I'm wasting time up here while he's going to get away," he muttered to himself, but he drew his sword and carefully prodded about the interior behind the clothes.

As he leaned to reach deeper into the wardrobe's interior, I caught a glimpse of his face in the mirror opposite me. My guts turned to water, and then hatred blazed up in me. I had no name for this one, but his mocking face had been forever etched into my memory. He had been part of Regal's personal guard, and had stood by to witness my death.

I think he saw my reflection at the same time I saw his. I did not give him time to react, but sprang on him from behind. The blade of his sword was still tangled inside Regal's wardrobe when my knife punched low into his belly. I clamped my forearm across his throat to give me leverage as I dragged up on the knife, gutting him like a fish. His mouth gaped open to scream, and I let go my knife to slap my hand over his mouth. I held him a moment as his entrails bulged out of the gash I'd made. When I let him go, he went down, his unvoiced bellow turned to a groan. He'd not let go of his sword, so I stamped on his hand, breaking his fingers around its hilt. He rolled slightly to one side, to stare up at me in agony and shock. I went down on one knee beside him, put my face close to his.

"FitzChivalry," I said quietly, meeting his eyes, making sure he knew. "FitzChivalry." For the second time that night, I cut a throat. It scarcely needed doing. I wiped my knife on his sleeve as he died. As I stood, I felt two things. Disappointment that he had died so swiftly. And a sensation as if a harp string had been plucked, letting out a sound I felt rather than heard.

In the next instant, I felt a wave of Skill inundate me. It was laden with terror, but this time I recognized it for what it was and knew its source. I stood firm before it, my defenses strong. I almost felt it part and go around me. Yet I sensed that even that act was read by someone, somewhere. I did not wonder who. Will felt the shape of my resistance. I felt the echo of his surge of triumph. For a moment it froze me with panic. Then I was moving, sheathing my knife, rising to slip out the door and into the still-empty hallway. I had but a short time to find a new hiding place. Will had been riding with the guardsman's mind, had seen that chamber and me just as clearly as the dying man had. Like the sounding of horns, I could sense him Skilling out, setting the guards in motion as if he were setting dogs to a fox's trail.

As I fled, a part of me knew with undeniable certainty that I was dead. I might be able to hide myself for a time, but Will knew I was within the mansion. All he had to do was block off every exit and begin a systematic search. I raced down a hall, turned a corner, and went up a staircase there. I held my Skill walls firm and clutched my tiny plan to myself as if it were a precious gem. I would find Regal's chambers and poison everything there. Then I would go seeking Regal himself. If the guards discovered me first, well, I'd lead them a merry chase. They couldn't kill me. Not with all the poison I was carrying. I'd take my own life first. It wasn't much of a plan, but the only alternative was surrendering.

So I raced on, past more doors, more statuary and flowers, more hangings. Every door I tried was locked. I turned another corner and was suddenly back at the top of the staircase. I felt a moment of dizzy disorientation. I attempted to brush it off but panic rose like a black tide inside my mind. It appeared to be the same staircase. I knew I had not turned enough corners to have come back to it. I hurried past the staircase, past the doors again, hearing the shouts of guardsmen below me as knowledge grew and squirmed queasily inside me.

Will leaned on my mind.

Dizziness and pressure inside my eyes. Grimly I set my mental walls yet again. I turned my head quickly and my vision doubled for a moment. Smoke, I wondered? I had no head for any of the fume intoxicants that Regal favored. Yet this felt like more to me than the giddiness of Smoke or the mellowness of merrybud.

The Skill is a powerful tool in the hand of a master. I had been with Verity when he had used it against the Red-Ships, to so muddle a helmsman that he turned his own ships onto the rocks, to convince a navigator that he had not yet passed a point of land when it was far behind him, to raise fears and doubts in a captain's heart before he went into battle, or to bolster the courage of a ship's crew so that they foolhardily set sail into the very teeth of a storm.

How long had Will been working on me? Had he lured me here, for this encounter, by subtly convincing me that he would never expect me to come?

I forced myself to halt at the next door. I held myself firm, focused myself on the latch of the door as I worked it. It was not locked. I slipped into it, closing the door behind me. Blue fabric was set out on a table before me, ready for sewing. I'd been in this room before. I knew a moment of relief, then checked it. No. This room had been on the ground floor. I was upstairs. Wasn't I? I crossed quickly to the window, stood to one side of it as I peered out. Far below me were the torchlit grounds of the King's Gardens. I could see the white of the great drive gleaming in the night. Carriages were coming up it and liveried servants darted here and there, opening doors. Ladies and gentlemen in extravagant red evening clothes were leaving in droves. I gathered that Verde's end had rather spoiled Regal's ball. There were liveried guards on the doors, regulating who might leave and who must wait. All this I took in at a glance, and realized also that I was up a lot higher than I thought.

Yet I had been sure that this table and the blue garments waiting to be sewn had been down in the servants' wing of the ground floor.

Well, it was not all that unlikely that Regal would be having two different sets of blue clothes sewn. No time to puzzle about it; I had to find his bedchamber. I felt a strange elation as I slipped out of the room and fled once more down the hallway, a thrill not unlike that of a good hunt. Let them catch me if they could.

I came suddenly to a T in the corridor and stood a moment, puzzled. It did not seem to fit in with what I had seen of the building from outside. I glanced left, then right. Right was noticeably grander, and the tall double doors at the end of the hall were emblazoned with the golden oak of Farrow. As if to put spurs to me, I heard a mutter of angry voices from a room somewhere off to my left. I went right, drawing my knife as I ran. When I came to the great double doors, I put my hand to the latch quietly, expecting to find it locked tight. Instead the door gave easily and swung forward silently. It was almost too easy. I set those apprehensions aside and slipped in, knife drawn.

The room before me was dark, save for two candles burning in silver candle holders on the mantlepiece. I slipped inside what was obviously Regal's sitting room. A second door stood ajar, revealing the corner of a magnificently curtained bed and beyond it a hearth with a rack of firewood laid ready in it. I pulled the door gently closed behind me and advanced into the room. On a low table a carafe of wine and two glasses awaited Regal's return, as did a platter of sweets. The censer beside it was heaped with powdered Smoke waiting to be ignited on his return. It was an assassin's fantasy. I could scarcely decide where to begin.

"That, you see, is how it is done."

I spun about, then experienced a distortion of my senses that dizzied me. I stood in the middle of a well-lit but rather bare room. Will sat, negligently relaxed, in a cushioned chair. A glass of white wine waited on a table beside him. Carrod and Burl flanked him, wearing expressions of irritation and discomfiture. Despite my longing, I dared not take my eyes off them.

"Go ahead, Bastard, look behind you. I shan't attack you. It would be a shame to spring such a trap as this on one such as you, and have you die before you appreciated the fullness of your failure. Go on. Look behind you."

I turned my whole body slowly, to allow me to glance back with a mere shifting of my eyes. Gone, it was all gone. No royal sitting room, no curtained bed or carafe of wine, nothing. A plain, simple room, probably for several lady's maids to share. Six liveried guards stood silent but attentive. All had drawn swords.

"My companions seem to feel that a drenching of fear will ferret out any man. But they, of course, have not experienced your strength of will as completely as I have. I do hope you appreciate the finesse I used, in simply assuring you that you were seeing exactly what you most wished to see." He gave a glance each to Carrod and Burl. "He has walls the like of which you have never experienced. But a wall that will not yield to a battering ram can still be breached by the gentle twining of ivy." He swung his attention back to me. "You would have been a worthy opponent, save that in your conceit you always underestimated me."

I still had not said a word. I stared at them all, letting the hatred that filled me strengthen my Skill walls. All three had changed since I had last seen them. Burl, once a well-muscled carpenter, showed the affects of a good appetite and lack of exercise. Carrod's attire outshone the man within it. Ribbons and charms festooned his garments like blossoms on a springtime apple tree. But Will, seated between them in his chair, showed the greatest change of all. He was dressed entirely in dark blue, in garments whose precise tailoring made them seem richer than Carrod's costume. A single chain of silver, a silver ring on his hand, silver earrings; these were his only ornaments. Of his dark eyes, once so terrifyingly piercing, only one remained. The other was sunken deep in its socket, showing cloudy in the depths like a dead fish in a dirty pool. He smiled at me as he saw me looking at it. He gestured at his eye.

"A memento of our last encounter. Whatever it was that you threw into my face."

"A pity," I said, quite sincerely. "I had meant those poisons to kill Regal, not half-blind you."

Will sighed lackadaisically. "Another admission of treason. As if we needed one. Ah, well. We shall be more thorough this time. First, of course, we will spend a bit of time ferreting out just how you escaped death. A bit of time for that, and however much longer King Regal finds you amusing. He will have no need for either haste or discretion this time." He gave a minuscule nod to the guards behind me.

I smiled at him as I set the poisoned blade of my own knife to my left arm. I clenched my teeth against the pain as I dragged it down the length of my arm, not deeply, but enough to open my skin and let the poison from the blade into my blood. Will leapt to his feet in shock, while Carrod and Burl looked horrified and disgusted. I passed my knife to my left hand, drew my sword with my right.

"I'm dying now," I told them, smiling. "Probably very soon. I've no time to waste, and nothing to lose."

But he had been correct. I had always underestimated him. Somehow I found myself facing, not the coterie members, but six guards with drawn blades. Killing myself was one thing. Being hacked to death while those I desired vengeance on watched was another. I spun about, and felt a wave of dizziness as I did so, as if the room moved rather than I myself. I lifted my eyes to find the swordsmen still confronting me. I turned again and again experienced a sensation of swinging. The thin line of blood along my arm had begun to burn. My chance to do anything about Will and Burl and Carrod was leaking away as the poison seeped through my blood.

The guards were advancing on me, unhurriedly, fanning out in a half circle and driving me before them as if I were an errant sheep. I backed up, glanced once over my shoulder and caught the most fleeting glimpse of the coterie members. Will stood, a step or so in front of the others, an annoyed look on his face. I had come here in the hope of killing Regal. I had barely succeeded in annoying his henchmen with my suicide.

Suicide? Somewhere deep within me, Verity was horrorstruck.

Better than torture. Less than a whisper of Skill on that thought, but I swear I felt Will go groping after it.

Boy, stop this insanity. Get out of there. Come to me.

I cannot. It's too late. There's no escape. Let go of me, you only reveal yourself to them.

Reveal myself? Verity's Skill boomed suddenly in my mind, like thunder on a summer night, like storm waves shaking a shale cliff. I had seen him do this before. Angered, he would expend all of his Skill-strength in one effort, with no thought to what might befall him afterward. I felt Will hesitate, then plunge into that Skilling, reaching after Verity and trying to leech onto him.

Study this revelation, you nest of adders! My king let forth his wrath.

Verity's Skilling was a blast, of a strength I had never encountered anywhere. It was not directed at me, but still I went to my knees. I heard Carrod and Burl cry out, guttural cries of terror. For a moment my head and perceptions cleared, and I saw the room as it had always been, with the guardsmen arrayed between me and the coterie. Will was stretched senseless on the floor. Perhaps I alone felt the great surge of strength it cost Verity to save me. The guards were staggering, wilting like candles in the sun. I spun, saw the door at my back as it opened to admit more guards. Three strides would carry me to the window.

COME TO ME!

There was no choice left for me in that command. It was impregnated with the Skill it rode on, and it burned into my brain, becoming one with my breathing and the beating of my heart. I had to go to Verity. It was a cry both of command and, now, of need. My king had sacrificed his reserves to save me.

There were heavy curtains over the window, and thick whorled glass behind them. Neither stopped me as I launched myself out into the air beyond, hoping there would at least be bushes below me to break some of my fall. Instead I slammed to the earth amid the shards of glass a fraction of a moment later. I had leaped, expecting to fall at least one story, from a ground-floor window. For a split second I appreciated the completeness of how Will had deceived me. Then I staggered to my feet, still clutching my knife and my sword, and ran.